100 GREAT SHORT STORIES

DOVER THRIFT EDITIONS

Edited by
James Daley

DOVER PUBLICATIONS, INC.
MINEOLA, NEW YORK

DOVER THRIFT EDITIONS

GENERAL EDITOR: MARY CAROLYN WALDREP
EDITOR OF THIS VOLUME: JANET BAINE KOPITO

Bibliographical Note

100 Great Short Stories, first published by Dover Publications, Inc., in 2015, is a new anthology of short stories reprinted from standard sources. James Daley has made the selection and provided a Note specially for this edition.

Library of Congress Cataloging-in-Publication Data

100 great short stories / edited by James Daley.
    p. cm. — (Dover thrift editions)
    Summary: "This treasury of 100 tales offers a volume of remarkable value to students and readers of short fiction. Selections by masters of the form from all over the world include Edgar Allan Poe, Jack London, Guy de Maupassant, Charles Dickens, Anton Chekhov, Mark Twain, Rudyard Kipling, and Saki."— Provided by publisher.
    ISBN-13: 978-0-486-79021-3 (pbk.)
    ISBN-10: 0-486-79021-5
    1. Short stories.   I. Daley, James, 1979–   editor.
PN6120.2.054 2015
808.83'1—dc23

2014034831

Manufactured in the United States by LSC Communications
79021505   2019
www.doverpublications.com

Note

ALTHOUGH THE MODERN short story arose primarily in the first quarter of the nineteenth century, its precursors can be traced back through the oldest forms of narrative. From the myths and legends of the ancient world to the ballads and parables of the Middle Ages, the short form of narrative has maintained a constant presence in nearly every culture, long before the term "short story" was used. While the reasons for the form's longevity are many, certainly one of the most overt explanations is that these brief narratives seem always to have had an amazing ability to provide commentary and insight on the society from which they were born.

With the rise of the modern short story, this inclination towards using fiction to express an author's perspective on the world-at-large became all the more prevalent, as the works contained in this collection demonstrate. From Daniel Defoe's *The Apparition of Mrs. Veal* (as much a commentary on society's penchant for superstition as it is a classic ghost story) to John Galsworthy's *The Broken Boot* (a poignant look at the gap between the social classes), we find examples of authors using their fiction as a means for social critique.

As it is today, humor has always been an effective tool for cloaking social commentary in the guise of entertainment. In Benjamin Franklin's wonderful *Alice Addertongue*, we find the famous Founding Father opining about colonial society through the voice of an invented town gossip. With Mark Twain's *Journalism in Tennessee* and John Kendrick Bangs' *The Idiot's Journalism Scheme*, we find authors providing hilarious visions of their own media landscapes in a way that rings very true today. Exploring the roles of women in society are such timeless tales as Charlotte Perkins Gilman's *If I Were a Man*, Kate Chopin's *A Pair of Silk Stockings*, and

Mary E. Wilkins Freeman's *A New England Nun*. O. Henry's classic *The Gift of the Magi* delves into society's relationship with money, as do Leo Tolstoy's *How Much Land Does a Man Need?* and Washington Irving's *The Devil and Tom Walker*. Family relationships acting as a microcosm of society are an enduring theme in short fiction and are prevalent in Franz Kafka's *The Judgment*, George W. Peck's *His Pa Gets Mad!*, and Luigi Pirandello's *Mrs. Frola and Mr. Ponza, Her Son-in-Law*. Throughout history, authors have been using narratives to make sense of war, and in this collection we see this theme explored through a wide variety of stories. *A Horseman in the Sky*, by Ambrose Bierce, and *The Veteran*, by Stephen Crane, explore the effects of the Civil War on the individual, while Ford Madox Ford's *Pink Flannel*, H. M. Tomlinson's *A Raid Night*, and Isaak Babel's *The Blind Ones* convey both the physical and emotional horrors of World War One.

With one hundred stories, spanning more than two centuries, this comprehensive collection provides a vision of the world over time that one could never find in a history book. It is only through short stories and longer fiction that one can experience such a diversity of perspectives, and it is aim of this anthology that its readers dive right in, lose themselves in the narratives and characters, and allow these hundred stories to deepen and expand their own view of the world—both as it has been, and as it is today.

JAMES DALEY

Contents

Daniel Defoe: The Apparition of Mrs. Veal (1705) 1

Benjamin Franklin: Alice Addertongue (1732) 9

Washington Irving: The Devil and Tom Walker (1824) . . . 14

Prosper Mérimée: Mateo Falcone (1829) 25

Charlotte Brontë: Napoleon and the Spectre (1833) 37

Mary Shelley: The Mortal Immortal: A Tale (1834) 41

Nathaniel Hawthorne: Young Goodman Brown (1835) . . . 54

Nathaniel Hawthorne: Dr. Heidegger's
Experiment (1837) 67

Edgar Allan Poe: The Masque of the Red Death (1841) . . 77

Edgar Allan Poe: The Tell-Tale Heart (1843) 83

Edgar Allan Poe: The Cask of Amontillado (1846) 88

Mary Anne Hoare: The Knitted Collar (1851) 95

Ivan S. Turgenev: The District Doctor (1852) 102

Charles Dickens: Nobody's Story (1853) 111

Herman Melville: The Fiddler (1854) 117

Herman Melville: The Lightning-Rod Man (1854) 123

Robert Carlton: Selecting the Faculty (1855) 130

Mary E. Braddon: The Cold Embrace (1861) 136

Alphonse Daudet: The Pope's Mule (1868) 145

Mark Twain: Journalism in Tennessee (1869) 155

Bret Harte: The Luck of Roaring Camp (1870) 162

Bill Arp: Bill Nations (1873) 172

Bret Harte: A Jersey Centenarian (1875) 175

Mark Twain: The Notorious Jumping Frog
          of Calaveras County (1875) 181

Mark Twain: A Literary Nightmare (1876) 187

Stephen Crane: The Bride Comes to Yellow Sky (1898) . 192

Lucretia P. Hale: The Peterkins Decide to Learn
          the Languages (1878) 203

Harriet Beecher Stowe: The Parson's
          Horse Race (1878) 210

Charles Dudley Warner: How I Killed a Bear (1878) . . . 218

Joel Chandler Harris: Uncle Remus and the
          Wonderful Tar-Baby Story (1881) 225

George W. Peck: His Pa Gets Mad! (1883) 231

Guy de Maupassant: The Necklace (1884) 234

Sarah Orne Jewett: A White Heron (1886) 243

Leo Tolstoy: How Much Land Does a Man Need? (1886) . 253

Charles Waddell Chesnutt: The Goophered
Grapevine (1887) 268

Bill Nye: John Adams' Diary (1887) 281

Oscar Wilde: The Sphinx Without a Secret (1887) 286

Oscar Wilde: The Happy Prince (1888) 291

Oscar Wilde: The Selfish Giant (1888) 300

Ambrose Bierce: A Horseman in the Sky (1889) 304

Mary E. Wilkins Freeman: A New England Nun (1891) . 311

Thomas Hardy: Squire Petrick's Lady (1891) 323

Jerome K. Jerome: A Ghost Story (1892). 332

Kate Chopin: Désirée's Baby (1893) 339

Jules Renard: The Dark Lantern (1893) 345

John Kendrick Bangs: The Idiot's
Journalism Scheme (1895). 351

Hayden Carruth: Active Colorado Real Estate (1895) . . 355

H. G. Wells: The Remarkable Case of
Davidson's Eyes (1895) 358

Stephen Crane: The Veteran (1896) 368

Joaquim Maria Machado de Assis:
The Fortune-Teller (1896) 373

Robert J. Burdette: Rollo Learning to Read (1897). . . . 383

Kate Chopin: A Pair of Silk Stockings (1897) 387

W. B. Yeats: The Tables of the Law (1897) 392

Anton Chekhov: Gooseberries (1898) 402

Kate Chopin: The Storm (1898) 411

Rudyard Kipling: Wee Willie Winkie (1899) 417

Jack London: The White Silence (1900) 427

Rainer Maria Rilke: How Old Timofei Died
with a Song (1900) 436

Thomas Mann: The Path to the Cemetery (1901) 442

Luigi Pirandello: With Other Eyes (1901) 451

Isabella Augusta, Lady Gregory: The Only Son
of Aoife (1902) 459

Jack London: The Leopard Man's Story (1903) 465

Guy de Maupassant: A Piece of String (trans. 1903). . . . 469

George Moore: Home Sickness (1903). 476

H. H. Munro, or Saki: The Open Window (1903). 488

Willa Cather: A Wagner Matinée (1905). 492

George Ade: The Set of Poe (1906) 499

O. Henry: The Furnished Room (1906) 504

O. Henry: The Gift of the Magi (1906) 511

O. Henry: The Last Leaf (1907) 517

Ambrose Bierce: An Occurrence
at Owl Creek Bridge (1891) 523

Willa Cather: The Enchanted Bluff (1909) 532

Charlotte Perkins Gilman: The Cottagette (1910) 541

Katherine Mansfield: Germans at Meat (1911) 550

H. H. Munro, or Saki: Tobermory (1911) 554

Katherine Mansfield: How Pearl Button
Was Kidnapped (1912) 562

Djuna Barnes: Smoke (1913) 566

James Stephens: The Blind Man (1913) 574

Charlotte Perkins Gilman: If I Were a Man (1914) 580

James Joyce: Araby (1914) 587

James Joyce: Eveline (1914) 593

D. H. Lawrence: Second Best (1914) 598

Vsevolod M. Garshin: The Signal (trans. 1915) 607

Theodor Sologub: The White Mother (trans. 1915) 616

Daniel Corkery: The Ploughing
of Leaca-na-Naomh (1916). . . . .: 625

Franz Kafka: The Judgment (1916) 636

Alexander Pushkin: The Coffin-Maker (trans. 1916) . . . 647

Luigi Pirandello: Mrs. Frola and Mr. Ponza,
Her Son-in-Law (1917) 655

Isaak Babel: The Blind Ones (1918). 664

Anton Chekhov: A Malefactor (trans. 1918) 668

Fyodor Dostoyevsky: A Christmas Tree
and a Wedding (trans. 1918). 672

Fyodor Dostoyevsky: The Peasant Marey (trans. 1918) . . 680

Ford Madox Ford: Pink Flannel (1919) 685

Franz Kafka: A Country Doctor (1919) 690

Sherwood Anderson: The Egg (1921) 696

Virginia Woolf: The Mark on the Wall (1921). 706

Franz Kafka: A Hunger Artist (1922) 713

Ring Lardner: The Golden Honeymoon (1922) 723

H. M. Tomlinson: A Raid Night (1922). 739

John Galsworthy: The Broken Boot (1923) 745

100
Great
Short Stories

THE APPARITION OF MRS. VEAL

Daniel Defoe

THIS THING IS so rare in all its circumstances, and on so good authority, that my reading and conversation have not given me anything like it. It is fit to gratify the most ingenious and serious inquirer. Mrs. Bargrave is the person to whom Mrs. Veal appeared after her death; she is my intimate friend, and I can avouch for her reputation for these fifteen or sixteen years, on my own knowledge; and I can confirm the good character she had from her youth to the time of my acquaintance. Though, since this relation, she is calumniated by some people that are friends to the brother of Mrs. Veal who appeared, who think the relation of this appearance to be a reflection, and endeavor what they can to blast Mrs. Bargrave's reputation and to laugh the story out of countenance. But by the circumstances thereof, and the cheerful disposition of Mrs. Bargrave, notwithstanding the ill usage of a very wicked husband, there is not yet the least sign of dejection in her face; nor did I ever hear her let fall a desponding or murmuring expression; nay, not when actually under her husband's barbarity, which I have been witness to, and several other persons of undoubted reputation.

Now you must know Mrs. Veal was a maiden gentlewoman of about thirty years of age, and for some years past had been troubled with fits, which were perceived coming on her by her going off from her discourse very abruptly to some impertinence. She was maintained by an only brother, and kept his house in Dover. She was a very pious woman, and her brother a very sober man to all appearance; but now he does all he can to null or quash the story. Mrs. Veal was intimately acquainted with Mrs. Bargrave from her childhood. Mrs. Veal's circumstances were then mean; her father did not take care of his children as he ought, so that they were exposed to hardships. And Mrs. Bargrave in those days had as unkind a father, though she wanted neither for food nor clothing; while Mrs. Veal wanted for both, insomuch that she would often say, "Mrs. Bargrave, you are not only the best, but the only friend I have in the world; and no circumstance of life shall ever dissolve my friendship." They would often condole each other's adverse fortunes, and read together *Drelincourt upon Death,* and other good books; and so, like two Christian friends, they comforted each other under their sorrow.

Some time after, Mr. Veal's friends got him a place in the custom-house at Dover, which occasioned Mrs. Veal, by little and little, to fall off from her intimacy with Mrs. Bargrave, though there was never any such thing as a quarrel; but an indifference came on by degrees, till at last Mrs. Bargrave had not seen her in two years and a half, though above a twelve-month of the time Mrs. Bargrave hath been absent from Dover, and this last half-year has been in Canterbury about two months of the time, dwelling in a house of her own.

In this house, on the eighth of September, one thousand seven hundred and five, she was sitting alone in the forenoon, thinking over her unfortunate life, and arguing herself into a due resignation to Providence, though her condition seemed hard: "And," said she, "I have been provided for hitherto, and doubt not but I shall be still, and am well satisfied that my afflictions shall end when it is most fit for me." And then took up her sewing work, which she had no sooner done but she hears a knocking at the door; she went to see who was there, and this proved to be Mrs. Veal, her old friend, who was in a riding-habit. At that moment of time the clock struck twelve at noon.

"Madam," says Mrs. Bargrave, "I am surprised to see you, you have been so long a stranger"; but told her she was glad to see her, and offered to salute her, which Mrs. Veal complied with, till their lips almost touched, and then Mrs. Veal drew her hand across her own eyes, and said, "I am not very well," and so waived it. She told Mrs. Bargrave she was going a journey, and had a great mind to see her first. "But," says Mrs. Bargrave, "how can you to take a journey alone? I am amazed at it, because I know you have a fond brother." "Oh!" says Mrs. Veal, "I gave my brother the slip, and came away, because I had so great a desire to see you before I took my journey."

So Mrs. Bargrave went in with her into another room within the first, and Mrs. Veal sat her down in an elbow-chair, in which Mrs. Bargrave was sitting when she heard Mrs. Veal knock. "Then," says Mrs. Veal, "my dear friend, I am come to renew our old friendship again, and beg your pardon for my breach of it; and if you can forgive me, you are the best of women." "Oh," says Mrs. Bargrave, "do not mention such a thing; I have not had an uneasy thought about it." "What did you think of me?" says Mrs. Veal. Says Mrs. Bargrave, "I thought you were like the rest of the world, and that prosperity had made you forget yourself and me." Then Mrs. Veal reminded Mrs. Bargrave of the many friendly offices she did her in former days, and much of the conversation they had with each other in the times of their adversity; what books they read, and what comfort in particular they received from Drelincourt's *Book of Death,* which was the best, she said, on the subject ever wrote. She also mentioned Doctor Sherlock, the two Dutch books, which were translated, wrote upon death, and several others. But Drelincourt, she said, had the clearest notions of death and of the future state of any who had handled that subject. Then she asked Mrs. Bargrave whether she had Drelincourt. She said, "Yes." Says Mrs. Veal, "Fetch it." And so Mrs. Bargrave goes up-stairs and brings it down. Says Mrs. Veal, "Dear Mrs. Bargrave, if the eyes of our faith were as open as the eyes of our body, we should see numbers of angels about us for our guard. The notions we have of Heaven now are nothing like what it is, as Drelincourt says; therefore be comforted under your afflictions, and believe that the Almighty has a particular regard to you, and that your afflictions are marks of God's favor; and when they have done the business they are sent for, they shall be removed from you. And believe me, my dear friend, believe what I say to you, one minute of future happiness will infinitely reward you for all your sufferings. For I can never believe" (and claps her hand upon her knee with great earnestness, which, indeed, ran through most of her discourse) "that ever God will suffer you to spend all your days in this afflicted state. But be assured that your afflictions shall leave you, or you them, in a short time." She spake in that pathetical and heavenly manner that Mrs. Bargrave wept several times, she was so deeply affected with it.

Then Mrs. Veal mentioned Dr. Kenrick's *Ascetic,* at the end of which he gives an account of the lives of the primitive Christians. Their pattern she recommended to our imitation, and said, "Their conversation was not like this of our age. For now," says she, "there is nothing but vain, frothy discourse, which is far different from theirs. Theirs was to edification, and to build one another up in faith, so that they were not as we are, nor are we as they were. But," said she, "we ought to do as they did; there was a hearty friendship among them; but where is it now to be found?" Says Mrs. Bargrave, "It is hard indeed to find a true friend in these days." Says Mrs. Veal, "Mr. Norris has a fine copy of verses, called *Friendship in Perfection*, which I wonderfully admire. Have you seen the book?" says Mrs. Veal. "No," says Mrs. Bargrave, "but I have the verses of my own writing out." "Have you?" says Mrs. Veal; "then fetch them"; which she did from above stairs, and offered them to Mrs. Veal to read, who refused, and waived the thing, saying, "holding down her head would make it ache"; and then desiring Mrs. Bargrave to read them to her, which she did. As they were admiring *Friendship*, Mrs. Veal said, "Dear Mrs. Bargrave, I shall love you forever." In these verses there is twice used the word "Elysian." "Ah!" says Mrs. Veal, "these poets have such names for Heaven." She would often draw her hand across her own eyes, and say, "Mrs. Bargrave, do not you think I am mightily impaired by my fits?" "No," says Mrs. Bargrave; "I think you look as well as ever I knew you."

After this discourse, which the apparition put in much finer words than Mrs. Bargrave said she could pretend to, and as much more than she can remember—for it cannot be thought that an hour and three quarters' conversation could all be retained, though the main of it she thinks she does—she said to Mrs. Bargrave she would have her write a letter to her brother, and tell him she would have him give rings to such and such; and that there was a purse of gold in her cabinet, and that she would have two broad pieces given to her cousin Watson.

Talking at this rate, Mrs. Bargrave thought that a fit was coming upon her, and so placed herself on a chair just before her knees, to keep her from falling to the ground, if her fits should occasion it; for the elbow-chair, she thought, would keep her from falling on either side. And to divert Mrs. Veal, as she thought, took hold of her gown-sleeve several times, and commended it. Mrs. Veal told her it was a scoured silk, and newly made up. But, for all this, Mrs. Veal persisted in her request, and told Mrs. Bargrave she must not deny her. And she would have her tell her brother all their conversation when she had the opportunity. "Dear Mrs. Veal," says Mrs. Bargrave, "this seems so impertinent that I cannot tell how to comply with it; and what a mortifying story will our conversation be to a young gentleman. "Why," says Mrs. Bargrave, "it is much better, methinks, to do it yourself." "No," says Mrs. Veal; "though it seems impertinent to you now, you will see more reasons for it hereafter." Mrs. Bargrave, then, to satisfy her importunity, was going to fetch a pen and ink, but Mrs. Veal said, "Let it alone now, but do it when I am gone; but you must be sure to do it"; which was one of the last things she enjoined her at parting, and so she promised her.

Then Mrs. Veal asked for Mrs. Bargrave's daughter. She said she was not at home. "But if you have a mind to see her," says Mrs. Bargrave, "I'll send for her." "Do," says Mrs. Veal; on which she left her, and went to a neighbor's to see her; and by the time Mrs. Bargrave was returning, Mrs. Veal was got without the door in the street, in the face of the beast-market, on a Saturday (which is market-day), and stood ready to part as soon as Mrs. Bargrave came to her. She asked her why she was in such haste. She said she must be going, though perhaps she might not go her journey till Monday; and told Mrs. Bargrave she hoped she should see her again at her cousin Watson's before she went whither she was going. Then she said she would take her leave of her, and walked from Mrs. Bargrave, in her view, till a turning interrupted the sight of her, which was three-quarters after one in the afternoon.

Mrs. Veal died the seventh of September, at twelve o'clock at noon, of her fits, and had not above four hours' senses before her death, in which time she received the sacrament. The next day after Mrs. Veal's appearance, being Sunday, Mrs. Bargrave was mightily indisposed with a cold and sore throat, that she could not go out that day; but on Monday morning she sends a person to Captain Watson's to know if Mrs. Veal was there. They wondered at Mrs. Bargrave's inquiry, and sent her word she was not there, nor was expected. At this answer, Mrs. Bargrave told the maid she had certainly mistook the name or made some blunder. And though she was ill, she put on her hood and went herself to Captain Watson's, though she knew none of the family, to see if Mrs. Veal was there or not. They said they wondered at her asking, for that she had not been in town; they were sure, if she had, she would have been there. Says Mrs. Bargrave, "I am sure she was with me on Saturday almost two hours." They said it was impossible, for they must have seen her if she had. In comes Captain Watson, while they were in dispute, and said that Mrs. Veal was certainly dead, and the escutcheons were making. This strangely surprised Mrs. Bargrave, when she sent to the person immediately who had the care of them, and found it true. Then she related the whole story to Captain Watson's family; and what gown she had on, and how striped; and that Mrs. Veal told her it was scoured. Then Mrs. Watson cried out, "You have seen her indeed, for none knew but Mrs. Veal and myself that the gown was scoured." And Mrs. Watson owned that she described the gown exactly; "for," said she, "I helped her to make it up." This Mrs. Watson blazed all about the town, and avouched the demonstration of truth of Mrs. Bargrave's seeing Mrs. Veal's apparition. And Captain Watson carried two gentlemen immediately to Mrs. Bargrave's house to hear the relation from her own mouth. And when it spread so fast that gentlemen and persons of quality, the judicious and sceptical part of the world, flocked in upon her, it at last became such a task that she was forced to go out of the way; for they were in general extremely satisfied of the truth of the thing, and plainly saw that Mrs. Bargrave was no hypochondriac, for she always appears with such a cheerful air and pleasing mien that she has gained the favor and esteem of all the gentry, and it is thought a great favor if they can but get the relation from her own mouth. I should have told you before that Mrs. Veal told Mrs. Bargrave that her sister and brother-in-law were just come down from London to see her. Says Mrs. Bargrave, "How came you to order matters so strangely?" "It could not be helped," said Mrs. Veal. And her brother and sister did come to see her, and entered the town of Dover just as Mrs. Veal was expiring. Mrs. Bargrave asked her whether she would drink some tea. Says Mrs. Veal, "I do not care if I do; but I'll warrant you this mad fellow"—meaning Mrs. Bargrave's husband—"has broke all your trinkets." "But," says Mrs. Bargrave, "I'll get something to drink in for all that"; but Mrs. Veal waived it, and said, "It is no matter; let it alone"; and so it passed.

All the time I sat with Mrs. Bargrave, which was some hours, she recollected fresh sayings of Mrs. Veal. And one material thing more she told Mrs. Bargrave, that old Mr. Bretton allowed Mrs. Veal ten pounds a year, which was a secret, and unknown to Mrs. Bargrave till Mrs. Veal told her.

Mrs. Bargrave never varies in her story, which puzzles those who doubt of the truth, or are unwilling to believe it. A servant in the neighbor's yard adjoining to Mrs. Bargrave's house heard her talking to somebody an hour of the time Mrs. Veal was with her.

Mrs. Bargrave went out to her next neighbor's the very moment she parted with Mrs. Veal, and told her what ravishing conversation she had had with an old friend, and told the whole of it. Drelincourt's *Book of Death* is, since this happened, bought up strangely. And it is to be observed that, notwithstanding all the trouble and fatigue Mrs. Bargrave has undergone upon this account, she never took the value of a farthing, nor suffered her daughter to take anything of anybody, and therefore can have no interest in telling the story.

But Mr. Veal does what he can to stifle the matter, and said he would see Mrs. Bargrave; but yet it is certain matter of fact that he has been at Captain Watson's since the death of his sister, and yet never went near Mrs. Bargrave; and some of his friends report her to be a liar, and that she knew of Mr. Bretton's ten pounds a year. But the person who pretends to say so has the reputation to be a notorious liar among persons whom I know to be of undoubted credit. Now, Mr. Veal is more of a gentleman than to say she lies, but says a bad husband has crazed her; but she needs only present herself, and it will effectually confute that pretence. Mr. Veal says he asked his sister on her death-bed whether she had a mind to dispose of anything. And she said no. Now the things which Mrs. Veal's apparition would have disposed of were so trifling, and nothing of justice aimed at in the disposal, that the design of it appears to me to be only in order to make Mrs. Bargrave satisfy the world of the reality thereof as to what she had seen and heard and to secure her reputation among the reasonable and understanding part of mankind. And then, again, Mr. Veal owns that there was a purse of gold; but it was not found in her cabinet, but in a comb-box. This looks improbable; for that Mrs. Watson owned that Mrs. Veal was so very careful of the key of her cabinet that she would trust nobody with it; and if so, no doubt she would not trust her gold out of it. And Mrs. Veal's often drawing her hands over her eyes, and asking Mrs. Bargrave whether her fits had not impaired her, looks to me as if she did it on purpose to remind Mrs. Bargrave of her fits, to prepare her not to think it strange that she should put her upon writing to her brother, to dispose of rings and gold, which look so much like a dying person's request; and it took accordingly with Mrs. Bargrave as the effect of her fits coming upon her, and was one of the many instances of her wonderful love to her and care of her, that she should not be affrighted, which, indeed, appears in her whole management, particularly in her coming to her in the daytime, waiving the salutation, and when she was alone; and then the manner of her parting, to prevent a second attempt to salute her.

Now, why Mr. Veal should think this relation a reflection—as it is plain he does, by his endeavoring to stifle it—I cannot imagine; because the generality believe her to be a good spirit, her discourse was so heavenly. Her two great errands were, to comfort Mrs. Bargrave in her affliction, and to ask her forgiveness for her breach of friendship, and with a pious discourse to encourage her. So that, after all, to suppose that Mrs. Bargrave could hatch such an invention as this, from Friday noon to Saturday noon—supposing that she knew of Mrs. Veal's death the very first moment—without jumbling circumstances, and without any interest, too, she must be more witty, fortunate, and wicked, too, than any indifferent person, I dare say, will allow. I asked Mrs. Bargrave several times if she was sure she felt the gown. She answered, modestly, "If my senses be to be relied on, I am sure of it." I asked her if she heard a sound when she clapped her hand upon her knee. She said she did not remember she did, but said she appeared to be as much a substance as I did who talked with her. "And I may," said she, "be as soon persuaded that your apparition is talking to me now as that I did not really see her; for I was under no manner of fear, and received her as a friend, and parted with her as such. I would not," says she, "give one farthing to make any one believe it; I have no interest in it; nothing but trouble is entailed upon me for a long time, for aught I know; and, had it not come to light by accident, it would never have been made public." But now she says she will make her own private use of it, and keep herself out of the way as much as she can; and so she has done since. She says she had a gentleman who came thirty miles to her to hear the relation; and that she had told it to a roomful of people at the time. Several particular gentlemen have had the story from Mrs. Bargrave's own mouth.

This thing has very much affected me, and I am as well satisfied as I am of the best-grounded matter of fact. And why we should dispute matter of fact, because we cannot solve things of which we can have no certain or demonstrative notions, seems strange to me; Mrs. Bargrave's authority and sincerity alone would have been undoubted in any other case.

ALICE ADDERTONGUE

Benjamin Franklin

MR. GAZETTEER,

I was highly pleased with your last Week's Paper upon SCANDAL, as the uncommon Doctrine therein preach'd is agreeable both to my Principles and Practice, and as it was published very seasonably to reprove the Impertinence of a Writer in the foregoing Thursday's *Mercury,* who at the Conclusion of one of his silly Paragraphs, laments, forsooth, that the Fair Sex are so peculiarly guilty of this enormous Crime: Every Blockhead ancient and modern, that could handle a Pen, has I think taken upon him to cant in the same sense-less Strain. If to scandalize be really a Crime, what do these Puppies mean? They describe it, they dress it up in the most odious frightful and detestable Colours, they represent it as the worst of Crimes, and then roundly and charitably charge the whole Race of Womankind with it. Are they not then guilty of what they con-demn, at the same time that they condemn it? If they accuse us of any other Crime, they must necessarily scandalize while they do it: But to scandalize us with being guilty of Scandal, is in itself an egregious Absurdity, and can proceed from nothing but the most consummate Impudence in Conjunction with the most profound Stupidity.

This, supposing, as they do, that to scandalize is a Crime; which you have convinc'd all reasonable People, is an Opinion absolutely erroneous. Let us leave then these Ideot Mock-Moralists, while I entertain you with some Account of my Life and Manners.

I am a young Girl of about thirty-five, and live at present with my Mother. I have no Care upon my Head of getting a Living, and therefore find it my Duty as well as Inclination, to exercise my

Talent at CENSURE, for the Good of my Country folks. There was, I am told, a certain generous Emperor, who if a Day had passed over his Head, in which he had conferred no Benefit on any Man, used to say to his Friends, in Latin, *Diem perdidi,* that is, it seems, I have lost a Day. I believe I should make use of the same Expression, if it were possible for a Day to pass in which I had not, or miss'd, an Opportunity to scandalize somebody: But, Thanks be praised, no such Misfortune has befel me these dozen Years.

Yet, whatever Good I may do, I cannot pretend that I first entred into the Practice of this Virtue from a Principle of Publick Spirit; for I remember that when a Child, I had a violent Inclination to be ever talking in my own Praise, and being continually told that it was ill Manners, and once severely whipt for it, the confin'd Stream form'd itself a new Channel, and I began to speak for the future in the Dispraise of others. This I found more agreable to Company, and almost as much so to my self: For what great Difference can there be, between putting your self up, or putting your Neighbour down? Scandal, like other Virtues, is in part its own Reward, as it gives us the Satisfaction of making our selves appear better than others, or others no better than ourselves.

My Mother, good Woman, and I, have heretofore differ'd upon this Account. She argu'd that Scandal spoilt all good Conversation, and I insisted that without it there could be no such Thing. Our Disputes once rose so high, that we parted Tea-Table, and I concluded to entertain my Acquaintance in the Kitchin. The first Day of this Separation we both drank Tea at the same Time, but she with her Visitors in the Parlor. She would not hear of the least Objection to any one's Character, but began a new sort of Discourse in some such queer philosophical Manner as this; I am mightily pleas'd sometimes, says she, when I observe and consider that the World is not so bad as People out of humour imagine it to be. There is something amiable, some good Quality or other in every body. If we were only to speak of People that are least respected, there is such a one is very dutiful to her Father, and methinks has a fine Set of Teeth; such a one is very respectful to her Husband; such a one is very kind to her poor Neighbours, and besides has a very handsome Shape; such a one is always ready to serve a Friend, and in my Opinion there is not a Woman in Town that has a more agreeable Air and Gait. This fine kind of Talk, which lasted near half an Hour, she concluded by saying, I do not doubt but every one of you have made the like Observations, and I should be glad to have the Conversation continu'd upon this Subject. Just at that Juncture I peep'd in at the Door, and never in my Life before saw such a Set of simple vacant Countenances; they looked somehow neither glad, nor sorry, nor angry, nor pleas'd, nor indifferent, nor attentive; but, (excuse the Simile) like so many blue wooden Images of Rie Doe. I in the Kitchin had already begun a ridiculous Story of Mr. —————'s Intrigue with his Maid, and his Wife's Behaviour upon the Discovery; at some Passages we laugh'd heartily, and one of the gravest of Mama's Company, without making any Answer to her Discourse, got up to go and see what the Girls were so merry about: She was follow'd by a Second, and shortly after by a Third, till at last the old Gentlewoman found herself quite alone, and being convinc'd that her Project was impracticable, came her self and finish'd her Tea with us; ever since which Saul also has been among the Prophets, and our Disputes lie dormant.

By Industry and Application, I have made my self the Center of all the Scandal in the Province, there is little stirring but I hear of it. I began the World with this Maxim, That no Trade can subsist without Returns; and accordingly, whenever I receiv'd a good Story, I endeavour'd to give two or a better in the Room of it. My Punctuality in this Way of Dealing gave such Encouragement, that it has procur'd me an incredible deal of Business, which without Diligence and good Method it would be impossible for me to go through. For besides the Stock of Defamation thus naturally flowing in upon me, I practice an Art by which I can pump Scandal out of People that are the least enclin'd that way. Shall I discover my Secret? Yes; to let it die with me would be inhuman.—If I have never heard Ill of some Person, I always impute it to defective Intelligence; for there are none without their Faults, no not one. If she is a Woman, I take the first Opportunity to let all her Acquaintance know I have heard that one of the handsomest or best Men in Town has said something in Praise either of her Beauty, her Wit, her Virtue, or her good Management. If you know any thing of Humane Nature, you perceive that this naturally introduces a Conversation turning upon all her Failings, past, present, and to come. To the same purpose, and with the same Success, I cause every Man of Reputation to be praised before his Competitors in Love, Business, or Esteem on Account of any particular Qualification.

Near the Times of Election, if I find it necessary, I commend every Candidate before some of the opposite Party, listning attentively to what is said of him in answer: (But Commendations in this latter Case are not always necessary, and should be used judiciously;) of late Years I needed only observe what they said of one another freely; and having for the Help of Memory taken Account of all Information & Accusations received, whoever peruses my Writings after my Death, may happen to think, that during a certain Term, the People of Pennsylvania chose into all their Offices of Honour and Trust, the veriest Knaves, Fools and Rascals in the whole Province. The Time of Election used to be a busy Time with me, but this Year, with Concern I speak it, People are grown so good natur'd, so intent upon mutual Feasting and friendly Entertainment, that I see no Prospect of much Employment from that Quarter.

I mention'd above, that without good Method I could not go thro' my Business: In my Father's Life-time I had some Instruction in Accompts, which I now apply with Advantage to my own Affairs. I keep a regular Set of Books, and can tell at an Hour's Warning how it stands between me and the World. In my Daybook I enter every Article of Defamation as it is transacted; for Scandals receiv'd in, I give Credit; and when I pay them out again, I make the Persons to whom they respectively relate Debtor. In my Journal, I add to each Story by Way of Improvement, such probable Circumstances as I think it will bear, and in my Ledger the whole is regularly posted.

I suppose the Reader already condemns me in his Heart, for this particular of adding Circumstances; but I justify that part of my Practice thus. 'Tis a Principle with me, that none ought to have a greater Share of Reputation than they really deserve; if they have, 'tis an Imposition upon the Publick: I know it is every one's Interest, and therefore believe they endeavour, to conceal all their Vices and Follies; and I hold, that those People are extraordinary foolish or careless who suffer a Fourth of their Failings to come to publick Knowledge: Taking then the common Prudence and Imprudence of Mankind in a Lump, I suppose none suffer above one Fifth to be discovered: Therefore when I hear of any Person's Misdoing, I think I keep within Bounds if in relating it I only make it three times worse than it is; and I reserve to my self the Privilege of charging them with one Fault in four, which, for aught I know, they may be entirely innocent of. You see there are but few so careful of doing Justice as my self; what Reason then have Mankind to complain of Scandal? In a general way, the worst that is said of us is only half what might be said, if all our Faults were seen.

But alas, two great Evils have lately befaln me at the same time; an extream Cold that I can scarce speak, and a most terrible Toothach that I dare hardly open my Mouth: For some Days past I have receiv'd ten Stories for one I have paid; and I am not able to ballance my Accounts without your Assistance. I have long thought that if you would make your Paper a Vehicle of Scandal, you would double the Number of your Subscribers. I send you herewith Account of 4 Knavish Tricks, 2 crackt M—n—ds, 5 Cu—ld—ms, 3 drub'd Wives, and 4 Henpeck'd Husbands, all within this Fortnight; which you may, as Articles of News, deliver to the Publick; and if my Toothach continues, shall send you more; being, in the mean time,

Your constant Reader,
ALICE ADDERTONGUE

I thank my Correspondent Mrs. Addertongue for her Good-Will; but desire to be excus'd inserting the Articles of News she has sent me; such Things being in Reality no News at all.

THE DEVIL AND TOM WALKER

Washington Irving

A FEW MILES from Boston in Massachusetts, there is a deep inlet, winding several miles into the interior of the country from Charles Bay, and terminating in a thickly-wooded swamp or morass. On one side of this inlet is a beautiful dark grove; on the opposite side the land rises abruptly from the water's edge into a high ridge, on which grow a few scattered oaks of great age and immense size. Under one of these gigantic trees, according to old stories, there was a great amount of treasure buried by Kidd the pirate. The inlet allowed a facility to bring the money in a boat secretly and at night to the very foot of the hill; the elevation of the place permitted a good lookout to be kept that no one was at hand; while the remarkable trees formed good landmarks by which the place might easily be found again. The old stories add, moreover, that the devil presided at the hiding of the money, and took it under his guardianship; but this, it is well known, he always does with buried treasure, particularly when it has been ill-gotten. Be that as it may, Kidd never returned to recover his wealth; being shortly after seized at Boston, sent out to England, and there hanged for a pirate.

About the year 1727, just at the time that earthquakes were prevalent in New England, and shook many tall sinners down upon their knees, there lived near this place a meagre, miserly fellow of the name of Tom Walker. He had a wife as miserly as himself: they were so miserly that they even conspired to cheat each other. Whatever the woman could lay hands on, she hid away; a hen could not cackle but she was on the alert to secure the new-laid egg. Her husband was continually prying about to detect her secret hoards, and many and fierce were the conflicts that took place about what ought to have been common property. They lived in a forlorn-looking house, that stood alone, and had an air of starvation. A few straggling savin-trees, emblems of sterility, grew near it; no smoke ever curled from its chimney; no traveller stopped at its door. A miserable horse, whose ribs were as articulate as the bars of a gridiron, stalked about a field where a thin carpet of moss, scarcely covering the ragged beds of pudding-stone, tantalized and balked his hunger; and sometimes he would lean his head over the fence, look piteously at the passer-by, and seem to petition deliverance from this land of famine.

The house and its inmates had altogether a bad name. Tom's wife was a tall termagant, fierce of temper, loud of tongue, and strong of arm. Her voice was often heard in wordy warfare with her husband; and his face sometimes showed signs that their conflicts were not confined to words. No one ventured, however, to interfere between them. The lonely wayfarer shrunk within himself at the horrid clamor and clapper-clawing; eyed the den of discord askance; and hurried on his way, rejoicing, if a bachelor, in his celibacy.

One day that Tom Walker had been to a distant part of the neighborhood, he took what he considered a short cut homeward, through the swamp. Like most short cuts, it was an ill-chosen route. The swamp was thickly grown with great gloomy pines and hemlocks, some of them ninety feet high, which made it dark at noonday, and a retreat for all the owls of the neighborhood. It was full of pits and quagmires, partly covered with weeds and mosses, where the green surface often betrayed the traveller into a gulf of black smothering mud: there were also dark and stagnant pools, the abodes of the tadpole, the bull-frog, and the water-snake, where the trunks of pines and hemlocks lay half-drowned, half-rotting, looking like alligators sleeping in the mire.

Tom had long been picking his way cautiously through this treacherous forest; stepping from tuft to tuft of rushes and roots, which afforded precarious foothold among deep sloughs; or pacing carefully, like a cat, along the prostrate trunks of trees; startled now and then by the sudden screaming of the bittern, or the quacking of a wild duck rising on the wing from some solitary pool. At length he arrived at a firm piece of ground, which ran out like a peninsula into the deep bosom of the swamp. It had been one of the strongholds of the Indians during their wars with the first colonists. Here they had thrown up a kind of fort, which they had looked upon as almost impregnable, and had used as a place of refuge for their squaws and children. Nothing remained of the old Indian fort but a few embankments, gradually sinking to the level of the surrounding earth, and already overgrown in part by oaks and other forest trees, the foliage of which formed a contrast to the dark pines and hemlocks of the swamp.

It was late in the dusk of evening that Tom Walker reached the old fort, and he paused there for awhile to rest himself. Any one but he would have felt unwilling to linger in this lonely, melancholy place, for the common people had a bad opinion of it, from the stories handed down from the time of the Indian wars; when it was asserted that the savages held incantations here, and made sacrifices to the evil spirit.

Tom Walker, however, was not a man to be troubled with any fears of the kind. He reposed himself for some time on the trunk of a fallen hemlock, listening to the boding cry of the tree-toad, and delving with his walking-staff into a mound of black mould at his feet. As he turned up the soil unconsciously, his staff struck against something hard. He raked it out of the vegetable mould, and lo! a cloven skull, with an Indian tomahawk buried deep in it, lay before him. The rust on the weapon showed the time that had elapsed since this death blow had been given. It was a dreary memento of the fierce struggle that had taken place in this last foothold of the Indian warriors.

"Humph!" said Tom Walker, as he gave it a kick to shake the dirt from it.

"Let that skull alone!" said a gruff voice. Tom lifted up his eyes, and beheld a great black man seated directly opposite him, on the stump of a tree. He was exceedingly surprised, having neither heard nor seen any one approach; and he was still more perplexed on observing, as well as the gathering gloom would permit, that the stranger was neither negro nor Indian. It is true he was dressed in a rude half Indian garb, and had a red belt or sash swathed round his body, but his face was neither black nor copper-color, but swarthy and dingy and begrimed with soot, as if he had been accustomed to toil among fires and forges. He had a shock of coarse black hair, that stood out from his head in all directions, and bore an axe on his shoulder.

He scowled for a moment at Tom with a pair of great red eyes.

"What are you doing in my grounds?" said the black man, with a hoarse growling voice.

"Your grounds!" said Tom, with a sneer, "no more your grounds than mine: they belong to Deacon Peabody."

"Deacon Peabody be d——d," said the stranger, "as I flatter myself he will be, if he does not look more to his own sins and less to those of his neighbors. Look yonder, and see how Deacon Peabody is faring."

Tom looked in the direction that the stranger pointed and beheld one of the great trees, fair and flourishing without, but rotten at the core, and saw that it had been nearly hewn through, so that the first high wind was likely to below it down. On the bark of the tree was scored the name of Deacon Peabody, an eminent man, who had waxed wealthy by driving shrewd bargains with the Indians. He now looked around, and found most of the tall trees marked with the name of some great man of the colony, and all more or less scored by the axe. The one on which he had been seated, and which had evidently just been hewn down, bore the name of Crowninshield; and he recollected a mighty rich man of that name, who made a vulgar display of wealth, which it was whispered he had acquired by buccaneering.

"He's just ready for burning!" said the black man with a growl of triumph. "You see I am likely to have a good stock of firewood for winter."

"But what right have you," said Tom, "to cut down Deacon Peabody's timber?"

"The right of a prior claim," said the other. "This woodland belonged to me long before one of your white-faced race put foot upon the soil."

"And pray, who are you, if I may be so bold?" said Tom.

"Oh, I go by various names. I am the wild huntsman in some countries; the black miner in others. In this neighborhood I am known by the name of the black woodsman. I am he to whom the red men devoted this spot, and in honor of whom they now and then roasted a white man, by way of sweet-smelling sacrifice. Since the red men have been exterminated by you white savages, I amuse myself by presiding at the persecutions of Quakers and Anabaptists; I am the great patron and prompter of slave-dealers, and the grand-master of the Salem witches."

"The upshot of all which is, that, if I mistake not," said Tom, sturdily, "you are he commonly called Old Scratch."

"The same at your service!" replied the black man, with a half civil nod.

Such was the opening of this interview, according to the old story; though it has almost too familiar an air to be credited. One would think that to meet with such a singular personage, in this wild lonely place, would have shaken any man's nerves; but Tom was a hard-minded fellow, not easily daunted, and he had lived so long with a termagant wife, that he did not even fear the devil.

It is said that after this commencement they had a long and earnest conversation together, as Tom returned homeward. The black man told him of great sums of money buried by Kidd the pirate, under the oak-trees on the high ridge, not far from the morass. All these were under his command and protected by his power, so that none could find them but such as propitiated his favour. These he offered to place within Tom Walker's reach, having conceived an especial kindness for him: but they were to be had only on certain conditions. What these conditions were may be easily surmised, though Tom never disclosed them publicly. They must have been very hard, for he required time to think of them, and he was not a man to stick at trifles where money was in view. When they had reached the edge of the swamp, the stranger paused. "What proof have I that all you have been telling me is true?" said Tom. "There's my signature," said the black man, pressing his finger on Tom's forehead. So saying, he turned off among the thickets of the swamp, and seemed, as Tom said, to go down, down, down, into the earth, until nothing but his head and shoulders could be seen, and so on until he totally disappeared.

When Tom reached home, he found the black print of a finger burnt, as it were, into his forehead, which nothing could obliterate.

The first news his wife had to tell him was the sudden death of Absalom Crowninshield, the rich buccaneer. It was announced in the papers with the usual flourish, that "A great man had fallen in Israel."

Tom recollected the tree which his black friend had just hewn down, and which was ready for burning. "Let the freebooter roast," said Tom, "who cares!" He now felt convinced that all he had heard and seen was no illusion.

He was not prone to let his wife into his confidence; but as this was an uneasy secret, he willingly shared it with her. All her avarice was awakened at the mention of hidden gold, and she urged her husband to comply with the black man's terms, and secure what would make them wealthy for life. However Tom might have felt disposed to sell himself to the Devil, he was determined not to do so to oblige his wife; so he flatly refused, out of the mere spirit of contradiction. Many and bitter were the quarrels they had on the subject, but the more she talked, the more resolute was Tom not to be damned to please her.

At length she determined to drive the bargain on her own account, and if she succeeded, to keep all the gain to herself. Being of the same fearless temper as her husband, she set off for the old Indian fort towards the close of a summer's day. She was many hours absent. When she came back, she was reserved and sullen in her replies. She spoke something of a black man, whom she had met about twilight hewing at the root of a tall tree. He was sulky, however, and would not come to terms: she was to go again with a propitiatory offering, but what it was she forebore to say.

The next evening she set off again for the swamp, with her apron heavily laden. Tom waited and waited for her, but in vain; midnight came, but she did not make her appearance: morning, noon, night returned, but still she did not come. Tom now grew uneasy for her safety, especially as he found she had carried off in her apron the silver tea-pot and spoons and every portable article of value. Another night elapsed, another morning came; but no wife. In a word, she was never heard of more.

What was her real fate nobody knows, in consequence of so many pretending to know. It is one of those facts which have become confounded by a variety of historians. Some asserted that she lost her way among the tangled mazes of the swamp, and sunk into some pit or slough; others, more uncharitable, hinted that she had eloped with the household booty, and made off to some other province; while others surmised that the tempter had decoyed her into a dismal quagmire, on top of which her hat was found lying. In confirmation of this, it was said a great black man, with an axe on his shoulder, was seen late that very evening coming out of the swamp, carrying a bundle tied in a check apron, with an air of surly triumph.

The most current and probable story, however, observes that Tom Walker grew so anxious about the fate of his wife and his property, that he set out at length to seek them both at the Indian fort. During a long summer's afternoon he searched about the gloomy place, but no wife was to be seen. He called her name repeatedly, but she was nowhere to be heard. The bittern alone responded to his voice, as he flew screaming by; or the bull-frog croaked dolefully from a neighboring pool. At length, it is said, just in the brown hour of twilight, when the owls began to hoot, and the bats to flit about, his attention was attracted by the clamor of carrion crows hovering about a cypress-tree. He looked up, and beheld a bundle tied in a check apron, and hanging in the branches of the tree, with a great vulture perched hard by, as if keeping watch upon it. He leaped with joy; for he recognized his wife's apron, and supposed it to contain the household valuables.

"Let us get hold of the property," said he, consolingly to himself, "and we will endeavor to do without the woman."

As he scrambled up the tree, the vulture spread its wide wings, and sailed off, screaming, into the deep shadows of the forest. Tom seized the check apron, but, woful sight! found nothing but a heart and liver tied up in it!

Such, according to the most authentic old story, was all that was to be found of Tom's wife. She had probably attempted to deal with the black man as she had been accustomed to deal with her husband; but though a female scold is generally considered a match for the devil, yet in this instance she appears to have had the worst of it. She must have died game, however; for it is said Tom noticed many prints of cloven feet deeply stamped about the tree, and found handfuls of hair, that looked as if they had been plucked from the coarse black shock of the woodman. Tom knew his wife's prowess by experience. He shrugged his shoulders, as he looked at the signs of a fierce clapper-clawing. "Egad," said he to himself, "Old Scratch must have had a tough time of it!"

Tom consoled himself for the loss of his property, with the loss of his wife, for he was a man of fortitude. He even felt something like gratitude towards the black woodman, who, he considered, had done him a kindness. He sought, therefore, to cultivate a further acquaintance with him, but for some time without success; the old black-legs played shy, for whatever people may think, he is not always to be had for calling for: he knows how to play his cards when pretty sure of his game.

At length, it is said, when delay had whetted Tom's eagerness to the quick, and prepared him to agree to anything rather than not gain the promised treasure, he met the black man one evening in his usual woodman's dress, with his axe on his shoulder, sauntering along the swamp, and humming a tune. He affected to receive Tom's advance with great indifference, made brief replies, and went on humming his tune.

By degrees, however, Tom brought him to business, and they began to haggle about the terms on which the former was to have the pirate's treasure. There was one condition which need not be mentioned, being generally understood in all cases where the devil grants favors; but there were others about which, though of less importance, he was inflexibly obstinate. He insisted that the money found through his means should be employed in his service. He proposed, therefore, that Tom should employ it in the black traffic; that is to say, that he should fit out a slave-ship. This, however, Tom resolutely refused; he was bad enough in all conscience; but the devil himself could not tempt him to turn slave-trader.

Finding Tom so squeamish on this point, he did not insist upon it, but proposed, instead, that he should turn usurer; the devil being extremely anxious for the increase of usurers, looking upon them as his peculiar people.

To this no objections were made, for it was just to Tom's taste.

"You shall open a broker's shop in Boston next month," said the black man.

"I'll do it to-morrow, if you wish," said Tom Walker.

"You shall lend money at two per cent. a month."

"Egad, I'll charge four!" replied Tom Walker.

"You shall extort bonds, foreclose mortgages, drive the merchant to bankruptcy—"

"I'll drive him to the d——l," cried Tom Walker.

"You are the usurer for my money!" said the black-legs, with delight. "When will you want the rhino?"

"This very night."

"Done!" said the devil.

"Done!" said Tom Walker.—So they shook hands and struck a bargain.

A few days' time saw Tom Walker seated behind his desk in a counting-house in Boston.

His reputation for a ready-moneyed man, who would lend money out for a good consideration, soon spread abroad. Everybody remembers the time of Governor Belcher, when money was particularly scarce. It was a time of paper credit. The country had been deluged with government bills, the famous Land Bank had been established; there had been a rage for speculating; the people had run mad with schemes for new settlements; for building cities in the wilderness; land-jobbers went about with maps of grants, and townships, and Eldorados, lying nobody knew where, but which everybody was ready to purchase. In a word, the great speculating fever which breaks out every now and then in the country, had raged to an alarming degree, and everybody was dreaming of making sudden fortunes from nothing. As usual the fever had subsided; the dream had gone off, and the imaginary fortunes with it; the patients were left in doleful plight, and the whole country resounded with the consequent cry of "hard times."

At this propitious time of public distress did Tom Walker set up as a usurer in Boston. His door was soon thronged by customers. The needy and adventurous; the gambling speculator; the dreaming land-jobber; the thriftless tradesman; the merchant with cracked credit; in short, every one driven to raise money by desperate means and desperate sacrifices, hurried to Tom Walker.

Thus Tom was the universal friend of the needy, and acted like a "friend in need"; that is to say, he always exacted good pay and good security. In proportion to the distress of the applicant was the hardness of his terms. He accumulated bonds and mortgages; gradually squeezed his customers closer and closer: and sent them at length, dry as a sponge from his door.

In this way he made money hand over hand; became a rich and mighty man, and exalted his cocked hat upon Change. He built himself, as usual, a vast house, out of ostentation; but left the greater part of it unfinished and unfurnished, out of parsimony. He even set up a carriage in the fullness of his vainglory, though he nearly starved the horses which drew it; and as the ungreased wheels groaned and screeched on the axletrees, you would have thought you heard the souls of the poor debtors he was squeezing.

As Tom waxed old, however, he grew thoughtful. Having secured the good things of this world, he began to feel anxious about those of the next. He thought with regret on the bargain he had made with his black friend, and set his wits to work to cheat him out of the conditions. He became, therefore, all of a sudden, a violent churchgoer. He prayed loudly and strenuously as if heaven were to be taken by force of lungs. Indeed, one might always tell when he had sinned most during the week, by the clamor of his Sunday devotion. The quiet Christians who had been modestly and steadfastly travelling Zionward, were struck with self-reproach at seeing themselves so suddenly outstripped in their career by this new-made convert. Tom was as rigid in religious as in money matters; he was a stern supervisor and censurer of his neighbors, and seemed to think every sin entered up to their account became a credit on his own side of the page. He even talked of the expediency of reviving the persecution of Quakers and Anabaptists. In a word, Tom's zeal became as notorious as his riches.

Still, in spite of all this strenuous attention to forms, Tom had a lurking dread that the devil, after all, would have his due. That he might not be taken unawares, therefore, it is said he always carried a small Bible in his coat-pocket. He had also a great folio Bible on his counting-house desk, and would frequently be found reading it when people called on business; on such occasions he would lay his green spectacles on the book, to mark the place, while he turned round to drive some usurious bargain.

Some say that Tom grew a little crack-brained in his old days, and that, fancying his end approaching, he had his horse new shod, saddled and bridled, and buried with his feet uppermost; because he supposed that at the last day the world would be turned upside down; in which case he should find his horse standing ready for mounting, and he was determined at the worst to give his old friend a run for it. This, however, is probably a mere old wives' fable. If he really did take such a precaution it was totally superfluous; at least so says the authentic old legend which closes his story in the following manner.

One hot summer afternoon in the dog-days, just as a terrible black thunder-gust was coming up, Tom sat in his counting-house in his white linen cap and India silk morning-gown. He was on the point of foreclosing a mortgage, by which he would complete the ruin of an unlucky land-speculator for whom he had professed the greatest friendship. The poor land-jobber begged him to grant a few months' indulgence. Tom had grown testy and irritated, and refused another day.

"My family will be ruined, and brought upon the parish," said the land-jobber. "Charity begins at home," replied Tom; "I must take care of myself in these hard times."

"You have made so much money out of me," said the speculator.

Tom lost his patience and his piety. "The devil take me," said he, "if I have made a farthing!"

Just then there were three loud knocks at the street-door. He stepped out to see who was there. A black man was holding a black horse, which neighed and stamped with impatience.

"Tom, you're come for," said the black fellow, gruffly. Tom shrunk back, but too late. He had left his little Bible at the bottom of his coat-pocket, and his big Bible on the desk buried under the mortgage he was about to foreclose: never was sinner taken more unawares. The black man whisked him like a child into the saddle, gave the horse the lash, and away he galloped, with Tom on his back, in the midst of a thunder-storm. The clerks stuck their pens behind their ears, and stared after him from the windows. Away went Tom Walker, dashing down the streets; his white cap bobbing up and down; his morning-gown fluttering in the wind, and his steed striking fire out of the pavement at every bound. When the clerks turned to look for the black man, he had disappeared.

Tom Walker never returned to foreclose the mortgage. A countryman who lived on the border of the swamp, reported that in the height of the thunder-gust he had heard a great clattering of hoofs and a howling along the road, and running to the window just caught sight of a figure, such as I have described, on a horse that galloped like mad across the fields, over the hills, and down into the black hemlock swamp towards the old Indian fort; and that shortly after a thunder-bolt fell in that direction which seemed to set the whole forest in a blaze.

The good people of Boston shook their heads and shrugged their shoulders, but had been so much accustomed to witches and goblins, and tricks of the devil, in all kinds of shapes, from the first settlement of the colony, that they were not so much horror struck as might have been expected. Trustees were appointed to take charge of Tom's effects. There was nothing, however, to administer upon. On searching his coffers, all his bonds and mortgages were found reduced to cinders. In place of gold and silver his iron chest was filled with chips and shavings; two skeletons lay in his stable instead of his half-starved horses, and the very next day his great house took fire and was burnt to the ground.

Such was the end of Tom Walker and his ill-gotten wealth. Let all griping money-brokers lay this story to heart. The truth of it is not to be doubted. The very hole under the oak-trees, from whence he dug Kidd's money, is to be seen to this day; and the neighboring swamp and old Indian fort are often haunted in stormy nights by a figure on horseback, in a morning-gown and white cap, which is doubtless the troubled spirit of the usurer. In fact, the story has resolved itself into a proverb, and is the origin of that popular saying, prevalent throughout New England, of "The Devil and Tom Walker."

PROSPER MÉRIMÉE

Mateo Falcone

LEAVING PORTO-VECCHIO AND heading northwest, toward the interior of the island, you see the terrain rising quite rapidly; and after walking three hours along twisting paths, obstructed by large boulders and sometimes intersected by ravines, you find yourself at the edge of a very extensive area of brushwood. This brush is the home of the Corsican shepherds and of anyone who has fallen afoul of the law. You must know that the Corsican farmer, to save himself the trouble of manuring his field, sets fire to a certain stretch of forest: it's just too bad if the flames spread farther than necessary—let things take their course!—hell be sure to have a good crop if he sows on that soil fertilized by the ashes of the trees that once grew on it. After the ears of grain are removed—they leave the stalks, which would be bothersome to gather—the roots that have remained in the soil without being burned put out shoots the following spring, very thick clusters that in a very few years reach a height of seven or eight feet. It is this type of dense underbrush that is called *maquis*. It is made up of various species of trees and bushes, mingled and confused as God wishes. A man can only open a passage through it with an axe in his hands, and you can find areas of brush so thick and close that even the wild sheep can't penetrate them.

If you've killed a man, go to the Porto-Vecchio *maquis,* and you'll be safe there with a good rifle, powder, and bullets; don't forget a brown cape furnished with a hood,[1] which serves as a blanket and a mattress. The shepherds will give you milk, cheese, and chestnuts, and you'll have nothing to fear from the law or the dead

---

[1] Pilone.

man's relatives, except when you have to go down to the town to get more ammunition there.

When I was in Corsica in 18—, Mateo Falcone's house was located half a league from this *maquis*. He was rather wealthy for that vicinity, living like a nobleman—that is, he did no work himself, but lived off the produce of his flocks, which shepherds of a nomadic type led out to graze here and there in the mountains. When I saw him, two years after the event I'm about to narrate, he seemed to me to be fifty at the very most. Picture a short but robust man with frizzy hair as black as jet, an aquiline nose, thin lips, large, alert eyes, and a complexion the color of boot tops. His skill with a rifle was deemed extraordinary, even in his country, where there are so many good shots. For example, Mateo would never have fired at a wild sheep with buckshot, but, at a hundred twenty paces, he would bring it down with a bullet in the head or shoulder, just as he chose. He used his weapons at night as easily as by day, and I've been told about a feat of his that may seem incredible to those who haven't visited Corsica. At eighty paces, a lighted candle was placed behind a sheet of translucent paper the width of a plate. He took aim, then the candle was extinguished, and after a minute in the most total darkness, he would fire, hitting the paper three times out of four.

With such transcendent merit, Mateo Falcone had acquired a great reputation. He was said to be as good to have as a friend as he was dangerous to have as an enemy: helpful and charitable besides, he lived at peace with everyone in the Porto-Vecchio district. But the story was told of him that, in Corte, where he had taken a wife, he had most vigorously gotten rid of a rival said to be as formidable in war as in love: at least, Mateo was credited with a certain rifle shot that took this rival by surprise as he was shaving in front of a small mirror hanging in his window. When the matter had quieted down, Mateo married. His wife, Giuseppa, had at first given him three daughters (which made him furious), but finally a son, whom he named Fortunato: he was the hope of the family, the heir to his name. The girls had made good marriages: their father could count on the daggers and blunder-busses of his sons-in-law in an emergency. The son was only ten, but he already gave promise of gratifying natural gifts.

On a certain autumn day, Mateo went out early with his wife to visit one of his flocks in a clearing in the *maquis*. Little Fortunato wanted to accompany him, but the clearing was too far; besides, it was necessary for someone to stay and guard the house; thus, his father refused: we shall see whether he didn't have occasion to regret it.

He had been gone for several hours, and little Fortunato was peacefully stretched out in the sun, looking at the blue mountains and thinking that, on the following Sunday, he would go and dine in town at the home of his uncle the *caporale*[2] when he was suddenly interrupted in his meditations by the report of a firearm. He got up and turned toward the direction in the plain from which that sound had come. Other rifle shots followed, fired at unequal intervals, and coming nearer and nearer all the time; at last, on the path that led from the plain to Mateo's house, there appeared a man wearing a pointed cap like those worn by mountaineers; he was bearded, covered with rags, and dragging himself along painfully, using his rifle for support. He had just been shot in the thigh.

This man was a bandit[3] who had set out at night to get gunpowder in town and, on the way, had fallen into an ambush laid by Corsican light infantrymen.[4] After defending himself vigorously, he had managed to beat a retreat, eagerly pursued and taking pot shots from one boulder to another. But he wasn't far ahead of the soldiers, and his wound made him incapable of reaching the *maquis* before they caught up with him.

He approached Fortunato and said:

"You're the son of Mateo Falcone?"

"Yes."

"I'm Gianetto Sanpiero. I'm being pursued by the yellow collars.[5] Hide me, because I can't go any farther."

"And what will my father say if I hide you without his permission?"

"He'll say you did the right thing."

"Who knows?"

---

[2] The *caporali* were formerly the chiefs appointed by the Corsican commoners when they revolted against their feudal lords. Today, this name is still sometimes given to a man who, through his property and his connections by marriage and in business, exerts an influence and a sort of *de facto* magistracy over a *pieve* or a canton. By ancient custom, Corsicans are divided into five castes: gentlemen (of whom some are *magnifici*, others *signori*), *caporali*, citizens, plebeians, and foreigners.

[3] Here this word is synonymous with "outlaw."

[4] This is a corps formed by the government only a few years ago; it polices the countryside concurrently with the gendarmerie.

[5] At the time the uniform of these *voltigeurs* was a brown outfit with a yellow collar.

"Hide me fast; they're coming."

"Wait for my father to get back."

"Wait? Damnation! They'll be here in five minutes. Come on, hide me, or I'll kill you."

Fortunato replied with the greatest coolness:

"Your rifle is unloaded and there are no more cartridges in your *carchera*."[6]

"I have my stiletto."

"But will you run as fast as me?"

He made a jump, placing himself out of reach.

"You're not the son of Mateo Falcone! So you'll let me be arrested in front of your house?"

The child seemed to be affected by this.

"What'll you give me if I hide you?" he asked, coming closer.

The bandit groped through a leather pouch that hung from his belt, and pulled out a five-franc piece that he had no doubt kept to buy powder with. Fortunato smiled when he saw the silver coin; he seized it, saying to Gianetto:

"Don't worry about a thing."

At once he made a large hole in a haystack located near the house. Gianetto huddled in it, and the child covered him up in such a way that he left him a little air to breathe, but it was nevertheless impossible to suspect that the hay concealed a man. On top of that, he thought of a primitive ruse that was quite ingenious. He went and got a cat and her kittens and placed them on the haystack to give the impression that it hadn't been touched recently. Next, noticing traces of blood on the path near the house, he carefully covered them with dust; after that, he lay down in the sun again as calmly as could be.

A few minutes later, six men in brown uniforms with yellow collars, commanded by a sergeant-major, stood in front of Mateo's door. This sergeant was very slightly related to Falcone. (As is well known, in Corsica degrees of kinship are traced much further than elsewhere.) His name was Tiodoro Gamba; he was an active man, much dreaded by the bandits, several of whom he had already tracked down.

"Hello, little cousin," he said to Fortunato, coming up to him, "My, but you've grown! Did you see a man go by a little while ago?"

---

[6] A leather belt that serves as a cartridge pouch and wallet.

"Oh! I'm still not as big as you, cousin," the child replied, playing the simpleton.

"You'll get there. But, tell me, didn't you see a man go by?"

"Did I see a man go by?"

"Yes, a man with a black-velvet pointed cap and a jacket embroidered in red and yellow."

"A man with a pointed cap and a jacket embroidered in red and yellow?"

"Yes, answer fast, and don't repeat my questions."

"This morning the parish priest passed by our door on his horse Piero. He asked me how Papa was feeling, and I told him . . ."

"Ah, you little scamp, you're trying to be smart! Tell me quickly which way Gianetto went—he's the one we're looking for—and I'm sure he took this path."

"Who knows?"

"Who knows? *I* know that you saw him."

"Do you see people pass by when you're sleeping?"

"You weren't sleeping, you scamp; the rifle shots woke you up."

"Cousin, do you really think your rifles make so much noise? My father's blunderbuss makes much more."

"The devil take you, you damned brat! I'm sure you saw Gianetto. Maybe you even hid him. Come on, men, go into this house and see if our man isn't there. He was walking on only one leg and he has too much good sense, the rogue, to have tried to reach the *maquis* hobbling along. Besides, the trail of blood stops here."

"And what will Papa say?" Fortunato asked, snickering. "What will he say if he finds out his house has been entered while he was out?"

"Rascal!" said Sergeant Gamba, taking him by the ear. "Do you realize it's only up to me to make you change your tune? Maybe if I give you twenty blows with the flat of my saber, you'll finally talk."

And Fortunato kept on snickering.

"My father is Mateo Falcone!" he said, significantly.

"Little scamp, do you realize that I can take you to Corte or Bastia? I'll stretch you out in a dungeon, on straw, with irons on your feet, and I'll have you guillotined if you don't tell me where Gianetto Sanpiero is."

The child burst out laughing at that ridiculous threat. He repeated:

"My father is Mateo Falcone!"

"Sergeant," one of the infantrymen said quietly, "let's not get on the wrong side of Mateo."

Gamba looked obviously embarrassed. He chatted in a low voice with his soldiers, who had already inspected the whole house. This wasn't a very long procedure, because a Corsican's hut consists of a single square room. The furniture is comprised of a table, benches, chests, and hunting and household utensils. Meanwhile, little Fortunato was petting his cat, seeming to take malicious satisfaction in the embarrassment of the infantrymen and his cousin.

A soldier approached the haystack. He saw the cat, and negligently stabbed the hay with his bayonet, shrugging his shoulders as if he felt his precaution was laughable. Nothing stirred: and the child's face betrayed not the slightest emotion.

The sergeant and his troop were in despair: by this time they were looking seriously in the direction of the plain, as if disposed to go back where they had come from—when their leader, convinced that threats would have no effect on Falcone's son, decided to make one last effort and try out the power of blandishments and presents.

"Little cousin," he said, "you look to me like a really sharp fellow! You'll go places. But the game you're playing with me is a nasty one; and if I weren't afraid of hurting my cousin Mateo, devil take me if I didn't lead you away with me."

"Bah!"

"But when my cousin is back, I'll tell him what happened, and to punish you for lying, he'll whip you till he draws blood."

"How's that?"

"You'll see . . . But wait . . . Be a good boy and I'll give you something."

"As for me, cousin, I'll give you a piece of advice: if you wait any longer, Gianetto will be in the *maquis,* and then it'll take more than one strapping fellow like you to go get him there."

The sergeant drew from his pocket a silver watch that was worth at least thirty francs; and, observing that little Fortunato's eyes sparkled when he looked at it, he dangled the watch from the end of its steel chain, saying:

"Scalawag! You'd surely like to have a watch like this hanging from your neck while you promenaded through the streets of Porto-Vecchio, proud as a peacock, with people asking you,' What time is it?' and you saying, 'Look at my watch and see.'"

"When I grow up, my uncle the *caporale* will give me a watch."

"Yes, but your uncle's son already has one . . . not as beautiful as this one, it's true . . . But he's younger than you."

The child sighed.

"Well, little cousin, do you want this watch?"

Fortunato, stealing sidelong glances at the watch from the corner of his eye, looked like a cat that was being offered a whole chicken. Since it feels it is being made fun of, it doesn't dare put its claws on it, and from time to time it turns away its eyes to avoid succumbing to the temptation; but every moment it licks its chops, seeming to say to its master:

"How cruel your joke is!"

And yet Sergeant Gamba appeared to be acting in good faith in offering his watch. Fortunato didn't reach out for it, but he said with a bitter smile:

"Why are you ribbing me?"[7]

"By God, I'm not ribbing you. Just tell me where Gianetto is, and this watch is yours."

Fortunato emitted a sigh of disbelief, and, with his dark eyes staring directly into the sergeant's, he strove to see how much trust he ought to repose in his words.

"May I lose my epaulets," the sergeant exclaimed, "if I don't give you the watch on those terms! My comrades are witnesses, and I can't go back on my word."

While saying this, he kept moving the watch nearer until it almost touched the child's pale cheek. The boy's face clearly showed the struggle being waged in his soul between greed and respect for the laws of hospitality. His bare chest was heaving mightily, and he seemed close to choking. Meanwhile the watch was swinging, turning, and at times striking the tip of his nose. Finally, little by little, his right hand rose in the direction of the watch; he touched it with his fingertips; and it was resting in his hand with its full weight, although the sergeant didn't release the end of the chain . . . The dial was blue . . . the case newly polished . . . in the sunlight, it seemed to be all ablaze . . . The temptation was too strong.

Fortunato raised his left hand, too, and with his thumb pointed over his shoulder at the haystack on which he was leaning. The sergeant understood him at once. He let go of the end of the chain;

---

[7] *Perchè me c . . . ?*

Fortunato realized he was sole possessor of the watch. He rose with the agility of a deer and moved ten paces away from the haystack, which the infantrymen immediately began to knock over.

Before long they saw the hay moving, and a bleeding man, dagger in hand, came out; but, when he tried to stand up, his stiffened wound made it impossible to keep his feet any longer. He fell. The sergeant pounced on him and tore his stiletto from him. At once he was tightly bound hand and foot despite his resistance.

Gianetto, lying on the ground, trussed up like a bundle of firewood, turned his head toward Fortunato, who had come up to him.

"Son of a . . .!" he said, with more contempt than anger.

The child threw at him the silver coin he had received from him, feeling that he no longer deserved it; but the outlaw seemed to pay no heed to that action. As calmly as possible he said to the sergeant:

"My friend Gamba, I can't walk; you're going to have to carry me to town."

"Just a while ago you were running faster than a roebuck," the cruel victor retorted; "but relax: I'm so happy over catching you that I'd carry you a league on my back without getting tired. Anyway, comrade, we're going to make you a litter out of branches and your cloak, and at the Crespoli farm we'll find horses."

"Good," said the prisoner, "and put a little straw on your litter so I'll be more comfortable."

While the infantrymen were busy, some making a sort of stretcher out of chestnut branches, and the others dressing Gianetto's wound, Mateo Falcone and his wife suddenly appeared at the bend of a path that led into the *maquis*. His wife was walking, painfully stooped under the weight of an enormous sack of chestnuts, while her husband was strutting at his ease, carrying nothing but a rifle in his hand and another slung across his back: because it's beneath a man's dignity to carry any burden other than his weapons.

At sight of the soldiers, Mateo's first thought was that they had come to arrest him. But why did he have that idea? Had Mateo had any run-ins with the law, after all? No. He enjoyed a good reputation. He was what is called "an individual of good repute"; but he was a Corsican and a mountaineer, and there are few Corsican mountaineers who, if they racked their memory, wouldn't discover some little peccadillo, in the nature of rifle shots, stiletto stabs, and other trifles. More than many another, Mateo had a clear conscience, because for over ten years he hadn't pointed his rifle at a man; but nevertheless he was cautious, and he now prepared to defend himself bravely if it should prove necessary.

"Wife," he said to Giuseppa, "put down your sack and be prepared."

She obeyed at once. He gave her the rifle he had been carrying on his back; it might have hampered his movements. He cocked the one he had in his hands and proceeded slowly toward his house, keeping close to the trees that lined the road and ready, at the least sign of hostility, to dash behind the thickest trunk and thus be able to fire from a position of cover. His wife was following at his heels, holding his spare rifle and his cartridge pouch. The duty of a good housewife, in times of combat, is to load her husband's guns.

On the other side, the sergeant was most distressed to see Mateo advancing that way, with measured tread, his rifle pointed forward and his finger on the trigger.

"If by chance," he thought, "Mateo was a relative of Gianetto, or if he was his friend, and wanted to defend him, the wads of his two rifles would reach two of us, just as sure as a letter in the mail, and if he aimed at me, despite our relationship . . . !"

In that perplexity, he made a very courageous decision: he advanced alone toward Mateo to tell him what was going on, greeting him like an old acquaintance; but the short space separating him from Mateo seemed terribly long to him.

"Hi there, old comrade!" he shouted. "How's it going, friend? It's me, it's Gamba, your cousin."

Without a word in reply, Mateo had stopped, and, while the other man was speaking, he gently raised the barrel of his rifle, so that, by the time the sergeant reached him, it was pointing to the sky.

"Hello, brother!"[8] the sergeant said, offering his hand. "I haven't seen you for quite a while."

"Hello, brother!"

"I had come to say hello to you as I passed by, and to my cousin Pepa. We've covered a lot of ground today; but you mustn't feel sorry for our being tired, because we've made a wonderful catch. We've just laid hands on Gianetto Sanpiero."

"God be praised!" exclaimed Giuseppa. "He stole a milk goat from us last week."

---

[8] *Buon giorno, fratello,* the customary greeting in Corsica.

Those words delighted Gamba.

"Poor devil!" said Mateo. "He was hungry."

"The scamp defended himself like a lion," continued the sergeant, a little mortified. "He killed one of my infantrymen, and, as if that wasn't enough, he broke Corporal Chardon's arm; but there's no great harm in that, he was only a Frenchman . . . After that, he hid so well that the devil couldn't have detected him. Without my little cousin Fortunato, I would never have been able to find him."

"Fortunato!" Mateo exclaimed.

"Fortunato!" Giuseppa repeated.

"Yes, Gianetto had concealed himself in that haystack over there; but my little cousin pointed out the trick to me. I'm also going to tell his uncle the *caporale* about it, so he'll send him a fine gift for his trouble. And his name and yours will be in the report I'll send to the public prosecutor."

"Damnation!" said Mateo quietly.

They had come up to the detachment. Gianetto was already lying on his litter and ready to leave. When he saw Mateo in company with Gamba, he smiled a strange smile; then, turning toward the door to the house, he spat on the threshold, saying:

"House of a betrayer!"

Only a man determined to die would have dared pronounce the word "betrayer" with reference to Falcone. A firm stiletto stab, which wouldn't need to be repeated, would have immediately repaid the insult. And yet Mateo made no other gesture than to raise his hand to his forehead like a man overwhelmed.

Fortunato had gone into the house on seeing his father arrive. He soon reappeared with a bowl of milk, which he offered to Gianetto with eyes cast down.

"Get away from me!" the outlaw shouted with a crushing voice.

Then, turning to one of the infantrymen, he said:

"Comrade, give me a drink."

The soldier put his canteen in his hands, and the bandit drank the water given to him by a man with whom he had just been exchanging rifle shots. Then he requested to have his hands tied so that they would be crossed over his chest instead of having them tied behind his back.

"I like to lie comfortably," he said.

They hastened to satisfy him; then the sergeant gave the signal for departure, said good-bye to Mateo, who didn't reply, and descended to the plain in quick time.

Nearly ten minutes went by before Mateo opened his mouth. With nervous eyes, the child was looking now at his mother and now at his father, who, leaning on his rifle, was observing him with an expression of concentrated anger.

"You're making a fine beginning!" Mateo finally said in a voice that was calm but frightening for anyone who knew him well.

"Father!" exclaimed the child, stepping forward with tears in his eyes, as if intending to go down on his knees to him.

But Mateo shouted to him:

"Stand back!"

And the child stopped, sobbing motionlessly a few paces away from his father.

Giuseppa approached. She had just caught sight of the watch chain, one end of which was protruding from Fortunato's shirt.

"Who gave you that watch?" she asked with a severe expression.

"My cousin the sergeant."

Falcone seized the watch and, hurling it violently against a rock, shattered it into bits.

"Wife," he said, "is this child mine?"

Giuseppa's brown cheeks turned brick-red.

"What are you saying, Mateo? And do you realize who you're talking to?"

"Well, then, this child is the first of his line to betray anyone."

Fortunato's sobs and hiccups redoubled, and Falcone kept his lynx eyes fixed on him. Finally he struck the ground with his rifle butt, then threw the rifle over his shoulder, and went back onto the road to the *maquis,* calling to Fortunato to follow him. The child obeyed.

Giuseppa ran after Mateo and took hold of his arm.

"He's your son," she said, her voice trembling and her dark eyes staring into her husband's, as if to detect what was going on in his soul.

"Let me go," Mateo replied. "I'm his father."

Giuseppa kissed her son and entered her hut, weeping. She fell on her knees in front of a statuette of the Virgin and prayed fervently. Meanwhile, Falcone walked some two hundred paces along the path, not stopping until he reached a small ravine, into which he descended. He tested the soil with his rifle butt and found it soft and easy to dig. The spot seemed suitable for his purpose.

"Fortunato, go over to that big rock."

The child did what he was ordered to, then knelt down.

"Say your prayers."

"Father, father, don't kill me!"

"Say your prayers!" Mateo repeated in fearsome tones.

The child, stammering and sobbing, recited the Lord's Prayer and the Apostles' Creed. His father loudly replied "Amen!" at the end of each prayer.

"Are those all the prayers you know?"

"Father, I also know the 'Hail, Mary' and the litany my aunt taught me."

"It's pretty long, but go ahead."

The child completed the litany in a toneless voice.

"Are you done?"

"Oh, father, mercy! Forgive me! I'll never do it again! I'll keep on begging my cousin the *caporale* until Gianetto is pardoned!"

He was still speaking; Mateo had cocked his rifle and was taking aim, saying:

"May God forgive you!"

The child made a desperate effort to get up and clasp his father's knees, but he didn't have the time. Mateo fired, and Fortunato fell down dead.

Without even glancing at the corpse, Mateo went back along the road to his house to fetch a spade so he could bury his son. He had scarcely taken a few steps when he met Giuseppa, who was running up, alarmed at the shot.

"What have you done?" she exclaimed.

"I've dealt out justice."

"Where is he?"

"In the ravine. I'm going to bury him. He died like a Christian; I'll have a Mass sung for him. Have my son-in-law Tiodoro Bianchi told to come and move in with us."

NAPOLEON AND THE SPECTRE

Charlotte Brontë

WELL, AS I was saying, the Emperor got into bed.

"Chevalier," says he to his valet, "let down those window-curtains, and shut the casement before you leave the room."

Chevalier did as he was told, and then, taking up his candlestick, departed.

In a few minutes the Emperor felt his pillow becoming rather hard, and he got up to shake it. As he did so a slight rustling noise was heard near the bed-head. His Majesty listened, but all was silent as he lay down again.

Scarcely had he settled into a peaceful attitude of repose, when he was disturbed by a sensation of thirst. Lifting himself on his elbow, he took a glass of lemonade from the small stand which was placed beside him. He refreshed himself by a deep draught. As he returned the goblet to its station a deep groan burst from a kind of closet in one corner of the apartment.

"Who's there?" cried the Emperor, seizing his pistols. "Speak, or I'll blow your brains out."

This threat produced no other effect than a short, sharp laugh, and a dead silence followed.

The Emperor started from his couch, and, hastily throwing on a *robe-de-chambre* which hung over the back of a chair, stepped courageously to the haunted closet. As he opened the door something rustled. He sprang forward sword in hand. No soul or even substance appeared, and the rustling, it was evident, proceeded from the falling of a cloak, which had been suspended by a peg from the door.

Half ashamed of himself he returned to bed.

Just as he was about once more to close his eyes, the light of the three wax tapers, which burned in a silver branch over the mantle-piece, was suddenly darkened. He looked up. A black, opaque shadow obscured it. Sweating with terror, the Emperor put out his hand to seize the bell-rope, but some invisible being snatched it rudely from his grasp, and at the same instant the ominous shade vanished.

"Pooh!" exclaimed Napoleon, "it was but an ocular delusion."

"Was it?" whispered a hollow voice, in deep mysterious tones, close to his ear. "Was it a delusion, Emperor of France? No! all thou hast heard and seen is sad forewarning reality. Rise, lifter of the Eagle Standard! Awake, swayer of the Lily Sceptre! Follow me, Napoleon, and thou shalt see more."

As the voice ceased, a form dawned on his astonished sight. It was that of a tall, thin man, dressed in a blue surtout edged with gold lace. It wore a black cravat very tightly round its neck, and confined by two little sticks placed behind each ear. The counte-nance was livid; the tongue protruded from between the teeth, and the eyes all glazed and bloodshot started with frightful prominence from their sockets.

"Mon Dieu!" exclaimed the Emperor, "what do I see? Spectre, whence cometh thou?"

The apparition spoke not, but gliding forward beckoned Napoleon with uplifted finger to follow.

Controlled by a mysterious influence, which deprived him of the capability of either thinking or acting for himself, he obeyed in silence.

The solid wall of the apartment fell open as they approached, and, when both had passed through, it closed behind them with a noise like thunder.

They would now have been in total darkness had it not been for a dim light which shone round the ghost and revealed the damp walls of a long, vaulted passage. Down this they proceeded with mute rapidity. Ere long a cool, refreshing breeze, which rushed wailing up the vault and caused the Emperor to wrap his loose nightdress closer round, announced their approach to the open air.

This they soon reached, and Nap found himself in one of the principal streets of Paris.

"Worthy Spirit," said he, shivering in the chill night air, "permit me to return and put on some additional clothing. I will be with you again presently."

"Forward," replied his companion sternly.

He felt compelled, in spite of the rising indignation which almost choked him, to obey.

On they went through the deserted streets till they arrived at a lofty house built on the banks of the Seine. Here the Spectre stopped, the gates rolled back to receive them, and they entered a large marble hall which was partly concealed by a curtain drawn across, through the half transparent folds of which a bright light might be seen burning with dazzling lustre. A row of fine female figures, richly attired, stood before this screen. They wore on their heads garlands of the most beautiful flowers, but their faces were concealed by ghastly masks representing death's-heads.

"What is all this mummery?" cried the Emperor, making an effort to shake off the mental shackles by which he was so unwillingly restrained, "Where am I, and why have I been brought here?"

"Silence," said the guide, lolling out still further his black and bloody tongue. "Silence, if thou wouldst escape instant death."

The Emperor would have replied, his natural courage overcoming the temporary awe to which he had at first been subjected, but just then a strain of wild, supernatural music swelled behind the huge curtain, which waved to and fro, and bellied slowly out as if agitated by some internal commotion or battle of waving winds. At the same moment an overpowering mixture of the scents of mortal corruption, blent with the richest Eastern odours, stole through the haunted hall.

A murmur of many voices was now heard at a distance, and something grasped his arm eagerly from behind.

He turned hastily round. His eyes met the well-known countenance of Marie Louise.

"What! are you in this infernal place, too?" said he. "What has brought you here?"

"Will your Majesty permit me to ask the same question of yourself?" said the Empress, smiling.

He made no reply; astonishment prevented him.

No curtain now intervened between him and the light. It had been removed as if by magic, and a splendid chandelier appeared suspended over his head. Throngs of ladies, richly dressed, but without death's-head masks, stood round, and a due proportion of gay cavaliers was mingled with them. Music was still sounding, but it was seen to proceed from a band of mortal musicians stationed in an orchestra near at hand. The air was yet redolent of incense, but it was incense unblended with stench.

"Mon dieu!" cried the Emperor, "how is all this come about? Where in the world is Piche?"

"Piche?" replied the Empress. "What does your Majesty mean? Had you not better leave the apartment and retire to rest?"

"Leave the apartment? Why, where am I?"

"In my private drawing-room, surrounded by a few particular persons of the Court whom I had invited this evening to a ball. You entered a few minutes since in your nightdress with your eyes fixed and wide open. I suppose from the astonishment you now testify that you were walking in your sleep."

The Emperor immediately fell into a fit of catalepsy, in which he continued during the whole of that night and the greater part of the next day.

THE MORTAL IMMORTAL: A TALE

Mary Shelley

JULY 16, 1833.—THIS is a memorable anniversary for me; on it I complete my three hundred and twenty-third year!

The Wandering Jew?—certainly not. More than eighteen centuries have passed over his head. In comparison with him, I am a very young Immortal.

Am I, then, immortal? This is a question which I have asked myself, by day and night, for now three hundred and three years, and yet cannot answer it. I detected a gray hair amidst my brown locks this very day—that surely signifies decay. Yet it may have remained concealed there for three hundred years—for some persons have become entirely white-headed before twenty years of age.

I will tell my story, and my reader shall judge for me. I will tell my story, and so contrive to pass some few hours of a long eternity, become so wearisome to me. For ever! Can it be? to live for ever! I have heard of enchantments, in which the victims were plunged into a deep sleep, to wake, after a hundred years, as fresh as ever: I have heard of the Seven Sleepers—thus to be immortal would not be so burthensome: but, oh! the weight of never-ending time—the tedious passage of the still-succeeding hours! How happy was the fabled Nourjahad!——But to my task.

All the world has heard of Cornelius Agrippa. His memory is as immortal as his arts have made me. All the world has also heard of his scholar, who, unawares, raised the foul fiend during his master's absence, and was destroyed by him. The report, true or false, of this accident, was attended with many inconveniences to the renowned philosopher. All his scholars at once deserted him—his servants disappeared. He had no one near him to put

41

coals on his ever-burning fires while he slept, or to attend to the changeful colours of his medicines while he studied. Experiment after experiment failed, because one pair of hands was insufficient to complete them: the dark spirits laughed at him for not being able to retain a single mortal in his service.

I was then very young—very poor—and very much in love. I had been for about a year the pupil of Cornelius, though I was absent when this accident took place. On my return, my friends implored me not to return to the alchymist's abode. I trembled as I listened to the dire tale they told; I required no second warning; and when Cornelius came and offered me a purse of gold if I would remain under his roof, I felt as if Satan himself tempted me. My teeth chattered—my hair stood on end—I ran off as fast as my trembling knees would permit.

My failing steps were directed whither for two years they had every evening been attracted—a gently bubbling spring of pure living waters, beside which lingered a dark-haired girl, whose beaming eyes were fixed on the path I was accustomed each night to tread. I cannot remember the hour when I did not love Bertha; we had been neighbours and playmates from infancy— her parents, like mine, were of humble life, yet respectable—our attachment had been a source of pleasure to them. In an evil hour, a malignant fever carried off both her father and mother, and Bertha became an orphan. She would have found a home beneath my paternal roof, but, unfortunately, the old lady of the near castle, rich, childless, and solitary, declared her intention to adopt her. Henceforth Bertha was clad in silk—inhabited a marble palace—and was looked on as being highly favoured by fortune. But in her new situation among her new associates, Bertha remained true to the friend of her humbler days; she often visited the cottage of my father, and when forbidden to go thither, she would stray towards the neighbouring wood, and meet me beside its shady fountain.

She often declared that she owed no duty to her new protectress equal in sanctity to that which bound us. Yet still I was too poor to marry, and she grew weary of being tormented on my account. She had a haughty but an impatient spirit, and grew angry at the obstacles that prevented our union. We met now after an absence, and she had been sorely beset while I was away; she complained bitterly, and almost reproached me for being poor. I replied hastily—

"I am honest, if I am poor!—were I not, I might soon become rich!"

This exclamation produced a thousand questions. I feared to shock her by owning the truth, but she drew it from me; and then, casting a look of disdain on me, she said—

"You pretend to love, and you fear to face the Devil for my sake!"

I protested that I had only dreaded to offend her—while she dwelt on the magnitude of the reward that I should receive. Thus encouraged—shamed by her—led on by love and hope, laughing at my late fears, with quick steps and a light heart, I returned to accept the offers of the alchymist, and was instantly installed in my office.

A year passed away. I became possessed of no insignificant sum of money. Custom had banished my fears. In spite of the most painful vigilance, I had never detected the trace of a cloven foot; nor was the studious silence of our abode ever disturbed by demoniac howls. I still continued my stolen interviews with Bertha, and Hope dawned on me—Hope—but not perfect joy; for Bertha fancied that love and security were enemies, and her pleasure was to divide them in my bosom. Though true of heart, she was somewhat of a coquette in manner; and I was jealous as a Turk. She slighted me in a thousand ways, yet would never acknowledge herself to be in the wrong. She would drive me mad with anger, and then force me to beg her pardon. Sometimes she fancied that I was not sufficiently submissive, and then she had some story of a rival, favoured by her protectress. She was surrounded by silk-clad youths—the rich and gay——What chance had the sad-robed scholar of Cornelius compared with these?

On one occasion, the philosopher made such large demands upon my time, that I was unable to meet her as I was wont. He was engaged in some mighty work, and I was forced to remain, day and night, feeding his furnaces and watching his chemical preparations. Bertha waited for me in vain at the fountain. Her haughty spirit fired at this neglect; and when at last I stole out during the few short minutes allotted to me for slumber, and hoped to be consoled by her, she received me with disdain, dismissed me in scorn, and vowed that any man should possess her hand rather than he who could not be in two places at once for her sake. She would be revenged!—And truly she was. In my dingy retreat I heard that she had been hunting, attended by Albert Hoffer. Albert Hoffer was favoured by her protectress, and the three passed in cavalcade before my smoky window. Methought that they mentioned my name—it was followed by a laugh of derision, as her dark eyes glanced contemptuously towards my abode.

Jealousy, with all its venom, and all its misery, entered my breast. Now I shed a torrent of tears, to think that I should never call her mine; and, anon, I imprecated a thousand curses on her inconstancy. Yet, still I must stir the fires of the alchymist, still attend on the changes of his unintelligible medicines.

Cornelius had watched for three days and nights, nor closed his eyes. The progress of his alembics was slower than he expected: in spite of his anxiety, sleep weighed upon his eyelids. Again and again he threw off drowsiness with more than human energy; again and again it stole away his senses. He eyed his crucibles wistfully. "Not ready yet," he murmured; "will another night pass before the work is accomplished? Winzy, you are vigilant—you are faithful—you have slept, my boy—you slept last night. Look at that glass vessel. The liquid it contains is of a soft rose-colour: the moment it begins to change its hue, awaken me—till then I may close my eyes. First, it will turn white, and then emit golden flashes; but wait not till then; when the rose-colour fades, rouse me." I scarcely heard the last words, muttered, as they were, in sleep. Even then he did not quite yield to nature. "Winzy, my boy," he again said, "do not touch the vessel—do not put it to your lips; it is a philter—a philter to cure love; you would not cease to love your Bertha—beware to drink!"

And he slept. His venerable head sunk on his breast, and I scarce heard his regular breathing. For a few minutes I watched the vessel—the rosy hue of the liquid remained unchanged. Then my thoughts wandered—they visited the fountain, and dwelt on a thousand charming scenes never to be renewed—never! Serpents and adders were in my heart as the word "Never!" half formed itself on my lips. False girl!—false and cruel! Never more would she smile on me as that evening she smiled on Albert. Worthless, detested woman! I would not remain unrevenged—she should see Albert expire at her feet—she should die beneath my vengeance. She had smiled in disdain and triumph—she knew my wretchedness and her power. Yet what power had she?—the power of exciting my hate—my utter scorn—my—oh, all but indifference! Could I attain that—could I regard her with careless eyes, transferring my rejected love to one fairer and more true, that were indeed a victory!

A bright flash darted before my eyes. I had forgotten the medicine of the adept; I gazed on it with wonder: flashes of admirable beauty, more bright than those which the diamond emits when the sun's rays are on it, glanced from the surface of the liquid; an odour the most fragrant and grateful stole over my sense; the vessel seemed one globe of living radiance, lovely to the eye, and most inviting to the taste. The first thought, instinctively inspired by the grosser sense, was, I will—I must drink. I raised the vessel to my lips. "It will cure me of love—of torture!" Already I had quaffed half of the most delicious liquor ever tasted by the palate of man, when the philosopher stirred. I started—I dropped the glass—the fluid flamed and glanced along the floor, while I felt Cornelius's gripe at my throat, as he shrieked aloud, "Wretch! you have destroyed the labour of my life!"

The philosopher was totally unaware that I had drunk any portion of his drug. His idea was, and I gave a tacit assent to it, that I had raised the vessel from curiosity, and that, frighted at its brightness, and the flashes of intense light it gave forth, I had let it fall. I never undeceived him. The fire of the medicine was quenched— the fragrance died away—he grew calm, as a philosopher should under the heaviest trials, and dismissed me to rest.

I will not attempt to describe the sleep of glory and bliss which bathed my soul in paradise during the remaining hours of that memorable night. Words would be faint and shallow types of my enjoyment, or of the gladness that possessed my bosom when I woke. I trod air—my thoughts were in heaven. Earth appeared heaven, and my inheritance upon it was to be one trance of delight. "This it is to be cured of love," I thought; "I will see Bertha this day, and she will find her lover cold and regardless: too happy to be disdainful, yet how utterly indifferent to her!"

The hours danced away. The philosopher, secure that he had once succeeded, and believing that he might again, began to concoct the same medicine once more. He was shut up with his books and drugs, and I had a holiday. I dressed myself with care; I looked in an old but polished shield, which served me for a mirror; methought my good looks had wonderfully improved. I hurried beyond the precincts of the town, joy in my soul, the beauty of heaven and earth around me. I turned my steps towards the castle— I could look on its lofty turrets with lightness of heart, for I was cured of love. My Bertha saw me afar off, as I came up the avenue.

I know not what sudden impulse animated her bosom, but at the sight, she sprung with a light fawn-like bound down the marble steps, and was hastening towards me. But I had been perceived by another person. The old high-born hag, who called herself her protectress, and was her tyrant, had seen me, also; she hobbled, panting, up the terrace; a page, as ugly as herself, held up her train, and fanned her as she hurried along, and stopped my fair girl with a "How, now, my bold mistress? whither so fast? Back to your cage—hawks are abroad!"

Bertha clasped her hands—her eyes were still bent on my approaching figure. I saw the contest. How I abhorred the old crone who checked the kind impulses of my Bertha's softening heart. Hitherto, respect for her rank had caused me to avoid the lady of the castle; now I disdained such trivial considerations. I was cured of love, and lifted above all human fears; I hastened forwards, and soon reached the terrace. How lovely Bertha looked! her eyes flashing fire, her cheeks glowing with impatience and anger, she was a thousand times more graceful and charming than ever—I no longer loved—Oh! no, I adored—worshipped—idolized her!

She had that morning been persecuted, with more than usual vehemence, to consent to an immediate marriage with my rival. She was reproached with the encouragement that she had shown him—she was threatened with being turned out of doors with disgrace and shame. Her proud spirit rose in arms at the threat; but when she remembered the scorn that she had heaped upon me, and how, perhaps, she had thus lost one whom she now regarded as her only friend, she wept with remorse and rage. At that moment I appeared. "O, Winzy!" she exclaimed, "take me to your mother's cot; swiftly let me leave the detested luxuries and wretchedness of this noble dwelling—take me to poverty and happiness."

I clasped her in my arms with transport. The old lady was speechless with fury, and broke forth into invective only when we were far on our road to my natal cottage. My mother received the fair fugitive, escaped from a gilt cage to nature and liberty, with tenderness and joy; my father, who loved her, welcomed her heartily; it was a day of rejoicing, which did not need the addition of the celestial potion of the alchymist to steep me in delight.

Soon after this eventful day, I became the husband of Bertha. I ceased to be the scholar of Cornelius, but I continued his friend. I always felt grateful to him for having, unawares, procured me that delicious draught of a divine elixir, which, instead of curing me of love (sad cure! solitary and joyless remedy for evils which seem blessings to the memory), had inspired me with courage and resolution, thus winning for me an inestimable treasure in my Bertha.

I often called to mind that period of trance-like inebriation with wonder. The drink of Cornelius had not fulfilled the task for which he affirmed that it had been prepared, but its effects were more potent and blissful than words can express. They had faded by degrees, yet they lingered long—and painted life in hues of splendour. Bertha often wondered at my lightness of heart and unaccustomed gaiety; for, before, I had been rather serious, or even sad, in my disposition. She loved me the better for my cheerful temper, and our days were winged by joy.

Five years afterwards I was suddenly summoned to the bedside of the dying Cornelius. He had sent for me in haste, conjuring my instant presence. I found him stretched on his pallet, enfeebled even to death; all of life that yet remained animated his piercing eyes, and they were fixed on a glass vessel, full of a roseate liquid.

"Behold," he said, in a broken and inward voice, "the vanity of human wishes! a second time my hopes are about to be crowned, a second time they are destroyed. Look at that liquor—you remember five years ago I had prepared the same, with the same success—then, as now, my thirsting lips expected to taste the immortal elixir—you dashed it from me! and at present it is too late."

He spoke with difficulty, and fell back on his pillow. I could not help saying—

"How, revered master, can a cure for love restore you to life?"

A faint smile gleamed across his face as I listened earnestly to his scarcely intelligible answer.

"A cure for love and for all things—the Elixir of Immortality. Ah! if now I might drink, I should live for ever!"

As he spoke, a golden flash gleamed from the fluid; a well-remembered fragrance stole over the air; he raised himself, all weak as he was—strength seemed miraculously to re-enter his frame—he stretched forth his hand—a loud explosion startled me—a ray of fire shot up from the elixir, and the glass vessel which contained it was shivered to atoms! I turned my eyes towards the philosopher; he had fallen back—his eyes were glassy—his features rigid—he was dead!

But I lived, and was to live for ever! So said the unfortunate alchymist, and for a few days I believed his words. I remembered the glorious drunkenness that had followed my stolen draught. I reflected on the change I had felt in my frame—in my soul. The bounding elasticity of the one—the buoyant lightness of the other. I surveyed myself in a mirror, and could perceive no change in my features during the space of the five years which had elapsed. I remembered the radiant hues and grateful scent of that delicious beverage—worthy the gift it was capable of bestowing———I was, then, IMMORTAL!

A few days after I laughed at my credulity. The old proverb, that "a prophet is least regarded in his own country," was true with respect to me and my defunct master. I loved him as a man—I respected him as a sage—but I derided the notion that he could command the powers of darkness, and laughed at the superstitious fears with which he was regarded by the vulgar. He was a wise philosopher, but had no acquaintance with any spirits but those clad in flesh and blood. His science was simply human; and human science, I soon persuaded myself, could never conquer nature's laws so far as to imprison the soul for ever within its carnal habitation. Cornelius had brewed a soul-refreshing drink—more inebriating than wine—sweeter and more fragrant than any fruit: it possessed probably strong medicinal powers, imparting gladness to the heart and vigor to the limbs; but its effects would wear out; already were they diminished in my frame. I was a lucky fellow to have quaffed health and joyous spirits, and perhaps long life, at my master's hands; but my good fortune ended there: longevity was far different from immortality.

I continued to entertain this belief for many years. Sometimes a thought stole across me—Was the alchymist indeed deceived? But my habitual credence was, that I should meet the fate of all the children of Adam at my appointed time—a little late, but still at a natural age. Yet it was certain that I retained a wonderfully youthful look. I was laughed at for my vanity in consulting the mirror so often, but I consulted it in vain—my brow was untrenched—my cheeks—my eyes—my whole person continued as untarnished as in my twentieth year.

I was troubled. I looked at the faded beauty of Bertha—I seemed more like her son. By degrees our neighbours began to make similar observations, and I found at last that I went by the name of the Scholar bewitched. Bertha herself grew uneasy. She became jealous and peevish, and at length she began to question me. We had no children; we were all in all to each other; and though, as she grew older, her vivacious spirit became a little allied to ill-temper, and her beauty sadly diminished, I cherished her in my heart as the mistress I had idolized, the wife I had sought and won with such perfect love.

At last our situation became intolerable: Bertha was fifty—I twenty years of age. I had, in very shame, in some measure adopted the habits of a more advanced age; I no longer mingled in the dance among the young and gay, but my heart bounded along with them while I restrained my feet; and a sorry figure I cut among the Nestors of our village. But before the time I mention, things were altered—we were universally shunned; we were—at least, I was— reported to have kept up an iniquitous acquaintance with some of my former master's supposed friends. Poor Bertha was pitied, but deserted. I was regarded with horror and detestation.

What was to be done? we sat by our winter fire—poverty had made itself felt, for none would buy the produce of my farm; and often I had been forced to journey twenty miles, to some place where I was not known, to dispose of our property. It is true we had saved something for an evil day—that day was come.

We sat by our lone fireside—the old-hearted youth and his anti-quated wife. Again Bertha insisted on knowing the truth; she reca-pitulated all she had ever heard said about me, and added her own observations. She conjured me to cast off the spell; she described how much more comely grey hairs were than my chestnut locks; she descanted on the reverence and respect due to age—how pref-erable to the slight regard paid to mere children: could I imagine that the despicable gifts of youth and good looks outweighed dis-grace, hatred, and scorn? Nay, in the end I should be burnt as a dealer in the black art, while she, to whom I had not deigned to communicate any portion of my good fortune, might be stoned as my accomplice. At length she insinuated that I must share my secret with her, and bestow on her like benefits to those I myself enjoyed, or she would denounce me—and then she burst into tears.

Thus beset, methought it was the best way to tell the truth. I revealed it as tenderly as I could, and spoke only of a *very long life,* not of immortality—which representation, indeed, coincided best with my own ideas. When I ended, I rose and said,

"And now, my Bertha, will you denounce the lover of your youth?—You will not, I know. But it is too hard, my poor wife, that you should suffer from my ill-luck and the accursed arts of Cornelius. I will leave you—you have wealth enough, and friends will return in my absence. I will go; young as I seem, and strong as I am, I can work and gain my bread among strangers, unsuspected and unknown. I loved you in youth; God is my witness that I would not desert you in age, but that your safety and happiness require it."

I took my cap and moved towards the door; in a moment Bertha's arms were round my neck, and her lips were pressed to mine. "No, my husband, my Winzy," she said, "you shall not go alone—take me with you; we will remove from this place, and, as you say, among strangers we shall be unsuspected and safe. I am not so very old as quite to shame you, my Winzy; and I dare say the charm will soon wear off, and, with the blessing of God, you will become more elderly-looking, as is fitting; you shall not leave me."

I returned the good soul's embrace heartily. "I will not, my Bertha; but for your sake I had not thought of such a thing. I will be your true, faithful husband while you are spared to me, and do my duty by you to the last."

The next day we prepared secretly for our emigration. We were obliged to make great pecuniary sacrifices—it could not be helped. We realised a sum sufficient, at least, to maintain us while Bertha lived; and, without saying adieu to anyone, quitted our native country to take refuge in a remote part of western France.

It was a cruel thing to transport poor Bertha from her native village, and the friends of her youth, to a new country, new language, new customs. The strange secret of my destiny rendered this removal immaterial to me; but I compassionated her deeply, and was glad to perceive that she found compensation for her misfortunes in a variety of little ridiculous circumstances. Away from all tell-tale chroniclers, she sought to decrease the apparent disparity of our ages by a thousand feminine arts—rouge, youthful dress, and assumed juvenility of manner. I could not be angry—Did not I myself wear a mask? Why quarrel with hers, because it was less successful? I grieved deeply when I remembered that this was my Bertha, whom I had loved so fondly, and won with such transport—the dark-eyed, dark-haired girl, with smiles of enchanting archness and a step like a fawn—this mincing, simpering, jealous old woman. I should have revered her gray locks and withered cheeks; but thus!——It was my work, I knew; but I did not the less deplore this type of human weakness.

Her jealousy never slept. Her chief occupation was to discover that, in spite of outward appearances, I was myself growing old. I verily believe that the poor soul loved me truly in her heart, but never had woman so tormenting a mode of displaying fondness. She would discern wrinkles in my face and decrepitude in my walk, while I bounded along in youthful vigour, the youngest looking of twenty youths. I never dared address another woman: on one occasion, fancying that the belle of the village regarded me with favouring eyes, she bought me a gray wig. Her constant discourse among her acquaintances was, that though I looked so young, there was ruin at work within my frame; and she affirmed that the worst symptom about me was my apparent health. My youth was a disease, she said, and I ought at all times to prepare, if not for a sudden and awful death, at least to awake some morning white-headed, and bowed down with all the marks of advanced years. I let her talk—I often joined in her conjectures. Her warnings chimed in with my never-ceasing speculations concerning my state, and I took an earnest, though painful, interest in listening to all that her quick wit and excited imagination could say on the subject.

Why dwell on these minute circumstances? We lived on for many long years. Bertha became bed-rid and paralytic: I nursed her as a mother might a child. She grew peevish, and still harped upon one string—of how long I should survive her. It has ever been a source of consolation to me, that I performed my duty scrupulously towards her. She had been mine in youth, she was mine in age, and at last, when I heaped the sod over her corpse, I wept to feel that I had lost all that really bound me to humanity.

Since then how many have been my cares and woes, how few and empty my enjoyments! I pause here in my history—I will pursue it no further. A sailor without rudder or compass, tossed on a stormy sea—a traveller lost on a wide-spread heath, without landmark or star to guide him—such have I been: more lost, more hopeless than either. A nearing ship, a gleam from some far cot, may save them; but I have no beacon except the hope of death.

Death! mysterious, ill-visaged friend of weak humanity! Why alone of all mortals have you cast me from your sheltering fold? O, for the peace of the grave! the deep silence of the iron-bound tomb! that thought would cease to work in my brain, and my heart beat no more with emotions varied only by new forms of sadness!

Am I immortal? I return to my first question. In the first place, is it not more probable that the beverage of the alchymist was fraught rather with longevity than eternal life? Such is my hope. And then be it remembered that I only drank *half* of the potion prepared by him. Was not the whole necessary to complete the charm? To have drained half the Elixir of Immortality is but to be half immortal—my For-ever is thus truncated and null.

But again, who shall number the years of the half of eternity? I often try to imagine by what rule the infinite may be divided. Sometimes I fancy age advancing upon me. One gray hair I have found. Fool! do I lament? Yes, the fear of age and death often creeps coldly into my heart; and the more I live, the more I dread death, even while I abhor life. Such an enigma is man— born to perish— when he wars, as I do, against the established laws of his nature.

But for this anomaly of feeling surely I might die: the medicine of the alchymist would not be proof against fire—sword—and the strangling waters. I have gazed upon the blue depths of many a placid lake, and the tumultuous rushing of many a mighty river, and have said, peace inhabits those waters; yet I have turned my steps away, to live yet another day. I have asked myself, whether suicide would be a crime in one to whom thus only the portals of the other world could be opened. I have done all, except presenting myself as a soldier or duellist, an object of destruction to my—no, *not* my fellow-mortals, and therefore I have shrunk away. They are not my fellows. The inextinguishable power of life in my frame, and their ephemeral existence, place us wide as the poles asunder. I could not raise a hand against the meanest or the most powerful among them.

Thus I have lived on for many a year—alone, and weary of myself—desirous of death, yet never dying—a mortal immortal. Neither ambition nor avarice can enter my mind, and the ardent love that gnaws at my heart, never to be returned—never to find an equal on which to expend itself—lives there only to torment me.

This very day I conceived a design by which I may end all— without self-slaughter, without making another man a Cain—an expedition, which mortal frame can never survive, even endued with the youth and strength that inhabits mine. Thus I shall put my immortality to the test, and rest for ever—or return, the wonder and benefactor of the human species.

Before I go, a miserable vanity has caused me to pen these pages. I would not die, and leave no name behind. Three centuries have passed since I quaffed the fatal beverage: another year shall not elapse before, encountering gigantic dangers—warring with the powers of frost in their home—beset by famine, toil, and tempest—I yield this body, too tenacious a cage for a soul which thirsts for freedom, to the destructive elements of air and water—or, if I survive, my name shall be recorded as one of the most famous among the sons of men; and, my task achieved, I shall adopt more resolute means, and, by scattering and annihilating the atoms that compose my frame, set at liberty the life imprisoned within, and so cruelly prevented from soaring from this dim earth to a sphere more congenial to its immortal essence.

YOUNG GOODMAN BROWN

Nathaniel Hawthorne

YOUNG GOODMAN BROWN came forth at sunset into the street of Salem village; but put his head back, after crossing the threshold, to exchange a parting kiss with his young wife. And Faith, as the wife was aptly named, thrust her own pretty head into the street, letting the wind play with the pink ribbons of her cap, while she called to Goodman Brown.

"Dearest heart," whispered she, softly and rather sadly, when her lips were close to his ear, "pr'ithee put off your journey until sunrise and sleep in your own bed to-night. A lone woman is troubled with such dreams and such thoughts that she's afeard of herself sometimes. Pray tarry with me this night, dear husband, of all nights in the year."

"My love and my Faith," replied young Goodman Brown, "of all nights in the year, this one night must I tarry away from thee. My journey, as thou callest it, forth and back again, must needs be done 'twixt now and sunrise. What, my sweet, pretty wife, dost thou doubt me already, and we but three months married?"

"Then God bless you!" said Faith, with the pink ribbons, "and may you find all well, when you come back."

"Amen!" cried Goodman Brown. "Say thy prayers, dear Faith, and go to bed at dusk, and no harm will come to thee."

So they parted; and the young man pursued his way until, being about to turn the corner by the meeting-house, he looked back and saw the head of Faith still peeping after him with a melancholy air, in spite of her pink ribbons.

"Poor little Faith!" thought he, for his heart smote him. "What a wretch am I to leave her on such an errand! She talks of dreams, too. Methought as she spoke, there was trouble in her face, as if a dream had warned her what work is to be done to-night. But, no, no; 't would kill her to think it. Well, she's a blessed angel on earth; and after this one night I'll cling to her skirts and follow her to heaven."

With this excellent resolve for the future, Goodman Brown felt himself justified in making more haste on his present evil purpose. He had taken a dreary road, darkened by all the gloomiest trees of the forest, which barely stood aside to let the narrow path creep through, and closed immediately behind. It was all as lonely as could be; and there is this peculiarity in such a solitude, that the traveller knows not who may be concealed by the innumerable trunks and the thick boughs overhead; so that with lonely footsteps he may yet be passing through an unseen multitude.

"There may be a devilish Indian behind every tree," said Goodman Brown to himself; and he glanced fearfully behind him as he added, "What if the devil himself should be at my very elbow!"

His head being turned back, he passed a crook of the road, and, looking forward again, beheld the figure of a man, in grave and decent attire, seated at the foot of an old tree. He arose at Goodman Brown's approach, and walked onward side by side with him.

"You are late, Goodman Brown," said he. "The clock of the Old South was striking as I came through Boston; and that is full fifteen minutes agone."

"Faith kept me back awhile," replied the young man, with a tremor in his voice, caused by the sudden appearance of his companion, though not wholly unexpected.

It was now deep dusk in the forest, and deepest in that part of it where these two were journeying. As nearly as could be discerned, the second traveller was about fifty years old, apparently in the same rank of life as Goodman Brown, and bearing a considerable resemblance to him, though perhaps more in expression than features. Still they might have been taken for father and son. And yet, though the elder person was as simply clad as the younger and as simple in manner too, he had an indescribable air of one who knew the world, and would not have felt abashed at the governor's dinner-table or in King William's court, were it possible that his affairs should call him thither. But the only thing about him that could be fixed upon as remarkable was his staff, which bore the likeness of a great black snake, so curiously wrought that it might almost be seen to twist and wriggle itself like a living serpent. This, of course, must have been an ocular deception, assisted by the uncertain light.

"Come, Goodman Brown," cried his fellow-traveller, "this is a dull pace for the beginning of a journey. Take my staff, if you are so soon weary."

"Friend," said the other, exchanging his slow pace for a full stop, "having kept covenant by meeting thee here, it is my purpose now to return whence I came. I have scruples, touching the matter thou wot'st of."

"Sayest thou so?" replied he of the serpent, smiling apart. "Let us walk on, nevertheless, reasoning as we go; and if I convince thee not, thou shalt turn back. We are but a little way in the forest yet."

"Too far! too far!" exclaimed the goodman, unconsciously resuming his walk. "My father never went into the woods on such an errand, nor his father before him. We have been a race of honest men and good Christians since the days of the martyrs; and shall I be the first of the name of Brown that ever took this path and kept—"

"Such company, thou wouldst say," observed the elder person, interpreting his pause. "Well said, Goodman Brown! I have been as well acquainted with your family as with ever a one among the Puritans; and that's no trifle to say. I helped your grandfather, the constable, when he lashed the Quaker woman so smartly through the streets of Salem; and it was I that brought your father a pitch-pine knot, kindled at my own hearth, to set fire to an Indian village, in King Philip's war. They were my good friends both; and many a pleasant walk have we had along this path, and returned merrily after midnight. I would fain be friends with you for their sake."

"If it be as thou sayest," replied Goodman Brown, "I marvel they never spoke of these matters; or, verily, I marvel not, seeing that the least rumor of the sort would have driven them from New England. We are a people of prayer, and good works to boot, and abide no such wickedness."

"Wickedness or not," said the traveller with the twisted staff, "I have a very general acquaintance here in New England. The deacons of many a church have drunk the communion wine with me; the selectmen of divers towns make me their chairman; and a majority of the Great and General Court are firm supporters of my interest. The governor and I, too—But these are state secrets."

"Can this be so?" cried Goodman Brown, with a stare of amazement at his undisturbed companion. "Howbeit, I have nothing to do with the governor and council; they have their own ways, and are no rule for a simple husbandman like me. But, were I to go on with thee, how should I meet the eye of that good old man, our minister, at Salem village? O, his voice would make me tremble both Sabbath day and lecture day!"

Thus far the elder traveller had listened with due gravity; but now burst into a fit of irrepressible mirth, shaking himself so violently that his snake-like staff actually seemed to wriggle in sympathy.

"Ha! ha! ha!" shouted he again and again; then composing himself, "Well, go on, Goodman Brown, go on; but, prithee, don't kill me with laughing."

"Well, then, to end the matter at once," said Goodman Brown, considerably nettled, "there is my wife, Faith. It would break her dear little heart; and I 'd rather break my own."

"Nay, if that be the case," answered the other, "e'en go thy ways, Goodman Brown. I would not, for twenty old women like the one hobbling before us that Faith should come to any harm."

As he spoke, he pointed his staff at a female figure on the path, in whom Goodman Brown recognized a very pious and exemplary dame, who had taught him his catechism in youth, and was still his moral and spiritual adviser, jointly with the minister and Deacon Gookin.

"A marvel, truly, that Goody Cloyse should be so far in the wilderness, at nightfall," said he. "But, with your leave, friend, I shall take a cut through the woods until we have left this Christian woman behind. Being a stranger to you, she might ask whom I was consorting with and whither I was going."

"Be it so," said his fellow-traveller. "Betake you to the woods, and let me keep the path."

Accordingly the young man turned aside, but took care to watch his companion, who advanced softly along the road until he had come within a staff's length of the old dame. She, meanwhile, was making the best of her way, with singular speed for so aged a woman, and mumbling some indistinct words—a prayer, doubtless—as she went. The traveller put forth his staff and touched her withered neck with what seemed the serpent's tail.

"The Devil!" screamed the pious old lady.

"Then Goody Cloyse knows her old friend?" observed the traveller, confronting her and leaning on his writing stick.

"Ah, forsooth, and is it your worship, indeed?" cried the good dame. "Yea, truly is it, and in the very image of my old gossip, Goodman Brown, the grandfather of the silly fellow that now is. But—would your worship believe it? —my broomstick hath strangely disappeared, stolen, as I suspect, by that unhanged witch, Goody Cory, and that, too, when I was all anointed with the juice of smallage, and cinquefoil, and wolf's-bane—"

"Mingled with fine wheat and the fat of a new-born babe," said the shape of old Goodman Brown.

"Ah, your worship knows the recipe," cried the old lady, cackling aloud. "So, as I was saying, being all ready for the meeting, and no horse to ride on, I made up my mind to foot it; for they tell me there is a nice young man to be taken into communion to-night. But now your good worship will lend me your arm, and we shall be there in a twinkling."

"That can hardly be," answered her friend. "I may not spare you my arm, Goody Cloyse, but here is my staff, if you will."

So saying, he threw it down at her feet, where, perhaps, it assumed life, being one of the rods which its owner had formerly lent to the Egyptian magi. Of this fact, however, Goodman Brown could not take cognizance. He had cast up his eyes in astonishment, and, looking down again, beheld neither Goody Cloyse nor the serpentine staff, but his fellow-traveller alone, who waited for him as calmly as if nothing had happened.

"That old woman taught me my catechism," said the young man; and there was a world of meaning in this simple comment.

They continued to walk onward, while the elder traveller exhorted his companion to make good speed and persevere in the path, discoursing so aptly that his arguments seemed rather to spring up in the bosom of his auditor than to be suggested by himself. As they went, he plucked a branch of maple to serve for a walking-stick, and began to strip it of the twigs and little boughs, which were wet with evening dew. The moment his fingers touched them they became strangely withered and dried up as with a week's sunshine. Thus the pair proceeded, at a good free pace, until suddenly, in a gloomy hollow of the road, Goodman Brown sat himself down on the stump of a tree and refused to go any farther.

"Friend," said he, stubbornly, "my mind is made up. Not another step will I budge on this errand. What if a wretched old woman do choose to go to the Devil when I thought she was going to heaven; is that any reason why I should quit my dear Faith and go after her?"

"You will think better of this by and by," said his acquaintance, composedly. "Sit here and rest yourself awhile; and when you feel like moving again, there is my staff to help you along."

Without more words, he threw his companion the maple-stick, and was as speedily out of sight as if he had vanished into the deepening gloom. The young man sat a few moments by the roadside, applauding himself greatly, and thinking with how clear a conscience he should meet the minister, in his morning walk, nor shrink from the eye of good old Deacon Gookin. And what calm sleep would be his that very night, which was to have been spent so wickedly, but so purely and sweetly now, in the arms of Faith! Amidst these pleasant and praiseworthy meditations, Goodman Brown heard the tramp of horses along the road, and deemed it advisable to conceal himself within the verge of the forest, conscious of the guilty purpose that had brought him thither, though now so happily turned from it.

On came the hoof-tramps and the voices of the riders, two grave old voices, conversing soberly as they drew near. These mingled sounds appeared to pass along the road, within a few yards of the young man's hiding-place; but, owing doubtless to the depth of the gloom at that particular spot, neither the travellers nor their steeds were visible. Though their figures brushed the small boughs by the wayside, it could not be seen that they intercepted, even for a moment, the faint gleam from the strip of bright sky athwart which they must have passed. Goodman Brown alternately crouched and stood on tiptoe, pulling aside the branches and thrusting forth his head as far as he durst without discerning so much as a shadow. It vexed him the more, because he could have sworn, were such a thing possible, that he recognized the voices of the minister and Deacon Gookin, jogging along quietly, as they were wont to do, when bound to some ordination or ecclesiastical council. While yet within hearing, one of the riders stopped to pluck a switch.

"Of the two, reverend sir," said the voice like the deacon's, "I had rather miss an ordination dinner than to-night's meeting. They tell me that some of our community are to be here from

Falmouth and beyond, and others from Connecticut and Rhode Island, besides several of the Indian powwows, who, after their fashion, know almost as much deviltry as the best of us. Moreover, there is a goodly young woman to be taken into communion."

"Mighty well, Deacon Gookin!" replied the solemn old tones of the minister. "Spur up, or we shall be late. Nothing can be done, you know, until I get on the ground."

The hoofs clattered again; and the voices, talking so strangely in the empty air, passed on through the forest, where no church had ever been gathered nor solitary Christian prayed. Whither, then, could these holy men be journeying so deep into the heathen wilderness? Young Goodman Brown caught hold of a tree for support, being ready to sink down on the ground, faint and overburdened with the heavy sickness of his heart. He looked up to the sky, doubting whether there really was a heaven above him. Yet, there was the blue arch, and the stars brightening in it.

"With heaven above, and Faith below, I will yet stand firm against the Devil!" cried Goodman Brown.

While he still gazed upward into the deep arch of the firmament and had lifted his hands to pray, a cloud, though no wind was stirring, hurried across the zenith and hid the brightening stars. The blue sky was still visible except directly overhead, where this black mass of cloud was sweeping swiftly northward. Aloft in the air, as if from the depths of the cloud, came a confused and doubtful sound of voices. Once the listener fancied that he could distinguish the accent of townspeople of his own, men and women, both pious and ungodly, many of whom he had met at the communion-table, and had seen others rioting at the tavern. The next moment, so indistinct were the sounds, he doubted whether he had heard aught but the murmur of the old forest, whispering without a wind. Then came a stronger swell of those familiar tones, heard daily in the sunshine at Salem village, but never until now from a cloud of night. There was one voice, of a young woman, uttering lamentations, yet with an uncertain sorrow, and entreating for some favor, which, perhaps, it would grieve her to obtain; and all the unseen multitude, both saints and sinners, seemed to encourage her onward.

"Faith!" shouted Goodman Brown, in a voice of agony and desperation; and the echoes of the forest mocked him, crying, "Faith! Faith!" as if bewildered wretches were seeking her all through the wilderness.

The cry of grief, rage, and terror was yet piercing the night, when the unhappy husband held his breath for a response. There was a scream, drowned immediately in a louder murmur of voices, fading into far-off laughter, as the dark cloud swept away, leaving the clear and silent sky above Goodman Brown. But something fluttered lightly down through the air and caught on the branch of a tree. The young man seized it, and beheld a pink ribbon.

"My Faith is gone!" cried he, after one stupefied moment. "There is no good on earth; and sin is but a name. Come, Devil; for to thee is this world given."

And, maddened with despair, so that he laughed loud and long, did Goodman Brown grasp his staff and set forth again, at such a rate that he seemed to fly along the forest path rather than to walk or run. The road grew wilder and drearier and more faintly traced, and vanished at length, leaving him in the heart of the dark wilderness, still rushing onward with the instinct that guides mortal man to evil. The whole forest was peopled with frightful sounds—the creaking of the trees, the howling of wild beasts, and the yell of Indians; while, sometimes the wind tolled like a distant church-bell, and sometimes gave a broad roar around the traveller, as if all Nature were laughing him to scorn. But he was himself the chief horror of the scene, and shrank not from its other horrors.

"Ha! ha! ha!" roared Goodman Brown when the wind laughed at him. "Let us hear which will laugh loudest! Think not to frighten me with your deviltry. Come witch, come wizard, come Indian powwow, come Devil himself! and here comes Goodman Brown. You may as well fear him as he fear you!"

In truth, all through the haunted forest there could be nothing more frightful than the figure of Goodman Brown. On he flew among the black pines, brandishing his staff with frenzied gestures, now giving vent to an inspiration of horrid blasphemy, and now shouting forth such laughter as set all the echoes of the forest laughing like demons around him. The fiend in his own shape is less hideous than when he rages in the breast of man. Thus sped the demoniac on his course, until, quivering among the trees, he saw a red light before him, as when the felled trunks and branches of a clearing have been set on fire, and throw up their lurid blaze against the sky, at the hour of midnight. He paused, in a lull of the tempest that had driven him onward, and heard the swell of what seemed a hymn rolling solemnly from a distance with the weight of many voices. He knew the tune; it was a familiar one in the choir of the village meeting-house. The verse died heavily away, and was lengthened by a chorus, not of human voices, but of all the sounds of the benighted wilderness pealing in awful harmony together. Goodman Brown cried out; and his cry was lost to his own ear by its unison with the cry of the desert.

In the interval of silence he stole forward until the light glared full upon his eyes. At one extremity of an open space, hemmed in by the dark wall of the forest, arose a rock, bearing some rude, natural resemblance either to an altar or a pulpit, and surrounded by four blazing pines, their tops aflame, their stems untouched, like candles at an evening meeting. The mass of foliage that had over-grown the summit of the rock was all on fire, blazing high into the night and fitfully illuminating the whole field. Each pendant twig and leafy festoon was in a blaze. As the red light arose and fell, a numerous congregation alternately shone forth, then disappeared in shadow, and again grew, as it were, out of the darkness, peopling the heart of the solitary woods at once.

"A grave and dark-clad company," quoth Goodman Brown.

In truth, they were such. Among them, quivering to and fro between gloom and splendor, appeared faces that would be seen next day at the council board of the province, and others which, Sabbath after Sabbath, looked devoutly heavenward, and benignantly over the crowded pews, from the holiest pulpits in the land. Some affirm that the lady of the governor was there. At least there were high dames well known to her, and wives of honored husbands, and widows, a great multitude, and ancient maidens, all of excellent repute, and fair young girls, who trembled lest their mothers should espy them. Either the sudden gleams of light flashing over the obscure field bedazzled Goodman Brown, or he recognized a score of the church-members of Salem village famous for their especial sanctity. Good old Deacon Gookin had arrived, and waited at the skirts of that venerable saint, his revered pastor. But, irreverently consorting with these grave, reputable, and pious people, these elders of the church, these chaste dames and dewy virgins, there were men of dissolute lives and women of spotted fame, wretches given over to all mean and filthy vice, and suspected even of horrid crimes. It was strange to see that the good shrank not from the wicked, nor were the sinners abashed by the saints. Scattered also among their pale-faced enemies were the Indian priests, or powwows, who had often scared their native forest with more hideous incantations than any known to English witchcraft.

"But, where is Faith?" thought Goodman Brown; and, as hope came into his heart, he trembled.

Another verse of the hymn arose, a slow and mournful strain, such as the pious love, but joined to words which expressed all that our nature can conceive of sin, and darkly hinted at far more. Unfathomable to mere mortals is the lore of fiends. Verse after verse was sung; and still the chorus of the desert swelled between like the deepest tone of a mighty organ; and with the final peal of that dreadful anthem, there came a sound, as if the roaring wind, the rushing streams, the howling beasts, and every other voice of the unconverted wilderness were mingling and according with the voice of guilty man in homage to the prince of all. The four blazing pines threw up a loftier flame, and obscurely discovered shapes and visages of horror on the smoke-wreaths above the impious assembly. At the same moment the fire on the rock shot redly forth and formed a glowing arch above its base, where now appeared a figure. With reverence be it spoken, the figure bore no slight similitude, both in garb and manner, to some grave divine of the New England churches.

"Bring forth the converts!" cried a voice that echoed through the field and rolled into the forest.

At the word, Goodman Brown stepped forth from the shadow of the trees and approached the congregation, with whom he felt a loathful brotherhood by the sympathy of all that was wicked in his heart. He could have well-nigh sworn that the shape of his own dead father beckoned him to advance, looking downward from a smoke-wreath, while a woman, with dim features of despair, threw out her hand to warn him back. Was it his mother? But he had no power to retreat one step, nor to resist, even in thought, when the minister and good old Deacon Gookin seized his arms and led him to the blazing rock. Thither came also the slender form of a veiled female, led between Goody Cloyse, that pious teacher of the catechism, and Martha Carrier, who had received the Devil's promise to be queen of hell. A rampant hag was she. And there stood the proselytes beneath the canopy of fire.

"Welcome, my children," said the dark figure, "to the communion of your race. Ye have found thus young your nature and your destiny. My children, look behind you!"

They turned; and flashing forth, as it were, in a sheet of flame, the fiend worshippers were seen; the smile of welcome gleamed darkly on every visage.

"There," resumed the sable form, "are all whom ye have reverenced from youth. Ye deemed them holier than yourselves, and shrank from your own sin, contrasting it with their lives of righteousness and prayerful aspirations heavenward. Yet here are they all in my worshipping assembly. This night it shall be granted you to know their secret deeds; how hoary-bearded elders of the church have whispered wanton words to the young maids of their households; how many a woman, eager for widow's weeds, has given her husband a drink at bedtime and let him sleep his last sleep in her bosom; how beardless youth have made haste to inherit their fathers' wealth; and how fair damsels—blush not, sweet ones—have dug little graves in the garden, and bidden me, the sole guest, to an infant's funeral. By the sympathy of your human hearts for sin ye shall scent out all the places—whether in church, bedchamber, street, field, or forest—where crime has been committed, and shall exult to behold the whole earth one stain of guilt, one mighty blood-spot. Far more than this. It shall be yours to penetrate, in every bosom, the deep mystery of sin, the fountain of all wicked arts, and which inexhaustibly supplies more evil impulses than human power—than my power at its utmost—can make manifest in deeds. And now, my children, look upon each other."

They did so; and, by the blaze of the hell-kindled torches, the wretched man beheld his Faith, and the wife her husband, trembling before that unhallowed altar.

"Lo, there ye stand, my children," said the figure, in a deep and solemn tone, almost sad, with its despairing awfulness, as if his once angelic nature could yet mourn for our miserable race. "Depending upon one another's hearts, ye had still hoped that virtue were not all a dream. Now are ye undeceived. Evil is the nature of mankind. Evil must be your only happiness. Welcome again, my children, to the communion of your race."

"Welcome," repeated the fiend worshippers, in one cry of despair and triumph.

And there they stood, the only pair, as it seemed, who were yet hesitating on the verge of wickedness in this dark world. A basin was hollowed, naturally, in the rock. Did it contain water, reddened by the lurid light? or was it blood? or, perchance, a liquid flame? Herein did the shape of evil dip his hand, and prepare to lay the mark of baptism upon their foreheads, that they might be partakers of the mystery of sin, more conscious of the secret guilt of others, both in deed and thought, than they could now be of their own. The husband cast one look at his pale wife, and Faith at him. What polluted wretches would the next glance show them to each other, shuddering alike at what they disclosed and what they saw!

"Faith! Faith!" cried the husband, "look up to Heaven, and resist the wicked one!"

Whether Faith obeyed, he knew not. Hardly had he spoken, when he found himself amid calm night and solitude, listening to a roar of the wind which died heavily away through the forest. He staggered against the rock, and felt it chill and damp; while a hanging twig, that had been all on fire, besprinkled his cheek with the coldest dew.

The next morning young Goodman Brown came slowly into the street of Salem village, staring around him like a bewildered man. The good old minister was taking a walk along the graveyard to get an appetite for breakfast and meditate his sermon, and bestowed a blessing, as he passed, on Goodman Brown. He shrank from the venerable saint as if to avoid an anathema. Old Deacon Gookin was at domestic worship, and the holy words of his prayer were heard through the open window. "What God doth the wizard pray to?" quoth Goodman Brown. Goody Cloyse, that excellent old Christian, stood in the early sunshine at her own lattice, catechising a little girl who had brought her a pint of morning's milk. Goodman Brown snatched away the child as from the grasp of the fiend himself. Turning the corner by the meeting-house, he spied the head of Faith, with the pink ribbons, gazing anxiously forth, and bursting into such joy at sight of him that she skipped along the street and almost kissed her husband before the whole village. But Goodman Brown looked sternly and sadly into her face, and passed on without a greeting.

Had Goodman Brown fallen asleep in the forest, and only dreamed a wild dream of a witch-meeting?

Be it so, if you will; but, alas! it was a dream of evil omen for young Goodman Brown. A stern, a sad, a darkly meditative, a distrustful, if not a desperate, man did he become from the night of that fearful dream. On the Sabbath day, when the congregation were singing a holy psalm, he could not listen, because an anthem of sin rushed loudly upon his ear, and drowned all the blessed strain. When the minister spoke from the pulpit, with power and fervid eloquence, and with his hand on the open Bible, of the sacred truths of our religion, and of saint-like lives and triumphant deaths, and of future bliss or misery unutterable, then did Goodman Brown turn pale, dreading lest the roof should thunder down upon the gray blasphemer and his hearers. Often, awaking suddenly at midnight, he shrank from the bosom of Faith, and at morning or eventide, when the family knelt down at prayer, he scowled, and muttered to himself, and gazed sternly at his wife, and turned away. And when he had lived long, and was borne to his grave, a hoary corpse, followed by Faith, an aged woman, and children and grandchildren, a goodly procession, besides neighbors, not a few, they carved no hopeful verse upon his tombstone; for his dying hour was gloom.

DR. HEIDEGGER'S EXPERIMENT

Nathaniel Hawthorne

THAT VERY SINGULAR man, old Dr. Heidegger, once invited four venerable friends to meet him in his study. There were three white-bearded gentlemen, Mr. Medbourne, Colonel Killigrew, and Mr. Gascoigne, and a withered gentlewoman, whose name was the Widow Wycherly. They were all melancholy old creatures, who had been unfortunate in life, and whose greatest misfortune it was that they were not long ago in their graves. Mr. Medbourne, in the vigor of his age, had been a prosperous merchant, but had lost his all by a frantic speculation, and was now little better than a mendicant. Colonel Killigrew had wasted his best years, and his health and sub-stance, in the pursuit of sinful pleasures, which had given birth to a brood of pains, such as the gout, and divers other torments of soul and body. Mr. Gascoigne was a ruined politician, a man of evil fame, or at least had been so, till time had buried him from the knowledge of the present generation, and made him obscure instead of infamous. As for the Widow Wycherly, tradition tells us that she was a great beauty in her day; but, for a long while past, she had lived in deep seclusion, on account of certain scandalous stories, which had prejudiced the gentry of the town against her. It is a circumstance worth mentioning, that each of these three old gentle-men, Mr. Medbourne, Colonel Killigrew, and Mr. Gascoigne, were early lovers of the Widow Wycherly, and had once been on the point of cutting each other's throats for her sake. And, before pro-ceeding further, I will merely hint, that Dr. Heidegger and all his four guests were sometimes thought to be a little beside themselves; as is not unfrequently the case with old people, when worried either by present troubles or woful recollections.

"My dear old friends," said Dr. Heidegger, motioning them to be seated, "I am desirous of your assistance in one of those little experiments with which I amuse myself here in my study."

If all stories were true, Dr. Heidegger's study must have been a very curious place. It was a dim, old-fashioned chamber, festooned with cobwebs, and besprinkled with antique dust. Around the walls stood several oaken bookcases, the lower shelves of which were filled with rows of gigantic folios and black-letter quartos, and the upper with little parchment-covered duodecimos. Over the central bookcase was a bronze bust of Hippocrates, with which, according to some authorities, Dr. Heidegger was accustomed to hold consultations, in all difficult cases of his practice. In the obscurest corner of the room stood a tall and narrow oaken closet, with its door ajar, within which doubtfully appeared a skeleton. Between two of the bookcases hung a looking-glass, presenting its high and dusty plate within a tarnished gilt frame. Among many wonderful stories related of this mirror, it was fabled that the spirits of all the doctor's deceased patients dwelt within its verge, and would stare him in the face whenever he looked thitherward. The opposite side of the chamber was ornamented with the full-length portrait of a young lady, arrayed in the faded magnificence of silk, satin, and brocade, and with a visage as faded as her dress. Above half a century ago, Dr. Heidegger had been on the point of marriage with this young lady; but, being affected with some slight disorder, she had swallowed one of her lover's prescriptions, and died on the bridal evening. The greatest curiosity of the study remains to be mentioned; it was a ponderous folio volume, bound in black leather, with massive silver clasps. There were no letters on the back, and nobody could tell the title of the book. But it was well known to be a book of magic; and once, when a chambermaid had lifted it, merely to brush away the dust, the skeleton had rattled in its closet, the picture of the young lady had stepped one foot upon the floor, and several ghastly faces had peeped forth from the mirror; while the brazen head of Hippocrates frowned, and said, "Forbear!"

Such was Dr. Heidegger's study. On the summer afternoon of our tale, a small round table, as black as ebony, stood in the centre of the room, sustaining a cut-glass vase, of beautiful form and elaborate workmanship. The sunshine came through the window, between the heavy festoons of two faded damask curtains, and fell directly across this vase; so that a mild splendor was reflected from it on the ashen visages of the five old people who sat around. Four champagne-glasses were also on the table.

"My dear old friends," repeated Dr. Heidegger, "may I reckon on your aid in performing an exceedingly curious experiment?"

Now Dr. Heidegger was a very strange old gentleman, whose eccentricity had become the nucleus for a thousand fantastic stories. Some of these fables, to my shame be it spoken, might possibly be traced back to mine own veracious self; and if any passages of the present tale should startle the reader's faith, I must be content to bear the stigma of a fiction-monger.

When the doctor's four guests heard him talk of his proposed experiment, they anticipated nothing more wonderful than the murder of a mouse in an air-pump, or the examination of a cobweb by the microscope, or some similar nonsense, with which he was constantly in the habit of pestering his intimates. But without waiting for a reply, Dr. Heidegger hobbled across the chamber, and returned with the same ponderous folio, bound in black leather, which common report affirmed to be a book of magic. Undoing the silver clasps, he opened the volume, and took from among its black-letter pages a rose, or what was once a rose, though now the green leaves and crimson petals had assumed one brownish hue, and the ancient flower seemed ready to crumble to dust in the doctor's hands.

"This rose," said Dr. Heidegger, with a sigh, "this same withered and crumbling flower, blossomed five-and-fifty years ago. It was given me by Sylvia Ward, whose portrait hangs yonder; and I meant to wear it in my bosom at our wedding. Five-and-fifty years it has been treasured between the leaves of this old volume. Now, would you deem it possible that this rose of half a century could ever bloom again?"

"Nonsense!" said the Widow Wycherly, with a peevish toss of her head. "You might as well ask whether an old woman's wrinkled face could ever bloom again."

"See!" answered Dr. Heidegger.

He uncovered the vase, and threw the faded rose into the water which it contained. At first, it lay lightly on the surface of the fluid, appearing to imbibe none of its moisture. Soon, however, a singular change began to be visible. The crushed and dried petals stirred, and assumed a deepening tinge of crimson, as if the flower were reviving from a death-like slumber; the slender stalk and twigs of foliage became green; and there was the rose of half a century, looking as fresh as when Sylvia Ward had first given it to her lover. It was scarcely full blown; for some of its delicate red leaves curled modestly around its moist bosom, within which two or three dew-drops were sparkling.

"That is certainly a very pretty deception," said the doctor's friends; carelessly, however, for they had witnessed greater miracles at a conjurer's show; "pray how was it effected?"

"Did you never hear of the 'Fountain of Youth?'" asked Dr. Heidegger, "which Ponce de Leon, the Spanish adventurer, went in search of, two or three centuries ago?"

"But did Ponce de Leon ever find it?" said the Widow Wycherly.

"No," answered Dr. Heidegger, "for he never sought it in the right place. The famous Fountain of Youth, if I am rightly informed, is situated in the southern part of the Floridian peninsula, not far from Lake Macaco. Its source is overshadowed by several gigantic magnolias, which, though numberless centuries old, have been kept as fresh as violets, by the virtues of this wonderful water. An acquaintance of mine, knowing my curiosity in such matters, has sent me what you see in the vase."

"Ahem!" said Colonel Killigrew, who believed not a word of the doctor's story; "and what may be the effect of this fluid on the human frame?"

"You shall judge for yourself, my dear Colonel," replied Dr. Heidegger; "and all of you, my respected friends, are welcome to so much of this admirable fluid as may restore to you the bloom of youth. For my own part, having had much trouble in growing old, I am in no hurry to grow young again. With your permission, therefore, I will merely watch the progress of the experiment."

While he spoke, Dr. Heidegger had been filling the four champagne-glasses with the water of the Fountain of Youth. It was apparently impregnated with an effervescent gas, for little bubbles were continually ascending from the depths of the glasses, and bursting in silvery spray at the surface. As the liquor diffused a pleas-ant perfume, the old people doubted not that it possessed cordial and comfortable properties; and, though utter sceptics as to its rejuvenescent power, they were inclined to swallow it at once. But Dr. Heidegger besought them to stay a moment.

"Before you drink, my respectable old friends," said he, "it would be well that, with the experience of a lifetime to direct you,

you should draw up a few general rules for your guidance, in passing a second time through the perils of youth. Think what a sin and shame it would be, if, with your peculiar advantages, you should not become patterns of virtue and wisdom to all the young people of the age."

The doctor's four venerable friends made him no answer, except by a feeble and tremulous laugh; so very ridiculous was the idea, that, knowing how closely repentance treads behind the steps of error, they should ever go astray again.

"Drink, then," said the doctor, bowing. "I rejoice that I have so well selected the subjects of my experiment."

With palsied hands, they raised the glasses to their lips. The liquor, if it really possessed such virtues as Dr. Heidegger imputed to it, could not have been bestowed on four human beings who needed it more wofully. They looked as if they had never known what youth or pleasure was, but had been the offspring of Nature's dotage, and always the gray, decrepit, sapless, miserable creatures who now sat stooping round the doctor's table, without life enough in their souls or bodies to be animated even by the prospect of growing young again. They drank off the water, and replaced their glasses on the table.

Assuredly there was an almost immediate improvement in the aspect of the party, not unlike what might have been produced by a glass of generous wine, together with a sudden glow of cheerful sunshine, brightening over all their visages at once. There was a healthful suffusion on their cheeks, instead of the ashen hue that had made them look so corpse-like. They gazed at one another, and fancied that some magic power had really begun to smooth away the deep and sad inscriptions which Father Time had been so long engraving on their brows. The Widow Wycherly adjusted her cap, for she felt almost like a woman again.

"Give us more of this wondrous water!" cried they, eagerly. "We are younger,—but we are still too old! Quick,—give us more!"

"Patience, patience!" quoth Dr. Heidegger, who sat watching the experiment, with philosophic coolness. "You have been a long time growing old. Surely, you might be content to grow young in half an hour! But the water is at your service."

Again he filled their glasses with the liquor of youth, enough of which still remained in the vase to turn half the old people in the city to the age of their own grandchildren. While the bubbles were yet sparkling on the brim, the doctor's four guests snatched their glasses from the table, and swallowed the contents at a single gulp. Was it delusion? even while the draught was passing down their throats, it seemed to have wrought a change on their whole systems. Their eyes grew clear and bright; a dark shade deepened among their silvery locks; they sat around the table, three gentlemen of middle age, and a woman, hardly beyond her buxom prime.

"My dear widow, you are charming!" cried Colonel Killigrew, whose eyes had been fixed upon her face, while the shadows of age were flitting from it like darkness from the crimson daybreak.

The fair widow knew, of old, that Colonel Killigrew's compliments were not always measured by sober truth; so she started up and ran to the mirror, still dreading that the ugly visage of an old woman would meet her gaze. Meanwhile, the three gentlemen behaved in such a manner, as proved that the water of the Fountain of Youth possessed some intoxicating qualities; unless, indeed, their exhilaration of spirits were merely a lightsome dizziness, caused by the sudden removal of the weight of years. Mr. Gascoigne's mind seemed to run on political topics, but whether relating to the past, present, or future, could not easily be determined, since the same ideas and phrases have been in vogue these fifty years. Now he rattled forth full-throated sentences about patriotism, national glory, and the people's right; now he muttered some perilous stuff or other, in a sly and doubtful whisper, so cautiously that even his own conscience could scarcely catch the secret; and now, again, he spoke in measured accents, and a deeply deferential tone, as if a royal ear were listening to his well-turned periods. Colonel Killigrew all this time had been trolling forth a jolly bottle-song, and ringing his glass in symphony with the chorus, while his eyes wandered toward the buxom figure of the Widow Wycherly. On the other side of the table, Mr. Medbourne was involved in a calculation of dollars and cents, with which was strangely intermingled a project for supplying the East Indies with ice, by harnessing a team of whales to the polar icebergs.

As for the Widow Wycherly, she stood before the mirror courtesying and simpering to her own image, and greeting it as the friend whom she loved better than all the world beside. She thrust her face close to the glass, to see whether some long-remembered wrinkle or crow's-foot had indeed vanished. She examined whether the snow had so entirely melted from her hair, that the venerable cap could be safely thrown aside. At last, turning briskly away, she came with a sort of dancing step to the table.

"My dear old doctor," cried she, "pray favor me with another glass!"

"Certainly, my dear madam, certainly!" replied the complaisant doctor; "see! I have already filled the glasses."

There, in fact, stood the four glasses, brimful of this wonderful water, the delicate spray of which, as it effervesced from the surface, resembled the tremulous glitter of diamonds. It was now so nearly sunset, that the chamber had grown duskier than ever; but a mild and moonlike splendor gleamed from within the vase, and rested alike on the four guests, and on the doctor's venerable figure. He sat in a high-backed, elaborately carved oaken armchair, with a gray dignity of aspect that might have well befitted that very Father Time, whose power had never been disputed, save by this fortunate company. Even while quaffing the third draught of the Fountain of Youth, they were almost awed by the expression of his mysterious visage.

But, the next moment, the exhilarating gush of young life shot through their veins. They were now in the happy prime of youth. Age, with its miserable train of cares, and sorrows, and diseases, was remembered only as the trouble of a dream, from which they had joyously awoke. The fresh gloss of the soul, so early lost, and without which the world's successive scenes had been but a gallery of faded pictures, again threw its enchantment over all their prospects. They felt like new-created beings, in a new-created universe.

"We are young! We are young!" they cried exultingly.

Youth, like the extremity of age, had effaced the strongly marked characteristics of middle life, and mutually assimilated them all. They were a group of merry youngsters, almost maddened with the exuberant frolicsomeness of their years. The most singular effect of their gayety was an impulse to mock the infirmity and decrepitude of which they had so lately been the victims. They laughed loudly at their old-fashioned attire, the wide-skirted coats and flapped waistcoats of the young men, and the ancient cap and gown of the blooming girl. One limped across the floor, like a gouty grandfather; one set a pair of spectacles astride of his nose, and pretended to pore over the black-letter pages of the book of magic; a third seated himself in an arm-chair, and strove to imitate the venerable dignity of Dr. Heidegger. Then all shouted mirthfully, and leaped about the room. The Widow Wycherly—if so fresh a damsel could be called a widow—tripped up to the doctor's chair, with a mischievous merriment in her rosy face.

"Doctor, you dear old soul," cried she, "get up and dance with me!" And then the four young people laughed louder than ever, to think what a queer figure the poor old doctor would cut.

"Pray excuse me," answered the doctor, quietly. "I am old and rheumatic, and my dancing days were over long ago. But either of these gay young gentlemen will be glad of so pretty a partner."

"Dance with me, Clara!" cried Colonel Killigrew.

"No, no, I will be her partner!" shouted Mr. Gascoigne.

"She promised me her hand, fifty years ago!" exclaimed Mr. Medbourne.

They all gathered round her. One caught both her hands in his passionate grasp,—another threw his arm about her waist,—the third buried his hand among the glossy curls that clustered beneath the widow's cap. Blushing, panting, struggling, chiding, laughing, her warm breath fanning each of their faces by turns, she strove to disengage herself, yet still remained in their triple embrace. Never was there a livelier picture of youthful rivalship, with bewitching beauty for the prize. Yet, by a strange deception, owing to the duskiness of the chamber, and the antique dresses which they still wore, the tall mirror is said to have reflected the figures of the three old, gray, withered grandsires, ridiculously contending for the skinny ugliness of a shrivelled grandam.

But they were young: their burning passions proved them so. Inflamed to madness by the coquetry of the girl-widow, who neither granted nor quite withheld her favors, the three rivals began to interchange threatening glances. Still keeping hold of the fair prize, they grappled fiercely at one another's throats. As they struggled to and fro, the table was overturned, and the vase dashed into a thousand fragments. The precious Water of Youth flowed in a bright stream across the floor, moistening the wings of a butterfly, which, grown old in the decline of summer, had alighted there to die. The insect fluttered lightly through the chamber, and settled on the snowy head of Dr. Heidegger.

"Come, come, gentlemen!—come, Madam Wycherly," exclaimed the doctor, "I really must protest against this riot."

They stood still and shivered; for it seemed as if gray Time were calling them back from their sunny youth, far down into the chill and darksome vale of years. They looked at old Dr. Heidegger, who sat in his carved arm-chair, holding the rose of half a century, which he had rescued from among the fragments of the shattered vase. At the motion of his hand, the four rioters resumed their seats; the more readily, because their violent exertions had wearied them, youthful though they were.

"My poor Sylvia's rose!" ejaculated Dr. Heidegger, holding it in the light of the sunset clouds; "it appears to be fading again."

And so it was. Even while the party were looking at it, the flower continued to shrivel up, till it became as dry and fragile as when the doctor had first thrown it into the vase. He shook off the few drops of moisture which clung to its petals.

"I love it as well thus, as in its dewy freshness," observed he, pressing the withered rose to his withered lips. While he spoke, the butterfly fluttered down from the doctor's snowy head, and fell upon the floor.

His guests shivered again. A strange chillness, whether of the body or spirit they could not tell, was creeping gradually over them all. They gazed at one another, and fancied that each fleeting moment snatched away a charm, and left a deepening furrow where none had been before. Was it an illusion? Had the changes of a lifetime been crowded into so brief a space, and were they now four aged people, sitting with their old friend, Dr. Heidegger?

"Are we grown old again, so soon?" cried they, dolefully.

In truth, they had. The Water of Youth possessed merely a virtue more transient than that of wine. The delirium which it created had effervesced away. Yes! they were old again. With a shuddering impulse, that showed her a woman still, the widow clasped her skinny hands before her face, and wished that the coffin-lid were over it, since it could be no longer beautiful.

"Yes, friends, ye are old again," said Dr. Heidegger, "and lo! the Water of Youth is all lavished on the ground. Well, I bemoan it not; for if the fountain gushed at my very doorstep, I would not stoop to bathe my lips in it; no, though its delirium were for years instead of moments. Such is the lesson ye have taught me!"

But the doctor's four friends had taught no such lesson to themselves. They resolved forthwith to make a pilgrimage to Florida, and quaff at morning, noon, and night from the Fountain of Youth.

Note.—In an English Review, not long since, I have been accused of plagiarizing the idea of this story from a chapter in one of the novels of Alexandre Dumas. There has undoubtedly been a plagiarism on one side or the other; but as my story was written a good deal more than twenty years ago, and as the novel is of considerably more recent date, I take pleasure in thinking that M. Dumas has done me the honor to appropriate one of the fanciful conceptions of my earlier days. He is heartily welcome to it; nor is it the only instance, by many, in which the great French romancer has exercised the privilege of commanding genius by confiscating the intellectual property of less famous people to his own use and behoof.

THE MASQUE OF THE RED DEATH

Edgar Allan Poe

THE "RED DEATH" had long devastated the country. No pestilence had ever been so fatal, or so hideous. Blood was its Avatar and its seal—the redness and the horror of blood. There were sharp pains, and sudden dizziness, and then profuse bleeding at the pores, with dissolution. The scarlet stains upon the body and especially upon the face of the victim, were the pest ban which shut him out from the aid and from the sympathy of his fellow-men. And the whole seizure, progress and termination of the disease, were the incidents of half an hour.

But the Prince Prospero was happy and dauntless and sagacious. When his dominions were half depopulated, he summoned to his presence a thousand hale and light-hearted friends from among the knights and dames of his court, and with these retired to the deep seclusion of one of his castellated abbeys. This was an extensive and magnificent structure, the creation of the prince's own eccentric yet august taste. A strong and lofty wall girdled it in. This wall had gates of iron. The courtiers, having entered, brought furnaces and massy hammers and welded the bolts. They resolved to leave means neither of ingress or egress to the sudden impulses of despair or of frenzy from within. The abbey was amply provisioned. With such precautions the courtiers might bid defiance to contagion. The external world could take care of itself. In the meantime it was folly to grieve, or to think. The prince had provided all the appliances of pleasure. There were buffoons, there were improvisatori, there were ballet-dancers, there were musicians, there was Beauty, there was wine. All these and security were within. Without was the "Red Death."

It was toward the close of the fifth or sixth month of his seclusion, and while the pestilence raged most furiously abroad, that the Prince Prospero entertained his thousand friends at a masked ball of the most unusual magnificence.

It was a voluptuous scene, that masquerade. But first let me tell of the rooms in which it was held. There were seven—an imperial suite. In many palaces, however, such suites form a long and straight vista, while the folding doors slide back nearly to the walls on either hand, so that the view of the whole extent is scarcely impeded. Here the case was very different; as might have been expected from the duke's love of the *bizarre*. The apartments were so irregularly disposed that the vision embraced but little more than one at a time. There was a sharp turn at every twenty or thirty yards, and at each turn a novel effect. To the right and left, in the middle of each wall, a tall and narrow Gothic window looked out upon a closed corridor which pursued the windings of the suite. These windows were of stained glass whose color varied in accordance with the prevailing hue of the decorations of the chamber into which it opened. That at the eastern extremity was hung, for example, in blue—and vividly blue were its windows. The second chamber was purple in its ornaments and tapestries, and here the panes were purple. The third was green throughout, and so were the casements. The fourth was furnished and lighted with orange—the fifth with white—the sixth with violet. The seventh apartment was closely shrouded in black velvet tapestries that hung all over the ceiling and down the walls, falling in heavy folds upon a carpet of the same material and hue. But in this chamber only, the color of the windows failed to correspond with the decorations. The panes here were scarlet—a deep blood color. Now in no one of the seven apartments was there any lamp or candelabrum, amid the profusion of golden ornaments that lay scattered to and fro or depended from the roof. There was no light of any kind emanating from lamp or candle within the suite of chambers. But in the corridors that followed the suite, there stood, opposite to each window, a heavy tripod, bearing a brazier of fire that projected its rays through the tinted glass and so glaringly illumined the room. And thus were produced a multitude of gaudy and fantastic appearances. But in the western or black chamber the effect of the fire-light that streamed upon the dark hangings through the blood-tinted panes, was ghastly in the extreme, and produced so wild a look upon the countenances of those who entered, that there were few of the company bold enough to set foot within its precincts at all.

It was in this apartment, also, that there stood against the western wall, a gigantic clock of ebony. Its pendulum swung to and fro with a dull, heavy, monotonous clang; and when the minute-hand made the circuit of the face, and the hour was to be stricken, there came from the brazen lungs of the clock a sound which was clear and loud and deep and exceedingly musical, but of so peculiar a note and emphasis that, at each lapse of an hour, the musicians of the orchestra were constrained to pause, momentarily, in their performance, to hearken to the sound; and thus the waltzers perforce ceased their evolutions; and there was a brief disconcert of the whole gay company; and, while the chimes of the clock yet rang, it was observed that the giddiest grew pale, and the more aged and sedate passed their hands over their brows as if in confused reverie or meditation. But when the echoes had fully ceased, a light laughter at once pervaded the assembly; the musicians looked at each other and smiled as if at their own nervousness and folly, and made whispering vows, each to the other, that the next chiming of the clock should produce in them no similar emotion; and then, after the lapse of sixty minutes, (which embrace three thousand and six hundred seconds of the Time that flies,) there came yet another chiming of the clock, and then were the same disconcert and tremulousness and meditation as before.

But, in spite of these things, it was a gay and magnificent revel. The tastes of the duke were peculiar. He had a fine eye for colors and effects. He disregarded the *decora* of mere fashion. His plans were bold and fiery, and his conceptions glowed with barbaric lustre. There are some who would have thought him mad. His followers felt that he was not. It was necessary to hear and see and touch him to be *sure* that he was not.

He had directed, in great part, the moveable embellishments of the seven chambers, upon occasion of this great *fête;* and it was his own guiding taste which had given character to the masqueraders. Be sure they were grotesque. There were much glare and glitter and piquancy and phantasm—much of what has been since seen in "Hernani." There were arabesque figures with unsuited limbs and appointments. There were delirious fancies such as the madman fashions. There was much of the beautiful, much of the wanton, much of the *bizarre,* something of the terrible, and not a little of that which might have excited disgust. To and fro in the seven chambers there stalked, in fact, a multitude of dreams. And these—the dreams—writhed in and about, taking hue from the rooms, and causing the wild music of the orchestra to seem as the echo of their steps. And, anon, there strikes the ebony clock which stands in the hall of the velvet. And then, for a moment, all is still, and all is silent save the voice of the clock. The dreams are stiff-frozen as they stand. But the echoes of the chime die away—they have endured but an instant—and a light, half-subdued laughter floats after them as they depart. And now again the music swells, and the dreams live, and writhe to and fro more merrily than ever, taking hue from the many-tinted windows through which stream the rays from the tripods. But to the chamber which lies most westwardly of the seven, there are now none of the maskers who venture; for the night is waning away; and there flows a ruddier light through the blood-colored panes; and the blackness of the sable drapery appals; and to him whose foot falls upon the sable carpet, there comes from the near clock of ebony a muffled peal more solemnly emphatic than any which reaches *their* ears who indulge in the more remote gaieties of the other apartments.

But these other apartments were densely crowded, and in them beat feverishly the heart of life. And the revel went whirlingly on, until at length there commenced the sounding of midnight upon the clock. And then the music ceased, as I have told; and the evolutions of the waltzers were quieted; and there was an uneasy cessation of all things as before. But now there were twelve strokes to be sounded by the bell of the clock; and thus it happened, perhaps, that more of thought crept, with more of time, into the meditations of the thoughtful among those who revelled. And thus, too, it happened, perhaps, that before the last echoes of the last chime had utterly sunk into silence, there were many individuals in the crowd who had found leisure to become aware of the presence of a masked figure which had arrested the attention of no single individual before. And the rumor of this new presence having spread itself whisperingly around, there arose at length from the whole company a buzz, or murmur, expressive of disapprobation and surprise—then, finally, of terror, of horror, and of disgust.

In an assembly of phantasms such as I have painted, it may well be supposed that no ordinary appearance could have excited such sensation. In truth the masquerade license of the night was nearly unlimited; but the figure in question had out-Heroded Herod, and gone beyond the bounds of even the prince's indefinite decorum. There are chords in the hearts of the most reckless which cannot be touched without emotion. Even with the utterly lost, to whom life and death are equally jests, there are matters of which no jest can be made. The whole company, indeed, seemed now deeply to feel that in the costume and bearing of the stranger neither wit nor propriety existed. The figure was tall and gaunt, and shrouded from head to foot in the habiliments of the grave. The mask which concealed the visage was made so nearly to resemble the countenance of a stiffened corpse that the closest scrutiny must have had difficulty in detecting the cheat. And yet all this might have been endured, if not approved, by the mad revellers around. But the mummer had gone so far as to assume the type of the Red Death. His vesture was dabbled in *blood*—and his broad brow, with all the features of the face, was besprinkled with the scarlet horror.

When the eyes of Prince Prospero fell upon this spectral image (which with a slow and solemn movement, as if more fully to sustain its *rôle,* stalked to and fro among the waltzers) he was seen to be convulsed, in the first moment with a strong shudder either of terror or distaste; but, in the next, his brow reddened with rage.

"Who dares?" he demanded hoarsely of the courtiers who stood near him—"who dares insult us with this blasphemous mockery? Seize him and unmask him—that we may know whom we have to hang at sunrise, from the battlements!"

It was in the eastern or blue chamber in which stood the Prince Prospero as he uttered these words. They rang throughout the seven rooms loudly and clearly—for the prince was a bold and robust man, and the music had become hushed at the waving of his hand.

It was in the blue room where stood the prince, with a group of pale courtiers by his side. At first, as he spoke, there was a slight rushing movement of this group in the direction of the intruder, who at the moment was also near at hand, and now, with deliberate and stately step, made closer approach to the speaker. But from a certain nameless awe with which the mad assumptions of the mummer had inspired the whole party, there were found none who put forth hand to seize him; so that, unimpeded, he passed within a yard of the prince's person; and, while the vast assembly, as if with one impulse, shrank from the centres of the rooms to the walls, he made his way uninterruptedly, but with the same solemn and measured step which had distinguished him from the first, through the blue chamber to the purple—through the purple to the green—through the green to the orange—through this again to the white—and even thence to the violet, ere a decided movement had been made to arrest him. It was then, however, that the Prince Prospero, maddening with rage and the shame of his own momentary cowardice, rushed hurriedly through the six chambers, while none followed him on account of a deadly terror that had seized upon all. He bore aloft a drawn dagger, and had approached, in rapid impetuosity, to within three or four feet of the retreating figure, when the latter, having attained the extremity of the velvet apartment, turned suddenly and confronted his pursuer. There was a sharp cry—and the dagger dropped gleaming upon the sable carpet, upon which, instantly afterwards, fell prostrate in death the Prince Prospero. Then, summoning the wild courage of despair, a throng of the revellers at once threw themselves into the black apartment, and, seizing the mummer, whose tall figure stood erect and motionless within the shadow of the ebony clock, gasped in unutterable horror at finding the grave-cerements and corpselike mask which they handled with so violent a rudeness, untenanted by any tangible form.

And now was acknowledged the presence of the Red Death. He had come like a thief in the night. And one by one dropped the revellers in the blood-bedewed halls of their revel, and died each in the despairing posture of his fall. And the life of the ebony clock went out with that of the last of the gay. And the flames of the tripods expired. And Darkness and Decay and the Red Death held illimitable dominion over all.

THE TELL-TALE HEART

Edgar Allan Poe

TRUE!—NERVOUS—VERY, VERY DREADFULLY nervous I had been and am; but why *will* you say that I am mad? The disease had sharpened my senses—not destroyed—not dulled them. Above all was the sense of hearing acute. I heard all things in the heaven and in the earth. I heard many things in hell. How, then, am I mad? Hearken! and observe how healthily—how calmly I can tell you the whole story.

It is impossible to say how first the idea entered my brain; but once conceived, it haunted me day and night. Object there was none. Passion there was none. I loved the old man. He had never wronged me. He had never given me insult. For his gold I had no desire. I think it was his eye! yes, it was this! One of his eyes resembled that of a vulture—a pale blue eye, with a film over it. Whenever it fell upon me, my blood ran cold; and so by degrees—very gradually—I made up my mind to take the life of the old man, and thus rid myself of the eye for ever.

Now this is the point. You fancy me mad. Madmen know nothing. But you should have seen *me*. You should have seen how wisely I proceeded—with what caution—with what foresight—with what dissimulation I went to work! I was never kinder to the old man than during the whole week before I killed him. And every night, about midnight, I turned the latch of his door and opened it—oh, so gently! And then, when I had made an opening sufficient for my head, I put in a dark lantern, all closed, closed, that no light shone out, and then I thrust in my head. Oh, you would have laughed to see how cunningly I thrust it in! I moved it slowly—very, very slowly, so that I might not disturb the old man's sleep. It took me an hour to place my whole head within the opening so far that I could see him as he lay upon his bed. Ha!—would a madman have been so wise as this? And then, when my head was well in the room, I undid the lantern cautiously—oh, so cautiously—cautiously (for the hinges creaked)—I undid it just so much that a single thin ray fell upon the vulture eye. And this I did for seven long nights— every night just at midnight—but I found the eye always closed; and so it was impossible to do the work; for it was not the old man who vexed me, but his Evil Eye. And every morning, when the day broke, I went boldly into the chamber, and spoke courageously to him, calling him by name in a hearty tone, and inquiring how he had passed the night. So you see he would have been a very profound old man, indeed, to suspect that every night, just at twelve, I looked in upon him while he slept.

Upon the eighth night I was more than usually cautious in open- ing the door. A watch's minute hand moves more quickly than did mine. Never before that night had I *felt* the extent of my own powers—of my sagacity. I could scarcely contain my feelings of triumph. To think that there I was, opening the door, little by little, and he not even to dream of my secret deeds or thoughts. I fairly chuckled at the idea; and perhaps he heard me; for he moved on the bed suddenly, as if startled. Now you may think that I drew back—but no. His room was as black as pitch with the thick dark- ness (for the shutters were close fastened, through fear of robbers), and so I knew that he could not see the opening of the door, and I kept pushing it on steadily, steadily.

I had my head in, and was about to open the lantern, when my thumb slipped upon the tin fastening, and the old man sprang up in bed, crying out—"Who's there?"

I kept quite still and said nothing. For a whole hour I did not move a muscle, and in the meantime I did not hear him lie down. He was still sitting up in the bed listening;—just as I have done, night after night, hearkening to the death watches in the wall.

Presently I heard a slight groan, and I knew it was the groan of mortal terror. It was not a groan of pain or of grief—oh, no!—it was the low stifled sound that arises from the bottom of the soul when overcharged with awe. I knew the sound well. Many a night, just at midnight, when all the world slept, it has welled up from my own bosom, deepening, with its dreadful echo, the terrors that distracted me. I say I knew it well. I knew what the old man felt, and pitied him, although I chuckled at heart. I knew that he had been lying awake ever since the first slight noise, when he had turned in the bed. His fears had been ever since growing upon him. He had been trying to fancy them causeless, but could not. He had been saying to himself—"It is nothing but the wind in the chimney—it is only a mouse crossing the floor," or "it is merely a cricket which has made a single chirp." Yes, he had been trying to comfort himself with these suppositions: but he had found all in vain. *All in vain;* because Death, in approaching him, had stalked with his black shadow before him, and enveloped the victim. And it was the mournful influence of the unperceived shadow that caused him to feel—although he neither saw nor heard—to *feel* the presence of my head within the room.

When I had waited a long time, very patiently, without hearing him lie down, I resolved to open a little—a very, very little crevice in the lantern. So I opened it—you cannot imagine how stealthily, stealthily—until, at length, a single dim ray, like the thread of the spider, shot from out the crevice and full upon the vulture eye.

It was open—wide, wide open—and I grew furious as I gazed upon it. I saw it with perfect distinctness—all a dull blue, with a hideous veil over it that chilled the very marrow in my bones; but I could see nothing else of the old man's face or person: for I had directed the ray as if by instinct, precisely upon the damned spot.

And now have I not told you that what you mistake for madness is but over-acuteness of the senses?—now, I say, there came to my ears a low, dull, quick sound, such as a watch makes when enveloped in cotton. I knew *that* sound well too. It was the beating of the old man's heart. It increased my fury, as the beating of a drum stimulates the soldier into courage.

But even yet I refrained and kept still. I scarcely breathed. I held the lantern motionless. I tried how steadily I could maintain the ray upon the eye. Meantime the hellish tattoo of the heart increased. It grew quicker and quicker, and louder and louder every instant. The old man's terror must have been extreme! It grew louder, I say, louder every moment!—do you mark me well? I have told you that I am nervous: so I am. And now at the dead hour of the night, amid the dreadful silence of that old house, so strange a noise as this excited me to uncontrollable terror. Yet, for some minutes longer I refrained and stood still. But the beating grew louder, louder! I thought the heart must burst. And now a new anxiety seized me—the sound would be heard by a neighbor! The old man's hour had come! With a loud yell, I threw open the lantern and leaped into the room. He shrieked once—once only. In an instant I dragged him to the floor, and pulled the heavy bed over him. I then smiled gaily, to find the deed so far done. But, for many minutes, the heart beat on with a muffled sound. This, however, did not vex me; it would not be heard through the wall. At length it ceased. The old man was dead. I removed the bed and examined the corpse. Yes, he was stone, stone dead. I placed my hand upon the heart and held it there many minutes. There was no pulsation. He was stone dead. His eye would trouble me no more.

If still you think me mad, you will think so no longer when I describe the wise precautions I took for the concealment of the body. The night waned, and I worked hastily, but in silence. First of all I dismembered the corpse. I cut off the head and the arms and the legs.

I then took up three planks from the flooring of the chamber, and deposited all between the scantlings. I then replaced the boards so cleverly, so cunningly, that no human eye—not even *his*—could have detected any thing wrong. There was nothing to wash out—no stain of any kind—no blood-spot whatever. I had been too wary for that. A tub had caught all—ha! ha!

When I had made an end of these labors, it was four o'clock—still dark as midnight. As the bell sounded the hour, there came a knocking at the street door. I went down to open it with a light heart,—for what had I *now* to fear? There entered three men, who introduced themselves, with perfect suavity, as officers of the police. A shriek had been heard by a neighbor during the night; suspicion of foul play had been aroused; information had been lodged at the police office, and they (the officers) had been deputed to search the premises.

I smiled,—for *what* had I to fear? I bade the gentlemen welcome. The shriek, I said, was my own in a dream. The old man, I mentioned, was absent in the country. I took my visitors all over the house. I bade them search—search *well*. I led them, at length, to *his* chamber. I showed them his treasures, secure, undisturbed. In the enthusiasm of my confidence, I brought chairs into the room, and desired them *here* to rest from their fatigues, while I myself, in the wild audacity of my perfect triumph, placed my own seat upon the very spot beneath which reposed the corpse of the victim.

The officers were satisfied. My *manner* had convinced them. I was singularly at ease. They sat, and while I answered cheerily, they chatted of familiar things. But, ere long, I felt myself getting pale and wished them gone. My head ached, and I fancied a ringing in my ears: but still they sat and still chatted. The ringing became more distinct:—it continued and became more distinct: I talked more freely to get rid of the feeling: but it continued and gained definitiveness—until, at length, I found that the noise was *not* within my ears.

No doubt I now grew *very* pale;—but I talked more fluently, and with a heightened voice. Yet the sound increased—and what could I do? It was *a low, dull, quick sound—much such a sound as a watch makes when enveloped in cotton.* I gasped for breath—and yet the officers heard it not. I talked more quickly—more vehemently; but the noise steadily increased. I arose and argued about trifles, in a high key and with violent gesticulations, but the noise steadily increased. Why *would* they not be gone? I paced the floor to and fro with heavy strides, as if excited to fury by the observation of the men—but the noise steadily increased. Oh God! what *could* I do? I foamed—I raved—I swore! I swung the chair upon which I had been sitting, and grated it upon the boards, but the noise arose over all and continually increased. It grew louder—louder—*louder!* And still the men chatted pleasantly, and smiled. Was it possible they heard not? Almighty God!—no, no! They heard!—they suspected!— they *knew!*—they were making a mockery of my horror!—this I thought, and this I think. But any thing was better than this agony! Any thing was more tolerable than this derision! I could bear those hypocritical smiles no longer! I felt that I must scream or die!—and now—again!—hark! louder! louder! louder! *louder!*—

"Villains!" I shrieked, "dissemble no more! I admit the deed!—tear up the planks! here, here!—it is the beating of his hideous heart!"

THE CASK OF AMONTILLADO

Edgar Allan Poe

THE THOUSAND INJURIES of Fortunato I had borne as I best could; but when he ventured upon insult, I vowed revenge. You, who so well know the nature of my soul, will not suppose, however, that I gave utterance to a threat. *At length* I would be avenged; this was a point definitively settled—but the very definitiveness with which it was resolved, precluded the idea of risk. I must not only punish, but punish with impunity. A wrong is unredressed when retribution overtakes its redresser. It is equally unredressed when the avenger fails to make himself felt as such to him who has done the wrong.

It must be understood, that neither by word nor deed had I given Fortunato cause to doubt my good-will. I continued, as was my wont, to smile in his face, and he did not perceive that my smile *now* was at the thought of his immolation.

He had a weak point—this Fortunato—although in other regards he was a man to be respected and even feared. He prided himself on his connoisseurship in wine. Few Italians have the true virtuoso spirit. For the most part their enthusiasm is adopted to suit the time and opportunity—to practise imposture upon the British and Austrian *millionaires*. In painting and gemmary Fortunato, like his countrymen, was a quack—but in the matter of old wines he was sincere. In this respect I did not differ from him materially: I was skilful in the Italian vintages myself, and bought largely whenever I could.

It was about dusk, one evening during the supreme madness of the carnival season, that I encountered my friend. He accosted me with excessive warmth, for he had been drinking much. The man wore motley. He had on a tight-fitting parti-striped dress, and his head was surmounted by the conical cap and bells. I was so pleased to see him, that I thought I should never have done wringing his hand.

I said to him: "My dear Fortunato, you are luckily met. How remarkably well you are looking to-day! But I have received a pipe of what passes for Amontillado, and I have my doubts."

"How?" said he. "Amontillado? A pipe? Impossible! And in the middle of the carnival!"

"I have my doubts," I replied; "and I was silly enough to pay the full Amontillado price without consulting you in the matter. You were not to be found, and I was fearful of losing a bargain."

"Amontillado!"

"I have my doubts."

"Amontillado!"

"And I must satisfy them."

"Amontillado!"

"As you are engaged, I am on my way to Luchesi. If any one has a critical turn, it is he. He will tell me—"

"Luchesi cannot tell Amontillado from Sherry."

"And yet some fools will have it that his taste is a match for your own."

"Come, let us go."

"Whither?"

"To your vaults."

"My friend, no; I will not impose upon your good nature. I perceive you have an engagement. Luchesi—"

"I have no engagement;—come."

"My friend, no. It is not the engagement, but the severe cold with which I perceive you are afflicted. The vaults are insufferably damp. They are encrusted with nitre."

"Let us go, nevertheless. The cold is merely nothing. Amontillado! You have been imposed upon. And as for Luchesi, he cannot distinguish Sherry from Amontillado."

Thus speaking, Fortunato possessed himself of my arm. Putting on a mask of black silk, and drawing a *roquelaire* closely about my person, I suffered him to hurry me to my palazzo.

There were no attendants at home; they had absconded to make merry in honor of the time. I had told them that I should not return until the morning, and had given them explicit orders not to stir from the house. These orders were sufficient, I well knew, to insure their immediate disappearance, one and all, as soon as my back was turned.

I took from their sconces two flambeaux, and giving one to Fortunato, bowed him through several suites of rooms to the archway that led into the vaults. I passed down a long and winding staircase, requesting him to be cautious as he followed. We came at length to the foot of the descent and stood together on the damp ground of the catacombs of the Montresors.

The gait of my friend was unsteady, and the bells upon his cap jingled as he strode.

"The pipe?" said he.

"It is farther on," said I; "but observe the white web-work which gleams from these cavern walls."

He turned toward me, and looked into my eyes with two filmy orbs that distilled the rheum of intoxication.

"Nitre?" he asked, at length.

"Nitre," I replied. "How long have you had that cough?"

"Ugh! ugh! ugh!—ugh! ugh! ugh!—ugh! ugh! ugh!—ugh! ugh! ugh!—ugh! ugh! ugh!"

My poor friend found it impossible to reply for many minutes.

"It is nothing," he said, at last.

"Come," I said, with decision, "we will go back; your health is precious. You are rich, respected, admired, beloved; you are happy, as once I was. You are a man to be missed. For me it is no matter. We will go back; you will be ill, and I cannot be responsible. Besides, there is Luchesi—"

"Enough," he said; "the cough is a mere nothing; it will not kill me. I shall not die of a cough."

"True—true," I replied; "and, indeed, I had no intention of alarming you unnecessarily; but you should use all proper caution. A draught of this Medoc will defend us from the damps."

Here I knocked off the neck of a bottle which I drew from a long row of its fellows that lay upon the mould.

"Drink," I said, presenting him the wine.

He raised it to his lips with a leer. He paused and nodded to me familiarly, while his bells jingled.

"I drink," he said, "to the buried that repose around us."

"And I to your long life."

He again took my arm, and we proceeded.

"These vaults," he said, "are extensive."

"The Montresors," I replied, "were a great and numerous family."

"I forget your arms."

"A huge human foot d'or, in a field azure; the foot crushes a serpent rampant whose fangs are imbedded in the heel."

"And the motto?"

"Nemo me impune lacessit."

"Good!" he said.

The wine sparkled in his eyes and the bells jingled. My own fancy grew warm with the Medoc. We had passed through walls of piled bones, with casks and puncheons intermingling, into the inmost recesses of the catacombs. I paused again, and this time I made bold to seize Fortunato by an arm above the elbow.

"The nitre!" I said; "see, it increases. It hangs like moss upon the vaults. We are below the river's bed. The drops of moisture trickle among the bones. Come, we will go back ere it is too late. Your cough—"

"It is nothing," he said; "let us go on. But first, another draught of the Medoc."

I broke and reached him a flagon of De Grâve. He emptied it at a breath. His eyes flashed with a fierce light. He laughed and threw the bottle upward with a gesticulation I did not understand.

I looked at him in surprise. He repeated the movement—a grotesque one.

"You do not comprehend?" he said.

"Not I," I replied.

"Then you are not of the brotherhood."

"How?"

"You are not of the masons."

"Yes, yes," I said; "yes, yes."

"You? Impossible! A mason?"

"A mason," I replied.

"A sign," he said.

"It is this," I answered, producing a trowel from beneath the folds of my *roquelaire*.

"You jest," he exclaimed, recoiling a few paces. "But let us proceed to the Amontillado."

"Be it so," I said, replacing the tool beneath the cloak, and again offering him my arm. He leaned upon it heavily. We continued our route in search of the Amontillado. We passed through a range of low arches, descended, passed on, and descending again, arrived at a deep crypt, in which the foulness of the air caused our flambeaux rather to glow than flame.

At the most remote end of the crypt there appeared another less spacious. Its walls had been lined with human remains, piled to the vault overhead, in the fashion of the great catacombs of Paris. Three sides of this interior crypt were still ornamented in this manner. From the fourth the bones had been thrown down, and lay promiscuously upon the earth, forming at one point a mound of some size. Within the wall thus exposed by the displacing of the bones, we perceived a still interior recess, in depth about four feet, in width three, in height six or seven. It seemed to have been constructed for no especial use within itself, but formed merely the interval between two of the colossal supports of the roof of the catacombs, and was backed by one of their circumscribing walls of solid granite.

It was in vain that Fortunato, uplifting his dull torch, endeavored to pry into the depth of the recess. Its termination the feeble light did not enable us to see.

"Proceed," I said; "herein is the Amontillado. As for Luchesi—"

"He is an ignoramus," interrupted my friend, as he stepped unsteadily forward, while I followed immediately at his heels. In an instant he had reached the extremity of the niche, and finding his progress arrested by the rock, stood stupidly bewildered. A moment more and I had fettered him to the granite. In its surface were two iron staples, distant from each other about two feet, horizontally. From one of these depended a short chain, from the other a padlock. Throwing the links about his waist, it was but the work of a few seconds to secure it. He was too much astounded to resist. Withdrawing the key I stepped back from the recess.

"Pass your hand," I said, "over the wall; you cannot help feeling the nitre. Indeed it is *very* damp. Once more let me *implore* you to return. No? Then I must positively leave you. But I must first render you all the little attentions in my power."

"The Amontillado!" ejaculated my friend, not yet recovered from his astonishment.

"True," I replied; "the Amontillado."

As I said these words I busied myself among the pile of bones of which I have before spoken. Throwing them aside, I soon uncovered a quantity of building stone and mortar. With these materials and with the aid of my trowel, I began vigorously to wall up the entrance of the niche.

I had scarcely laid the first tier of the masonry when I discovered that the intoxication of Fortunato had in a great measure worn off.

The earliest indication I had of this was a low moaning cry from the depth of the recess. It was *not* the cry of a drunken man. There was then a long and obstinate silence. I laid the second tier, and the third, and the fourth; and then I heard the furious vibrations of the chain. The noise lasted for several minutes, during which, that I might hearken to it with the more satisfaction, I ceased my labors and sat down upon the bones. When at last the clanking subsided, I resumed the trowel, and finished without interruption the fifth, the sixth, and the seventh tier. The wall was now nearly upon a level with my breast. I again paused, and holding the flambeaux over the mason-work, threw a few feeble rays upon the figure within.

A succession of loud and shrill screams, bursting suddenly from the throat of the chained form, seemed to thrust me violently back. For a brief moment I hesitated—I trembled. Unsheathing my rapier, I began to grope with it about the recess; but the thought of an instant reassured me. I placed my hand upon the solid fabric of the catacombs, and felt satisfied. I reapproached the wall. I replied to the yells of him who clamored. I reechoed—I aided—I surpassed them in volume and in strength. I did this, and the clamorer grew still.

It was now midnight, and my task was drawing to a close. I had completed the eighth, the ninth, and the tenth tier. I had finished a portion of the last and the eleventh; there remained but a single stone to be fitted and plastered in. I struggled with its weight; I placed it partially in its destined position. But now there came from out the niche a low laugh that erected the hairs upon my head. It was succeeded by a sad voice, which I had difficulty in recognizing as that of the noble Fortunato. The voice said—

"Ha! ha! ha!—he! he!—a very good joke indeed—an excellent jest. We will have many a rich laugh about it at the palazzo—he! he! he!—over our wine—he! he! he!"

"The Amontillado!" I said.

"He! he! he!—he! he! he!—yes, the Amontillado. But is it not getting late? Will not they be awaiting us at the palazzo, the Lady Fortunato and the rest? Let us be gone."

"Yes," I said, "let us be gone."

"For the love of God, Montresor!"

"Yes," I said, "for the love of God!"

But to these words I hearkened in vain for a reply. I grew impatient. I called aloud:

"Fortunato!"

No answer. I called again:

"Fortunato!"

No answer still. I thrust a torch through the remaining aperture and let it fall within. There came forth in return only a jingling of the bells. My heart grew sick—on account of the dampness of the catacombs. I hastened to make an end of my labor. I forced the last stone into its position; I plastered it up. Against the new masonry I re-erected the old rampart of bones. For the half of a century no mortal has disturbed them. *In pace requiescat!*

THE KNITTED COLLAR

Mary Anne Hoare

ONE DARK DISMAL morning in the month of November, 1846, a miserable group of human beings were assembled in the attic of an old crumbling house, situated in a filthy obscure lane in a large Irish city. The room contained no furniture save an old empty box, a broken pitcher, and a bundle of damp straw, on which lay a man pale and ghastly. His wife and four children were crouching on the ground, near a fireless grate; their tatted rags and famine-stricken faces testifying too surely the dreadful extremity to which they were reduced.

"Nelly," said the man, "give me a drink of water. Oh, then, if 'twas *that* I always drank, 't isn't this way we'd be now?"

"Denis, agra, don't fret yourself," replied the poor woman, rising feebly, and holding the jug to his parched lips. "If I had anything at all to give you, darling, you'd do well yet; but where to get even one halfpenny to buy a grain of meal, I don't know."

The eldest daughter, a girl of fourteen, who had been holding one of her little brothers in her wasted arms, and trying gently to hush the plaintive cries of the starving child, looked up, and said eagerly, "Oh! mother, I had the collar that Jane Brown gave me thread to knit, nearly finished, when little Denny began to cry; maybe I could put the last stitch to it now, if you'd take him in your arms, and then I might be able to sell it in the streets."

"Do, darling," said her mother, "in the name of God, though He knows this blessed minute that 'tis badly able you are either to work or to walk."

Mary Sullivan, like many Irish girls, had much taste and facility in executing fine knitting; she had learned the art in happier days, while attending an excellent charity-school, and now she tried to make her talent available for the support of her family. They had once been well off. Denis Sullivan was a journeyman shoemaker, and earned a sufficiency for their wants. In an evil hour he was persuaded by a fellow workman to enter a public-house and take a glass of whiskey; then the common oft-repeated fate was his—his earnings squandered, his family reduced to want, and finally his own health totally destroyed. Things were in this state, when bitter famine visited the land in 1846. Then the Sullivans were literally left to perish, for those who had charity to dispense could scarcely reach one half the cases of heartrending misery which they witnessed; and therefore justly selected as objects of relief those who were brought to destitution by the pressure of the times, and not by any fault of their own. A drunken journeyman shoemaker could not hope for assistance while so many sober industrious men were perishing; and Sullivan's unfortunate family of course suffered with him. His wife, a poor weakly woman, in a spirit of almost Turkish apathy, was content to lie down and die; and when all their little articles of clothing and furniture had been pawned, the three young children pined away from hunger in slow but sure decay.

Mary alone of all the family tried *to do something*. She was a gentle, dark-eyed girl, with a look of patient suffering in her thin pale face, and a soft low voice which few, one would think, could listen to unmoved. The sale of work, however, had become almost hopeless; so many were trying to live by it, and so few had money to buy. The delicate fabrics, both in knitting and embroidery, which many a bony finger worked at till the hollow eye grew dim, were often disposed of for two or three pence beyond the price of the materials. The collar which poor Mary had now finished was beautifully fine, and had cost her many hours of toil; yet she almost despaired of selling it, as she sallied forth at eleven o'clock, shivering with cold and hunger.

About four o'clock the same day, as a fashionably dressed lady was walking along a road at the western end of the city, she heard a plaintive voice behind her saying, "Will you please, ma'am, to buy a knitted collar?"

She turned, and poor Mary, now almost fainting from exhaustion, offered the lace-like piece of work for her inspection.

"What do you ask for it, child?"

"Two shillings, ma'am."

"Oh, that's much too dear! I'll give you one for it."

"It took me several days to knit, and my parents and brothers are starving," said poor Mary, bursting into tears.

"Oh, yes; I suppose the old story. Well, child, if you don't like to give it for a shilling, you can sell it elsewhere."

"Take it, ma'am," said Mary, giving it to the lady, and eagerly seizing the offered shilling. There was life to her and those she loved in that bit of silver, that paltry coin which its former possessors would have squandered without a thought for any unneeded trifle, yet now considered well-spent in securing a *bargain*.

Let us change the scene to a baker's shop, in——street. It was a large establishment, and the deep shelves were piled with the crisp, fresh loaves of every shape, size, and quality, from the fine light French roll, to the dark, compact "household brick;" and the wide window displayed biscuits, cakes, and confectionery, in various tempting forms. It was half-past four o'clock, and the space outside the counter was filled with purchasers, very different in their rank and appearance. Two richly dressed ladies, whose carriage was in waiting, were selecting, with jewelled fingers, some of the prettiest *bon-bons* which the attentive master of the shop produced, and mirthfully discussing which kind "baby" was likely to prefer; near them stood a stout, fresh-coloured country-woman, wrapped in a blue cloak, and holding up her checked apron, while she impatiently called out—"Ah, then, good luck to you, honest man, and don't be keeping me this way, but just give me them two lumps, and three bricks I axed you for: here's the money ready, and 'tis three miles of the road home I ought to have over me by this."

The master of the shop had but two boys to assist him behind the counter, and though they hurried and toiled and "did the impossible" to content their clamorous customers, the latter were by no means satisfied to wait for their turn to be served. There were but two individuals in the shop who appeared to possess the very un-Irish quality of patience. One of them seemed to have learned it in a hard school; she was a thin, pale girl, barefooted, and clothed in miserable, scanty rags, which, however, were clean, and as tidily put on as they would admit of. She held a shilling tightly grasped in her slender fingers, and advancing through an opening in the crowd, asked the youngest shop-boy for a stale loaf of "thirds"—(the coarsest kind of bread manufactured). He had just finished serving a farmer, and hastily giving her what she wanted, took the shilling, and returned her the change. There had been standing next the girl, a pleasing-looking, neatly-dressed lady, who now advanced, and asked for some Naples biscuits.—The boy was busy weighing them, when the girl came back, and said to him, "If you please, what did you charge for the loaf?"

"Threepence, and I gave you the change."

"But you gave me sixpence and a fourpence, so you kept a penny too little."

The boy looked vexed at his blunder, which he probably feared his master might observe; so hastily taking the silver fourpence, and giving the girl threepence, he said, "'Tis all right now, you may go."

She was hastening away, when the gentle-looking lady next her said, "Stay, you have been very honest; good principle may be shown as well about a penny as a pound—here is a shilling for you."

The girl involuntarily raised her clasped hands.

"Oh, thank you, thank you, ma'am," she said, "God for ever bless you!" and then hastened out of the shop, before the lady could again address her.

Miss Saville had only moderate means, but possessed a truly benevolent heart. She usually resided in a remote part of the country, with her brother, who was a clergyman, and who was wont to assert, that in attention to the schools, and visiting the sick in his parish, his sister Sarah was worth two curates, "aye, and hardworking ones, too."

She was now staying on a visit with a married sister, who resided near——; and who, although blessed with an excellent husband, and several fine children, could not be called as truly happy as her maiden sister; for though, in the main, a good-natured woman, she lacked that generous, thoughtful benevolence of spirit which distinguished Miss Saville. On this day, however, the latter walked home to dinner in a self-reproaching frame of mind.

"How very thoughtless I was," she said to herself, "not to ask that poor child where she lives, and something of her history. I'm sure she's in great distress, and she seemed so honest and so grateful. I wish very much I could find her out."

A few hours afterwards, a happy family party were assembled in Mr. Elliott's drawing-room.—His sister-in-law, Miss Saville, held her youngest nephew on her knee, and was surrounded by four other bright-eyed little ones, among whom she had just distributed her purchase of Naples biscuits; and as they ate, they listened with much interest to Aunt Sarah's account of the honest girl, who, "though she looked so very poor, would not keep a penny which did not belong to her."

Mrs. Elliott, who was seated at her work-table, arranging some lace trimming on a cap, now got up, and handing a small collar to her sister, said—

"Look, Sarah, did you ever see any knitting so fine as that?"

"It is, indeed, beautiful—quite like lace; where did you get it, Eliza?"

"I bought it to-day in the street—such a bargain! Just fancy—the girl who had it asked two shillings; and when I offered her one, seemed quite glad to take it. Really, there's no knowing what to offer; for now money is so scarce, people who live by knitting and needlework, are willing to take almost anything. I dare say Miss Wilson, the milliner, would charge me five shillings for that collar."

Miss Saville looked very grave, and was silent, but Mr. Elliott, who had been reading the newspaper, now laid it down, and said—

"Do you think it honest, Eliza, to take the fruit of a poor girl's industry for one-fifth of its value?"

"Really, James, you men have the strangest notions!—why should it not be honest to purchase an article for the price at which its owner is willing to sell it?"

"Not *willing,* Eliza. By your own account it is wrung from them by the direst want; and perhaps the other shilling which you with-held from the poor maker of that little article, and which to you is nothing, might have given food and comfort to a starving family."

Mrs. Elliott blushed, but did not speak. Her conscience told her her husband was right, yet she did not like—what woman does?—to own herself in the wrong.

Mr. Elliott did not wish to give his wife pain; and her sister felt glad to see that an impression, which she hoped might prove lasting, had been made on her mind; so, after a momentary pause, the conversation turned on other subjects, and the evening concluded happily. In the silence of night, however, ere they fell asleep, perhaps the last reflection of each was something of this kind:

"How I wish," thought Miss Saville, "I knew where that poor girl lives. I shall not forget her pale face and gentle voice for some time."

"Well," thought her brother, "I blamed Eliza for not being charitable, and I fear I'm not half enough so myself. When I'm paying my subscriptions next week, I think I'll double them."

"I wish I had given the shilling to that poor girl," was Mrs. Elliott's reflection. "James is right. I'll never again bargain with a poor work-woman."

Let us now return to the wretched attic inhabited by the Sullivans.

A month had elapsed since the day when our story commenced, and their miserable resources were utterly exhausted. Denis and his youngest child lay dead; they had both expired of hunger the preceding day, and as yet no one came to bury them. The wife lay gasping at the corpses' feet, and a low, dull moaning proceeded from the white, drawn lips of the two little skeletons lying on the floor, who, but for that sign of life, could scarcely be distinguished from their dead brother.

Where was Mary? Day after day, when the last halfpenny was expended, had she crawled forth to beg alms for her perishing family: often she returned to them empty. Her failing strength and eyesight, together with the long December nights, unlighted by fire or candle, forbade her resuming her ill-rewarded knitting. This day she went out, almost frantically, to beseech a morsel of bread; for she felt that ere another sun went down, they must all perish. We will leave her tottering towards a crowded thoroughfare, where she thought, perchance, even one halfpenny might be obtained.

About two o'clock, that day, Mr. and Mrs. Elliott, and their sister, emerged from a haberdasher's shop, in a street where the ladies had been making various purchases, and the gentleman—as gentlemen always have done and always will do—amused himself by commenting on their proceedings, and thanking his stars that masculine costume is so much more easily arranged than that pertaining to the softer portion of the creation. They were about to cross the street, when Mr. Elliott said—

"There's a crowd on the opposite footpath; we had better wait till it disperses."

"'Tis only a poor hungry crathur that fainted," said a man who was passing, "and she's lying now like dead."

"Let us go," said Miss Saville, "and see what can be done." And on she went, followed by her brother and sister.

There lay poor Mary, apparently lifeless, her head resting against a lamp post. Miserably death-like as she looked, Miss Saville immediately recognised the girl she had met at the baker's; and her sister the same moment knew the poor seller of the knitted collar.

No time was lost by Mr. Elliott in getting her conveyed to the nearest apothecary's shop; where, after some time, she was restored to consciousness. A few words sufficed to make known her story, and to direct her benefactor to the miserable dwelling where her parents lay. Thither Mr. Elliott went, and found that Nelly Sullivan had breathed her last since morning. The little boys were still alive, and able to swallow the cordial he offered them. He summoned some of the neighbours to his assistance, and provided for the decent burial of the dead. He then had the poor children wrapped up, and conveyed to a house inhabited by an old woman who had nursed his family, and who readily undertook the charge of them and of Mary. After some time, they all recovered their bodily health, but it was long before Mary could be roused from a state of deep dejection. At length Miss Saville took her to the country, and there the grateful girl lives with her as a servant, each day become more useful. The boys, through Mr. Elliott's interest, have been placed at school, where they promise to do well. Their benefactors found that such giving was indeed "twice blessed," for they experienced an abundant enlargement of their own hearts, while doing good to others. Mrs. Elliott especially, though thrifty, as a housewife should be, in buying from rich tradespeople, has never been known to cheapen the work of the poor, since the day on which she purchased the *knitted collar*.

THE DISTRICT DOCTOR

Ivan S. Turgenev

ONE DAY IN autumn on my way back from a remote part of the country I caught cold and fell ill. Fortunately the fever attacked me in the district town at the inn; I sent for the doctor. In half-an-hour the district doctor appeared, a thin, dark-haired man of middle height. He prescribed me the usual sudorific, ordered a mustard-plaster to be put on, very deftly slid a five-ruble note up his sleeve, coughing drily and looking away as he did so, and then was getting up to go home, but somehow fell into talk and remained. I was exhausted with feverishness; I foresaw a sleepless night, and was glad of a little chat with a pleasant companion. Tea was served. My doctor began to converse freely. He was a sensible fellow, and expressed himself with vigor and some humor. Queer things happen in the world: you may live a long while with some people, and be on friendly terms with them, and never once speak openly with them from your soul; with others you have scarcely time to get acquainted, and all at once you are pouring out to him—or he to you—all your secrets, as though you were at confession. I don't know how I gained the confidence of my new friend—anyway, with nothing to leap up to it, he told me a rather curious incident; and here I will report his tale for the information of the indulgent reader. I will try to tell it in the doctor's own words.

"You don't happen to know," he began in a weak and quavering voice (the common result of the use of unmixed Berezov snuff); "you don't happen to know the judge here, Mylov, Pavel Lukich? . . . You don't know him? . . . Well, it's all the same." (He cleared his throat and rubbed his eyes.) "Well, you see, the thing happened, to tell you exactly without mistake, in Lent, at the very time of the thaws.

I was sitting at his house—our judge's, you know—playing preference. Our judge is a good fellow, and fond of playing preference.
Suddenly" (the doctor made frequent use of this word, suddenly)
"they tell me, 'There's a servant asking for you.' I say, 'What does
he want?' They say, 'He has brought a note—it must be from a
patient.' 'Give me the note,' I say. So it is from a patient—well and
good—you understand—it's our bread and butter. . . . But this is
how it was: a lady, a widow, writes to me; she says, 'My daughter
is dying. Come, for God's sake!' she says, 'and the horses have been
sent for you.' . . . Well, that's all right. But she was twenty miles
from the town, and it was midnight out of doors, and the roads in
such a state, my word! And as she was poor herself, one could not
expect more than two silver rubles, and even that problematic; and
perhaps it might only be a matter of a roll of linen and a sack of
oatmeal in payment. However, duty, you know, before everything:
a fellow-creature may be dying. I hand over my cards at once to
Kalliopin, the member of the provincial commission, and return
home. I look; a wretched little trap was standing at the steps, with
peasant's horses, fat—too fat—and their coat as shaggy as felt; and the
coachman sitting with his cap off out of respect. Well, I think to
myself, 'It's clear, my friend, these patients aren't rolling in riches.' . . .
You smile; but I tell you, a poor man like me has to take everything
into consideration. . . . If the coachman sits like a prince, and
doesn't touch his cap, and even sneers at you behind his beard, and
flicks his whip—then you may bet on six rubles. But this case, I
saw, had a very different air. However, I think there's no help for
it; duty before everything. I snatch up the most necessary drugs,
and set off. Will you believe it? I only just managed to get there at
all. The road was infernal: streams, snow, watercourses, and the
dyke had suddenly burst there—that was the worst of it! However,
I arrived at last. It was a little thatched house. There was a light in
the windows; that meant they expected me. I was met by an old
lady, very venerable, in a cap. 'Save her!' she says; 'she is dying.' I
say, 'Pray don't distress yourself—Where is the invalid?' 'Come this
way.' I see a clean little room, a lamp in the corner; on the bed a
girl of twenty, unconscious. She was in a burning heat, and breathing heavily—it was fever. There were two other girls, her sisters,
scared and in tears. 'Yesterday,' they tell me, 'she was perfectly well
and had a good appetite; this morning she complained of her head,
and this evening, suddenly, you see, like this.' I say again: 'Pray

don't be uneasy.' It's a doctor's duty, you know—and I went up to her and bled her, told them to put on a mustard-plaster, and prescribed a mixture. Meantime I looked at her; I looked at her, you know—there, by God! I had never seen such a face!—she was a beauty, in a word! I felt quite shaken with pity. Such lovely features; such eyes! . . . But, thank God! she became easier; she fell into a perspiration, seemed to come to her senses, looked round, smiled, and passed her hand over her face. . . . Her sisters bent over her. They ask, 'How are you?' 'All right,' she says, and turns away. I looked at her; she had fallen asleep. 'Well,' I say, 'now the patient should be left alone.' So we all went out on tiptoe; only a maid remained, in case she was wanted. In the parlor there was a samovar standing on the table, and a bottle of rum; in our profession one can't get on without it. They gave me tea; asked me to stop the night. . . . I consented: where could I go, indeed, at that time of night? The old lady kept groaning. 'What is it?' I say; 'she will live; don't worry yourself; you had better take a little rest yourself; it is about two o'clock.' 'But will you send to wake me if anything happens?' 'Yes, yes.' The old lady went away, and the girls too went to their own room; they made up a bed for me in the parlor. Well, I went to bed—but I could not get to sleep, for a wonder! for in reality I was very tired. I could not get my patient out of my head. At last I could not put up with it any longer; I got up suddenly; I think to myself, 'I will go and see how the patient is getting on.' Her bedroom was next to the parlor. Well, I got up, and gently opened the door—how my heart beat! I looked in: the servant was asleep, her mouth wide open, and even snoring, the wretch! but the patient lay with her face towards me, and her arms flung wide apart, poor girl! I went up to her . . . when suddenly she opened her eyes and stared at me! 'Who is it? who is it?' I was in confusion. 'Don't be alarmed, madam,' I say; 'I am the doctor; I have come to see how you feel.' 'You the doctor?' 'Yes, the doctor; your mother sent for me from the town; we have bled you, madam; now pray go to sleep, and in a day or two, please God! we will set you on your feet again.' 'Ah, yes, yes, doctor, don't let me die. . . please, please.' 'Why do you talk like that? God bless you!' She is in a fever again, I think to myself; I felt her pulse; yes, she was feverish. She looked at me, and then took me by the hand. 'I will tell you why I don't want to die; I will tell you. . . . Now we are alone; and only, please don't you . . . not to any one . . . Listen. . . .' I bent down;

she moved her lips quite to my ear; she touched my cheek with her hair—I confess my head went round—and began to whisper. . . . I could make out nothing of it. . . . Ah, she was delirious! . . . She whispered and whispered, but so quickly, and as if it were not in Russian; at last she finished, and shivering dropped her head on the pillow, and threatened me with her finger: 'Remember, doctor, to no one.' I calmed her somehow, gave her something to drink, waked the servant, and went away."

At this point the doctor again took snuff with exasperated energy, and for a moment seemed stupefied by its effects.

"However," he continued, "the next day, contrary to my expectations, the patient was no better. I thought and thought, and suddenly decided to remain there, even though my other patients were expecting me. . . . And you know one can't afford to disregard that; one's practice suffers if one does. But, in the first place, the patient was really in danger; and secondly, to tell the truth, I felt strongly drawn to her. Besides, I liked the whole family. Though they were really badly off, they were singularly, I may say, cultivated people. . . . Their father had been a learned man, an author; he died, of course, in poverty, but he had managed before he died to give his children an excellent education; he left a lot of books too. Either because I looked after the invalid very carefully, or for some other reason; anyway, I can venture to say all the household loved me as if I were one of the family. . . . Meantime the roads were in a worse state than ever; all communications, so to say, were cut off completely; even medicine could with difficulty be got from the town. . . . The sick girl was not getting better. . . . Day after day, and day after day . . . but. . . here. . . ." (The doctor made a brief pause.) "I declare I don't know how to tell you." . . . (He again took snuff, coughed, and swallowed a little tea.) "I will tell you without beating about the bush. My patient. . . how should I say? . . . Well she had fallen in love with me . . .or, no, it was not that she was in love . . . however. . . really, how should one say?" (The doctor looked down and grew red.) "No," he went on quickly, "in love, indeed! A man should not over-estimate himself. She was an educated girl, clever and well-read, and I had even forgotten my Latin, one may say, completely. As to appearance" (the doctor looked himself over with a smile) "I am nothing to boast of there either. But God Almighty did not make me a fool; I don't take black for white; I know a thing or two; I could see very clearly, for instance that Aleksandra Andreyevna—that was her name—did not feel love for me, but had a friendly, so to say, inclination—a respect or something for me. Though she herself perhaps mistook this sentiment, anyway this was her attitude; you may form your own judgment of it. But," added the doctor, who had brought out all these disconnected sentences without taking breath, and with obvious embarrassment, "I seem to be wandering rather—you won't understand anything like this. . . . There, with your leave, I will relate it all in order."

He drank off a glass of tea, and began in a calmer voice.

"Well, then. My patient kept getting worse and worse. You are not a doctor, my good sir; you cannot understand what passes in a poor fellow's heart, especially at first, when he begins to suspect that the disease is getting the upper hand of him. What becomes of his belief in himself? You suddenly grow so timid; it's indescribable. You fancy then that you have forgotten everything you knew, and that the patient has no faith in you, and that other people begin to notice how distracted you are, and tell you the symptoms with reluctance; that they are looking at you suspiciously, whispering . . . Ah! it's horrid! There must be a remedy, you think, for this disease, if one could find it. Isn't this it? You try—no, that's not it! You don't allow the medicine the necessary time to do good . . . You clutch at one thing, then at another. Sometimes you take up a book of medical prescriptions—here it is, you think! Sometimes, by Jove, you pick one out by chance, thinking to leave it to fate. . . . But meantime a fellow-creature's dying, and another doctor would have saved him. 'We must have a consultation,' you say; 'I will not take the responsibility on myself.' And what a fool you look at such times! Well, in time you learn to bear it; it's nothing to you. A man has died—but it's not your fault; you treated him by the rules. But what's still more torture to you is to see blind faith in you, and to feel yourself that you are not able to be of use. Well, it was just this blind faith that the whole of Aleksandra Andreyevna's family had in me; they had forgotten to think that their daughter was in danger. I, too, on my side assure them that it's nothing, but meantime my heart sinks into my boots. To add to our troubles, the roads were in such a state that the coachman was gone for whole days together to get medicine. And I never left the patient's room; I could not tear myself away; I tell her amusing stories, you know, and play cards with her. I watch by her side at night. The old mother thanks me with tears in her eyes; but I think to myself, 'I don't deserve your gratitude.' I frankly confess to you—there is no object in concealing it now—I was in love with my patient. And Aleksandra Andreyevna had grown fond of me; she would not sometimes let any one be in her room but me. She began to talk to me, to ask me questions; where I had studied, how I lived, who are my people, whom I go to see. I feel that she ought not to talk; but to forbid her to—to forbid her resolutely, you know—I could not. Sometimes I held my head in my hands, and asked myself, 'What are you doing, villain?'. . . And she would take my hand and hold it, give me a long, long look, and turn away, sigh, and say, 'How good you are!' Her hands were so feverish, her eyes so large and languid. . . . 'Yes,' she says, 'you are a good, kind man; you are not like our neighbors. . . . No, you are not like that. . . . Why did I not know you till now!' 'Aleksandra Andreyevna, calm yourself,' I say. . . . 'I feel, believe me, I don't know how I have gained . . . but there, calm yourself. . . . All will be right; you will be well again.' And meanwhile I must tell you," continued the doctor, bending forward and raising his eyebrows, "that they associated very little with the neighbors, because the smaller people were not on their level, and pride hindered them from being friendly with the rich. I tell you, they were an exceptionally cultivated family so you know it was gratifying for me. She would only take her medicine from my hands . . . she would lift herself up, poor girl, with my aid, take it, and gaze at me. . . . My heart felt as if it were bursting. And meanwhile she was growing worse and worse, worse and worse, all the time; she will die, I think to myself; she must die. Believe me, I would sooner have gone to the grave myself; and here were her mother and sisters watching me, looking into my eyes . . . and their faith in me was wearing away. 'Well? how is she?' 'Oh, all right, all right!' All right, indeed! My mind was failing me. Well, I was sitting one night alone again by my patient. The maid was sitting there too, and snoring away in full swing; I can't find fault with the poor girl, though! she was worn out too. Aleksandra Andreyevna had felt very unwell all the evening; she was very feverish. Until midnight she kept tossing about; at last she seemed to fall asleep; at least, she lay still without stirring. The lamp was burning in the corner before the holy image. I sat there you know, with my head bent; I even dozed a little. Suddenly it seemed as though some one touched me in the side; I turned round. . . .

Good God! Aleksandra Andreyevna was gazing with intent eyes at me . . . her lips parted, her cheeks seemed burning. 'What is it?' 'Doctor, shall I die?' 'Merciful Heavens!' 'No, doctor, no; please don't tell me I shall live . . . don't say so. . . . If you knew. . . . Listen! for God's sake don't conceal my real position,' and her breath came so fast. 'If I can know for certain that I must die . . . then I will tell you all—all!' 'Aleksandra Andreyevna, I beg!' 'Listen; I have not been asleep at all . . . I have been looking at you a long while. . . . For God's sake! . . . I believe in you; you are a good man, an honest man; I entreat you by all that is sacred in the world—tell me the truth! If you knew how important it is for me. . . . Doctor, for God's sake tell me. . . . Am I in danger?' 'What can I tell you, Aleksandra Andreyevna pray?' 'For God's sake, I beseech you!' 'I can't disguise from you,' I say, 'Aleksandra Andreyevna; you are certainly in danger; but God is merciful.' 'I shall die, I shall die.' And it seemed as though she were pleased; her face grew so bright; I was alarmed. 'Don't be afraid, don't be afraid! I am not frightened of death at all.' She suddenly sat up and leaned on her elbow. 'Now . . . yes, now I can tell you that I thank you with my whole heart. . . that you are kind and good—that I love you!' I stare at her, like one possessed; it was terrible for me, you know. 'Do you hear, I love you!' 'Aleksandra Andreyevna, how have I deserved—' 'No, no, you don't—you don't understand me.'. . . And suddenly she stretched out her arms, and taking my head in her hands, she kissed it. . . . Believe me, I almost screamed aloud. . . . I threw myself on my knees, and buried my head in the pillow. She did not speak; her fingers trembled in my hair; I listen; she is weeping. I began to soothe her, to assure her. . . . I really don't know what I did say to her. 'You will wake up the girl,' I say to her; 'Aleksandra Andreyevna, I thank you . . . believe me . . . calm yourself.' 'Enough, enough!' she persisted; 'never mind all of them; let them wake, then; let them come in—it does not matter; I am dying, you see. . . . And what do you fear? why are you afraid? Lift up your head. . . . Or, perhaps, you don't love me; perhaps I am wrong. . . . In that case, forgive me.' 'Aleksandra Andreyevna, what are you saying!. . . I love you, Aleksandra Andreyevna.' She looked straight into my eyes, and opened her arms wide. 'Then take me in your arms.' I tell you frankly, I don't know how it was I did not go mad that night. I feel that my patient is killing herself; I see that she is not fully herself; I understand, too, that if she did not consider herself on the point of death, she would never have thought of me; and, indeed, say what you will, it's hard to die at twenty without having known love; this was what was torturing her; this was why, in despair, she caught at me—do you understand now? But she held me in her arms, and would not let me go. 'Have pity on me, Aleksandra Andreyevna, and have pity on yourself,' I say. 'Why,' she says; 'what is there to think of? You know I must die.' . . . This she repeated incessantly. . . . 'If I knew that I should return to life, and be a proper young lady again, I should be ashamed . . . of course, ashamed . . . but why now?' 'But who has said you will die?' 'Oh, no, leave off! you will not deceive me; you don't know how to lie—look at your face.' . . . 'You shall live, Aleksandra Andreyevna; I will cure you; we will ask your mother's blessing . . . we will be united—we will be happy.' 'No, no, I have your word; I must die . . . you have promised me . . . you have told me.'. . . It was cruel for me—cruel for many reasons. And see what trifling things can do sometimes; it seems nothing at all, but it's painful. It occurred to her to ask me, what is my name; not my surname, but my first name. I must needs be so unlucky as to be called Trifon. Yes, indeed; Trifon Ivanich. Every one in the house called me doctor. However, there's no help for it. I say, 'Trifon, madam.' She frowned, shook her head, and muttered something in French—ah, something unpleasant, of course!—and then she laughed—disagreeably too. Well, I spent the whole night with her in this way. Before morning I went away, feeling as though I were mad. When I went again into her room it was daytime, after morning tea. Good God! I could scarcely recognize her; people are laid in their grave looking better than that. I swear to you, on my honor, I don't understand—I absolutely don't understand—now, how I lived through that experience. Three days and nights my patient still lingered on. And what nights! What things she said to me! And on the last night—only imagine to yourself—I was sitting near her, and kept praying to God for one thing only: 'Take her,' I said, 'quickly, and me with her.' Suddenly the old mother comes unexpectedly into the room. I had already the evening before told her—the mother—there was little hope, and it would be well to send for a priest. When the sick girl saw her mother she said: 'It's very well you have come; look at us, we love one another—we have given each other our word.' 'What does she say, doctor? what does she say?' I turned livid. 'She is wandering,' I say; 'the fever.'

But she: 'Hush, hush; you told me something quite different just now, and have taken my ring. Why do you pretend? My mother is good—she will forgive—she will understand—and I am dying. . . . I have no need to tell lies; give me your hand.' I jumped up and ran out of the room. The old lady, of course, guessed how it was.

"I will not, however, weary you any longer, and to me too, of course, it's painful to recall all this. My patient passed away the next day. God rest her soul!" the doctor added, speaking quickly and with a sigh. "Before her death she asked her family to go out and leave me alone with her."

"'Forgive me,' she said; 'I am perhaps to blame towards you . . . my illness . . . but believe me, I have loved no one more than you . . . do not forget me . . . keep my ring.'"

The doctor turned away; I took his hand.

"Ah!" he said, "let us talk of something else, or would you care to play preference for a small stake? It is not for people like me to give way to exalted emotions. There's only one thing for me to think of; how to keep the children from crying and the wife from scolding. Since then, you know, I have had time to enter into law- ful wedlock, as they say. . . . Oh . . . I took a merchant's daugh- ter—seven thousand for her dowry. Her name's Akulina; it goes well with Trifon. She is an ill-tempered woman, I must tell you, but luckily she's asleep all day. . . . Well, shall it be preference?"

We sat down to preference for halfpenny points. Trifon Ivanich won two rubles and a half from me, and went home late, well pleased with his success.

NOBODY'S STORY

Charles Dickens

HE LIVED ON the bank of a mighty river, broad and deep, which was always silently rolling on to a vast undiscovered ocean. It had rolled on, ever since the world began. It had changed its course sometimes, and turned into new channels, leaving its old ways dry and barren; but it had ever been upon the flow, and ever was to flow until Time should be no more. Against its strong, unfathomable stream, nothing made head. No living creature, no flower, no leaf, no particle of animate or inanimate existence ever strayed back from the undiscovered ocean. The tide of the river set resistlessly towards it; and the tide never stopped, any more than the earth stops in its circling round the sun.

He lived in a busy place, and he worked very hard to live. He had no hope of ever being rich enough to live a month without hard work, but he was quite content, God knows, to labor with a cheerful will. He was one of an immense family, all of whose sons and daughters gained their daily bread by daily work, prolonged from their rising up betimes until their lying down at night. Beyond this destiny he had no prospect, and he sought none.

There was over-much drumming, trumpeting, and speech-making, in the neighborhood where he dwelt; but he had nothing to do with that. Such clash and uproar came from the Bigwig family, at the unaccountable proceedings of which race, he marveled much. They set up the strangest statues, in iron, marble, bronze, and brass, before his door; and darkened his house with the legs and tails of uncouth images of horses. He wondered what it all meant, smiled in a rough good-humored way he had, and kept at his hard work.

The Bigwig family (composed of all the stateliest people there-abouts, and all the noisiest) had undertaken to save him the trouble of thinking for himself, and to manage him and his affairs. "Why truly," said he, "I have little time upon my hands; and if you will be so good as to take care of me, in return for the money I pay over"—for the Bigwig family were not above his money—"I shall be relieved and much obliged, considering that you know best." Hence the drumming, trumpeting, and speech-making, and the ugly images of horses which he was expected to fall down and worship.

"I don't understand all this," said he, rubbing his furrowed brow confusedly. "But it *has* a meaning, maybe, if I could find it out."

"It means," returned the Bigwig family, suspecting something of what he said, "honor and glory in the highest, to the highest merit."

"Oh!" said he. And he was glad to hear that.

But, when he looked among the images in iron, marble, bronze, and brass, he failed to find a rather meritorious countryman of his, once the son of a Warwickshire wool-dealer, or any single country-man whomsoever of that kind. He could find none of the men whose knowledge had rescued him and his children from terrific and disfiguring disease, whose boldness had raised his forefathers from the condition of serfs, whose wise fancy had opened a new and high existence to the humblest, whose skill had filled the work-ingman's world with accumulated wonders. Whereas, he did find others whom he knew no good of, and even others whom he knew much ill of.

"Humph!" said he. "I don't quite understand it."

So, he went home, and sat down by his fireside to get it out of his mind.

Now, his fireside was a bare one, all hemmed in by blackened streets; but it was a precious place to him. The hands of his wife were hardened with toil, and she was old before her time; but she was dear to him. His children, stunted in their growth, bore traces of unwholesome nurture; but they had beauty in his sight. Above all other things, it was an earnest desire of this man's soul that his children should be taught. "If I am sometimes misled," said he, "for want of knowledge, at least let them know better, and avoid my mistakes. If it is hard to me to reap the harvest of pleasure and instruction that is stored in books, let it be easier to them."

But, the Bigwig family broke out into violent family quarrels concerning what it was lawful to teach to this man's children.

Some of the family insisted on such a thing being primary and indispensable above all other things; and others of the family insisted on such another thing being primary and indispensable above all other things; and the Bigwig family, rent into factions, wrote pamphlets, held convocations, delivered charges, orations, and all varieties of discourses; impounded one another in courts Lay and courts Ecclesiastical; threw dirt, exchanged pummelings, and fell together by the ears in unintelligible animosity. Meanwhile, this man, in his short evening snatches at his fireside, saw the demon Ignorance arise there, and take his children to itself. He saw his daughter perverted into a heavy slatternly drudge; he saw his son go moping down the ways of low sensuality, to brutality and crime; he saw the dawning light of intelligence in the eyes of his babies so changing into cunning and suspicion, that he could have rather wished them idiots.

"I don't understand this any the better," said he; "but I think it cannot be right. Nay, by the clouded Heaven above me, I protest against this as my wrong!"

Becoming peaceable again (for his passion was usually short-lived, and his nature kind), he looked about him on his Sundays and holidays, and he saw how much monotony and weariness there was, and thence how drunkenness arose with all its train of ruin. Then he appealed to the Bigwig family, and said, "We are a laboring people, and I have a glimmering suspicion in me that laboring people of whatever condition were made—by a higher intelligence than yours, as I poorly understand it—to be in need of mental refreshment and recreation. See what we fall into, when we rest without it. Come! Amuse me harmlessly, show me something, give me an escape!"

But, here the Bigwig family fell into a state of uproar absolutely deafening. When some few voices were faintly heard, proposing to show him the wonders of the world, the greatness of creation, the mighty changes of time, the workings of nature and the beauties of art—to show him these things, that is to say, at any period of his life when he could look upon them—there arose among the Bigwigs such roaring and raving, such pulpiting and petitioning, such maundering and memorializing, such name-calling and dirt-throwing, such a shrill wind of parliamentary questioning and feeble replying—where "I dare not" waited on "I would"—that the poor fellow stood aghast, staring wildly around.

"Have I provoked all this," said he, with his hands to his affrighted ears, "by what was meant to be an innocent request, plainly arising out of my familiar experience, and the common knowledge of all men who choose to open their eyes? I don't understand, and I am not understood. What is to come of such a state of things?"

He was bending over his work, often asking himself the question, when the news began to spread that a pestilence had appeared among the laborers, and was slaying them by thousands. Going forth to look about him, he soon found this to be true. The dying and the dead were mingled in the close and tainted houses among which his life was passed. New poison was distilled into the always murky, always sickening air. The robust and the weak, old age and infancy, the father and the mother, all were stricken down alike.

What means of flight had he? He remained there, where he was, and saw those who were dearest to him die. A kind preacher came to him, and would have said some prayers to soften his heart in his gloom, but he replied:

"O what avails it, missionary, to come to me, a man condemned to residence in this fetid place, where every sense bestowed upon me for my delight becomes a torment, and where every minute of my numbered days is new mire added to the heap under which I lie oppressed! But, give me my first glimpse of Heaven, through a little of its light and air; give me pure water; help me to be clean; lighten this heavy atmosphere and heavy life, in which our spirits sink, and we become the indifferent and callous creatures you too often see us; gently and kindly take the bodies of those who die among us, out of the small room where we grow to be so familiar with the awful change that even ITS sanctity is lost to us; and, Teacher, then I will hear—none know better than you, how willingly—of Him whose thoughts were so much with the poor, and who had compassion for all human sorrow!"

He was at work again, solitary and sad, when his Master came and stood near to him dressed in black. He, also, had suffered heavily. His young wife, his beautiful and good young wife, was dead; so, too, his only child.

"Master, 'tis hard to bear—I know it—but be comforted. I would give you comfort, if I could."

The Master thanked him from his heart, but, said he, "O you laboring men! The calamity began among you. If you had but lived more healthily and decently, I should not be the widowed and bereft mourner that I am this day."

"Master," returned the other, shaking his head, "I have begun to understand a little that most calamities will come from us, as this one did, and that none will stop at our poor doors, until we are united with that great squabbling family yonder, to do the things that are right. We cannot live healthily and decently, unless they who undertook to manage us provide the means. We cannot be instructed unless they will teach us; we cannot be rationally amused, unless they will amuse us; we cannot but have some false gods of our own, while they set up so many of theirs in all the public places. The evil consequences of imperfect instruction, the evil consequences of pernicious neglect, the evil consequences of unnatural restraint and the denial of humanizing enjoyments, will all come from us, and none of them will stop with us. They will spread far and wide. They always do; they always have done—just like the pestilence. I understand so much, I think, at last."

But the Master said again, "O you laboring men! How seldom do we ever hear of you, except in connection with some trouble!"

"Master," he replied, "I am Nobody, and little likely to be heard of (nor yet much wanted to be heard of, perhaps), except when there *is* some trouble. But it never begins with me, and it never can end with me. As sure as Death, it comes down to me, and it goes up from me."

There was so much reason in what he said, that the Bigwig family, getting wind of it, and being horribly frightened by the late desolation, resolved to unite with him to do the things that were right—at all events, so far as the said things were associated with the direct prevention, humanly speaking, of another pestilence. But, as their fear wore off, which it soon began to do, they resumed their falling out among themselves, and did nothing. Consequently the scourge appeared again—low down as before— and spread avengingly upward as before, and carried off vast numbers of the brawlers. But not a man among them ever admitted, if in the least degree he ever perceived, that he had anything to do with it.

So Nobody lived and died in the old, old, old way; and this, in the main, is the whole of Nobody's story.

Had he no name, you ask? Perhaps it was Legion. It matters little what his name was. Let us call him Legion.

If you were ever in the Belgian villages near the field of Waterloo, you will have seen, in some quiet little church, a monument erected by faithful companions in arms to the memory of Colonel A, Major B, Captains C, D and E, Lieutenants F and G, Ensigns H, I and J, seven noncommissioned officers, and one hundred and thirty rank and file, who fell in the discharge of their duty on the memorable day. The story of Nobody is the story of the rank and file of the earth. They bear their share of the battle; they have their part in the victory; they fall; they leave no name but in the mass. The march of the proudest of us, leads to the dusty way by which they go. O! Let us think of them this year at the Christmas fire, and not forget them when it is burned out.

THE FIDDLER

Herman Melville

So my poem is damned, and immortal fame is not for me! I am nobody forever and ever. Intolerable fate!

Snatching my hat, I dashed down the criticism, and rushed out into Broadway, where enthusiastic throngs were crowding to a circus in a side-street near by, very recently started, and famous for a capital clown.

Presently my old friend Standard rather boisterously accosted me.

"Well met, Helmstone, my boy! Ah! what's the matter? Haven't been committing murder? Ain't flying justice? You look wild!"

"You have seen it, then?" said I, of course referring to the criticism.

"Oh yes; I was there at the morning performance. Great clown, I assure you. But here comes Hautboy. Hautboy—Helmstone."

Without having time or inclination to resent so mortifying a mistake, I was instantly soothed as I gazed on the face of the new acquaintance so unceremoniously introduced. His person was short and full, with a juvenile, animated cast to it. His complexion rurally ruddy; his eye sincere, cheery, and gray. His hair alone betrayed that he was not an overgrown boy. From his hair I set him down as forty or more.

"Come, Standard," he gleefully cried to my friend, "are you not going to the circus? The clown is inimitable, they say. Come; Mr. Helmstone, too—come both; and circus over, we'll take a nice stew and punch at Taylor's."

The sterling content, good humor, and extraordinary ruddy, sincere expression of this most singular new acquaintance acted upon me like magic. It seemed mere loyalty to human nature to

117

accept an invitation from so unmistakably kind and honest a heart.

During the circus performance I kept my eye more on Hautboy than on the celebrated clown. Hautboy was the sight for me. Such genuine enjoyment as his struck me to the soul with a sense of the reality of the thing called happiness. The jokes of the clown he seemed to roll under his tongue as ripe magnum bonums. Now the foot, now the hand, was employed to attest his grateful applause. At any hit more than ordinary, he turned upon Standard and me to see if his rare pleasure was shared. In a man of forty I saw a boy of twelve; and this too without the slightest abatement of my respect. Because all was so honest and natural, every expression and attitude so graceful with genuine good-nature, that the marvelous juvenility of Hautboy assumed a sort of divine and immortal air, like that of some forever youthful god of Greece.

But much as I gazed upon Hautboy, and much as I admired his air, yet that desperate mood in which I had first rushed from the house had not so entirely departed as not to molest me with momentary returns. But from these relapses I would rouse myself, and swiftly glance round the broad amphitheatre of eagerly interested and all-applauding human faces. Hark! claps, thumps, deafening huzzas; the vast assembly seemed frantic with acclamation; and what, mused I, has caused all this? Why, the clown only comically grinned with one of his extra grins.

Then I repeated in my mind that sublime passage in my poem, in which Cleothemes the Argive vindicates the justice of the war. Aye, aye, thought I to myself, did I now leap into the ring there, and repeat that identical passage, nay, enact the whole tragic poem before them, would they applaud the poet as they applaud the clown? No! They would hoot me, and call me doting or mad. Then what does this prove? Your infatuation or their insensibility? Perhaps both; but indubitably the first. But why wail? Do you seek admiration from the admirers of a buffoon? Call to mind the saying of the Athenian, who, when the people vociferously applauded in the forum, asked his friend in a whisper, what foolish thing had he said?

Again my eye swept the circus, and fell on the ruddy radiance of the countenance of Hautboy. But its clear honest cheeriness disdained my disdain. My intolerant pride was rebuked. And yet Hautboy dreamed not what magic reproof to a soul like mine sat on his laughing brow. At the very instant I felt the dart of the

censure, his eye twinkled, his hand waved, his voice was lifted in
jubilant delight at another joke of the inexhaustible clown.

Circus over, we went to Taylor's. Among crowds of others, we
sat down to our stews and punches at one of the small marble tables.
Hautboy sat opposite to me. Though greatly subdued from its former hilarity, his face still shone with gladness. But added to this was
a quality not so prominent before: a certain serene expression of
leisurely, deep good sense. Good sense and good humor in him
joined hands. As the conversation proceeded between the brisk
Standard and him—for I said little or nothing—I was more and
more struck with the excellent judgment he evinced. In most of his
remarks upon a variety of topics Hautboy seemed intuitively to hit
the exact line between enthusiasm and apathy. It was plain that
while Hautboy saw the world pretty much as it was, yet he did not
theoretically espouse its bright side nor its dark side. Rejecting all
solutions, he but acknowledged facts. What was sad in the world he
did not superficially gainsay; what was glad in it he did not cynically
slur; and all which was to him personally enjoyable, he gratefully
took to his heart. It was plain, then—so it seemed at that moment,
at least—that his extraordinary cheerfulness did not arise either
from deficiency of feeling or thought.

Suddenly remembering an engagement, he took up his hat,
bowed pleasantly, and left us.

"Well, Helmstone," said Standard, inaudibly drumming on the
slab, "what do you think of your new acquaintance?"

The two last words tingled with a peculiar and novel significance.

"New acquaintance indeed," echoed I. "Standard, I owe you a
thousand thanks for introducing me to one of the most singular
men I have ever seen. It needed the optical sight of such a man to
believe in the possibility of his existence."

"You rather like him, then," said Standard, with ironical dryness.

"I hugely love and admire him, Standard. I wish I were Hautboy."

"Ah? That's a pity, now. There's only one Hautboy in the world."

This last remark set me to pondering again, and somehow it
revived my dark mood.

"His wonderful cheerfulness, I suppose," said I, sneering with
spleen, "originates not less in a felicitous fortune than in a felicitous
temper. His great good sense is apparent; but great good sense may
exist without sublime endowments. Nay, I take it, in certain cases,
that good sense is simply owing to the absence of those. Much

more, cheerfulness. Unpossessed of genius, Hautboy is eternally blessed."

"Ah? You would not think him an extraordinary genius, then?"

"Genius? What! such a short, fat fellow a genius! Genius, like Cassius, is lank."

"Ah? But could you not fancy that Hautboy might formerly have had genius, but luckily getting rid of it, at last fatted up?"

"For a genius to get rid of his genius is as impossible as for a man in the galloping consumption to get rid of that."

"Ah? You speak very decidedly."

"Yes, Standard," cried I, increasing in spleen, "your cheery Hautboy, after all, is no pattern, no lesson for you and me. With average abilities; opinions clear, because circumscribed; passions docile, because they are feeble; a temper hilarious, because he was born to it—how can your Hautboy be made a reasonable example to a handy fellow like you, or an ambitious dreamer like me? Nothing tempts him beyond common limit; in himself he has nothing to restrain. By constitution he is exempted from all moral harm. Could ambition but prick him; had he but once heard applause, or endured contempt, a very different man would your Hautboy be. Acquiescent and calm from the cradle to the grave, he obviously slides through the crowd."

"Ah?"

"Why do you say Ah to me so strangely whenever I speak?"

"Did you ever hear of Master Betty?"

"The great English prodigy, who long ago ousted the Siddons and the Kembles from Drury Lane, and made the whole town run mad with acclamation?"

"The same," said Standard, once more inaudibly drumming on the slab.

I looked at him perplexed. He seemed to be holding the master-key of our theme in mysterious reserve; seemed to be throwing out his Master Betty, too, to puzzle me only the more.

"What under heaven can Master Betty, the great genius and prodigy, an English boy twelve years old, have to do with the poor commonplace plodder, Hautboy, an American of forty?"

"Oh, nothing in the least. I don't imagine that they ever saw each other. Besides, Master Betty must be dead and buried long ere this."

"Then why cross the ocean, and rifle the grave to drag his remains into this living discussion?"

"Absent-mindedness, I suppose. I humbly beg pardon. Proceed with your observations on Hautboy. You think he never had genius, quite too contented, and happy and fat for that—ah? You think him no pattern for men in general? affording no lesson of value to neglected merit, genius ignored, or impotent presumption rebuked?—all of which three amount to much the same thing. You admire his cheerfulness, while scorning his commonplace soul. Poor Hautboy, how sad that your very cheerfulness should, by a by-blow, bring you despite!"

"I don't say I scorn him; you are unjust. I simply declare that he is no pattern for me."

A sudden noise at my side attracted my ear. Turning, I saw Hautboy again, who very blithely reseated himself on the chair he had left.

"I was behind time with my engagement," said Hautboy, "so thought I would run back and rejoin you. But come, you have sat long enough here. Let us go to my rooms. It is only a five minutes' walk."

"If you will promise to fiddle for us, we will," said Standard.

Fiddle! thought I—he's a jiggumbob *fiddler,* then? No wonder genius declines to measure its pace to a fiddler's bow. My spleen was very strong on me now.

"I will gladly fiddle you your fill," replied Hautboy to Standard. "Come on."

In a few minutes we found ourselves in the fifth story of a sort of storehouse, in a lateral street to Broadway. It was curiously furnished with all sorts of odd furniture which seemed to have been obtained, piece by piece, at auctions of old-fashioned household stuff. But all was charmingly clean and cozy.

Pressed by Standard, Hautboy forthwith got out his dented old fiddle and, sitting down on a tall rickety stool, played away right merrily at "Yankee Doodle" and other off-handed, dashing, and disdainfully care-free airs. But common as were the tunes, I was transfixed by something miraculously superior in the style. Sitting there on the old stool, his rusty hat sideways cocked on his head, one foot dangling adrift, he plied the bow of an enchanter. All my moody discontent, every vestige of peevishness, fled. My whole splenetic soul capitulated to the magical fiddle.

"Something of an Orpheus, ah?" said Standard, archly nudging me beneath the left rib.

"And I, the charmed Bruin," murmured I.

The fiddle ceased. Once more, with redoubled curiosity, I gazed upon the easy, indifferent Hautboy. But he entirely baffled inquisition.

When, leaving him, Standard and I were in the street once more, I earnestly conjured him to tell me who, in sober truth, this marvelous Hautboy was.

"Why, haven't you seen him? And didn't you yourself lay his whole anatomy open on the marble slab at Taylor's? What more can you possibly learn? Doubtless, your own masterly insight has already put you in possession of all."

"You mock me, Standard. There is some mystery here. Tell me, I entreat you, who is Hautboy?"

"An extraordinary genius, Helmstone," said Standard, with sudden ardor, "who in boyhood drained the whole flagon of glory; whose going from city to city was a going from triumph to triumph. One who has been an object of wonder to the wisest, been caressed by the loveliest, received the open homage of thousands on thousands of the rabble. But to-day he walks Broadway and no man knows him. With you and me, the elbow of the hurrying clerk, and the pole of the remorseless omnibus, shove him. He who has a hundred times been crowned with laurels, now wears, as you see, a bunged beaver. Once fortune poured showers of gold into his lap, as showers of laurel leaves upon his brow. To-day, from house to house he hies, teaching fiddling for a living. Crammed once with fame, he is now hilarious without it. *With* genius and *without* fame, he is happier than a king. More a prodigy now than ever."

"His true name?"

"Let me whisper it in your ear."

"What! Oh, Standard, myself, as a child, have shouted myself hoarse applauding that very name in the theatre."

"I have heard your poem was not very handsomely received," said Standard, now suddenly shifting the subject.

"Not a word of that, for Heaven's sake!" cried I. "If Cicero, traveling in the East, found sympathetic solace for his grief in beholding the arid overthrow of a once gorgeous city, shall not my petty affair be as nothing, when I behold in Hautboy the vine and the rose climbing the shattered shafts of his tumbled temple of Fame?"

Next day I tore all my manuscripts, bought me a fiddle, and went to take regular lessons of Hautboy.

THE LIGHTNING-ROD MAN

Herman Melville

WHAT GRAND IRREGULAR thunder, thought I, standing on my hearthstone among the Acroceraunian hills, as the scattered bolts boomed overhead, and crashed down among the valleys, every bolt followed by zigzag irradiations, and swift slants of sharp rain, which audibly rang, like a charge of spear-points, on my low shingled roof. I suppose, though, that the mountains hereabouts break and churn up the thunder, so that it is far more glorious here than on the plain. Hark!—some one at the door. Who is this that chooses a time of thunder for making calls? And why don't he, man-fashion, use the knocker, instead of making that doleful undertaker's clatter with his fist against the hollow panel? But let him in. Ah, here he comes. "Good day, sir:" an entire stranger. "Pray be seated." What is that strange-looking walking-stick he carries: "A fine thunderstorm, sir."

"Fine?—Awful!"

"You are wet. Stand here on the hearth before the fire."

"Not for worlds!"

The stranger still stood in the exact middle of the cottage, where he had first planted himself. His singularity impelled a closer scrutiny. A lean, gloomy figure. Hair dark and lank, mattedly streaked over his brow. His sunken pitfalls of eyes were ringed by indigo halos, and played with an innocuous sort of lightning: the gleam without the bolt. The whole man was dripping. He stood in a puddle on the bare oak floor: his strange walking-stick vertically resting at his side.

It was a polished copper rod, four feet long, lengthwise attached to a neat wooden staff, by insertion into two balls of greenish glass, ringed with copper bands. The metal rod terminated at the top tripodwise, in three keen tines, brightly gilt. He held the thing by the wooden part alone.

"Sir," said I, bowing politely, "have I the honor of a visit from that illustrious God, Jupiter Tonans? So stood he in the Greek statue of old, grasping the lightning-bolt. If you be he, or his viceroy, I have to thank you for this noble storm you have brewed among our mountains. Listen: that was a glorious peal. Ah, to a lover of the majestic, it is a good thing to have the Thunderer himself in one's cottage. The thunder grows finer for that. But pray be seated. This old rush-bottomed arm-chair, I grant, is a poor substitute for your evergreen throne on Olympus; but, condescend to be seated."

While I thus pleasantly spoke, the stranger eyed me, half in wonder, and half in a strange sort of horror; but did not move a foot.

"Do, sir, be seated; you need to be dried ere going forth again."

I planted the chair invitingly on the broad hearth, where a little fire had been kindled that afternoon to dissipate the dampness, not the cold; for it was early in the month of September.

But without heeding my solicitation, and still standing in the middle of the floor, the stranger gazed at me portentously and spoke.

"Sir," said he, "excuse me; but instead of my accepting your invitation to be seated on the hearth there, I solemnly warn *you,* that you had best accept *mine,* and stand with me in the middle of the room. Good Heavens!" he cried, starting—"there is another of those awful crashes. I warn you, sir, quit the hearth."

"Mr. Jupiter Tonans," said I, quietly rolling my body on the stone, "I stand very well here."

"Are you so horridly ignorant, then," he cried, "as not to know, that by far the most dangerous part of a house, during such a terrific tempest as this, is the fire-place?"

"Nay, I did not know that," involuntarily stepping upon the first board next to the stone.

The stranger now assumed such an unpleasant air of successful admonition, that—quite involuntarily again—I stepped back upon the hearth, and threw myself into the erectest, proudest posture I could command. But I said nothing.

"For Heaven's sake," he cried, with a strange mixture of alarm and intimidation—"for Heaven's sake, get off the hearth! Know you not, that the heated air and soot are conductors;—to say nothing of those immense iron fire-dogs? Quit the spot—I con-jure—I command you."

"Mr. Jupiter Tonans, I am not accustomed to be commanded in my own house."

"Call me not by that pagan name. You are profane in this time of terror."

"Sir, will you be so good as to tell me your business? If you seek shelter from the storm, you are welcome, so long as you be civil; but if you come on business, open it forthwith. Who are you?"

"I am a dealer in lightning-rods," said the stranger, softening his tone; "my special business is—Merciful Heaven! what a crash!—Have you ever been struck—your premises, I mean? No? It's best to be provided,"—significantly rattling his metallic staff on the floor,—"by nature, there are no castles in thunder-storms; yet, say but the word, and of this cottage I can make a Gibraltar by a few waves of this wand. Hark, what Himalayas of concussions!"

"You interrupted yourself; your special business you were about to speak of."

"My special business is to travel the country for orders for light-ning-rods. This is my specimen rod;" tapping his staff; "I have the best of references"—fumbling in his pockets. "In Criggan last month, I put up three-and-twenty rods on only five buildings."

"Let me see. Was it not at Criggan last week, about midnight on Saturday, that the steeple, the big elm, and the assembly-room cupola were struck? Any of your rods there?"

"Not on the tree and cupola, but on the steeple."

"Of what use is your rod, then?"

"Of life-and-death use. But my workman was heedless. In fitting the rod at top to the steeple, he allowed a part of the metal to graze the tin sheeting. Hence the accident. Not my fault, but his. Hark!"

"Never mind. That clap burst quite loud enough to be heard without finger-pointing. Did you hear of the event at Montreal last year? A servant-girl struck at her bedside with a rosary in her hand; the beads being metal. Does your beat extend into the Canadas?"

"No. And I hear that there, iron rods only are in use. They should have *mine,* which are copper. Iron is easily fused. Then they draw out the rod so slender, that it has not body enough to conduct the full electric current. The metal melts; the building is destroyed. My copper rods never act so. Those Canadians are fools. Some of them knob the rod at the top, which risks a deadly explosion, instead of imperceptibly carrying down the current into the earth, as this sort of rod does. *Mine* is the only true rod. Look at it. Only one dollar a foot."

"This abuse of your own calling in another might make one distrustful with respect to yourself."

"Hark! The thunder becomes less muttering. It is nearing us, and nearing the earth, too. Hark! One crammed crash! All the vibrations made one by nearness. Another flash. Hold."

"What do you?" I said, seeing him now instantaneously relinquishing his staff, lean intently forward towards the window, with his right fore and middle fingers on his left wrist.

But ere the words had well escaped me, another exclamation escaped him.

"Crash! only three pulses—less than a third of a mile off—yonder, somewhere in that wood. I passed three stricken oaks there, ripped out new and glittering. The oak draws lightning more than other timber, having iron in solution in its sap. Your floor here seems oak."

"Heart-of-oak. From the peculiar time of your call upon me, I suppose you purposely select stormy weather for your journeys. When the thunder is roaring, you deem it an hour peculiarly favorable for producing impressions favorable to your trade."

"Hark—Awful!"

"For one who would arm others with fearlessness, you seem unbeseemingly timorous yourself. Common men choose fair weather for their travels; you choose thunder-storms; and yet——"

"That I travel in thunder-storms, I grant; but not without particular precautions, such as only a lightning-rod man may know. Hark! Quick—look at my specimen rod. Only one dollar a foot."

"A very fine rod, I dare say. But what are these particular precautions of yours? Yet first let me close yonder shutters; the slanting rain is beating through the sash. I will bar up."

"Are you mad? Know you not that yon iron bar is a swift conductor? Desist."

"I will simply close the shutters, then, and call my boy to bring me a wooden bar. Pray, touch the bell-pull there."

"Are you frantic? That bell-wire might blast you. Never touch bell-wire in a thunder-storm, nor ring a bell of any sort."

"Nor those in belfries? Pray, will you tell me where and how one may be safe in a time like this? Is there any part of my house I may touch with hopes of my life?"

"There is; but not where you now stand. Come away from the wall. The current will sometimes run down a wall, and—a man being a better conductor than a wall—it would leave the wall and run into him. Swoop! *That* must have fallen very nigh. That must have been globular lightning."

"Very probably. Tell me at once, which is, in your opinion, the safest part of this house?"

"This room, and this one spot in it where I stand. Come hither."

"The reasons first."

"Hark!—after the flash the gust—the sashes shiver—the house, the house!—Come hither to me!"

"The reasons, if you please."

"Come hither to me!"

"Thank you again, I think I will try my old stand—the hearth. And now, Mr Lightning-rod man, in the pauses of the thunder, be so good as to tell me your reasons for esteeming this one room of the house the safest, and your own one stand-point there the safest spot in it."

There was now a little cessation of the storm for a while. The Lightning-rod man seemed relieved, and replied:—

"Your house is a one-storied house, with an attic and a cellar; this room is between. Hence its comparative safety. Because lightning sometimes passes from the clouds to the earth, and sometimes from the earth to the clouds. Do you comprehend?—and I choose the middle of the room, because, if the lightning should strike the house at all, it would come down the chimney or walls; so, obviously, the further you are from them, the better. Come hither to me, now."

"Presently. Something you just said, instead of alarming me, has strangely inspired confidence."

"What have I said?"

"You said that sometimes lightning flashes from the earth to the clouds."

"Aye, the returning-stroke, as it is called; when the earth, being overcharged with the fluid, flashes its surplus upward."

"The returning-stroke; that is, from earth to sky. Better and better. But come here on the hearth, and dry yourself."

"I am better here, and better wet."

"How?"

"It is the safest thing you can do—Hark, again!—to get yourself thoroughly drenched in a thunder-storm. Wet clothes are better conductors than the body; and so, if the lightning strike, it might pass down the wet clothes without touching the body. The storm deepens again. Have you a rug in the house? Rugs are non-conductors. Get one, that I may stand on it here, and you, too. The skies blacken—it is dusk at noon. Hark!—the rug, the rug!"

I gave him one; while the hooded mountains seemed closing and tumbling into the cottage.

"And now, since our being dumb will not help us," said I, resuming my place, "let me hear your precautions in traveling during thunder-storms."

"Wait till this one is passed."

"Nay, proceed with the precautions. You stand in the safest possible place according to your own account. Go on."

"Briefly, then. I avoid pine-trees, high houses, lonely barns, upland pastures, running water, flocks of cattle and sheep, a crowd of men. If I travel on foot—as to-day—I do not walk fast; if in my buggy, I touch not its back or sides; if on horseback, I dismount and lead the horse. But of all things, I avoid tall men."

"Do I dream? Man avoid man? and in danger-time, too."

"Tall men in a thunder-storm I avoid. Are you so grossly ignorant as not to know, that the height of a six-footer is sufficient to discharge an electric cloud upon him? Are not lonely Kentuckians, ploughing, smit in the unfinished furrow? Nay, if the six-footer stand by running water, the cloud will sometimes *select* him as its conductor to that running water. Hark! Sure, yon black pinnacle is split. Yes, a man is a good conductor. The lightning goes through and through a man, but only peels a tree. But sir, you have kept me so long answering your questions, that I have not yet come to business. Will you order one of my rods? Look at this specimen one? See: it is of the best of copper. Copper's the best conductor. Your house is low; but being upon the mountains, that lowness does not one whit depress it. You mountaineers are most exposed. In mountainous countries the lightning-rod man should have most business. Look at the specimen, sir. One rod will answer for a house so small as this. Look over these recommendations. Only one rod, sir; cost, only twenty dollars. Hark! There go all the granite Taconics and Hoosics dashed together like pebbles. By the sound, that must have struck something. An elevation of five feet above the house, will protect twenty feet radius all about the rod. Only twenty dollars, sir—a dollar a foot. Hark—Dreadful!—Will you order? Will you buy? Shall I put down your name? Think of being a heap of charred offal, like a haltered horse burnt in his stall; and all in one flash!"

"You pretended envoy extraordinary and minister plenipoten-tiary to and from Jupiter Tonans," laughed I; "you mere man who come here to put you and your pipestem between clay and sky, do you think that because you can strike a bit of green light from the Leyden jar, that you can thoroughly avert the supernal bolt? Your rod rusts, or breaks, and where are you? Who has empowered you, you Tetzel, to peddle round your indulgences from divine ordinations? The hairs of our heads are numbered, and the days of our lives. In thunder as in sunshine, I stand at ease in the hands of my God. False negotiator, away! See, the scroll of the storm is rolled back; the house is unharmed; and in the blue heavens I read in the rainbow, that the Deity will not, of purpose, make war on man's earth."

"Impious wretch!" foamed the stranger, blackening in the face as the rainbow beamed. "I will publish your infidel notions."

"Begone! move quickly! if quickly you can, you that shine forth into sight in moist times like the worm."

The scowl grew blacker on his face; the indigo-circles enlarged round his eyes as the storm rings round the midnight moon. He sprang upon me; his tri-forked thing at my heart.

I seized it; I snapped it; I dashed it; I trod it; and dragging the dark lightning-king out of my door, flung his elbowed, copper sceptre after him.

But spite of my treatment, and spite of my dissuasive talk of him to my neighbors, the Lightning-rod man still dwells in the land; still travels in storm-time, and drives a brave trade with the fears of man.

SELECTING THE FACULTY

Robert Carlton (Baynard Rush Hall)

OUR BOARD OF Trustees, it will be remembered, had been directed by the Legislature to procure, as the ordinance called it, "Teachers for the commencement of the State College at Woodville." That business, by the Board, was committed to Dr. Sylvan and Robert Carlton—the most learned gentlemen of the body, and of—the New Purchase! Our honourable Board will be more specially introduced hereafter; at present we shall bring forward certain rejected candidates, that, like rejected prize essays, they may be published, and *thus* have their revenge.

None can tell us how plenty good things are till he looks for them; and hence, to the great surprise of the Committee, there seemed to be a sudden growth and a large crop of persons even in and around Woodville, either already qualified for the "Professorships," as we named them in our publications, or who *could* "qualify" by the time of election. As to the "chair" named also in our publications, one very worthy and disinterested schoolmaster offered, as a great collateral inducement for his being elected, "*to find his own chair!*"—a vast saving to the State, if the same chair I saw in Mr. Whackum's school-room. For his chair there was one with a hickory bottom; and doubtless he would have filled it, and even lapped over its edges, with equal dignity in the recitation room of Big College.

The Committee had, at an early day, given an invitation to the Rev. Charles Clarence, A. M., of New Jersey, and his answer had been affirmative; yet for political reasons we had been obliged to invite competitors, or *make* them, and we found and created "a right smart sprinkle."

130

Hopes of success were built on many things—for instance, on poverty; a plea being entered that some thing ought to be done for the poor fellow—on one's having taught a common school all his born days, who now deserved to rise a peg—on political, or religious, or fanatical partisan qualifications—and on pure patriotic principles, such as a person's having been "born in a canebrake and rocked in a sugar trough." On the other hand, a fat, dull-headed, and modest Englishman asked for a place, because he had been born in Liverpool! and had seen the world beyond the woods and waters too! And another fussy, talkative, pragmatical little gentleman, rested his pretensions on his ability to draw and paint maps!—not projecting them in roundabout scientific processes, but in that speedy and elegant style in which young ladies *copy* maps at first chop boarding schools! Nay, so transcendent seemed Mr. Merchator's claims, when his *show* or *sample* maps were exhibited to us, that some in our Board, and nearly everybody out of it, were confident he would do for Professor of Mathematics and even Principal.

But of all our unsuccessful candidates, we shall introduce by name only two—Mr. James Jimmey, A.S.S., and Mr. Solomon Rapid, A. to Z.

Mr. Jimmey, who aspired to the mathematical chair, was master of a small school of all sexes, near Woodville. At the first, he was kindly, yet honestly told, his knowledge was too limited and inaccurate; yet, notwithstanding this, and some almost rude repulses afterwards, he persisted in his application and his hopes. To give evidence of competency, he once told me he was arranging a new spelling-book, the publication of which would make him known as a literary man, and be an unspeakable advantage to "the rising generation." And this naturally brought on the following colloquy about the work:—

"Ah! indeed! Mr. Jimmey?"

"Yes, indeed, Mr. Carlton."

"On what new principle do you go, sir?"

"Why, sir, on the principles of nature and common sense. I allow school-books for schools are all too powerful obstruse and hard-like to be understood without exemplifying illustrations."

"Yes, but Mr. Jimmey, how is a child's spelling-book to be made any plainer?"

"Why, sir, by clear explifications of the words in one column, by exemplifying illustrations in the other."

"I do not understand you, Mr. Jimmey, give me a specimen."

"Sir?"

"An example."

"To be sure—here's a spes-a-example; you see, for instance, I put in the spelling column, C-r-e-a-m, *cream,* and here in the explification column, I put the exemplifying illustration—*Unctious part of milk!*"

We had asked, at our first interview, if our candidate was an algebraist, and his reply was *negative;* but, "he allowed he could *'qualify'* by the time of election, as he was powerful good at figures, and had cyphered clean through every arithmetic he had ever seen, the rule of promiscuous questions and all!" Hence, some weeks after, as I was passing his door, on my way to a squirrel hunt, with a party of friends, Mr. Jimmey, hurrying out with a slate in his hand, begged me to stop a moment, and thus addressed me:—

"Well, Mr. Carlton, this algebra is a most powerful thing—aint it?"

"Indeed it is, Mr. Jimmey—have you been looking into it?"

"Looking into it! I have been all through this here fust part; and by election time, I allow I'll be ready for examination."

"Indeed!"

"Yes, sir! but it is such a pretty thing! Only to think of cyphering by letters! Why, sir, the sums come out, and bring the answers exactly like figures. Jist stop a minute—look here; a stands for 6, and b stands for 8, and c stands for 4, and d stands for figure 10; now if I say $a + b - c = d$, it is all the same as if I said, 6 is 6 and 8 makes 14, and 4 subtracted, leaves 10! Why, sir, I done a whole slate full of letters and signs; and afterwards, when I tried by figures, they every one of them came out right and brung the answer! I mean to cypher by letters altogether."

"Mr. Jimmey, my company is nearly out of sight—if you can get along this way through simple and quadratic equations by our meeting, your chance will not be so bad—good morning, sir."

But our man of "letters" quit cyphering the new way, and returned to plain figures long before reaching equations; and so he could not become our professor. Yet anxious to do us all the good in his power, after our college opened, he waited on me, a leading trustee, with a proposal to board our students, and authorized me to publish—"as how Mr. James Jimmey will take strange students—students not belonging to Woodville—to board, at one dollar a week, and find every thing, washing included, and will black their *shoes* three times a week to *boot,* and—*give them their dog-wood and cherry-bitters every morning into the bargain!"*

The most extraordinary candidate, however, was Mr. Solomon Rapid. He was now somewhat advanced into the shaving age, and was ready to assume offices the most opposite in character; although justice compels us to say Mr. Rapid was as fit for one thing as another. Deeming it waste of time to prepare for any station till he was certain of obtaining it, he wisely demanded the place first, and then set to work to become qualified for its duties, being, I suspect, the very man, or some relation of his, who is recorded as not knowing whether he could read Greek, as he had never tried. And, beside, Mr. Solomon Rapid contended that all offices, from president down to fence-viewer, were open to every white American citizen; and that every republican had a blood-bought right to seek any that struck his fancy; and if the profits were less, or the duties more onerous than had been anticipated, that a man ought to resign and try another.

Naturally, therefore, Mr. Rapid, thought he would like to sit in our chair of languages, or have some employment in the State college; and hence he called for that purpose on Dr. Sylvan, who, knowing the candidate's character, maliciously sent him to me. Accordingly, the young gentleman presented himself, and without ceremony, instantly made known his business thus:—

"I heerd, sir, you wanted somebody to teach the State school, and I'm come to let you know I'm willing to take the place."

"Yes, sir, we are going to elect a professor of languages who is to be the principal, and a professor."

"Well, I don't care which I take, but I'm willing to be the principal. I can teach sifring, reading, writing, joggerfree, surveying, grammur, spelling, definitions, parsin—"

"Are you a linguist?"

"Sir?"

"You of course understand the dead languages?"

"Well, can't say I ever seed much of them, though I have heerd tell of them; but I can soon larn them—they aint more than a few of them I allow?"

"Oh! my dear sir, it is not possible—we—can't—"

"Well, I never seed what I couldn't larn about as smart as any body—"

"Mr. Rapid, I do not mean to question your abilities; but if you are now wholly unacquainted with the dead languages, it is impossible for you or any other talented man to learn them under four or five years."

"Pshoo! foo! I'll bet I larn one in three weeks! Try me, sir,—let's have the furst one furst—how many are there?"

"Mr. Rapid, it is utterly impossible; but if you insist, I will loan you a Latin book—"

"That's your sorts, let's have it, that's all I want, fair play."

Accordingly, I handed him a copy of *Historiae Sacrae,* with which he soon went away, saying, he "didn't allow it would take long to git through Latin, if 'twas only sich a thin patch of a book as that."

In a few weeks to my no small surprise, Mr. Solomon Rapid again presented himself; and drawing forth the book began with a triumphant expression of countenance: "Well, sir, I have done the Latin."

"Done the Latin!"

"Yes, I can read it as fast as English."

"Read it as fast as English!"

"Yes, as fast as English—and I didn't find it hard at all."

"May I try you on a page?"

"Try away, try away; that's what I've come for."

"Please read here then, Mr. Rapid"; and in order to give him a fair chance, I pointed to the first lines of the first chapter, viz: *"In principio Deus creavit coelum et terram intra sex dies; primo die fecit lucem,"* etc.

"That, sir?" and then he read thus, "in prinspo duse creevit kalelum et terrum intra sex dyes—primmo dye fe-fe-sit looseum," etc.

"That will do, Mr. Rapid—"

"Aha! I told you so."

"Yes, yes—but translate."

"Translate!" (eyebrows elevating).

"Yes, translate, render it."

"Render it! how's that?" (forehead more wrinkled).

"Why, yes, render it into English—give me the meaning of it."

"MEANING!" (staring full in my face, his eyes like saucers, and forehead wrinkled with the furrows of eighty)—"MEANING! I didn't know it *had* any meaning. I thought it was a DEAD language!"

Well, reader, I am glad you are *not* laughing at Mr. Rapid; for how should any thing *dead* speak out so as to be understood? And indeed, does not his definition suit the vexed feelings of some young gentlemen attempting to read Latin without any interlinear translation? and who inwardly, cursing both book and teacher, blast their souls "if they can make any sense out of it." The ancients may yet speak in their own languages to a few; but to most who boast the honour of their acquaintance, they are certainly dead in the sense of Solomon Rapid.

Our honourable board of trustees at last met; and after a real attempt by some, and a pretended one by others, to elect one and another out of the three dozen candidates, the Reverend Charles Clarence, A. M., was chosen our principal and professor of languages; and that to the chagrin of Mr. Rapid and other disappointed persons, who all from that moment united in determined and active hostility towards the college, Mr. Clarence, Dr. Sylvan, Mr. Carlton, and, in short, towards "every puss proud aristocrat big-bug, and blasted Yankee in the New Purchase."

THE COLD EMBRACE

Mary E. Braddon

HE WAS AN artist—such things as happened to him happen sometimes to artists.

He was a German—such things as happened to him happen sometimes to Germans.

He was young, handsome, studious, enthusiastic, metaphysical, reckless, unbelieving, heartless.

And being young, handsome and eloquent, he was beloved.

He was an orphan, under the guardianship of his dead father's brother, his uncle Wilhelm, in whose house he had been brought up from a little child; and she who loved him was his cousin—his cousin Gertrude, whom he swore he loved in return.

Did he love her? Yes, when he first swore it. It soon wore out, this passionate love; how threadbare and wretched a sentiment it became at last in the selfish heart of the student! But in its first golden dawn, when he was only nineteen, and had just returned from his apprenticeship to a great painter at Antwerp, and they wandered together in the most romantic outskirts of the city at rosy sunset, by holy moonlight, or bright and joyous morning, how beautiful a dream!

They keep it a secret from Wilhelm, as he has the father's ambition of a wealthy suitor for his only child—a cold and dreary vision beside the lover's dream.

So they are betrothed; and standing side by side when the dying sun and the pale rising moon divide the heavens, he puts the betrothal ring upon her finger, the white and taper finger whose slender shape he knows so well. This ring is a peculiar one, a massive golden serpent, its tail in its mouth, the symbol of eternity; it had been his mother's, and he would know it amongst a thousand. If he were to become blind tomorrow, he could select it from amongst a thousand by the touch alone.

He places it on her finger, and they swear to be true to each other for ever and ever—through trouble and danger—sorrow and change—in wealth or poverty. Her father must needs be won to consent to their union by-and-by, for they were now betrothed, and death alone could part them.

But the young student, the scoffer at revelation, yet the enthusiastic adorer of the mystical, asks:

"Can death part us? I would return to you from the grave, Gertrude. My soul would come back to be near my love. And you—you, if you died before me—the cold earth would not hold you from me; if you loved me, you would return, and again these fair arms would be clasped round my neck as they are now."

But she told him, with a holier light in her deep-blue eyes than had ever shone in his—she told him that the dead who die at peace with God are happy in heaven, and cannot return to the troubled earth; and that it is only the suicide—the lost wretch on whom sorrowful angels shut the door of Paradise—whose unholy spirit haunts the footsteps of the living.

The first year of their betrothal is passed, and she is alone, for he has gone to Italy, on a commission for some rich man, to copy Raphaels, Titians, Guidos, in a gallery at Florence. He has gone to win fame, perhaps; but it is not the less bitter—he is gone!

Of course her father misses his young nephew, who has been as a son to him; and he thinks his daughter's sadness no more than a cousin should feel for a cousin's absence.

In the meantime, the weeks and months pass. The lover writes—often at first, then seldom—at last, not at all.

How many excuses she invents for him! How many times she goes to the distant little post-office, to which he is to address his letters! How many times she hopes, only to be disappointed! How many times she despairs, only to hope again!

But real despair comes at last, and will not be put off any more. The rich suitor appears on the scene, and her father is determined. She is to marry at once. The wedding-day is fixed—the fifteenth of June.

The date seems to burn into her brain.

The date, written in fire, dances for ever before her eyes.

The date, shrieked by the Furies, sounds continually in her ears.

But there is time yet—it is the middle of May—there is time for a letter to reach him at Florence; there is time for him to come to Brunswick, to take her away and marry her, in spite of her father—in spite of the whole world.

But the days and the weeks fly by, and he does not write—he does not come. This is indeed despair which usurps her heart, and will not be put away.

It is the fourteenth of June. For the last time she goes to the little post-office; for the last time she asks the old question, and they give her for the last time the dreary answer, "No; no letter."

For the last time—for tomorrow is the day appointed for the bridal. Her father will hear no entreaties; her rich suitor will not listen to her prayers. They will not be put off a day—an hour; to-night alone is hers—this night, which she may employ as she will.

She takes another path than that which leads home; she hurries through some by-streets of the city, out on to a lonely bridge, where he and she had stood so often in the sunset, watching the rose-coloured light glow, fade, and die upon the river.

He returns from Florence. He had received her letter. That letter, blotted with tears, entreating, despairing—he had received it, but he loved her no longer. A young Florentine, who has sat to him for a model, had bewitched his fancy—that fancy which with him stood in place of a heart—and Gertrude had been half-forgotten. If she had a rich suitor, good; let her marry him; better for her, better far for himself. He had no wish to fetter himself with a wife. Had he not his art always?—his eternal bride, his unchanging mistress.

Thus he thought it wiser to delay his journey to Brunswick, so that he should arrive when the wedding was over—arrive in time to salute the bride.

And the vows—the mystical fancies—the belief in his return, even after death, to the embrace of his beloved? O, gone out of his life; melted away for ever, those foolish dreams of his boyhood.

So on the fifteenth of June he enters Brunswick, by that very bridge on which she stood, the stars looking down on her, the night before. He strolls across the bridge and down by the water's edge, a great rough dog at his heels, and the smoke from his short meerschaum-pipe curling in blue wreaths fantastically in the pure morning air. He has his sketch-book under his arm, and attracted now and then by some object that catches his artist's eye, stops to draw: a few weeds and pebbles on the river's brink—a crag on the opposite shore—a group of pollard willows in the distance. When he has done, he admires his drawing, shuts his sketch-book, empties the ashes from his pipe, refills from his tobacco-pouch, sings the refrain of a gay drinking-song, calls to his dog, smokes again, and walks on. Suddenly he opens his sketch-book again; this time that which attracts him is a group of figures: but what is it?

It is not a funeral, for there are no mourners.

It is not a funeral, but a corpse lying on a rude bier, covered with an old sail, carried between two bearers.

It is not a funeral, for the bearers are fishermen—fishermen in their everyday garb.

About a hundred yards from him they rest their burden on a bank—one stands at the head of the bier, the other throws himself down at the foot of it.

And thus they form the perfect group; he walks back two or three paces, selects his point of sight, and begins to sketch a hurried outline. He has finished it before they move; he hears their voices, though he cannot hear their words, and wonders what they can be talking of. Presently he walks on and joins them.

"You have a corpse there, my friends?" he says.

"Yes; a corpse washed ashore an hour ago."

"Drowned?"

"Yes, drowned. A young girl, very handsome."

"Suicides are always handsome," says the painter; and then he stands for a little while idly smoking and meditating, looking at the sharp outline of the corpse and the stiff folds of the rough canvas covering.

Life is such a golden holiday for him—young, ambitious, clever—that it seems as though sorrow and death could have no part in his destiny.

At last he says that, as this poor suicide is so handsome, he should like to make a sketch of her.

He gives the fishermen some money, and they offer to remove the sailcloth that covers her features.

No; he will do it himself. He lifts the rough, coarse, wet canvas from her face. What face?

The face that shone on the dreams of his foolish boyhood; the face which once was the light of his uncle's home. His cousin Gertrude—his betrothed!

He sees, as in one glance, while he draws one breath, the rigid features—the marble arms—the hands crossed on the cold bosom; and, on the third finger of the left hand, the ring which had been his mother's—the golden serpent; the ring which, if he were to become blind, he could select from a thousand others by the touch alone.

But he is a genius and a metaphysician—grief, true grief, is not for such as he. His first thought is flight—flight anywhere out of that accursed city—anywhere far from the brink of that hideous river—anywhere away from remorse—anywhere to forget.

He is miles on the road that leads away from Brunswick before he knows that he has walked a step.

It is only when his dog lies down panting at his feet that he feels how exhausted he is himself, and sits down upon a bank to rest. How the landscape spins round and round before his dazzled eyes, while his morning's sketch of the two fishermen and the canvas-covered bier glares redly at him out of the twilight!

At last, after sitting a long time by the roadside, idly playing with his dog, idly smoking, idly lounging, looking as any idle, light-hearted travelling student might look, yet all the while acting over that morning's scene in his burning brain a hundred times a minute; at last he grows a little more composed, and tries presently to think of himself as he is, apart from his cousin's suicide. Apart from that, he was no worse off than he was yesterday. His genius was not gone; the money he had earned at Florence still lined his pocket-book; he was his own master, free to go whither he would.

And while he sits on the roadside, trying to separate himself from the scene of that morning—trying to put away the image of the corpse covered with the damp canvas sail—trying to think of what he should do next, where he should go, to be farthest away from Brunswick and remorse, the old diligence comes rumbling and jingling along. He remembers it; it goes from Brunswick to Aix-la-Chapelle.

He whistles to the dog, shouts to the postillion to stop, and springs into the *coupé*.

During the whole evening, through the long night, though he does not once close his eyes, he never speaks a word; but when morning dawns, and the other passengers awake and begin to talk to each other, he joins in the conversation. He tells them that he is an artist, that he is going to Cologne and to Antwerp to copy Rubenses, and the great picture by Quentin Matsys, in the museum. He remembered afterwards that he talked and laughed boisterously, and that when he was talking and laughing loudest, a passenger, older and graver than the rest, opened the window near him, and told him to put his head out. He remembered the fresh air blowing in his face, the singing of the birds in his ears, and the flat fields and roadside reeling before his eyes. He remembered this, and then falling in a lifeless heap on the floor of the diligence.

It is a fever that keeps him for six long weeks on a bed at a hotel in Aix-la-Chapelle.

He gets well, and, accompanied by his dog, starts on foot for Cologne. By this time he is his former self once more. Again the blue smoke from his short meerschaum curls upwards in the morning air—again he sings some old university drinking-song—again stops here and there, meditating and sketching.

He is happy, and has forgotten his cousin—and so on to Cologne.

It is by the great cathedral he is standing, with his dog at his side. It is night, the bells have just chimed the hour, and the clocks are striking eleven; the moonlight shines full upon the magnificent pile, over which the artist's eye wanders, absorbed in the beauty of form.

He is not thinking of his drowned cousin, for he has forgotten her and is happy.

Suddenly someone, something from behind him, puts two cold arms round his neck, and clasps its hands on his breast.

And yet there is no one behind him, for on the flags bathed in the broad moonlight there are only two shadows, his own and his dog's. He turns quickly round—there is no one—nothing to be seen in the broad square but himself and his dog; and though he feels, he cannot see the cold arms clasped round his neck.

It is not ghostly, this embrace, for it is palpable to the touch— it cannot be real, for it is invisible.

He tries to throw off the cold caress. He clasps the hands in his own to tear them asunder, and to cast them off his neck. He can feel the long delicate fingers cold and wet beneath his touch, and on the third finger of the left hand he can feel the ring which was his mother's—the golden serpent—the ring which he has always said he would know among a thousand by the touch alone. He knows it now!

His dead cousin's cold arms are round his neck—his dead cousin's wet hands are clasped upon his breast. He asks himself if he is mad. "Up, Leo!" he shouts. "Up, up, boy!" and the Newfoundland leaps to his shoulders—the dog's paws are on the dead hands, and the animal utters a terrific howl, and springs away from his master.

The student stands in the moonlight, the dead arms around his neck, and the dog at a little distance moaning piteously.

Presently a watchman, alarmed by the howling of the dog, comes into the square to see what is wrong.

In a breath the cold arms are gone.

He takes the watchman home to the hotel with him and gives him money; in his gratitude he could have given that man half his little fortune.

Will it ever come to him again, this embrace of the dead?

He tries never to be alone; he makes a hundred acquaintances, and shares the chamber of another student. He starts up if he is left by himself in the public room of the inn where he is staying, and runs into the street. People notice his strange actions, and begin to think that he is mad.

But, in spite of all, he is alone once more; for one night the public room being empty for a moment, when on some idle pretence he strolls into the street, the street is empty too, and for the second time he feels the cold arms round his neck, and for the second time, when he calls his dog, the animal shrinks away from him with a piteous howl.

After this he leaves Cologne, still travelling on foot—of necessity now, for his money is getting low. He joins travelling hawkers, he walks side by side with labourers, he talks to every foot-passenger he falls in with, and tries from morning till night to get company on the road.

At night he sleeps by the fire in the kitchen of the inn at which he stops; but do what he will, he is often alone, and it is now a common thing for him to feel the cold arms around his neck.

Many months have passed since his cousin's death—autumn, winter, early spring. His money is nearly gone, his health is utterly broken, he is the shadow of his former self, and he is getting near to Paris. He will reach that city at the time of the Carnival. To this he looks forward. In Paris, in Carnival time, he need never, surely, be alone, never feel that deadly caress; he may even recover his lost gaiety, his lost health, once more resume his profession, once more earn fame and money by his art.

How hard he tries to get over the distance that divides him from Paris, while day by day he grows weaker, and his step slower and more heavy!

But there is an end at last; the long dreary roads are passed. This is Paris, which he enters for the first time—Paris, of which he has dreamed so much—Paris, whose million voices are to exorcise his phantom.

To him to-night Paris seems one vast chaos of lights, music, and confusion—lights which dance before his eyes and will not be still—music that rings in his ears and deafens him—confusion which makes his head whirl round and round.

But, in spite of all, he finds the opera-house, where there is a masked ball. He has enough money left to buy a ticket of admission, and to hire a domino to throw over his shabby dress. It seems only a moment after his entering the gates of Paris that he is in the very midst of all the wild gaiety of the opera-house ball.

No more darkness, no more loneliness, but a mad crowd, shouting and dancing, and a lovely Débardeuse hanging on his arm.

The boisterous gaiety he feels surely is his old light-heartedness come back. He hears the people round him talking of the outrageous conduct of some drunken student, and it is to him they point when they say this—to him, who has not moistened his lips since yesterday at noon, for even now he will not drink; though his lips are parched, and his throat burning, he cannot drink. His voice is thick and hoarse, and his utterance indistinct; but still this must be his old light-heartedness come back that makes him so wildly gay.

The little Débardeuse is wearied out—her arm rests on his shoulder heavier than lead—the other dancers one by one drop off.

The lights in the chandeliers one by one die out.

The decorations look pale and shadowy in that dim light which is neither night nor day.

A faint glimmer from the dying lamps, a pale streak of cold grey light from the new-born day, creeping in through half-opened shutters.

And by this light the bright-eyed Débardeuse fades sadly. He looks her in the face. How the brightness of her eyes dies out!

Again he looks her in the face. How white that face has grown! Again—and now it is the shadow of a face alone that looks in his.

Again—and they are gone—the bright eyes, the face, the shadow of the face. He is alone; alone in that vast saloon.

Alone, and, in the terrible silence, he hears the echoes of his own footsteps in that dismal dance which has no music.

No music but the beating of his breast. Then the cold arms are round his neck—they whirl him round, they will not be flung off, or cast away; he can no more escape from their icy grasp than he can escape from death. He looks behind him—there is nothing but himself in the great empty *salle;* but he can feel— cold, deathlike, but O, how palpable!—the long slender fingers, and the ring which was his mother's.

He tries to shout, but he has no power in his burning throat. The silence of the place is only broken by the echoes of his own footsteps in the dance from which he cannot extricate himself. Who says he has no partner? The cold hands are clasped on his breast, and now he does not shun their caress. No! One more polka, if he drops down dead.

The lights are all out, and, half an hour after, the *gendarmes* come in with a lantern to see that the house is empty; they are followed by a great dog that they have found seated howling on the steps of the theatre. Near the principal entrance they stumble over—

The body of a student, who has died from want of food, exhaustion, and the breaking of a blood-vessel.

Alphonse Daudet

THE POPE'S MULE

La Mule du Pape

OF ALL THE pretty sayings, proverbs, and adages with which our peasants in Provence lace their speech, I don't know any that are more picturesque or more unusual than this one. In a radius of fifteen leagues around my windmill, whenever they talk about a grudge-bearing, vindictive man, they say: "That man! Watch out! . . . He's like the Pope's she-mule, and holds back his kick for seven years."

I searched for a long time to see where that proverb might come from, and the story of that papal mule and that kick held in reserve for seven years. No one here has been able to give me information on that subject, not even Francet Mamaï, my fife player, even though he has his Provençal legends at his fingertips. Francet agrees with me that, at the bottom of it, there's some old chronicle of the Avignon region; but he's never heard talk of it except by way of the proverb.

"You'll only find that in the cicadas' library," the old fifer said to me, laughing.

That sounded like a good idea, and, seeing that the cicadas' library is right outside my door, I went and shut myself up in it for a week.

It's a wonderful library, admirably fitted out, open to poets day and night, and staffed by little librarians with cymbals who make music for you the whole time. I spent a few delightful days there, and after a week of research—on my back—I finally found what I wanted; that is, the history of my mule and that notorious kick held in reserve for seven years. The tale is a pretty one, though somewhat naïve, and I'll try to tell it to you just as I read it yesterday

145

morning in a sky-blue manuscript that had a good smell of dry lavender, with big threads of gossamer for bookmarks.

★ ★ ★

If you didn't see Avignon when the Popes were there, you've never seen a thing. For merriment, liveliness, animation, the busy series of festivals, there's never been a city like it. From morning to evening there were processions, pilgrimages, the streets strewn with flowers and overhung by high-warp tapestries, arrivals of cardinals on the Rhône, banners in the wind, galleys decked with flags, the Pope's soldiers chanting in Latin on the squares, the rattles of the monks collecting alms. And then, from top to bottom of the houses that huddled around the great Palace of the Popes, buzzing like bees around the hive, there was, besides, the click-clack of the lace frames, the to-and-fro of shuttles weaving the gold for chasubles, the little hammers of the engravers of altar cruets, the soundboards being finished in the lute makers' shops, the hymns sung by the women setting up the warp on looms; and, above all the rest, the sound of the bells, and always a few Provençal drums that could be heard rumbling there, toward the bridge. Because, where we live, when the populace is happy, it must dance, it must dance; and, since in those days the city streets were too narrow for the farandole, fife and drum players took up their station on the bridge of Avignon, in the cool breeze from the Rhone, and day and night "people danced there, people danced there" . . . Oh, the happy time! The happy city! Halberds that did not strike; prisons of the state in which wine was placed to cool. Never a food shortage; never a war . . . That's how the Popes of the County of Avignon knew how to govern their people; that's why their people missed them so when they left! . . .

There's one especially, a good old man, who was called Boniface . . . Oh, how many tears were shed in Avignon for *him* when he died! He was such an amiable and pleasing ruler! How kindly he smiled at you while seated on his mule! And whenever you passed by him—whether you were a poor little extractor of madder dye or the chief justice of the city—he gave you a blessing so politely! A true Pope of Yvetot,[1] but of an Yvetot in Provence,

---

[1] A word play with reference to a humorous song text by Pierre-Jean de Béranger (1780–1857), "Le roi d'Yvetot," about a very plain-living, jolly king with a sweetheart named Jeanneton. (Yvetot is a small town in Normandy.)—Trans.

with something delicate in his laughter, a sprig of marjoram in his biretta, and not the slightest Jeanneton . . . The only "sweetheart Jeanneton" that that kindly father ever had was his vineyard—a little vineyard he had planted himself, three leagues from Avignon, among the myrtles of Châteauneuf.

Every Sunday, on leaving vespers, the worthy man went to pay his court to it, and when he was up there, sitting in the beneficent sunshine, his mule nearby, his cardinals all around stretched out at the feet of the vinestocks, then he had a flagon of the local wine uncorked—that beautiful, ruby-colored wine which, ever since, has been called Châteauneuf-du-Pape—and he would taste it in little sips, looking at his vineyard tenderly. Then, the flagon emptied, the sun setting, he would return joyously to his city, followed by his entire chapter of canons; and, when he crossed the bridge of Avignon,[2] in the midst of the drums and the farandoles, his mule, enlivened by the music, would go into a little hopping amble, while the Pope himself beat time to the dance music with his biretta, which greatly shocked his cardinals but caused all the plain people to say: "Oh, what a good ruler! Oh, what a fine Pope!"

★ ★ ★

After his vineyard at Châteauneuf, what the Pope loved most in the world was his she-mule. The dear old man was crazy about that animal. Every night before going to bed, he went to see whether her stable was properly closed, whether there was nothing lacking in her feeding trough; and he would never have risen from his table without seeing prepared before his eyes a large bowl of French-style wine,[3] with plenty of sugar and spices, which he himself brought to the mule, despite his cardinals' remarks. . . . It must also be said that the animal was worth all of this. She was a beautiful black mule with red spots, surefooted, with a gleaming coat and wide, full hindquarters; she carried with pride her small, lean head that was lavishly accoutred with pompoms, bows, silver jingle bells, and tassels. In addition, she was as gentle as an angel, with candid eyes and two long ears that were always in motion, giving her

---

[2] Every French commentator gleefully points out that Châteauneuf and Avignon are on the same side of the Rhone, so that this crossing of the bridge is an error (or a fantasy?).—Trans.

[3] Warmed-up red wine with sugar, cinnamon, and other flavorings.—Trans.

a good-natured appearance. All Avignon esteemed her and, when she wandered through the streets, everyone treated her as courteously as possible; because everyone knew that that was the best way to be in good standing at the papal court, and that, with her innocent appearance, the Pope's mule had led more than one person to good fortune—as a proof, Tistet Védène and his prodigious adventure.

This Tistet Védène was basically a brazen-faced young rascal whom his father, Guy Védène, a goldsmith, had been forced to throw out of his house because he refused to do any work and was keeping the apprentices from doing theirs. For six months he was to be seen dragging his coat through every gutter in Avignon, but especially in the vicinity of the papal palace; because for some time the rogue had had a plan concerning the Pope's mule, and you're about to see that it was pretty shrewd. . . . One day, when His Holiness was on an outing, all alone with his mount, alongside the city walls, there was our Tistet, greeting him and saying, with his hands joined together in admiration:

"Oh, my heavens! Great Holy Father, what a fine mule you have there! . . . Let me look at her for a while. . . . Oh, Pope, such a beautiful mule! . . . The Emperor of Germany doesn't have one like her."

And he patted her, and spoke gently to her as if addressing a well-born young lady.

"Come here, my jewel, my treasure, my precious pearl . . ."

And the good Pope, sincerely touched, said to himself:

"What a good little boy! . . . How nice he is to my mule!"

And then, the next day, do you know what happened? Tistet Védène swapped his old yellow coat for a beautiful lace alb, a violet silk short cape such as priests wear, and buckled shoes, and he joined the Pope's choir school, where never before that time had anyone been received but noblemen's sons and cardinals' nephews. Just see what intrigue will do! . . . But Tistet didn't stop there.

Once in the Pope's service, the rogue continued the game that had stood him in such good stead. Insolent with everybody, he lavished his cares and kindness only on the mule, and was always to be found in the palace courtyards with a handful of oats or a little bunch of sainfoin, amiably shaking its clusters of pink flowers while looking at the Holy Father's balcony, as if to say: "Well? . . . Who is this for? . . ." So much so, that the good Pope, who felt he was growing old, finally assigned him the task of taking care of the stable and bringing the mule her bowl of French-style wine; this did not make the cardinals happy.

★ ★ ★

Nor was the mule happy about it, either. . . . Now, when the time for her wine arrived, she always saw arriving in her stable five or six young clerics from the choir school, who quickly nestled in the straw with their short capes and their laces; a moment later, a pleasant, warm aroma of burnt sugar and spices filled the stable, and Tistet Védène appeared, carefully carrying the bowl of French-style wine. Then the martyrdom of the poor animal would begin.

That flavored wine she loved so much, which kept her warm, which lent her wings—they were so cruel as to bring it over to her, there in her feeding trough, to let her inhale it; then, when her nostrils were filled with it—presto, vanished! The beautiful, fiery-pink beverage would completely disappear into the gullets of those little brats. . . . And, as if stealing her wine wasn't enough, all those little clerics were like devils when they were drunk! . . . One of them pulled her ears, another, her tail; Quiquet climbed on her back, Béluguet tried out his biretta on her, and not one of those rascals imagined that, with a flick of her crupper or a kick, the good animal could have sent them all to the pole star, or even farther. . . But no! It's not for nothing that you're the Pope's mule, the mule of benedictions and indulgences. . . . No matter how the youngsters irritated her, she didn't get angry; and her rancor was directed only at Tistet Védène. . . . Now, when she sensed that *he* was behind her, her hooves itched her, and truly she had good reasons. That good-for-nothing Tistet played such nasty tricks on her! He thought up such cruel things to do when he got drunk! . . .

Didn't he get the idea one day to make her climb up with him to the bell tower of the choir school, up there, way up there, at the pinnacle of the palace? . . . And what I'm now telling you isn't a fairy tale; two hundred thousand inhabitants of Provence saw it happen. Picture the terror of that unhappy mule when, after twisting her way up a spiral staircase blindly for an hour, and after climbing heaven knows how many steps, she suddenly found herself on a platform inundated with dazzling light, and caught sight, at a thousand feet below her, of an entire fantastic Avignon, the market stalls no bigger than hazelnuts, the Pope's soldiers in front of their barracks like red ants, and, over yonder, on a silver thread, a little, microscopic bridge on which "people were dancing, people were dancing." . . . Oh, the poor animal! What panic she felt! The cry she uttered made all the windows in the palace shake.

"What's wrong? What are they doing to her?" exclaimed the good Pope, dashing out onto his balcony.

Tistet Védène was already in the courtyard, pretending to weep and pull out his hair:

"Oh, great Holy Father, you ask what's wrong? Your mule has climbed the bell tower."

"All by herself?"

"Yes, great Holy Father, all by herself. . . . See! Look at her up there. . . . Do you see the tips of her ears sticking out? . . . They look like a pair of swallows . . ."

"Mercy!" cried the poor Pope, raising his eyes. "But she must have gone crazy! But she's going to get killed. . . . Will you come down from there, you wretched thing?! . . ."

Alas![4] As for her, she would have liked nothing better than to go down . . . but which way? The staircase wasn't even to be thought of; those contraptions can be climbed up, at best; but going down them, you could break your legs a hundred times. . . . And the poor mule was in misery; while walking around the platform, her large eyes glazed over with dizziness, she kept thinking about Tistet Védène.

"Oh, you villain, if I get out of this . . . what a kick you'll get tomorrow morning!"

That thought of the kick put a little heart back into her; otherwise, she wouldn't have been able to stick it out. . . . Finally they managed to get her down from there, but it was quite a job. She had to be let down with a winch, ropes, and a litter. Just imagine how humiliating it was for a Pope's mule to see herself hanging up so high, swimming with her feet in the air like a June bug at the end of a string! And with everyone in Avignon watching her!

The unhappy animal didn't sleep all night. She kept thinking she was still turning to and fro on that accursed platform, with the laughter of the city below her; then she thought about that vile Tistet Védène and the neat kick she was going to treat him to on

---

[4] The French word here, *"pécaïre!,"* is a typically Provençal exclamation.— Trans.

the following morning. Oh, my friends, what a kick! They'd see
the smoke from it all the way to Pampérigouste.[5] . . . Now, while
this lovely reception was being planned for him in the stable, do
you know what Tistet Védène was doing? He was going down the
Rhone, singing, on a papal galley, on his way to the court of Naples
as one of the company of young noblemen that the city used to
send annually to Queen Jeanne[6] to perfect themselves in diplomacy
and fine manners. Tistet wasn't a nobleman, but the Pope desired
to reward him for the attentions he had shown his animal, particularly for his active participation on the day when she was rescued.

Wasn't the mule disappointed the next day!

"Oh, the villain! He suspected something!" she thought, shaking
her jingle bells in a rage. "But it's all the same; go on, you rat!
You'll find your kick when you get back. . . . I'll save it for you!"

And she saved it for him.

After Tistet's departure, the Pope's mule regained her calm life
style and her former ways. No more Quiquet, no more Béluguet
in the stable. The good old days of the French-style wine had
returned and, with them, her good humor, her long siestas, and her
little gavotte step whenever she crossed the bridge of Avignon. And
yet, ever since her adventure, people in town always showed a little
coolness toward her. There were whispers when she passed by; old
folks shook their heads, children laughed and pointed to the bell
tower. The good Pope himself no longer had as much confidence
in his friend as formerly, and when he allowed himself to take a
little nap on her back on Sundays on his way back from the vineyard, he always had this thought in the back of his mind: "What if
I were to wake up up there, on the platform?" The mule noticed
all this, and suffered from it, but said nothing; it was only when
Tistet Védène's name was pronounced in her presence that her
long ears quivered, and she sharpened the iron of her shoes on the
pavement with a little laugh.

Seven years went by in that way; then, at the end of those seven
years, Tistet Védène returned from the court of Naples. His
appointed time there was not yet over, but he had learned that the

---

[5] A fictitious village mentioned in several of the *Letters from My Windmill*
stories.—Trans.

[6] Jeanne I of Anjou, ruler of the Kingdom of Naples from 1343 to
1382.—Trans.

chief purveyor of mustard to the Pope had just died suddenly in Avignon, and, since the office seemed like a good one to him, he had arrived in great haste to apply for it.

When that intriguer Védène entered the great hall of the palace, the Holy Father had trouble recognizing him, he was so much taller and had filled out so much. It must also be said that, on his part, the good Pope had grown old and didn't see well without his spectacles.

Tistet wasn't intimidated.

"What! Great Holy Father, you no longer recognize me? It's I, Tistet Védène! . . ."

"Védène? . . ."

"Yes, yes, you know . . . the one who used to bring the French-style wine to your mule."

"Oh, yes . . . yes . . . I remember. . . . A good little boy, that Tistet Védène! . . . And now, what does he ask of us?"

"Oh, not much, great Holy Father. . . . I've come to request of you . . . By the way, do you still have her, your mule? And is she in good health? . . . Oh, good! . . . I've come to request of you the office of the chief purveyor of mustard, who has just died."

"Chief purveyor of mustard—you! But you're too young. How old are you, anyway?"

"Twenty years and two months old, illustrious Pontiff, exactly five years older than your mule. . . . Ah, by heaven, that fine animal! . . . If you only knew how I loved that mule! . . . How I missed her when I was in Italy! . . . Won't you let me see her?"

"Yes, my child, you'll see her," said the good Pope, deeply touched. "And since you love that fine animal so much, I don't want you to be separated from her any longer. From this day forward, I attach you to my person as chief purveyor of mustard. . . . My cardinals will raise the roof, but I don't care! I'm used to it. . . . Come see us tomorrow when vespers are over, and we'll hand over to you the insignia of your office in the presence of our chapter of canons; and then . . . I'll take you to see the mule, and you'll come to the vineyard with both of us. . . . Ho, ho! Go now . . ."

I have no need to tell you how happy Tistet Védène was on leaving the great hall, or how impatiently he awaited the ceremony on the following day. And yet there was someone in the palace who was even happier and more impatient than he: it was the mule. From the moment of Védène's return until vespers on the following day, the awesome beast didn't stop stuffing herself with oats and kicking out at the wall with her hind hooves. She, too, was getting ready for the ceremony.

And thus, the next day, after vespers had been recited, Tistet Védène made his entry into the courtyard of the papal palace. All of the high clergymen were there, the cardinals in red robes, the devil's advocate[7] in black velvet, the abbots of the monastery with their little miters, the church wardens of Saint-Agrico, the violet short capes of the choir school, as well as the minor clergymen, the Pope's soldiers in dress uniform, the three brotherhoods of penitents, the hermits from Mont Ventoux[8] with their fierce expressions, the young cleric walking behind them carrying the handbell, the flagellant monks stripped to the waist, the florid sacristans in judges' robes, everyone, everyone, down to the people who hand out holy water, who light candles and put them out. . . there wasn't a single one missing. . . . Oh, what a beautiful ordination it was! Bells, firecrackers, sunshine, music, and constantly those rabid drummers leading the dance over yonder on the bridge of Avignon.

When Védène made his appearance in the midst of the assembly, his noble bearing and good looks touched off a murmur of admiration. He was a magnificent Provençal, but one of the blond type, with plentiful hair curling at the tips and a little wisp of beard, which seemed to be made of the filings of fine metal that had fallen from the graving tool of his father, the goldsmith. A rumor was afloat that the fingers of Queen Jeanne had sometimes toyed with that blond beard; and, indeed "Lord" Védène had the boastful air and absentminded gaze of men whom queens have loved. . . . On that day, to honor his native land, he had exchanged his Neapolitan garments for a Provençal-style coat edged with pink, and on his headgear there waved a large ibis plume from the Camargue.[9]

As soon as he came in, the chief purveyor of mustard greeted the assembly gallantly and made his way to the high flight of steps where the Pope was waiting to hand over the insignia of his office: the yellow boxwood spoon and the saffron outfit. The mule was at

---

[7] The theologian appointed to plead against a candidate for canonization; the entire ceremony here is wildly exaggerated in a spirit of burlesque.—Trans.

[8] A mountain in the same modern *départment* as Avignon (Vaucluse).—Trans.

[9] Wetlands in the delta of the Rhône.—Trans.

the foot of the steps, completely harnessed and ready to leave for the vineyard. . . . When he came near her, Tistet Védène had a kind smile for her, and stopped to give her two or three little friendly taps on the back, looking out of the corner of his eye to see whether the Pope was watching. The position was a good one. . . . The mule started into motion:

"Here you are! Take this, villain! I've been saving it for you for seven years now!"

And she launched an awesome kick at him, so awesome that, even as far off as Pampérigouste, they could see the smoke from it, a whirlwind of blond smoke in which an ibis feather was whirling: all that was left of the unfortunate Tistet Védène! . . .

Kicks from mules aren't usually that overwhelming; but this mule belonged to a Pope, and besides, just imagine: she had been saving it for him for seven years. . . . There's no finer example of an ecclesiastical grudge.

JOURNALISM IN TENNESSEE

Mark Twain

THE EDITOR OF the Memphis *Avalanche* swoops thus mildly down upon a correspondent who posted him as a Radical: "While he was writing the first word, the middle word, dotting his i's, crossing his t's, and punching his period, he knew he was concocting a sentence that was saturated with infamy and reeking with falsehood."—*Exchange*.

I was told by the physician that a Southern climate would improve my health, and so I went down to Tennessee and got a berth on the *Morning Glory and Johnson County War-Whoop,* as associate editor. When I went on duty I found the chief editor sitting tilted back in a three-legged chair with his feet on a pine table. There was another pine table in the room, and another afflicted chair, and both were half buried under newspapers and scraps and sheets of manuscript. There was a wooden box of sand, sprinkled with cigar stubs and "old soldiers," and a stove with a door hanging by its upper hinge. The chief editor had a long-tailed black cloth frock coat on, and white linen pants. His boots were small and neatly blacked. He wore a ruffled shirt, a large seal ring, a standing collar of obsolete pattern and a checkered neckerchief with the ends hanging down. Date of costume, about 1848. He was smoking a cigar and trying to think of a word. And in trying to think of a word, and in pawing his hair for it, he had rumpled his locks a good deal. He was scowling fearfully, and I judged that he was concocting a particularly knotty editorial. He told me to take the exchanges and skim through them and write up the "Spirit of the Tennessee Press," condensing into the article all of their contents that seemed of interest.

I wrote as follows:

"SPIRIT OF THE TENNESSEE PRESS.

"The editors of the *Semi-Weekly Earthquake* evidently labor under a misapprehension with regard to the Ballyhack railroad. It is not the object of the company to leave Buzzardville off to one side. On the contrary they consider it one of the most important points along the line, and consequently can have no desire to slight it. The gentlemen of the *Earthquake* will of course take pleasure in making the correction.

"John W. Blossom, Esq., the able editor of the Higginsville *Thunderbolt and Battle-Cry of Freedom,* arrived in the city yesterday. He is stopping at the Van Buren House.

"We observe that our contemporary of the Mud Springs *Morning Howl* has fallen into the error of supposing that the election of Van Werter is not an established fact, but he will have discovered his mistake before this reminder reaches him, no doubt. He was doubtless misled by incomplete election returns.

"It is pleasant to note that the city of Blathersville is endeavoring to contract with some New York gentlemen to pave its well nigh impassable streets with the Nicholson pavement. But it is difficult to accomplish a desire like this since Memphis got some New Yorkers to do a like service for her and then declined to pay for it. However the *Daily Hurrah* still urges the measure with ability, and seems confident of ultimate success.

"We are pained to learn that Col. Bascom, chief editor of the *Dying Shriek for Liberty,* fell in the street a few evenings since and broke his leg. He has lately been suffering with debility, caused by overwork and anxiety on account of sickness in his family, and it is supposed that he fainted from the exertion of walking too much in the sun."

I passed my manuscript over to the chief editor for acceptance, alteration or destruction. He glanced at it and his face clouded. He ran his eye down the pages, and his countenance grew portentous. It was easy to see that something was wrong. Presently he sprang up and said:

"Thunder and lightning! Do you suppose I am going to speak of those cattle that way? Do you suppose my subscribers are going to stand such gruel as that? Give me the pen!"

I never saw a pen scrape and scratch its way so viciously, or plough through another man's verbs and adjectives so relentlessly.

While he was in the midst of his work somebody shot at him through the open window and marred the symmetry of his ear.

"Ah," said he, "that is that scoundrel Smith, of the *Moral Volcano*—he was due yesterday." And he snatched a navy revolver from his belt and fired. Smith dropped, shot in the thigh. The shot spoiled Smith's aim, who was just taking a second chance, and he crippled a stranger. It was me. Merely a finger shot off.

Then the chief editor went on with his erasures and interlineations. Just as he finished them a hand-grenade came down the stove-pipe, and the explosion shivered the stove into a thousand fragments. However, it did no further damage, except that a vagrant piece knocked a couple of my teeth out.

"That stove is utterly ruined," said the chief editor.

I said I believed it was.

"Well, no matter—don't want it this kind of weather. I know the man that did it. I'll get him. Now *here* is the way this stuff ought to be written."

I took the manuscript. It was scarred with erasures and interlineations till its mother wouldn't have known it, if it had had one. It now read as follows:

"SPIRIT OF THE TENNESSEE PRESS.

"The inveterate liars of the *Semi-Weekly Earthquake* are evidently endeavoring to palm off upon a noble and chivalrous people another of their vile and brutal falsehoods with regard to that most glorious conception of the nineteenth century, the Ballyhack railroad. The idea that Buzzardville was to be left off at one side originated in their own fulsome brains—or rather in the settlings which *they* regard as brains. They had better swallow this lie, and not stop to chew it, either, if they want to save their abandoned, reptile carcasses the cowhiding they so richly deserve.

"That ass, Blossom of the Higginsville *Thunderbolt and Battle-Cry of Freedom,* is down here again, bumming his board at the Van Buren.

"We observe that the besotted blackguard of the Mud Springs *Morning Howl* is giving out, with his usual propensity for lying, that Van Werter is not elected. The heaven-born mission of journalism is to disseminate truth—to eradicate error—to educate, refine and elevate the tone of public morals and manners, and make all men more gentle, more virtuous, more charitable, and in all ways better, and holier and happier—and yet this black-hearted villain, this hell-spawned miscreant, prostitutes his great office persistently to the dissemination of falsehood, calumny, vituperation and degrading vulgarity. His paper is notoriously unfit to take into the people's homes, and ought to be banished to the gambling hells and brothels where the mass of reeking pollution which does duty as its editor, lives and moves, and has his being.

"Blathersville wants a Nicholson pavement—it wants a jail and a poor-house more. The idea of a pavement in a one-horse town with two gin-mills and a blacksmith shop in it, and that mustard-plaster of a newspaper, the *Daily Hurrah!* Better borrow of Memphis, where the article is cheap. The crawling insect, Buckner, who edits the *Hurrah,* is braying about this pavement business with his customary loud-mouthed imbecility, and imagining that he is talking sense. Such foul, mephitic scum as this verminous Buckner, are a disgrace to journalism.

"That degraded ruffian Bascom, of the *Dying Shriek for Liberty,* fell down and broke his leg yesterday—pity it wasn't his neck. He says it was 'debility caused by overwork and anxiety!' It was debility caused by trying to lug six gallons of forty-rod whisky around town when his hide is only gauged for four, and anxiety about where he was going to bum another six. He 'fainted from the exertion of walking too much in the sun!' And well he might say that—but if he would walk *straight* he would get just as far and not have to walk half as much. For years the pure air of this town has been rendered perilous by the deadly breath of this perambulating pestilence, this pulpy bloat, this steaming, animated tank of mendacity, gin and profanity, this Bascom! Perish all such from out the sacred and majestic mission of journalism!"

"Now *that* is the way to write—peppery and to the point. Mush-and-milk journalism gives me the fan-tods."

About this time a brick came through the window with a splintering crash, and gave me a considerable of a jolt in the middle of the back. I moved out of range—I began to feel in the way. The chief said:

"That was the Colonel, likely, I've been expecting him for two days. He will be up, now, right away."

He was correct. The "Colonel" appeared in the door a moment afterward, with a dragoon revolver in his hand. He said:

"Sir, have I the honor of addressing the white-livered poltroon who edits this mangy sheet?"

"You have—be seated, Sir—be careful of the chair, one of the legs is gone. I believe I have the pleasure of addressing the blatant, black-hearted scoundrel, Col. Blatherskite Tecumseh?"

"The same. I have a little account to settle with you. If you are at leisure, we will begin."

"I have an article on the 'Encouraging Progress of Moral and Intellectual Development in America,' to finish, but there is no hurry. Begin."

Both pistols rang out their fierce clamor at the same instant. The chief lost a lock of hair, and the Colonel's bullet ended its career in the fleshy part of my thigh. The Colonel's left shoulder was clipped a little. They fired again. Both missed their men this time, but I got my share, a shot in the arm. At the third fire both gentlemen were wounded slightly, and I had a knuckle chipped. I then said I believed I would go out and take a walk, as this was a private matter and I had a delicacy about participating in it further. But both gentlemen begged me to keep my seat and assured me that I was not in the way. I had thought differently, up to this time.

They then talked about the elections and the crops a while, and I fell to tying up my wounds. But presently they opened fire again with animation, and every shot took effect—but it is proper to remark that five out of the six fell to my share. The sixth one mortally wounded the Colonel, who remarked, with fine humor, that he would have to say good morning, now, as he had business up town. He then inquired the way to the undertaker's and left. The chief turned to me and said:

"I am expecting company to dinner and shall have to get ready. It will be a favor to me if you will read proof and attend to the customers."

I winced a little at the idea of attending to the customers, but I was too bewildered by the fusillade that was still ringing in my ears to think of anything to say. He continued:

"Jones will be here at 3. Cowhide him. Gillespie will call earlier, perhaps—throw him out of the window. Ferguson will be along about 4—kill him. That is all for to-day, I believe. If you have any odd time, you may write a blistering article on the police—give the

Chief Inspector rats. The cowhides are under the table; weapons in the drawer—ammunition there in the corner—lint and bandages up there in the pigeonholes. In case of accident, go to Lancet, the surgeon, down stairs. He advertises—we take it out in trade."

He was gone. I shuddered. At the end of the next three hours I had been through perils so awful that all peace of mind and all cheerfulness had gone from me. Gillespie had called, and thrown *me* out of the window. Jones arrived promptly, and when I got ready to do the cowhiding, he took the job off my hands. In an encounter with a stranger, not in the bill of fare, I had lost my scalp. Another stranger, by the name of Thompson, left me a mere wreck and ruin of chaotic rags. And at last, at bay in the corner, and beset by an infuriated mob of editors, blacklegs, politicians and desperadoes, who raved and swore and flourished their weapons about my head till the air shimmered with glancing flashes of steel, I was in the act of resigning my berth on the paper when the chief arrived, and with him a rabble of charmed and enthusiastic friends. Then ensued a scene of riot and carnage such as no human pen, or steel one either, could describe. People were shot, probed, dismembered, blown up, thrown out of the window. There was a brief tornado of murky blasphemy, with a confused and frantic war-dance glimmering through it, and then all was over. In five minutes there was silence, and the gory chief and I sat alone and surveyed the sanguinary ruin that strewed the floor around us. He said:

"You'll like this place when you get used to it." I said:

"I'll have to get you to excuse me. I think maybe I might write to suit you, after a while, as soon as I had had some practice and learned the language—I am confident I could. But to speak the plain truth, that sort of energy of expression has its inconveniences, and a man is liable to interruption. You see that, yourself. Vigorous writing is calculated to elevate the public, no doubt, but then I do not like to attract so much attention as it calls forth. I can't write with comfort when I am interrupted so much as I have been to-day. I like this berth well enough, but I don't like to be left here to wait on the customers. The experiences are novel, I grant you, and entertaining, too, after a fashion, but they are not judiciously distributed. A gentleman shoots at you, through the window, and cripples *me*; a bomb-shell comes down the stove-pipe for your gratification, and sends the stove door down *my* throat; a friend drops in to swap compliments with you, and freckles *me* with bullet holes till my skin won't hold my principles; you go to dinner, and Jones comes with his cowhide, Gillespie throws me out of the window, Thompson tears all my clothes off, and an entire stranger takes my scalp with the easy freedom of an old acquaintance; and in less than five minutes all the blackguards in the country arrive in their war paint and proceed to scare the rest of me to death with their tomahawks. Take it altogether, I never have had such a spirited time in all my life as I have had to-day. No. I like you, and I like your calm, unruffled way of explaining things to the customers, but you see I am not used to it. The Southern heart is too impulsive— Southern hospitality is too lavish with the stranger. The paragraphs which I have written to-day, and into whose cold sentences your masterly hand has infused the fervent spirit of Tennesseean journalism, will wake up another nest of hornets. All that mob of editors will come—and they will come hungry, too, and want somebody for breakfast. I shall have to bid you adieu. I decline to be present at these festivities. I came South for my health—I will go back on the same errand, and suddenly. Tennessee journalism is too stirring for me." After which, we parted, with mutual regret, and I took apartments at the hospital.

THE LUCK OF ROARING CAMP

Bret Harte

THERE WAS COMMOTION in Roaring Camp. It could not have been a fight, for in 1850 that was not novel enough to have called together the entire settlement. The ditches and claims were not only deserted, but "Tuttle's grocery" had contributed its gamblers, who, it will be remembered, calmly continued their game the day that French Pete and Kanaka Joe shot each other to death over the bar in the front room. The whole camp was collected before a rude cabin on the outer edge of the clearing. Conversation was carried on in a low tone, but the name of a woman was frequently repeated. It was a name familiar enough in the camp,—"Cherokee Sal."

Perhaps the less said of her the better. She was a coarse, and, it is to be feared, a very sinful woman. But at that time she was the only woman in Roaring Camp, and was just then lying in sore extremity, when she most needed the ministration of her own sex. Dissolute, abandoned, and irreclaimable, she was yet suffering a martyrdom hard enough to bear even when veiled by sympathizing womanhood, but now terrible in her loneliness. The primal curse had come to her in that original isolation which must have made the punishment of the first transgression so dreadful. It was, perhaps, part of the expiation of her sin, that, at a moment when she most lacked her sex's intuitive tenderness and care, she met only the half-contemptuous faces of her masculine associates. Yet a few of the spectators were, I think, touched by her sufferings. Sandy Tipton thought it was "rough on Sal," and, in the contemplation of her condition, for a moment rose superior to the fact that he had an ace and two bowers in his sleeve.

It will be seen, also, that the situation was novel. Deaths were by no means uncommon in Roaring Camp, but a birth was a new thing. People had been dismissed from the camp effectively, finally, and with no possibility of return; but this was the first time that anybody had been introduced *ab initio*. Hence the excitement.

"You go in there, Stumpy," said a prominent citizen known as "Kentuck," addressing one of the loungers. "Go in there, and see what you kin do. You've had experience in them things."

Perhaps there was a fitness in the selection. Stumpy, in other climes, had been the putative head of two families; in fact, it was owing to some legal informality in these proceedings that Roaring Camp—a city of refuge—was indebted to his company. The crowd approved the choice, and Stumpy was wise enough to bow to the majority. The door closed on the extempore surgeon and midwife, and Roaring Camp sat down outside, smoked its pipe, and awaited the issue.

The assemblage numbered about a hundred men. One or two of these were actual fugitives from justice, some were criminal, and all were reckless. Physically, they exhibited no indication of their past lives and character. The greatest scamp had a Raphael face, with a profusion of blond hair; Oakhurst, a gambler, had the melancholy air and intellectual abstraction of a Hamlet; the coolest and most courageous man was scarcely over five feet in height, with a soft voice and an embarrassed, timid manner. The term "roughs" applied to them was a distinction rather than a definition. Perhaps in the minor details of fingers, toes, ears, &c., the camp may have been deficient; but these slight omissions did not detract from their aggregate force. The strongest man had but three fingers on his right hand; the best shot had but one eye.

Such was the physical aspect of the men that were dispersed around the cabin. The camp lay in a triangular valley, between two hills and a river. The only outlet was a steep trail over the summit of a hill that faced the cabin, now illuminated by the rising moon. The suffering woman might have seen it from the rude bunk whereon she lay,—seen it winding like a silver thread until it was lost in the stars above.

A fire of withered pine-boughs added sociability to the gathering. By degrees the natural levity of Roaring Camp returned. Bets were freely offered and taken regarding the result. Three to five that "Sal would get through with it"; even that the child would survive; side bets as to the sex and complexion of the coming stranger. In the midst of an excited discussion an exclamation came from those nearest the door, and the camp stopped to listen. Above the swaying and moaning of the pines, the swift rush of the river, and the crackling of the fire, rose a sharp, querulous cry—a cry unlike anything heard before in the camp. The pines stopped moaning, the river ceased to rush, and the fire to crackle. It seemed as if Nature had stopped to listen too.

The camp rose to its feet as one man! It was proposed to explode a barrel of gunpowder, but, in consideration of the situation of the mother, better counsels prevailed, and only a few revolvers were discharged; for, whether owing to the rude surgery of the camp, or some other reason, Cherokee Sal was sinking fast. Within an hour she had climbed, as it were, that rugged road that led to the stars, and so passed out of Roaring Camp, its sin and shame, for ever. I do not think that the announcement disturbed them much, except in speculation as to the fate of the child. "Can he live now?" was asked of Stumpy. The answer was doubtful. The only other being of Cherokee Sal's sex and maternal condition in the settlement was an ass. There was some conjecture as to fitness, but the experiment was tried. It was less problematical than the ancient treatment of Romulus and Remus, and apparently as successful.

When these details were completed, which exhausted another hour, the door was opened, and the anxious crowd of men who had already formed themselves into a queue, entered in single file. Beside the low bunk or shelf, on which the figure of the mother was starkly outlined below the blankets stood a pine table. On this a candle-box was placed, and within it, swathed in staring red flannel, lay the last arrival at Roaring Camp. Beside the candle-box was placed a hat. Its use was soon indicated. "Gentlemen," said Stumpy, with a singular mixture of authority and *ex officio* complacency,— "Gentlemen will please pass in at the front door, round the table, and out at the back door. Them as wishes to contribute anything toward the orphan will find a hat handy." The first man entered with his hat on; he uncovered, however, as he looked about him, and so, unconsciously, set an example to the next. In such communities good and bad actions are catching. As the procession filed in, comments were audible,—criticisms addressed, perhaps, rather to Stumpy, in the character of showman,—"Is that him?" "mighty small specimen"; "hasn't mor'n got the color"; "ain't bigger nor a derringer." The contributions were as characteristic: A silver tobacco-box; a doubloon; a navy revolver, silver mounted; a gold specimen; a very beautifully embroidered lady's handkerchief from Oakhurst (the gambler); a diamond breastpin; a diamond ring (suggested by the pin, with the remark from the giver that he "saw that pin and went two diamonds better"); a slung shot; a Bible (contributor not detected); a golden spur; a silver teaspoon (the initials, I regret to say, were not the giver's); a pair of surgeon's shears; a lancet; a Bank of England note for £5; and about $200 in loose gold and silver coin. During these proceedings Stumpy maintained a silence as impassive as the dead on his left, a gravity as inscrutable as that of the newly born on his right. Only one incident occurred to break the monotony of the curious procession. As Kentuck bent over the candle-box half curiously, the child turned, and, in a spasm of pain, caught at his groping finger, and held it fast for a moment. Kentuck looked foolish and embarrassed. Something like a blush tried to assert itself in his weather-beaten cheek. "The d—d little cuss!" he said, as he extricated his finger, with, perhaps, more tenderness and care than he might have been deemed capable of showing. He held that finger a little apart from its fellows as he went out, and examined it curiously. The examination provoked the same original remark in regard to the child. In fact, he seemed to enjoy repeating it. "He rastled with my finger," he remarked to Tipton, holding up the member, "the d—d little cuss!"

It was four o'clock before the camp sought repose. A light burnt in the cabin where the watchers sat, for Stumpy did not go to bed that night. Nor did Kentuck. He drank quite freely, and related with great gusto his experience, invariably ending with his characteristic condemnation of the new-comer. It seemed to relieve him of any unjust implication of sentiment, and Kentuck had the weaknesses of the nobler sex. When everybody else had gone to bed, he walked down to the river, and whistled reflectingly. Then he walked up the gulch, past the cabin, still whistling with demonstrative unconcern. At a large redwood tree he paused and retraced his steps, and again passed the cabin. Half-way down to the river's bank he again paused, and then returned and knocked at the door. It was opened by Stumpy. "How goes it?" said Kentuck, looking past Stumpy toward the candle-box. "All serene," replied Stumpy. "Anything up?" "Nothing." There was a pause—an embarrassing one—Stumpy still holding the door. Then Kentuck had recourse to his finger, which he held up to Stumpy. "Rastled with it,—the d—d little cuss," he said, and retired.

The next day Cherokee Sal had such rude sepulture as Roaring Camp afforded. After her body had been committed to the hill-side, there was a formal meeting of the camp to discuss what should be done with her infant. A resolution to adopt it was unanimous and enthusiastic. But an animated discussion in regard to the manner and feasibility of providing for its wants at once sprang up. It was remarkable that the argument partook of none of those fierce personalities with which discussions were usually conducted at Roaring Camp. Tipton proposed that they should send the child to Red Dog,—a distance of forty miles,—where female attention could be procured. But the unlucky suggestion met with fierce and unanimous opposition. It was evident that no plan which entailed parting from their new acquisition would for a moment be entertained. "Besides," said Tom Ryder, "them fellows at Red Dog would swap it, and ring in somebody else on us." A disbelief in the honesty of other camps prevailed at Roaring Camp as in other places.

The introduction of a female nurse in the camp also met with objection. It was argued that no decent woman could be prevailed to accept Roaring Camp as her home, and the speaker urged that "they didn't want any more of the other kind." This unkind allusion to the defunct mother, harsh as it may seem, was the first spasm of propriety,—the first symptom of the camp's regeneration. Stumpy advanced nothing. Perhaps he felt a certain delicacy in interfering with the selection of a possible successor in office. But when questioned, he averred stoutly that he and "Jinny"—the mammal before alluded to—could manage to rear the child. There was something original, independent, and heroic about the plan that pleased the camp. Stumpy was retained. Certain articles were sent for to Sacramento. "Mind," said the treasurer, as he pressed a bag of gold-dust into the expressman's hand, "the best that can be got,—lace, you know, and filigree-work and frills,—d—n the cost!"

Strange to say, the child thrived. Perhaps the invigorating climate of the mountain camp was compensation for material deficiencies. Nature took the foundling to her broader breast. In that rare atmo-sphere of the Sierra foothills,—that air pungent with balsamic odour, that ethereal cordial at once bracing and exhilarating,—he may have found food and nourishment, or a subtle chemistry that transmuted asses' milk to lime and phosphorus. Stumpy inclined to the belief that it was the latter, and good nursing. "Me and that ass," he would say, "has been father and mother to him! Don't you," he would add, apostrophizing the helpless bundle before him, "never go back on us."

By the time he was a month old, the necessity of giving him a name became apparent. He had generally been known as "the Kid," "Stumpy's boy," "the Cayote" (an allusion to his vocal powers), and even by Kentuck's endearing diminutive of "the d—d little cuss." But these were felt to be vague and unsatisfactory, and were at last dismissed under another influence. Gamblers and adventurers are generally superstitious, and Oakhurst one day declared that the baby had brought "the luck" to Roaring Camp. It was certain that of late they had been successful. "Luck" was the name agreed upon, with the prefix of Tommy for greater convenience. No allusion was made to the mother, and the father was unknown. "It's better," said the philosophical Oakhurst, "to take a fresh deal all round. Call him Luck, and start him fair." A day was accordingly set apart for the christening. What was meant by this ceremony the reader may imagine, who has already gathered some idea of the reckless irreverence of Roaring Camp. The master of ceremonies was one "Boston," a noted wag, and the occasion seemed to promise the greatest facetiousness. This ingenious satirist had spent two days in preparing a burlesque of the church service, with pointed local allusions. The choir was properly trained, and Sandy Tipton was to stand godfather. But after the procession had marched to the grove with music and banners, and the child had been deposited before a mock altar, Stumpy stepped before the expectant crowd. "It ain't my style to spoil fun, boys," said the little man, stoutly, eying the faces around him, "but it strikes me that this thing ain't exactly on the squar. It's playing it pretty low down on this yer baby to ring in fun on him that he ain't going to understand. And ef there's going to be any godfathers round, I'd like to see who's got any better rights than me." A silence followed Stumpy's speech. To the credit of all humorists be it said, that the first man to acknowledge its justice was the satirist, thus stopped of his fun. "But," said Stumpy, quickly, following up his advantage, "we're here for a christening, and we'll have it. I proclaim you Thomas Luck, according to the laws of the United States and the State of California, so help me God." It was the first time that the name of the Deity had been uttered otherwise than profanely in the camp. The form of christening was perhaps even more ludicrous than the satirist had conceived; but, strangely enough, nobody saw it, and nobody laughed. "Tommy" was christened as seriously as he would have been under a Christian roof, and cried and was comforted in as orthodox fashion.

And so the work of regeneration began in Roaring Camp. Almost imperceptibly a change came over the settlement. The cabin assigned to "Tommy Luck"—or "The Luck," as he was more frequently called—first showed signs of improvement. It was kept scrupulously clean and whitewashed. Then it was boarded, clothed, and papered. The rosewood cradle—packed eighty miles by mule—had, in Stumpy's way of putting it, "sorter killed the rest of the furniture." So the rehabilitation of the cabin became a necessity. The men who were in the habit of lounging in at Stumpy's to see "how 'The Luck' got on" seemed to appreciate the change, and, in self-defense, the rival establishment of "Tuttle's grocery" bestirred itself, and imported a carpet and mirrors. The reflections of the latter on the appearance of Roaring Camp tended to produce stricter habits of personal cleanliness. Again, Stumpy imposed a kind of quarantine upon those who aspired to the honor and privilege of holding "The Luck." It was a cruel mortification to Kentuck—who, in the carelessness of a large nature and the habits of frontier life, had begun to regard all garments as a second cuticle, which, like a snake's, only sloughed off through decay—to be debarred this privilege from certain prudential reasons. Yet such was the subtle influence of innovation that he thereafter appeared regularly every afternoon in a clean shirt, and face still shining from his ablutions. Nor were moral and social sanitary laws neglected. "Tommy," who was supposed to spend his whole existence in a persistent attempt to repose, must not be disturbed by noise. The shouting and yelling which had gained the camp its infelicitous title were not permitted within hearing distance of Stumpy's. The men conversed in whispers, or smoked with Indian gravity. Profanity was tacitly given up in these sacred precincts, and throughout the camp a popular form of expletive, known as "D—n the luck!" and "Curse the luck!" was abandoned, as having a new personal bearing. Vocal music was not interdicted, being supposed to have a soothing, tranquillizing quality, and one song, sung by "Man-o'-war Jack," an English sailor, from her Majesty's Australian colonies, was quite popular as a lullaby. It was a lugubrious recital of the

exploits of "the Arethusa, Seventy-four," in a muffled minor, ending with a prolonged dying fall at the burden of each verse, "On
b-o-o-o-ard of the Arethusa." It was a fine sight to see Jack holding
The Luck, rocking from side to side as if with the motion of a ship,
and crooning forth this naval ditty. Either through the peculiar
rocking of Jack or the length of his song—it contained ninety stanzas, and was continued with conscientious deliberation to the bitter
end—the lullaby generally had the desired effect. At such times the
men would lie at full length under the trees, in the soft summer
twilight, smoking their pipes and drinking in the melodious utter-
ances. An indistinct idea that this was pastoral happiness pervaded
the camp. "This 'ere kind o' think," said the Cockney Simmons,
meditatively reclining on his elbow, "is 'evingly." It reminded him
of Greenwich.

On the long summer days The Luck was usually carried to the
gulch, from whence the golden store of Roaring Camp was taken.
There, on a blanket spread over pine-boughs, he would lie while
the men were working in the ditches below. Latterly there was a
rude attempt to decorate this bower with flowers and sweet-
smelling shrubs, and generally someone would bring him a cluster
of wild honeysuckles, azaleas, or the painted blossoms of Las
Mariposas. The men had suddenly awakened to the fact that there
were beauty and significance in these trifles, which they had so long
trodden carelessly beneath their feet. A flake of glittering mica, a
fragment of variegated quartz, a bright pebble from the bed of the
creek, became beautiful to eyes thus cleared and strengthened, and
were invariably put aside for "The Luck." It was wonderful how
many treasures the woods and hill-sides yielded that "would do for
Tommy." Surrounded by playthings such as never child out of
fairy-land had before, it is to be hoped that Tommy was content.
He appeared to be securely happy, albeit there was an infantine
gravity about him, a contemplative light in his round gray eyes, that
sometimes worried Stumpy. He was always tractable and quiet, and
it is recorded that once, having crept beyond his "corral,"—a hedge
of tessellated pine-boughs, which surrounded his bed,—he dropped
over the bank on his head in the soft earth, and remained with his
mottled legs in the air in that position for at least five minutes with
unflinching gravity. He was extricated without a murmur. I hesitate
to record the many other instances of his sagacity, which rest,
unfortunately, upon the statements of prejudiced friends. Some of

them were not without a tinge of superstition. "I crep' up the bank just now," said Kentuck one day, in a breathless state of excitement, "and dern my skin if he wasn't a talking to a jay-bird as was a sittin' on his lap. There they was, just as free and sociable as anything you please, a jawin' at each other just like two cherrybums." Howbeit, whether creeping over the pine-boughs or lying lazily on his back blinking at the leaves above him, to him the birds sang, the squirrels chattered, and the flowers bloomed. Nature was his nurse and play-fellow. For him she would let slip between the leaves golden shafts of sunlight that fell just within his grasp; she would send wandering breezes to visit him with the balm of bay and resinous gums; to him the tall redwoods nodded familiarly and sleepily, the bumble-bees buzzed, and the rooks cawed a slumbrous accompaniment.

Such was the golden summer of Roaring Camp. They were "flush times,"—and the luck was with them. The claims had yielded enormously. The camp was jealous of its privileges and looked suspiciously on strangers. No encouragement was given to immigration, and, to make their seclusion more perfect, the land on either side of the mountain wall that surrounded the camp they duly pre-empted. This, and a reputation for singular proficiency with the revolver, kept the reserve of Roaring Camp inviolate. The expressman—their only connecting link with the surrounding world—sometimes told wonderful stories of the camp. He would say, "They've a street up there in 'Roaring,' that would lay over any street in Red Dog. They've got vines and flowers round their houses, and they wash themselves twice a day. But they're mighty rough on strangers, and they worship an Ingin baby."

With the prosperity of the camp came a desire for further improvement. It was proposed to build a hotel in the following spring, and to invite one or two decent families to reside there for the sake of "The Luck,"—who might perhaps profit by female companionship. The sacrifice that this concession to the sex cost these men, who were fiercely skeptical in regard to its general virtue and usefulness, can only be accounted for by their affection for Tommy. A few still held out. But the resolve could not be carried into effect for three months, and the minority meekly yielded in the hope that something might turn up to prevent it. And it did.

The winter of 1851 will long be remembered in the foot-hills. The snow lay deep on the Sierras, and every mountain creek became a river, and every river a lake. Each gorge and gulch was transformed into a tumultuous water-course that descended the hill-sides, tearing down giant trees and scattering its drift and débris along the plain. Red Dog had been twice under water, and Roaring Camp had been forewarned. "Water put the gold into them gulches," said Stumpy, "it's been here once and will be here again!" And that night the North Fork suddenly leaped over its banks, and swept up the triangular valley of Roaring Camp.

In the confusion of rushing water, crushing trees, and crackling timber, and the darkness which seemed to flow with the water and blot out the fair valley, but little could be done to collect the scattered camp. When the morning broke, the cabin of Stumpy nearest the river-bank was gone. Higher up the gulch they found the body of its unlucky owner; but the pride, the hope, the joy, the Luck, of Roaring Camp had disappeared. They were returning with sad hearts, when a shout from the bank recalled them.

It was a relief-boat from down the river. They had picked up, they said, a man and an infant, nearly exhausted, about two miles below. Did anybody know them, and did they belong here?

It needed but a glance to show them Kentuck lying there, cruelly crushed and bruised, but still holding the Luck of Roaring Camp in his arms. As they bent over the strangely assorted pair, they saw that the child was cold and pulseless. "He is dead," said one. Kentuck opened his eyes. "Dead?" he repeated, feebly. "Yes, my man, and you are dying too." A smile lit the eyes of the expiring Kentuck. "Dying," he repeated, "he's a taking me with him,—tell the boys I've got the Luck with me now"; and the strong man, clinging to the frail babe as a drowning man is said to cling to a straw, drifted away into the shadowy river that flows forever to the unknown sea.

BILL NATIONS

Bill Arp (Charles Henry Smith)

YOU NEVER KNOWD Bill, I rekun. Hes gone to Arkensaw, and I don't know whether hes ded or alive. He was a good feller, Bill was, as most all whisky drinkers are. Me and him both used to love it powerful—especially Bill. We soaked it when we could git it, and when we coudent we hankered after it amazingly. I must tell you a little antidote on Bill, tho I dident start to tell you about that.

We started on a little jurney one day in June, and took along a bottle of "old rye," and there was so many springs and wells on the road that it was mighty nigh gone before dinner. We took our snack, and Bill drained the last drop, for he said we would soon git to Joe Paxton's, and that Joe always kept some.

Shore enuff Joe dident have a drop, and we concluded, as we was mighty dry, to go on to Jim Alford's, and stay all night. We knew that Jim had it, for he always had it. So we whipped up, and the old Bay had to travel, for I tell you when a man wants whiskey everything has to bend to the gittin' of it. Shore enuff Jim had some. He was mity glad to see us, and he knowd what we wanted, for he knowd how it was hisself. So he brought out an old-fashend glass decanter, and a shugar bowl, and a tumbler, and a spoon, and says he, "Now, boys, jest wait a minit till you git rested sorter, for it ain't good to take whiskey on a hot stomack. I've jest been readin' a piece in Grady's newspaper about a frog—the darndest frog that perhaps ever come from a tadpole. It was found up in Kanetucky, and is as big as a peck measure. Bill, do you take this paper and read it aloud to us. I'm a poor hand to read, and I want to hear it. I'll be hanged if it ain't the darndest frog I ever hearn of."

He laid the paper on my knees, and I begun to read, thinkin' it was a little short anticdote, but as I turned the paper over *I* found it was mighty nigh a column. I took a side glance at Bill, and I saw the little dry twitches a jumpin' about on his countenance. He was mighty nigh dead for a drink. I warent so bad off myself, and I was about half mad with him for drainin' the bottle before dinner; so I just read along slow, and stopped two or three times to clear my throat just to consume time. Pretty soon Bill got up and commenced walkin' about, and he would look at the dekanter like he would give his daylights to choke the corn juice out of it. I read along slowly. Old Alford was a listnin' and chawin' his tobakker and spittin' out of the door. Bill come up to me, his face red and twitchin', and leanin' over my shoulder he seed the length of the story, and I will never forgit his pitiful tone as he whispered, "Skip some, Bill, for heaven's sake skip some."

My heart relented, and I did skip some, and hurried through, and we all jined in a drink; but I'll never forgit how Bill looked when he whispered to me to "skip some, Bill, skip some." I've got over the like of that, boys, and I hope Bill has, too, but I don't know. I wish in my soul that everybody had quit it, for you may talk about slavery, and penitentiary, and chain-gangs, and the Yankees, and General Grant, and a devil of a wife, but whiskey is the worst master that ever a man had over him. I know how it is myself.

But there is one good thing about drinkin'. I almost wish every man was a reformed drunkard. No man who hasn't drank liker knows what a luxury cold water is. I have got up in the night in cold wether after I had been spreein' around, and gone to the well burnin' up with thirst, feeling like the gallows, and the grave, and the infernal regions was too good for me, and when I took up the bucket in my hands, and with my elbows a tremblin' like I had the shakin' ager, put the water to my lips; it was the most delicious, satisfying luxurius draft that ever went down my throat. I have stood there and drank and drank until I could drink no more, and gone back to bed thankin' God for the pure, innocent, and coolin' beverig, and cursin' myself from my inmost soul for ever touchin' the accursed whisky. In my torture of mind and body I have made vows and promises, and broken 'em within a day. But if you want to know the luxury of cold water, get drunk, and keep at it until you get on fire, and then try a bucket full with your shirt on at the well in the middle of the night. You won't want a gourd full—you'll feel like the bucket ain't big enuf, and when you begin to drink an earthquake couldn't stop you. My fathers, how good it was! I know a hundred men who will swear to the truth of what I say: but you see it's a thing they don't like to talk about. It's too humiliatin'.

But I dident start to talk about drinkin'. In fact, I've forgot what I did start to tell you. My mind is sorter addled now a days, anyhow, and I hav to jes let my tawkin' tumble out permiskuous. I'll take another whet at it afore long, and fill up the gaps.

Yours trooly,
BILL ARP.

A JERSEY CENTENARIAN

Bret Harte

I HAVE SEEN her at last. She is a hundred and seven years old, and remembers George Washington quite distinctly. It is somewhat confusing, however, that she also remembers a contemporaneous Josiah W. Perkins, of Basking Ridge, N.J., and, I think, has the impression that Perkins was the better man. Perkins, at the close of the last century, paid her some little attention. There are a few things that a really noble woman of a hundred and seven never forgets.

It was Perkins, who said to her in 1795, in the streets of Philadelphia, "Shall I show thee General Washington?" Then she said, carelesslike (for you know, child, at that time it wasn't what it is now to see General Washington)—she said, "So do, Josiah, so do!" Then he pointed to a tall man who got out of a carriage, and went into a large house. He was larger than you be. He wore his own hair—not powdered; had a flowered chintz vest, with yellow breeches and blue stockings, and a broad-brimmed hat. In summer he wore a white straw hat, and at his farm at Basking Ridge he always wore it. At this point, it became too evident that she was describing the clothes of the all-fascinating Perkins: so I gently but firmly led her back to Washington.

Then it appeared that she did not remember exactly what he wore. To assist her, I sketched the general historic dress of that period. She said she thought he was dressed like that. Emboldened by my success, I added a hat of Charles II, and pointed shoes of the eleventh century. She endorsed these with such cheerful alacrity that I dropped the subject.

The house upon which I had stumbled, or, rather, to which my horse—a Jersey hack, accustomed to historic research—had

175

brought me, was low and quaint. Like most old houses, it had the appearance of being encroached upon by the surrounding glebe, as if it were already half in the grave, with a sod or two, in the shape of moss, thrown on it, like ashes on ashes, and dust on dust. A wooden house, instead of acquiring dignity with age, is apt to lose its youth and respectability together. A porch, with scant, sloping seats, from which even the winter's snow must have slid uncomfortably, projected from a doorway that opened most unjustifiably into a small sitting-room. There was no vestibule, or locus poenitentiae, for the embarrassed or bashful visitor: he passed at once from the security of the public road into shameful privacy. And here, in the mellow autumnal sunlight, that, streaming through the maples and sumach on the opposite bank, flickered and danced upon the floor, she sat and discoursed of George Washington, and thought of Perkins. She was quite in keeping with the house and the season, albeit a little in advance of both; her skin being of a faded russet, and her hands so like dead November leaves, that I fancied they even rustled when she moved them.

For all that, she was quite bright and cheery; her faculties still quite vigorous, although performing irregularly and spasmodically. It was somewhat discomposing, I confess, to observe that at times her lower jaw would drop, leaving her speechless, until one of the family would notice it, and raise it smartly into place with a slight snap—an operation always performed in such an habitual, perfunctory manner, generally in passing to and fro in their household duties, that it was very trying to the spectator. It was still more embarrassing to observe that the dear old lady had evidently no knowledge of this, but believed she was still talking, and that, on resuming her actual vocal utterance, she was often abrupt and incoherent, beginning always in the middle of a sentence, and often in the middle of a word.

"Sometimes," said her daughter, a giddy, thoughtless young thing of eighty-five—"sometimes just moving her head sort of unhitches her jaw; and, if we don't happen to see it, she'll go on talking for hours without ever making a sound."

Although I was convinced, after this, that during my interview I had lost several important revelations regarding George Washington through these peculiar lapses, I could not help reflecting how beneficent were these provisions of the Creator—how, if properly studied and applied, they might be fraught with happiness to mankind—how a slight jostle or jar at a dinner-party might make the post-prandial eloquence of garrulous senility satisfactory to itself, yet harmless to others—how a more intimate knowledge of anatomy, introduced into the domestic circle, might make a home tolerable at least, if not happy—how a long-suffering husband, under the pretense of a conjugal caress, might so unhook his wife's condyloid process as to allow the flow of expostulation, criticism or denunciation to go on with gratification to her, and perfect immunity to himself.

But this was not getting back to George Washington and the early struggles of the Republic. So I returned to the commander-in-chief, but found, after one or two leading questions, that she was rather inclined to resent his re-appearance on the stage. Her reminiscences here were chiefly social and local, and more or less flavored with Perkins. We got back as far as the Revolutionary epoch, or, rather, her impressions of that epoch, when it was still fresh in the public mind. And here I came upon an incident, purely personal and local, but, withal, so novel, weird and uncanny, that for a while I fear it quite displaced George Washington in my mind, and tinged the autumnal fields beyond with a red that was not of the sumach. I do not remember to have read of it in the books. I do not know that it is entirely authentic. It was attested to me by mother and daughter, as an uncontradicted tradition.

In the little field beyond, where the plough still turns up musket-balls and cartridge-boxes, took place one of those irregular skirmishes between the militiamen and Knyphausen's stragglers, that made the retreat historical. A Hessian soldier, wounded in both legs and utterly helpless, dragged himself to the cover of a hazel-copse, and lay there hidden for two days. On the third day, maddened by thirst, he managed to creep to the rail-fence of an adjoining farm-house, but found himself unable to mount it or pass through. There was no one in the house but a little girl of six or seven years. He called to her, and in a faint voice asked for water. She returned to the house, as if to comply with his request, but, mounting a chair, took from the chimney a heavily loaded Queen Anne musket, and, going to the door, took deliberate aim at the helpless intruder, and fired. The man fell back dead, without a groan. She replaced the musket, and, returning to the fence, covered the body with boughs and leaves, until it was hidden. Two or three days after, she related the occurrence in a careless, casual way, and leading the way to the fence, with a piece of bread and butter in her guileless little fingers, pointed out the result of her simple, unsophisticated effort. The Hessian was decently buried, but I could not find out what became of the little girl. Nobody seemed to remember. I trust that, in after years, she was happily married; that no Jersey Lovelace attempted to trifle with a heart whose impulses were so prompt, and whose purposes were so sincere. They did not seem to know if she had married or not. Yet it does not seem probable that such simplicity of conception, frankness of expression, and deftness of execution, were lost to posterity, or that they failed, in their time and season, to give flavor to the domestic felicity of the period. Beyond this, the story perhaps has little value, except as an offset to the usual anecdotes of Hessian atrocity.

They had their financial panics even in Jersey, in the old days. She remembered when Dr. White married your cousin Mary—or was it Susan?—yes, it was Susan. She remembers that your Uncle Harry brought in an armful of bank-notes—paper money, you know—and threw them in the corner, saying they were no good to anybody. She remembered playing with them, and giving them to your Aunt Anna—no, child, it was your own mother, bless your heart! Some of them was marked as high as a hundred dollars. Everybody kept gold and silver in a stocking, or in a "chancy" vase, like that. You never used money to buy anything. When Josiah went to Springfield to buy anything, he took a cartload of things with him to exchange. That yaller picture-frame was paid for in greenings. But then people knew jest what they had. They didn't fritter their substance away in unchristian trifles, like your father, Eliza Jane, who doesn't know that there is a God who will smite him hip and thigh; for vengeance is mine, and those that believe in me. But here, singularly enough, the inferior maxillaries gave out, and her jaw dropped. (I noticed that her giddy daughter of eighty-five was sitting near her, but I do not pretend to connect this fact with the arrested flow of personal disclosure.) Howbeit, when she recovered her speech again, it appeared that she was complaining of the weather.

The seasons had changed very much since your father went to sea. The winters used to be terrible in those days. When she went over to Springfield, in June, she saw the snow still on Watson's Ridge. There were whole days when you couldn't get over to William Henry's, their next neighbor, a quarter of a mile away.

It was that drefful winter that the Spanish sailor was found. You don't remember the Spanish sailor, Eliza Jane—it was before your time. There was a little personal skirmishing here, which I feared, at first, might end in a suspension of maxillary functions, and the loss of the story: but here it is. Ah, me! it is a pure white winter idyl: how shall I sing it this bright, gay autumnal day?

It was a terrible night, that winter's night, when she and the century were young together. The sun was lost at three o'clock: the snowy night came down like a white sheet, that flapped around the house, beat at the windows with its edges, and at last wrapped it in a close embrace. In the middle of the night, they thought they heard above the wind a voice crying, "Christus, Christus!" in a foreign tongue. They opened the door—no easy task in the north wind that pressed its strong shoulders against it—but nothing was to be seen but the drifting snow. The next morning dawned on fences hidden, and a landscape changed and obliterated with drift. During the day, they again heard the cry of "Christus!" this time faint and hidden, like a child's voice. They searched in vain: the drifted snow hid its secret. On the third day they broke a path to the fence, and then they heard the cry distinctly. Digging down, they found the body of a man—a Spanish sailor, dark and bearded, with earrings in his ears. As they stood gazing down at his cold and pulseless figure, the cry of "Christus!" again rose upon the wintry air; and they turned and fled in superstitious terror to the house. And then one of the children, bolder than the rest, knelt down, and opened the dead man's rough peajacket, and found—what think you!—a little blue-and-green parrot, nestling against his breast. It was the bird that had echoed mechanically the last despairing cry of the life that was given to save it. It was the bird, that ever after, amid outlandish oaths and wilder sailor-songs, that I fear often shocked the pure ears of its gentle mistress, and brought scandal into the Jerseys, still retained that one weird and mournful cry.

The sun meanwhile was sinking behind the steadfast range beyond, and I could not help feeling that I must depart with my wants unsatisfied. I had brought away no historic fragment: I absolutely knew little or nothing new regarding George Washington. I had been addressed variously by the names of different members of the family who were dead and forgotten; I had stood for an hour in the past: yet I had not added to my historical knowledge, nor the practical benefit of your readers. I spoke once more of Washington, and she replied with a reminiscence of Perkins.

Stand forth, O Josiah W. Perkins, of Basking Ridge, N.J.! Thou wast of little account in thy life, I warrant; thou didst not even feel the greatness of thy day and time; thou didst criticise thy superiors; thou wast small and narrow in thy ways; thy very name and grave are unknown and uncared for: but thou wast once kind to a woman who survived thee, and, lo! thy name is again spoken of men, and for a moment lifted up above thy betters.

THE NOTORIOUS JUMPING FROG OF CALAVERAS COUNTY

Mark Twain

IN COMPLIANCE WITH the request of a friend of mine, who wrote me from the East, I called on good-natured, garrulous old Simon Wheeler, and inquired after my friend's friend, Leonidas W. Smiley, as requested to do, and I hereunto append the result. I have a lurking suspicion that *Leonidas* W. Smiley is a myth; that my friend never knew such a personage; and that he only conjectured that if I asked old Wheeler about him, it would remind him of his infamous *Jim* Smiley, and he would go to work and bore me to death with some exasperating reminiscence of him as long and as tedious as it should be useless to me. If that was the design, it succeeded.

I found Simon Wheeler dozing comfortably by the bar-room stove of the dilapidated tavern in the decayed mining camp of Angel's, and I noticed that he was fat and bald-headed, and had an expression of winning gentleness and simplicity upon his tranquil countenance. He roused up, and gave me good day. I told him that a friend of mine had commissioned me to make some inquiries about a cherished companion of his boyhood named *Leonidas* W. Smiley—*Rev. Leonidas* W. Smiley, a young minister of the Gospel, who he had heard was at one time a resident of Angel's Camp. I added that if Mr. Wheeler could tell me anything about this Rev. Leonidas W. Smiley, I would feel under many obligations to him.

Simon Wheeler backed me into a corner and blockaded me there with his chair, and then sat down and reeled off the monotonous narrative which follows this paragraph. He never smiled, he never frowned, he never changed his voice from the gentle-flowing

181

key to which he tuned his initial sentence, he never betrayed the slightest suspicion of enthusiasm; but all through the interminable narrative there ran a vein of impressive earnestness and sincerity, which showed me plainly that, so far from his imagining that there was anything ridiculous or funny about his story, he regarded it as a really important matter, and admired its two heroes as men of transcendent genius in *finesse*. I let him go on in his own way, and never interrupted him once.

"Rev. Leonidas W. H'm, Reverend Le—well, there was a feller here once by the name *of Jim* Smiley, in the winter of '49—or maybe it was the spring of '50—I don't recollect exactly, somehow, though what makes me think it was one or the other is because I remember the big flume warn't finished when he first come to the camp; but anyway, he was the curiousest man about always betting on anything that turned up you ever see, if he could get anybody to bet on the other side; and if he couldn't he'd change sides. Any way that suited the other man would suit *him*— any way just so's he got a bet, *he* was satisfied. But still he was lucky, uncommon lucky; he most always come out winner. He was always ready and laying for a chance; there couldn't be no solit'ry thing mentioned but that feller'd offer to bet on it, and take ary side you please, as I was just telling you. If there was a horse-race, you'd find him flush or you'd find him busted at the end of it; if there was a dog-fight, he'd bet on it; if there was a cat-fight, he'd bet on it; if there was a chicken-fight, he'd bet on it; why, if there was two birds setting on a fence, he would bet you which one would fly first; or if there was a camp-meeting, he would be there reg'lar to bet on Parson Walker, which he judged to be the best exhorter about here, and so he was too, and a good man. If he even see a straddle-bug start to go anywheres, he would bet you how long it would take him to get to—to wherever he was going to, and if you took him up, he would foller that straddle-bug to Mexico but what he would find out where he was bound for and how long he was on the road. Lots of the boys here has seen that Smiley, and can tell you about him. Why, it never made no difference to *him*—he'd bet on *any* thing—the dangdest feller. Parson Walker's wife laid very sick once, for a good while, and it seemed as if they warn't going to save her; but one morning he come in, and Smiley up and asked him how she was, and he said she was considerable better—thank the Lord for his inf'nite mercy—and coming on so smart that with the blessing of Prov'dence she'd get well yet; and Smiley, before he thought, says, 'Well, I'll resk two-and-a-half she don't anyway.'

"Thish-yer Smiley had a mare—the boys called her the fifteen-minute nag, but that was only in fun, you know, because of course she was faster than that—and he used to win money on that horse, for all she was so slow and always had the asthma, or the distemper, or the consumption, or something of that kind. They used to give her two or three hundred yards' start, and then pass her under way; but always at the fag end of the race she'd get excited and desperate like, and come cavorting and straddling up, and scattering her legs around limber, sometimes in the air, and sometimes out to one side among the fences, and kicking up m-o-r-e dust and raising m-o-r-e racket with her coughing and sneezing and blowing her nose—and *always* fetch up at the stand just about a neck ahead, as near as you could cipher it down.

"And he had a little small bull-pup, that to look at him you'd think he warn't worth a cent but to set around and look ornery and lay for a chance to steal something. But as soon as money was up on him he was a different dog; his under-jaw'd begin to stick out like the fo'castle of a steamboat, and his teeth would uncover and shine like the furnaces. And a dog might tackle him and bully-rag him, and bite him, and throw him over his shoulder two or three times, and Andrew Jackson—which was the name of the pup—Andrew Jackson would never let on but what *he* was satisfied, and hadn't expected nothing else—and the bets being doubled and doubled on the other side all the time, till the money was all up; and then all of a sudden he would grab that other dog jest by the j'int of his hind leg and freeze to it—not chaw, you understand, but only just grip and hang on till they throwed up the sponge, if it was a year. Smiley always come out winner on that pup, till he harnessed a dog once that didn't have no hind legs, because they'd been sawed off in a circular saw, and when the thing had gone along far enough, and the money was all up, and he come to make a snatch for his pet holt, he see in a minute how he'd been imposed on, and how the other dog had him in the door, so to speak, and he 'peared surprised, and then he looked sorter discouraged-like, and didn't try no more to win the fight, and so he got shucked out bad. He give Smiley a look, as much as to say his heart was broke, and it was *his* fault, for putting up a dog that hadn't no hind legs for

him to take holt of, which was his main dependence in a fight, and
then he limped off a piece and laid down and died. It was a good
pup, was that Andrew Jackson, and would have made a name for
hisself if he'd lived, for the stuff was in him and he had genius—I
know it, because he hadn't no opportunities to speak of, and it
don't stand to reason that a dog could make such a fight as he could
under them circumstances if he hadn't no talent. It always makes
me feel sorry when I think of that last fight of his'n, and the way it
turned out.

"Well, thish-yer Smiley had rat-tarriers, and chicken cocks, and
tomcats and all them kind of things, till' you couldn't rest, and you
couldn't fetch nothing for him to bet on but he'd match you. He
ketched a frog one day, and took him home, and said he cal'lated
to educate him; and so he never done nothing for three months but
set in his back yard and learn that frog to jump. And you bet you
he *did* learn him, too. He'd give him a little punch behind, and the
next minute you'd see that frog whirling in the air like a
doughnut—see him turn one summerset, or maybe a couple, if he
got a good start, and come down flat-footed and all right, like a cat.
He got him up so in the matter of ketching flies, and kep' him in
practice so constant, that he'd nail a fly every time as fur as he could
see him. Smiley said all a frog wanted was education, and he could
do 'most anything—and I believe him. Why, I've seen him set
Dan'l Webster down here on this floor—Dan'l Webster was the
name of the frog—and sing out, 'Flies, Dan'l, flies!' and quicker'n
you could wink he'd spring straight up and snake a fly off'n the
counter there, and flop down on the floor ag'in as solid as a gob of
mud, and fall to scratching the side of his head with his hind foot
as indifferent as if he hadn't no idea he'd been doin' any more'n any
frog might do. You never see a frog so modest and straightfor'ard
as he was, for all he was so gifted. And when it come to fair and
square jumping on a dead level, he could get over more ground at
one straddle than any animal of his breed you ever see. Jumping on
a dead level was his strong suit, you understand; and when it come
to that, Smiley would ante up money on him as long as he had a
red. Smiley was monstrous proud of his frog, and well he might be,
for fellers that had traveled and been everywheres all said he laid
over any frog that ever *they* see.

"Well, Smiley kep' the beast in a little lattice box, and he used
to fetch him down-town sometimes and lay for a bet. One day a

feller—a stranger in the camp, he was—come acrost him with his box, and says:

"'What might it be that you've got in the box?'

"And Smiley says, sorter indifferent-like, 'It might be a parrot, or it might be a canary, maybe, but it ain't—it's only just a frog.'

"And the feller took it, and looked at it careful, and turned it round this way and that, and says, 'H'm—so 'tis. Well, what's *he* good for?'

"'Well,' Smiley says, easy and careless, 'he's good enough for *one* thing, I should judge—he can outjump any frog in Calaveras County.'

"The feller took the box again, and took another long, particular look, and give it back to Smiley, and says, very deliberate, 'Well,' he says, 'I don't see no p'ints about that frog that's any better'n any other frog.'

"'Maybe you don't,' Smiley says. 'Maybe you understand frogs and maybe you don't understand 'em; maybe you've had experience, and maybe you ain't only a amature, as it were. Anyways, I've got *my* opinion, and I'll resk forty dollars that he can outjump any frog in Calaveras County.'

"And the feller studied a minute, and then says, kinder sad-like, 'Well, I'm only a stranger here, and I ain't got no frog; but if I had a frog, I'd bet you.'

"And then Smiley says, 'That's all right—that's all right—if you'll hold my box a minute, I'll go and get you a frog.' And so the feller took the box, and put up his forty dollars along with Smiley's, and set down to wait.

"So he set there a good while thinking and thinking to himself, and then he got the frog out and prized his mouth open and took a teaspoon and filled him full of quail-shot—filled him pretty near up to his chin—and set him on the floor. Smiley he went to the swamp and slopped around in the mud for a long time, and finally he ketched a frog, and fetched him in, and give him to this feller, and says:

"'Now, if you're ready, set him alongside of Dan'l, with his fore paws just even with Dan'l's, and I'll give the word.' Then he says, 'One—two —three—*git!*' and him and the feller touched up the frogs from behind, and the new frog hopped off lively, but Dan'l give a heave, and hysted up his shoulders—so—like a Frenchman, but it warn't no use—he couldn't budge; he was planted as solid as a church, and he couldn't no more stir than if he was anchored out. Smiley was a good deal surprised, and he was disgusted too, but he didn't have no idea what the matter was, of course.

"The feller took the money and started away; and when he was going out at the door, he sorter jerked his thumb over his shoulder—so—at Dan'l, and says again, very deliberate, 'Well,' he says, '*I* don't see no p'ints about that frog that's any better'n any other frog.'

"Smiley he stood scratching his head and looking down at Dan'l a long time, and at last he says, 'I do wonder what in the nation that frog throw'd off for—I wonder if there ain't something the matter with him—he 'pears to look mighty baggy, somehow.' And he ketched Dan'l by the nap of the neck, and hefted him, and says, 'Why blame my cats if he don't weigh five pound!' and turned him upside down and he belched out a double handful of shot. And then he see how it was, and he was the maddest man—he set the frog down and took out after that feller, but he never ketched him. And—"

[Here Simon Wheeler heard his name called from the front yard, and got up to see what was wanted.] And turning to me as he moved away, he said: "Just set where you are, stranger, and rest easy—I ain't going to be gone a second."

But, by your leave, I did not think that a continuation of the history of the enterprising vagabond *Jim* Smiley would be likely to afford me much information concerning the Rev. *Leonidas* W. Smiley, and so I started away.

At the door I met the sociable Wheeler returning, and he buttonholed me and recommenced:

"Well, thish-yer Smiley had a yaller one-eyed cow that didn't have no tail, only just a short stump like a bannanner, and—"

However, lacking both time and inclination, I did not wait to hear about the afflicted cow, but took my leave.

A LITERARY NIGHTMARE

Mark Twain

WILL THE READER please to cast his eye over the following verses, and see if he can discover anything harmful in them?

> "Conductor, when you receive a fare,
> Punch in the presence of the passenjare!
> A blue trip slip for an eight-cent fare,
> A buff trip slip for a six-cent fare,
> A pink trip slip for a three-cent fare,
> Punch in the presence of the passenjare!
> CHORUS.
> Punch, brothers! punch with care!
> Punch in the presence of the passenjare!"

I came across these jingling rhymes in a newspaper, a little while ago, and read them a couple of times. They took instant and entire possession of me. All through breakfast they went waltzing through my brain; and when, at last, I rolled up my napkin, I could not tell whether I had eaten anything or not. I had carefully laid out my day's work the day before—a thrilling tragedy in the novel which I am writing. I went to my den to begin my deed of blood. I took up my pen, but all I could get it to say was, "Punch in the presence of the passenjare." I fought hard for an hour, but it was useless. My head kept humming, "A blue trip slip for an eight-cent fare, a buff trip slip for a six-cent fare," and so on and so on, without peace or respite. The day's work was ruined—I could see that plainly enough. I gave up and drifted down town, and presently discovered that my feet were keeping time to that relentless jingle. When

I could stand it no longer I altered my step. But it did no good; those rhymes accommodated themselves to the new step and went on harassing me just as before. I returned home, and suffered all the afternoon; suffered all through an unconscious and unrefreshing dinner; suffered, and cried, and jingled all through the evening; went to bed and rolled, tossed, and jingled right along, the same as ever; got up at midnight frantic, and tried to read; but there was nothing visible upon the whirling page except "Punch! punch in the presence of the passenjare." By sunrise I was out of my mind, and everybody marveled and was distressed at the idiotic burden of my ravings,—"Punch! oh, punch! punch in the presence of the passenjare!"

Two days later, on Saturday morning, I arose, a tottering wreck, and went forth to fulfill an engagement with a valued friend, the Rev. Mr. ——, to walk to the Talcott Tower, ten miles distant. He stared at me, but asked no questions. We started. Mr. —— talked, talked, talked—as is his wont. I said nothing; I heard nothing. At the end of a mile, Mr. —— said,—

"Mark, are you sick? I never saw a man look so haggard and worn and absent-minded. Say something; do!"

Drearily, without enthusiasm, I said: "Punch, brothers, punch with care! Punch in the presence of the passenjare!"

My friend eyed me blankly, looked perplexed, then said,—

"I do not think I get your drift, Mark. There does not seem to be any relevancy in what you have said, certainly nothing sad; and yet—maybe it was the way you *said* the words—I never heard anything that sounded so pathetic. What is"—

But I heard no more. I was already far away with my pitiless, heartbreaking "blue trip slip for an eight-cent fare, buff trip slip for a six-cent fare, pink trip slip for a three-cent fare; punch in the presence of the passenjare." I do not know what occurred during the other nine miles. However, all of a sudden Mr. —— laid his hand on my shoulder and shouted,—

"Oh, wake up! wake up! wake up! Don't sleep all day! Here we are at the Tower, man! I have talked myself deaf and dumb and blind, and never got a response. Just look at this magnificent autumn landscape! Look at it! look at it! Feast your eyes on it! You have traveled; you have seen boasted landscapes elsewhere. Come, now, deliver an honest opinion. What do you say to this?"

I sighed wearily, and murmured,—

"A buff trip slip for a six-cent fare, a pink trip slip for a three-cent fare, punch in the presence of the passenjare."

Rev. Mr. —— stood there, very grave, full of concern, apparently, and looked long at me; then he said,—

"Mark, there is something about this that I cannot understand. Those are about the same words you said before; there does not seem to be anything in them, and yet they nearly break my heart when you say them. Punch in the—how is it they go?"

I began at the beginning and repeated all the lines. My friend's face lighted with interest. He said,—

"Why, what a captivating jingle it is! It is almost music. It flows along so nicely. I have nearly caught the rhymes myself. Say them over just once more, and then I'll have them, sure."

I said them over. Then Mr. —— said them. He made one little mistake, which I corrected. The next time and the next he got them right. Now a great burden seemed to tumble from my shoulders. That torturing jingle departed out of my brain, and a grateful sense of rest and peace descended upon me. I was light-hearted enough to sing; and I did sing for half an hour, straight along, as we went jogging homeward. Then my freed tongue found blessed speech again, and the pent talk of many a weary hour began to gush and flow. It flowed on and on, joyously, jubilantly, until the fountain was empty and dry. As I wrung my friend's hand at parting, I said,—

"Have n't we had a royal good time! But now I remember, you have n't said a word for two hours. Come, come, out with something!"

The Rev. Mr. —— turned a lacklustre eye upon me, drew a deep sigh, and said, without animation, without apparent consciousness,—

"Punch, brothers, punch with care! Punch in the presence of the passenjare!"

A pang shot through me as I said to myself, "Poor fellow, poor fellow! *he* has got it, now."

I did not see Mr. —— for two or three days after that. Then, on Tuesday evening, he staggered into my presence and sank dejectedly into a seat. He was pale, worn; he was a wreck. He lifted his faded eyes to my face and said,—

"Ah, Mark, it was a ruinous investment that I made in those heartless rhymes. They have ridden me like a nightmare, day and night, hour after hour, to this very moment. Since I saw you I have suffered the torments of the lost. Saturday evening I had a sudden call, by telegraph, and took the night train for Boston. The occasion was the death of a valued old friend who had requested that I should preach his funeral sermon. I took my seat in the cars and set myself to framing the discourse. But I never got beyond the opening paragraph; for then the train started and the car-wheels began their 'clack–clack–clack–clack! clack–clack–clack–clack!' and right away those odious rhymes fitted themselves to that accompaniment. For an hour I sat there and set a syllable of those rhymes to every separate and distinct clack the car-wheels made. Why, I was as fagged out, then, as if I had been chopping wood all day. My skull was splitting with headache. It seemed to me that I must go mad if I sat there any longer; so I undressed and went to bed. I stretched myself out in my berth, and—well, you know what the result was. The thing went right along, just the same. 'Clack-clack-clack, a blue trip slip, clack-clack-clack, for an eight-cent fare; clack-clack-clack, a buff trip slip, clack-clack-clack, for a six-cent fare, and so on, and so on, and so on—*punch,* in the presence of the passenjare!' Sleep? Not a single wink! I was almost a lunatic when I got to Boston. Don't ask me about the funeral. I did the best I could, but every solemn individual sentence was meshed and tangled and woven in and out with 'Punch, brothers, punch with care, punch in the presence of the passenjare.' And the most distressing thing was that my *delivery* dropped into the undulating rhythm of those pulsing rhymes, and I could actually catch absent-minded people nodding *time* to the swing of it with their stupid heads. And, Mark, you may believe it or not, but before I got through, the entire assemblage were placidly bobbing their heads in solemn unison, mourners, undertaker, and all. The moment I had finished, I fled to the anteroom in a state bordering on frenzy. Of course it would be my luck to find a sorrowing and aged maiden aunt of the deceased there, who had arrived from Springfield too late to get into the church. She began to sob, and said,—

" 'Oh, oh, he is gone, he is gone, and I did n't see him before he died!'

" 'Yes!' I said, 'he *is* gone, he *is* gone, he *is* gone—oh, *will* this suffering never cease!'

" '*You* loved him, then! Oh, you too loved him!'

" 'Loved him! Loved *who?*'

" 'Why, my poor George! my poor nephew!'

"'Oh—*him!* Yes—oh, yes, yes. Certainly—certainly. Punch—punch—oh, this misery will kill me!'

"'Bless you! bless you, sir, for these sweet words! *I*, too, suffer in this dear loss. Were you present during his last moments?'

"'Yes! I—*whose* last moments?'

"'*His.* The dear departed's.'

"'Yes! Oh, yes—yes—*yes!* I suppose so, I think so, *I* don't know! Oh, certainly—I was there—*I* was there!'

"'Oh, what a privilege! what a precious privilege! And his last words—oh, tell me, tell me his last words! What did he say?'

"'He said—he said—oh, my head, my head, my head! He said—he said—he never said *anything* but Punch, punch, *punch* in the presence of the passenjare! Oh, leave me, madam! In the name of all that is generous, leave me to my madness, my misery, my despair!—a buff trip slip for a six-cent fare, a pink trip slip for a three-cent fare—endur-ance *can* no fur-ther go!—PUNCH in the presence of the passenjare!'"

My friend's hopeless eyes rested upon mine a pregnant minute, and then he said impressively,—

"Mark, you do not say anything. You do not offer me any hope. But, ah me, it is just as well—it is just as well. You could not do me any good. The time has long gone by when words could comfort me. Something tells me that my tongue is doomed to wag forever to the jigger of that remorseless jingle. There—there it is coming on me again: a blue trip slip for an eight-cent fare, a buff trip slip for a"—

Thus murmuring faint and fainter, my friend sank into a peaceful trance and forgot his sufferings in a blessed respite.

How did I finally save him from the asylum? I took him to a neighboring university and made him discharge the burden of his persecuting rhymes into the eager ears of the poor, unthinking students. How is it with *them,* now? The result is too sad to tell. Why did I write this article? It was for a worthy, even a noble, purpose. It was to warn you, reader, if you should come across those merciless rhymes, to avoid them—avoid them as you would a pestilence!

THE BRIDE COMES TO YELLOW SKY

Stephen Crane

I

THE GREAT PULLMAN was whirling onward with such dignity of motion that a glance from the window seemed simply to prove that the plains of Texas were pouring eastward. Vast flats of green grass, dull-hued spaces of mesquite and cactus, little groups of frame houses, woods of light and tender trees, all were sweeping into the east, sweeping over the horizon, a precipice.

A newly married pair had boarded this coach at San Antonio. The man's face was reddened from many days in the wind and sun, and a direct result of his new black clothes was that his brick-colored hands were constantly performing in a most conscious fashion. From time to time he looked down respectfully at his attire. He sat with a hand on each knee, like a man waiting in a barber's shop. The glances he devoted to other passengers were furtive and shy.

The bride was not pretty, nor was she very young. She wore a dress of blue cashmere, with small reservations of velvet here and there, and with steel buttons abounding. She continually twisted her head to regard her puff sleeves, very stiff, straight, and high. They embarrassed her. It was quite apparent that she had cooked, and that she expected to cook, dutifully. The blushes caused by the careless scrutiny of some passengers as she had entered the car were strange to see upon this plain, underclass countenance, which was drawn in placid, almost emotionless lines.

They were evidently very happy. "Ever been in a parlor car before?" he asked, smiling with delight.

"No," she answered, "I never was. It's fine, ain't it?"

"Great! And then after a while we'll go forward to the diner, and get a big layout. Finest meal in the world. Charge a dollar."

"Oh, do they?" cried the bride. "Charge a dollar? Why, that's too much—for us—ain't it, Jack?"

"Not this trip, anyhow," he answered bravely. "We're going to go the whole thing."

Later, he explained to her about the trains. "You see, it's a thousand miles from one end of Texas to the other; and this train runs right across it and never stops but four times." He had the pride of an owner. He pointed out to her the dazzling fittings of the coach; and in truth her eyes opened wider as she contemplated the sea-green figured velvet, the shining brass, silver, and glass, the wood that gleamed as darkly brilliant as the surface of a pool of oil. At one end a bronze figure sturdily held a support for a separated chamber, and at convenient places on the ceiling were frescoes in olive and silver.

To the minds of the pair, their surroundings reflected the glory of their marriage that morning in San Antonio. This was the environment of their new estate, and the man's face in particular beamed with an elation that made him appear ridiculous to the negro porter. This individual at times surveyed them from afar with an amused and superior grin. On other occasions he bullied them with skill in ways that did not make it exactly plain to them that they were being bullied. He subtly used all the manners of the most unconquerable kind of snobbery. He oppressed them; but of this oppression they had small knowledge, and they speedily forgot that infrequently a number of travelers covered them with stares of derisive enjoyment. Historically there was supposed to be something infinitely humorous in their situation.

"We are due in Yellow Sky at 3:42," he said, looking tenderly into her eyes.

"Oh, are we?" she said, as if she had not been aware of it. To evince surprise at her husband's statement was part of her wifely amiability. She took from a pocket a little silver watch, and as she held it before her, and stared at it with a frown of attention, the new husband's face shone.

"I bought it in San Anton' from a friend of mine," he told her gleefully.

"It's seventeen minutes past twelve," she said, looking up at him with a kind of shy and clumsy coquetry. A passenger, noting this play, grew excessively sardonic, and winked at himself in one of the numerous mirrors.

At last they went to the dining car. Two rows of negro waiters, in glowing white suits, surveyed their entrance with the interest, and also the equanimity, of men who had been forewarned. The pair fell to the lot of a waiter who happened to feel pleasure in steering them through their meal. He viewed them with the manner of a fatherly pilot, his countenance radiant with benevolence. The patronage, entwined with the ordinary deference, was not plain to them. And yet, as they returned to their coach, they showed in their faces a sense of escape.

To the left, miles down a long purple slope, was a little ribbon of mist where moved the keening Rio Grande. The train was approaching it at an angle, and the apex was Yellow Sky. Presently it was apparent that, as the distance from Yellow Sky grew shorter, the husband became commensurately restless. His brick-red hands were more insistent in their prominence. Occasionally he was even rather absent-minded and faraway when the bride leaned forward and addressed him.

As a matter of truth, Jack Potter was beginning to find the shadow of a deed weigh upon him like a leaden slab. He, the town marshal of Yellow Sky, a man known, liked, and feared in his corner, a prominent person, had gone to San Antonio to meet the girl he believed he loved, and there, after the usual prayers, had actually induced her to marry him, without consulting Yellow Sky for any part of the transaction. He was now bringing his bride before an innocent and unsuspecting community.

Of course, people in Yellow Sky married as it pleased them, in accordance with a general custom; but such was Potter's thought of his duty to his friends, or of their idea of his duty, or of an unspoken form which does not control men in these matters, that he felt he was heinous. He had committed an extraordinary crime. Face to face with this girl in San Antonio, and spurred by his sharp impulse, he had gone headlong over all the social hedges. At San Antonio he was like a man hidden in the dark. A knife to sever any friendly duty, any form, was easy to his hand in that remote city. But the hour of Yellow Sky—the hour of daylight—was approaching.

He knew full well that his marriage was an important thing to his town. It could only be exceeded by the burning of the new hotel. His friends could not forgive him. Frequently he had reflected on the advisability of telling them by telegraph, but a new cowardice had been upon him. He feared to do it. And now the train was hurrying him toward a scene of amazement, glee, and reproach. He glanced out of the window at the line of haze swinging slowly in towards the train.

Yellow Sky had a kind of brass band, which played painfully, to the delight of the populace. He laughed without heart as he thought of it. If the citizens could dream of his prospective arrival with his bride, they would parade the band at the station and escort them, amid cheers and laughing congratulations, to his adobe home.

He resolved that he would use all the devices of speed and plains-craft in making the journey from the station to his house. Once within that safe citadel, he could issue some sort of a vocal bulletin, and then not go among the citizens until they had time to wear off a little of their enthusiasm.

The bride looked anxiously at him. "What's worrying you, Jack?"

He laughed again. "I'm not worrying, girl. I'm only thinking of Yellow Sky."

She flushed in comprehension.

A sense of mutual guilt invaded their minds and developed a finer tenderness. They looked at each other with eyes softly aglow. But Potter often laughed the same nervous laugh. The flush upon the bride's face seemed quite permanent.

The traitor to the feelings of Yellow Sky narrowly watched the speeding landscape. "We're nearly there," he said.

Presently the porter came and announced the proximity of Potter's home. He held a brush in his hand, and, with all his airy superiority gone, he brushed Potter's new clothes as the latter slowly turned this way and that way. Potter fumbled out a coin and gave it to the porter, as he had seen others do. It was a heavy and muscle-bound business, as that of a man shoeing his first horse.

The porter took their bag, and as the train began to slow they moved forward to the hooded platform of the car. Presently the two engines and their long string of coaches rushed into the station of Yellow Sky.

"They have to take water here," said Potter, from a constricted throat and in mournful cadence, as one announcing death. Before the train stopped, his eye had swept the length of the platform, and he was glad and astonished to see there was none upon it but the station-agent, who, with a slightly hurried and anxious air, was walking toward the water tanks. When the train had halted, the porter alighted first and placed in position a little temporary step.

"Come on, girl," said Potter, hoarsely. As he helped her down they each laughed on a false note. He took the bag from the negro, and bade his wife cling to his arm. As they slunk rapidly away, his hangdog glance perceived that they were unloading the two trunks, and also that the station-agent far ahead near the baggage car, had turned and was running toward him, making gestures. He laughed, and groaned as he laughed, when he noted the first effect of his marital bliss upon Yellow Sky. He gripped his wife's arm firmly to his side, and they fled. Behind them the porter stood chuckling fatuously.

II

The California Express on the Southern Railway was due at Yellow Sky in twenty-one minutes. There were six men at the bar of the Weary Gentleman saloon. One was a drummer who talked a great deal and rapidly; three were Texans who did not care to talk at that time; and two were Mexican sheepherders who did not talk as a general practice in the Weary Gentleman saloon. The barkeeper's dog lay on the boardwalk that crossed in front of the door. His head was on his paws, and he glanced drowsily here and there with the constant vigilance of a dog that is kicked on occasion. Across the sandy street were some vivid green grass-plots, so wonderful in appearance amid the sands that burned near them in a blazing sun that they caused a doubt in the mind. They exactly resembled the grass mats used to represent lawns on the stage. At the cooler end of the railway station, a man without a coat sat in a tilted chair and smoked his pipe. The fresh-cut bank of the Rio Grande circled near the town, and there could be seen beyond it a great, plum-colored plain of mesquite.

Save for the busy drummer and his companions in the saloon, Yellow Sky was dozing. The newcomer leaned gracefully upon the bar, and recited many tales with the confidence of a bard who has come upon a new field.

"——and at the moment that the old man fell downstairs with the bureau in his arms, the old woman was coming up with two scuttles of coal, and of course——"

The drummer's tale was interrupted by a young man who suddenly appeared in the open door. He cried: "Scratchy Wilson's drunk, and has turned loose with both hands." The two Mexicans at once set down their glasses and faded out of the rear entrance of the saloon.

The drummer, innocent and jocular, answered: "All right, old man. S'pose he has? Come in and have a drink, anyhow."

But the information had made such an obvious cleft in every skull in the room that the drummer was obliged to see its importance. All had become instantly solemn. "Say," said he, mystified, "what is this?" His three companions made the introductory gesture of eloquent speech, but the young man at the door forestalled them.

"It means, my friend," he answered, as he came into the saloon, "that for the next two hours this town won't be a health resort."

The barkeeper went to the door and locked and barred it. Reaching out of the window, he pulled in heavy wooden shutters and barred them. Immediately a solemn, chapel-like gloom was upon the place. The drummer was looking from one to another.

"But, say," he cried, "what is this, anyhow? You don't mean there is going to be a gunfight?"

"Don't know whether there'll be a fight or not," answered one man, grimly. "But there'll be some shootin'—some good shootin'."

The young man who had warned them waved his hand. "Oh, there'll be a fight fast enough, if anyone wants it. Anybody can get a fight out there in the street. There's a fight just waiting."

The drummer seemed to be swayed between the interest of a foreigner and a perception of personal danger.

"What did you say his name was?" he asked.

"Scratchy Wilson," they answered in chorus.

"And will he kill anybody? What are you going to do? Does this happen often? Does he rampage around like this once a week or so? Can he break in that door?"

"No, he can't break down that door," replied the barkeeper. "He's tried it three times. But when he comes you'd better lay down on the floor, stranger. He's dead sure to shoot at it, and a bullet may come through."

Thereafter the drummer kept a strict eye upon the door. The time had not yet been called for him to hug the floor, but, as a minor precaution, he sidled near to the wall. "Will he kill anybody?" he said again.

The men laughed low and scornfully at the question.

"He's out to shoot, and he's out for trouble. Don't see any good in experimentin' with him."

"But what do you do in a case like this? What do you do?"

A man responded: "Why, he and Jack Potter——"

"But," in chorus, the other men interrupted, "Jack Potter's in San Anton'."

"Well, who is he? What's he got to do with it?"

"Oh, he's the town marshal. He goes out and fights Scratchy when he gets on one of these tears."

"Wow," said the drummer, mopping his brow. "Nice job he's got."

The voices had toned away to mere whisperings. The drummer wished to ask further questions, which were born of an increasing anxiety and bewilderment; but when he attempted them, the men merely looked at him in irritation and motioned him to remain silent. A tense waiting hush was upon them. In the deep shadows of the room their eyes shone as they listened for sounds from the street. One man made three gestures at the barkeeper; and the latter, moving like a ghost, handed him a glass and a bottle. The man poured a full glass of whisky, and set down the bottle noiselessly. He gulped the whisky in a swallow, and turned again toward the door in immovable silence. The drummer saw that the barkeeper, without a sound, had taken a Winchester from beneath the bar. Later he saw this individual beckoning to him, so he tiptoed across the room.

"You better come with me back of the bar."

"No, thanks," said the drummer, perspiring. "I'd rather be where I can make a break for the back door."

Whereupon the man of bottles made a kindly but peremptory gesture. The drummer obeyed it, and, finding himself seated on a box with his head below the level of the bar, balm was laid upon his soul at sight of various zinc and copper fittings that bore a resemblance to armor plate. The barkeeper took a seat comfortably upon an adjacent box.

"You see," he whispered, "this here Scratchy Wilson is a wonder with a gun—a perfect wonder—and when he goes on the war trail, we hunt our holes—naturally. He's about the last one of the old gang that used to hang out along the river here. He's a terror when he's drunk. When he's sober he's all right—kind of simple—wouldn't hurt a fly—nicest fellow in town. But when he's drunk—whoo!"

There were periods of stillness. "I wish Jack Potter was back from San Anton'," said the barkeeper. "He shot Wilson up once—in the leg—and he would sail in and pull out the kinks in this thing."

Presently they heard from a distance the sound of a shot, followed by three wild yowls. It instantly removed a bond from the men in the darkened saloon. There was a shuffling of feet. They looked at each other. "Here he comes," they said.

III

A man in a maroon-colored flannel shirt, which had been purchased for purposes of decoration, and made principally by some
Jewish women on the East Side of New York, rounded a corner
and walked into the middle of the main street of Yellow Sky. In
either hand the man held a long, heavy, blue-black revolver.
Often he yelled, and these cries rang through a semblance of a
deserted village, shrilly flying over the roofs in a volume that
seemed to have no relation to the ordinary vocal strength of a
man. It was as if the surrounding stillness formed the arch of a
tomb over him. These cries of ferocious challenge rang against
walls of silence. And his boots had red tops with gilded imprints,
of the kind beloved in winter by little sledding boys on the
hillsides of New England.

The man's face flamed in a rage begot of whiskey. His eyes, rolling and yet keen for ambush, hunted the still doorways and windows. He walked with the creeping movement of the midnight cat.
As it occurred to him, he roared menacing information. The long
revolvers in his hands were as easy as straws; they were moved with
an electric swiftness. The little fingers of each hand played sometimes in a musician's way. Plain from the low collar of the shirt, the
cords of his neck straightened and sank, straightened and sank, as
passion moved him. The only sounds were his terrible invitations.
The calm adobes preserved their demeanor at the passing of this
small thing in the middle of the street.

There was no offer of fight—no offer of fight. The man called
to the sky. There were no attractions. He bellowed and fumed and
swayed his revolvers here and everywhere.

The dog of the barkeeper of the Weary Gentleman saloon had
not appreciated the advance of events. He yet lay dozing in front
of his master's door. At sight of the dog, the man paused and raised
his revolver humorously. At sight of the man, the dog sprang up
and walked diagonally away, with a sullen head, and growling. The
man yelled, and the dog broke into a gallop. As it was about to
enter an alley, there was a loud noise, a whistling, and something
spat the ground directly before it. The dog screamed, and, wheeling
in terror, galloped headlong in a new direction. Again there was a
noise, a whistling, and sand was kicked viciously before it. Fear-
stricken, the dog turned and flurried like an animal in a pen. The
man stood laughing, his weapons at his hips.

Ultimately the man was attracted by the closed door of the Weary Gentleman saloon. He went to it and, hammering with a revolver, demanded drink.

The door remaining imperturbable, he picked a bit of paper from the walk and nailed it to the framework with a knife. He then turned his back contemptuously upon this popular resort and, walking to the opposite side of the street, and spinning there on his heel quickly and lithely, fired at the bit of paper. He missed it by a half-inch. He swore at himself, and went away. Later, he comfortably fusilladed the windows of his most intimate friend. The man was playing with this town. It was a toy for him.

But still there was no offer of fight. The name of Jack Potter, his ancient antagonist, entered his mind, and he concluded that it would be a glad thing if he should go to Potter's house and by bombardment induce him to come out and fight. He moved in the direction of his desire, chanting Apache scalp-music.

When he arrived at it, Potter's house presented the same still front as had the other adobes. Taking up a strategic position, the man howled a challenge. But this house regarded him as might a great stone god. It gave no sign. After a decent wait, the man howled further challenges, mingling with them wonderful epithets.

Presently there came the spectacle of a man churning himself into deepest rage over the immobility of a house. He fumed at it as the winter wind attacks a prairie cabin in the North. To the distance there should have gone the sound of a tumult like the fighting of two hundred Mexicans. As necessity bade him, he paused for breath or to reload his revolvers.

IV

Potter and his bride walked sheepishly and with speed. Sometimes they laughed together shamefacedly and low.

"Next corner, dear," he said finally.

They put forth the efforts of a pair walking bowed against a strong wind. Potter was about to raise a finger to point the first appearance of the new home when, as they circled the corner, they came face to face with a man in a maroon-colored shirt who was feverishly pushing cartridges into a large revolver. Upon the instant the man dropped his revolver to the ground, and, like lightning, whipped another from its holster. The second weapon was aimed at the bridegroom's chest.

There was a silence. Potter's mouth seemed to be merely a grave for his tongue. He exhibited an instinct to at once loosen his arm from the woman's grip, and he dropped the bag to the sand. As for the bride, her face had gone as yellow as old cloth. She was a slave to hideous rites gazing at the apparitional snake.

The two men faced each other at a distance of three paces. He of the revolver smiled with a new and quiet ferocity.

"Tried to sneak up on me," he said. "Tried to sneak up on me!" His eyes grew more baleful. As Potter made a slight movement, the man thrust his revolver venomously forward. "No; don't you do it, Jack Potter. Don't you move a finger toward a gun just yet. Don't you move an eyelash. The time has come for me to settle with you, and I'm goin' to do it my own way and loaf along with no inter- ferin'. So if you don't want a gun bent on you, just mind what I tell you."

Potter looked at his enemy. "I ain't got a gun on me, Scratchy," he said. "Honest, I ain't." He was stiffening and steadying, but yet somewhere at the back of his mind a vision of the Pullman floated: the sea-green figured velvet, the shining brass, silver, and glass, the wood that gleamed as darkly brilliant as the surface of a pool of oil—all the glory of the marriage, the environment of the new estate. "You know I fight when it comes to fighting, Scratchy Wilson; but I ain't got a gun on me. You'll have to do all the shootin' yourself."

His enemy's face went livid. He stepped forward, and lashed his weapon to and fro before Potter's chest. "Don't you tell me you ain't got no gun on you, you whelp. Don't tell me no lie like that. There ain't a man in Texas ever seen you without no gun. Don't take me for no kid." His eyes blazed with light, and his throat worked like a pump.

"I ain't takin' you for no kid," answered Potter. His heels had not moved an inch backward. "I'm takin' you for a damn fool. I tell you I ain't got a gun, and I ain't. If you're goin' to shoot me up, you better begin now. You'll never get a chance like this again."

So much enforced reasoning had told on Wilson's rage. He was calmer. "If you ain't got a gun, why ain't you got a gun?" he sneered. "Been to Sunday school?"

"I ain't got a gun because I've just come from San Anton' with my wife. I'm married," said Potter. "And if I'd thought there was going to be any galoots like you prowling around when I brought my wife home, I'd had a gun, and don't you forget it."

"Married!" said Scratchy, not at all comprehending.

"Yes, married. I'm married," said Potter, distinctly.

"Married?" said Scratchy. Seemingly for the first time, he saw the drooping, drowning woman at the other man's side. "No!" he said. He was like a creature allowed a glimpse of another world. He moved a pace backward, and his arm, with the revolver dropped to his side. "Is this the lady?" he asked.

"Yes; this is the lady," answered Potter.

There was another period of silence.

"Well," said Wilson at last, slowly, "I s'pose it's all off now."

"It's all off if you say so, Scratchy. You know I didn't make the trouble." Potter lifted his valise.

"Well, I 'low it's off, Jack," said Wilson. He was looking at the ground. "Married!" He was not a student of chivalry; it was merely that in the presence of this foreign condition he was a simple child of the earlier plains. He picked up his starboard revolver, and, placing both weapons in their holsters, he went away. His feet made funnel-shaped tracks in the heavy sand.

THE PETERKINS DECIDE TO LEARN THE LANGUAGES

Lucretia Peabody Hale

CERTAINLY NOW WAS the time to study the languages. The Peterkins had moved into a new house, far more convenient than their old one, where they would have a place for everything, and everything in its place. Of course they would then have more time.

Elizabeth Eliza recalled the troubles of the old house; how for a long time she was obliged to sit outside of the window upon the piazza, when she wanted to play on her piano.

Mrs. Peterkin reminded them of the difficulty about the table-cloths. The upper table-cloth was kept in a trunk that had to stand in front of the door to the closet under the stairs. But the under tablecloth was kept in a drawer in the closet. So, whenever the cloths were changed, the trunk had to be pushed away under some projecting shelves to make room for opening the closet door (as the under table-cloth must be taken out first), then the trunk was pushed back to make room for it to be opened for the upper table-cloth, and, after all, it was necessary to push the trunk away again to open the closet-door for the knife-tray. This always consumed a great deal of time.

Now that the china-closet was large enough, everything could find a place in it.

Agamemnon especially enjoyed the new library. In the old house there was no separate room for books. The dictionaries were kept upstairs, which was very inconvenient, and the volumes of the Encyclopaedia could not be together. There was not room for all in one place. So from A to P were to be found downstairs, and from Q to Z were scattered in different rooms upstairs. And the worst of it was, you could never remember whether from A to P included P. "I always went upstairs after P," said Agamemnon, "and then always found it downstairs, or else it was the other way."

Of course, now there were more conveniences for study. With the books all in one room there would be no time wasted in looking for them.

Mr. Peterkin suggested they should each take a separate language. If they went abroad, this would prove a great convenience. Elizabeth Eliza could talk French with the Parisians; Agamemnon, German with the Germans; Solomon John, Italian with the Italians; Mrs. Peterkin, Spanish in Spain; and perhaps he could himself master all the Eastern languages and Russian.

Mrs. Peterkin was uncertain about undertaking the Spanish; but all the family felt very sure they should not go to Spain (as Elizabeth Eliza dreaded the Inquisition), and Mrs. Peterkin felt more willing.

Still she had quite an objection to going abroad. She had always said she would not go till a bridge was made across the Atlantic, and she was sure it did not look like it now.

Agamemnon said there was no knowing. There was something new every day, and a bridge was surely not harder to invent than a telephone, for they had bridges in the very earliest days.

Then came up the question of the teachers. Probably these could be found in Boston. If they could all come the same day, three could be brought out in the carry-all. Agamemnon could go in for them, and could learn a little on the way out and in.

Mr. Peterkin made some inquiries about the Oriental languages. He was told that Sanskrit was at the root of all. So he proposed they should all begin with Sanskrit. They would thus require but one teacher, and could branch out into the other languages afterward.

But the family preferred learning the separate languages. Elizabeth Eliza already knew something of the French. She had tried to talk it, without much success, at the Centennial Exhibition, at one of the side stands. But she found she had been talking with a Moorish gentleman who did not understand French. Mr. Peterkin feared they might need more libraries if all the teachers came at the same hour; but Agamemnon reminded him that they would be using different dictionaries. And Mr. Peterkin thought something might be learned by having them all at once. Each one might pick up something besides the language he was studying, and it was a great thing to learn to talk a foreign language while others were talking about you. Mrs. Peterkin was afraid it would be like the Tower of Babel, and hoped it was all right.

Agamemnon brought forward another difficulty. Of course, they ought to have foreign teachers who spoke only their native languages. But, in this case, how could they engage them to come, or explain to them about the carry-all, or arrange the proposed hours? He did not understand how anybody ever began with a foreigner, because he could not even tell him what he wanted.

Elizabeth Eliza thought a great deal might be done by signs and pantomime. Solomon John and the little boys began to show how it might be done. Elizabeth Eliza explained how "*langues*" meant both "languages" and "tongues," and they could point to their tongues. For practice, the little boys represented the foreign teachers talking in their different languages, and Agamemnon and Solomon John went to invite them to come out and teach the family by a series of signs.

Mr. Peterkin thought their success was admirable, and that they might almost go abroad without any study of the languages, and trust to explaining themselves by signs. Still, as the bridge was not yet made, it might be as well to wait and cultivate the languages.

Mrs. Peterkin was afraid the foreign teachers might imagine they were invited out to lunch. Solomon John had constantly pointed to his mouth as he opened it and shut it, putting out his tongue, and it looked a great deal more as if he were inviting them to eat than asking them to teach. Agamemnon suggested that they might carry the separate dictionaries when they went to see the teachers, and that would show that they meant lessons, and not lunch.

Mrs. Peterkin was not sure but she ought to prepare a lunch for them, if they had come all that way; but she certainly did not know what they were accustomed to eat.

Mr. Peterkin thought this would be a good thing to learn of the foreigners. It would be a good preparation for going abroad, and they might get used to the dishes before starting. The little boys were delighted at the idea of having new things cooked. Agamemnon had heard that beer-soup was a favorite dish with the Germans, and he would inquire how it was made in the first lesson. Solomon John had heard they were all very fond of garlic, and thought it would be a pretty attention to have some in the house the first day, that they might be cheered by the odor.

Elizabeth Eliza wanted to surprise the lady from Philadelphia by her knowledge of French, and hoped to begin on her lessons before the Philadelphia family arrived for their annual visit.

There were still some delays. Mr. Peterkin was very anxious to obtain teachers who had been but a short time in this country. He did not want to be tempted to talk any English with them. He wanted the latest and freshest languages, and at last came home one day with a list of "brand-new foreigners."

They decided to borrow the Bromwicks' carry-all to use, besides their own, for the first day, and Mr. Peterkin and Agamemnon drove into town to bring all the teachers out. One was a Russian gentleman, traveling, who came with no idea of giving lessons, but perhaps would consent to do so. He could not yet speak English. Mr. Peterkin had his card-case and the cards of the several gentlemen who had recommended the different teachers, and he went with Agamemnon from hotel to hotel collecting them. He found them all very polite and ready to come, after the explanation by signs agreed upon. The dictionaries had been forgotten, but Agamemnon had a directory, which looked the same and seemed to satisfy the foreigners.

Mr. Peterkin was obliged to content himself with the Russian instead of one who could teach Sanskrit, as there was no new teacher of that language lately arrived.

But there was an unexpected difficulty in getting the Russian gentleman into the same carriage with the teacher of Arabic, for he was a Turk, sitting with a fez on his head, on the back seat! They glared at each other, and began to assail each other in every language they knew, none of which Mr. Peterkin could understand. It might be Russian; it might have been Arabic. It was easy to understand that they would never consent to sit in the same carriage. Mr. Peterkin was in despair; he had forgotten about the Russian war! What a mistake to have invited the Turk!

Quite a crowd collected on the sidewalk in front of the hotel. But the French gentleman politely, but stiffly, invited the Russian to go with him in the first carry-all. Here was another difficulty. For the German professor was quietly ensconced on the back seat! As soon as the French gentleman put his foot on the step and saw him, he addressed him in such forcible language that the German professor got out of the door the other side, and came round on the sidewalk and took him by the collar. Certainly the German and

French gentlemen could not be put together, and more crowd collected!

Agamemnon, however, had happily studied up the German word "Herr," and he applied it to the German, inviting him by signs to take a seat in the other carry-all. The German consented to sit by the Turk, as they neither of them could understand the other; and at last they started, Mr. Peterkin with the Italian by his side, and the French and Russian teachers behind, vociferating to each other in languages unknown to Mr. Peterkin, while he feared they were not perfectly in harmony; so he drove home as fast as possible. Agamemnon had a silent party. The Spaniard at his side was a little moody, while the Turk and the German behind did not utter a word.

At last they reached the house, and were greeted by Mrs. Peterkin and Elizabeth Eliza, Mrs. Peterkin with her llama lace shawl over her shoulders, as a tribute to the Spanish teacher. Mr. Peterkin was careful to take his party in first, and deposit them in a distant part of the library, far from the Turk or the German, even putting the Frenchman and Russian apart.

Solomon John found the Italian dictionary, and seated himself by his Italian; Agamemnon, with the German dictionary, by the German. The little boys took their copy of the *Arabian Nights* to the Turk. Mr. Peterkin attempted to explain to the Russian that he had no Russian dictionary, as he had hoped to learn Sanskrit of him, while Mrs. Peterkin was trying to inform her teacher that she had no books in Spanish. She got over all fears of the Inquisition, he looked so sad, and she tried to talk a little, using English words, but very slowly, and altering the accent as far as she knew how. The Spaniard bowed, looked gravely interested, and was very polite.

Elizabeth Eliza, meanwhile, was trying her grammar phrases with the Parisian. She found it easier to talk French than to understand him. But he understood perfectly her sentences. She repeated one of her vocabularies, and went on with, "*J'ai le livre.*" "*As-tu le pain?*" "*L'enfant a une poire.*" He listened with great attention, and replied slowly. Suddenly she started, after making out one of his sentences, and went to her mother to whisper, "They have made the mistake you feared. They think they are invited to lunch! *He* has just been thanking me for our politeness in inviting them to *dejeuner,*—that means breakfast!"

"They have not had their breakfast!" exclaimed Mrs. Peterkin, looking at her Spaniard; "he does look hungry! What shall we do?"

Elizabeth Eliza was consulting her father. What should they do? How should they make them understand that they invited them to teach, not lunch. Elizabeth Eliza begged Agamemnon to look out "*apprendre*" in the dictionary. It must mean to teach. Alas, they found it means both to teach and to learn! What should they do? The foreigners were now sitting silent in their different corners. The Spaniard grew more and more sallow. What if he should faint? The Frenchman was rolling up each of his mustaches to a point as he gazed at the German. What if the Russian should fight the Turk? What if the German should be exasperated by the airs of the Parisian?

"We must give them something to eat," said Mr. Peterkin, in a low tone. "It would calm them."

"If I only knew what they were used to eating!" said Mrs. Peterkin.

Solomon John suggested that none of them knew what the others were used to eating, and they might bring in anything.

Mrs. Peterkin hastened out with hospitable intents. Amanda could make good coffee. Mr. Peterkin had suggested some American dish. Solomon John sent a little boy for some olives.

It was not long before the coffee came in, and a dish of baked beans. Next, some olives and a loaf of bread, and some boiled eggs, and some bottles of beer. The effect was astonishing. Every man spoke his own tongue, and fluently. Mrs. Peterkin poured out coffee for the Spaniard, while he bowed to her. They all liked beer; they all liked olives. The Frenchman was fluent about "*les moeurs Americaines.*" Elizabeth Eliza supposed he alluded to their not having set any table. The Turk smiled; the Russian was voluble. In the midst of the clang of the different languages, just as Mr. Peterkin was again repeating, under cover of the noise of many tongues, "How shall we make them understand that we want them to teach?"—at this moment the door was flung open, and there came in the lady from Philadelphia, that day arrived, her first call of the season.

She started back in terror at the tumult of so many different languages. The family, with joy, rushed to meet her. All together they called upon her to explain for them. Could she help them? Could she tell the foreigners that they wanted to take lessons? Lessons?

They had no sooner uttered the word than their guests all started up with faces beaming with joy. It was the one English word they all knew! They had come to Boston to give lessons! The Russian traveler had hoped to learn English in this way. The thought pleased them more than the dejeuner. Yes, gladly would they give lessons. The Turk smiled at the idea. The first step was taken. The teachers knew they were expected to teach.

THE PARSON'S HORSE RACE

Harriet Beecher Stowe

"WAL, NOW, THIS 'ere does beat all! I wouldn'ta thought it o' the deacon."

So spoke Sam Lawson, drooping in a discouraged, contemplative attitude in front of an equally discouraged-looking horse, that had just been brought to him by the Widow Simpkins for medical treatment. Among Sam's many accomplishments, he was reckoned in the neighborhood an oracle in all matters of this kind, especially by women, whose helplessness in meeting such emergencies found unfailing solace under his compassionate willingness to attend to any business that did not strictly belong to him, and from which no pecuniary return was to be expected.

The Widow Simpkins had bought this horse of Deacon Atkins, apparently a fairly well-appointed brute, and capable as he was good-looking. A short, easy drive, when the Deacon held the reins, had shown off his points to advantage; and the widow's small stock of ready savings had come forth freely in payment for what she thought was a bargain. When, soon after coming into possession, she discovered that her horse, if driven with any haste, panted in a fearful manner, and that he appeared to be growing lame, she waxed wroth, and went to the Deacon in anger, to be met only with the smooth reminder that the animal was all right when she took him; that she had seen him tried herself. The widow was of a nature somewhat spicy, and expressed herself warmly: "It's a cheat and a shame, and I'll take the law on ye!"

"What law will you take?" said the unmoved Deacon. "Wasn't it a fair bargain?"

"I'll take the law of God," said the widow, with impotent indignation; and she departed to pour her cares and trials into the ever ready ear of Sam. Having assumed the care of the animal, he now sat contemplating it in a sort of trance of melancholy reflection.

"Why, boys," he broke out, "why didn't she come to me afore she bought this crittur? Why, I knew all about him! That 'ere crittur was jest ruined a year ago last summer, when Tom, the Deacon's boy there, come home from college. Tom driv him over to Sherburn and back that 'ere hot Fourth of July. 'Member it, 'cause I saw the crittur when he come home. I sot up with Tom takin' care of him all night. That 'ere crittur had the thumps all night, and he hain't never been good for nothin' since. I telled the Deacon he was a gone hoss then, and wouldn't never be good for nothin'. The Deacon, he took off his shoes, and let him run to pastur' all summer, and he's ben a-feedin' and nussin' on him up; and now he's put him off on the widder. I wouldn't'a thought it o' the Deacon! Why, this hoss'll never be no 'good to her! That 'ere's a used-up crittur, any fool may see! He'll mabbe do for about a quarter of an hour on a smooth road; but come to drive him as a body wants to drive, why, he blows like my bellowsis; and the Deacon knew it—musta known it!"

"Why, Sam!" we exclaimed, "ain't the Deacon a good man?"

"Wal, now, there's where the shoe pinches! In a gin'al way the Deacon is a good man—he's consid'able more than middlin' good; gin'ally he adorns his perfession. On most p'ints I don't hev nothin' agin the Deacon; and this 'ere ain't a bit like him. But there 'tis! Come to hosses, there's where the unsanctified natur' comes out. Folks will cheat about hosses when they won't about 'most nothin' else." And Sam leaned back on his cold forge, now empty of coal, and seemed to deliver himself to a mournful train of general reflection. "Yes, hosses does seem to be sort o' unregenerate critturs," he broke out: "there's suthin about hosses that deceives the very elect. The best o' folks gets tripped up when they come to deal in hosses."

"Why, Sam, is there anything bad in horses?" we interjected timidly.

"'Tain't the hosses," said Sam with solemnity. "Lordy massy! the hosses is all right enough! Hosses is scriptural animals. Elijah went up to heaven in a chari't with hosses, and then all them lots o' hosses in the Ravelations—black and white and red, and all sorts o' colors. That 'ere shows hosses goes to heaven; but it's more'n the folks that hev 'em is likely to, ef they don't look out.

"Ministers, now," continued Sam, in a soliloquizing vein—"folks allers thinks it's suthin' sort o' shaky in a minister to hev much to do with hosses—sure to get 'em into trouble. There was old Parson Williams of North Billriky got into a drefful mess about a hoss. Lordy massy! he wern't to blame, neither; but he got into the dreffulest scrape you ever heard on—come nigh to unsettlin' him."

"O Sam, tell us all about it!" we boys shouted, delighted with the prospect of a story.

"Wal, wait now till I get off this crittur's shoes, and we'll take him up to pastur', and then we can kind o' set by the river, and fish. Hepsy wanted a mess o' fish for supper, and I was cal'latin' to git some for her. You boys go and be digging bait, and git yer lines."

And so, as we were sitting tranquilly beside the Charles River, watching our lines, Sam's narrative began:

"Ye see, boys, Parson Williams—he's dead now, but when I was a boy he was one of the gret men round here. He writ books. He writ a tract agin the Armenians, and put 'em down; and he writ a big book on the millennium (I've got that 'ere book now); and he was a smart preacher. Folks said he had invitations to settle in Boston, and there ain't no doubt he mighta hed a Boston parish ef he'd'a ben a mind ter take it; but he'd got a good settlement and a handsome farm in North Billriky, and didn't care to move; thought, I s'pose, that 'twas better to be number one in a little place than number two in a big un. Anyway, he carried all before him where he was.

"Parson Williams was a tall, straight, personable man; come of good family—father and grand'ther before him all ministers. He was putty up and down, and commandin' in his ways, and things had to go putty much as he said. He was a good deal sot by, Parson Williams was, and his wife was a Derby—one o' them rich Salem Derbys—and brought him a lot o' money; and so they lived putty easy and comfortable so fur as this world's goods goes. Well, now, the parson wa'n't reely what you call worldly-minded; but then he was one o' them folks that knows what's good in temporals as well as sperituals, and allers liked to hev the best that there was goin'; and he allers had an eye to a good hoss.

"Now, there was Parson Adams and Parson Scranton, and most of the other ministers: they didn't know and didn't care what hoss they hed; jest jogged round with these 'ere poundin', potbellied, sleepy critturs that ministers mostly hes—good enough to crawl around to funerals and ministers' meetin's and 'sociations and sich; but Parson Williams, he allers would hev a hoss as was a hoss. He looked out for blood; and, when these 'ere Vermont fellers would come down with a drove, the person he hed his eyes open, and knew what was what. Couldn't none of 'em cheat him on hoss flesh! And so one time when Zach Buel was down with a drove, the doctor he bought the best hoss in the lot. Zach said he never see a parson afore that he couldn't cheat; but he said the doctor reely knew as much as he did, and got the very one he'd meant to 'a kept for himself.

"This 'ere hoss was a peeler, I'll tell you! They'd called him Tamerlane, from some heathen feller or other: the boys called him Tam, for short. Tam was a great character. All the fellers for miles round knew the doctor's Tam, and used to come clear over from the other parishes to see him.

"Wal, this 'ere sot up Cuff's back high, I tell you! Cuff was the doctor's nigger man, and he was nat'lly a dreffal proud crittur. The way he would swell and strut and brag about the doctor and his folks and his things! The doctor used to give Cuff his cast-off clothes: and Cuff would prance round in 'em, and seem to think he was a doctor of divinity himself, and had the charge of all natur'.

"Well, Cuff he reely made an idol o' that 'ere hoss—a reg'lar graven image—and bowed down and worshiped him. He didn't think nothin' was too good for him. He washed and brushed and curried him, and rubbed him down till he shone like a lady's satin dress; and he took pride in ridin' and drivin' him, 'cause it was what the doctor wouldn't let nobody else do but himself. You see, Tam wern't no lady's hoss. Miss Williams was 'afraid as death of him; and the parson he hed to git her a sort o' low-sperited crittur that she could drive herself. But he liked to drive Tam; and he liked to go round the country on his back, and a fine figure of a man he was on him, too. He didn't let nobody else back him or handle the reins but Cuff; and Cuff was dreffal set up about it, and he swelled and bragged about that ar hoss all round the country. Nobody couldn't put in a word 'bout any other hoss, without Cuff's feathers would be all up stiff as a tomturkey's tail; and that's how Cuff got the doctor into trouble.

"Ye see, there nat'lly was others that thought they'd got horses, and didn't want to be crowed over. There was Bill Atkins, out to the west parish, and Ike Sanders, that kep' a stable up to Pequot Holler: they was down a-lookin' at the parson's hoss, and a-bettin' on their'n, and a darin' Cuff to race with 'em.

"Wal, Cuff, he couldn't stan' it, and, when the doctor's back was turned, he'd be off on the sly, and they'd hev their race; and Tam he beat 'em all. Tam, ye see, boys, was a hoss that couldn't and wouldn't hev a hoss ahead of him—he jest wouldn't! Ef he dropped down dead in his tracks the next minit, he would be ahead; and he allers got ahead. And so his name got up, and fellers kep' comin' to try their horses; and Cuff'd take Tam out to race with fust one and then another till this 'ere got to be a reg'lar thing, and begun to be talked about.

"Folks sort o' wondered if the doctor knew: but Cuff was sly as a weasel, and allers had a story ready for every turn. Cuff was one of them fellers that could talk a bird off a bush—master hand he was to slick things over!

"There was folks as said they believed the doctor was knowin' to it, and that he felt a sort o' carnal pride sech as a minister oughtn't fer to hev, and so shet his eyes to what was a-goin' on. Aunt Sally Nickerson said she was sure on't. 'Twas all talked over down to old Miss Bummiger's funeral, and Aunt Sally she said the church ought to look into't. But everybody knew Aunt Sally: she was allers watchin' for folks' haltin's, and settin' on herself up to jedge her neighbors.

"Wal, I never believed nothin' agin Parson Williams: it was all Cuff's contrivances. But the fact was, the fellers all got their blood up, and there was hoss-racin' in all the parishes; and it got so they'd even race hosses a Sunday.

"Wal, of course they never got the doctor's hoss out a Sunday. Cuff wouldn'ta durst to do that, Lordy massy, no! He was allers there in church, settin' up in the doctor's clothes, rollin' up his eyes, and lookin' as pious as ef he never thought o' racin' hosses. He was an awful solemn-lookin' nigger in church, Cuff was.

"But there was a lot o' them fellers up to Pequot Holler— Bill Atkins, and Ike Sanders, and Tom Peters, and them Hokum boys— used to go out arter meetin' Sunday arternoon, and race hosses. Ye see, it was jest close to the State-line, and, if the s'lectmen was to come down on 'em, they could jest whip over the line, and they couldn't take 'em.

"Wal, it got to be a great scandal. The fellers talked about it up to the tavern; and the deacons and the tithingman, they took it up and went to Parson Williams about it; and the parson he told 'em jest to keep still, not let the fellers know that they was bein' watched, and next Sunday he and the tithingman and the constable, they'd ride over, and catch 'em in the very act.

"So next Sunday arternoon Parson Williams and Deacon Popkins and Ben Bradley (he was constable that year), they got on to their hosses, and rode over to Pequot Holler. The doctor's blood was up, and he meant to come down on 'em strong; for that was his way o' doin' in his parish. And they was in a sort o' day-o'-jedgment frame o' mind, and jogged along solemn as a hearse, till, come to rise the hill above the holler, they see three or four fellers with their hosses gittin' ready to race; and the parson says he, 'Let's come on quiet, and get behind these bushes, and we'll see what they're up to, and catch 'em in the act.'

"But the mischief on't was, that Ike Sanders see 'em comin', and he knowed Tam in a minit—Ike knowed Tam of old—and he jest tipped the wink to the rest. 'Wait, boys,' says he: 'let 'em git close up, and then I'll give the word, and the doctor's hoss will be racin' ahead like thunder.'

"Wal, so the doctor and his folks they drew up behind the bushes, and stood there innocent as could be, and saw 'em gittin' ready to start. Tam, he begun to snuffle and paw, but the doctor never mistrusted what he was up to till Ike sung out, 'Go it, boys!' and the hosses all started, when, sure as you live, boys! Tam give one fly, and was over the bushes, and in among 'em, goin' it like chain-lightnin' ahead of 'em all.

"Deacon Popkins and Ben Bradley jest stood and held their breath to see 'em all goin' it so like thunder; and the doctor, he was took so sudden it was all he could do to jest hold on anyway: so away he went, and trees and bushes and fences streaked by him like ribbins. His hat flew off behind him, and his wig arter, and got catched in a barberry-bush; but Lordy massy! he couldn't stop to think o' them. He jest leaned down, and caught Tam round the neck, and held on for dear life till they come to the stopping-place.

"Wal, Tam was ahead of them all, sure enough, and was snorting and snuffling as if he'd got the very old boy in him, and was up to racing some more on the spot.

"That 'ere Ike Sanders was the impudentest feller that ever you see, and he roared and rawhawed at the doctor. 'Good for you, parson!' says he. 'You beat us all holler,' says he. 'Takes a parson for that, don't it, boys?' he said. And then he and Ike and Tom, and the two Hokum boys, they jest roared, and danced round like wild critturs. Wal, now, only think on't, boys, what a situation that 'ere was for a minister—a man that had come out with the best of motives to put a stop to Sabbath-breakin'! There he was all rumpled up and dusty, and his wig hangin' in the bushes, and these 'ere ungodly fellers gettin' the laugh on him, and all acause o' that 'ere hoss. There's times, boys, when ministers must be tempted to swear, if there ain't preventin' grace, and this was one o' them times to Parson Williams. They say he got red in the face, and looked as if he should bust, but he didn't say nothin': he scorned to answer. The sons o' Zeruiah was too hard for him, and he let 'em hev their say. But when they'd got through, and Ben had brought him his hat and wig, and brushed and settled him ag'in, the parson he says, 'Well, boys, ye've had your say and your laugh; but I warn you now I won't have this thing goin' on here any more,' says he; 'so mind yourselves.'

"Wal, the boys see that the doctor's blood was up, and they rode off pretty quiet; and I believe they never raced no more in that spot.

"But there ain't no tellin' the talk this 'ere thing made. Folks will talk, you know; and there wer'n't a house in all Billriky, nor in the south parish nor center, where it wer'n't had over and discussed. There was the deacon, and Ben Bradley was there, to witness and show jest how the thing was, and that the doctor was jest in the way of his duty; but folks said it made a great scandal; that a minister hadn't no business to hev that kind o' hoss, and that he'd give the enemy occasion to speak reproachfully. It reely did seem as if Tam's sins was imputed to the doctor; and folks said he ought to sell Tam right away, and get a sober minister's hoss.

"But others said it was Cuff that had got Tam into bad ways; and they do say that Cuff had to catch it pretty lively when the doctor come to settle with him. Cuff thought his time had come, sure enough, and was so scairt that he turned blacker'n ever: he got enough to cure him o' hoss-racin' for one while. But Cuff got over it arter a while, and so did the doctor. Lordy massy! there ain't nothin' lasts forever! Wait long enough, and 'most every thing blows over. So it turned out about the doctor. There was a rumpus and a fuss, and folks talked and talked, and advised; everybody had their say: but the doctor kep' right straight on, and kep' his hoss all the same.

"The ministers, they took it up in the 'sociation; but, come to tell the story, it sot 'em all a-laughin', so they couldn't be very hard on the doctor.

"The doctor felt sort o' streaked at fust when they told the story on him; he didn't jest like it: but he got used to it, and finally, when he was twitted on't, he'd sort o' smile, and say, 'Anyway, Tam beat 'em: that's one comfort.'"

HOW I KILLED A BEAR

Charles Dudley Warner

So many conflicting accounts have appeared about my casual encounter with an Adirondack bear last summer, that in justice to the public, to myself and to the bear, it is necessary to make a plain statement of the facts. Besides, it is so seldom I have occasion to kill a bear, that the celebration of the exploit may be excused.

The encounter was unpremeditated on both sides. I was not hunting for a bear, and I have no reason to suppose that a bear was looking for me. The fact is, that we were both out blackberrying and met by chance—the usual way. There is among the Adirondack visitors always a great deal of conversation about bears—a general expression of the wish to see one in the woods, and much speculation as to how a person would act if he or she chanced to meet one. But bears are scarce and timid, and appear only to a favored few.

It was a warm day in August, just the sort of a day when an adventure of any kind seemed impossible. But it occurred to the housekeepers at our cottage—there were four of them—to send me to the clearing, on the mountain back of the house, to pick blackberries. It was, rather, a series of small clearings, running up into the forest, much overgrown with bushes and briers, and not unromantic. Cows pastured there, penetrating through the leafy passages from one opening to another, and browsing among the bushes. I was kindly furnished with a six-quart pail, and told not to be gone long.

Not from any predatory instinct, but to save appearances, I took a gun. It adds to the manly aspect of a person with a tin pail if he also carries a gun. It was possible I might start up a partridge; though how I was to hit him, if he started up instead of standing still, puzzled me. Many people use a shot-gun for partridges.

I prefer the rifle: it makes a clean job of death, and does not prematurely stuff the bird with globules of lead. The rifle was a Sharps, carrying a ball cartridge (ten to the pound)—an excellent weapon belonging to a friend of mine, who had intended, for a good many years back, to kill a deer with it. He could hit a tree with it—if the wind did not blow, and the atmosphere was just right, and the tree was not too far off—nearly every time. Of course, the tree must have some size. Needless to say that I was at that time no sportsman. Years ago I killed a robin under the most humiliating circumstances. The bird was in a low cherry-tree. I loaded a big shotgun pretty full, crept up under the tree, rested the gun on the fence, with the muzzle more than ten feet from the bird, shut both eyes and pulled the trigger. When I got up to see what had happened, the robin was scattered about under the tree in more than a thousand pieces, no one of which was big enough to enable a naturalist to decide from it to what species it belonged. This disgusted me with the life of a sportsman. I mention the incident to show, that although I went blackberrying armed, there was not much inequality between me and the bear.

In this blackberry-patch bears had been seen. The summer before, our colored cook, accompanied by a little girl of the vicinage, was picking berries there one day, when a bear came out of the woods and walked towards them. The girl took to her heels, and escaped. Aunt Chloe was paralyzed with terror. Instead of attempting to run, she sat down on the ground where she was standing, and began to weep and scream, giving herself up for lost. The bear was bewildered by this conduct. He approached and looked at her; he walked around and surveyed her. Probably he had never seen a colored person before, and did not know whether she would agree with him: at any rate, after watching her a few moments, he turned about and went into the forest. This is an authentic instance of the delicate consideration of a bear, and is much more remarkable than the forbearance towards the African slave of the well-known lion, because the bear had no thorn in his foot.

When I had climbed the hill, I set up my rifle against a tree, and began picking berries, lured on from bush to bush by the black gleam of fruit (that always promises more in the distance than it realizes when you reach it); penetrating farther and farther, through leaf-shaded cow-paths flecked with sunlight, into clearing after clearing. I could hear on all sides the tinkle of bells, the crack-ing of sticks, and the stamping of cattle that were taking refuge in the thicket from the flies. Occasionally, as I broke through a covert, I encountered a meek cow, who stared at me stupidly for a second, and then shambled off into the brush. I became accus-tomed to this dumb society, and picked on in silence, attributing all the wood-noises to the cattle, thinking nothing of any real bear. In point of fact, however, I was thinking all the time of a nice romantic bear, and, as I picked, was composing a story about a generous she-bear who had lost her cub, and who seized a small girl in this very wood, carried her tenderly off to a cave, and brought her up on bear's milk and honey. When the girl got big enough to run away, moved by her inherited instincts, she escaped, and came into the valley to her father's house (this part of the story was to be worked out, so that the child would know her father by some family resemblance, and have some language in which to address him), and told him where the bear lived. The father took his gun, and, guided by the unfeeling daughter, went into the woods and shot the bear, who never made any resistance, and only, when dying, turned reproachful eyes upon her murderer. The moral of the tale was to be, kindness to animals.

I was in the midst of this tale, when I happened to look some rods away to the other edge of the clearing, and there was a bear! He was standing on his hind-legs, and doing just what I was doing—picking blackberries. With one paw he bent down the bush, while with the other he clawed the berries into his mouth—green ones and all. To say that I was astonished is inside the mark. I suddenly discovered that I didn't want to see a bear, after all. At about the same moment the bear saw me, stopped eating berries, and regarded me with a glad surprise. It is all very well to imagine what you would do under such circumstances. Probably you wouldn't do it: I didn't. The bear dropped down on his forefeet, and came slowly towards me. Climbing a tree was of no use, with so good a climber in the rear. If I started to run, I had no doubt the bear would give chase; and although a bear cannot run down hill as fast as he can run uphill, yet I felt that he could get over this rough, brush-tangled ground faster than I could.

The bear was approaching. It suddenly occurred to me how I could divert his mind until I could fall back upon my military base.

My pail was nearly full of excellent berries—much better than the bear could pick himself. I put the pail on the ground, and slowly backed away from it, keeping my eye, as beast tamers do, on the bear. The ruse succeeded.

The bear came up to the berries, and stopped. Not accustomed to eat out of a pail, he tipped it over, and nosed about in the fruit, "gorming" (if there is such a word) it down, mixed with leaves and dirt, like a pig. The bear is a worse feeder than the pig. Whenever he disturbs a maple-sugar camp in the spring, he always upsets the buckets of syrup, and tramples round in the sticky sweets, wasting more than he eats. The bear's manners are thoroughly disagreeable.

As soon as my enemy's head was down, I started and ran. Somewhat out of breath, and shaky, I reached my faithful rifle. It was not a minute too soon. I heard the bear crashing through the brush after me. Enraged at my duplicity, he was now coming on with blood in his eye. I felt that the time of one of us was probably short. The rapidity of thought at such moments of peril is well known. I thought an octavo volume, had it illustrated and published, sold fifty thousand copies, and went to Europe on the proceeds, while that bear was loping across the clearing. As I was cocking the gun, I made a hasty and unsatisfactory review of my whole life. I noted that, even in such a compulsory review, it is almost impossible to think of any good thing you have done. The sins come out uncommonly strong.

I recollected a newspaper subscription I had delayed paying years and years ago, until both editor and newspaper were dead, and which now never could be paid to all eternity.

The bear was coming on.

I tried to remember what I had read about encounters with bears. I couldn't recall an instance in which a man had run away from a bear in the woods and escaped, although I recalled plenty where the bear had run from the man and got off. I tried to think what is the best way to kill a bear with a gun, when you are not near enough to club him with the stock. My first thought was to fire at his head; to plant the ball between his eyes: but this is a dangerous experiment. The bear's brain is very small; and, unless you hit that, the bear does not mind a bullet in his head; that is, not at the time. I remembered that the instant death of the bear would follow a bullet planted just back of his foreleg, and sent into his heart. This spot is also difficult to reach, unless the bear stands off, side towards you, like a target. I finally determined to fire at him generally.

The bear was coming on.

The contest seemed to me very different from anything at Creedmoor. 1 had carefully read the reports of the shooting there; but it was not easy to apply the experience I had thus acquired. I hesitated whether I had better fire lying on my stomach; or lying on my back, and resting the gun on my toes. But in neither position, I reflected, could I see the bear until he was upon me. The range was too short; and the bear wouldn't wait for me to examine the thermometer, and note the direction of the wind. Trial of the Creedmoor method, therefore, had to be abandoned; and I bitterly regretted that I had not read more accounts of off-hand shooting.

For the bear was coming on.

I tried to fix my last thoughts upon my family. As my family is small, this was not difficult. Dread of displeasing my wife, or hurting her feelings, was uppermost in my mind. What would be her anxiety as hour after hour passed on, and I did not return! What would the rest of the household think as the afternoon passed, and no blackberries came! What would be my wife's mortification when the news was brought that her husband had been eaten by a bear! I cannot imagine anything more ignominious than to have a husband eaten by a bear. And this was not my only anxiety. The mind at such times is not under control. With the gravest fears the most whimsical ideas will occur. I looked beyond the mourning friends, and thought what kind of an epitaph they would be compelled to put upon the stone. Something like this:

HERE LIE THE REMAINS
OF_____ _____,
EATEN BY A BEAR
Aug. 20, 1877.

It is a very unheroic and even disagreeable epitaph. That "eaten by a bear" is intolerable. It is grotesque. And then I thought what an inadequate language the English is for compact expression. It would not answer to put upon the stone simply "eaten," for that is indefinite, and requires explanation: it might mean eaten by a cannibal. This difficulty could not occur in the German, where *essen* signifies the act of feeding by a man, and *fressen* by a beast. How simple the thing would be in German!—

HIER LIEGT
HOCHWOHLGEBOREN
HERR_____ _____,
GEFRESSEN
Aug. 20, 1877.

That explains itself. The well-born one was eaten by a beast, and presumably by a bear—an animal that has a bad reputation since the days of Elisha.

The bear was coming on; he had, in fact, come on. I judged that he could see the whites of my eyes. All my subsequent reflections were confused. I raised the gun, covered the bear's breast with the sight, and let drive. Then I turned, and ran like a deer. I did not hear the bear pursuing. I looked back. The bear had stopped. He was lying down. I then remembered that the best thing to do after having fired your gun is to reload it. I slipped in a charge, keeping my eyes on the bear. He never stirred. I walked back suspiciously. There was a quiver in the hind-legs, but no other motion. Still, he might be shamming: bears often sham. To make sure, I approached, and put a ball into his head. He didn't mind it now; he minded nothing. Death had come to him with a merciful suddenness. He was calm in death. In order that he might remain so, I blew his brains out, and then started for home. I had killed a bear!

Notwithstanding my excitement, I managed to saunter into the house with an unconcerned air. There was a chorus of voices:

"Where are your blackberries?"

"Why were you gone so long?"

"Where's your pail?"

"I left the pail."

"Left the pail? What for?"

"A bear wanted it."

"Oh, nonsense!"

"Well, the last I saw of it a bear had it."

"Oh, come! You didn't really see a bear?"

"Yes, but I did really see a real bear."

"Did he run?"

"Yes; he ran after me."

"I don't believe a word of it! What did you do?"

"Oh! nothing particular—except kill the bear."

Cries of "Gammon!" "Don't believe it!" "Where's the bear?"

"If you want to see the bear, you must go up into the woods. I couldn't bring him down alone."

Having satisfied the household that something extraordinary had occurred, and excited the posthumous fear of some of them for my own safety, I went down into the valley to get help. The great bear-hunter, who keeps one of the summer boarding-houses, received my story with a smile of incredulity; and the incredulity spread to the other inhabitants and to the boarders, as soon as the story was known. However, as I insisted in all soberness, and offered to lead them to the bear, a party of forty or fifty people at last started off with me to bring the bear in. Nobody believed there was any bear in the case; but everybody who could get a gun carried one; and we went into the woods, armed with guns, pistols, pitchforks and sticks, against all contingencies or surprises—a crowd made up mostly of scoffers and jeerers.

But when I led the way to the fatal spot, and pointed out the bear, lying peacefully wrapped in his own skin, something like terror seized the boarders, and genuine excitement the natives. It was a no-mistake bear, by George! and the hero of the fight—well, I will not insist upon that. But what a procession that was, carrying the bear home! and what a congregation was speedily gathered in the valley to see the bear! Our best preacher up there never drew anything like it on Sunday.

And I must say that my particular friends, who were sportsmen, behaved very well on the whole. They didn't deny that it was a bear, although they said it was small for a bear. Mr. Deane, who is equally good with a rifle and a rod, admitted that it was a very fair shot. He is probably the best salmon-fisher in the United States, and he is an equally good hunter. I suppose there is no person in America who is more desirous to kill a moose than he. But he needlessly remarked, after he had examined the wound in the bear, that he had seen that kind of a shot made by a cow's horn.

This sort of talk affected me not. When I went to sleep that night, my last delicious thought was, "I've killed a bear!"

UNCLE REMUS AND THE WONDERFUL TAR-BABY STORY

Joel Chandler Harris

ONE EVENING RECENTLY, the lady whom Uncle Remus calls "Miss Sally" missed her little seven-year-old. Making search for him through the house and through the yard, she heard the sound of voices in the old man's cabin, and, looking through the window, saw the child sitting by Uncle Remus. His head rested against the old man's arm, and he was gazing with an expression of the most intense interest into the rough, weather-beaten face that beamed so kindly upon him. This is what "Miss Sally" heard:

"Bimeby, one day, arter Brer Fox bin doin' all dat he could fer ter ketch Brer Rabbit, en Brer Rabbit bin doin' all he could fer ter keep 'im fum it, Brer Fox say to hisse'f dat Uncle Remus, he'd put up a game on Brer Rabbit, en he ain't mo'n got de wuds out'n his mout twel Brer Rabbit come a lopin' up de big road, lookin' des ez plump en ez fat en ez sassy ez a Moggin hoss in a barley-patch.

"'Hol' on, dar, Brer Rabbit,' sez Brer Fox, sezee.

"'I ain't got time, Brer Fox,' sez Brer Rabbit, sezee, sorter mendin' his licks.

"'I wanter have some confab wid you, Brer Rabbit,' sez Brer Fox, sezee.

"'All right, Brer Fox; but you better holler fum whar you stan'. I'm monstus full er fleas dis mawnin',' sez Brer Rabbit, sezee.

"'I seed Brer B'ar yistiddy,' sez Brer Fox, sezee, "en he sorter rake me over de coals kaze you en me ain't make frens en live naberly; en I tole 'im dat I'd see you.'

"Den Brer Rabbit scratch one year wid his off hine-foot sorter jub'usly, en den he ups en sez, sezee:

"'All a settin', Brer Fox. Spose'n you drap roun' ter-morrer en take dinner wid me. We ain't got no great doin's at our house, but I speck de ole 'oman en de chilluns kin sorter scramble roun' en git up somp'n fer ter stay yo' stummuck.'

"'I'm 'gree'ble, Brer Rabbit,' sez Brer Fox, sezee.

"'Den I'll 'pen' on you,' sez Brer Rabbit, sezee.

"Nex' day, Mr. Rabbit an' Miss Rabbit got up soon, 'fo' day, en raided on a gyarden, like Miss Sally's out dar, en got some cabbiges, en some roas'n years, en some sparrer-grass, en dey fix up a smashin' dinner. Bimeby, one er de little Rabbits playin' out in de back-yard, come runnin' in, hollerin', 'Oh, ma! oh, ma! I seed Mr. Fox a comin'!' En den Brer Rabbit he tuck de chilluns by der years en make um set down; en den him en Miss Rabbit sorter dally roun' waitin' for Brer Fox. En dey keep on waitin', but no Brer Fox ain't come. Atter 'while Brer Rabbit goes to de do', easy like, en peep out, en dar, stickin' out fum behine de cornder, wuz de tip-een' er Brer Fox's tail. Den Brer Rabbit shot de do' en sot down, en put his paws behime his years en begin fer ter sing:

> "*De place wharbouts you spill de grease,*
> *Right dar youer boun' ter slide,*
> *An' whar you fine a bunch er hay,*
> *You'll sholy fine de hide.*

"Nex' day, Brer Fox sent word by Mr. Mink, en skuze hisse'f, kase he wuz too sick fer ter come, en he ax Brer Rabbit fer ter come en take dinner wid him, en Brer Rabbit say he wuz 'gree'ble.

"Bimeby, w'en de shadders wuz at der shortes', Brer Rabbit he sorter brush up en santer down ter Brer Fox's house, en w'en he got dar, he yer somebody groanin', en he look in de do' en dar he see Brer Fox settin' up in a rockin'-cheer all wrop up wid flannil, en he look mighty weak. Brer Rabbit look all 'roun', he did, but he ain't see no dinner. De dish-pan wuz settin' on de table, en close by wuz a kyarvin'-knife.

"'Look like you gwinter have chicken fer dinner, Brer Fox,' sez Brer Rabbit, sezee.

"'Yes, Brer Rabbit, deyer nice en fresh en tender,' sez Brer Fox, sezee.

"Den Brer Rabbit sorter pull his mustarsh, en say: 'You ain't got no calamus root, is you, Brer Fox? I done got so now dat I can't eat no chicken 'ceptin she's seasoned up wid calamus root.' En wid dat, Brer Rabbit lipt out er de do' and dodge 'mong de bushes, en sot dar watchin' fer Brer Fox; en he ain't watch long, nudder, kaze Brer Fox flung off de flannel en crope out er de house en got whar he could close in on Brer Rabbit, en bimeby Brer Rabbit holler out: 'Oh, Brer Fox! I'll des put yo' calamus root out yer on dish yer stump. Better come git it while it's fresh,' an' wid dat Brer Rabbit gallop off home. En Brer Fox ain't never kotch 'imyit, en w'at's mo', honey, he ain't gwineter."

"Didn't the fox *never* catch the rabbit, Uncle Remus?" asked the little boy the next evening.

"He come mighty nigh it, honey, sho's you bawn—Brer Fox did. One day, alter Brer Rabbit fool 'im wid dat calamus root, Brer Fox went ter wuk en got 'im some tar, en mix it wid some turken-time, en fix up a contrapshun wat he call a Tar-Baby, en he tuck dish yer Tar-Baby en he sot 'er in de big road, en den he lay off in de bushes fer ter see wat de news wuz gwineter be. En he didn't hatter wait long, nudder, kaze bimeby here come Brer Rabbit pacin' down de road—lippity-clippity, clippitylippity—dez ez sassy ez a jay-bird. Brer Fox, he lay low. Brer Rabbit come prancin' long twel he spy de Tar-Baby, en den he fotch up on his behine legs like he was 'stonished. De Tar-Baby, she sot dar, she did, en Brer Fox, he lay low.

"'Mawnin'!' sez Brer Rabbit, sezee—'nice wedder dis mawnin',' sezee.

"Tar-Baby ain't sayin' nuthin', en Brer Fox, he lay low.

"'How duz yo' sym'tums seem ter segashuate?' sez Brer Rabbit, sezee.

"Brer Fox, he wink his eye slow, en lay low, en de Tar-Baby, she ain't sayin' nuthin'.

"'How you come on, den? Is you deaf?' sez Brer Rabbit, sezee. 'Kaze if you is, I kin holler louder,' sezee.

"Tar-Baby stay still, en Brer Fox, he lay low.

"'Youer stuck up, dat's what you is,' says Brer Rabbit, sezee, 'and I'm gwineter kyore you, dat's w'at I'm a gwineter do,' sezee.

"Brer Fox, he sorter chuckle in his stummock, he did, but Tar-Baby aint' sayin' nuthin'.

"'I'm gwineter larn you howter talk ter 'specttubble fokes ef hit's de las' ack,' sez Brer Rabbit, sezee. 'Ef you don't take off dat hat en tell me howdy, I'm gwineter bus' you wide open,' sezee.

"Tar-Baby stay still, en Brer Fox, he lay low.

"Brer Rabbit keep on axin' 'im, en de Tar-Baby, she keep on sayin' nuthin', twel present'y Brer Rabbit draw back wid his fis', he did, en blip he tuck 'er side 'er de head. Right dar's whar he broke his merlasses jug. His fis' stuck, en he can't pull loose. De tar hilt 'im. But Tar-Baby, she stay still, en Brer Fox, he lay low.

"'Ef you don't lemme loose, I'll knock you agin,' sez Brer Rabbit, sezee, en wid dat he fotch 'er a wipe wid de udder han', en dat stuck. Tar-Baby, she ain't sayin' nuthin', en Brer Fox, he lay low.

"'Tu'n me loose, fo' I kick de natal stuffin' outen you,' sez Brer Rabbit, sezee, but de Tar-Baby, she ain't sayin' nuthin'. She des hilt on, en den Brer Rabbit lose de use er his feet in de same way. Brer Fox, he lay low. Den Brer Rabbit squall out dat ef de Tar-Baby don't tu'n 'im loose he butt 'er cranksided. En den he butted, en his head got stuck. Den Brer Fox, he sa'ntered fort', lookin' des ez innercent ez wunner yo' mammy's mockin'-birds.

"'Howdy, Brer Rabbit,' sez Brer Fox, sezee. 'You look sorter stuck up dis mawnin',' sezee, en den he rolled on de groun', en laft en laft twel he couldn't laff no mo'. 'I speck you'll take dinner wid me dis time, Brer Rabbit. I done laid in some calamus root, en I ain't gwineter take no skuse,' sez Brer Fox, sezee."

Here Uncle Remus paused, and drew a two-pound yam out of the ashes.

"Did the fox eat the rabbit?" asked the little boy to whom the story had been told.

"Dat's all de fur de tale goes," replied the old man. "He mout, en den agin he mountent. Some say Jedge B'ar come 'long en loosed 'im—some say he didn't. I hear Miss Sally callin'. You better run 'long."

"Uncle Remus," said the little boy one evening, when he had found the old man with little or nothing to do, "did the fox kill and eat the rabbit when he caught him with the Tar-Baby?"

"Law, honey, ain't I tell you 'bout dat?" replied the old darkey, chuckling slyly. "I 'clar ter grashus I ought er tole you dat, but ole man Nod wuz ridin' on my eyeleds 'twel a leetle mo'n I'd a dis'member'd my own name, en den on to dat here come yo' mammy hollerin' after you.

"Wat I tell you w'en I fus' begin? I tole you Brer Rabbit wuz a monstus soon beas'; leas'ways- dat's w'at I laid out fer ter tell you.

Well, den, honey, don't you go en make no udder kalkalashuns, kaze in dem days Brer Rabbit en his fambly wuz at de head er de gang w'en enny racket wuz on han', en dar dey stayed. 'Fo' you begins fer ter wipe yo' eyes 'bout Brer Rabbit, you wait en see whar'bouts Brer Rabbit gwineter fetch up at. But dat's needer yer ner dar.

"Wen Brer Fox fine Brer Rabbit mixt up wid de Tar-Baby, he feel mighty good, en he roll on de groun' en laff. Bimeby he up'n say, sezee:

"'Well, I speck I got you dis time, Brer Rabbit,' sezee; 'maybe I ain't, but I speck I is. You been runnin' roun' here sassin' atter me a mighty long time, but I speck you done come ter de een' er de row. You bin cuttin' up yo' capers en bouncin' 'roun' in dis naberhood ontwel you come ter b'leeve yo'se'f de boss er de whole gang. En den youer allers some'rs whar you got no bizness,' sez Brer Fox, sezee. 'Who ax you fer ter come en strike up a 'quaintence wid dish yer Tar-Baby? En who stuck you up dar whar you iz? Nobody in de roun' worril. You des tuck en jam yo'se'f on dat Tar-Baby widout waitin' fer enny invite,' sez Brer Fox, sezee, 'en dar you is, en dar you'll stay twel I fixes up a bresh-pile and fires her up, kaze I'm gwineter bobbycue you dis day, sho,' sez Brer Fox, sezee.

"Den Brer Rabbit talk mighty 'umble.

"'I don't keer w'at you do wid me, Brer Fox,' sezee, 'so you don't fling me in dat brier-patch. Roas' me, Brer Fox,' sezee, 'but don't fling me in dat brier-patch,' sezee.

"'Hit's so much trouble fer ter kindle a fier,' sez Brer Fox, sezee, 'dat I speck I'll hatter hang you,' sezee.

"'Hang me des ez high as you please, Brer Fox,' sez Brer Rabbit, sezee, 'but do fer de Lord's sake don't fling me in dat brier-patch,' sezee.

"'I ain't got no string,' sez Brer Fox, sezee, 'en now I speck I'll hatter drown you,' sezee.

"'Drown me des ez deep ez you please, Brer Fox,' sez Brer Rabbit, sezee, 'but do don't fling me in dat brier-patch,' sezee.

"'Dey ain't no water nigh,' sez Brer Fox, sezee, 'en now I speck I'll hatter skin you,' sezee.

"'Skin me, Brer Fox,' sez Brer Rabbit, sezee, 'snatch out my eyeballs, tar out my years by de roots, en cut off my legs,' sezee, 'but do please, Brer Fox, don't fling me in dat brier-patch,' sezee.

"Co'se Brer Fox wanter hurt Brer Rabbit bad ez he kin, so he cotch 'im by de bchime legs en slung 'im right in de middle er de brier-patch. Dar wuz a considerbul flutter whar Brer Rabbit struck de bushes, en Brer Fox sorter hang 'roun' fer ter see w'at wuz gwineter happen. Bimeby he hear somebody call 'im, en way up de hill he see Brer Rabbit settin' cross-legged on a chinkapin log koamin' de pitch outen his har wid a chip. Den Brer Fox know dat he bin swop off mighty bad. Brer Rabbit wuz bleedzed fer ter fling back some er his sass, en he holler out:

"'Bred en bawn in a brier-patch, Brer Fox—bred en bawn in a brier-patch!' en wid dat he skip out des ez lively ez a cricket in de embers."

HIS PA GETS MAD!

George W. Peck

"I WAS DOWN to the drug store this morning and saw your Ma buying a lot of court-plaster, enough to make a shirt I should think. What's she doing with so much court-plaster?" asked the grocery man of the bad boy, as he came in and pulled off his boots by the stove and emptied out a lot of snow that had collected as he walked through a drift, which melted and made a bad smell.

"O, I guess she was going to patch Pa up so he will hold water. Pa's temper got him into the worst muss you ever see, last night. If that museum was here now they would hire Pa and exhibit him as the tattooed man. I tell you, I have got too old to be mauled as though I was a kid, and any man who attacks me from this out, wants to have his peace made with the insurance companies, and know that his calling and election is sure, because I am a bad man and don't you forget it." And the boy pulled on his boots and looked so cross and desperate that the grocer-man asked him if he wouldn't try a little new cider.

"Good heavens!" said the grocery man, as the boy swallowed the cider, and his face resumed its natural look, and the piratical frown disappeared with the cider. "You have not stabbed your father have you? I have feared that one thing would bring on another, with you, and that you would yet be hung."

"Naw, I haven't stabbed him. It was another cat that stabbed him. You see, Pa wants me to do all the work around the house. The other day he bought a load of kindling wood, and told me to carry it into the basement. I had not been educated up to kindling wood, and I didn't do it. When supper time came, and Pa found that I had not carried in the kindling wood, he had a hot box, and told me if that wood was not in when he came back from the lodge, that he would warm my jacket. Well, I tried to hire someone to carry it in, and got a man to promise to come in the morning and carry it in and take his pay in groceries, and I was going to buy the groceries here and have them charged to Pa. But that wouldn't help me out that night. I knew when Pa came home he would search for me. So I slept in the back hall on a cot. But I didn't want Pa to have all his trouble for nothing, so I borrowed an old torn cat that my chum's old maid aunt owns, and put the cat in my bed. I thought if Pa came into my room after me, and found that by his unkindness I had changed to a torn cat, he would be sorry. That is the biggest cat you ever see, and the worst fighter in our ward. It isn't afraid of anything, and can whip a New Foundland dog quicker than you could put sand in a barrel of sugar.

"Well, about eleven o'clock I heard Pa tumble over the kindling wood, and I knew by the remark he made as the wood slid around under him, that there was going to be a cat fight real quick. He came up to Ma's room, and sounded Ma as to whether Hennery had retired to his virtuous couch. Pa is awful sarcastic when he tries to be. I could hear him take off his clothes, and hear him say, as he picked up a trunk strap, 'I guess I will go up to his room and watch the smile on his face, as he dreams of angels. I yearn to press him to my aching bosom.' I thought to myself, mebbe you won't yearn so much directly. He come up stairs, and I could hear him breathing hard. I looked around the corner and could see he just had on his shirt and pants, and his suspenders were hanging down, and his bald head shown like a calcium light just before it explodes.

"Pa went into my room, and up to the bed, and I could hear him say, 'Come out here and bring in that kindling wood or I will start a fire on your base burner with this strap.' And then there was a yowling such as I never heard before, and Pa said, 'Helen Blazes,' and the furniture in my room began to fall around and break. O, *my*! I think Pa took the torn cat right by the neck, the way he does me, and that left the cat's feet free to get in their work. By the way the cat squawled as though it was being choked I know Pa had him by the neck. I suppose the cat thought Pa was a whole flock of New Foundland dogs, and the cat had a record on dogs, and it kicked awful. Pa's shirt was no protection at all in a cat fight, and the cat just walked all around Pa's stomach, and Pa yelled 'police,' and 'fire,' and 'turn on the hose,' and he called Ma, and the cat yowled. If Pa had had presence of mind enough to have dropped the cat, or rolled it up in the mattrass, it would have been all right, but a man always gets rattled in time of danger, and he held on to the cat and started down stairs yelling murder, and he met Ma coming up.

"I guess Ma's night cap or something frightened the cat more, cause he stabbed Ma on the night-shirt with one hind foot, and Ma said 'mercy on us,' and she went back, and Pa stumbled on a hand-sled that was on the stairs, and they all fell down, and the cat got away and went down in the coal bin and yowled all night. Pa and Ma went into their room, and I guess they annointed themselves with vasaline, and Pond's extract, and I went and got into my bed, cause it was cold out in the hall, and the cat had warmed my bed as well as it had warmed Pa. It was all I could do to go to sleep, with Pa and Ma talking all night, and this morning I came down the back stairs, and haven't been to breakfast, cause I don't want to see Pa when he is vexed. You let the man that carries in the kindling wood have six shillings worth of groceries, and charge them to Pa. I have passed the kindling wood period in a boy's life, and have arrived at the coal period. I will carry in coal, but I draw the line at kindling wood."

"Well, you are a cruel, bad boy," said the grocery man, as he went to the book and charged the six shillings.

"O, I don't know. I think Pa is cruel. A man who will take a poor kitty by the neck, that hasn't done any harm, and tries to chastise the poor thing with a trunk strap, ought to be looked after by the humane society. And if it is cruel to take a cat by the neck, how much more cruel is it to take a boy by the neck, that had diphtheria only a few years ago, and whose throat is tender? Say, I guess I will accept your invitation to take breakfast with you," and the boy cut off a piece of bologna and helped himself to the crackers, and while the grocery man was out shoveling off the snow from the sidewalk, the boy filled his pockets with raisins and loaf sugar, and then went out to watch the man carry in his kindling wood.

THE NECKLACE

Guy de Maupassant

SHE WAS ONE of those pretty, charming young ladies, born, as if through an error of destiny, into a family of clerks. She had no dowry, no hopes, no means of becoming known, appreciated, loved, and married by a man either rich or distinguished; and she allowed herself to marry a petty clerk in the office of the Board of Education.

She was simple, not being able to adorn herself; but she was unhappy, as one out of her class; for women belong to no caste, no race; their grace, their beauty, and their charm serving them in the place of birth and family. Their inborn finesse, their instinctive elegance, their suppleness of wit are their only aristocracy, making some daughters of the people the equal of great ladies.

She suffered incessantly, feeling herself born for all delicacies and luxuries. She suffered from the poverty of her apartment, the shabby walls, the worn chairs, and the faded stuffs. All these things, which another woman of her station would not have noticed, tortured and angered her. The sight of the little Breton, who made this humble home, awoke in her sad regrets and desperate dreams. She thought of quiet antechambers, with their Oriental hangings, lighted by high, bronze torches, and of the two great footmen in short trousers who sleep in the large armchairs, made sleepy by the heavy air from the heating apparatus. She thought of large drawing-rooms, hung in old silks, of graceful pieces of furniture carrying bric-a-brac of inestimable value, and of the little perfumed coquettish apartments, made for five o'clock chats with most intimate friends, men known and sought after, whose attention all women envied and desired.

When she seated herself for dinner, before the round table where the tablecloth had been used three days, opposite her husband who uncovered the tureen with a delighted air, saying: "Oh! the good potpie! I know nothing better than that—" she would think of the elegant dinners, of the shining silver, of the tapestries peopling the walls with ancient personages and rare birds in the midst of fairy forests; she thought of the exquisite food served on marvelous dishes, of the whispered gallantries, listened to with the smile of the sphinx, while eating the rose-colored flesh of the trout or a chicken's wing.

She had neither frocks nor jewels, nothing. And she loved only those things. She felt that she was made for them. She had such a desire to please, to be sought after, to be clever, and courted.

She had a rich friend, a schoolmate at the convent, whom she did not like to visit, she suffered so much when she returned. And she wept for whole days from chagrin, from regret, from despair, and disappointment.

* * *

One evening her husband returned elated bearing in his hand a large envelope.

"Here," he said, "here is something for you."

She quickly tore open the wrapper and drew out a printed card on which were inscribed these words:

> "The Minister of Public Instruction and Madame George Ramponneau ask the honor of Mr. and Mrs. Loisel's company Monday evening, January 18, at the Minister's residence."

Instead of being delighted, as her husband had hoped, she threw the invitation spitefully upon the table murmuring:

"What do you suppose I want with that?"

"But, my dearie, I thought it would make you happy. You never go out, and this is an occasion, and a fine one! I had a great deal of trouble to get it. Everybody wishes one, and it is very select; not many are given to employees. You will see the whole official world there."

She looked at him with an irritated eye and declared impatiently:

"What do you suppose I have to wear to such a thing as that?"

He had not thought of that; he stammered:

"Why, the dress you wear when we go to the theater. It seems very pretty to me—"

He was silent, stupefied, in dismay, at the sight of his wife weeping. Two great tears fell slowly from the corners of her eyes toward the corners of her mouth; he stammered:

"What is the matter? What is the matter?"

By a violent effort, she had controlled her vexation and responded in a calm voice, wiping her moist cheeks:

"Nothing. Only I have no dress and consequently I cannot go to this affair. Give your card to some colleague whose wife is better fitted out than I."

He was grieved, but answered:

"Let us see, Matilda. How much would a suitable costume cost, something that would serve for other occasions, something very simple?"

She reflected for some seconds, making estimates and thinking of a sum that she could ask for without bringing with it an immediate refusal and a frightened exclamation from the economical clerk.

Finally she said, in a hesitating voice:

"I cannot tell exactly, but it seems to me that four hundred francs ought to cover it."

He turned a little pale, for he had saved just this sum to buy a gun that he might be able to join some hunting parties the next summer, on the plains at Nanterre, with some friends who went to shoot larks up there on Sunday. Nevertheless, he answered:

"Very well. I will give you four hundred francs. But try to have a pretty dress."

★ ★ ★

The day of the ball approached and Mme. Loisel seemed sad, disturbed, anxious. Nevertheless, her dress was nearly ready. Her husband said to her one evening:

"What is the matter with you? You have acted strangely for two or three days."

And she responded: "I am vexed not to have a jewel, not one stone, nothing to adorn myself with. I shall have such a poverty-laden look. I would prefer not to go to this party."

He replied: "You can wear some natural flowers. At this season they look very *chic*. For ten francs you can have two or three magnificent roses."

She was not convinced. "No," she replied, "there is nothing more humiliating than to have a shabby air in the midst of rich women."

Then her husband cried out: "How stupid we are! Go and find your friend Mrs. Forestier and ask her to lend you her jewels. You are well enough acquainted with her to do this."

She uttered a cry of joy: "It is true!" she said. "I had not thought of that."

The next day she took herself to her friend's house and related her story of distress. Mrs. Forestier went to her closet with the glass doors, took out a large jewel-case, brought it, opened it, and said: "Choose, my dear."

She saw at first some bracelets, then a collar of pearls, then a Venetian cross of gold and jewels and of admirable workmanship. She tried the jewels before the glass, hesitated, but could neither decide to take them nor leave them. Then she asked:

"Have you nothing more?"

"Why, yes. Look for yourself. I do not know what will please you."

Suddenly she discovered, in a black satin box, a superb necklace of diamonds, and her heart beat fast with an immoderate desire. Her hands trembled as she took them up. She placed them about her throat against her dress, and remained in ecstasy before them. Then she asked, in a hesitating voice, full of anxiety:

"Could you lend me this? Only this?"

"Why, yes, certainly."

She fell upon the neck of her friend, embraced her with passion, then went away with her treasure.

★ ★ ★

The day of the ball arrived. Mme. Loisel was a great success. She was the prettiest of all, elegant, gracious, smiling, and full of joy. All the men noticed her, asked her name, and wanted to be presented. All the members of the Cabinet wished to waltz with her. The Minister of Education paid her some attention.

She danced with enthusiasm, with passion, intoxicated with pleasure, thinking of nothing, in the triumph of her beauty, in the glory of her success, in a kind of cloud of happiness that came of all this homage, and all this admiration, of all these awakened desires, and this victory so complete and sweet to the heart of woman.

She went home toward four o'clock in the morning. Her husband had been half asleep in one of the little salons since midnight, with three other gentlemen whose wives were enjoying themselves very much.

He threw around her shoulders the wraps they had carried for the coming home, modest garments of everyday wear, whose poverty clashed with the elegance of the ball costume. She felt this and wished to hurry away in order not to be noticed by the other women who were wrapping themselves in rich furs.

Loisel retained her: "Wait," said he. "You will catch cold out there. I am going to call a cab."

But she would not listen and descended the steps rapidly. When they were in the street, they found no carriage; and they began to seek for one, hailing the coachmen whom they saw at a distance.

They walked along toward the Seine, hopeless and shivering. Finally they found on the quay one of those old, nocturnal *coupés* that one sees in Paris after nightfall, as if they were ashamed of their misery by day.

It took them as far as their door in Martyr street, and they went wearily up to their apartment. It was all over for her. And on his part, he remembered that he would have to be at the office by ten o'clock.

She removed the wraps from her shoulders before the glass, for a final view of herself in her glory. Suddenly she uttered a cry. Her necklace was not around her neck.

Her husband, already half undressed, asked: "What is the matter?"

She turned toward him excitedly:

"I have—I have—I no longer have Mrs. Forestier's necklace."

He arose in dismay: "What! How is that? It is not possible."

And they looked in the folds in the dress, in the folds of the mantle, in the pockets, everywhere. They could not find it.

He asked: "You are sure you still had it when we left the house?"

"Yes, I felt it in the vestibule as we came out."

"But if you had lost it in the street, we should have heard it fall. It must be in the cab."

"Yes. It is probable. Did you take the number?"

"No. And you, did you notice what it was?"

"No."

They looked at each other utterly cast down. Finally, Loisel dressed himself again.

"I am going," said he, "over the track where we went on foot, to see if I can find it."

And he went. She remained in her evening gown, not having the force to go to bed, stretched upon a chair, without ambition or thoughts.

Toward seven o'clock her husband returned. He had found nothing.

He went to the police and to the cab offices, and put an advertisement in the newspapers, offering a reward; he did everything that afforded them a suspicion of hope.

She waited all day in a state of bewilderment before this frightful disaster. Loisel returned at evening with his face harrowed and pale; and had discovered nothing.

"It will be necessary," said he, "to write to your friend that you have broken the clasp of the necklace and that you will have it repaired. That will give us time to turn around."

She wrote as he dictated.

★ ★ ★

At the end of a week, they had lost all hope. And Loisel, older by five years, declared:

"We must take measures to replace this jewel."

The next day they took the box which had inclosed it, to the jeweler whose name was on the inside. He consulted his books:

"It is not I, Madame," said he, "who sold this necklace; I only furnished the casket."

Then they went from jeweler to jeweler seeking a necklace like the other one, consulting their memories, and ill, both of them, with chagrin and anxiety.

In a shop of the Palais-Royal, they found a chaplet of diamonds which seemed to them exactly like the one they had lost. It was valued at forty thousand francs. They could get it for thirty-six thousand.

They begged the jeweler not to sell it for three days. And they made an arrangement by which they might return it for thirty-four thousand francs if they found the other one before the end of February.

Loisel possessed eighteen thousand francs which his father had left him. He borrowed the rest.

He borrowed it, asking for a thousand francs of one, five hundred of another, five louis of this one, and three louis of that one. He gave notes, made ruinous promises, took money of usurers and the whole race of lenders. He compromised his whole existence, in fact, risked his signature, without even knowing whether he could make it good or not, and, harassed by anxiety for the future, by the black misery which surrounded him, and by the prospect of all physical privations and moral torture, he went to get the new necklace, depositing on the merchant's counter thirty-six thousand francs.

When Mrs. Loisel took back the jewels to Mrs. Forestier, the latter said to her in a frigid tone:

"You should have returned them to me sooner, for I might have needed them."

She did open the jewel-box as her friend feared she would. If she should perceive the substitution, what would she think? What should she say? Would she take her for a robber?

★ ★ ★

Mrs. Loisel now knew the horrible life of necessity. She did her part, however, completely, heroically. It was necessary to pay this frightful debt. She would pay it. They sent away the maid; they changed their lodgings; they rented some rooms under a mansard roof.

She learned the heavy cares of a household, the odious work of a kitchen. She washed the dishes, using her rosy nails upon the greasy pots and the bottoms of the stewpans. She washed the soiled linen, the chemises and dishcloths, which she hung on the line to dry; she took down the refuse to the street each morning and brought up the water, stopping at each landing to breathe. And, clothed like a woman of the people, she went to the grocers, the butcher's, and the fruiterer's, with her basket on her arm, shopping, haggling to the last sou her miserable money.

Every month it was necessary to renew some notes, thus obtaining time, and to pay others.

The husband worked evenings, putting the books of some merchants in order, and nights he often did copying at five sous a page.

And this life lasted for ten years.

At the end of ten years, they had restored all, all, with interest of the usurer, and accumulated interest besides.

Mrs. Loisel seemed old now. She had become a strong, hard woman, the crude woman of the poor household. Her hair badly dressed, her skirts awry, her hands red, she spoke in a loud tone, and washed the floors in large pails of water. But sometimes, when her husband was at the office, she would seat herself before the window and think of that evening party of former times, of that ball where she was so beautiful and so flattered.

How could it have been if she had not lost that necklace? Who knows? Who knows? How singular is life, and how full of changes! How small a thing will ruin or save one!

★ ★ ★

One Sunday, as she was taking a walk in the Champs-Elysées to rid herself of the cares of the week, she suddenly perceived a woman walking with a child. It was Mrs. Forestier, still young, still pretty, still attractive. Mrs. Loisel was affected. Should she speak to her? Yes, certainly. And now that she had paid, she would tell her all. Why not?

She approached her. "Good morning, Jeanne."

Her friend did not recognize her and was astonished to be so familiarly addressed by this common personage. She stammered:

"But, Madame—I do not know—You must be mistaken—"

"No, I am Matilda Loisel."

Her friend uttered a cry of astonishment: "Oh! my poor Matilda! How you have changed—"

"Yes, I have had some hard days since I saw you; and some miserable ones—and all because of you—"

"Because of me? How is that?"

"You recall the diamond necklace that you loaned me to wear to the Commissioner's ball?"

"Yes, very well."

"Well, I lost it."

"How is that, since you returned it to me?"

"I returned another to you exactly like it. And it has taken us ten years to pay for it. You can understand that it was not easy for us who have nothing. But it is finished and I am decently content."

Madame Forestier stopped short. She said:

"You say that you bought a diamond necklace to replace mine?"

"Yes. You did not perceive it then? They were just alike."

And she smiled with a proud and simple joy. Madame Forestier was touched and took both her hands as she replied:

"Oh! my poor Matilda! Mine were false. They were not worth over five hundred francs!"

A WHITE HERON

Sarah Orne Jewett

I

THE WOODS WERE already filled with shadows one June evening, just before eight o'clock, though a bright sunset still glimmered faintly among the trunks of the trees. A little girl was driving home her cow, a plodding, dilatory, provoking creature in her behavior, but a valued companion for all that. They were going away from whatever light there was, and striking deep into the woods, but their feet were familiar with the path, and it was no matter whether their eyes could see it or not.

There was hardly a night the summer through when the old cow could be found waiting at the pasture bars; on the contrary, it was her greatest pleasure to hide herself away among the huckleberry bushes, and though she wore a loud bell she had made the discovery that if one stood perfectly still it would not ring. So Sylvia had to hunt for her until she found her, and call Co'! Co'! with never an answering Moo, until her childish patience was quite spent. If the creature had not given good milk and plenty of it, the case would have seemed very different to her owners. Besides, Sylvia had all the time there was, and very little use to make of it. Sometimes in pleasant weather it was a consolation to look upon the cow's pranks as an intelligent attempt to play hide and seek, and as the child had no playmates she lent herself to this amusement with a good deal of zest. Though this chase had been so long that the wary animal herself had given an unusual signal of her whereabouts, Sylvia had only laughed when she came upon Mistress Moolly at the swampside, and urged her affectionately homeward with a twig of birch leaves. The old cow was not inclined to wander farther, she even turned in the right direction for once as they left the pasture, and stepped along the road at a good pace. She was quite ready to be milked now, and seldom stopped to browse. Sylvia wondered what her grandmother would say because they were so late. It was a great while since she had left home at half-past five o'clock, but everybody knew the difficulty of making this errand a short one. Mrs. Tilley had chased the hornéd torment too many summer evenings herself to blame any one else for lingering, and was only thankful as she waited that she had Sylvia, nowadays, to give such valuable assistance. The good woman suspected that Sylvia loitered occasionally on her own account; there never was such a child for straying about out-of-doors since the world was made! Everybody said that it was a good change for a little maid who had tried to grow for eight years in a crowded manufacturing town, but, as for Sylvia herself, it seemed as if she never had been alive at all before she came to live at the farm. She thought often with wistful compassion of a wretched geranium that belonged to a town neighbor.

"'Afraid of folks,'" old Mrs. Tilley said to herself, with a smile, after she had made the unlikely choice of Sylvia from her daughter's houseful of children, and was returning to the farm. "'Afraid of folks,' they said! I guess she won't be troubled no great with 'em up to the old place!" When they reached the door of the lonely house and stopped to unlock it, and the cat came to purr loudly, and rub against them, a deserted pussy, indeed, but fat with young robins, Sylvia whispered that this was a beautiful place to live in, and she never should wish to go home.

The companions followed the shady woodroad, the cow taking slow steps and the child very fast ones. The cow stopped long at the brook to drink, as if the pasture were not half a swamp, and Sylvia stood still and waited, letting her bare feet cool themselves in the shoal water, while the great twilight moths struck softly against her. She waded on through the brook as the cow moved away, and listened to the thrushes with a heart that beat fast with pleasure. There was a stirring in the great boughs overhead. They were full of little birds and beasts that seemed to be wide awake, and going about their world, or else saying good-night to each other in sleepy twitters. Sylvia herself felt sleepy as she walked along. However, it was not much farther to the house, and the air was soft and sweet. She was not often in the woods so late as this, and it made her feel as if she were a part of the gray shadows and the moving leaves. She was just thinking how long it seemed since she first came to the farm a year ago, and wondering if everything went on in the noisy town just the same as when she was there; the thought of the great red-faced boy who used to chase and frighten her made her hurry along the path to escape from the shadow of the trees.

Suddenly this little woods-girl is horror-stricken to hear a clear whistle not very far away. Not a bird's-whistle, which would have a sort of friendliness, but a boy's whistle, determined, and somewhat aggressive. Sylvia left the cow to whatever sad fate might await her, and stepped discreetly aside into the bushes, but she was just too late. The enemy had discovered her, and called out in a very cheerful and persuasive tone, "Halloa, little girl, how far is it to the road?" and trembling Sylvia answered almost inaudibly, "A good ways."

She did not dare to look boldly at the tall young man, who carried a gun over his shoulder, but she came out of her bush and again followed the cow, while he walked alongside.

"I have been hunting for some birds," the stranger said kindly, "and I have lost my way, and need a friend very much. Don't be afraid," he added gallantly. "Speak up and tell me what your name is, and whether you think I can spend the night at your house, and go out gunning early in the morning."

Sylvia was more alarmed than before. Would not her grandmother consider her much to blame? But who could have foreseen such an accident as this? It did not seem to be her fault, and she hung her head as if the stem of it were broken, but managed to answer "Sylvy," with much effort when her companion again asked her name.

Mrs. Tilley was standing in the doorway when the trio came into view. The cow gave a loud moo by way of explanation.

"Yes, you'd better speak up for yourself, you old trial! Where'd she tucked herself away this time, Sylvy?" But Sylvia kept an awed silence; she knew by instinct that her grandmother did not comprehend the gravity of the situation. She must be mistaking the stranger for one of the farmer-lads of the region.

The young man stood his gun beside the door, and dropped a lumpy game-bag beside it; then he bade Mrs. Tilley good-evening, and repeated his wayfarer's story, and asked if he could have a night's lodging.

"Put me anywhere you like," he said. "I must be off early in the morning, before day; but I am very hungry, indeed. You can give me some milk at any rate, that's plain."

"Dear sakes, yes," responded the hostess, whose long slumbering hospitality seemed to be easily awakened. "You might fare better if you went out to the main road a mile or so, but you're welcome to what we've got. I'll milk right off, and you make yourself at home. You can sleep on husks or feathers," she proffered graciously. "I raised them all myself. There's good pasturing for geese just below here towards the ma'sh. Now step round and set a plate for the gentleman, Sylvy!" And Sylvia promptly stepped. She was glad to have something to do, and she was hungry herself.

It was a surprise to find so clean and comfortable a little dwelling in this New England wilderness. The young man had known the horrors of its most primitive housekeeping, and the dreary squalor of that level of society which does not rebel at the companionship of hens. This was the best thrift of an old-fashioned farmstead, though on such a small scale that it seemed like a hermitage. He listened eagerly to the old woman's quaint talk, he watched Sylvia's pale face and shining gray eyes with ever growing enthusiasm, and insisted that this was the best supper he had eaten for a month, and afterward the new-made friends sat down in the door-way together while the moon came up.

Soon it would be berry-time, and Sylvia was a great help at picking. The cow was a good milker, though a plaguy thing to keep track of, the hostess gossiped frankly, adding presently that she had buried four children, so Sylvia's mother, and a son (who might be dead) in California were all the children she had left. "Dan, my boy, was a great hand to go gunning," she explained sadly. "I never wanted for pa'tridges or gray squer'ls while he was to home. He's been a great wand'rer, I expect, and he's no hand to write letters. There, I don't blame him, I'd ha' seen the world myself if it had been so I could."

"Sylvy takes after him," the grandmother continued affectionately, after a minute's pause. "There ain't a foot o' ground she don't know her way over, and the wild creatur's counts her one o' themselves. Squer'ls she'll tame to come an' feed right out o' her hands, and all sorts o' birds. Last winter she got the jaybirds to bangeing[1]

---

[1] *bangeing* regional term meaning lounging around, loafing.

here, and I believe she'd 'a' scanted herself of her own meals to
have plenty to throw out amongst 'em, if I hadn't kep' watch.
Anything but crows, I tell her, I'm willin' to help support—though
Dan he had a tamed one o' them that did seem to have reason same
as folks. It was round here a good spell after he went away. Dan an'
his father they didn't hitch,—but he never held up his head ag'in
after Dan had dared him an' gone off."

The guest did not notice this hint of family sorrows in his eager
interest in something else.

"So Sylvy knows all about birds, does she?" he exclaimed, as he
looked round at the little girl who sat, very demure but increasingly
sleepy, in the moonlight. "I am making a collection of birds myself.
I have been at it ever since I was a boy." (Mrs. Tilley smiled.)
"There are two or three very rare ones I have been hunting for
these five years. I mean to get them on my own ground if they can
be found."

"Do you cage 'em up?" asked Mrs. Tilley doubtfully, in response
to this enthusiastic announcement.

"Oh no, they're stuffed and preserved, dozens and dozens of
them," said the ornithologist, "and I have shot or snared every one
myself. I caught a glimpse of a white heron a few miles from here
on Saturday, and I have followed it in this direction. They have
never been found in this district at all. The little white heron, it is,"
and he turned again to look at Sylvia with the hope of discovering
that the rare bird was one of her acquaintances.

But Sylvia was watching a hop-toad in the narrow footpath.

"You would know the heron if you saw it," the stranger continued eagerly "A queer tall white bird with soft feathers and long thin
legs. And it would have a nest perhaps in the top of a high tree,
made of sticks, something like a hawk's nest."

Sylvia's heart gave a wild beat; she knew that strange white bird,
and had once stolen softly near where it stood in some bright green
swamp grass, away over at the other side of the woods. There was
an open place where the sunshine always seemed strangely yellow
and hot, where tall, nodding rushes grew, and her grandmother had
warned her that she might sink in the soft black mud underneath
and never be heard of more. Not far beyond were the salt marshes
just this side the sea itself, which Sylvia wondered and dreamed
much about, but never had seen, whose great voice could sometimes be heard above the noise of the woods on stormy nights.

"I can't think of anything I should like so much as to find that heron's nest," the handsome stranger was saying. "I would give ten dollars to anybody who could show it to me," he added desperately, "and I mean to spend my whole vacation hunting for it if need be. Perhaps it was only migrating, or had been chased out of its own region by some bird of prey."

Mrs. Tilley gave amazed attention to all this, but Sylvia still watched the toad, not divining, as she might have done at some calmer time, that the creature wished to get to its hole under the door-step, and was much hindered by the unusual spectators at that hour of the evening. No amount of thought, that night, could decide how many wished-for treasures the ten dollars, so lightly spoken of, would buy.

The next day the young sportsman hovered about the woods, and Sylvia kept him company, having lost her first fear of the friendly lad, who proved to be most kind and sympathetic. He told her many things about the birds and what they knew and where they lived and what they did with themselves. And he gave her a jack-knife, which she thought as great a treasure as if she were a desert-islander. All day long he did not once make her troubled or afraid except when he brought down some unsuspecting singing creature from its bough. Sylvia would have liked him vastly better without his gun; she could not understand why he killed the very birds he seemed to like so much. But as the day waned, Sylvia still watched the young man with loving admiration. She had never seen anybody so charming and delightful; the woman's heart, asleep in the child, was vaguely thrilled by a dream of love. Some premonition of that great power stirred and swayed these young creatures who traversed the solemn woodlands with soft-footed silent care. They stopped to listen to a bird's song; they pressed forward again eagerly, parting the branches—speaking to each other rarely and in whispers; the young man going first and Sylvia following, fascinated, a few steps behind, with her gray eyes dark with excitement.

She grieved because the longed-for white heron was elusive, but she did not lead the guest, she only followed, and there was no such thing as speaking first. The sound of her own unquestioned voice would have terrified her—it was hard enough to answer yes or no when there was need of that. At last evening began to fall, and they drove the cow home together, and Sylvia smiled with pleasure when they came to the place where she heard the whistle and was afraid only the night before.

II

Half a mile from home, at the farther edge of the woods, where the land was highest, a great pine-tree stood, the last of its generation. Whether it was left for a boundary mark, or for what reason, no one could say; the wood-choppers who had felled its mates were dead and gone long ago, and a whole forest of sturdy trees, pines and oaks and maples, had grown again. But the stately head of this old pine towered above them all and made a landmark for sea and shore miles and miles away. Sylvia knew it well. She had always believed that whoever climbed to the top of it could see the ocean; and the little girl had often laid her hand on the great rough trunk and looked up wistfully at those dark boughs that the wind always stirred, no matter how hot and still the air might be below. Now she thought of the tree with a new excitement, for why, if one climbed it at break of day could not one see all the world, and easily discover from whence the white heron flew, and mark the place, and find the hidden nest?

What a spirit of adventure, what wild ambition! What fancied triumph and delight and glory for the later morning when she could make known the secret! It was almost too real and too great for the childish heart to bear.

All night the door of the little house stood open and the whip-poorwills came and sang upon the very step. The young sportsman and his old hostess were sound asleep, but Sylvia's great design kept her broad awake and watching. She forgot to think of sleep. The short summer night seemed as long as the winter darkness, and at last when the whippoorwills ceased, and she was afraid the morning would after all come too soon, she stole out of the house and followed the pasture path through the woods, hastening toward the open ground beyond, listening with a sense of comfort and companionship to the drowsy twitter of a half-awakened bird, whose perch she had jarred in passing. Alas, if the great wave of human interest which flooded for the first time this dull little life should sweep away the satisfactions of an existence heart to heart with nature and the dumb life of the forest!

There was the huge tree asleep yet in the paling moonlight, and small and silly Sylvia began with utmost bravery to mount to the top of it, with tingling, eager blood coursing the channels of her whole frame, with her bare feet and fingers, that pinched and held like bird's claws to the monstrous ladder reaching up, up, almost to the sky itself. First she must mount the white oak tree that grew alongside, where she was almost lost among the dark branches and the green leaves heavy and wet with dew; a bird fluttered off its nest, and a red squirrel ran to and fro and scolded pettishly at the harmless housebreaker. Sylvia felt her way easily. She had often climbed there, and knew that higher still one of the oak's upper branches chafed against the pine trunk, just where its lower boughs were set close together. There, when she made the dangerous pass from one tree to the other, the great enterprise would really begin.

She crept out along the swaying oak limb at last, and took the daring step across into the old pine-tree. The way was harder than she thought; she must reach far and hold fast, the sharp dry twigs caught and held her and scratched her like angry talons, the pitch made her thin little fingers clumsy and stiff as she went round and round the tree's great stem, higher and higher upward. The sparrows and robins in the woods below were beginning to wake and twitter to the dawn, yet it seemed much lighter there aloft in the pine-tree, and the child knew she must hurry if her project were to be of any use.

The tree seemed to lengthen itself out as she went up, and to reach farther and farther upward. It was like a great main-mast to the voyaging earth; it must truly have been amazed that morning through all its ponderous frame as it felt this determined spark of human spirit wending its way from higher branch to branch. Who knows how steadily the least twigs held themselves to advantage this light, weak creature on her way! The old pine must have loved his new dependent. More than all the hawks, and bats, and moths, and even the sweet voiced thrushes, was the brave, beating heart of the solitary gray-eyed child. And the tree stood still and frowned away the winds that June morning while the dawn grew bright in the east.

Sylvia's face was like a pale star, if one had seen it from the ground, when the last thorny bough was past, and she stood trembling and tired but wholly triumphant, high in the treetop. Yes, there was the sea with the dawning sun making a golden dazzle over it, and toward that glorious east flew two hawks with

slow-moving pinions. How low they looked in the air from that
height when one had only seen them before far up, and dark against
the blue sky. Their gray feathers were as soft as moths; they seemed
only a little way from the tree, and Sylvia felt as if she too could go
flying away among the clouds. Westward, the woodlands and farms
reached miles and miles into the distance; here and there were
church steeples, and white villages, truly it was a vast and awesome
world!

The birds sang louder and louder. At last the sun came up bewil-
deringly bright. Sylvia could see the white sails of ships out at sea,
and the clouds that were purple and rose-colored and yellow at first
began to fade away. Where was the white heron's nest in the sea of
green branches, and was this wonderful sight and pageant of the
world the only reward for having climbed to such a giddy height?
Now look down again, Sylvia, where the green marsh is set among
the shining birches and dark hemlocks; there where you saw the
white heron once you will see him again; look, look! a white spot
of him like a single floating feather comes up from the dead hemlock and grows larger, and rises, and comes close at last, and goes
by the landmark pine with steady sweep of wing and outstretched
slender neck and crested head. And wait! wait! do not move a foot
or a finger, little girl, do not send an arrow of light and consciousness from your two eager eyes, for the heron has perched on a pine
bough not far beyond yours, and cries back to his mate on the nest
and plumes his feathers for the new day!

The child gives a long sigh a minute later when a company of
shouting cat-birds comes also to the tree, and vexed by their fluttering and lawlessness the solemn heron goes away. She knows his
secret now, the wild, light, slender bird that floats and wavers, and
goes back like an arrow presently to his home in the green world
beneath. Then Sylvia, well satisfied, makes her perilous way down
again, not daring to look far below the branch she stands on, ready
to cry sometimes because her fingers ache and her lamed feet slip.
Wondering over and over again what the stranger would say to her,
and what he would think when she told him how to find his way
straight to the heron's nest.

"Sylvy, Sylvy!" called the busy old grandmother again and again,
but nobody answered, and the small husk bed was empty and Sylvia
had disappeared.

The guest waked from a dream, and remembering his day's pleasure hurried to dress himself that it might sooner begin. He was sure from the way the shy little girl looked once or twice yesterday that she had at least seen the white heron, and now she must really be made to tell. Here she comes now, paler than ever, and her worn old frock is torn and tattered, and smeared with pine pitch. The grandmother and the sportsman stand in the door together and question her, and the splendid moment has come to speak of the dead hemlock-tree by the green marsh.

But Sylvia does not speak after all, though the old grandmother fretfully rebukes her, and the young man's kind, appealing eyes are looking straight in her own. He can make them rich with money; he has promised it, and they are poor now. He is so well worth making happy, and he waits to hear the story she can tell.

No, she must keep silence! What is it that suddenly forbids her and makes her dumb? Has she been nine years growing and now, when the great world for the first time puts out a hand to her, must she thrust it aside for a bird's sake? The murmur of the pine's green branches is in her ears, she remembers how the white heron came flying through the golden air and how they watched the sea and the morning together, and Sylvia cannot speak; she cannot tell the heron's secret and give its life away.

Dear loyalty, that suffered a sharp pang as the guest went away disappointed later in the day, that could have served and followed him and loved him as a dog loves! Many a night Sylvia heard the echo of his whistle haunting the pasture path as she came home with the loitering cow. She forgot even her sorrow at the sharp report of his gun and the sight of thrushes and sparrows dropping silent to the ground, their songs hushed and their pretty feathers stained and wet with blood. Were the birds better friends than their hunter might have been,—who can tell? Whatever treasures were lost to her, woodlands and summer-time, remember! Bring your gifts and graces and tell your secrets to this lonely country child!

HOW MUCH LAND DOES A MAN NEED?

Leo Tolstoy

I

AN ELDER SISTER came to visit her younger sister in the country. The elder was married to a tradesman in town, the younger to a peasant in the village. As the sisters sat over their tea talking, the elder began to boast of the advantages of town life: saying how comfortably they lived there, how well they dressed, what fine clothes her children wore, what good things they ate and drank, and how she went to the theater, promenades, and entertainments.

The younger sister was piqued, and in turn disparaged the life of a tradesman, and stood up for that of a peasant.

"I would not change my way of life for yours," said she. "We may live roughly, but at least we are free from anxiety. You live in better style than we do, but though you often earn more than you need, you are very likely to lose all you have. You know the proverb, 'Loss and gain are brothers twain.' It often happens that people who are wealthy one day are begging their bread the next. Our way is safer. Though a peasant's life is not a fat one, it is a long one. We shall never grow rich, but we shall always have enough to eat."

The elder sister said sneeringly:

"Enough? Yes, if you like to share with the pigs and the calves! What do you know of elegance or manners! However much your goodman may slave, you will die as you are living—on a dung heap—and your children the same."

"Well, what of that?" replied the younger. "Of course our work is rough and coarse. But, on the other hand, it is sure, and we need not bow to anyone. But you, in your towns, are surrounded by temptations; to-day all may be right, but to-morrow the Evil One may tempt your husband with cards, wine, or women, and all will go to ruin. Don't such things happen often enough?"

Pahóm, the master of the house, was lying on the top of the stove and he listened to the women's chatter.

"It is perfectly true," thought he. "Busy as we are from child-hood tilling mother earth, we peasants have no time to let any nonsense settle in our heads. Our only trouble is that we haven't land enough. If I had plenty of land, I shouldn't fear the Devil himself!"

The women finished their tea, chatted a while about dress, and then cleared away the tea-things and lay down to sleep.

But the Devil had been sitting behind the stove, and had heard all that was said. He was pleased that the peasant's wife had led her husband into boasting, and that he had said that if he had plenty of land he would not fear the Devil himself.

"All right," thought the Devil. "We will have a tussle. I'll give you land enough; and by means of that land I will get you into my power."

II

Close to the village there lived a lady, a small landowner who had an estate of about three hundred acres.[1] She had always lived on good terms with the peasants until she engaged as her steward an old soldier, who took to burdening the people with fines. However careful Pahom tried to be, it happened again and again that now a horse of his got among the lady's oats, now a cow strayed into her garden, now his calves found their way into her meadows—and he always had to pay a fine.

Pahom paid up, but grumbled and, going home in a temper, was rough with his family. All through that summer, Pahom had much trouble because of this steward, and he was even glad when winter came and the cattle had to be stabled. Though he grudged the fod-der when they could no longer graze on the pasture-land, at least he was free from anxiety about them.

---

[1] 120 desyatins. The desyatina is properly 2.7 acres; but in this story round numbers are used.

In the winter the news got about that the lady was going to sell her land and that the keeper of the inn on the high road was bargaining for it. When the peasants heard this they were very much alarmed.

"Well," thought they, "if the innkeeper gets the land, he will worry us with fines worse than the lady's steward. We all depend on that estate."

So the peasants went on behalf of their Commune, and asked the lady not to sell the land to the innkeeper, offering her a better price for it themselves. The lady agreed to let them have it. Then the peasants tried to arrange for the Commune to buy the whole estate, so that it might be held by them all in common. They met twice to discuss it, but could not settle the matter; the Evil One sowed discord among them and they could not agree. So they decided to buy the land individually, each according to his means; and the lady agreed to this plan as she had to the other.

Presently Pahom heard that a neighbor of his was buying fifty acres, and that the lady had consented to accept one half in cash and to wait a year for the other half. Pahom felt envious.

"Look at that," thought he, "the land is all being sold, and I shall get none of it." So he spoke to his wife.

"Other people are buying," said he, "and we must also buy twenty acres or so. Life is becoming impossible. That steward is simply crushing us with his fines."

So they put their heads together and considered how they could manage to buy it. They had one hundred rubles laid by. They sold a colt and one half of their bees, hired out one of their sons as a laborer and took his wages in advance; borrowed the rest from a brother-in-law, and so scraped together half the purchase money.

Having done this, Pahom chose out a farm of forty acres, some of it wooded, and went to the lady to bargain for it. They came to an agreement, and he shook hands with her upon it and paid her a deposit in advance. Then they went to town and signed the deeds; he paying half the price down, and undertaking to pay the remainder within two years.

So now Pahom had land of his own. He borrowed seed, and sowed it on the land he had bought. The harvest was a good one, and within a year he had managed to pay off his debts both to the lady and to his brother-in-law. So he became a landowner, ploughing and sowing his own land, making hay on his own land, cutting

his own trees, and feeding his cattle on his own pasture. When he
went out to plough his fields, or to look at his growing corn, or at
his grass-meadows, his heart would fill with joy. The grass that
grew and the flowers that bloomed there seemed to him unlike any
that grew elsewhere. Formerly, when he had passed by that land, it
had appeared the same as any other land, but now it seemed quite
different.

III

So Pahom was well-contented, and everything would have been
right if the neighboring peasants would only not have trespassed on
his cornfields and meadows. He appealed to them most civilly, but
they still went on: now the Communal herdsmen would let the village cows stray into his meadows, then horses from the night pasture
would get among his corn. Pahom turned them out again and again,
and forgave their owners, and for a long time he forbore to prose-
cute any one. But at last he lost patience and complained to the
District Court. He knew it was the peasants' want of land, and no
evil intent on their part, that caused the trouble, but he thought:

"I cannot go on overlooking it or they will destroy all I have.
They must be taught a lesson."

So he had them up, gave them one lesson, and then another, and
two or three of the peasants were fined. After a time Pahom's
neighbors began to bear him a grudge for this, and would now and
then let their cattle on to his land on purpose. One peasant even
got into Pahom's wood at night and cut down five young lime trees
for their bark. Pahom passing through the wood one day noticed
something white. He came nearer and saw the stripped trunks lying
on the ground, and close by stood the stumps where the trees had
been. Pahom was furious.

"If he had only cut one here and there it would have been bad
enough," thought Pahom, "but the rascal has actually cut down a
whole clump. If I could only find out who did this, I would pay
him out."

He racked his brain as to who it could be. Finally he decided: "It
must be Simon—no one else could have done it." So he went to
Simon's homestead to have a look round, but he found nothing,
and only had an angry scene. However, he now felt more certain
than ever that Simon had done it, and he lodged a complaint.

Simon was summoned. The case was tried, and retried, and at the end of it all Simon was acquitted, there being no evidence against him. Pahom felt still more aggrieved, and let his anger loose upon the Elder and the Judges.

"You let thieves grease your palms," said he. "If you were honest folk yourselves you would not let a thief go free."

So Pahom quarreled with the Judges and with his neighbors. Threats to burn his building began to be uttered. So though Pahom had more land, his place in the Commune was much worse than before.

About this time a rumor got about that many people were moving to new parts.

"There's no need for me to leave my land," thought Pahom. "But some of the others might leave our village and then there would be more room for us. I would take over their land myself and make my estate a bit bigger. I could then live more at ease. As it is, I am still too cramped to be comfortable."

One day Pahom was sitting at home when a peasant, passing through the village, happened to call in. He was allowed to stay the night, and supper was given him. Pahom had a talk with this peasant and asked him where he came from. The stranger answered that he came from beyond the Volga, where he had been working. One word led to another, and the man went on to say that many people were settling in those parts. He told how some people from his village had settled there. They had joined the Commune, and had had twenty-five acres per man granted them. The land was so good, he said, that the rye sown on it grew as high as a horse, and so thick that five cuts of a sickle made a sheaf. One peasant, he said, had brought nothing with him but his bare hands, and now he had six horses and two cows of his own.

Pahom's heart kindled with desire. He thought:

"Why should I suffer in this narrow hole, if one can live so well elsewhere? I will sell my land and my homestead here, and with the money I will start afresh over there and get everything new. In this crowded place one is always having trouble. But I must first go and find out all about it myself."

Towards summer he got ready and started. He went down the Volga on a steamer to Samara, then walked another three hundred miles on foot, and at last reached the place. It was just as the stranger had said. The peasants had plenty of land: every man had twenty-five acres of Communal land given him for his use, and any one who had money could buy, besides, at a ruble an acre as much good freehold land as he wanted.

Having found out all he wished to know, Pahom returned home as autumn came on, and began selling off his belongings. He sold his land at a profit, sold his homestead and all his cattle, and withdrew from membership in the Commune. He only waited till the spring, and then started with his family for the new settlement.

IV

As soon as Pahom and his family reached their new abode, he applied for admission into the Commune of a large village. He stood treat to the Elders and obtained the necessary documents. Five shares of Communal land were given him for his own and his sons' use: that is to say—125 acres (not all together, but in different fields) besides the use of the Communal pasture. Pahom put up the buildings he needed, and bought cattle. Of the Communal land alone he had three times as much as at his former home, and the land was good corn-land. He was ten times better off than he had been. He had plenty of arable land and pasturage, and could keep as many head of cattle as he liked.

At first, in the bustle of building and settling down, Pahom was pleased with it all, but when he got used to it he began to think that even here he had not enough land. The first year, he sowed wheat on his share of the Communal land and had a good crop. He wanted to go on sowing wheat, but had not enough Communal land for the purpose, and what he had already used was not available; for in those parts wheat is only sown on virgin soil or on fallow land. It is sown for one or two years, and then the land lies fallow till it is again overgrown with prairie grass. There were many who wanted such land and there was not enough for all; so that people quarreled about it. Those who were better off wanted it for growing wheat, and those who were poor wanted it to let to dealers, so that they might raise money to pay their taxes. Pahom wanted to sow more wheat, so he rented land from a dealer for a year. He sowed much wheat and had a fine crop, but the land was too far from the village—the wheat had to be carted more than ten miles. After a time Pahom noticed that some peasant-dealers were living on separate farms and were growing wealthy; and he thought:

"If I were to buy some freehold land and have a homestead on it, it would be a different thing altogether. Then it would all be nice and compact."

The question of buying freehold land recurred to him again and again.

He went on in the same way for three years, renting land and sowing wheat. The seasons turned out well and the crops were good, so that he began to lay money by. He might have gone on living contentedly, but he grew tired of having to rent other people's land every year, and having to scramble for it. Wherever there was good land to be had, the peasants would rush for it and it was taken up at once, so that unless you were sharp about it you got none. It happened in the third year that he and a dealer together rented a piece of pasture-land from some peasants; and they had already ploughed it up, when there was some dispute and the peasants went to law about it, and things fell out so that the labor was all lost.

"If it were my own land," thought Pahom, "I should be independent, and there would not be all this unpleasantness."

So Pahom began looking out for land which he could buy; and he came across a peasant who had bought thirteen hundred acres, but having got into difficulties was willing to sell again cheap. Pahom bargained and haggled with him, and at last they settled the price at 1,500 rubles, part in cash and part to be paid later. They had all but clinched the matter when a passing dealer happened to stop at Pahom's one day to get a feed for his horses. He drank tea with Pahom and they had a talk. The dealer said that he was just returning from the land of the Bashkirs,[2] far away, where he had bought thirteen thousand acres of land, all for 1,000 rubles. Pahom questioned him further, and the tradesman said:

"All one need do is to make friends with the chiefs. I gave away about one hundred rubles' worth of silk robes and carpets, besides a case of tea, and I gave wine to those who would drink it; and I got the land for less than a penny an acre."[3] And he showed Pahom the title-deeds, saying:

"The land lies near a river, and the whole prairie is virgin soil."

Pahom plied him with questions, and the tradesman said:

---

[2] [Turkic people dwelling on both sides of the Urals.]
[3] Five kopeks for a desyatina.

"There is more land there than you could cover if you walked a year, and it all belongs to the Bashkirs. They are as simple as sheep, and land can be got almost for nothing."

"There now," thought Pahom, "with my one thousand rubles, why should I get only thirteen hundred acres, and saddle myself with a debt besides? If I take it out there, I can get more than ten times as much for the money."

V

Pahom inquired how to get to the place, and as soon as the trades-man had left him, he prepared to go there himself. He left his wife to look after the homestead, and started on his journey taking his man with him. They stopped at a town on their way and bought a case of tea, some wine, and other presents, as the tradesman had advised. On and on they went until they had gone more than three hundred miles, and on the seventh day they came to a place where the Bashkirs had pitched their tents. It was all just as the tradesman had said. The people lived on the steppes, by a river, in felt-covered tents.[4] They neither tilled the ground, nor ate bread. Their cattle and horses grazed in herds on the steppe. The colts were tethered behind the tents, and the mares were driven to them twice a day. The mares were milked, and from the milk kumiss[5] was made. It was the women who prepared kumiss, and they also made cheese. As far as the men were concerned, drinking kumiss and tea, eating mutton, and playing on their pipes, was all they cared about. They were all stout and merry, and all the summer long they never thought of doing any work. They were quite ignorant, and knew no Russian, but were good-natured enough.

As soon as they saw Pahom, they came out of their tents and gathered round their visitor. An interpreter was found, and Pahom told them he had come about some land. The Bashkirs seemed very glad; they took Pahom and led him into one of the best tents, where they made him sit on some down cushions placed on a car-pet, while they sat round him. They gave him some tea and kumiss,

---

[4] A kibitka is a movable dwelling, made up of detachable wooden frames, forming a round, and covered over with felt.

[5] [A fermented drink.]

and had a sheep killed, and gave him mutton to eat. Pahom took presents out of his cart and distributed them among the Bashkirs, and divided the tea amongst them. The Bashkirs were delighted. They talked a great deal among themselves, and then told the interpreter to translate.

"They wish to tell you," said the interpreter, "that they like you, and that it is our custom to do all we can to please a guest and to repay him for his gifts. You have given us presents, now tell us which of the things we possess please you best, that we may present them to you."

"What pleases me best here," answered Pahom, "is your land. Our land is crowded and the soil is exhausted; but you have plenty of land and it is good land. I never saw the like of it."

The interpreter translated. The Bashkirs talked among themselves for a while. Pahom could not understand what they were saying, but saw that they were much amused and that they shouted and laughed. Then they were silent and looked at Pahom while the interpreter said:

"They wish me to tell you that in return for your presents they will gladly give you as much land as you want. You have only to point it out with your hand and it is yours."

The Bashkirs talked again for a while and began to dispute. Pahom asked what they were disputing about, and the interpreter told him that some of them thought they ought to ask their Chief about the land and not act in his absence, while others thought there was no need to wait for his return.

VI

While the Bashkirs were disputing, a man in a large fox-fur cap appeared on the scene. They all became silent and rose to their feet. The interpreter said, "This is our Chief himself."

Pahom immediately fetched the best dressing-gown and five pounds of tea, and offered these to the Chief. The Chief accepted them, and seated himself in the place of honor. The Bashkirs at once began telling him something. The Chief listened for a while, then made a sign with his head for them to be silent, and addressing himself to Pahom, said in Russian:

"Well, let it be so. Choose whatever piece of land you like; we have plenty of it."

"How can I take as much as I like?" thought Pahom. "I must get a deed to make it secure, or else they may say, 'It is yours,' and afterwards may take it away again."

"Thank you for your kind words," he said aloud. "You have much land, and I only want a little. But I should like to be sure which bit is mine. Could it not be measured and made over to me? Life and death are in God's hands. You good people give it to me, but your children might wish to take it away again."

"You are quite right," said the Chief. "We will make it over to you."

"I heard that a dealer had been here," continued Pahom, "and that you gave him a little land, too, and signed title-deeds to that effect. I should like to have it done in the same way."

The Chief understood.

"Yes," replied he, "that can be done quite easily. We have a scribe, and we will go to town with you and have the deed properly sealed."

"And what will be the price?" asked Pahom.

"Our price is always the same: one thousand rubles a day."

Pahom did not understand.

"A day? What measure is that? How many acres would that be?"

"We do not know how to reckon it out," said the Chief. "We sell it by the day. As much as you can go round on your feet in a day is yours, and the price is one thousand rubles a day."

Pahom was surprised.

"But in a day you can get round a large tract of land," he said.

The Chief laughed.

"It will all be yours!" said he. "But there is one condition: If you don't return on the same day to the spot whence you started, your money is lost."

"But how am I to mark the way that I have gone?"

"Why, we shall go to any spot you like, and stay there. You must start from that spot and make your round, taking a spade with you. Wherever you think necessary, make a mark. At every turning, dig a hole and pile up the turf; then afterwards we will go round with a plough from hole to hole. You may make as large a circuit as you please, but before the sun sets you must return to the place you started from. All the land you cover will be yours."

Pahom was delighted. It was decided to start early next morning. They talked a while, and after drinking some more kumiss and eating some more mutton, they had tea again, and then the night came on. They gave Pahom a feather-bed to sleep on, and the Bashkirs dispersed for the night, promising to assemble the next morning at daybreak and ride out before sunrise to the appointed spot.

VII

Pahom lay on the feather-bed, but could not sleep. He kept thinking about the land.

"What a large tract I will mark off!" thought he. "I can easily do thirty-five miles in a day. The days are long now, and within a circuit of thirty-five miles what a lot of land there will be! I will sell the poorer land, or let it to peasants, but I'll pick out the best and farm it. I will buy two oxteams, and hire two more laborers. About a hundred and fifty acres shall be plough-land, and I will pasture cattle on the rest."

Pahom lay awake all night, and dozed off only just before dawn. Hardly were his eyes closed when he had a dream. He thought he was lying in that same tent and heard somebody chuckling outside. He wondered who it could be, and rose and went out, and he saw the Bashkir Chief sitting in front of the tent holding his sides and rolling about with laughter. Going nearer to the Chief, Pahom asked: "What are you laughing at?" But he saw that it was no longer the Chief, but the dealer who had recently stopped at his house and had told him about the land. Just as Pahom was going to ask, "Have you been here long?" he saw that it was not the dealer, but the peasant who had come up from the Volga, long ago, to Pahom's old home. Then he saw that it was not the peasant either, but the Devil himself with hoofs and horns, sitting there and chuckling, and before him lay a man barefoot, prostrate on the ground, with only trousers and a shirt on. And Pahom dreamt that he looked more attentively to see what sort of a man it was that was lying there, and he saw that the man was dead, and that it was himself! He awoke horror-struck.

"What things one does dream," thought he.

Looking round he saw through the open door that the dawn was breaking.

"It's time to wake them up," thought he. "We ought to be starting."

He got up, roused his man (who was sleeping in his cart), bade him harness; and went to call the Bashkirs.

"It's time to go to the steppe to measure the land," he said.

The Bashkirs rose and assembled, and the Chief came too. Then they began drinking kumiss again, and offered Pahom some tea, but he would not wait.

"If we are to go, let us go. It is high time," said he.

VIII

The Bashkirs got ready and they all started: some mounted on horses, and some in carts. Pahom drove in his own small cart with his servant and took a spade with him. When they reached the steppe, the morning red was beginning to kindle. They ascended a hillock (called by the Bashkirs a *shikhan*) and dismounting from their carts and their horses, gathered in one spot. The Chief came up to Pahom and stretching out his arm towards the plain:

"See," said he, "all this, as far as your eye can reach, is ours. You may have any part of it you like."

Pahom's eyes glistened: it was all virgin soil, as flat as the palm of your hand, as black as the seed of a poppy, and in the hollows different kinds of grasses grew breast high.

The Chief took off his fox-fur cap, placed it on the ground and said:

"This will be the mark. Start from here, and return here again. All the land you go round shall be yours."

Pahom took out his money and put it on the cap. Then he took off his outer coat, remaining in his sleeveless under-coat. He unfastened his girdle and tied it tight below his stomach, put a little bag of bread into the breast of his coat, and tying a flask of water to his girdle, he drew up the tops of his boots, took the spade from his man, and stood ready to start. He considered for some moments which way he had better go —it was tempting everywhere.

"No matter," he concluded, "I will go towards the rising sun."

He turned his face to the east, stretched himself, and waited for the sun to appear above the rim.

"I must lose no time," he thought, "and it is easier walking while it is still cool."

The sun's rays had hardly flashed above the horizon, before Pahom, carrying the spade over his shoulder, went down into the steppe.

Pahom started walking neither slowly nor quickly. After having gone a thousand yards he stopped, dug a hole, and placed pieces of turf one on another to make it more visible. Then he went on; and now that he had walked off his stiffness he quickened his pace. After a while he dug another hole.

Pahom looked back. The hillock could be distinctly seen in the sunlight, with the people on it, and the glittering tires of the cart-wheels. At a rough guess Pahom concluded that he had walked three miles. It was growing warmer; he took off his under-coat, flung it across his shoulder, and went on again. It had grown quite warm now; he looked at the sun, it was time to think of breakfast.

"The first shift is done, but there are four in a day, and it is too soon yet to turn. But I will just take off my boots," said he to himself.

He sat down, took off his boots, stuck them into his girdle, and went on. It was easy walking now.

"I will go on for another three miles," thought he, "and then turn to the left. This spot is so fine, that it would be a pity to lose it. The further one goes, the better the land seems."

He went straight on for a while, and when he looked round, the hillock was scarcely visible and the people on it looked like black ants, and he could just see something glistening there in the sun.

"Ah," thought Pahom, "I have gone far enough in this direction, it is time to turn. Besides I am in a regular sweat, and very thirsty."

He stopped, dug a large hole, and heaped up pieces of turf. Next he untied his flask, had a drink, and then turned sharply to the left. He went on and on; the grass was high, and it was very hot.

Pahom began to grow tired: he looked at the sun and saw that it was noon.

"Well," he thought, "I must have a rest."

He sat down, and ate some bread and drank some water; but he did not lie down, thinking that if he did he might fall asleep. After sitting a little while, he went on again. At first he walked easily: the food had strengthened him; but it had become terribly hot and he felt sleepy, still he went on, thinking: "An hour to suffer, a life-time to live."

He went a long way in this direction also, and was about to turn to the left again, when he perceived a damp hollow: "It would be a pity to leave that out," he thought. "Flax would do well there."

So he went on past the hollow, and dug a hole on the other side of it before he turned the corner. Pahom looked towards the hillock. The heat made the air hazy: it seemed to be quivering, and through the haze the people on the hillock could scarcely be seen.

"Ah!" thought Pahom, "I have made the sides too long; I must make this one shorter." And he went along the third side, stepping faster. He looked at the sun: it was nearly half-way to the horizon, and he had not yet done two miles of the third side of the square. He was still ten miles from the goal.

"No," he thought, "though it will make my land lop-sided, I must hurry back in a straight line now. I might go too far, and as it is I have a great deal of land."

So Pahom hurriedly dug a hole, and turned straight towards the hillock.

IX

Pahom went straight towards the hillock, but he now walked with difficulty. He was done up with the heat, his bare feet were cut and bruised, and his legs began to fail. He longed to rest, but it was impossible if he meant to get back before sunset. The sun waits for no man, and it was sinking lower and lower.

"Oh dear," he thought, "if only I have not blundered trying for too much! What if I am too late?"

He looked towards the hillock and at the sun. He was still far from his goal, and the sun was already near the rim.

Pahom walked on and on; it was very hard walking but he went quicker and quicker. He pressed on, but was still far from the place. He began running, threw away his coat, his boots, his flask, and his cap, and kept only the spade which he used as a support.

"What shall I do," he thought again, "I have grasped too much and ruined the whole affair. I can't get there before the sun sets."

And this fear made him still more breathless. Pahom went on running, his soaking shirt and trousers stuck to him and his mouth was parched. His breast was working like a blacksmith's bellows, his heart was beating like a hammer, and his legs were giving way as if they did not belong to him. Pahom was seized with terror lest he should die of the strain.

Though afraid of death, he could not stop. "After having run all that way they will call me a fool if I stop now," thought he. And he ran on and on, and drew near and heard the Bashkirs yelling and shouting to him, and their cries inflamed his heart still more. He gathered his last strength and ran on.

The sun was close to the rim, and cloaked in mist looked large, and red as blood. Now, yes now, it was about to set! The sun was quite low, but he was also quite near his aim. Pahom could already see the people on the hillock waving their arms to hurry him up. He could see the fox-fur cap on the ground and the money on it, and the Chief sitting on the ground holding his sides. And Pahom remembered his dream.

"There is plenty of land," thought he, "but will God let me live on it? I have lost my life, I have lost my life! I shall never reach that spot!"

Pahom looked at the sun, which had reached the earth: one side of it had already disappeared. With all his remaining strength he rushed on, bending his body forward so that his legs could hardly follow fast enough to keep him from falling. Just as he reached the hillock it suddenly grew dark. He looked up—the sun had already set! He gave a cry: "All my labor has been in vain," thought he, and was about to stop, but he heard the Bashkirs still shouting, and remembered that though to him, from below, the sun seemed to have set, they on the hillock could still see it. He took a long breath and ran up the hillock. It was still light there. He reached the top and saw the cap. Before it sat the Chief laughing and holding his sides. Again Pahom remembered his dream, and he uttered a cry: his legs gave way beneath him, he fell forward and reached the cap with his hands.

"Ah, that's a fine fellow!" exclaimed the Chief. "He has gained much land!"

Pahom's servant came running up and tried to raise him, but he saw that blood was flowing from his nostril. Pahom was dead!

The Bashkirs clicked their tongues to show their pity.

His servant picked up the spade and dug a grave long enough for Pahom to lie in, and buried him in it. Six feet from his head to his heels was all he needed.

THE GOOPHERED GRAPEVINE

Charles Waddell Chesnutt

SOME YEARS AGO my wife was in poor health, and our family doctor, in whose skill and honesty I had implicit confidence, advised a change of climate. I shared, from an unprofessional standpoint, his opinion that the raw winds, the chill rains, and the violent changes of temperature that characterized the winters in the region of the Great Lakes tended to aggravate my wife's difficulty, and would undoubtedly shorten her life if she remained exposed to them. The doctor's advice was that we seek, not a temporary place of sojourn, but a permanent residence, in a warmer and more equable climate. I was engaged at the time in grape-culture in northern Ohio, and, as I liked the business and had given it much study, I decided to look for some other locality suitable for carrying it on. I thought of sunny France, of sleepy Spain, of Southern California, but there were objections to them all. It occurred to me that I might find what I wanted in some one of our own Southern States. It was a sufficient time after the war for conditions in the South to have become somewhat settled; and I was enough of a pioneer to start a new industry, if I could not find a place where grape-culture had been tried. I wrote to a cousin who had gone into the turpentine business in central North Carolina. He assured me, in response to my inquiries, that no better place could be found in the South than the State and neighborhood where he lived; the climate was perfect for health, and, in conjunction with the soil, ideal for grape-culture; labor was cheap, and land could be bought for a mere song. He gave us a cordial invitation to come and visit him while we looked into the matter. We accepted the invitation, and after several days of leisurely travel, the last hundred miles of which were up a river on a sidewheel steamer, we reached our destination, a quaint old town, which I shall call Patesville, because, for one reason, that is not its name. There was a red brick market-house in the public square, with a tall tower, which held a four-faced clock that struck the hours, and from which there pealed out a curfew at nine o'clock. There were two or three hotels, a court-house, a jail, stores, offices, and all the appurtenances of a county seat and a commercial emporium; for while Patesville numbered only four or five thousand inhabitants, of all shades of complexion, it was one of the principal towns in North Carolina, and had a considerable trade in cotton and naval stores. This business activity was not immediately apparent to my unaccustomed eyes. Indeed, when I first saw the town, there brooded over it a calm that seemed almost sabbatic in its restfulness, though I learned later on that underneath its somnolent exterior the deeper currents of life—love and hatred, joy and despair, ambition and avarice, faith and friendship—flowed not less steadily than in livelier latitudes.

We found the weather delightful at that season, the end of summer, and were hospitably entertained. Our host was a man of means and evidently regarded our visit as a pleasure, and we were therefore correspondingly at our ease, and in a position to act with the coolness of judgment desirable in making so radical a change in our lives. My cousin placed a horse and buggy at our disposal, and himself acted as our guide until I became somewhat familiar with the country.

I found that grape-culture, while it had never been carried on to any great extent, was not entirely unknown in the neighborhood. Several planters thereabouts had attempted it on a commercial scale, in former years, with greater or less success; but like most Southern industries, it had felt the blight of war and had fallen into desuetude.

I went several times to look at a place that I thought might suit me. It was a plantation of considerable extent, that had formerly belonged to a wealthy man by the name of McAdoo. The estate had been for years involved in litigation between disputing heirs, during which period shiftless cultivation had well-nigh exhausted the soil. There had been a vineyard of some extent on the place, but it had not been attended to since the war, and had lapsed into utter neglect. The vines—here partly supported by decayed and broken-down trellises, there twining themselves among the branches of the slender saplings which had sprung up among them—grew in wild and unpruned luxuriance, and the few scattered grapes they bore were the undisputed prey of the first comer. The site was admirably adapted to grape-raising; the soil, with a little attention, could not have been better; and with the native grape, the luscious scuppernong, as my main reliance in the beginning, I felt sure that I could introduce and cultivate successfully a number of other varieties.

One day I went over with my wife to show her the place. We drove out of the town over a long wooden bridge that spanned a spreading mill-pond, passed the long whitewashed fence surrounding the county fair-ground, and struck into a road so sandy that the horse's feet sank to the fetlocks. Our route lay partly up hill and partly down, for we were in the sand-hill country; we drove past cultivated farms, and then by abandoned fields grown up in scrub-oak and short-leaved pine, and once or twice through the solemn aisles of the virgin forest, where the tall pines, well-nigh meeting over the narrow road, shut out the sun, and wrapped us in cloistral solitude. Once, at a crossroads, I was in doubt as to the turn to take, and we sat there waiting ten minutes—we had already caught some of the native infection of restfulness—for some human being to come along, who could direct us on our way. At length a little negro girl appeared, walking straight as an arrow, with a piggin full of water on her head. After a little patient investigation, necessary to overcome the child's shyness, we learned what we wished to know, and at the end of about five miles from the town reached our destination.

We drove between a pair of decayed gateposts—the gate itself had long since disappeared—and up a straight sandy lane, between two lines of rotting rail fence, partly concealed by jimson-weeds and briers, to the open space where a dwelling-house had once stood, evidently a spacious mansion, if we might judge from the ruined chimneys that were still standing, and the brick pillars on which the sills rested. The house itself, we had been informed, had fallen a victim to the fortunes of war.

We alighted from the buggy, walked about the yard for a while, and then wandered off into the adjoining vineyard. Upon Annie's complaining of weariness I led the way back to the yard, where a pine log, lying under a spreading elm, afforded a shady though somewhat hard seat. One end of the log was already occupied by a venerable-looking colored man. He held on his knees a hat full of grapes, over which he was smacking his lips with great gusto, and a pile of grapeskins near him indicate that the performance was no new thing. We approached him at an angle from the rear, and were close to him before he perceived us. He respectfully rose as we drew near, and was moving away, when I begged him to keep his seat.

"Don't let us disturb you," I said. "There is plenty of room for us all."

He resumed his seat with somewhat of embarrassment. While he had been standing, I had observed that he was a tall man, and, though slightly bowed by the weight of years, apparently quite vigorous. He was not entirely black, and this fact, together with the quality of his hair, which was about six inches long and very bushy, except on the top of his head, where he was quite bald, suggested a slight strain of other than negro blood. There was a shrewdness in his eyes, too, which was not altogether African, and which, as we afterwards learned from experience, was indicative of a corresponding shrewdness in his character. He went on eating the grapes, but did not seem to enjoy himself quite so well as he had apparently done before he became aware of our presence.

"Do you live around here?" I asked, anxious to put him at his ease.

"Yas, suh. I lives des ober yander, behine de nex' san'-hill, on de Lumberton plank-road."

"Do you know anything about the time when this vineyard was cultivated?"

"Lawd bless you, suh, I knows all about it. Dey ain' na'er a man in dis settlement w'at won' tell you ole Julius McAdoo 'uz bawn en raise' on dis yer same plantation. Is you de Norv'n gemman w'at's gwine ter buy de ole vimya'd?"

"I am looking at it," I replied; "but I don't know that I shall care to buy unless I can be reasonably sure of making something out of it."

"Well, suh, you is a stranger ter me, en I is a stranger ter you, en we is bofe strangers ter one anudder, but 'f I 'uz in yo' place, I wouldn' buy dis vimya'd."

"Why not?" I asked.

"Well, I dunno whe'r you b'lieves in cunj'in 'er not,—some er de w'ite folks don't, er says dey don't,—but de truf er de matter is dat dis yer ole vimya'd is goophered."

"Is what?" I asked, not grasping the meaning of this unfamiliar word.

"Is goophered,—cunju'd, bewitch'."

He imparted this information with such solemn earnestness, and with such an air of confidential mystery, that I felt somewhat interested, while Annie was evidently much impressed, and drew closer to me.

"How do you know it is bewitched?" I asked.

"I wouldn' spec' fer you ter b'lieve me 'less you know all 'bout de fac's. But ef you en young miss dere doan' min' lis'nin' ter a ole nigger run on a minute er two w'ile you er restin', I kin 'splain to you how it all happen'."

We assured him that we would be glad to hear how it all happened, and he began to tell us. At first the current of his memory—or imagination—seemed somewhat sluggish; but as his embarrassment wore off, his language flowed more freely, and the story acquired perspective and coherence. As he became more and more absorbed in the narrative, his eyes assumed a dreamy expression, and he seemed to lose sight of his auditors, and to be living over again in monologue his life on the old plantation.

"Ole Mars Dugal' McAdoo," he began, "bought dis place long many years befo' de wah, en I 'member well w'en he sot out all dis yer part er de plantation in scuppernon's. De vimes growed monst'us fas', en Mars Dugal' made a thousan' gallon er scuppernon' wine eve'y year.

"Now, ef dey's an'thing a nigger lub, nex' ter 'possum, en chick'n, en watermillyums, it's scuppernon's. Dey ain' nuffin dat kin stan' up side'n de scuppernon' for sweetness; sugar ain't a suckumstance ter scuppernon'. W'en de season is nigh 'bout ober, en de grapes begin ter swivel up des a little wid de wrinkles er ole age,—w'en de skin git sof' en brown,—den de scuppernon' make you smack yo' lip en roll yo' eye en wush fer mo'; so I reckon it ain' very 'stonishin' dat niggers lub scuppernon'.

"Dey wuz a sight er niggers in de naberhood er de vimya'd. Dere wuz ole Mars Henry Brayboy's niggers, en ol Mars Jeems McLean's niggers, en Mars Dugal's own niggers; den dey wuz a settlement er free niggers en po' buckrahs down by de Wim'l'ton Road, en Mars Dugal' had de only vimya'd in de naberhood. I reckon it ain' so much so nowadays, but befo' de wah, in slab'ry times, a nigger didn' mine goin' fi' er ten mile in a night, w'en dey wuz sump'n good ter eat at de yuther een'.

"So atter a w'ile Mars Dugal' begin ter miss his scuppernon's. Co'se he 'cuse' de niggers er it, but dey all 'nied it ter de las'. Mars Dugal' sot spring guns en steel traps, en he en de oberseah sot up nights once't er twice't, tel one night Mars Dugal'—he 'uz a monst'us keerless man—got his leg shot full er cow-peas. But somehow er nudder dey couldn' nebber ketch none er de niggers. I dunner how it happen, but it happen des like I tell you, en de grapes kep' on a-goin' des de same.

"But bimeby ole Mars Dugal' fix' up a plan ter stop it. Dey wuz a cunjuh 'oman livin' down 'mongs' de free niggers on de Wim'l'ton Road, en all de darkies fum Rockfish ter Beaver Crick wuz feared er her. She could wuk de mos' powerfulles' kin' er goopher,—could make people hab fits, er rheumatiz, er make 'em des dwinel away en die; en dey say she went out ridin' de niggers at night, fer she wuz a witch 'sides bein' a cunjuh 'oman. Mars Dugal' hearn 'bout Aun' Peggy's doin's, en begun ter 'flect whe'r er no he couldn' git her ter he'p him keep de niggers off'n de grapevimes. One day in de spring er de year, ole miss pack' up a basket er chick'n en poun'-cake, en a bottle er scuppernon' wine, en Mars Dugal' tuk it in his buggy en driv ober ter Aun' Peggy's cabin. He tuk de basket in, en had a long talk wid Aun' Peggy.

"De nex' day Aun' Peggy come up ter de vimya'd. De niggers seed her slippin' 'roun', en dey soon foun' out what she 'uz doin' dere. Mars Dugal' had hi'ed her ter goopher de grapevimes, She sa'ntered 'roun' 'mongs' de vimes, en tuk a leaf fum dis one, en a grape-hull fum dat one, en a grape-seed fum anudder one; en den a little twig fum here, en a little pinch er dirt fum dere,—en put it all in a big black bottle, wid a snake's toof en a speckle' hen's gall en some ha'rs fum a black cat's tail, en den fill' de bottle wid scuppernon' wine. W'en she got de goopher all ready en fix', she tuk 'n went out in de woods en buried it under de root uv a red oak tree, en den come back en tole one er de niggers she done goopher de grapevimes, en a'er a nigger w'at eat dem grapes 'ud be sho ter die inside'n twel' mont's.

"Atter dat de niggers let de scuppernon's 'lone, en Mars Dugal' didn' hab no 'casion ter fine no mo' fault; en de season wuz mos' gone, w'en a strange gemman stop at de plantation one night ter see Mars Dugal' on some business; en his coachman, seein' de scuppernon's growin' so nice en sweet, slip 'roun' behine de smoke-house, en et all de scuppernon's he could hole. Nobody didn' notice it at de time, but dat night, on de way home, de gemman's hoss runned away en kill' de coachman. W'en we hearn de noos, Aun' Lucy, de cook, she up 'n say she seed de strange nigger eat'n' er de scuppemon's behine de smoke-house; en den we knowed de goopher had b'en er wukkin'. Den one er de nigger chilluns runned away fum de quarters one day, en got in de scupper-non's, en died de nex' week. W'ite folks say he die' er de fevuh, but de niggers knowed it wuz de goopher. So you k'n be sho de darkies didn' hab much ter do wid dem scuppernon' vimes.

"W'en de scuppernon' season 'uz ober fer dat year, Mars Dugal' foun' he had made fifteen hund'ed gallon er wine; en one er de niggers hearn him laffin' wid de oberseah fit ter kill, en sayin dem fifteen hund'ed gallon er wine wuz monst'us good intrus' on de ten dollars he laid out on de vimya'd. So I 'low ez he paid Aun' Peggy ten dollars fer to goopher de grapevimes.

"De goopher didn' wuk no mo' tel de nex' summer, w'en 'long to'ds de middle er de season one er de fiel' han's died; en ez dat lef' Mars Dugal' sho't er han's, he went off ter town fer ter buy anudder. He fotch de noo nigger home wid 'im. He wuz er ole nigger, er de color er a gingy-cake, en ball ez a hoss-apple on de top er his head. He wuz a peart ole nigger, do', en could do a big day's wuk.

"Now it happen dat one er de niggers on de nex' plantation, one er old Mars Henry Brayboy's niggers, had runned away de day befo', en tuk ter de swamp, en ole Mars Dugal' en some er de yuther nabor w'ite folks had gone out wid dere guns en dere dogs fer ter he'p 'em hunt fer de nigger; en de han's on our own plantation wuz all so flusterated dat we fuhgot ter tell de noo han' 'bout de goopher on de scuppernon' vimes. Co'se he smell de grapes en see de vimes, an atter dahk de fus' thing he done wuz ter slip off ter de grapevimes 'dout sayin' nuffin ter nobody. Nex' mawnin' he tole some er de niggers 'bout de fine bait er scuppernon' he et de night befo'.

"W'en dey tole 'im 'bout de goopher on de grapevimes, he 'uz dat tarrified dat he turn pale, en look des like he gwine ter die right in his tracks. De oberseah come up en axed w'at 'uz de matter; en w'en dey tole 'im Henry be'n eatin' er de scuppernon's, en got de goopher on 'im, he gin Henry a big drink er w'iskey, en 'low dat de nex' rainy day he take 'im ober ter Aun' Peggy's, en see ef she wouldn' take de goopher off'n him, seein' ez he didn' know nuffin erbout it tel he done et de grapes.

"Sho nuff, it rain de nex' day, en de oberseah went ober ter Aun' Peggy's wid Henry. En Aun' Peggy say dat bein' ez Henry didn' know 'bout de goopher, en et de grapes in ign'ance er de conseq'ences, she reckon she mought be able fer ter take de goopher off'n him. So she fotch out er bottle wid some cunjuh medicine in it, en po'd some out in a go'd for Henry ter drink. He manage ter git it down; he say it tas'e like whiskey wid sump'n bitter in it. She 'lowed dat 'ud keep de goopher off'n him tel de spring: but w'en de sap begin ter rise in de grape-vimes he ha' ter come en see her ag'in, en she tell him w'at e's ter do.

"Nex' spring, w'en de sap commence' ter rise in de scuppernon' vime, Henry tuk a ham one night. Whar'd he git de ham? *I* doan know; dey wa'n't no hams on de plantation 'cep'n' w'at 'uz in de smokehouse, but *I* never see Henry 'bout de smoke-house. But ez I wuz a–sayin', he tuk de ham ober ter Aun' Peggy's; en Aun' Peggy tole 'im dat w'en Mars Dugal' begin ter prune de grapevimes, he mus' go en take 'n scrape off de sap whar it ooze out'n de cut een's er de vimes, en 'n'int his ball head wid it; en ef he do dat once't a year de goopher wouldn' wuk agin 'im long ez he done it. En bein' ez he fotch her de ham, she fix' it so he kin eat all de scuppernon' he want.

"So Henry 'n'int his head wid de sap out'n de big grapevime des ha'f way 'twix' de quarters en de big house, en de goopher nebber wuk agin him dat summer. But de beatenes' thing you eber see happen ter Henry. Up ter dat time he wuz ez ball ez a sweeten' 'tater, but des ez soon ez de young leaves begun ter come out on de grapevimes, de ha'r begun ter grow out on Henry's head, en by de middle er de summer he had de bigges' head er ha'r on de plantation. Befo' dat, Henry had tol'able good ha'r 'roun' de aidges, but soon ez de young grapes begun ter come, Henry's ha'r begun to quirl all up in little balls, de like dis yer reg'lar grapy ha'r, en by de time de grapes got ripe his head look des like a bunch er grapes. Combin' it didn' do no good; he wuk at it ha'f de night wid er Jim Crow,[1] en think he git it straighten' out, but in de mawnin' de grapes 'ud be dere des de same. So he gin it up, en tried ter keep de grapes down by havin' his hair cut sho't.

"But dat wa'n't de quares' thing 'bout de goopher. When Henry come ter de plantation, he wuz gittin' a little ole an stiff in de j'ints. But dat summer he got des ez spry en libely ez any young nigger

---

[1] A small card, resembling a currycomb in construction, and used by negroes in the rural districts instead of a comb.

on de plantation; fac', he got so biggity dat Mars Jackson, de oberseah, ha' ter th'eaten ter whip 'im, ef he didn' stop cuttin' up his
didos en behave hisse'f. But de mos' cur'ouses' thing happen' in de
fall, when de sap begin ter go down in de grapevimes. Fus', when
de grapes 'uz gethered, de knots begun ter straighten out'n Henry's
ha'r; en w'en de leaves begin ter fall, Henry's ha'r 'mence' ter drap
out; en when de vimes 'uz bar', Henry's head wuz baller'n it wuz
in de spring, en he begin ter git ole en stiff in de j'ints ag'in, en paid
no mo' 'tention ter de gals dyoin' er de whole winter. En nex'
spring, w'en he rub de sap on ag'in, he got young ag'in, en so soopl
en libely dat none er de young niggers on de plantation couldn'
jump, ner dance, ner hoe ez much cotton ez Henry. But in de fall
er de year his grapes 'mence' ter straighten out, en his j'ints ter git
stiff, en his ha'r drap off, en de rheumatiz begin ter wrastle wid 'im.

"Now, ef you'd 'a' knowed ole Mars Dugal' McAdoo, you'd 'a'
knowed dat it ha' ter be a mighty rainy day when he couldn' fine
sump'n fer his niggers ter do, en it ha' ter be a mighty little hole he
could n' crawl thoo, en ha' ter be a monst'us cloudy night when a
dollar git by him in de dahkness; en w'en he see how Henry git
young in de spring en ole in de fall, he 'lowed ter hisse'f ez how he
could make mo' money out'n Henry dan by wukkin' him in de
cotton-fiel'. 'Long de nex' spring, atter de sap 'mence' ter rise, en
Henry 'n'int 'is head en sta'ted fer ter git young en soopl, Mars
Dugal' up 'n tuk Henry ter town, en sole 'im fer fifteen hunder'
dollars. Co'se de man w'at bought Henry didn' know nuffin 'bout
de goopher, en Mars Dugal' didn' see no 'casion fer ter tell 'im.
Long to'ds de fall, w'en de sap went down, Henry begin ter git ole
agin same ez yuzhal, en his noo marster begin ter git skeered les'n
he gwine ter lose his fifteen-hunder'-dollar nigger. He sent fer a
mighty fine doctor, but de med'cine didn' 'pear ter do no good; de
goopher had a good holt. Henry tole de doctor 'bout de goopher,
but de doctor des laff at 'im.

"One day in de winter Mars Dugal' went ter town, en wuz san-
terin' 'long de Main Street, when who should he meet but Henry's
noo marster. Dey said 'Hoddy,' en Mars Dugal' ax 'im ter hab a
seegyar; en atter dey run on awhile 'bout de craps en de weather,
Mars Dugal' ax 'im, sorter keerless, like ez ef he des thought of it,—

"'How you like de nigger I sole you las' spring?'

"Henry's marster shuck his head en knock de ashes off'n his
seegyar.

" 'Spec' I made a bad bahgin when I bought dat nigger. Henry done good wuk all de summer, but sence de fall set in he 'pears ter be sorter pinin' away. Dey ain' nuffin pertickler de matter wid 'im—leastways de doctor say so—'cep'n' a tech er de rheumatiz; but his ha'r is all fell out, en ef he don't pick up his strenk mighty soon, I spec' I'm gwine ter lose 'im.'

"Dey smoked on awhile, en bimeby ole mars say, 'Well, a bahgin's a bahgin, but you en me is good fren's, en I doan wan' ter see you lose all de money you paid fer dat nigger; en ef w'at you say is so, en I ain't 'sputin' it, he ain't wuf much now. I 'spec's you wukked him too ha'd dis summer, er e'se de swamps down here don't agree wid de san'-hill nigger. So you des lemme know, en ef he gits any wusser I'll be willin' ter gib yer five hund'ed dollars fer 'im, en take my chances on his livin'.'

"Sho 'nuff, when Henry begun ter draw up wid de rheumatiz en it look like he gwine ter die fer sho, his noo marster sen' fer Mars Dugal', en Mars Dugal' gin him what he promus, en brung Henry home ag'in. He tuk good keer uv 'im dyoin' er de winter,—give 'im w'iskey ter rub his rheumatiz, en terbacker ter smoke, en all he want ter eat,—'caze a nigger w'at he could make a thousan' dollars a year off'n didn' grow on eve'y huckleberry bush.

"Nex' spring, w'en de sap ris en Henry's ha'r commence' ter sprout, Mars Dugal' sole 'im ag'in, down in Robeson County dis time; en he kep' dat sellin' business up fer five year er mo'. Henry nebber say nuffin 'bout de goopher ter his noo marsters, 'caze he know he gwine ter be tuk good keer uv de nex' winter, w'en Mars Dugal' buy him back. En Mars Dugal' made 'nuff money off'n Henry ter buy anudder plantation ober on Beaver Crick.

"But 'long 'bout de een' er dat five year dey come a stranger ter stop at de plantation. De fus' day he 'uz dere he went out wid Mars Dugal' en spent all de mawnin' lookin' ober de vimya'd, en atter dinner dey spent all de evenin' playin' kya'ds. De niggers soon 'skiver' dat he wuz a Yankee, en dat he come down ter Norf C'lina fer ter l'arn de w'ite folks how to raise grapes en make wine. He promus Mars Dugal' he c'd make de grapevimes b'ar twice't ez many grapes, en dat de noo winepress he wuz a-sellin' would make mo' d'n twice't ez many gallons er wine. En ole Mars Dugal' des drunk it all in, des 'peared ter be bewitch' wid dat Yankee. W'en de darkies see dat Yankee runnin' 'roun' de vimya'd en diggin' under de grapevimes, dey shuk dere heads, en

'lowed dat dey feared Mars Dugal' losin' his min'. Mars Dugal'
had all de dirt dug away fum under de roots er all de scuppernon'
vimes, an' let 'em stan' dat away fer a week er mo'. Den dat
Yankee made de niggers fix up a mixtry er lime en ashes en
manyo, en po' it 'roun' de roots er de grapevimes. Den he 'vise
Mars Dugal' fer ter trim de vimes close't, en Mars Dugal' tuck 'n
done eve'ything de Yankee tole him ter do. Dyoin' all er dis time,
mind yer, dis yer Yankee wuz libbin' off'n de fat er de lan', at de
big house, en playin' kya'ds wid Mars Dugal' eve'y night; en dey
say Mars Dugal' los' mo'n a thousan' dollars dyoin' er de week dat
Yankee wuz a-ruinin' de grapevimes.

"Wen de sap ris nex' spring, ole Henry 'n'inted his head ez
yuzhal, en his ha'r 'mence' ter grow des de same ez it done eve'y
year. De scuppernon' vimes growed monst'us fas', en de leaves wuz
greener en thicker den dey eber be'n dyoin' my rememb'ance; en
Henry's ha'r growed out thicker den eber, en he 'peared ter git
younger 'n younger, en soopler 'n soopler; en seein' ez he wuz
sho't er han's dat spring, havin' tuk in con-sid'able noo groun',
Mars Dugal' 'cluded he wouldn' sell Henry 'tel he git de crap in en
de cotton chop'. So he kep' Henry on de plantation.

"But 'long 'bout time fer de grapes ter come on de scuppernon'
vimes, dey 'peared ter come a change ober 'em; de leaves withered
en swivel' up, en de young grapes turn' yaller, en bimeby eve'ybody
on de plantation could see dat de whole vimya'd wuz dyin'. Mars
Dugal' tuk 'n water de vimes en done all he could, but't wa'n' no
use: dat Yankee had done bus' de watermillyum. One time de
vimes picked up a bit, en Mars Dugal' 'lowed dey wuz gwine ter
come out ag'in; but dat Yankee done dug too close under de roots,
en prune de branches too close ter de vime, en all dat lime en ashes
done burn' de life out'n de vimes, en dey des kep' a-with'in' en
a-swivelin'.

"All dis time de goopher wuz a-wukkin'. When de vimes sta'ted
ter wither, Henry 'mence' ter complain er his rheumatiz; en when
de leaves begin ter dry up, his ha'r 'mence' ter drap out. When de
vimes fresh' up a bit, Henry'd git peart ag'in, en when de vimes
wither' ag'in, Henry'd git ole ag'in, en des kep' gittin' mo' en mo'
fitten fer nufffin; he des pined away, en pined away, en fine'ly tuk
ter his cabin; en when de big vime whar he got de sap ter 'n'int his
head withered en turned yaller en died, Henry died too,—des went
out sorter like a cannel. Dey didn't 'pear ter be nuffin de matter wid

'im, 'cep'n' de rheumatiz, but his strenk des dwinel' away 'tel he didn' hab ernuff lef' ter draw his bref. De goopher had got de under holt, en th'owed Henry dat time fer good en all.

"Mars Dugal' tuk on might'ly 'bout losin' his vimes en his nigger in de same year; en he swo' dat ef he could git holt er dat Yankee he'd wear 'im ter a frazzle, en den chaw up de frazzle; en he'd done it, too, for Mars Dugal' 'uz a monst'us brash man w'en he once git started. He sot de vimya'd out ober ag'in, but it wuz th'ee er fo' year befo' de vimes got ter b'arin' any scuppernon's.

"W'en de wah broke out, Mars Dugal' raise' a comp'ny, en went off ter fight de Yankees. He say he wuz mighty glad dat wah come, en he des want ter kill a Yankee fer eve'y dollar he los' 'long er dat grape-raisin' Yankee. En I 'spec' he would 'a' done it, too, ef de Yankees hadn' s'picioned sump'n en killed him fus'. Atter de s'render ole miss move' ter town, de niggers all scattered 'way fum de plantation, en de vimya'd ain' be'n cultervated sence."

"Is that story true?" asked Annie doubtfully, but seriously, as the old man concluded his narrative.

"It's des ez true ez I'm a-settin' here, miss. Dey's a easy way ter prove it: I kin lead de way right ter Henry's grave ober yander in de plantation buryin'-groun'. En I tell yer w'at, marster, I wouldn' 'vise you to buy dis yer ole vimya'd, 'caze de goopher's on it yit, en dey ain' no tellin' w'en it's gwine ter crap out."

"But I thought you said all the old vines died."

"Dey did 'pear ter die, but a few un 'em come out ag'in, en is mixed in 'mongs' de yuthers. I ain' skeered ter eat de grapes, 'caze I knows de old vimes fum de noo ones; but wid strangers dey ain' no tellin' w'at mought happen. I wouldn' 'vise yer ter buy dis vimya'd."

I bought the vineyard, nevertheless, and it has been for a long time in a thriving condition, and is often referred to by the local press as a striking illustration of the opportunities open to Northern capital in the development of Southern industries. The luscious scuppernong holds first rank among our grapes, though we cultivate a great many other varieties, and our income from grapes packed and shipped to the Northern markets is quite considerable. I have not noticed any developments of the goopher in the vineyard, although I have a mild suspicion that our colored assistants do not suffer from want of grapes during the season.

I found, when I bought the vineyard, that Uncle Julius had occupied a cabin on the place for many years, and derived a respectable revenue from the product of the neglected grapevines. This, doubtless, accounted for his advice to me not to buy the vineyard, though whether it inspired the goopher story I am unable to state. I believe, however, that the wages I paid him for his services as coachman, for I gave him employment in that capacity, were more than an equivalent for anything he lost by the sale of the vineyard.

JOHN ADAMS' DIARY
Bill Nye

DECEMBER 3, 1764.—I am determined to keep a diary, if possible, the rest of my life. I fully realize how difficult it will be to do so. Many others of my acquaintance have endeavored to maintain a diary, but have only advanced so far as the second week in January. It is my purpose to write down each evening the events of the day as they occur to my mind, in order that in a few years they may be read and enjoyed by my family. I shall try to deal truthfully with all matters that I may refer to in these pages, whether they be of national or personal interest, and I shall seek to avoid anything bitter or vituperative, trying rather to cool my temper before I shall submit my thoughts to paper.

December 4.—This morning we have had trouble with the hired girl. It occurred in this wise: We had fully two-thirds of a pumpkin pie that had been baked in a square tin. This major portion of the pie was left over from our dinner yesterday, and last night, before retiring to rest, I desired my wife to suggest something in the cold pie line, which she did. I lit a candle and explored the pantry in vain.

The pie was no longer visible. I told Mrs. Adams that I had not been successful, whereupon we sought out the hired girl, whose name is Tootie Tooterson, a foreign damsel, who landed in this country Nov. 7, this present year. She does not understand our language, apparently, especially when we refer to pie. The only thing she does without a strong foreign accent is to eat pumpkin pie and draw her salary. She landed on our coast six weeks ago, after a tedious voyage across the heaving billows. It was a close fight between Tootie and the ocean, but when they quit, the heaving billows were one heave ahead by the log.

Miss Tooterson landed in Massachusetts in a woolen dress and hollow clear down into the ground. A strong desire to acquire knowledge and cold, handmade American pie seems to pervade her entire being.

She has only allowed Mrs. Adams and myself to eat what she did not want herself.

Miss Tooterson has also introduced into my household various European eccentricities and strokes of economy which deserve a brief notice here. Among other things she has made pie crust with castor oil in it, and lubricated the pancake griddle with a pork rind that I had used on my lame neck. She is thrifty and saving in this way, but rashly extravagant in the use of doughnuts, pie and Medford rum, which we keep in the house for visitors who are so unfortunate as to be addicted to the doughnut, pie or rum habit.

It is discouraging, indeed, for two young people like Mrs. Adams and myself, who have just begun to keep house, to inherit a famine, and such a robust famine, too. It is true that I should not have set my heart upon such a transitory and evanescent terrestrial object like a pumpkin pie so near to T. Tooterson, imported pie soloist, doughnut maestro and feminine virtuoso, but I did, and so I returned from the pantry desolate.

I told Abigail that unless we poisoned a few pies for Tootie the Adams family would be a short-lived race. I could see with my prophetic eye that unless the Tootersons yielded the Adamses would be wiped out. Abigail would not consent to this, but decided to relieve Miss Tooterson from duty in this department, so this morning she went away. Not being at all familiar with the English language, she took four of Abigail's sheets and quite a number of towels, handkerchiefs and collars. She also erroneously took a pair of my night-shirts in her poor, broken way. Being entirely ignorant of American customs, I presume that she will put a belt around them and wear them externally to church. I trust that she will not do this, however, without mature deliberation. I also had a bottle of lung medicine of a very powerful nature which the doctor had prepared for me. By some oversight, Miss Tooterson drank this the first day that she was in our service. This was entirely wrong, as I did not intend to use it for the foreign trade, but mostly for home consumption.

This is a little piece of drollery that I thought of myself. I do not think that a joke impairs the usefulness of a diary, as some do. A diary with a joke in it is just as good to fork over to posterity as one that is not thus disfigured. In fact, what has posterity ever done for me that I should hesitate about socking a little humor into a diary? When has posterity ever gone out of its way to do me a favor? Never! I defy the historian to show a single instance where posterity has ever been the first to recognize and remunerate ability.

December 6.—It is with great difficulty that I write this entry in my diary, for this morning Abigail thought best for me to carry the oleander down into the cellar, as the nights have been growing colder of late.

I do not know which I dislike most, foreign usurpation or the oleander. I have carried that plant up and down stairs every time the weather has changed, and the fickle elements of New England have kept me rising and falling with the thermometer, and whenever I raised or fell I most always had that scrawny oleander in my arms.

Richly has it repaid us, however, with its long, green, limber branches and its little yellow nubs on the end. How full of promises to the eye that are broken to the heart. The oleander is always just about to meet its engagements, but later on it peters out and fails to materialize.

I do not know what we would do if it were not for our house plants. Every fall I shall carry them cheerfully down cellar, and in the spring I will bring up the pots for Mrs. Adams to weep softly into. Many a night at the special instance and request of my wife I have risen, clothed in one simple, clinging garment, to go and see if the speckled, double and twisted Rise-up-William-Riley geranium was feeling all right.

Last summer Abigail brought home a slip of English ivy. I do not like things that are English very much, but I tolerated this little sickly thing because it seemed to please Abigail. I asked her what were the salient features of the English ivy. What did the English ivy do? What might be its specialty? Mrs. Adams said that it made a specialty of climbing. It was a climber from away back. "All right," I then to her did straightway say, "let her climb." It was a good early climber. It climbed higher than Jack's beanstalk. It climbed the golden stair. Most of our plants are actively engaged in descending the cellar stairs or in ascending the golden stair most all the time,

I descended the stairs with the oleander this morning, though the oleander got there a little more previously than I did. Parties desiring a good, second-hand oleander tub, with castors on it, will do well to give us a call before going elsewhere. Purchasers desiring a good set of second-hand ear muffs for tulips will find something to their advantage by addressing the subscriber.

We also have two very highly ornamental green dogoods for ivy vines to ramble over. We could be induced to sell these dogoods at a sacrifice, in order to make room for our large stock of new and attractive dogoods. These articles are as good as ever. We bought them during the panic last fall for our vines to climb over, but, as our vines died of membranous croup in November, these dogoods still remain unclum.

Second-hand dirt always on hand. Ornamental geranium stumps at bed-rock prices. Highest cash prices paid for slips of black-and-tan foliage plants. We are headquarters for the century plant that draws a salary for ninety-nine years and then dies.

I do not feel much like writing in my diary today, but the physician says that my arm will be better in a day or two, so that it will be more of a pleasure to do business.

We are still without a servant girl, so I do some of the cooking. I make a fire each day and boil the tea-kettle. People who have tried my boiled tea-kettle say it is very fine.

Some of my friends have asked me to run for the Legislature here next election. Somehow I feel that I might, in public life, rise to distinction some day, and perhaps at some future time figure prominently in the affairs of a one-horse republic at a good salary.

I have never done anything in the statesman line, but it does not look difficult to me. It occurs to me that success in public life is the result of a union of several great primary elements, to-wit:

Firstly—Ability to whoop in a felicitous manner.

Secondly—Promptness in improving the proper moment in which to whoop.

Thirdly—Ready and correct decision in the matter of which side to whoop on.

Fourthly—Ability to cork up the whoop at the proper moment and keep it in a cool place till needed.

And this last is one of the most important of all. It is the amateur statesman who talks the most. Fearing that he will conceal his identity as a fool, he babbles in conversation and slashes around in his shallow banks in public.

As soon as I get the house plants down cellar and get their overshoes on for the winter, I will more seriously consider the question of our political affairs here in this new land where we have to tie our scalps on at night and where every summer is an Indian summer.

THE SPHINX WITHOUT A SECRET

Oscar Wilde

AN ETCHING

ONE AFTERNOON I was sitting outside the Café de la Paix, watching the splendour and shabbiness of Parisian life, and wondering over my vermouth at the strange panorama of pride and poverty that was passing before me, when I heard some one call my name. I turned round and saw Lord Murchison. We had not met since we had been at college together, nearly ten years before, so I was delighted to come across him again, and we shook hands warmly. At Oxford we had been great friends. I had liked him immensely, he was so handsome, so high-spirited, and so honourable. We used to say of him that he would be the best of fellows, if he did not always speak the truth, but I think we really admired him all the more for his frankness. I found him a good deal changed. He looked anxious and puzzled, and seemed to be in doubt about something. I felt it could not be modern scepticism, for Murchison was the stoutest of Tories, and believed in the Pentateuch as firmly as he believed in the House of Peers; so I concluded that it was a woman, and asked him if he was married yet.

"I don't understand women well enough," he answered.

"My dear Gerald," I said, "women are meant to be loved, not to be understood."

"I cannot love where I cannot trust," he replied.

"I believe you have a mystery in your life, Gerald," I exclaimed; "tell me about it."

"Let us go for a drive," he answered, "it is too crowded here. No, not a yellow carriage, any other colour—there, that dark green one will do"; and in a few moments we were trotting down the boulevard in the direction of the Madeleine.

"Where shall we go to?" I said.

"Oh, anywhere you like!" he answered—"to the restaurant in the Bois; we will dine there, and you shall tell me all about yourself."

"I want to hear about you first," I said. "Tell me your mystery."

He took from his pocket a little silver-clasped morocco case, and handed it to me. I opened it. Inside there was the photograph of a woman. She was tall and slight, and strangely picturesque with her large vague eyes and loosened hair. She looked like a clairvoyante, and was wrapped in rich furs.

"What do you think of that face?" he said; "is it truthful?"

I examined it carefully. It seemed to me the face of some one who had a secret, but whether that secret was good or evil I could not say. Its beauty was a beauty moulded out of many mysteries—the beauty, in fact, which is psychological, not plastic—and the faint smile that just played across the lips was far too subtle to be really sweet.

"Well," he cried impatiently, "what do you say?"

"She is the Gioconda in sables," I answered. "Let me know all about her."

"Not now," he said; "after dinner," and began to talk of other things.

When the waiter brought us our coffee and cigarettes I reminded Gerald of his promise. He rose from his seat, walked two or three times up and down the room, and, sinking into an arm-chair, told me the following story:

"One evening," he said, "I was walking down Bond Street about five o'clock. There was a terrific crush of carriages, and the traffic was almost stopped. Close to the pavement was standing a little yellow brougham, which, for some reason or other, attracted my attention. As I passed by there looked out from it the face I showed you this afternoon. It fascinated me immediately. All that night I kept thinking of it, and all the next day. I wandered up and down that wretched Row, peering into every carriage, and waiting for the yellow brougham; but I could not find *ma belle inconnue,* and at last I began to think she was merely a dream. About a week afterwards I was dining with Madame de Rastail. Dinner was for eight o'clock; but at half-past eight we were still waiting in the drawing-room. Finally the servant threw open the door, and announced Lady Alroy. It was the woman I had been looking for. She came in very slowly, looking like a moonbeam in grey lace, and, to my intense delight, I was asked to take her in to dinner. After we had sat down, I remarked quite innocently, 'I think I caught sight of you in Bond Street some time ago, Lady Alroy.' She grew very pale, and said to me in a low voice, 'Pray do not talk so loud; you may be overheard.' I felt miserable at having made such a bad beginning, and plunged recklessly into the subject of the French plays. She spoke very little, always in the same low musical voice, and seemed as if she was afraid of some one listening. I fell passionately, stupidly in love, and the indefinable atmosphere of mystery that surrounded her excited my most ardent curiosity. When she was going away, which she did very soon after dinner, I asked her if I might call and see her. She hesitated for a moment, glanced round to see if any one was near us, and then said, 'Yes; to-morrow at a quarter to five.' I begged Madame de Rastail to tell me about her; but all that I could learn was that she was a widow with a beautiful house in Park Lane, and as some scientific bore began a dissertation on widows, as exemplifying the survival of the matrimonially fittest, I left and went home.

"The next day I arrived at Park Lane punctual to the moment, but was told by the butler that Lady Alroy had just gone out. I went down to the club quite unhappy and very much puzzled, and after long consideration wrote her a letter, asking if I might be allowed to try my chance some other afternoon. I had no answer for several days, but at last I got a little note saying she would be at home on Sunday at four and with this extraordinary postscript: 'Please do not write to me here again; I will explain when I see you.' On Sunday she received me, and was perfectly charming; but when I was going away she begged of me, if I ever had occasion to write to her again, to address my letter to 'Mrs. Knox, care of Whittaker's Library, Green Street.' 'There are reasons,' she said, 'why I cannot receive letters in my own house.'

"All through the season I saw a great deal of her, and the atmosphere of mystery never left her. Sometimes I thought she was in the power of some man, but she looked so unapproachable that I could not believe it. It was really very difficult for me to come to any conclusion, for she was like one of those strange crystals that one sees in museums, which are at one moment clear, and at another clouded. At last I determined to ask her to be my wife: I was sick and tired of the incessant secrecy that she imposed on all my visits, and on the few letters I sent her. I wrote to her at the library to ask her if she could see me the following Monday at six. She answered yes, and I was in the seventh heaven of delight. I was infatuated with her: in spite of the mystery, I thought then—in consequence of it, I see now. No; it was the woman herself I loved. The mystery troubled me, maddened me. Why did chance put me in its track?"

"You discovered it, then?" I cried.

"I fear so," he answered. "You can judge for yourself."

"When Monday came round I went to lunch with my uncle, and about four o'clock found myself in the Marylebone Road. My uncle, you know, lives in Regent's Park. I wanted to get to Piccadilly, and took a short cut through a lot of shabby little streets. Suddenly I saw in front of me Lady Alroy, deeply veiled and walking very fast. On coming to the last house in the street, she went up the steps, took out a latch-key, and let herself in. 'Here is the mystery,' I said to myself; and I hurried on and examined the house. It seemed a sort of place for letting lodgings. On the doorstep lay her handkerchief, which she had dropped. I picked it up and put it in my pocket. Then I began to consider what I should do. I came to the conclusion that I had no right to spy on her, and I drove down to the club. At six I called to see her. She was lying on a sofa, in a tea-gown of silver tissue looped up by some strange moonstones that she always wore. She was looking quite lovely. 'I am so glad to see you,' she said; 'I have not been out all day' I stared at her in amazement, and pulling the handkerchief out of my pocket, handed it to her. 'You dropped this in Cumnor Street this afternoon, Lady Alroy,' I said very calmly. She looked at me in terror, but made no attempt to take the handkerchief. 'What were you doing there?' I asked. 'What right have you to question me?' she answered. 'The right of a man who loves you,' I replied; 'I came here to ask you to be my wife.' She hid her face in her hands, and burst into floods of tears. 'You must tell me,' I continued. She stood up, and, looking me straight in the face, said, 'Lord Murchison, there is nothing to tell you.'—'You went to meet some one,' I cried; 'this is your mystery.' She grew dreadfully white, and said, 'I went to meet no one.'—'Can't you tell the truth?' I exclaimed. 'I have told it,' she replied. I was mad, frantic; I don't know what I said, but I said terrible things to her. Finally I rushed out of the house. She wrote me a letter the next day; I sent it back unopened, and started for Norway with Alan Colville. After a month I came back, and the first thing I saw in the *Morning Post* was the death of Lady Alroy. She had caught a chill at the Opera, and had died in five days of congestion of the lungs. I shut myself up and saw no one. I had loved her so much, I had loved her so madly. Good God! how I had loved that woman!"

"You went to the street, to the house in it?" I said.

"Yes," he answered.

"One day I went to Cumnor Street. I could not help it; I was tortured with doubt. I knocked at the door, and a respectable-looking woman opened it to me. I asked her if she had any rooms to let. 'Well, sir,' she replied, 'the drawing-rooms are supposed to be let; but I have not seen the lady for three months, and as rent is owing on them, you can have them.'—'Is this the lady?' I said, showing the photograph. 'That's her, sure enough,' she exclaimed; 'and when is she coming back, sir?'—'The lady is dead,' I replied. 'Oh, sir, I hope not!' said the woman; 'she was my best lodger. She paid me three guineas a week merely to sit in my drawing-rooms now and then.'—'She met some one here?' I said; but the woman assured me that it was not so, that she always came alone, and saw no one. 'What on earth did she do here?' I cried. 'She simply sat in the drawing-room, sir, reading books, and sometimes had tea,' the woman answered. I did not know what to say, so I gave her a sovereign and went away. Now, what do you think it all meant? You don't believe the woman was telling the truth?"

"I do."

"Then why did Lady Alroy go there?"

"My dear Gerald," I answered, "Lady Alroy was simply a woman with a mania for mystery. She took these rooms for the pleasure of going there with her veil down, and imagining she was a heroine. She had a passion for secrecy, but she herself was merely a Sphinx without a secret."

"Do you really think so?"

"I am sure of it," I replied.

He took out the morocco case, opened it, and looked at the photograph. "I wonder?" he said at last.

THE HAPPY PRINCE

Oscar Wilde

HIGH ABOVE THE city, on a tall column, stood the statue of the Happy Prince. He was gilded all over with thin leaves of fine gold, for eyes he had two bright sapphires, and a large red ruby glowed on his sword-hilt.

He was very much admired indeed. "He is as beautiful as a weathercock," remarked one of the Town Councillors who wished to gain a reputation for having artistic tastes; "only not quite so useful," he added, fearing lest people should think him unpractical, which he really was not.

"Why can't you be like the Happy Prince?" asked a sensible mother of her little boy who was crying for the moon. "The Happy Prince never dreams of crying for anything."

"I am glad there is some one in the world who is quite happy," muttered a disappointed man as he gazed at the wonderful statue.

"He looks just like an angel," said the Charity Children as they came out of the cathedral in their bright scarlet cloaks and their clean white pinafores.

"How do you know?" said the Mathematical Master, "you have never seen one."

"Ah! but we have, in our dreams," answered the children; and the Mathematical Master frowned and looked very severe, for he did not approve of children dreaming.

One night there flew over the city a little Swallow. His friends had gone away to Egypt six weeks before, but he had stayed behind, for he was in love with the most beautiful Reed. He had met her early in the spring as he was flying down the river after a big yellow moth, and had been so attracted by her slender waist that he had stopped to talk to her.

"Shall I love you?" said the Swallow, who liked to come to the point at once, and the Reed made him a low bow. So he flew round and round her, touching the water with his wings, and making silver ripples. This was his courtship, and it lasted all through the summer.

"It is a ridiculous attachment," twittered the other Swallows; "she has no money, and far too many relations"; and indeed the river was quite full of Reeds. Then, when the autumn came they all flew away.

After they had gone he felt lonely, and began to tire of his lady-love. "She has no conversation," he said, "and I am afraid that she is a coquette, for she is always flirting with the wind." And certainly, whenever the wind blew, the Reed made the most graceful curtsies. "I admit that she is domestic," he continued, "but I love travelling, and my wife, consequently, should love travelling also."

"Will you come away with me?" he said finally to her; but the Reed shook her head, she was so attached to her home.

"You have been trifling with me," he cried. "I am off to the Pyramids. Good-bye!" and he flew away.

All day long he flew, and at night-time he arrived at the city. "Where shall I put up?" he said; "I hope the town has made preparations."

Then he saw the statue on the tall column. "I will put up there," he cried; "it is a fine position, with plenty of fresh air." So he alighted just between the feet of the Happy Prince.

"I have a golden bedroom," he said softly to himself as he looked round, and he prepared to go to sleep; but just as he was putting his head under his wing a large drop of water fell on him. "What a curious thing!" he cried, "there is not a single cloud in the sky, the stars are quite clear and bright, and yet it is raining. The climate in the north of Europe is really dreadful. The Reed used to like the rain, but that was merely her selfishness."

Then another drop fell.

"What is the use of a statue if it cannot keep the rain off?" he said; "I must look for a good chimney-pot," and he determined to fly away.

But before he had opened his wings, a third drop fell, and he looked up, and saw—Ah! what did he see?

The eyes of the Happy Prince were filled with tears, and tears were running down his golden cheeks. His face was so beautiful in the moonlight that the little Swallow was filled with pity.

"Who are you?" he said.

"I am the Happy Prince."

"Why are you weeping then?" asked the Swallow; "you have quite drenched me."

"When I was alive and had a human heart," answered the statue, "I did not know what tears were, for I lived in the Palace of Sans-Souci where sorrow is not allowed to enter. In the daytime I played with my companions in the garden, and in the evening I led the dance in the Great Hall. Round the garden ran a very lofty wall, but I never cared to ask what lay beyond it, everything about me was so beautiful. My courtiers called me the Happy Prince, and happy indeed I was, if pleasure be happiness. So I lived, and so I died. And now that I am dead they have set me up here so high that I can see all the ugliness and all the misery of my city, and though my heart is made of lead yet I cannot choose but weep."

"What! is he not solid gold?" said the Swallow to himself. He was too polite to make any personal remarks out loud.

"Far away," continued the statue in a low musical voice, "far away in a little street there is a poor house. One of the windows is open, and through it I can see a woman seated at a table. Her face is thin and worn, and she has coarse, red hands, all pricked by the needle, for she is a seamstress. She is embroidering passion-flowers on a satin gown for the loveliest of the Queen's maids-of-honour to wear at the next Court-ball. In a bed in the corner of the room her little boy is lying ill. He has a fever, and is asking for oranges. His mother has nothing to give him but river water, so he is crying. Swallow, Swallow, little Swallow, will you not bring her the ruby out of my sword-hilt? My feet are fastened to this pedestal and I cannot move."

"I am waited for in Egypt," said the Swallow. "My friends are flying up and down the Nile, and talking to the large lotus-flowers. Soon they will go to sleep in the tomb of the great King. The King is there himself in his painted coffin. He is wrapped in yellow linen, and embalmed with spices. Round his neck is a chain of pale green jade, and his hands are like withered leaves."

"Swallow, Swallow, little Swallow," said the Prince, "will you not stay with me for one night, and be my messenger? The boy is so thirsty, and the mother so sad."

"I don't think I like boys," answered the Swallow. "Last summer, when I was staying on the river, there were two rude boys, the miller's sons, who were always throwing stones at me. They never hit me, of course; we swallows fly far too well for that, and besides, I come of a family famous for its agility; but still, it was a mark of disrespect."

But the Happy Prince looked so sad that the little Swallow was sorry. "It is very cold here," he said; "but I will stay with you for one night, and be your messenger."

"Thank you, little Swallow," said the Prince.

So the Swallow picked out the great ruby from the Prince's sword, and flew away with it in his beak over the roofs of the town.

He passed by the cathedral tower, where the white marble angels were sculptured. He passed by the palace and heard the sound of dancing. A beautiful girl came out on the balcony with her lover. "How wonderful the stars are," he said to her, "and how wonderful is the power of love!" "I hope my dress will be ready in time for the State-ball," she answered; "I have ordered passion-flowers to be embroidered on it; but the seamstresses are so lazy."

He passed over the river, and saw the lanterns hanging to the masts of the ships. He passed over the Ghetto, and saw the old Jews bargaining with each other, and weighing out money in copper scales. At last he came to the poor house and looked in. The boy was tossing feverishly on his bed, and the mother had fallen asleep, she was so tired. In he hopped, and laid the great ruby on the table beside the woman's thimble. Then he flew gently round the bed, fanning the boy's forehead with his wings. "How cool I feel," said the boy, "I must be getting better"; and he sank into a delicious slumber.

Then the Swallow flew back to the Happy Prince, and told him what he had done. "It is curious," he remarked, "but I feel quite warm now, although it is so cold."

"That is because you have done a good action," said the Prince. And the little Swallow began to think, and then he fell asleep. Thinking always made him sleepy.

When day broke he flew down to the river and had a bath.

"What a remarkable phenomenon," said the Professor of Ornithology as he was passing over the bridge. "A swallow in winter!" And he wrote a long letter about it to the local newspaper. Every one quoted it, it was full of so many words that they could not understand.

"To-night I go to Egypt," said the Swallow, and he was in high spirits at the prospect. He visited all the public monuments, and sat a long time on top of the church steeple. Wherever he went the Sparrows chirruped, and said to each other, "What a distinguished stranger!" so he enjoyed himself very much.

When the moon rose he flew back to the Happy Prince. "Have you any commissions for Egypt?" he cried; "I am just starting."

"Swallow, Swallow, little Swallow," said the Prince, "will you not stay with me one night longer?"

"I am waited for in Egypt," answered the Swallow. "To-morrow my friends will fly up to the Second Cataract. The river-horse couches there among the bulrushes, and on a great granite throne sits the God Memnon. All night long he watches the stars, and when the morning star shines he utters one cry of joy, and then he is silent. At noon the yellow lions come down to the water's edge to drink. They have eyes like green beryls, and their roar is louder than the roar of the cataract."

"Swallow, Swallow, little Swallow," said the Prince, "far away across the city I see a young man in a garret. He is leaning over a desk covered with papers, and in a tumbler by his side there is a bunch of withered violets. His hair is brown and crisp, and his lips are red as a pomegranate, and he has large and dreamy eyes. He is trying to finish a play for the Director of the Theatre, but he is too cold to write any more. There is no fire in the grate, and hunger has made him faint."

"I will wait with you one night longer," said the Swallow, who really had a good heart. "Shall I take him another ruby?"

"Alas! I have no ruby now," said the Prince; "my eyes are all that I have left. They are made of rare sapphires, which were brought out of India a thousand years ago. Pluck out one of them and take it to him. He will sell it to the jeweller, and buy food and firewood, and finish his play."

"Dear Prince," said the Swallow, "I cannot do that"; and he began to weep.

"Swallow, Swallow, little Swallow," said the Prince, "do as I command you."

So the Swallow plucked out the Prince's eye, and flew away to the student's garret. It was easy enough to get in, as there was a hole in the roof. Through this he darted, and came into the room. The young man had his head buried in his hands, so he did not hear the flutter of the bird's wings, and when he looked up he found the beautiful sapphire lying on the withered violets.

"I am beginning to be appreciated," he cried; "this is from some great admirer. Now I can finish my play," and he looked quite happy.

The next day the Swallow flew down to the harbour. He sat on the mast of a large vessel and watched the sailors hauling big chests out of the hold with ropes. "Heave a-hoy!" they shouted as each chest came up. "I am going to Egypt!" cried the Swallow, but nobody minded, and when the moon rose he flew back to the Happy Prince.

"I am come to bid you good-bye," he cried.

"Swallow, Swallow, little Swallow," said the Prince, "will you not stay with me one night longer?"

"It is winter," answered the Swallow, "and the chill snow will soon be here. In Egypt the sun is warm on the green palm-trees, and the crocodiles lie in the mud and look lazily about them. My companions are building a nest in the Temple of Baalbec, and the pink and white doves are watching them, and cooing to each other. Dear Prince, I must leave you, but I will never forget you, and next spring I will bring you back two beautiful jewels in place of those you have given away. The ruby shall be redder than a red rose, and the sapphire shall be as blue as the great sea."

"In the square below," said the Happy Prince, "there stands a little match-girl. She has let her matches fall in the gutter, and they are all spoiled. Her father will beat her if she does not bring home some money, and she is crying. She has no shoes or stockings, and her little head is bare. Pluck out my other eye, and give it to her, and her father will not beat her."

"I will stay with you one night longer," said the Swallow, "but I cannot pluck out your eye. You would be quite blind then."

"Swallow, Swallow, little Swallow," said the Prince, "do as I command you."

So he plucked out the Prince's other eye, and darted down with it. He swooped past the match-girl, and slipped the jewel into the palm of her hand. "What a lovely bit of glass," cried the little girl; and she ran home, laughing.

Then the Swallow came back to the Prince. "You are blind now," he said, "so I will stay with you always."

"No, little Swallow," said the poor Prince, "you must go away to Egypt."

"I will stay with you always," said the Swallow, and he slept at the Prince's feet.

All the next day he sat on the Prince's shoulder, and told him stories of what he had seen in strange lands. He told him of the red ibises, who stand in long rows on the banks of the Nile, and catch gold fish in their beaks; of the Sphinx, who is as old as the world itself, and lives in the desert, and knows everything; of the merchants, who walk slowly by the side of their camels, and carry amber beads in their hands; of the King of the Mountains of the Moon, who is as black as ebony, and worships a large crystal; of the great green snake that sleeps in a palm-tree, and has twenty priests to feed it with honey-cakes; and of the pygmies who sail over a big lake on large flat leaves, and are always at war with the butterflies.

"Dear little Swallow," said the Prince, "you tell me of marvellous things, but more marvellous than anything is the suffering of men and of women. There is no Mystery so great as Misery. Fly over my city, little Swallow, and tell me what you see there."

So the Swallow flew over the great city, and saw the rich making merry in their beautiful houses, while the beggars were sitting at the gates. He flew into dark lanes, and saw the white faces of starving children looking out listlessly at the black streets. Under the archway of a bridge two little boys were lying in one another's arms to try and keep themselves warm. "How hungry we are!" they said. "You must not lie here," shouted the Watchman, and they wandered out into the rain.

Then he flew back and told the Prince what he had seen.

"I am covered with fine gold," said the Prince, "you must take it off, leaf by leaf, and give it to my poor; the living always think that gold can make them happy."

Leaf after leaf of the fine gold the Swallow picked off, till the Happy Prince looked quite dull and grey. Leaf after leaf of the fine gold he brought to the poor, and the children's faces grew rosier, and they laughed and played games in the street. "We have bread now!" they cried.

Then the snow came, and after the snow came the frost. The streets looked as if they were made of silver, they were so bright and glistening; long icicles like crystal daggers hung down from the eaves of the houses, everybody went about in furs, and the little boys wore scarlet caps and skated on the ice.

The poor little Swallow grew colder and colder, but he would not leave the Prince, he loved him too well. He picked up crumbs outside the baker's door when the baker was not looking and tried to keep himself warm by flapping his wings.

But at last he knew that he was going to die. He had just strength to fly up to the Prince's shoulder once more. "Good-bye, dear Prince!" he murmured, "will you let me kiss your hand?"

"I am glad that you are going to Egypt at last, little Swallow," said the Prince, "you have stayed too long here; but you must kiss me on the lips, for I love you."

"It is not to Egypt that I am going," said the Swallow. "I am going to the House of Death. Death is the brother of Sleep, is he not?"

And he kissed the Happy Prince on the lips, and fell down dead at his feet.

At that moment a curious crack sounded inside the statue, as if something had broken. The fact is that the leaden heart had snapped right in two. It certainly was a dreadfully hard frost.

Early the next morning the Mayor was walking in the square below in company with the Town Councillors. As they passed the column he looked up at the statue: "Dear me! how shabby the Happy Prince looks!" he said.

"How shabby indeed!" cried the Town Councillors, who always agreed with the Mayor; and they went up to look at it.

"The ruby has fallen out of his sword, his eyes are gone, and he is golden no longer," said the Mayor; "in fact, he is little better than a beggar!"

"Little better than a beggar," said the Town Councillors.

"And here is actually a dead bird at his feet!" continued the Mayor. "We must really issue a proclamation that birds are not to be allowed to die here." And the Town Clerk made a note of the suggestion.

So they pulled down the statue of the Happy Prince. "As he is no longer beautiful he is no longer useful," said the Art Professor at the University.

Then they melted the statue in a furnace, and the Mayor held a meeting of the Corporation to decide what was to be done with the metal. "We must have another statue, of course," he said, "and it shall be a statue of myself."

"Of myself," said each of the Town Councillors, and they quarrelled. When I last heard of them they were quarrelling still.

"What a strange thing!" said the overseer of the workmen at the foundry. "This broken lead heart will not melt in the furnace. We must throw it away." So they threw it on a dust-heap where the dead Swallow was also lying.

"Bring me the two most precious things in the city," said God to one of His Angels; and the Angel brought Him the leaden heart and the dead bird.

"You have rightly chosen," said God, "for in my garden of Paradise this little bird shall sing for evermore, and in my city of gold the Happy Prince shall praise me."

THE SELFISH GIANT

Oscar Wilde

EVERY AFTERNOON, AS they were coming from school, the children used to go and play in the Giant's garden.

It was a large lovely garden, with soft green grass. Here and there over the grass stood beautiful flowers like stars, and there were twelve peach-trees that in the spring-time broke out into delicate blossoms of pink and pearl, and in the autumn bore rich fruit. The birds sat on the trees and sang so sweetly that the children used to stop their games in order to listen to them. "How happy we are here!" they cried to each other.

One day the Giant came back. He had been to visit his friend the Cornish ogre, and had stayed with him for seven years. After the seven years were over he had said all that he had to say, for his conversation was limited, and he determined to return to his own castle. When he arrived he saw the children playing in the garden.

"What are you doing here?" he cried in a very gruff voice, and the children ran away.

"My own garden is my own garden," said the Giant; "any one can understand that, and I will allow nobody to play in it but myself." So he built a high wall all round it, and put up a notice-board.

> TRESPASSERS
> WILL BE
> PROSECUTED

He was a very selfish Giant.

The poor children had now nowhere to play. They tried to play on the road, but the road was very dusty and full of hard stones, and they did not like it. They used to wander round the high wall when their lessons were over, and talk about the beautiful garden inside.

"How happy we were there," they said to each other.

Then the Spring came, and all over the country there were little blossoms and little birds. Only in the garden of the Selfish Giant it was still Winter. The birds did not care to sing in it as there were no children, and the trees forgot to blossom. Once a beautiful flower put its head out from the grass, but when it saw the notice-board it was so sorry for the children that it slipped back into the ground again, and went off to sleep. The only people who were pleased were the Snow and the Frost. "Spring has forgotten this garden," they cried, "so we will live here all the year round." The Snow covered up the grass with her great white cloak, and the Frost painted all the trees silver. Then they invited the North Wind to stay with them, and he came. He was wrapped in furs, and he roared all day about the garden, and blew the chimney-pots down. "This is a delightful spot," he said, "we must ask the Hail on a visit." So the Hail came. Every day for three hours he rattled on the roof of the castle till he broke most of the slates, and then he ran round and round the garden as fast as he could go. He was dressed in grey, and his breath was like ice.

"I cannot understand why the Spring is so late in coming," said the Selfish Giant, as he sat at the window and looked out at his cold white garden; "I hope there will be a change in the weather."

But the Spring never came, nor the Summer. The Autumn gave golden fruit to every garden, but to the Giant's garden she gave none. "He is too selfish," she said. So it was always Winter there, and the North Wind, and the Hail, and the Frost, and the Snow danced about through the trees.

One morning the Giant was lying awake in bed when he heard some lovely music. It sounded so sweet to his ears that he thought it must be the King's musicians passing by. It was really only a little linnet singing outside his window, but it was so long since he had heard a bird sing in his garden that it seemed to him to be the most beautiful music in the world. Then the Hail stopped dancing over his head, and the North Wind ceased roaring, and a delicious perfume came to him through the open casement. "I believe the Spring has come at last," said the Giant; and he jumped out of bed and looked out.

What did he see?

He saw a most wonderful sight. Through a little hole in the wall the children had crept in, and they were sitting in the branches of the trees. In every tree that he could see there was a little child. And the trees were so glad to have the children back again that they had covered themselves with blossoms, and were waving their arms gently above the children's heads. The birds were flying about and twittering with delight, and the flowers were looking up through the green grass and laughing. It was a lovely scene, only in one corner it was still Winter. It was the farthest corner of the garden, and in it was standing a little boy. He was so small that he could not reach up to the branches of the tree, and he was wandering all round it, crying bitterly. The poor tree was still quite covered with frost and snow, and the North Wind was blowing and roaring above it. "Climb up! little boy," said the Tree, and it bent its branches down as low as it could; but the boy was too tiny.

And the Giant's heart melted as he looked out. "How selfish I have been!" he said; "now I know why the Spring would not come here. I will put that poor little boy on the top of the tree, and then I will knock down the wall, and my garden shall be the children's playground for ever and ever." He was really very sorry for what he had done.

So he crept downstairs and opened the front door quite softly, and went out into the garden. But when the children saw him they were so frightened that they all ran away, and the garden became Winter again. Only the little boy did not run, for his eyes were so full of tears that he did not see the Giant coming. And the Giant stole up behind him and took him gently in his hand, and put him up into the tree. And the tree broke at once into blossom, and the birds came and sang on it, and the little boy stretched out his two arms and flung them round the Giant's neck, and kissed him. And the other children, when they saw that the Giant was not wicked any longer, came running back, and with them came the Spring. "It is your garden now, little children," said the Giant, and he took a great axe and knocked down the wall. And when the people were going to market at twelve o'clock they found the Giant playing with the children in the most beautiful garden they had ever seen.

All day long they played, and in the evening they came to the Giant to bid him good-bye.

"But where is your little companion?" he said: "the boy I put into the tree." The Giant loved him the best because he had kissed him.

"We don't know," answered the children; "he has gone away."

"You must tell him to be sure and come here to-morrow," said the Giant. But the children said that they did not know where he lived, and had never seen him before; and the Giant felt very sad.

Every afternoon, when school was over, the children came and played with the Giant. But the little boy whom the Giant loved was never seen again. The Giant was very kind to all the children, yet he longed for his first little friend, and often spoke of him. "How I would like to see him!" he used to say.

Years went over, and the Giant grew very old and feeble. He could not play about any more, so he sat in a huge armchair, and watched the children at their games, and admired his garden. "I have many beautiful flowers," he said; "but the children are the most beautiful flowers of all."

One winter morning he looked out of his window as he was dressing. He did not hate the Winter now, for he knew that it was merely the Spring asleep, and that the flowers were resting.

Suddenly he rubbed his eyes in wonder, and looked and looked. It certainly was a marvellous sight. In the farthest corner of the garden was a tree quite covered with lovely white blossoms. Its branches were all golden, and silver fruit hung down from them, and underneath it stood the little boy he had loved.

Downstairs ran the Giant in great joy, and out into the garden. He hastened across the grass, and came near to the child. And when he came quite close his face grew red with anger, and he said, "Who hath dared to wound thee?" For on the palms of the child's hands were the prints of two nails, and the prints of two nails were on the little feet.

"Who hath dared to wound thee?" cried the Giant; "tell me, that I may take my big sword and slay him."

"Nay!" answered the child; "but these are the wounds of Love."

"Who art thou?" said the Giant, and a strange awe fell on him, and he knelt before the little child.

And the child smiled on the Giant, and said to him, "You let me play once in your garden, to-day you shall come with me to my garden, which is Paradise."

And when the children ran in that afternoon, they found the Giant lying dead under the tree, all covered with white blossoms.

A HORSEMAN IN THE SKY

Ambrose Bierce

I

ONE SUNNY AFTERNOON in the autumn of the year 1861 a soldier lay in a clump of laurel by the side of a road in western Virginia. He lay at full length upon his stomach, his feet resting upon the toes, his head upon the left forearm. His extended right hand loosely grasped his rifle. But for the somewhat methodical disposition of his limbs and a slight rhythmic movement of the cartridge-box at the back of his belt he might have been thought to be dead. He was asleep at his post of duty. But if detected he would be dead shortly afterward, death being the just and legal penalty of his crime.

The clump of laurel in which the criminal lay was in the angle of a road which after ascending southward a steep acclivity to that point turned sharply to the west, running along the summit for perhaps one hundred yards. There it turned southward again and went zigzagging downward through the forest. At the salient of that second angle was a large flat rock, jutting out northward, overlooking the deep valley from which the road ascended. The rock capped a high cliff; a stone dropped from its outer edge would have fallen sheer downward one thousand feet to the tops of the pines. The angle where the soldier lay was on another spur of the same cliff. Had he been awake he would have commanded a view, not only of the short arm of the road and the jutting rock, but of the entire profile of the cliff below it. It might well have made him giddy to look.

The country was wooded everywhere except at the bottom of the valley to the northward, where there was a small natural meadow, through which flowed a stream scarcely visible from the valley's rim. This open ground looked hardly larger than an ordinary door-yard, but was really several acres in extent. Its green was more vivid than that of the inclosing forest. Away beyond it rose a line of giant cliffs similar to those upon which we are supposed to stand in our survey of the savage scene, and through which the road had somehow made its climb to the summit. The configuration of the valley, indeed, was such that from this point of observation it seemed entirely shut in, and one could but have wondered how the road which found a way out of it had found a way into it, and whence came and whither went the waters of the stream that parted the meadow more than a thousand feet below.

No country is so wild and difficult but men will make it a theatre of war; concealed in the forest at the bottom of that military rat-trap, in which half a hundred men in possession of the exits might have starved an army to submission, lay five regiments of Federal infantry. They had marched all the previous day and night and were resting. At nightfall they would take to the road again, climb to the place where their unfaithful sentinel now slept, and descending the other slope of the ridge fall upon a camp of the enemy at about midnight. Their hope was to surprise it, for the road led to the rear of it. In case of failure, their position would be perilous in the extreme; and fail they surely would should accident or vigilance apprise the enemy of the movement.

II

The sleeping sentinel in the clump of laurel was a young Virginian named Carter Druse. He was the son of wealthy parents, an only child, and had known such ease and cultivation and high living as wealth and taste were able to command in the mountain country of western Virginia. His home was but a few miles from where he now lay. One morning he had risen from the breakfast-table and said, quietly but gravely: "Father, a Union regiment has arrived at Grafton. I am going to join it."

The father lifted his leonine head, looked at the son a moment in silence, and replied: "Well, go, sir, and whatever may occur do what you conceive to be your duty. Virginia, to which you are a traitor, must get on without you. Should we both live to the end of the war, we will speak further of the matter. Your mother, as the physician has informed you, is in a most critical condition; at the best she cannot be with us longer than a few weeks, but that time is precious. It would be better not to disturb her."

So Carter Druse, bowing reverently to his father, who returned the salute with a stately courtesy that masked a breaking heart, left the home of his childhood to go soldiering. By conscience and courage, by deeds of devotion and daring, he soon commended himself to his fellows and his officers; and it was to these qualities and to some knowledge of the country that he owed his selection for his present perilous duty at the extreme outpost. Nevertheless, fatigue had been stronger than resolution and he had fallen asleep. What good or bad angel came in a dream to rouse him from his state of crime, who shall say? Without a movement, without a sound, in the profound silence and the languor of the late afternoon, some invisible messenger of fate touched with unsealing finger the eyes of his consciousness—whispered into the ear of his spirit the mysterious awakening word which no human lips ever have spoken, no human memory ever has recalled. He quietly raised his forehead from his arm and looked between the masking stems of the laurels, instinctively closing his right hand about the stock of his rifle.

His first feeling was a keen artistic delight. On a colossal pedestal, the cliff,—motionless at the extreme edge of the capping rock and sharply outlined against the sky,—was an equestrian statue of impressive dignity. The figure of the man sat the figure of the horse, straight and soldierly, but with the repose of a Grecian god carved in the marble which limits the suggestion of activity. The gray costume harmonized with its aerial background; the metal of accoutrement and caparison was softened and subdued by the shadow; the animal's skin had no points of high light. A carbine strikingly foreshortened lay across the pommel of the saddle, kept in place by the right hand grasping it at the "grip"; the left hand, holding the bridle rein, was invisible. In silhouette against the sky the profile of the horse was cut with the sharpness of a cameo; it looked across the heights of air to the confronting cliffs beyond. The face of the rider, turned slightly away, showed only an outline of temple and beard; he was looking downward to the bottom of the valley. Magnified by its lift against the sky and by the soldier's testifying sense of the formidableness of a near enemy the group appeared of heroic, almost colossal, size.

For an instant Druse had a strange, half-defined feeling that he had slept to the end of the war and was looking upon a noble work of art reared upon that eminence to commemorate the deeds of an heroic past of which he had been an inglorious part. The feeling was dispelled by a slight movement of the group: the horse, without moving its feet, had drawn its body slightly backward from the verge; the man remained immobile as before. Broad awake and keenly alive to the significance of the situation, Druse now brought the butt of his rifle against his cheek by cautiously pushing the barrel forward through the bushes, cocked the piece, and glancing through the sights covered a vital spot of the horseman's breast. A touch upon the trigger and all would have been well with Carter Druse. At that instant the horseman turned his head and looked in the direction of his concealed foeman—seemed to look into his very face, into his eyes, into his brave, compassionate heart.

Is it then so terrible to kill an enemy in war—an enemy who has surprised a secret vital to the safety of one's self and comrades—an enemy more formidable for his knowledge than all his army for its numbers? Carter Druse grew pale; he shook in every limb, turned faint, and saw the statuesque group before him as black figures, rising, falling, moving unsteadily in arcs of circles in a fiery sky. His hand fell away from his weapon, his head slowly dropped until his face rested on the leaves in which he lay. This courageous gentleman and hardy soldier was near swooning from intensity of emotion.

It was not for long; in another moment his face was raised from earth, his hands resumed their places on the rifle, his forefinger sought the trigger; mind, heart, and eyes were clear, conscience and reason sound. He could not hope to capture that enemy; to alarm him would but send him dashing to his camp with his fatal news. The duty of the soldier was plain: the man must be shot dead from ambush—without warning, without a moment's spiritual preparation, with never so much as an unspoken prayer, he must be sent to his account. But no—there is a hope; he may have discovered nothing—perhaps he is but admiring the sublimity of the landscape. If permitted, he may turn and ride carelessly away in the direction whence he came. Surely it will be possible to judge at the instant of his withdrawing whether he knows. It may well be that his fixity of attention—Druse turned his head and looked through the deeps of air downward, as from the surface to the bottom of a translucent sea. He saw creeping across the green meadow a sinuous line of figures of men and horses—some foolish commander was permitting the soldiers of his escort to water their beasts in the open, in plain view from a dozen summits!

Druse withdrew his eyes from the valley and fixed them again upon the group of man and horse in the sky, and again it was through the sights of his rifle. But this time his aim was at the horse. In his memory, as if they were a divine mandate, rang the words of his father at their parting: "Whatever may occur, do what you conceive to be your duty." He was calm now. His teeth were firmly but not rigidly closed; his nerves were as tranquil as a sleeping babe's—not a tremor affected any muscle of his body; his breathing, until suspended in the act of taking aim, was regular and slow. Duty had conquered; the spirit had said to the body: "Peace, be still." He fired.

III

An officer of the Federal force, who in a spirit of adventure or in quest of knowledge had left the hidden bivouac in the valley, and with aimless feet had made his way to the lower edge of a small open space near the foot of the cliff, was considering what he had to gain by pushing his exploration further. At a distance of a quarter-mile before him, but apparently at a stone's throw, rose from its fringe of pines the gigantic face of rock, towering to so great a height above him that it made him giddy to look up to where its edge cut a sharp, rugged line against the sky. It presented a clean, vertical profile against a background of blue sky to a point half the way down, and of distant hills, hardly less blue, thence to the tops of the trees at its base. Lifting his eyes to the dizzy altitude of its summit the officer saw an astonishing sight—a man on horseback riding down into the valley through the air!

Straight upright sat the rider, in military fashion, with a firm seat in the saddle, a strong clutch upon the rein to hold his charger from too impetuous a plunge. From his bare head his long hair streamed upward, waving like a plume. His hands were concealed in the cloud of the horse's lifted mane. The animal's body was as level as if every hoof-stroke encountered the resistant earth. Its motions were those of a wild gallop, but even as the officer looked they ceased, with all the legs thrown sharply forward as in the act of alighting from a leap. But this was a flight!

Filled with amazement and terror by this apparition of a horse-man in the sky—half believing himself the chosen scribe of some new Apocalypse, the officer was overcome by the intensity of his emotions; his legs failed him and he fell. Almost at the same instant he heard a crashing sound in the trees—a sound that died without an echo—and all was still.

The officer rose to his feet, trembling. The familiar sensation of an abraded shin recalled his dazed faculties. Pulling himself together he ran rapidly obliquely away from the cliff to a point distant from its foot; thereabout he expected to find his man; and thereabout he naturally failed. In the fleeting instant of his vision his imagination had been so wrought upon by the apparent grace and ease and intention of the marvelous performance that it did not occur to him that the line of march of aerial cavalry is directly downward, and that he could find the objects of his search at the very foot of the cliff. A half-hour later he returned to camp.

This officer was a wise man; he knew better than to tell an incredible truth. He said nothing of what he had seen. But when the commander asked him if in his scout he had learned anything of advantage to the expedition he answered:

"Yes, sir; there is no road leading down into this valley from the southward."

The commander, knowing better, smiled.

IV

After firing his shot, Private Carter Druse reloaded his rifle and resumed his watch. Ten minutes had hardly passed when a Federal sergeant crept cautiously to him on hands and knees. Druse neither turned his head nor looked at him, but lay without motion or sign of recognition.

"Did you fire?" the sergeant whispered.

"Yes."

"At what?"

"A horse. It was standing on yonder rock—pretty far out. You see it is no longer there. It went over the cliff."

The man's face was white, but he showed no other sign of emo-tion. Having answered, he turned away his eyes and said no more. The sergeant did not understand.

"See here, Druse," he said, after a moment's silence, "it's no use making a mystery. I order you to report. Was there anybody on the horse?"

"Yes."

"Well?"

"My father."

The sergeant rose to his feet and walked away. "Good God!" he said.

A NEW ENGLAND NUN

Mary E. Wilkins Freeman

IT WAS LATE in the afternoon, and the light was waning. There was a difference in the look of the tree shadows out in the yard. Somewhere in the distance cows were lowing and a little bell was tinkling; now and then a farm-wagon tilted by, and the dust flew; some blue-shirted laborers with shovels over their shoulders plodded past; little swarms of flies were dancing up and down before the people's faces in the soft air. There seemed to be a gentle stir arising over everything for the mere sake of subsidence—a very premonition of rest and hush and night.

This soft diurnal commotion was over Louisa Ellis also. She had been peacefully sewing at her sitting-room window all the afternoon. Now she quilted her needle carefully into her work, which she folded precisely, and laid in a basket with her thimble and thread and scissors. Louisa Ellis could not remember that ever in her life she had mislaid one of these little feminine appurtenances, which had become, from long use and constant association, a very part of her personality.

Louisa tied a green apron round her waist, and got out a flat straw hat with a green ribbon. Then she went into the garden with a little blue crockery bowl, to pick some currants for her tea. After the currants were picked she sat on the back door-step and stemmed them, collecting the stems carefully in her apron, and afterwards throwing them into the hen-coop. She looked sharply at the grass beside the step to see if any had fallen there.

Louisa was slow and still in her movements; it took her a long time to prepare her tea; but when ready it was set forth with as much grace as if she had been a veritable guest to her own self. The little square table stood exactly in the centre of the kitchen, and was covered with a starched linen cloth whose border pattern of flowers glistened. Louisa had a damask napkin on her tea-tray, where were arranged a cut-glass tumbler full of teaspoons, a silver cream-pitcher, a china sugar-bowl, and one pink china cup and saucer. Louisa used china every day—something which none of her neighbors did. They whispered about it among themselves. Their daily tables were laid with common crockery, their sets of best china stayed in the parlor closet, and Louisa Ellis was no richer nor better bred than they. Still she would use the china. She had for her supper a glass dish full of sugared currants, a plate of little cakes, and one of light white biscuits. Also a leaf or two of lettuce, which she cut up daintily. Louisa was very fond of lettuce, which she raised to perfection in her little garden. She ate quite heartily, though in a delicate, pecking way; it seemed almost surprising that any considerable bulk of the food should vanish.

After tea she filled a plate with nicely baked thin corn-cakes, and carried them out into the back-yard.

"Caesar!" she called. "Caesar! Caesar!"

There was a little rush, and the clank of a chain, and a large yellow-and-white dog appeared at the door of his tiny hut, which was half hidden among the tall grasses and flowers. Louisa patted him and gave him the corn-cakes. Then she returned to the house and washed the tea-things, polishing the china carefully. The twilight had deepened; the chorus of the frogs floated in at the open window wonderfully loud and shrill, and once in a while a long sharp drone from a tree-toad pierced it. Louisa took off her green gingham apron, disclosing a shorter one of pink-and-white print. She lighted her lamp, and sat down again with her sewing.

In about half an hour Joe Dagget came. She heard his heavy step on the walk, and rose and took off her pink-and-white apron. Under that was still another—white linen with a little cambric edging on the bottom; that was Louisa's company apron. She never wore it without her calico sewing apron over it unless she had a guest. She had barely folded the pink-and-white one with methodical haste and laid it in a table-drawer when the door opened and Joe Dagget entered.

He seemed to fill up the whole room. A little yellow canary that had been asleep in his green cage at the south window woke up and fluttered wildly, beating his little yellow wings against the wires. He always did so when Joe Dagget came into the room.

"Good-evening," said Louisa. She extended her hand with a kind of solemn cordiality.

"Good-evening, Louisa," returned the man, in a loud voice.

She placed a chair for him, and they sat facing each other, with the table between them. He sat bolt-upright, toeing out his heavy feet squarely, glancing with a good-humored uneasiness around the room. She sat gently erect, folding her slender hands in her white-linen lap.

"Been a pleasant day," remarked Dagget.

"Real pleasant," Louisa assented, softly. "Have you been haying?" she asked, after a little while.

"Yes, I've been haying all day, down in the ten-acre lot. Pretty hot work."

"It must be."

"Yes, it's pretty hot work in the sun."

"Is your mother well to-day?"

"Yes, mother's pretty well."

"I suppose Lily Dyer's with her now?"

Dagget colored. "Yes, she's with her," he answered, slowly.

He was not very young, but there was a boyish look about his large face. Louisa was not quite as old as he, her face was fairer and smoother, but she gave people the impression of being older.

"I suppose she's a good deal of help to your mother," she said, further.

"I guess she is; I don't know how mother'd get along without her," said Dagget, with a sort of embarrassed warmth.

"She looks like a real capable girl. She's pretty-looking too," remarked Louisa.

"Yes, she is pretty fair-looking."

Presently Dagget began fingering the books on the table. There was a square red autograph album, and a Young Lady's Gift-Book which had belonged to Louisa's mother. He took them up one after the other and opened them; then laid them down again, the album on the Gift-Book.

Louisa kept eying them with mild uneasiness. Finally she rose and changed the position of the books, putting the album underneath. That was the way they had been arranged in the first place.

Dagget gave an awkward little laugh. "Now what difference did it make which book was on top?" said he.

Louisa looked at him with a deprecating smile. "I always keep them that way," murmured she.

"You do beat everything," said Dagget, trying to laugh again. His large face was flushed.

He remained about an hour longer, then rose to take leave. Going out, he stumbled over a rug, and trying to recover himself, hit Louisa's work-basket on the table, knocking it on the floor.

He looked at Louisa, then at the rolling spools; he ducked himself awkwardly toward them, but she stopped him. "Never mind," said she; "I'll pick them up after you're gone."

She spoke with a mild stiffness. Either she was a little disturbed, or his nervousness affected her, and made her seem constrained in her effort to reassure him.

When Joe Dagget was outside he drew in the sweet evening air with a sigh, and felt much as an innocent and perfectly well-intentioned bear might after his exit from a china shop.

Louisa, on her part, felt much as the kind-hearted, long-suffering owner of the china shop might have done after the exit of the bear.

She tied on the pink, then the green apron, picked up all the scattered treasures and replaced them in her work-basket, and straightened the rug. Then she set the lamp on the floor, and began sharply examining the carpet. She even rubbed her fingers over it, and looked at them.

"He's tracked in a good deal of dust," she murmured. "I thought he must have."

Louisa got a dust-pan and brush, and swept Joe Dagget's track carefully.

If he could have known it, it would have increased his perplexity and uneasiness, although it would not have disturbed his loyalty in the least. He came twice a week to see Louisa Ellis, and every time, sitting there in her delicately sweet room, he felt as if surrounded by a hedge of lace. He was afraid to stir lest he should put a clumsy foot or hand through the fairy web, and he had always the consciousness that Louisa was watching fearfully lest he should.

Still the lace and Louisa commanded perforce his perfect respect and patience and loyalty. They were to be married in a month, after a singular courtship which had lasted for a matter of fifteen years. For fourteen out of the fifteen years the two had not once seen each other, and they had seldom exchanged letters. Joe had been all those years in Australia, where he had gone to make his fortune, and where he had stayed until he made it. He would have stayed fifty years if it had taken so long, and come home feeble and tottering, or never come home at all, to marry Louisa.

But the fortune had been made in the fourteen years, and he had come home now to marry the woman who had been patiently and unquestioningly waiting for him all that time.

Shortly after they were engaged he had announced to Louisa his determination to strike out into new fields, and secure a competency before they should be married. She had listened and assented with the sweet serenity which never failed her, not even when her lover set forth on that long and uncertain journey. Joe, buoyed up as he was by his sturdy determination, broke down a little at the last, but Louisa kissed him with a mild blush, and said good-by.

"It won't be for long," poor Joe had said, huskily; but it was for fourteen years.

In that length of time much had happened. Louisa's mother and brother had died, and she was all alone in the world. But greatest happening of all—a subtle happening which both were too simple to understand—Louisa's feet had turned into a path, smooth maybe under a calm, serene sky, but so straight and unswerving that it could only meet a check at her grave, and so narrow that there was no room for any one at her side.

Louisa's first emotion when Joe Dagget came home (he had not apprised her of his coming) was consternation, although she would not admit it to herself, and he never dreamed of it. Fifteen years ago she had been in love with him—at least she considered herself to be. Just at that time, gently acquiescing with and falling into the natural drift of girlhood, she had seen marriage ahead as a reasonable feature and a probable desirability of life. She had listened with calm docility to her mother's views upon the subject. Her mother was remarkable for her cool sense and sweet, even temperament. She talked wisely to her daughter when Joe Dagget presented himself, and Louisa accepted him with no hesitation. He was the first lover she had ever had.

She had been faithful to him all these years. She had never dreamed of the possibility of marrying any one else. Her life, especially for the last seven years, had been full of a pleasant peace, she had never felt discontented nor impatient over her lover's absence; still she had always looked forward to his return and their marriage as the inevitable conclusion of things. However, she had fallen into a way of placing it so far in the future that it was almost equal to placing it over the boundaries of another life.

When Joe came she had been expecting him, and expecting to be married, for fourteen years, but she was as much surprised and taken aback as if she had never thought of it.

Joe's consternation came later. He eyed Louisa with an instant confirmation of his old admiration. She had changed but little. She still kept her pretty manner and soft grace, and was, he considered, every whit as attractive as ever. As for himself, his stent was done; he had turned his face away from fortune-seeking, and the old winds of romance whistled as loud and sweet as ever through his ears. All the song which had been wont to hear in them was Louisa; he had for a long time a loyal belief that he heard it still, but finally it seemed to him that although the winds sang always that one song, it had another name. But for Louisa the wind had never more than murmured; now it had gone down, and everything was still. She listened for a little while with half-wistful attention; then she turned quietly away and went to work on her wedding-clothes.

Joe had made some extensive and quite magnificent alterations in his house. It was the old homestead; the newly-married couple would live there, for Joe could not desert his mother, who refused to leave her old home. So Louisa must leave hers. Every morning, rising and going about among her neat maidenly possessions, she felt as one looking her last upon the faces of dear friends. It was true that in a measure she could take them with her, but, robbed of their old environments, they would appear in such new guises that they would almost cease to be themselves. Then there were some peculiar features of her happy solitary life which she would probably be obliged to relinquish altogether. Sterner tasks than these graceful but half-needless ones would probably devolve upon her. There would be a larger house to care for; there would be company to entertain; there would be Joe's rigorous and feeble old mother to wait upon; and it would be contrary to all thrifty village traditions for her to keep more than one servant. Louisa had a little still, and she used to occupy herself pleasantly in summer weather with distilling the sweet and aromatic essences from roses and peppermint and spearmint. By-and-by her still must be laid away. Her store of essences was already considerable, and there would be no time for her to distil for the mere pleasure of it. Then Joe's mother would think it foolishness; she had already hinted her opinion in the matter. Louisa dearly loved to sew a linen seam, not always for use, but for the simple, mild pleasure which she took in it. She would have been loath to confess how more than once she had ripped a seam for the mere delight of sewing it together again. Sitting at her window during long sweet afternoons, drawing her needle gently through the dainty fabric, she was peace itself. But there was small chance of such foolish comfort in the future. Joe's mother, domineering, shrewd old matron that she was even in her old age, and very likely even Joe himself, with his honest masculine rudeness, would laugh and frown down all these pretty but senseless old maiden ways.

Louisa had almost the enthusiasm of an artist over the mere order and cleanliness of her solitary home. She had throbs of genuine triumph at the sight of the window-panes which she had polished until they shone like jewels. She gloated gently over her orderly bureau-drawers, with their exquisitely folded contents redolent with lavender and sweet clover and very purity. Could she be sure of the endurance of even this? She had visions, so startling that she half repudiated them as indelicate, of coarse masculine belongings strewn about in endless litter; of dust and disorder arising necessarily from a coarse masculine presence in the midst of all this delicate harmony.

Among her forebodings of disturbance, not the least was with regard to Caesar. Caesar was a veritable hermit of a dog. For the greater part of his life he had dwelt in his secluded hut, shut out from the society of his kind and all innocent canine joys. Never had Caesar since his early youth watched at a woodchuck's hole; never had he known the delights of a stray bone at a neighbor's kitchen door. And it was all on account of a sin committed when hardly out of his puppyhood. No one knew the possible depth of remorse of which this mild-visaged, altogether innocent-looking old dog might be capable; but whether or not he had encountered remorse, he had encountered a full measure of righteous retribution. Old Caesar seldom lifted up his voice in a growl or a bark; he was fat and sleepy; there were yellow rings which looked like spectacles around his dim old eyes; but there was a neighbor who bore on his hand the imprint of several of Caesar's sharp white youthful teeth, and for that he had lived at the end of a chain, all alone in a little hut, for fourteen years. The neighbor, who was choleric and smarting with pain of his wound, had demanded either Caesar's death or complete ostracism. So Louisa's brother, to whom the dog had belonged, had built him his little kennel and tied him up. It was now fourteen years since, in a flood of youthful spirits, he had inflicted that memorable bite, and with the exception of short excursions, always at the end of the chain, under the strict guardianship of his master or Louisa, the old dog had remained a close prisoner. It is doubtful if, with his limited ambition, he took much pride in the fact, but it is certain that he was possessed of considerable cheap fame. He was regarded by all the children in the village and by many adults as a very monster of ferocity. St. George's dragon could hardly have surpassed in evil repute Louisa Ellis's old yellow dog. Mothers charged their children with solemn emphasis not to go too near to him, and the children listened and believed greedily, with a fascinated appetite for terror, and ran by Louisa's house stealthily, with many sidelong and backward glances at the terrible dog. If perchance he sounded a hoarse bark, there was a panic. Wayfarers chancing into Louisa's yard eyed him with respect, and inquired if the chain were stout. Caesar at large might have seemed a very ordinary dog, and excited no comment whatever; chained, his reputation overshadowed him, so that he lost his own proper outlines and looked darkly vague and enormous. Joe Dagget, however, with his good-humored sense and shrewdness, saw him as he was. He strode valiantly up to him and patted him on the head, in spite of Louisa's soft clamor of warning, and even attempted to set him loose. Louisa grew so alarmed that he desisted, but kept announcing his opinion in the matter quite forcibly at intervals. "There ain't a better-natured dog in town," he would say, "and it's downright cruel to keep him tied up there. Some day I'm going to take him out."

Louisa had very little hope that he would not, one of these days, when their interests and possessions should be more completely fused in one. She pictured to herself Caesar on the rampage through the quiet and unguarded village. She saw innocent children bleeding in his path. She was herself very fond of the old dog, because he had belonged to her dead brother, and he was always very gentle with her; still she had great faith in his ferocity. She always warned people not to go too near him. She fed him on ascetic fare of corn-mush and cakes, and never fired his dangerous temper with heating and sanguinary diet of flesh and bones. Louisa looked at the old dog munching his simple fare, and thought of her approaching marriage and trembled. Still no anticipation of disorder and confusion in lieu of sweet peace and harmony, no forebodings of Caesar on the rampage, no wild fluttering of her little yellow canary, were sufficient to turn her a hair's-breadth. Joe Dagget had been fond of her and working for her all these years. It was not for her, whatever came to pass, to prove untrue and break his heart. She put the exquisite little stitches into her wedding-garments, and the time went on until it was only a week before her wedding-day. It was a Tuesday evening, and the wedding was to be a week from Wednesday.

There was a full moon that night. About nine o'clock Louisa strolled down the road a little way. There were harvest-fields on either hand, bordered by low stone walls. Luxuriant clumps of bushes grew beside the wall, and trees—wild cherry and old apple-trees—at intervals. Presently Louisa sat down on the wall and looked about her with mildly sorrowful reflectiveness. Tall shrubs of blueberry and meadow-sweet, all woven together and tangled with blackberry vines and horsebriers, shut her in on either side. She had a little clear space between them. Opposite her, on the other side of the road, was a spreading tree; the moon shone between its boughs, and the leaves twinkled like silver. The road was bespread with a beautiful shifting dapple of silver and shadow; the air was full of a mysterious sweetness. "I wonder if it's wild grapes?" murmured Louisa. She sat there some time. She was just thinking of rising, when she heard footsteps and low voices, and remained quiet. It was a lonely place, and she felt a little timid. She thought she would keep still in the shadow and let the persons, whoever they might be, pass her.

But just before they reached her the voices ceased, and the foot-steps. She understood that their owners had also found seats upon the stone wall. She was wondering if she could not steal away unobserved, when a voice broke the stillness. It was Joe Dagget's. She sat still and listened.

The voice was announced by a loud sigh, which was as familiar as itself. "Well," said Dagget, "you've made up your mind, then, I suppose?"

"Yes," returned the other voice; "I'm going day after to-morrow."

"That's Lily Dyer," thought Louisa to herself. The voice embodied itself in her mind. She saw a girl tall and full-figured, with a firm, fair face, looking fairer and firmer in the moonlight, her strong yellow hair braided in a close knot. A girl full of a calm rustic strength and bloom, with a masterful way which might have beseemed a princess. Lily Dyer was a favorite with the village folk; she had just the qualities to arouse the admiration. She was good and handsome and smart. Louisa had often heard her praises sounded.

"Well," said Joe Dagget, "I ain't got a word to say."

"I don't know what you could say," returned Lily Dyer.

"Not a word to say," repeated Joe, drawing out the words heavily. Then there was a silence. "I ain't sorry," he began at last, "that that happened yesterday—that we kind of let on how we felt to each other. I guess it's just as well we knew. Of course I can't do anything any different. I'm going right on an' get married next week. I ain't going back on a woman that's waited for me fourteen years, an' break her heart."

"If you should jilt her to-morrow, I wouldn't have you," spoke up the girl, with sudden vehemence.

"Well, I ain't going to give you the chance," said he; "but I don't believe you would, either."

"You'd see I wouldn't. Honor's honor, an' right's right. An' I'd never think anything of any man that went against 'em for me or any other girl; you'd find that out, Joe Dagget."

"Well, you'll find out fast enough that I ain't going against 'em for you or any other girl," returned he. Their voices sounded almost as if they were angry with each other. Louisa was listening eagerly.

"I'm sorry you feel as if you must go away," said Joe, "but I don't know but it's best."

"Of course it's best. I hope you and I have got common-sense."

"Well, I suppose you're right." Suddenly Joe's voice got an undertone of tenderness. "Say, Lily," said he, "I'll get along well enough myself, but I can't bear to think—You don't suppose you're going to fret much over it?"

"I guess you'll find out I sha'n't fret much over a married man."

"Well, I hope you won't—I hope you won't, Lily. God knows I do. And—I hope—one of these days—you'll—come across somebody else—"

"I don't see any reason why I shouldn't." Suddenly her tone changed. She spoke in a sweet, clear voice, so loud that she could have been heard across the street. "No, Joe Dagget," said she, "I'll never marry any other man as long as I live. I've got good sense, an' I ain't going to break my heart nor make a fool of myself; but I'm never going to be married, you can be sure of that. I ain't that sort of a girl to feel this way twice."

Louisa heard an exclamation and a soft commotion behind the bushes; then Lily spoke again—the voice sounded as if she had risen. "This must be put a stop to," said she. "We've stayed here long enough. I'm going home."

Louisa sat there in a daze, listening to their retreating steps. After a while she got up and slunk softly home herself. The next day she did her housework methodically; that was as much a matter of course as breathing; but she did not sew on her wedding-clothes. She sat at her window and meditated. In the evening Joe came. Louisa Ellis had never known that she had any diplomacy in her, but when she came to look for it that night she found it, although meek of its kind, among her little feminine weapons. Even now she could hardly believe that she had heard aright, and that she would not do Joe a terrible injury should she break her troth-plight. She wanted to sound him without betraying too soon her own inclinations in the matter. She did it successfully, and they finally came to an understanding; but it was a difficult thing, for he was as afraid of betraying himself as she.

She never mentioned Lily Dyer. She simply said that while she had no cause of complaint against him, she had lived so long in one way that she shrank from making a change.

"Well, I never shrank, Louisa," said Dagget. "I'm going to be honest enough to say that I think maybe it's better this way; but if you'd wanted to keep on, I'd have stuck to you till my dying day. I hope you know that."

"Yes, I do," said she.

That night she and Joe parted more tenderly than they had done for a long time. Standing in the door, holding each other's hands, a last great wave of regretful memory swept over them.

"Well, this ain't the way we've thought it was all going to end, is it, Louisa?" said Joe.

She shook her head. There was a little quiver on her placid face.

"You let me know if there's ever anything I can do for you," said he. "I ain't ever going to forget you, Louisa." Then he kissed her, and went down the path.

Louisa, all alone by herself that night, wept a little, she hardly knew why; but the next morning, on waking, she felt like a queen who, after fearing lest her domain be wrested away from her, sees it firmly insured in her possession.

Now the tall weeds and grasses might cluster around Caesar's little hermit hut, the snow might fall on its roof year in and year out, but he never would go on a rampage through the unguarded village. Now the little canary might turn itself into a peaceful yellow ball night after night, and have no need to wake and flutter with wild terror against its bars. Louisa could sew linen seams, and distil roses, and dust and polish and fold away in lavender, as long as she listed. That afternoon she sat with her needle-work at the window, and felt fairly steeped in peace. Lily Dyer, tall and erect and blooming, went past; but she felt no qualm. If Louisa Ellis had sold her birthright she did not know it, the taste of the pottage was so delicious, and had been her sole satisfaction for so long. Serenity and placid narrowness had become to her as the birthright itself. She gazed ahead through a long reach of future days strung together like pearls in a rosary, every one like the others, and all smooth and flawless and innocent, and her heart went up in thankfulness. Outside was the fervid summer afternoon; the air was filled with the sounds of the busy harvest of men and birds and bees; there were halloos, metallic clatterings, sweet calls, and long hummings. Louisa sat, prayerfully numbering her days, like an uncloistered nun.

SQUIRE PETRICK'S LADY

Thomas Hardy

FOLK WHO ARE at all acquainted with the traditions of Stapleford Park will not need to be told that in the middle of the last century it was owned by that trump of mortgagees, Timothy Petrick, whose skill in gaining possession of fair estates by granting sums of money on their title-deeds has seldom if ever been equaled in our part of England. Timothy was a lawyer by profession, and agent to several noblemen, by which means his special line of business became opened to him by a sort of revelation. It is said that a relative of his, a very deep thinker, who afterwards had the misfortune to be transported for life for mistaken notions on the signing of a will, taught him considerable legal lore, which he creditably resolved never to throw away for the benefit of other people, but to reserve it entirely for his own.

However, I have nothing in particular to say about his early and active days, but rather of the time when, an old man, he had become the owner of vast estates by the means I have signified—among them the great manor of Stapleford, on which he lived, in the splendid old mansion now pulled down; likewise estates at Marlott, estates near Sherton Abbas, nearly all the borough of Millpool, and many properties near Ivell. Indeed, I can't call to mind half his landed possessions, and I don't know that it matters much at this time of day, seeing that he's been dead and gone many years. It is said that when he bought an estate he would not decide to pay the price till he had walked over every single acre with his own two feet, and prodded the soil at every point with his own spud, to test its quality, which, if we regard the extent of his properties, must have been a stiff business for him.

At the time I am speaking of he was a man over eighty, and his son was dead; but he had two grandsons, the eldest of whom, his namesake, was married, and was shortly expecting issue. Just then the grandfather was taken ill, for death, as it seemed, considering his age. By his will the old man had created an entail (as I believe the lawyers call it), devising the whole of the estates to his elder grandson and his issue male, failing which, to his younger grandson and his issue male, failing which, to remoter relatives, who need not be mentioned now.

While old Timothy Petrick was lying ill, his elder grandson's wife, Annetta, gave birth to her expected child, who, as fortune would have it, was a son. Timothy, her husband, though sprung of a scheming family, was no great schemer himself; he was the single one of the Petricks then living whose heart had ever been greatly moved by sentiments which did not run in the groove of ambition; and on this account he had not married well, as the saying is, his wife having been the daughter of a family of no better beginnings than his own; that is to say, her father was a country townsman of the professional class. But she was a very pretty woman, by all accounts, and her husband had seen, courted, and married her in a high tide of infatuation, after a very short acquaintance, and with very little knowledge of her heart's history. He had never found reason to regret his choice as yet, and his anxiety for her recovery was great.

She was supposed to be out of danger, and herself and the child progressing well, when there was a change for the worse, and she sank so rapidly that she was soon given over. When she felt that she was about to leave him, Annetta sent for her husband, and, on his speedy entry and assurance that they were alone, she made him solemnly vow to give the child every care in any circumstances that might arise, if it should please Heaven to take her. This, of course, he readily promised. Then, after some hesitation, she told him that she could not die with a falsehood upon her soul, and dire deceit in her life; she must make a terrible confession to him before her lips were sealed forever. She thereupon related an incident concerning the baby's parentage which was not as he supposed.

Timothy Petrick, though a quick-feeling man, was not of a sort to show nerves outwardly; and he bore himself as heroically as he possibly could do in this trying moment of his life. That same night his wife died; and while she lay dead, and before her funeral, he hastened to the bedside of his sick grandfather, and revealed to him all that had happened—the baby's birth, his wife's confession, and her death, beseeching the aged man, as he loved him, to bestir himself now, at the eleventh hour, and alter his will so as to dish the intruder. Old Timothy, seeing matters in the same light as his grandson, required no urging against allowing anything to stand in the way of legitimate inheritance; he executed another will, limiting the entail to Timothy, his grandson, for life, and his male heirs thereafter to be born; after them to his other grandson, Edward, and Edward's heirs. Thus the newly born infant, who had been the center of so many hopes, was cut off and scorned as none of the elect.

The old mortgagee lived but a short time after this, the excitement of the discovery having told upon him considerably, and he was gathered to his fathers like the most charitable man in his neighborhood. Both wife and grandparent being buried, Timothy settled down to his usual life as well as he was able, mentally satisfied that he had, by prompt action, defeated the consequences of such dire domestic treachery as had been shown towards him, and resolving to marry a second time as soon as he could satisfy himself in the choice of a wife.

But men do not always know themselves. The imbittered state of Timothy Petrick's mind bred in him by degrees such a hatred and mistrust of womankind that, though several specimens of high attractiveness came under his eyes, he could not bring himself to the point of proposing marriage. He dreaded to take up the position of husband a second time, discerning a trap in every petticoat, and a Slough of Despond in possible heirs. "What has happened once, when all seemed so fair, may happen again," he said to himself. "I'll risk my name no more." So he abstained from marriage, and overcame his wish for a lineal descendant to follow him in the ownership of Stapleford.

Timothy had scarcely noticed the unfortunate child that his wife had borne, after arranging for a meager fulfilment of his promise to her to take care of the boy, by having him brought up in his house. Occasionally, remembering his promise, he went and glanced at the child, saw that he was doing well, gave a few special directions, and again went his solitary way. Thus he and the child lived on in the Stapleford mansion-house till two or three years had passed by. One day he was walking in the garden, and by some accident left his snuff-box on a bench. When he came back to find it he saw the little boy standing there; he had escaped his nurse, and was making a plaything of the box, in spite of the convulsive sneezings which the game brought in its train. Then the man with the incrusted heart became interested in the little fellow's persistence in his play under such discomforts; he looked in the child's face, saw there his wife's countenance, though he did not see his own, and fell into thought on the piteousness of childhood—particularly of despised and rejected childhood, like this before him.

From that hour, try as he would to counteract the feeling, the human necessity to love something or other got the better of what he had called his wisdom, and shaped itself in a tender anxiety for the youngster Rupert. This name had been given him by his dying mother when, at her request, the child was baptized in her chamber, lest he should not survive for public baptism; and her husband had never thought of it as a name of any significance till, about this time, he learned by accident that it was the name of the young Marquis of Christminster, son of the Duke of Southwesterland, for whom Annetta had cherished warm feelings before her marriage. Recollecting some wandering phrases in his wife's last words, which he had not understood at the time, he perceived at last that this was the person to whom she had alluded when affording him a clew to little Rupert's history.

He would sit in silence for hours with the child, being no great speaker at the best of times; but the boy, on his part, was too ready with his tongue for any break in discourse to arise because Timothy Petrick had nothing to say. After idling away his mornings in this manner, Petrick would go to his own room and swear in long, loud whispers, and walk up and down, calling himself the most ridiculous dolt that ever lived, and declaring that he would never go near the little fellow again; to which resolve he would adhere for the space, perhaps, of a day. Such cases are happily not new to human nature, but there never was a case in which a man more completely befooled his former self than in this.

As the child grew up, Timothy's attachment to him grew deeper, till Rupert became almost the sole object for which he lived. There had been enough of the family ambition latent in him for Timothy Petrick to feel a little envy when, some time before this date, his brother Edward had been accepted by the Honorable Harriet Mountclere, daughter of the second viscount of that name and title;

but having discovered, as I have before stated, the paternity of his boy Rupert to lurk in even a higher stratum of society, those envious feelings speedily dispersed. Indeed, the more he reflected thereon, after his brother's aristocratic marriage, the more content did he become. His late wife took softer outline in his memory, as he thought of the lofty taste she had displayed, though only a plain burgher's daughter, and the justification for his weakness in loving the child—the justification that he had longed for—was afforded now in the knowledge that the boy was by nature, if not by name, a representative of one of the noblest houses in England.

"She was a woman of grand instincts, after all," he said to himself, proudly. "To fix her choice upon the immediate successor in that ducal line—it was finely conceived! Had he been of low blood like myself or my relations she would scarce have deserved the harsh measure that I have dealt out to her and her offspring. How much less, then, when such groveling tastes were farthest from her soul! The man Annetta loved was noble, and my boy is noble in spite of me."

The after-clap was inevitable, and it soon came. "So far," he reasoned, "from cutting off this child from inheritance of my estates, as I have done, I should have rejoiced in the possession of him! He is of pure stock on one side at least, while in the ordinary run of affairs he would have been a commoner to the bone."

Being a man, whatever his faults, of good old beliefs in the divinity of kings and those about 'em, the more he overhauled the case in this light the more strongly did his poor wife's conduct in improving the blood and breed of the Petrick family win his heart. He considered what ugly, idle, hard-drinking scamps many of his own relations had been; the miserable scriveners, usurers, and pawnbrokers that he had numbered among his forefathers, and the probability that some of their bad qualities would have come out in a merely corporeal child, to give him sorrow in his old age, turn his black hairs gray, his gray hairs white, cut down every stick of timber, and Heaven knows what all, had he not, like a skilful gardener, minded his grafting and changed the sort; till at length this right-minded man fell down on his knees every night and morning and thanked God that he was not as other meanly descended fathers in such matters.

It was in the peculiar disposition of the Petrick family that the satisfaction which ultimately settled in Timothy's breast found nourishment. The Petricks had adored the nobility, and plucked them at the same time. That excellent man Izaak Walton's feelings about fish were much akin to those of old Timothy Petrick, and of his descendants in a lesser degree, concerning the landed aristocracy. To torture and to love simultaneously is a proceeding strange to reason, but possible to practise, as these instances show.

Hence, when Timothy's brother Edward said slightingly one day that Timothy's son was well enough, but that he had nothing but shops and offices in his backward perspective, while his own children, should he have any, would be far different, in possessing such a mother as the Honorable Harriet, Timothy felt a bound of triumph within him at the power he possessed of contradicting that statement if he chose.

So much was he interested in his boy in this new aspect that he now began to read up chronicles of the illustrious house ennobled as the Dukes of Southwesterland, from their very beginning in the glories of the Restoration of the blessed Charles till the year of his own time. He mentally noted their gifts from royalty, grants of lands, purchases, intermarriages, plantings, and buildings; more particularly their political and military achievements, which had been great, and their performances in arts and letters, which had been by no means contemptible. He studied prints of the portraits of that family, and then, like a chemist watching a crystallization, began to examine young Rupert's face for the unfolding of those historic curves and shades that the painters Vandyke and Lely had perpetuated on canvas.

When the boy reached the most fascinating age of childhood, and his shouts of laughter rang through Stapleford House from end to end, the remorse that oppressed Timothy Petrick knew no bounds. Of all people in the world this Rupert was the one on whom he could have wished the estates to devolve; yet Rupert, by Timothy's own desperate strategy at the time of his birth, had been ousted from all inheritance of them; and, since he did not mean to remarry, the manors would pass to his brother and his brother's children, who would be nothing to him, whose boasted pedigree on one side would be nothing to his Rupert's.

Had he only left the first will of his grandfather alone!

His mind ran on the wills continually, both of which were in existence, and the first, the canceled one, in his own possession. Night after night, when the servants were all abed, and the click of safety-locks sounded as loud as a crash, he looked at that first will, and wished it had been the second and not the first.

The crisis came at last. One night, after having enjoyed the boy's company for hours, he could no longer bear that his beloved Rupert should be dispossessed, and he committed the felonious deed of altering the date of the earlier will to a fortnight later, which made its execution appear subsequent to the date of the second will already proved. He then boldly propounded the first will as the second.

His brother Edward submitted to what appeared to be not only incontestible fact, but a far more likely disposition of old Timothy's property; for, like many others, he had been much surprised at the limitations defined in the other will, having no clew to their cause. He joined his brother Timothy in setting aside the hitherto accepted document, and matters went on in their usual course, there being no dispositions in the substituted will differing from those in the other, except such as related to a future which had not yet arrived.

The years moved on. Rupert had not yet revealed the anxiously expected historic lineaments which should foreshadow the political abilities of the ducal family aforesaid, when it happened on a certain day that Timothy Petrick made the acquaintance of a well-known physician of Budmouth, who had been the medical adviser and friend of the late Mrs. Petrick's family for many years, though after Annetta's marriage, and consequent removal to Stapleford, he had seen no more of her, the neighboring practitioner who attended the Petricks having then become her doctor as a matter of course. Timothy was impressed by the insight and knowledge disclosed in the conversation of the Budmouth physician, and the acquaintance ripening to intimacy, the physician alluded to a form of hallucination to which Annetta's mother and grandmother had been subject—that of believing in certain dreams as realities. He delicately inquired if Timothy had ever noticed anything of the sort in his wife during her lifetime; he, the physician, had fancied that he discerned germs of the same peculiarity in Annetta when he attended her in her girlhood. One explanation begat another, till the dumbfounded Timothy Petrick was persuaded in his own mind that Annetta's confession to him had been based on a delusion.

"You look down in the mouth!" said the doctor, pausing.

"A bit unmanned. 'Tis unexpected-like," sighed Timothy.

But he could hardly believe it possible; and, thinking it best to be frank with the doctor, told him the whole story which, till now, he had never related to living man, save his dying grandfather. To his surprise, the physician informed him that such a form of delusion was precisely what he would have expected from Annetta's antecedents at such a physical crisis in her life.

Petrick prosecuted his inquiries elsewhere; and the upshot of his labors was, briefly, that a comparison of dates and places showed irrefutably that his poor wife's assertion could not possibly have foundation in fact. The young Marquis of her tender passion—a highly moral and brightminded nobleman—had gone abroad the year before Annetta's marriage, and had not returned until after her death. The young girl's love for him had been a delicate ideal dream—no more.

Timothy went home, and the boy ran out to meet him; whereupon a strangely dismal feeling of discontent took possession of his soul. After all, then, there was nothing but plebeian blood in the veins of the heir to his name and estates; he was not to be succeeded by a noble-natured line. To be sure, Rupert was his son; but that glory and halo he believed him to have inherited from the ages, outshining that of his brother's children, had departed from Rupert's brow forever; he could no longer read history in the boy's face and centuries of domination in his eyes.

His manner towards his son grew colder and colder from that day forward; and it was with bitterness of heart that he discerned the characteristic features of the Petricks unfolding themselves by degrees. Instead of the elegant knife-edged nose, so typical of the Dukes of Southwesterland, there began to appear on his face the broad nostril and hollow bridge of his grandfather Timothy. No illustrious line of politicians was promised a continuator in that graying blue eye, for it was acquiring the expression of the orb of a particularly objectionable cousin of his own; and, instead of the mouth-curves which had thrilled Parliamentary audiences in speeches now bound in calf in every well-ordered library, there was the bull-lip of that very uncle of his who had had the misfortune with the signature of a gentleman's will, and had been transported for life in consequence.

To think how he himself, too, had sinned in this same matter of a will for this mere fleshly reproduction of a wretched old uncle whose very name he wished to forget! The boy's Christian name, even, was an imposture and an irony, for it implied hereditary force and brilliancy to which he plainly would never attain. The consolation of real sonship was always left him certainly; but he could not help groaning to himself, "Why cannot a son be one's own and somebody else's likewise?"

The Marquis was shortly afterwards in the neighborhood of Stapleford, and Timothy Petrick met him, and eyed his noble countenance admiringly. The next day, when Petrick was in his study, somebody knocked at the door.

"Who's there?"

"Rupert."

"I'll Rupert thee, you young impostor! Say, only a poor commonplace Petrick!" his father grunted. "Why didn't you have a voice like the Marquis I saw yesterday!" he continued, as the lad came in. "Why haven't you his looks, and a way of commanding as if you'd done it for centuries—hey?"

"Why? How can you expect it, father, when I'm not related to him?"

"Ugh! Then you ought to be!" growled his father.

A GHOST STORY

Jerome K. Jerome

I MET A man in the Strand one day that I knew very well, as I thought, though I had not seen him for years. We walked together to Charing Cross, and there we shook hands and parted. Next morning, I spoke of this meeting to a mutual friend, and then I learnt, for the first time, that the man had died six months before.

The natural inference was that I had mistaken one man for another, an error that, not having a good memory for faces, I frequently fall into. What was remarkable about the matter, however, was that throughout our walk I had conversed with the man under the impression that he was that other dead man, and, whether by coincidence or not, his replies had never once suggested to me my mistake.

As soon as I finished speaking, Jephson, who had been listening very thoughtfully, asked me if I believed in spiritualism "to its fullest extent."

"That is rather a large question," I answered. "What do you mean by 'spiritualism to its fullest extent?'"

"Well, do you believe that the spirits of the dead have not only the power of revisiting this earth at their will, but that, when here, they have the power of action, or rather, of exciting to action. Let me put a definite case. A spiritualist friend of mine, a sensible and by no means imaginative man, once told me that a table, through the medium of which the spirit of a friend had been in the habit of communicating with him, came slowly across the room towards him, of its own accord, one night as he sat alone, and pinioned him against the wall. Now can any of you believe that, or can't you?"

"I could," Brown took it upon himself to reply; "but, before doing so, I should wish for an introduction to the friend who told you the story. Speaking generally," he continued, "it seems to me that the difference between what we call the natural and the super-natural is merely the difference between frequency and rarity of occurrence. Having regard to the phenomena we are compelled to admit, I think it illogical to disbelieve anything that we are not able to disprove."

"For my part," remarked MacShaugnassy, "I can believe in the ability of our spirit friends to give the quaint entertainments cred-ited to them much easier than I can in their desire to do so."

"You mean," added Jephson, "that you cannot understand why a spirit, not compelled as we are by the exigencies of society, should care to spend its evenings carrying on a laboured and childish con-versation with a room full of abnormally uninteresting people."

"That is precisely what I cannot understand," MacShaugnassy agreed.

"Nor I, either," said Jephson. "But I was thinking of something very different altogether. Suppose a man died with the dearest wish of his heart unfulfilled, do you believe that his spirit might have power to return to earth and complete the interrupted work?"

"Well," answered MacShaugnassy, "if one admits the possibility of spirits retaining any interest in the affairs of this world at all, it is certainly more reasonable to imagine them engaged upon a task such as you suggest, than to believe that they occupy themselves with the performance of mere drawing-room tricks. But what are you leading up to?"

"Why to this," replied Jephson, seating himself straddle-legged across his chair, and leaning his arms upon the back. "I was told a story this morning at the hospital by an old French doctor. The actual facts are few and simple; all that is known can be read in the Paris police records of forty-two years ago.

"The most important part of the case, however, is the part that is not known, and that never will be known.

"The story begins with a great wrong done by one man unto another man. What the wrong was I do not know. I am inclined to think, however, it was connected with a woman. I think that because he who had been wronged hated him who had wronged with a hate such as does not often burn in a man's brain unless it be fanned by the memory of a woman's breath.

"Still that is only conjecture, and the point is immaterial. The man who had done the wrong fled, and the other man followed him. It became a point to point race, the first man having the advantage of a day's start. The course was the whole world, and the stakes were the first man's life.

"Travellers were few and far between in those days, and this made the trail easy to follow. The first man, never knowing how far or how near the other was behind him, and hoping now and again that he might have baffled him, would rest for a while. The second man, knowing always just how far the first one was before him, never paused, and thus each day the man who was spurred by Hate drew nearer to the man who was spurred by Fear.

"At this town the answer to the never-varied question would be:

"'At seven o'clock last evening, M'sieur.'

"'Seven—ah; eighteen hours. Give me something to eat, quick, while the horses are being put to.'

"At the next the calculation would be sixteen hours.

"Passing a lonely châlet, Monsieur puts his head out of the window:

"'How long since a carriage passed this way, with a tall, fair man inside?'

"'Such a one passed early this morning, M'sieur.'

"'Thanks, drive on, a hundred francs apiece if you are through the pass before daybreak.'

"'And what for dead horses, M'sieur?'

"'Twice their value when living.'

"One day the man who was ridden by Fear looked up, and saw before him the open door of a cathedral, and, passing in, knelt down and prayed. He prayed long and fervently, for men, whey they are in sore straits, clutch eagerly at the straws of faith. He prayed that he might be forgiven his sin, and, more important still, that he might be pardoned the consequences of his sin, and be delivered from his adversary; and a few chairs from him, facing him, knelt his enemy, praying also.

"But the second man's prayer, being a thanksgiving merely, was short, so that when the first man raised his eyes, he saw the face of his enemy gazing at him across the chair tops, with a mocking smile upon it.

"He made no attempt to rise, but remained kneeling, fascinated by the look of joy that shone out of the other man's eyes. And the other man moved the high-backed chairs one by one, and came towards him softly.

"Then, just as the man who had been wronged stood beside the man who had wronged him, full of gladness that his opportunity had come, there burst from the cathedral tower a sudden clash of bells, and the man whose opportunity had come broke his heart and fell back dead, with that mocking smile of his still playing round his mouth.

"And so he lay there.

"Then the man who had done the wrong rose up and passed out, praising God.

"What became of the body of the other man is not known. It was the body of a stranger who had died suddenly in the cathedral. There was none to identify it, none to claim it.

"Years passed away, and the survivor in the tragedy became a worthy and useful citizen, and a noted man of science.

"In his laboratory were many objects necessary to him in his researches, and prominent among them, stood in a certain corner, a human skeleton. It was a very old and much-mended skeleton, and one day the long-expected end arrived, and it tumbled to pieces.

"Thus it became necessary to purchase another.

"The man of science visited a dealer he well knew; a little parchment-faced old man who kept a dingy shop, where nothing was ever sold, within the shadow of the towers of Notre Dame.

"The little parchment-faced old man had just the very thing that Monsieur wanted—a singularly fine and well-proportioned "study." It should be sent round and set up in Monsieur's laboratory that very afternoon.

"The dealer was as good as his word. When Monsieur entered his laboratory that evening, the thing was in its place.

"Monsieur seated himself in his high-backed chair, and tried to collect his thoughts. But Monsieur's thoughts were unruly, and inclined to wander, and to wander always in one direction.

"Monsieur opened a large volume and commenced to read. He read of a man who had wronged another and fled from him, the other man following. Finding himself reading this, he closed the book angrily, and went and stood by the window and looked out. He saw before him the sun-pierced nave of a great cathedral, and on the stones lay a dead man with a mocking smile upon his face.

"Cursing himself for a fool, he turned away with a laugh. But his laugh was short-lived, for it seemed to him that something else in the room was laughing also. Stuck suddenly still, with his feet glued to the ground, he stood listening for awhile: then sought with starting eyes the corner from where the sound had seemed to come. But the white thing standing there was only grinning.

"Monsieur wiped the damp sweat from his head and hands, and stole out.

"For a couple of days he did not enter the room again. On the third, telling himself that his fears were those of a hysterical girl, he opened the door and went in. To shame himself, he took his lamp in his hand, and crossing over to the far corner where the skeleton stood, examined it. A set of bones bought for a hundred francs. Was he a child, to be scared by such a bogey!

"He held his lamp up in front of the thing's grinning head. The flame of the lamp flickered as though a faint breath had passed over it.

"The man explained this to himself by saying that the walls of the house were old and cracked, and that the wind might creep in anywhere. He repeated this explanation to himself as he recrossed the room, walking backwards, with his eyes fixed on the thing. When he reached his desk, he sat down and gripped the arms of his chair till his fingers turned white.

"He tried to work, but the empty sockets in that grinning head seemed to be drawing him towards them. He rose and battled with his inclination to fly screaming from the room. Glancing fearfully about him, his eye fell upon a high screen, standing before the door. He dragged it forward, and placed it between himself and the thing, so that he could not see it—nor it see him. Then he sat down again to his work. For awhile he forced himself to look at the book in front of him, but at last, unable to control himself any longer, he suffered his eyes to follow their own bent.

"It may have been an hallucination. He may have accidentally placed the screen so as to favour such an illusion. But what he saw was a bony hand coming round the corner of the screen, and, with a cry, he fell to the floor in a swoon.

"The people of the house came running in, and lifting him up, carried him out, and laid him upon his bed. As soon as he recovered, his first question was, where had they found the thing—where was it when they entered the room? and when they told him they had seen it standing where it always stood, and had gone down into the room to look again, because of his frenzied entreaties, and returned trying to hide their smiles, he listened to their talk about overwork, and the necessity for change and rest, and said they might do with him as they would.

"So for many months the laboratory door remained locked. Then there came a chill autumn evening when the man of science opened it again, and closed it behind him.

"He lighted his lamp, and gathered his instruments and books around him, and sat down before them in his high-backed chair. And the old terror returned to him.

"But this time he meant to conquer himself. His nerves were stronger now, and his brain clearer; he would fight his unreasoning fear. He crossed to the door and locked himself in, and flung the key to the other end of the room, where it fell among jars and bottles with an echoing clatter.

"Later on, his old housekeeper, going her final round, tapped at his door and wished him good night, as was her custom. She received no response, at first, and, growing nervous, tapped louder and called again; and at length an answering "good night" came back to her.

"She thought little about it at the time, but afterwards she remembered that the voice that had replied to her had been strangely grating and mechanical. Trying to describe it, she likened it to such a voice as she would imagine coming from a statue.

"Next morning his door remained still locked. It was no unusual thing for him to work all night, and far into the next day, so no one thought to be surprised. When, however, evening came, and yet he did not appear, his servants gathered outside the room and whispered, remembering what had happened once before.

"They listened, but could hear no sound. They shook the door and called to him, then beat with their fists upon the wooden panels. But still no sound came from the room.

"Becoming alarmed, they decided to burst open the door, and, after many blows, it gave way and flew back, and they crowded in.

"He sat bolt upright in his high-backed chair. They thought at first he had died in his sleep. But when they drew nearer and the light fell upon him, they saw the livid marks of bony fingers round his throat; and in his eyes there was a terror such as is not often seen in human eyes."

Brown was the first to break the silence that followed. He asked me if I had any brandy on board. He said he felt he should like just a nip of brandy before going to bed. That is one of the chief charms of Jephson's stories: they always make you feel you want a little brandy.

DÉSIRÉE'S BABY

Kate Chopin

As THE DAY was pleasant, Madame Valmondé drove over to L'Abri to see Désirée and the baby.

It made her laugh to think of Désirée with a baby. Why, it seemed but yesterday that Désirée was little more than a baby herself; when Monsieur in riding through the gateway of Valmondé had found her lying asleep in the shadow of the big stone pillar.

The little one awoke in his arms and began to cry for "Dada." That was as much as she could do or say. Some people thought she might have strayed there of her own accord, for she was of the toddling age. The prevailing belief was that she had been purposely left by a party of Texans, whose canvas-covered wagon, late in the day, had crossed the ferry that Coton Maïs kept, just below the plantation. In time Madame Valmondé abandoned every speculation but the one that Désirée had been sent to her by a beneficent Providence to be the child of her affection, seeing that she was without child of the flesh. For the girl grew to be beautiful and gentle, affectionate and sincere,—the idol of Valmondé.

It was no wonder, when she stood one day against the stone pillar in whose shadow she had lain asleep, eighteen years before, that Armand Aubigny riding by and seeing her there, had fallen in love with her. That was the way all the Aubignys fell in love, as if struck by a pistol shot. The wonder was that he had not loved her before; for he had known her since his father brought him home from Paris, a boy of eight, after his mother died there. The passion that awoke in him that day, when he saw her at the gate, swept along like an avalanche, or like a prairie fire, or like anything that drives headlong over all obstacles.

Monsieur Valmondé grew practical and wanted things well considered: that is, the girl's obscure origin. Armand looked into her eyes and did not care. He was reminded that she was nameless. What did it matter about a name when he could give her one of the oldest and proudest in Louisiana? He ordered the *corbeille* from Paris, and contained himself with what patience he could until it arrived; then they were married.

Madame Valmondé had not seen Désirée and the baby for four weeks. When she reached L'Abri she shuddered at the first sight of it, as she always did. It was a sad looking place, which for many years had not known the gentle presence of a mistress, old Monsieur Aubigny having married and buried his wife in France, and she having loved her own land too well ever to leave it. The roof came down steep and black like a cowl, reaching out beyond the wide galleries that encircled the yellow stuccoed house. Big, solemn oaks grew close to it, and their thick-leaved, far-reaching branches shadowed it like a pall. Young Aubigny's rule was a strict one, too, and under it his negroes had forgotten how to be gay, as they had been during the old master's easy-going and indulgent lifetime.

The young mother was recovering slowly, and lay full length, in her soft white muslins and laces, upon a couch. The baby was beside her, upon her arm, where he had fallen asleep, at her breast. The yellow nurse woman sat beside a window fanning herself.

Madame Valmondé bent her portly figure over Désirée and kissed her, holding her an instant tenderly in her arms. Then she turned to the child.

"This is not the baby!" she exclaimed, in startled tones. French was the language spoken at Valmondé in those days.

"I knew you would be astonished," laughed Désirée, "at the way he has grown. The little *cochon de lait!* Look at his legs, mamma, and his hands and finger-nails—real finger-nails. Zandrine had to cut them this morning. Isn't it true, Zandrine?"

The woman bowed her turbaned head majestically, "Mais si, Madame."

"And the way he cries," went on Désirée, "is deafening. Armand heard him the other day as far away as La Blanche's cabin."

Madame Valmondé had never removed her eyes from the child. She lifted it and walked with it over to the window that was lightest. She scanned the baby narrowly, then looked as searchingly at Zandrine, whose face was turned to gaze across the fields.

"Yes, the child has grown, has changed," said Madame Valmondé, slowly, as she replaced it beside its mother. "What does Armand say?"

Désirée's face became suffused with a glow that was happiness itself.

"Oh, Armand is the proudest father in the parish, I believe, chiefly because it is a boy, to bear his name; though he says not,—that he would have loved a girl as well. But I know it isn't true. I know he says that to please me. And mamma," she added, drawing Madame Valmondé's head down to her, and speaking in a whisper, "he hasn't punished one of them—not one of them—since baby is born. Even Négrillon, who pretended to have burnt his leg that he might rest from work—he only laughed, and said Négrillon was a great scamp. Oh, mamma, I'm so happy; it frightens me."

What Désirée said was true. Marriage, and later the birth of his son had softened Armand Aubigny's imperious and exacting nature greatly. This was what made the gentle Désirée so happy, for she loved him desperately. When he frowned she trembled, but loved him. When he smiled, she asked no greater blessing of God. But Armand's dark, handsome face had not often been disfigured by frowns since the day he fell in love with her.

When the baby was about three months old, Désirée awoke one day to the conviction that there was something in the air menacing her peace. It was at first too subtle to grasp. It had only been a disquieting suggestion; an air of mystery among the blacks; unexpected visits from far-off neighbors who could hardly account for their coming. Then a strange, an awful change in her husband's manner, which she dared not ask him to explain. When he spoke to her, it was with averted eyes, from which the old love-light seemed to have gone out. He absented himself from home; and when there, avoided her presence and that of her child, without excuse. And the very spirit of Satan seemed suddenly to take hold of him in his dealings with the slaves. Désirée was miserable enough to die.

She sat in her room, one hot afternoon, in her *peignoir,* listlessly drawing through her fingers the strands of her long, silky brown hair that hung about her shoulders. The baby, half naked, lay asleep upon her own great mahogany bed, that was like a sumptuous throne, with its satin-lined half-canopy. One of La Blanche's little quadroon boys—half naked too—stood fanning the child slowly with a fan of peacock feathers. Désirée's eyes had been fixed absently and sadly upon the baby, while she was striving to penetrate the threatening

mist that she felt closing about her. She looked from her child to the
boy who stood beside him, and back again; over and over. "Ah!" It
was a cry that she could not help; which she was not conscious of
having uttered. The blood turned like ice in her veins, and a
clammy moisture gathered upon her face.

She tried to speak to the little quadroon boy; but no sound
would come, at first. When he heard his name uttered, he looked
up, and his mistress was pointing to the door. He laid aside the
great, soft fan, and obediently stole away, over the polished floor,
on his bare tiptoes.

She stayed motionless, with gaze riveted upon her child, and her
face the picture of fright.

Presently her husband entered the room, and without noticing
her, went to a table and began to search among some papers which
covered it.

"Armand," she called to him, in a voice which must have
stabbed him, if he was human. But he did not notice. "Armand,"
she said again. Then she rose and tottered towards him. "Armand,"
she panted once more, clutching his arm, "look at our child. What
does it mean? Tell me."

He coldly but gently loosened her fingers from about his arm and
thrust the hand away from him. "Tell me what it means!" she cried
despairingly.

"It means," he answered lightly, "that the child is not white; it
means that you are not white."

A quick conception of all that this accusation meant for her
nerved her with unwonted courage to deny it. "It is a lie; it is not
true, I am white! Look at my hair, it is brown; and my eyes are
gray, Armand, you know they are gray. And my skin is fair," seizing his wrist. "Look at my hand; whiter than yours, Armand," she
laughed hysterically.

"As white as La Blanche's," he returned cruelly; and went away
leaving her alone with their child.

When she could hold a pen in her hand, she sent a despairing
letter to Madame Valmondé.

"My mother, they tell me I am not white. Armand has told me
I am not white. For God's sake tell them it is not true. You must
know it is not true. I shall die. I must die. I cannot be so unhappy,
and live."

The answer that came was as brief:

"My own Désirée: Come home to Valmondé; back to your mother who loves you. Come with your child."

When the letter reached Désirée she went with it to her husband's study, and laid it open upon the desk before which he sat. She was like a stone image: silent, white, motionless after she placed it there.

In silence he ran his cold eyes over the written words.

He said nothing. "Shall I go, Armand?" she asked in tones sharp with agonized suspense.

"Yes, go."

"Do you want me to go?"

"Yes, I want you to go."

He thought Almighty God had dealt cruelly and unjustly with him; and felt, somehow, that he was paying Him back in kind when he stabbed thus into his wife's soul. Moreover he no longer loved her, because of the unconscious injury she had brought upon his home and his name.

She turned away like one stunned by a blow, and walked slowly towards the door, hoping he would call her back.

"Good-by, Armand," she moaned.

He did not answer her. That was his last blow at fate.

Désirée went in search of her child. Zandrine was pacing the sombre gallery with it. She took the little one from the nurse's arms with no word of explanation, and descending the steps, walked away, under the live-oak branches.

It was an October afternoon; the sun was just sinking. Out in the still fields the negroes were picking cotton.

Désirée had not changed the thin white garment nor the slippers which she wore. Her hair was uncovered and the sun's rays brought a golden gleam from its brown meshes. She did not take the broad, beaten road which led to the far-off plantation of Valmondé. She walked across a deserted field, where the stubble bruised her tender feet, so delicately shod, and tore her thin gown to shreds.

She disappeared among the reeds and willows that grew thick along the banks of the deep, sluggish bayou; and she did not come back again.

★ ★ ★

Some weeks later there was a curious scene enacted at L'Abri. In the centre of the smoothly swept back yard was a great bonfire.

Armand Aubigny sat in the wide hallway that commanded a view of the spectacle; and it was he who dealt out to a half dozen negroes the material which kept this fire ablaze.

A graceful cradle of willow, with all its dainty furbishings, was laid upon the pyre, which had already been fed with the richness of a priceless *layette*. Then there were silk gowns, and velvet and satin ones added to these; laces, too, and embroideries; bonnets and gloves; for the *corbeille* had been of rare quality.

The last thing to go was a tiny bundle of letters; innocent little scribblings that Désirée had sent to him during the days of their espousal. There was the remnant of one back in the drawer from which he took them. But it was not Désirée's; it was part of an old letter from his mother to his father. He read it. She was thanking God for the blessing of her husband's love:—

"But, above all," she wrote, "night and day, I thank the good God for having so arranged our lives that our dear Armand will never know that his mother, who adores him, belongs to the race that is cursed with the brand of slavery."

THE DARK LANTERN

La Lanterne Sourde

Jules Renard

I. Crazy Tiennette

CHRIST PUNISHED

As she passes the foot of the cross set outside the village, apparently to protect it from surprises, crazy Tiennette notices that the Christ has fallen down.

No doubt, that night, a heavy wind has weakened the nails and thrown him to the ground.

Tiennette blesses herself and rights the Christ with many precautions, as she would a person still alive. She cannot set him back upon the tall cross; she cannot leave him all alone, at the side of the path.

What is more, he has hurt himself in the fall and some of his fingers are off.

"I must bring the Christ to the carpenter," she says, "and he will mend them."

She hugs him reverently around the middle and bears him off, not running. But he is so heavy he slips through her arms, and she must often hoist him up again with a rough jolt.

And when she does, the nails that pierce the Christ's feet hook to Tiennette's skirt and raise it a little and uncover her legs.

"Will you stop that now, Lord!" she says to him.

And Tiennette, simple, gives the Christ's cheeks a few light slaps, but delicately, with all respect.

THE SNOWCHILD

Snow is falling, and through the streets, bareheaded, crazy Tiennette is running like a crazy woman. She plays all alone, catches the white flies as they fall in her violet hands, sticks out her tongue to dissolve the light candy she can just taste, and, with the tip of her finger, draws sticks and rings on the bright sheet.

Farther on she guesses that this little star print has fallen from a bird, this big one from a goose, and this other strange one from the sky maybe.

Then the shoes that made her as tall as the roof thatch and dizzied her so come loose. She topples and stays on the ground a long while, making a cross, being good, until her portrait sinks in.

Then she makes herself a snowchild.

His limbs are twisted and shrunken from the cold. His eyes have been gouged out, his nose has one hole to take the place of two, his mouth has no teeth, and his skull has no hair, because hair and teeth are too hard.

"The poor little thing!" says Tiennette.

She clasps him to her heart and whistles a lullaby, then, once he starts to melt, she changes him quickly and give him a maternal roll in the fresh snow so the bed that envelops him will be clean.

TIENNETTE LOST

Tiennette goes out at her pleasure, walks where she will; and her innocence protects her. She walks hurriedly, never strolls, always seems in flight.

This morning, having left home one hour ago by the clock, she stops and says:

"Oh God! I've lost myself!"

She searches, reflects, worried, hunting for herself.

The countryside has vanished under snow. It fills the tree branches; this one seems to have dressed as a traveler waiting for the coach.

But Tiennette spies her own tracks, still fresh, in the snow, and the idea comes to her: she will follow and find herself again.

Sometimes she softly sets her feet inside the deep prints, and if other tracks cross hers she stoops and sets them right. Sometimes she runs, losing her breath, as if there were wolves at her back.

When she reaches the village and recognizes her house among the crouching shapes:

"I probably went back home," she thinks.

She stops hurrying. She takes a breath, drops her anxiety from her shoulders like a shawl grown too heavy, pushes open the door, and says calmly:

"I knew it; there I am!"

THE STICK

Tiennette rolls a stick between her fingers, scratches it with her nails, bites it with the tips of her teeth, strips its bark off. She moves on down the road and says to the trees:

"You must have heard that this is my wedding day. I'm serious, I mean it. He loves me, I expect him soon."

She gives them smiles left and right, already rehearsing the ceremony.

But a voice from among the trees gives her an order:

"Take off your cap, Tiennette."

She pauses, looks at the trees, hears breathing among them, and asks, trembling:

"Is it really you this time?"

"Yes, Tiennette; take off your cap."

Reassured, she throws away her cap, just as she threw away the leaves she pulled from her stick.

"Take off your jacket, Tiennette."

She obeys, throws away her jacket just as she threw away the thin branches she pulled from her stick.

"Take off your skirt, Tiennette."

She reaches a hand around to undo the knotted strings, but she sees the stick in her other hand, naked, its bark pulled off, and, abruptly waking up, Tiennette shamefacedly picks up her cap and jacket and runs away, far from the libertine who wanted to trap her again and who stays there, behind the trees, laughing.

II. Tiennot

THE CHERRY MAN

Tiennot, walking through the market place, sees baskets filled with cherries so fat and red they cannot be real. He says to the owner:

"Let me eat as many cherries as I want, and we'll settle for ten pennies."

The owner agrees, sure of a profit, because cherries aren't scarce this year and he could afford to give away a barrowful for ten pennies, at the price they bring in.

Tiennot lies down on his right side among the baskets.

Not hurrying, he chooses the finest cherries and eats them one by one.

Slowly he empties the first basket, then the second.

The owner smiles. Now and then some market people come to watch. The druggist shows up, then the café owner. Everyone gives Tiennot encouragement.

He carefully keeps from answering. Without moving he methodically opens and closes his mouth. At times, when a passing cherry is more juicy than the others, he seems to be asleep.

The owner, already uneasy, thinks:

"I may not lose anything on this, but I won't gain much by it."

And the ten-cent piece clenched between his teeth shrinks in value.

Suddenly reviving, he says:

"Well?"

Tiennot stirs, tries to lift himself, but the effort seems painful. In the end he only changes position, rolls over on his left side, gropes for another basket.

But he has worked up an appetite, and now he begins to devour the cherry stones as well.

The Spring and the Sugar

Tiennot is quenching his thirst with spring water. His hand serves as a cup at first; later he prefers a straight drink and he lies down over the spring, wetting his chin and nose. When he stops to breathe, he looks around at the animals and the water's white plume as it rises.

"It tastes good," he says, "but I know it would taste better with sugar."

He runs to the village, buys a piece of sugar, and steals back at nightfall to drop it into the spring.

"Tomorrow morning," he says just for himself, "I will have a feast."

All the people are still asleep when Tiennot leaves his bed and hurries to the spring.

Before he tastes the water, he says, sucking with his lips:

"Oh! What a fine taste!"

He bends down, tastes, and says, letting his lips relax:

"Yes. No. There's no more sugar in it than there was yesterday."

He is baffled, he fixes his eyes on his crestfallen reflection.

"My God! What a fool I am!" he shouts. "A child would know: water runs, and my melted sugar ran along with it. It left the spring behind and ran away across the field; it can't be going fast, I can catch it."

And Tiennot departs, walking beside the brook. He carefully counts out twenty paces and then stops. He takes a mouthful of water and savors it. But then he tosses his head, suddenly, and departs again in pursuit of his sugar.

THE FIST OF GOD

In a short smock and a shaggy top hat Tiennot is coming home from the fair. All he had to sell is sold, his pig, his cheese, and his two old hens, but the hens were sold for pullets, after he gave them wine and made them drunk.

They were full of life, their eyes glittered, they had fever in their wings and claws, they deceived a trusting woman who may be weighing them again, surprised and angry to see them dangling, cold, broken. Tiennot smiles; he feels no remorse; he has put it over many times. He zigzags, his legs give, he wanders all over the road, for while the hens were picking up drops of wine out of a bowl, he was drinking the rest of the bottle.

Then a cyclist shouts, a bell sounds, a horn trumpets right behind him. He hears nothing. He goes back and forth across the road, waving his arms, gesticulating, feeling compassion, as if he were selling his hens a second time.

And suddenly a fist blow crushes down his shaggy top hat.

Tiennot stops, bends double, his head a prisoner, surrounded by night down to the ears. He tries to lift his hat off; he tries for some time; but his head is caught, the circle around his skull hurts him. Tiennot struggles, heaves, bellows, finally frees himself.

He looks around: nobody on the road, nobody ahead, nobody behind. He looks over the hedge, first left, then right.

He sees nothing.

And Tiennot, who got his hens drunk and sold them, mechanically makes the sign of the cross.

THE FINE CORN

On the dry road, under the burning sun, Tiennot and Baptiste are driving back home in their donkey cart. They pass near a field of ripe corn, and Baptiste, who knows all about corn, says:

"What fine corn!"

Tiennot is driving and says nothing; he bows his back. Baptiste bows his own in imitation, and their necks, exposed, tough, slowly broil, shine like copper pans.

Like a machine, Tiennot pulls or shakes the reins. Sometimes he raises a stick and aims a lively blow at the donkey's buttocks, as if they were a bespattered pair of breeches. The donkey never changes pace; he bends his head, probably to watch the play of his hoofs as they move in and out, one after another, never mistaking. The cart follows along after him as best it can; a roundish shadow drags after; Tiennot and Baptiste bend down still farther.

They pass through villages that look deserted because of the heat. They meet a few scarce people who give only a single sign. They close their eyes against the road's white glare.

And yet they arrive that night, very late. In the end one always arrives. The donkey halts before the door, perks its ears. Baptiste and Tiennot, sluggish, stir themselves, and Tiennot answers Baptiste:

"Yes, it is fine corn."

THE IDIOT'S JOURNALISM SCHEME

John Kendrick Bangs

THE IDIOT WAS unusually thoughtful—a fact which made the School-Master and the Bibliomaniac unusually nervous. Their stock criticism of him was that he was thoughtless; and yet when he so far forgot his natural propensities as to meditate, they did not like it. It made them uneasy. They had a haunting fear that he was conspiring with himself against them, and no man, not even a callous school-master or a confirmed bibliomaniac, enjoys feeling that he is the object of a conspiracy. The thing to do, then, upon this occasion, seemed obviously to interrupt his train of thought—to put obstructions upon his mental track, as it were, and ditch the express, which they feared was getting up steam at that moment to run them down.

"You don't seem quite yourself this morning, sir," said the Bibliomaniac.

"Don't I?" queried the Idiot. "And whom do I seem to be?"

"I mean that you seem to have something on your mind that worries you," said the Bibliomaniac.

"No, I haven't anything on my mind," returned the Idiot. "I was thinking about you and Mr. Pedagog—which implies a thought not likely to use up much of my gray matter."

"Do you think your head holds any gray matter?" put in the Doctor.

"Rather verdant, I should say," said Mr. Pedagog.

"Green, gray, or pink," said the Idiot, "choose your color. It does not affect the fact that I was thinking about the Bibliomaniac and Mr. Pedagog. I have a great scheme in hand, which only requires capital and the assistance of those two gentlemen to launch it on the sea of prosperity. If any of you gentlemen want to get rich and die in comfort as the owner of your homes, now is your chance."

"In what particular line of business is your scheme?" asked Mr. Whitechoker. He had often felt that he would like to die in comfort, and to own a little house, even if it had a large mortgage on it.

"Journalism," said the Idiot. "There is a pile of money to be made out of journalism, particularly if you happen to strike a new idea. Ideas count."

"How far up do your ideas count—up to five?" questioned Mr. Pedagog, with a tinge of sarcasm in his tone.

"I don't know about that," returned the Idiot. "The idea I have hold of now, however, will count up into the millions if it can only be set going, and before each one of those millions will stand a big capital S with two black lines drawn vertically through it—in other words, my idea holds dollars, but to get the crop you've got to sow the seed. Plant a thousand dollars in my idea, and next year you'll reap two thousand. Plant that, and next year you'll have four thousand, and so on. At that rate millions come easy."

"I'll give you a dollar for the idea," said the Bibliomaniac.

"No, I don't want to sell. You'll do to help develop the scheme. You'll make a first-rate tool, but you aren't the workman to manage the tool. I will go as far as to say, however, that without you and Mr. Pedagog, or your equivalents in the animal kingdom, the idea isn't worth the fabulous sum you offer."

"You have quite aroused my interest," said Mr. Whitechoker. "Do you propose to start a new paper?"

"You are a good guesser," replied the Idiot. "That is a part of the scheme—but it isn't the idea. I propose to start a newspaper in accordance with the plan which the idea contains."

"Is it to be a magazine, or a comic paper, or what?" asked the Bibliomaniac.

"Neither. It's a daily."

"That's nonsense," said Mr. Pedagog, putting his spoon into the condensed-milk can by mistake. "There isn't a single scheme in daily journalism that hasn't been tried—except printing an evening paper in the morning."

"That's been tried," said the Idiot. "I know of an evening paper the second edition of which is published at mid-day. That's an old dodge, and there's money in it, too—money that will never be got out of it. But I really have a grand scheme. So many of our dailies, you know, go in for every horrid detail of daily events that people are beginning to tire of them. They contain practically the same things day after day. So many columns of murder, so many beautiful suicides, so much sport, a modicum of general intelligence, plenty of fires, no end of embezzlements, financial news, advertisements, and headlines. Events, like history, repeat themselves, until people have grown weary of them. They want something new. For instance, if you read in your morning paper that a man has shot another man, you know that the man who was shot was an inoffensive person who never injured a soul, stood high in the community in which he lived, and leaves a widow with four children. On the other hand, you know without reading the account that the murderer shot his victim in self-defense, and was apprehended by the detectives late last night; that his counsel forbid him to talk to the reporters, and that it is rumored that he comes of a good family living in New England.

"If a breach of trust is committed, you know that the defaulter was the last man of whom such an act would be suspected, and, except in the one detail of its location and sect, that he was prominent in some church. You can calculate to a cent how much has been stolen by a glance at the amount of space devoted to the account of the crime. Loaf of bread, two lines. Thousand dollars, ten lines. Hundred thousand dollars, half-column. Million dollars, a full column. Five million dollars, half the front page, wood-cut of the embezzler, and two editorials, one leader and one paragraph.

"And so with everything. We are creatures of habit. The expected always happens, and newspapers are dull because the events they chronicle are dull."

"Granting the truth of this," put in the School-Master, "what do you propose to do?"

"Get up a newspaper that will devote its space to telling what hasn't happened."

"That's been done," said the Bibliomaniac.

"To a much more limited extent than we think," returned the Idiot. "It has never been done consistently and truthfully."

"I fail to see how a newspaper can be made to prevaricate truthfully," asserted Mr. Whitechoker. To tell the truth, he was greatly disappointed with the idea, because he could not in the nature of things become one of its beneficiaries.

"I haven't suggested prevarication," said the Idiot. "Put on your front page, for instance, an item like this: 'George Bronson, colored, aged twenty-nine, a resident of Thompson Street, was caught cheating at poker last night. He was not murdered.' There you tell what has not happened. There is a variety about it. It has the charm of the unexpected. Then you might say: 'Curious incident on Wall Street yesterday. So-and-so, who was caught on the bear side of the market with 10,000 shares of J. B. & S. K. W., paid off all his obligations in full, and retired from business with 11,000,000 clear.' Or we might say, 'Superintendent Smithers, of the St. Goliath's Sunday-school, who is also cashier in the Forty-eighth National Bank, has not absconded with $4,000,000.'"

"Oh, that's a rich idea," put in the SchoolMaster. "You'd earn $1,000,000 in libel suits the first year."

"No, you wouldn't, either," said the Idiot. "You don't libel a man when you say he hasn't murdered anybody. Quite the contrary, you call attention to his conspicuous virtue. You are in reality commending those who refrain from criminal practice, instead of delighting those who are fond of departing from the paths of Christianity by giving them notoriety."

"But I fail to see in what respect Mr. Pedagog and I are essential to your scheme," said the Bibliomaniac.

"I must confess to some curiosity on my own part on that point," added the School-Master.

"Why, it's perfectly clear," returned the Idiot, with a conciliating smile as he prepared to depart. "You both know so much that isn't so, that I rather rely on you to fill up."

ACTIVE COLORADO REAL ESTATE

Hayden Carruth

"When I was visiting at my uncle's in Wisconsin last fall, I went out to Lake Kinnikinnic and caught a shovel-nose sturgeon which weighed eighty-five pounds."

It was Jackson Peters who spoke, and he did it rapidly and with an apprehensive air, for Jones was watching him closely. As he finished, Peters drew a long breath, and seemed much relieved that he had got through the story without an interruption.

"Eighty-five pounds," mused Jones.

"Yes, eighty-five pounds and ten ounces, to be exact, but I called it eighty-five."

"Exactness does not help your story in the least, Jackson," continued Jones. "You might give us the fractions of the ounce, and your story would still remain a crude production. I am in the habit of speaking plainly, and I will do so now. I take it that we are to consider your story simply as an exaggeration—that the fish probably didn't weigh ten pounds. Simple exaggeration, Jackson, is not art, and is unworthy of a man of brains. Anybody can exaggerate— the street laborer as easily as the man in Congress. But artistic storytelling is another thing, and the greatest may well hope for distinction in it. Why did you not, Jackson, tell an artistic lie, and say that when you pulled your fish out of the water the level of the lake fell two feet?"

Peters moved about uneasily, but made no reply.

"You never tell fish-stories, Jones?" observed Robinson, in an inquiring tone.

"Seldom, Robinson. The trail of gross exaggeration is over them all. Fish stories have become the common property of the inartistic multitude. Of course I do not for this reason suppress facts having a scientific or commercial value. For instance, last winter I went before the legislative committee on fisheries, and laid before it an account of my experience when I had a farm near Omaha, on the Missouri River bottoms, and baited two miles of barbed-wire fence with fresh pork just before the June rise, and after the water receded removed thirty-eight thousand four hundred fish from the barbs, weighing, in the aggregate, over ninety-six tons. The Legislature passed a special vote of thanks for the facts."

Jones was becoming warmed up. "You have observed, Robinson," he went on, "that I seldom relate the marvellous. That is because it is too easy. I prefer to have the reputation of telling a plain tale artistically to that of telling a fabulous one like a realistic novelist. That is the reason I never told any one of my experience at breaking one hundred and sixty acres of land to ride."

"Tell us, by all means, Jones," said Robinson.

"Yes, go ahead," added Smith. Jackson Peters hid himself behind a cloud of cigar smoke.

"It was an exciting experience," said Jones, thoughtfully, as he gazed into the fire, "and one which I have never mentioned to anybody, although it happened twenty years ago. There is nothing so easy to lose as a reputation for truthfulness. I have my own to maintain. More men have lost their good names by telling the plain, straightforward truth than by indulging in judicious lying. However, I will venture this time. It was, as I said, twenty years ago. There was a great mining boom in Colorado, and I closed my defective-flue factory in Chicago, to the intense joy of the insurance companies, and went out. I saw more money in hens than I did in mines, and decided to start a hen ranch. Eggs sold at five dollars a dozen. The hen, you know, requires a great amount of gravel for her digestion, and she also thrives best at a high altitude; so I went about two miles up Pike's Peak and selected a quarter-section of land good for my purpose. There was gravel in plenty, and I put up a small house and turned loose my three hundred hens. I became so interested in getting settled that I forgot all about establishing my right to the land before the United States Land Office at Colorado Springs.

"One day a large, red-headed man came along and erected a small house on one corner of my ranch, and said that he had as much right to the land as I. He turned out two hundred head of goats, and started for Colorado Springs to file his claim. He had a good horse, while I had none. It was ten miles to the town by the road, and only five in a straight line down the mountain, but this five was impassable on foot or in any other ordinary way. But I did not despair. I had studied the formation of the land, and knew what I could do. I took a half-dozen sticks of giant powder and went over to a small ridge of rocks which held my farm in place. I inserted the powder, gentlemen, and blew those rocks over into the next county. I then lay down on my back and clung to a root while I rode that one hundred and sixty acres of good hen-land down the mountain to Colorado Springs. It felt very much like an earthquake, and I made the five miles in a little over four minutes. Probably ten acres of my farm around the edges were knocked off along on the grand Colorado scenery, and most of the goats jolted off, but the hens, gentlemen, clung, the hens and myself. The corner of my front yard struck the Land Office and knocked it off its foundation. The register and receiver came running out, and I said:

"'Gentlemen, I desire to make claim entry on the northeast quarter of section twenty-seven, township fourteen south, of range sixty-nine, and to prevent mistake I have brought it with me.' The business was all finished by the time the red-headed man came lumbering along, and I gave him ten minutes to get the rest of his goats off my land. He seemed considerably surprised, and looked at me curiously."

Jackson Peters was the first to speak after Jones paused. "It is one of the saddest things in this life," he said, "that the man who always adheres to the exact truth often gets the reputation of being a liar."

"You are right, Jackson," said Jones. "I know of nothing sadder, unless it be, perhaps, to see a young man forget the respect he owes his elders. This life, Jackson, is full of sad things."

THE REMARKABLE CASE OF DAVIDSON'S EYES

H. G. Wells

I

THE TRANSITORY MENTAL aberration of Sidney Davidson, remarkable enough in itself, is still more remarkable if Wade's explanation is to be credited. It sets one dreaming of the oddest possibilities of intercommunication in the future, of spending an intercalary five minutes on the other side of the world, or being watched in our most secret operations by unsuspected eyes. It happened that I was the immediate witness of Davidson's seizure, and so it falls naturally to me to put the story upon paper.

When I say that I was the immediate witness of his seizure, I mean that I was the first on the scene. The thing happened at the Harlow Technical College just beyond the Highgate Archway. He was alone in the larger laboratory when the thing happened. I was in the smaller room, where the balances are, writing up some notes. The thunderstorm had completely upset my work, of course. It was just after one of the louder peals that I thought I heard some glass smash in the other room. I stopped writing, and turned round to listen. For a moment I heard nothing; the hail was playing the devil's tattoo on the corrugated zinc of the roof. Then came another sound, a smash—no doubt of it this time. Something heavy had been knocked off the bench. I jumped up at once and went and opened the door leading into the big laboratory.

I was surprised to hear a queer sort of laugh, and saw Davidson standing unsteadily in the middle of the room, with a dazzled look on his face. My first impression was that he was drunk. He did not notice me. He was clawing out at something invisible a yard in front of his face. He put out his hand, slowly, rather hesitatingly, and then clutched nothing. "What's come to it?" he said. He held up his hands to his face, fingers spread out. "Great Scott!" he said. The thing happened three or four years ago, when every one swore by that personage. Then he began raising his feet clumsily, as though he had expected to find them glued to the floor.

"Davidson!" cried I. "What's the matter with you?" He turned round in my direction and looked about for me. He looked over me and at me and on either side of me, without the slightest sign of seeing me. "Waves," he said; "and a remarkably neat schooner. I'd swear that was Bellow's voice. *Hullo!*" He shouted suddenly at the top of his voice.

I thought he was up to some foolery. Then I saw littered about his feet the shattered remains of the best of our electrometers. "What's up, man?" said I. "You've smashed the electrometer!"

"Bellows again!" said he. "Friends left, if my hands are gone. Something about electrometers. Which way *are* you, Bellows?" He suddenly came staggering towards me. "The damned stuff cuts like butter," he said. He walked straight into the bench and recoiled. "None so buttery, that!" he said, and stood swaying.

I felt scared. "Davidson," said I, "what on earth's come over you?"

He looked round him in every direction. "I could swear that was Bellows. Why don't you show yourself like a man, Bellows?"

It occurred to me that he must be suddenly struck blind. I walked round the table and laid my hand upon his arm. I never saw a man more startled in my life. He jumped away from me, and came round into an attitude of self-defence, his face fairly distorted with terror. "Good God!" he cried. "What was that?"

"It's I—Bellows. Confound it, Davidson!"

He jumped when I answered him and stared—how can I express it?—right through me. He began talking, not to me, but to himself. "Here in broad daylight on a clear beach. Not a place to hide in." He looked about him wildly. "Here! I'm *off*." He suddenly turned and ran headlong into the big electro-magnet—so violently that, as we found afterwards, he bruised his shoulder and jawbone cruelly. At that he stepped back a pace, and cried out with almost a whimper, "What, in Heaven's name, has come over me?" He stood, blanched with terror and trembling violently, with his right arm clutching his left, where that had collided with the magnet.

By that time I was excited, and fairly scared. "Davidson," said I, "don't be afraid."

He was startled at my voice, but not so excessively as before. I repeated my words in as clear and firm a tone as I could assume. "Bellows," he said, "is that you?"

"Can't you see it's me?"

He laughed. "I can't even see it's myself. Where the devil are we?"

"Here," said I, "in the laboratory."

"The laboratory!" he answered, in a puzzled tone, and put his hand to his forehead. "I *was* in the laboratory—till that flash came, but I'm hanged if I'm there now. What ship is that?"

"There's no ship," said I. "Do be sensible, old chap."

"No ship!" he repeated, and seemed to forget my denial forthwith. "I suppose," said he, slowly, "we're both dead. But the rummy part is I feel just as though I still had a body. Don't get used to it all at once, I suppose. The old shop was struck by lightning, I suppose. Jolly quick thing, Bellows—eigh?"

"Don't talk nonsense. You're very much alive. You are in the laboratory, blundering about. You've just smashed a new electrometer. I don't envy you when Boyce arrives."

He stared away from me towards the diagrams of cryohydrates. "I must be deaf," said he. "They've fired a gun, for there goes the puff of smoke, and I never heard a sound."

I put my hand on his arm again, and this time he was less alarmed. "We seem to have a sort of invisible bodies," said he. "By Jove! there's a boat coming round the headland! It's very much like the old life after all—in a different climate."

I shook his arm. "Davidson," I cried, "wake up!"

II

It was just then that Boyce came in. So soon as he spoke Davidson exclaimed: "Old Boyce! Dead too! What a lark!" I hastened to explain that Davidson was in a kind of somnambulistic trance. Boyce was interested at once. We both did all we could to rouse the fellow out of his extraordinary state. He answered our questions, and asked us some of his own, but his attention seemed distracted by his hallucination about a beach and a ship. He kept interpolating observations concerning some boat and the davits and sails filling with the wind. It made one feel queer, in the dusky laboratory, to hear him saying such things.

He was blind and helpless. We had to walk him down the passage, one at each elbow, to Boyce's private room, and while Boyce talked to him there, and humoured him about this ship idea, I went along the corridor and asked old Wade to come and look at him. The voice of our Dean sobered him a little, but not very much. He asked where his hands were, and why he had to walk about up to his waist in the ground. Wade thought over him a long time—you know how he knits his brows—and then made him feel the couch, guiding his hands to it. "That's a couch," said Wade. "The couch in the private room of Professor Boyce. Horse-hair stuffing."

Davidson felt about, and puzzled over it, and answered presently that he could feel it all right, but he couldn't see it.

"What *do* you see?" asked Wade. Davidson said he could see nothing but a lot of sand and broken-up shells. Wade gave him some other things to feel, telling him what they were, and watching him keenly.

"The ship is almost hull down," said Davidson, presently, *apropos* of nothing.

"Never mind the ship," said Wade. "Listen to me, Davidson. Do you know what hallucination means?"

"Rather," said Davidson.

"Well, everything you see is hallucinatory."

"Bishop Berkeley," said Davidson.

"Don't mistake me," said Wade. "You are alive, and in this room of Boyce's. But something has happened to your eyes. You cannot see; you can feel and hear, but not see. Do you follow me?"

"It seems to me that I see too much." Davidson rubbed his knuckles into his eyes. "Well?" he said.

"That's all. Don't let it perplex you. Bellows, here, and I will take you home in a cab."

"Wait a bit." Davidson thought. "Help me to sit down," said he, presently; "and now—I'm sorry to trouble you—but will you tell me all that over again?"

Wade repeated it very patiently. Davidson shut his eyes, and pressed his hands upon his forehead. "Yes," said he. "It's quite right. Now my eyes are shut I know you're right. That's you, Bellows, sitting by me on the couch. I'm in England again. And we're in the dark."

Then he opened his eyes. "And there," said he, "is the sun just rising, and the yards of the ship, and a tumbled sea, and a couple of birds flying. I never saw anything so real. And I'm sitting up to my neck in a bank of sand."

He bent forward and covered his face with his hands. Then he opened his eyes again. "Dark sea and sunrise! And yet I'm sitting on a sofa in old Boyce's room!—God help me!"

III

That was the beginning. For three weeks this strange affection of Davidson's eyes continued unabated. It was far worse than being blind. He was absolutely helpless, and had to be fed like a newly-hatched bird, and led about and undressed. If he attempted to move he fell over things or struck himself against walls or doors. After a day or so he got used to hearing our voices without seeing us, and willingly admitted he was at home, and that Wade was right in what he told him. My sister, to whom he was engaged, insisted on coming to see him, and would sit for hours every day while he talked about this beach of his. Holding her hand seemed to comfort him immensely. He explained that when we left the College and drove home,—he lived in Hampstead Village,—it appeared to him as if we drove right through a sandhill—it was perfectly black until he emerged again—and through rocks and trees and solid obstacles, and when he was taken to his own room it made him giddy and almost frantic with the fear of falling, because going upstairs seemed to lift him thirty or forty feet above the rocks of his imaginary island. He kept saying he should smash all the eggs. The end was that he had to be taken down into his father's consulting room and laid upon a couch that stood there.

He described the island as being a bleak kind of place on the whole, with very little vegetation, except some peaty stuff, and a lot of bare rock. There were multitudes of penguins, and they made the rocks white and disagreeable to see. The sea was often rough, and once there was a thunderstorm, and he lay and shouted at the silent flashes. Once or twice seals pulled up on the beach, but only on the first two or three days. He said it was very funny the way in which the penguins used to waddle right through him, and how he seemed to lie among them without disturbing them.

I remember one odd thing, and that was when he wanted very badly to smoke. We put a pipe in his hands—he almost poked his eye out with it—and lit it. But he couldn't taste anything. I've since found it's the same with me—I don't know if it's the usual case—that I cannot enjoy tobacco at all unless I can see the smoke.

But the queerest part of his vision came when Wade sent him out in a bath-chair to get fresh air. The Davidsons hired a chair, and got that deaf and obstinate dependant of theirs, Widgery, to attend to it. Widgery's ideas of healthy expeditions were peculiar. My sister, who had been to the Dogs' Home, met them in Camden Town, towards King's Cross, Widgery trotting along complacently, and Davidson evidently most distressed, trying in his feeble, blind way to attract Widgery's attention.

He positively wept when my sister spoke to him. "Oh, get me out of this horrible darkness!" he said, feeling for her hand. "I must get out of it, or I shall die." He was quite incapable of explaining what was the matter, but my sister decided he must go home, and presently, as they went up the hill towards Hampstead, the horror seemed to drop from him. He said it was good to see the stars again, though it was then about noon and a blazing day.

"It seemed," he told me afterwards, "as if I was being carried irresistibly towards the water. I was not very much alarmed at first. Of course it was night there—a lovely night."

"Of course?" I asked, for that struck me as odd.

"Of course," said he. "It's always night there when it is day here—Well, we went right into the water, which was calm and shining under the moonlight—just a broad swell that seemed to grow broader and flatter as I came down into it. The surface glistened just like a skin—it might have been empty space underneath for all I could tell to the contrary. Very slowly, for I rode slanting into it, the water crept up to my eyes. Then I went under, and the skin seemed to break and heal again about my eyes. The moon gave a jump up in the sky and grew green and dim, and fish, faintly glowing, came darting round me—and things that seemed made of luminous glass, and I passed through a tangle of seaweeds that shone with an oily lustre. And so I drove down into the sea, and the stars went out one by one, and the moon grew greener and darker, and the seaweed became a luminous purple-red. It was all very faint and mysterious, and everything seemed to quiver. And all the while 1 could hear the wheels of the bath-chair creaking, and the footsteps of people going by, and a man with a bell crying coals.

"I kept sinking down deeper and deeper into the water. It became inky black about me, not a ray from above came down into that darkness, and the phosphorescent things grew brighter and brighter. The snaky branches of the deeper weeds flickered like the flames of spirit lamps; but, after a time, there were no more weeds. The fishes came staring and gaping towards me, and into me and through me. I never imagined such fishes before. They had lines of fire along the sides of them as though they had been outlined with a luminous pencil. And there was a ghastly thing swimming backwards with a lot of twining arms. And then I saw, coming very slowly towards me through the gloom, a hazy mass of light that resolved itself as it drew nearer into multitudes of fishes, struggling and darting round something that drifted. I drove on straight towards it, and presently I saw in the midst of the tumult, and by the light of the fish, a bit of splintered spar looming over me, and a dark hull tilting over, and some glowing phosphorescent forms that were shaken and writhed as the fish bit at them. Then it was I began to try to attract Widgery's attention. A horror came upon me. Ugh! I should have driven right into those half-eaten—things. If your sister had not come! They had great holes in them, Bellows, and—Never mind. But it was ghastly!"

IV

For three weeks Davidson remained in this singular state, seeing what at the time we imagined was an altogether phantasmal world, and stone blind to the world around him. Then, one Tuesday, when I called, I met old Davidson in the passage. "He can see his thumb!" the old gentleman said, in a perfect transport. He was struggling into his overcoat. "He can see his thumb, Bellows!" he said, with the tears in his eyes. "The lad will be all right yet."

I rushed in to Davidson. He was holding up a little book before his face, and looking at it and laughing in a weak kind of way.

"It's amazing," said he. "There's a kind of patch come there." He pointed with his finger. "I'm on the rocks as usual, and the penguins are staggering and flapping about as usual, and there's been a whale showing every now and then, but it's got too dark now to make him out. But put something *there,* and I see it—I do see it. It's very dim and broken in places, but I see it all the same, like a faint spectre of itself. I found it out this morning while they were dressing me. It's like a hole in this infernal phantom world. Just put your hand by mine. No—not there. Ah! Yes! I see it. The base of your thumb and a bit of cuff! It looks like the ghost of a bit of your hand sticking out of the darkening sky. Just by it there's a group of stars like a cross coming out."

From that time Davidson began to mend. His account of the change, like his account of the vision, was oddly convincing. Over patches of his field of vision the phantom world grew fainter, grew transparent, as it were, and through these translucent gaps he began to see dimly the real world about him. The patches grew in size and number, ran together and spread until only here and there were blind spots left upon his eyes. He was able to get up and steer himself about, feed himself once more, read, smoke, and behave like an ordinary citizen again. At first it was very confusing to him to have these two pictures overlapping each other like the changing views of a lantern, but in a little while he began to distinguish the real from the illusory.

At first he was unfeignedly glad, and seemed only too anxious to complete his cure by taking exercise and tonics. But as that odd island of his began to fade away from him, he became queerly interested in it. He wanted particularly to go down into the deep sea again, and would spend half his time wandering about the low-lying parts of London, trying to find the water-logged wreck he had seen drifting. The glare of real daylight very soon impressed him so vividly as to blot out everything of his shadowy world, but of a night-time, in a darkened room, he could still see the white-splashed rocks of the island, and the clumsy penguins staggering to and fro. But even these grew fainter and fainter, and, at last, soon after he married my sister, he saw them for the last time.

V

And now to tell of the queerest thing of all. About two years after his cure, I dined with the Davidsons, and after dinner a man named Atkins called in. He is a lieutenant in the Royal Navy, and a pleasant, talkative man. He was on friendly terms with my brother-in-law, and was soon on friendly terms with me. It came out that he was engaged to Davidson's cousin, and incidentally he took out a kind of pocket photograph case to show us a new rendering of his *fiancée*. "And, by-the-by," said he, "here's the old *Fulmar.*"

Davidson looked at it casually Then suddenly his face lit up. "Good heavens!" said he. "I could almost swear—"

"What?" said Atkins.

"That I had seen that ship before."

"Don't see how you can have. She hasn't been out of the South Seas for six years, and before then—"

"But," began Davidson, and then, "Yes—that's the ship I dreamt of. I'm sure that's the ship I dreamt of. She was standing off an island that swarmed with penguins, and she fired a gun."

"Good Lord!" said Atkins, who had never heard the particulars of the seizure. "How the deuce could you dream that?"

And then, bit by bit, it came out that on the very day Davidson was seized, H.M.S. *Fulmar* had actually been off a little rock to the south of Antipodes Island. A boat had landed overnight to get penguins' eggs, had been delayed, and a thunderstorm drifting up, the boat's crew had waited until the morning before rejoining the ship. Atkins had been one of them, and he corroborated, word for word, the descriptions Davidson had given of the island and the boat. There is not the slightest doubt in any of our minds that Davidson has really seen the place. In some unaccountable way, while he moved hither and thither in London, his sight moved hither and thither in a manner that corresponded, about this distant island. *How* is absolutely a mystery.

That completes the remarkable story of Davidson's eyes. It is perhaps the best authenticated case in existence of real vision at a distance. Explanation there is none forthcoming, except what Professor Wade has thrown out. But his explanation invokes the Fourth Dimension, and a dissertation on theoretical kinds of space. To talk of there being "a kink in space" seems mere nonsense to me; it may be because I am no mathematician. When I said that nothing would alter the fact that the place is eight thousand miles away, he answered that two points might be a yard away on a sheet of paper and yet be brought together by bending the paper round. The reader may grasp his argument, but I certainly do not. His idea seems to be that Davidson, stooping between the poles of the big electro-magnet, had some extraordinary twist given to his retinal elements through the sudden change in the field of force due to the lightning.

He thinks, as a consequence of this, that it may be possible to live visually in one part of the world, while one lives bodily in another. He has even made some experiments in support of his views; but, so far, he has simply succeeded in blinding a few dogs. I believe that is the net result of his work, though I have not seen him for some weeks. Latterly, I have been so busy with my work in connection with the Saint Pancras installation that I have had little opportunity of calling to see him. But the whole of his theory seems fantastic to me. The facts concerning Davidson stand on an altogether different footing, and I can testify personally to the accuracy of every detail I have given.

THE VETERAN

Stephen Crane

OUT OF THE low window could be seen three hickory trees placed irregularly in a meadow that was resplendent in springtime green. Farther away, the old, dismal belfry of the village church loomed over the pines. A horse meditating in the shade of one of the hickories lazily swished his tail. The warm sunshine made an oblong of vivid yellow on the floor of the grocery.

"Could you see the whites of their eyes?" said the man who was seated on a soap box.

"Nothing of the kind," replied old Henry warmly "Just a lot of flitting figures, and I let go at where they 'peared to be the thickest. Bang!"

"Mr. Fleming," said the grocer—his deferential voice expressed somehow the old man's exact social weight—"Mr. Fleming, you never was frightened much in them battles, was you?"

The veteran looked down and grinned. Observing his manner, the entire group tittered. "Well, I guess I was," he answered finally. "Pretty well scared, sometimes. Why, in my first battle I thought the sky was falling down. I thought the world was coming to an end. You bet I was scared."

Every one laughed. Perhaps it seemed strange and rather wonderful to them that a man should admit the thing, and in the tone of their laughter there was probably more admiration than if old Fleming had declared that he had always been a lion. Moreover, they knew that he had ranked as an orderly sergeant, and so their opinion of his heroism was fixed. None, to be sure, knew how an orderly sergeant ranked, but then it was understood to be somewhere just shy of a major general's stars. So,

368

when old Henry admitted that he had been frightened, there was a laugh.

"The trouble was," said the old man, "I thought they were all shooting at me. Yes, sir, I thought every man in the other army was aiming at me in particular, and only me. And it seemed so darned unreasonable, you know. I wanted to explain to 'em what an almighty good fellow I was, because I thought then they might quit all trying to hit me. But I couldn't explain, and they kept on being unreasonable—blim!—blam! bang! So I run!"

Two little triangles of wrinkles appeared at the corners of his eyes. Evidently he appreciated some comedy in this recital. Down near his feet, however, little Jim, his grandson, was visibly horror-stricken. His hands were clasped nervously, and his eyes were wide with astonishment at this terrible scandal, his most magnificent grandfather telling such a thing.

"That was at Chancellorsville. Of course, afterward I got kind of used to it. A man does. Lots of men, though, seem to feel all right from the start. I did, as soon as I 'got on to it,' as they say now; but at first I was pretty well flustered. Now, there was young Jim Conklin, old Si Conklin's son—that used to keep the tannery—you none of you recollect him—well, he went into it from the start just as if he was born to it. But with me it was different. I had to get used to it."

When little Jim walked with his grandfather he was in the habit of skipping along on the stone pavement in front of the three stores and the hotel of the town and betting that he could avoid the cracks. But upon this day he walked soberly, with his hand gripping two of his grandfather's fingers. Sometimes he kicked abstractedly at dandelions that curved over the walk. Any one could see that he was much troubled.

"There's Sickles's colt over the medder, Jimmie," said the old man. "Don't you wish you owned one like him?"

"Um," said the boy, with a strange lack of interest. He continued his reflections. Then finally he ventured, "Grandpa—now—was that true what you was telling those men?"

"What?" asked the grandfather. "What was I telling them?"

"Oh, about your running."

"Why, yes, that was true enough, Jimmie. It was my first fight, and there was an awful lot of noise, you know."

Jimmie seemed dazed that this idol, of its own will, should so totter. His stout boyish idealism was injured.

Presently the grandfather said: "Sickles's colt is going for a drink. Don't you wish you owned Sickles's colt, Jimmie?"

The boy merely answered, "He ain't as nice as our'n." He lapsed then into another moody silence.

★ ★ ★

One of the hired men, a Swede, desired to drive to the county seat for purposes of his own. The old man loaned a horse and an unwashed buggy. It appeared later that one of the purposes of the Swede was to get drunk.

After quelling some boisterous frolic of the farm hands and boys in the garret, the old man had that night gone peacefully to sleep, when he was aroused by clamouring at the kitchen door. He grabbed his trousers, and they waved out behind as he dashed forward. He could hear the voice of the Swede, screaming and blubbering. He pushed the wooden button, and, as the door flew open, the Swede, a maniac, stumbled inward, chattering, weeping, still screaming: "De barn fire! Fire! Fire! De barn fire! Fire! Fire! Fire!"

There was a swift and indescribable change in the old man. His face ceased instantly to be a face; it became a mask, a gray thing, with horror written about the mouth and eyes. He hoarsely shouted at the foot of the little rickety stairs, and immediately, it seemed, there came down an avalanche of men. No one knew that during this time the old lady had been standing in her night clothes at the bedroom door, yelling: "What's th' matter? What's th' matter? What's th' matter?"

When they dashed toward the barn it presented to their eyes its usual appearance, solemn, rather mystic in the black night. The Swede's lantern was overturned at a point some yards in front of the barn doors. It contained a wild little conflagration of its own, and even in their excitement some of those who ran felt a gentle secondary vibration of the thrifty part of their minds at sight of this overturned lantern. Under ordinary circumstances it would have been a calamity.

But the cattle in the barn were trampling, trampling, trampling, and above this noise could be heard a humming like the song of innumerable bees. The old man hurled aside the great doors, and a yellow flame leaped out at one corner and sped and wavered frantically up the old gray wall. It was glad, terrible, this single flame, like the wild banner of deadly and triumphant foes.

The motley crowd from the garret had come with all the pails of the farm. They flung themselves upon the well. It was a leisurely old machine, long dwelling in indolence. It was in the habit of giving out water with a sort of reluctance. The men stormed at it, cursed it; but it continued to allow the buckets to be filled only after the wheezy windlass had howled many protests at the mad-handed men.

With his opened knife in his hand old Fleming himself had gone headlong into the barn, where the stifling smoke swirled with the air currents, and where could be heard in its fulness the terrible chorus of the flames, laden with tones of hate and death, a hymn of wonderful ferocity.

He flung a blanket over an old mare's head, cut the halter close to the manger, led the mare to the door, and fairly kicked her out to safety. He returned with the same blanket, and rescued one of the work horses. He took five horses out, and then came out himself, with his clothes bravely on fire. He had no whiskers, and very little hair on his head. They soused five pailfuls of water on him. His eldest son made a clean miss with the sixth pailful, because the old man had turned and was running down the decline and around to the basement of the barn, where were the stanchions of the cows. Some one noticed at the time that he ran very lamely, as if one of the frenzied horses had smashed his hip.

The cows, with their heads held in the heavy stanchions, had thrown themselves, strangled themselves, tangled themselves: done everything which the ingenuity of their exuberant fear could suggest to them.

Here, as at the well, the same thing happened to every man save one. Their hands went mad. They became incapable of everything save the power to rush into dangerous situations.

The old man released the cow nearest the door, and she, blind drunk with terror, crashed into the Swede. The Swede had been running to and fro babbling. He carried an empty milk pail, to which he clung with an unconscious, fierce enthusiasm. He shrieked like one lost as he went under the cow's hoofs, and the milk pail, rolling across the floor, made a flash of silver in the gloom.

Old Fleming took a fork, beat off the cow, and dragged the paralyzed Swede to the open air. When they had rescued all the cows save one, which had so fastened herself that she could not be moved an inch, they returned to the front of the barn and stood sadly, breathing like men who had reached the final point of human effort.

Many people had come running. Some one had even gone to the church, and now, from the distance, rang the tocsin note of the old bell. There was a long flare of crimson on the sky, which made remote people speculate as to the whereabouts of the fire.

The long flames sang their drumming chorus in voices of the heaviest bass. The wind whirled clouds of smoke and cinders into the faces of the spectators. The form of the old barn was outlined in black amid these masses of orange-hued flames.

And then came this Swede again, crying as one who is the weapon of the sinister fates. "De colts! De colts! You have forgot de colts!"

Old Fleming staggered. It was true; they had forgotten the two colts in the box stalls at the back of the barn. "Boys," he said, "I must try to get 'em out." They clamoured about him then, afraid for him, afraid of what they should see. Then they talked wildly each to each. "Why, it's sure death!" "He would never get out!" "Why, it's suicide for a man to go in there!" Old Fleming stared absent-mindedly at the open doors. "The poor little things!" he said. He rushed into the barn.

When the roof fell in, a great funnel of smoke swarmed toward the sky, as if the old man's mighty spirit, released from its body—a little bottle—had swelled like the genie of fable. The smoke was tinted rose-hue from the flames, and perhaps the unutterable mid-nights of the universe will have no power to daunt the colour of this soul.

THE FORTUNE-TELLER

Joaquim Maria Machado de Assis

HAMLET OBSERVES TO Horatio that there are more things in heaven and earth than are dreamt of in our philosophy. This was the self-same explanation that was given by beautiful Rita to her lover, Camillo, on a certain Friday of November, 1869, when Camillo laughed at her for having gone, the previous evening, to consult a fortune-teller. The only difference is that she made her explanation in other words.

"Laugh, laugh. That's just like you men; you don't believe in anything. Well, let me tell you, I went there and she guessed the reason for my coming before I ever spoke a word. Scarcely had she begun to lay out the cards when she said to me: The lady likes a certain person . . .' I confessed that it was so, and then she continued to re-arrange the cards in various combinations, finally telling me that I was afraid you would forget me, but that there were no grounds for my fear."

"She was wrong!" interrupted Camillo with a laugh.

"Don't say that, Camillo. If you only realized in what anguish I went there, all on account of you. You know. I've told you before. Don't laugh at me; don't poke fun at me . . ."

Camillo seized her hands and gazed into her eyes earnestly and long. He swore that he loved her ever so much, that her fears were childish; in any case, should she ever harbor a fear, the best fortune-teller to consult was he himself. Then he reproved her, saying that it was imprudent to visit such houses. Villela might learn of it, and then . . .

"Impossible! I was exceedingly careful when I entered the place."

"Where is the house?"

"Near here. On Guarda-Velha street. Nobody was passing by at the time. Rest easy. I'm not a fool."

Camillo laughed again.

"Do you really believe in such things?" he asked.

It was at this point that she translated Hamlet into every-day speech, assuring her lover that there was many a true, mysterious thing in this world. If he was skeptical, let him have patience. One thing, however, was certain: the card reader had guessed everything. What more could he desire? The best proof was that at this moment she was at ease and content.

He was about to speak, but he restrained himself. He did not wish to destroy her illusions. He, too, when a child, and even later, had been superstitious, filled with an arsenal of beliefs which his mother had instilled, and which had disappeared by the time he reached twenty. The day on which he rid himself of all this parasitic vegetation, leaving behind only the trunk of religion, he wrapped his superstition and his religion (which had both been inculcated by his mother) in the same doubt, and soon arrived at a single, total negation. Camillo believed in nothing. Why? He could not have answered; he had not a solitary reason; he was content simply to deny everything. But I express myself ill, for to deny is in a sense to affirm, and he did not formulate his unbelief. Before the great mystery he simply shrugged his shoulders and went on.

The lovers parted in good spirits, he more happy than she. Rita was sure that she was loved; but Camillo was not only sure that she loved him, but saw how she trembled for him and even took risks, running to fortune-tellers. However much he had reproved her for this, he could not help feeling flattered by it. Their secret meeting-place was in the old Barbonos street at the home of a woman that came from Rita's province. Rita went off through Mangueiras street, in the direction of Botafogo, where she resided; Camillo entered Guarda-Velha street, keeping his eye open, as he passed, for the home of the card reader.

Villela, Camillo and Rita: three names, one adventure and no explanation of how it all began. Let us proceed to explain. The first two were friends since earliest childhood. Villela had entered the magistracy. Camillo found employment with the government, against the will of his father, who desired him to embrace the medical profession. But his father had died, and Camillo preferred to be nothing at all, until his mother had procured him a departmental position. At the beginning of the year 1869 Villela returned from the interior, where he had married a silly beauty; he abandoned the magistracy and came hither to open a lawyer's office. Camillo had secured a house for him near Botafogo and had welcomed him home.

"Is this the gentleman?" exclaimed Rita, offering Camillo her hand. "You can't imagine how highly my husband thinks of you. He was always talking about you."

Camillo and Villela looked at each other tenderly. They were true friends. Afterwards, Camillo confessed to himself that Villela's wife did not at all belie the enthusiastic letters her husband had written to him. Really, she was most prepossessing, lively in her movements, her eyes burning, her mouth plastic and piquantly inquiring. Rita was a trifle older than both the men: she was thirty, Villela twenty-nine and Camillo twenty-six. The grave bearing of Villela gave him the appearance of being much older than his wife, while Camillo was but a child in moral and practical life. . . . He possessed neither experience nor intuition.

The three became closely bound. Propinquity bred intimacy. Shortly afterwards Camillo's mother died, and in this catastrophe, for such it was, the other two showed themselves to be genuine friends of his. Villela took charge of the interment, of the church services and the settlement of the affairs of the deceased; Rita dispensed consolation, and none could do it better.

Just how this intimacy between Camillo and Rita grew to love he never knew. The truth is that he enjoyed passing the hours at her side; she was his spiritual nurse, almost a sister,—but most of all she was a woman, and beautiful. The aroma of femininity: this is what he yearned for in her, and about her, seeking to incorporate it into himself. They read the same books, they went together to the theatre or for walks. He taught her cards and chess, and they played of nights;—she badly,—he, to make himself agreeable, but little less badly. Thus much, as far as external things are concerned. And now came personal intimacies, the timorous eyes of Rita, that so often sought his own, consulting them before they questioned those of her own husband,—the touches of cold hands, and unwonted communion. On one of his birthdays he received from Villela a costly cane, and from Rita, a hastily penciled, ordinary note expressing good wishes. It was then that he learned to read within his own heart; he could not tear his eyes away from the missive. Commonplace words, it is true; but there are sublime commonplaces,—or at least, delightful ones. The old chaise in which for the first time you rode with your beloved, snuggled together, is as good as the chariot of Apollo. Such is man, and such are the circumstances that surround him.

Camillo sincerely wished to flee the situation, but it was already beyond his power. Rita, like a serpent, was charming him, winding her coils about him; she was crushing his bones, darting her venomous fangs into his lips. He was helpless, overcome. Vexation, fear, remorse, desire,—all this he felt, in a strange confusion. But the battle was short and the victory deliriously intoxicating. Farewell, all scruple! The shoe now fitted snugly enough upon the foot, and there they were both, launched upon the high road, arm in arm, joyfully treading the grass and the gravel, without suffering anything more than lonesomeness when they were away from each other. As to Villela, his confidence in his wife and his esteem for his friend continued the same as before.

One day, however, Camillo received an anonymous letter, which called him immoral and perfidious, and warned him that his adventure was known to all. Camillo took fright, and, in order to ward off suspicion, began to make his visits to Villela's house more rare. The latter asked him the reason for his prolonged absence. Camillo answered that the cause was a youthful flirtation. Simplicity evolved into cunning. Camillo's absences became longer and longer, and then his visits ceased entirely. Into this course there may have entered a little self-respect,—the idea of diminishing his obligations to the husband in order to make his own actions appear less treacherous.

It was at this juncture that Rita, uncertain and in fear, ran to the fortune-teller to consult her upon the real reason for Camillo's actions. As we have seen, the card reader restored the wife's confidence and the young man reproved her for having done what she did. A few weeks passed. Camillo received two or three more anonymous letters, written with such passionate anger that they could not have been prompted by mere regard for virtue; surely they came from some violent rival of his. In this opinion Rita concurred, formulating, in ill-composed words of her own, this thought: virtue is indolent and niggardly, wasting neither time nor paper; only self-interest is alert and prodigal.

But this did not help to ease Camillo; he now feared lest the anonymous writer should inform Villela, in which case the catastrophe would follow fast and implacably. Rita agreed that this was possible.

"Very well," she said. "Give me the envelopes in which the letters came, so that I may compare the handwriting with that of the mail which comes to him. If any arrives with writing resembling the anonymous script, I'll keep it and tear it up . . ."

But no such letter appeared. A short time after this, however, Villela commenced to grow grave, speaking very little, as if something weighed upon his mind. Rita hurried to communicate the change to her lover, and they discussed the matter earnestly. Her opinion was that Camillo should renew his visits to their home, and sound her husband; it might be that Villela would confide to him some business worry. With this Camillo disagreed; to appear after so many months was to confirm the suspicions and denunciations of the anonymous letters. It was better to be very careful, to give each other up for several weeks. They arranged means for communicating with each other in case of necessity and separated, in tears.

On the following day Camillo received at his department this letter from Villela: "Come immediately to our house; I must talk to you without delay." It was past noon. Camillo left at once; as he reached the street it occurred to him that it would have been much more natural for Villela to have called him to his office; why to his house? All this betokened a very urgent matter; moreover, whether it was reality or illusion, it seemed to Camillo that the letter was written in a trembling hand. He sought to establish a connection between all these things and the news Rita had brought him the night before.

"Come immediately to our house; I must talk to you without delay," he repeated, his eyes staring at the note.

In his mind's eye he beheld the climax of a drama,—Rita cowed, weeping; Villela indignant, seizing his pen and dashing off the letter, certain that he, Camillo, would answer in person, and waiting to kill him as he entered. Camillo shuddered with terror; then he smiled weakly; in any event the idea of drawing back was repugnant to him. So he continued on his way. As he walked it occurred to him to step into his rooms; he might find there a message from Rita explaining everything. But he found nothing, nobody. He returned to the street, and the thought that they had been discovered grew every moment more convincing; yes, the author of the previous anonymous communications must have denounced him to the husband; perhaps by now Villela knew all. The very suspension of his calls without any apparent reason, with the flimsiest of pretexts, would confirm everything else.

Camillo walked hastily along, agitated, nervous. He did not read the letter again, but the words hovered persistently before his eyes; or else,—which was even worse—they seemed to be murmured into his ears by the voice of Villela himself. "Come immediately to our house; I must talk to you without delay." Spoken thus by the voice of the other they seemed pregnant with mystery and menace. Come immediately,—why? It was now nearly one o'clock. Camillo's agitation waxed greater with each passing moment. So clearly did he imagine what was about to take place that he began to believe it a reality, to see it before his very eyes. Yes, without a doubt, he was afraid. He even considered arming himself, thinking that if nothing should happen he would lose nothing by this useful precaution. But at once he rejected the idea, angry with himself, and hastened his step towards Carioca square, there to take a tilbury. He arrived, entered and ordered the driver to be off at full speed.

"The sooner the better," he thought. "I can't stand this uncertainty."

But the very sound of the horse's clattering hoofs increased his agitation. Time was flying, and he would be face to face with danger soon enough. When they had come almost to the end of Guarda-Velha street the tilbury had to come to a stop; the thoroughfare was blocked by a coach that had broken down. Camillo surveyed the obstruction and decided to wait. After five minutes had gone by, he noticed that there at his left, at the very foot of the tilbury, was the fortunate-teller's house,—the very same as Rita had once consulted. Never, as at this moment, had he so desired to believe in card-reading. He looked closer, saw that the windows were closed, while all the others on the street were opened, filled with folks curious to see what was the matter. It looked for all the world like the dwelling of indifferent Fate.

Camillo leaned back in his seat so as to shut all this from view. His excitement was intense, extraordinary, and from the deep, hidden recesses of his mind there began to emerge spectres of early

childhood, old beliefs, banished superstitions. The coachman proposed another route; he shook his head and said that he would wait.
He leaned forward to get a better look at the card-reader's house . . .
Then he made a gesture of self-ridicule: it had entered his mind to
consult the fortune-teller, who seemed to be hovering over him, far,
far above, with vast, ash-colored wings; she disappeared, reappeared,
and then her image was lost; then, in a few moments, the ash-
colored wings stirred again, nearer, flying about him in narrowing
circles . . . In the street men were shouting, dragging away the
coach.

"There! Now! Push! That's it! Now!"

In a short while the obstruction was removed. Camillo closed his
eyes, trying to think of other things; but the voice of Rita's husband
whispered into his ears the words of the letter: "Come immediately. . ."
And he could behold the anguish of the drama. He trembled. The
house seemed to look right at him. His feet instinctively moved as if
to leave the carriage and go in . . . Camillo found himself before a
long, opaque veil . . . he thought rapidly of the inexplicability of so
many things. The voice of his mother was repeating to him a host of
extraordinary happenings; and the very sentence of the Prince of
Denmark kept echoing within him:

> "There are more things in heaven and earth, Horatio,
> Than are dreamt of in our philosophy."

What could he lose by it, if. . .?

He jumped out to the pavement, just before the fortune-teller's
door; he told the driver to wait for him, and hastened into the
entry, ascending the stairs. There was little light, the stairs were
worn away from the many feet that had sought them, the banister
was smooth and sticky; but he saw and felt nothing. He stumbled
up the stairs and knocked. Nobody appearing, he was about to go
down; but it was too late now,—curiosity was whipping his blood
and his heart beat with violent throbs; he turned back to the door,
and knocked once, twice, three times. He beheld a woman: it was
the card-reader. Camillo said that he had come to consult her, and
she bade him enter. Thence they climbed to the attic by a staircase
even worse than the first and buried in deeper gloom. At the top
there was a garret, ill lighted by a small window. Old furniture,

somber walls, and an air of poverty augmented, rather than destroyed, the prestige of the occupant.

The fortune-teller told him to be seated before the table, and she sat down on the opposite side with her back to the window, so that whatever little light came from without fell full upon Camillo's face. She opened a drawer and took out a pack of worn, filthy cards. While she rapidly shuffled them she peered at him closely, not so much with a direct gaze as from under her eyes. She was a woman of forty, Italian, thin and swarthy, with large, sharp, cunning eyes. She placed three cards upon the table, and said:

"Let us first see what has brought you here. The gentleman has just received a severe shock and is in great fear . . ."

Camillo, astonished, nodded affirmatively.

"And he wishes to know," she continued, "whether anything will happen to him or not . . ."

"To me and to her," he explained, excitedly.

The fortune-teller did not smile; she simply told him to wait. She took the cards hastily once more and shuffled them with her long tapering fingers whose nails were so long and unclean from neglect; she shuffled them well, once, twice, thrice; then she began to lay them out. Camillo's eyes were riveted upon her in anxious curiosity.

"The cards tell me . . ."

Camillo leaned forward to drink in her words one by one. Then she told him to fear nothing. Nothing would happen to him or to the other. He, the third, was aware of naught. Nevertheless, great caution was indispensable; envy and rivalry were at work. She spoke to him of the love that bound them, of Rita's beauty . . . Camillo was bewildered. The fortune-teller stopped talking, gathered the cards and locked them in the drawer.

"The lady has restored peace to my spirit," he said, offering her his hand across the table and pressing that of the card-reader.

She arose, laughing.

"Go," she said, "Go, *ragazzo innamorato* . . ."

And arising, she touched his head with her index finger. Camillo shuddered, as if it were the hand of one of the original sybils, and he, too, arose. The fortune-teller went to the bureau, upon which lay a plate of raisins, took a cluster of them and commenced to eat them, showing two rows of teeth that were as white as her nails were black. Even in this common action the woman possessed an air all her own. Camillo, anxious to leave, was at a loss how much to pay; he did not know her fee.

"Raisins cost money," he said, at length, taking out his pocketbook. "How much do you want to send for?"

"Ask your heart," she replied.

Camillo took out a note for ten milreis' and gave it to her. The eyes of the card-reader sparkled. Her usual fee was two milreis.

"I can see easily that the gentleman loves his lady very much . . . And well he may. For she loves the gentleman very deeply, too. Go, go in peace, with your mind at ease. And take care as you descend the staircase,—it's dark. Don't forget your hat . . ."

The fortune-teller had already placed the note in her pocket, and accompanied him down the stairs, chatting rather gaily. At the bottom of the first flight Camillo bid her good-bye and ran down the stairs that led to the street, while the card-reader, rejoicing in her large fee, turned back to the garret, humming a barcarolle. Camillo found the tilbury waiting for him; the street was now clear. He entered and the driver whipped his horse into a fast trot.

To Camillo everything had now changed for the better and his affairs assumed a brighter aspect; the sky was clear and the faces of the people he passed were all so merry. He even began to laugh at his fears, which he now saw were puerile; he recalled the language of Villela's letter and perceived at once that it was most friendly and familiar. How in the world had he ever been able to read any threat of danger into those words! He suddenly realized that they were urgent, however, and that he had done ill to delay so long; it might be some very serious business affair.

"Faster, faster!" he cried to the driver.

And he began to think of a plausible explanation of his delay; he even contemplated taking advantage of this incident to re-establish his former intimacy in Villela's household . . . Together with his plans there kept echoing in his soul the words of the fortune-teller. In truth, she had guessed the object of his visit, his own state of mind, and the existence of a third; why, then, wasn't it reasonable to suppose that she had guessed the rest correctly, too? For, the unknown present is the same as the future. And thus, slowly and persistently the young man's childhood superstitions attained the upper hand and mystery clutched him in its iron claws. At times he was ready to burst into laughter, and with a certain vexation he did laugh at himself. But the woman, the cards, her dry, reassuring words, and her good-bye—"Go, go, *ragazzo innamorato,*" and finally, that farewell barcarolle, so lively and gracious,—such were the new elements which, together with the old, formed within him a new and abiding faith.

The truth is that his heart was happy and impatient, recalling the happy hours of the past and anticipating those yet to come. As he passed through Gloria street Camillo gazed across the sea, far across where the waters and the heaven meet in endless embrace, and the sight gave him a sensation of the future,—long, long and infinite.

From here it was but a moment's drive to Villela's home. He stepped out, thrust the iron garden gate open and entered. The house was silent. He ran up the six stone steps and scarcely had he had time to knock when the door opened and Villela loomed before him.

"Pardon my delay. It was impossible to come sooner. What is the matter?"

Villela made no reply. His features were distorted; he beckoned Camillo to step within. As he entered, Camillo could not repress a cry of horror:—there upon the sofa lay Rita, dead in a pool of blood. Villela seized the lover by the throat and, with two bullets, stretched him dead upon the floor.

ROLLO LEARNING TO READ

Robert J. Burdette

WHEN ROLLO WAS five years young, his father said to him one evening: "Rollo, put away your roller skates and bicycle, carry that rowing machine out into the hall, and come to me. It is time for you to learn to read."

Then Rollo's father opened the book which he had sent home on a truck and talked to the little boy about it. It was Bancroft's *History of the United States,* half complete in twenty-three volumes. Rollo's father explained to Rollo and Mary his system of education, with special reference to Rollo's learning to read. His plan was that Mary should teach Rollo fifteen hours a day for ten years, and by that time Rollo would be half through the beginning of the first volume, and would like it very much indeed.

Rollo was delighted at the prospect. He cried aloud: "Oh, papa! thank you very much. When I read this book clear through, all the way to the end of the last volume, may I have another little book to read?"

"No," replied his father, "that may not be; because you will never get to the last volume of this one. For as fast as you read one volume, the author of this history, or his heirs, executors, administrators, or assigns, will write another as an appendix. So even though you should live to be a very old man, like the boy preacher, this history will always be twenty-three volumes ahead of you. Now, Mary and Rollo, this will be a hard task (pronounced *tawsk)* for both of you, and Mary must remember that Rollo is a very little boy, and must be very patient and gentle."

The next morning after the one preceding it, Mary began the first lesson. In the beginning she was so gentle and patient that her mother went away and cried, because she feared her dear little daughter was becoming too good for this sinful world, and might soon spread her wings and fly away and be an angel.

But in the space of a short time, the novelty of the expedition wore off, and Mary resumed running her temper—which was of the old-fashioned, low-pressure kind, just forward of the firebox—on its old schedule. When she pointed to "A" for the seventh time, and Rollo said "W," she tore the page out by the roots, hit her little brother such a whack over the head with the big book that it set his birthday back six weeks, slapped him twice, and was just going to bite him, when her mother came in. Mary told her that Rollo had fallen down stairs and torn his book and raised that dreadful lump on his head. This time Mary's mother restrained her emotion, and Mary cried. But it was not because she feared her mother was pining away. Oh, no; it was her mother's rugged health and virile strength that grieved Mary, as long as the seance lasted, which was during the entire performance.

That evening Rollo's father taught Rollo his lesson and made Mary sit by and observe his methods, because, he said, that would be normal instruction for her. He said: "Mary, you must learn to control your temper and curb your impatience if you want to wear low-neck dresses, and teach school. You must be sweet and patient, or you will never succeed as a teacher. Now, Rollo, what is this letter?"

"I dunno," said Rollo, resolutely.

"That is A," said his father, sweetly.

"Huh," replied Rollo, "I knowed that."

"Then why did you not say so?" replied his father, so sweetly that Jonas, the hired boy, sitting in the corner, licked his chops.

Rollo's father went on with the lesson: "What is this, Rollo?"

"I dunno," said Rollo, hesitatingly.

"Sure?" asked his father. "You do not know what it is?"

"Nuck," said Rollo.

"It is A," said his father.

"A what?" asked Rollo.

"A nothing," replied his father, "it is just A. Now, what is it?"

"Just A," said Rollo.

"Do not be flip, my son," said Mr. Holliday, "but attend to your lesson. What letter is this?"

"I dunno," said Rollo.

"Don't fib to me," said his father, gently, "you said a minute ago that you knew. That is N."

"Yes, sir," replied Rollo, meekly. Rollo, although he was a little boy, was no slouch, if he did wear bibs; he knew where he lived without looking at the door-plate. When it came time to be meek, there was no boy this side of the planet Mars who could be meeker, on shorter notice. So he said, "Yes, sir," with that subdued and well pleased alacrity of a boy who has just been asked to guess the answer to the conundrum, "Will you have another piece of pie?"

"Well," said his father, rather suddenly, "what is it?"

"M," said Rollo, confidently.

"N!" yelled his father, in three-line Gothic.

"N," echoed Rollo, in lower case nonpareil.

"B-a-n," said his father, "what does that spell?"

"Cat?" suggested Rollo, a trifle uncertainly.

"Cat?" snapped his father, with a sarcastic inflection, "b-a-n, cat! Where were you raised? Ban! B-a-n—Ban! Say it! Say it, or I'll get at you with a skate-strap!"

"B-a-m, ban'd," said Rollo, who was beginning to wish that he had a rain-check and could come back and see the remaining innings some other day.

"Ba-a-a-an!" shouted his father, "B-a-n, Ban, Ban, Ban! Now say Ban!"

"Ban," said Rollo, with a little gasp.

"That's right," his father said, in an encouraging tone; "you will learn to read one of these years if you give your mind to it. All he needs, you see, Mary, is a teacher who doesn't lose patience with him the first time he makes a mistake. Now, Rollo, how do you spell, B-a-n—Ban?"

Rollo started out timidly on c-a—then changed to d-o—and finally compromised on h-e-n.

Mr. Holiday made a pass at him with Volume I, but Rollo saw it coming and got out of the way.

"B-a-n!" his father shouted, "B-a-n, Ban! Ban! Ban! Ban! Ban! Now go on, if you think you know how to spell that! What comes next? Oh, you're enough to tire the patience of Job! I've a good mind to make you learn by the Pollard system, and begin where you leave off! Go ahead, why don't you? Whatta you waiting for? Read on! What comes next? Why, croft, of course; anybody ought to know that—c-r-o-f-t, croft, Bancroft! What does that apostrophe mean? I mean, what does that punctuation mark between t and s stand for? You don't know? Take that, then! *(whack)*. What comes after Bancroft? Spell it! Spell it, I tell you, and don't be all night about it! Can't, eh? Well, read it then; if you can't spell it, read it. H–i–s–t–o–r–y–ry, history; Bancroft's *History of the United States!* Now what does that spell? I mean, spell that! Spell it! Oh, go away! Go to bed! Stupid, stupid child," he added as the little boy went weeping out of the room, "he'll never learn anything so long as he lives. I declare he has tired me all out, and I used to teach school in Trivoli township, too. Taught one whole winter in district number three when Nick Worthington was county superintendent, and had my salary— . . . Look here, Mary, what do you find in that English grammar to giggle about? You go to bed, too, and listen to me—if Rollo can't read that whole book clear through without making a mistake tomorrow night, you'll wish you had been born without a back, that's all."

The following morning, when Rollo's father drove away to business, he paused a moment as Rollo stood at the gate for a final goodbye kiss—for Rollo's daily goodbyes began at the door and lasted as long as his father was in sight—Mr. Holliday said: "Some day, Rollo, you will thank me for teaching you to read."

"Yes, sir," replied Rollo, respectfully, and then added, "but not this day."

Rollo's head, though it had here and there transient bumps consequent upon football practice, was not naturally or permanently hilly. On the contrary, it was quite level.

A PAIR OF SILK STOCKINGS

Kate Chopin

LITTLE MRS. SOMMERS one day found herself the unexpected possessor of fifteen dollars. It seemed to her a very large amount of
money, and the way in which it stuffed and bulged her worn old
porte-monnaie gave her a feeling of importance such as she had not
enjoyed for years.

The question of investment was one that occupied her greatly.
For a day or two she walked about apparently in a dreamy state, but
really absorbed in speculation and calculation. She did not wish to
act hastily, to do anything she might afterward regret. But it was
during the still hours of the night when she lay awake revolving
plans in her mind that she seemed to see her way clearly toward a
proper and judicious use of the money.

A dollar or two should be added to the price usually paid for
Janie's shoes, which would insure their lasting an appreciable time
longer than they usually did. She would buy so and so many yards
of percale for new shirt waists for the boys and Janie and Mag. She
had intended to make the old ones do by skilful patching. Mag
should have another gown. She had seen some beautiful patterns,
veritable bargains in the shop windows. And still there would be
left enough for new stockings—two pairs apiece—and what darning that would save for a while! She would get caps for the boys
and sailor-hats for the girls. The vision of her little brood looking
fresh and dainty and new for once in their lives excited her and
made her restless and wakeful with anticipation.

The neighbors sometimes talked of certain "better days" that
little Mrs. Sommers had known before she had ever thought of
being Mrs. Sommers. She herself indulged in no such morbid

retrospection. She had no time—no second of time to devote to the past. The needs of the present absorbed her every faculty. A vision of the future like some dim, gaunt monster sometimes appalled her, but luckily to-morrow never comes.

Mrs. Sommers was one who knew the value of bargains; who could stand for hours making her way inch by inch toward the desired object that was selling below cost. She could elbow her way if need be; she had learned to clutch a piece of goods and hold it and stick to it with persistence and determination till her turn came to be served, no matter when it came.

But that day she was a little faint and tired. She had swallowed a light luncheon—no! when she came to think of it, between getting the children fed and the place righted, and preparing herself for the shopping bout, she had actually forgotten to eat any luncheon at all!

She sat herself upon a revolving stool before a counter that was comparatively deserted, trying to gather strength and courage to charge through an eager multitude that was besieging breast-works of shirting and figured lawn. An all-gone limp feeling had come over her and she rested her hand aimlessly upon the counter. She wore no gloves. By degrees she grew aware that her hand had encountered something very soothing, very pleasant to touch. She looked down to see that her hand lay upon a pile of silk stockings. A placard near by announced that they had been reduced in price from two dollars and fifty cents to one dollar and ninety-eight cents; and a young girl who stood behind the counter asked her if she wished to examine their line of silk hosiery. She smiled, just as if she had been asked to inspect a tiara of diamonds with the ultimate view of purchasing it. But she went on feeling the soft, sheeny luxurious things—with both hands now, holding them up to see them glisten, and to feel them glide serpent-like through her fingers.

Two hectic blotches came suddenly into her pale cheeks. She looked up at the girl.

"Do you think there are any eights-and-a-half among these?"

There were any number of eights-and-a-half. In fact, there were more of that size than any other. Here was a light-blue pair; there were some lavender, some all black and various shades of tan and gray. Mrs. Sommers selected a black pair and looked at them very long and closely. She pretended to be examining their texture, which the clerk assured her was excellent.

"A dollar and ninety-eight cents," she mused aloud. "Well, I'll take this pair." She handed the girl a five-dollar bill and waited for her change and for her parcel. What a very small parcel it was! It seemed lost in the depths of her shabby old shopping-bag.

Mrs. Sommers after that did not move in the direction of the bargain counter. She took the elevator, which carried her to an upper floor into the region of the ladies' waiting-rooms. Here, in a retired corner, she exchanged her cotton stockings for the new silk ones which she had just bought. She was not going through any acute mental process or reasoning with herself, nor was she striving to explain to her satisfaction the motive of her action. She was not thinking at all. She seemed for the time to be taking a rest from that laborious and fatiguing function and to have abandoned herself to some mechanical impulse that directed her actions and freed her of responsibility.

How good was the touch of the raw silk to her flesh! She felt like lying back in the cushioned chair and reveling for a while in the luxury of it. She did for a little while. Then she replaced her shoes, rolled the cotton stockings together and thrust them into her bag. After doing this she crossed straight over to the shoe department and took her seat to be fitted.

She was fastidious. The clerk could not make her out; he could not reconcile her shoes with her stockings, and she was not too easily pleased. She held back her skirts and turned her feet one way and her head another way as she glanced down at the polished, pointed-tipped boots. Her foot and ankle looked very pretty. She could not realize that they belonged to her and were a part of herself. She wanted an excellent and stylish fit, she told the young fellow who served her, and she did not mind the difference of a dollar or two more in the price so long as she got what she desired.

It was a long time since Mrs. Sommers had been fitted with gloves. On rare occasions when she had bought a pair they were always "bargains," so cheap that it would have been preposterous and unreasonable to have expected them to be fitted to the hand.

Now she rested her elbow on the cushion of the glove counter, and a pretty, pleasant young creature, delicate and deft of touch, drew a long-wristed "kid" over Mrs. Sommers' hand. She smoothed it down over the wrist and buttoned it neatly, and both lost themselves for a second or two in admiring contemplation of the little symmetrical gloved hand. But there were other places where money might be spent.

There were books and magazines piled up in the window of a stall a few paces down the street. Mrs. Sommers bought two high-priced magazines such as she had been accustomed to read in the days when she had been accustomed to other pleasant things. She carried them without wrapping. As well as she could she lifted her skirts at the crossings. Her stockings and boots and well fitting gloves had worked marvels in her bearing—had given her a feeling of assurance, a sense of belonging to the well-dressed multitude.

She was very hungry. Another time she would have stilled the cravings for food until reaching her own home, where she would have brewed herself a cup of tea and taken a snack of anything that was available. But the impulse that was guiding her would not suffer her to entertain any such thought.

There was a restaurant at the corner. She had never entered its doors; from the outside she had sometimes caught glimpses of spotless damask and shining crystal, and soft-stepping waiters serving people of fashion.

When she entered her appearance created no surprise, no consternation, as she had half feared it might. She seated herself at a small table alone, and an attentive waiter at once approached to take her order. She did not want a profusion; she craved a nice and tasty bite—a half dozen blue-points,[1] a plump chop with cress, a something sweet—a crème-frappée, for instance; a glass of Rhine wine, and after all a small cup of black coffee.

While waiting to be served she removed her gloves very leisurely and laid them beside her. Then she picked up a magazine and glanced through it, cutting the pages with a blunt edge of her knife. It was all very agreeable. The damask was even more spotless than it had seemed through the window, and the crystal more sparkling. There were quiet ladies and gentlemen, who did not notice her, lunching at the small tables like her own. A soft, pleasing strain of music could be heard, and a gentle breeze, was blowing through the window. She tasted a bite, and she read a word or two, and she sipped the amber wine and wiggled her toes in the silk stockings. The price of it made no difference. She counted the money out to

---

[1] *blue-points:* a type of oyster from Blue Point, Long Island.

the waiter and left an extra coin on his tray, whereupon he bowed before her as before a princess of royal blood.

There was still money in her purse, and her next temptation presented itself in the shape of a matinée poster.

It was a little later when she entered the theatre, the play had begun and the house seemed to her to be packed. But there were vacant seats here and there, and into one of them she was ushered, between brilliantly dressed women who had gone there to kill time and eat candy and display their gaudy attire. There were many others who were there solely for the play and acting. It is safe to say there was no one present who bore quite the attitude which Mrs. Sommers did to her surroundings. She gathered in the whole—stage and players and people in one wide impression, and absorbed it and enjoyed it. She laughed at the comedy and wept—she and the gaudy woman next to her wept over the tragedy. And they talked a little together over it. And the gaudy woman wiped her eyes and sniffled on a tiny square of filmy, perfumed lace and passed little Mrs. Sommers her box of candy.

The play was over, the music ceased, the crowd filed out. It was like a dream ended. People scattered in all directions. Mrs. Sommers went to the corner and waited for the cable car.

A man with keen eyes, who sat opposite to her, seemed to like the study of her small, pale face. It puzzled him to decipher what he saw there. In truth, he saw nothing—unless he were wizard enough to detect a poignant wish, a powerful longing that the cable car would never stop anywhere, but go on and on with her forever.

THE TABLES OF THE LAW

W. B. Yeats

I

"WILL YOU PERMIT me, Aherne," I said, "to ask you a question, which I have wanted to ask you for years, and have not asked because we have grown nearly strangers? Why did you refuse the biretta, and almost at the last moment? When you and I lived together, you cared neither for wine, women, nor money, and had thoughts for nothing but theology and mysticism." I had watched through dinner for a moment to put my question, and ventured now, because he had thrown off a little of the reserve and indifference which, ever since his last return from Italy, had taken the place of our once close friendship. He had just questioned me, too, about certain private and almost sacred things, and my frankness had earned, I thought, a like frankness from him.

When I began to speak he was lifting a glass of that wine which he could choose so well and valued to little; and while I spoke, he set it slowly and meditatively upon the table and held it there, its deep red light dyeing his long delicate fingers. The impression of his face and form, as they were then, is still vivid with me, and is inseparable from another and fanciful impression: the impression of a man holding a flame in his naked hand. He was to me, at that moment, the supreme type of our race, which, when it has risen above, or is sunken below, the formalisms of half-education and the rationalisms of conventional affirmation and denial, turns away, unless my hopes for the world and for the Church have made me blind, from practicable desires and intuitions towards desires so unbounded that no human vessel can contain them, intuitions so immaterial that their sudden and far-off fire leaves heavy darkness about hand and foot. He had the nature, which is half monk, half soldier of fortune, and must needs turn action into dreaming, and dreaming into action; and for such there is no order, no finality, no contentment in this world. When he and I had been students in Paris, we had belonged to a little group which devoted itself to speculations about alchemy and mysticism. More orthodox in most of his beliefs than Michael Robartes, he had surpassed him in a fanciful hatred of all life, and this hatred had found expression in the curious paradox—half borrowed from some fanatical monk, half invented by himself—that the beautiful arts were sent into the world to overthrow nations, and finally life herself, by sowing everywhere unlimited desires, like torches thrown into a burning city. This idea was not at the time, I believe, more than a paradox, a plume of the pride of youth; and it was only after his return to Ireland that he endured the fermentation of belief which is coming upon our people with the reawakening of their imaginative life.

Presently he stood up, saying, "Come, and I will show you why; you at any rate will understand," and taking candles from the table, he lit the way into the long paved passage that led to his private chapel. We passed between the portraits of the Jesuits and priests—some of no little fame—his family had given to the Church; and engravings and photographs of pictures that had especially moved him; and the few paintings his small fortune, eked out by an almost penurious abstinence from the things most men desire, had enabled him to buy in his travels. The photographs and engravings were from the masterpieces of many schools; but in all the beauty, whether it was a beauty of religion, of love, or of some fantastical vision of mountain and wood, was the beauty achieved by temperaments which seek always an absolute emotion, and which have their most continual, though not most perfect, expression in the legends and vigils and music of the Celtic peoples. The certitude of a fierce or gracious fervour in the enraptured faces of the angels of Francesca, and in the august faces of the sibyls of Michaelangelo; and the incertitude, as of souls trembling between the excitement of the spirit and the excitement of the flesh, in wavering faces from frescoes in the churches of Siena, and in the faces like thin flames, imagined by the modern symbolists and Pre-Raphaelites, had often made that long, grey, dim, empty, echoing passage become to my eyes a vestibule of eternity.

Almost every detail of the chapel, which we entered by a narrow Gothic door, whose threshold had been worn smooth by the secret worshippers of the penal times, was vivid in my memory; for it was in this chapel that I had first, and when but a boy, been moved by the mediaevalism which is now, I think, the governing influence in my life. The only thing that seemed new was a square bronze box which stood upon the altar before the six unlighted candles and the ebony crucifix, and was like those made in ancient times of more precious substances to hold the sacred books. Aherne made me sit down on an oak bench, and having bowed very low before the crucifix, took the bronze box from the altar, and sat down beside me with the box upon his knees.

"You will perhaps have forgotten," he said, "most of what you have read about Joachim of Flora, for he is little more than a name to even the well-read. He was an abbot in Cortale in the twelfth century, and is best known for his prophecy, in a book called *Expositio in Apocalypsin,* that the Kingdom of the Father was past, the Kingdom of the Son passing, the Kingdom of the Spirit yet to come. The Kingdom of the Spirit was to be a complete triumph of the Spirit, the *spiritualis intelligentia* he called it, over the dead letter. He had many followers among the more extreme Franciscans, and these were accused of possessing a secret book of his called the *Liber inducens in Evangelium aeternum.* Again and again groups of visionaries were accused of possessing this terrible book, in which the freedom of the Renaissance lay hidden, until at last Pope Alexander IV. had it found and cast into the flames. I have here the greatest treasure the world contains. I have a copy of that book; and see what great artists have made the robes in which it is wrapped. This bronze box was made by Benvenuto Cellini, who covered it with gods and demons, whose eyes are closed to signify an absorption in the inner light." He lifted the lid and took out a book bound in leather, covered with filigree work of tarnished silver. "And this cover was bound by one of the binders that bound for Canevari; while Giulio Clovio, an artist of the later Renaissance, whose work is soft and gentle, took out the beginning page of every chapter of the old copy, and set in its place a page surmounted by an elaborate letter and a miniature of some one of the great whose example was cited in the chapter; and wherever the writing left a little space elsewhere, he put some delicate emblem or intricate pattern."

I took the book in my hands and began turning over the gilded, many-coloured pages, holding it close to the candle to discover the texture of the paper.

"Where did you get this amazing book?" I said. "If genuine, and I cannot judge by this light, you have discovered one of the most precious things in the world."

"It is certainly genuine," he replied. "When the original was destroyed, one copy alone remained, and was in the hands of a lute-player of Florence, and from him it passed to his son, and so from generation to generation until it came to the lute-player who was father to Benvenuto Cellini, and from him it passed to Giulio Clovio, and from Giulio Clovio to a Roman engraver; and then from generation to generation, the story of its wandering passing on with it, until it came into the possession of the family of Aretino, and so Giulio Aretino, an artist and worker in metals, and student of the cabalistic reveries of Pico della Mirandola. He spent many nights with me at Rome, discussing philosophy; and at last I won his confidence so perfectly that he showed me this, his greatest treasure; and, finding how much I valued it, and feeling that he himself was growing old and beyond the help of its teaching, he sold it to me for no great sum, considering its great preciousness."

"What is the doctrine?" I said. "Some mediaeval straw-splitting about the nature of the Trinity, which is only useful to-day to show how many things are unimportant to us, which once shook the world?"

"I could never make you understand," he said with a sigh, "that nothing is unimportant in belief, but even you will admit that this book goes to the heart. Do you see the tables on which the commandments were written in Latin?" I looked to the end of the room, opposite to the altar, and saw that the two marble tablets were gone, and that two large empty tablets of ivory, like large copies of the little tablets we set over our desks, had taken their place. "It has swept the commandments of the Father away," he went on, "and displaced the commandments of the Son by the commandments of the Holy Spirit. The first book is called *Fractura Tabularum*. In the first chapter it mentions the names of the great artists who made them graven things and the likeness of many things, and adored them and served them; and the second the names of the great wits who took the name of the Lord their God in vain; and that long third chapter, set with the emblems of sanctified faces, and having wings upon its borders, is the praise of breakers of the seventh day and wasters of the six days, who yet lived comely and pleasant days. Those two chapters tell of men and women who railed upon their parents, remembering that their god was older than the god of their parents; and that which has the sword of Michael for an emblem commends the kings that wrought secret murder and so won for their people a peace that was *amore somnoque gravata et vestibus versicoloribus,* "heavy with love and sleep and many-coloured raiment"; and that with the pale star at the closing has the lives of the noble youths who loved the wives of others and were transformed into memories, which have transformed many poorer hearts into sweet flames; and that with the winged head is the history of the robbers who lived upon the sea or in the desert, lives which it compares to the twittering of the string of a bow, *nervi stridentis instar;* and those two last, that are fire and gold, and devoted to the satirists who bore false witness against their neighbours and yet illustrated eternal wrath, and to those that have coveted more than other men wealth and women, and have thereby and therefore mastered and magnified great empires.

"The second book, which is called *Straminis Deflagratio,* recounts the conversations Joachim of Flora held in his monastery at Cortale, and afterwards in his monastery in the mountains of La Sila, with travellers and pilgrims, upon the laws of many countries; how chastity was a virtue and robbery a little thing in such a land, and robbery a crime and unchastity a little thing in such a land; and of the persons who had flung themselves upon these laws and become *decussa veste Dei sidera,* stars shaken out of the raiment of God.

"The third book, which is the close, is called *Lex Secreta,* and describes the true inspiration of action, the only Eternal Evangel; and ends with a vision, which he saw among the mountains of La Sila, of his disciples sitting throned in the blue deep of the air, and laughing aloud, with a laughter that was like the rustling of the wings of Time: *Coelis in coeruleis ridentes sedebant discipuli mei super thronos: talis erat risus, qualis temporis pennati susurrus.*"

"I know little of Joachim of Flora," I said, "except that Dante set him in Paradise among the great doctors. If he held a heresy so singular, I cannot understand how no rumours of it came to the ears of Dante; and Dante made no peace with the enemies of the Church."

"Joachim of Flora acknowledged openly the authority of the Church, and even asked that all his published writings, and those to be published by his desire after his death, should be submitted to the censorship of the Pope. He considered that those whose work was to live and not to reveal were children and that the Pope was their father; but he taught in secret that certain others, and in always increasing numbers, were elected, not to live, but to reveal that hidden substance of God which is colour and music and softness and a sweet odour; and that these have no father but the Holy Spirit. Just as poets and painters and musicians labour at their works, building them with lawless and lawful things alike, so long as they embody the beauty that is beyond the grave, these children of the Holy Spirit labour at their moments with eyes upon the shining substance on which Time has heaped the refuse of creation; for the world only exists to be a tale in the ears of coming generations; and terror and content, birth and death, love and hatred, and the fruit of the Tree, are but instruments for that supreme art which is to win us from life and gather us into eternity like doves into their dove-cots.

"I shall go away in a little while and travel into many lands, that I may know all accidents and destinies, and when I return, will write my secret law upon those ivory tablets, just as poets and romance-writers have written the principles of their art in prefaces; and will gather pupils about me that they may discover their law in the study of my law, and the Kingdom of the Holy Spirit be more widely and firmly established."

He was pacing up and down, and I listened to the fervour of his words and watched the excitement of his gestures with not a little concern. I had been accustomed to welcome the most singular speculations, and had always found them as harmless as the Persian cat, who half closes her meditative eyes and stretches out her long claws, before my fire. But now I would battle in the interests of orthodoxy, even of the commonplace; and yet could find nothing better to say than: "It is not necessary to judge every one by the law, for we have also Christ's commandment of love."

He turned and said, looking at me with shining eyes:

"Jonathan Swift made a soul for the gentlemen of this city by hating his neighbour as himself."

"At any rate, you cannot deny that to teach so dangerous a doctrine is to accept a terrible responsibility."

"Leonardo da Vinci," he replied, "has this noble sentence: 'The hope and desire of returning home to one's former state is like the

moth's desire for the light; and the man who with constant longing
awaits each new month and new year, deeming that the things he
longs for are ever too late in coming, does not perceive that he is
longing for his own destruction.' How then can the pathway which
will lead us into the heart of God be other than dangerous? Why
should you, who are no materialist, cherish the continuity and
order of the world as those do who have only the world? You do
not value the writers who will express nothing unless their reason
understands how it will make what is called the right more easy;
why, then, will you deny a like freedom to the supreme art, the art
which is the foundation of all arts? Yes, I shall send out of this chapel saints, lovers, rebels, and prophets: souls that will surround
themselves with peace, as with a nest made with grass; and others
over whom I shall weep. The dust shall fall for many years over this
little box; and then I shall open it; and the tumults which are, perhaps, the flames of the Last Day shall come from under the lid."

I did not reason with him that night, because his excitement was
great and I feared to make him angry; and when I called at his
house a few days later, he was gone and his house was locked up
and empty. I have deeply regretted my failure both to combat his
heresy and to test the genuineness of his strange book. Since my
conversion I have indeed done penance for an error which I was
only able to measure after some years.

II

I was walking along one of the Dublin quays, on the side nearest
the river, about ten years after our conversation, stopping from
time to time to turn over the works upon an old bookstall, and
thinking, curiously enough, of the terrible destiny of Michael
Robartes, and his brotherhood, when I saw a tall and bent man
walking slowly along the other side of the quay. I recognised, with
a start, in a lifeless mask with dim eyes, the once resolute and delicate face of Owen Aherne. I crossed the quay quickly, but had not
gone many yards before he turned away, as though he had seen me,
and hurried down a side street; I followed, but only to lose him
among the intricate streets on the north side of the river. During
the next few weeks I inquired of everybody who had once known
him, but he had made himself known to nobody; and I knocked,
without result, at the door of his old house; and had nearly

persuaded myself that I was mistaken, when I saw him again in a narrow street behind the Four Courts, and followed him to the door of his house.

I laid my hand on his arm; he turned quite without surprise; and indeed it is possible that to him, whose inner life had soaked up the outer life, a parting of years was a parting from forenoon to afternoon. He stood holding the door half open, as though he would keep me from entering; and would perhaps have parted from me without further words had I not said: "Owen Aherne, you trusted me once, will you not trust me again, and tell me what has come of the ideas we discussed in this house ten years ago?—but perhaps you have already forgotten them."

"You have a right to hear," he said, "for since I have told you the ideas, I should tell you the extreme danger they contain, or rather the boundless wickedness they contain; but when you have heard this we must part, and part for ever, because I am lost, and must be hidden!"

I followed him through the paved passage, and saw that its corners were choked with dust and cobwebs; and that the pictures were grey with dust and shrouded with cobwebs; and that the dust and cobwebs which covered the ruby and sapphire of the saints on the window had made it very dim. He pointed to where the ivory tablets glimmered faintly in the dimness, and I saw that they were covered with small writing, and went up to them and began to read the writing. It was in Latin, and was an elaborate casuistry, illustrated with many examples, but whether from his own life or from the lives of others I do not know. I had read but a few sentences when I imagined that a faint perfume had begun to fill the room, and turning round asked Owen Aherne if he were lighting the incense.

"No," he replied, and pointed where the thurible lay rusty and empty on one of the benches; as he spoke the faint perfume seemed to vanish, and I was persuaded I had imagined it.

"Has the philosophy of the *Liber inducens in Evangelium aeternum* made you very unhappy?" I said.

"At first I was full of happiness," he replied, "for I felt a divine ecstasy, an immortal fire in every passion, in every hope, in every desire, in every dream; and I saw, in the shadows under leaves, in the hollow waters, in the eyes of men and women, its image, as in a mirror; and it was as though I was about to touch the Heart of

God. Then all changed and I was full of misery; and in my misery it was revealed to me that man can only come to that Heart through the sense of separation from it which we call sin, and I understood that I could not sin, because I had discovered the law of my being, and could only express or fail to express my being, and I understood that God has made a simple and an arbitrary law that we may sin and repent!"

He had sat down on one of the wooden benches and now became silent, his bowed head and hanging arms and listless body having more of dejection than any image I have met with in life or in any art. I went and stood leaning against the altar, and watched him, not knowing what I should say; and I noticed his black closely-buttoned coat, his short hair, and shaven head, which preserved a memory of his priestly ambition, and understood how Catholicism had seized him in the midst of the vertigo he called philosophy; and I noticed his lightless eyes and his earth-coloured complexion, and understood how she had failed to do more than hold him on the margin; and I was full of an anguish of pity.

"It may be," he went on, "that the angels who have hearts of the Divine Ecstasy, and bodies of the Divine Intellect, need nothing but a thirst for the immortal element, in hope, in desire, in dreams; but we whose hearts perish every moment, and whose bodies melt away like a sigh, must bow and obey!"

I went nearer to him and said, "Prayer and repentance will make you like other men."

"No, no," he said, "I am not among those for whom Christ died, and this is why I must be hidden. I have a leprosy that even eternity cannot cure. I have seen the whole, and how can I come again to believe that a part is the whole? I have lost my soul because I have looked out of the eyes of the angels."

Suddenly I saw, or imagined that I saw, the room darken, and faint figures robed in purple, and lifting faint torches with arms that gleamed like silver, bending above Owen Aherne; and I saw, or imagined that I saw, drops, as of burning gum, fall from the torches, and a heavy purple smoke, as of incense, come pouring from the flames and sweeping about us. Owen Aherne, more happy than I who have seen half initiated into the Order of the Alchemical Rose, or protected perhaps by his great piety, had sunk again into dejection and listlessness, and saw none of these things; but my knees shook under me, for the purple-robed figures were less faint every moment, and now I could hear the hissing of the gum in the torches. They did not appear to see me, for their eyes were upon Owen Aherne; now and again I could hear them sigh as though with sorrow for his sorrow, and presently I heard words which I could not understand except that they were words of sorrow, and sweet as though immortal was talking to immortal. Then one of them waved her torch, and all the torches waved, and for a moment it was as though some great bird made of flames had fluttered its plumage, and a voice cried as from far up in the air, "He has charged even his angels with folly, and they also bow and obey; but let your heart mingle with our hearts, which are wrought of Divine Ecstasy, and your body with our bodies, which are wrought of Divine Intellect." And at that cry I understood that the Order of the Alchemical Rose was not of this earth, and that it was still seeking over this earth for whatever souls it could gather within its glittering net; and when all the faces turned towards me, as I saw the mild eyes and the unshaken eyelids, I was full of terror, and thought they were about to fling their torches upon me, so that all I held dear, all that bound me to spiritual and social order, would be burnt up, and my soul left naked and shivering among the winds that blow from beyond this world and from beyond the stars; and then a voice cried, "Why do you fly from our torches that were made out of the trees under which Christ wept in the Garden of Gethsemane? Why do you fly from our torches that were made out of sweet wood, after it had perished from the world?"

It was not until the door of the house had closed behind my flight, and the noise of the street was breaking on my ears, that I came back to myself and to a little of my courage; and I have never dared to pass the house of Owen Aherne from that day, even though I believe him to have been driven into some distant country by the spirits whose name is legion, and whose throne is in the indefinite abyss, and whom he obeys and cannot see.

GOOSEBERRIES

Anton Chekhov

FROM EARLY MORNING the sky had been overcast with clouds; the day was still, cool, and wearisome, as usual on grey, dull days when the clouds hang low over the fields and it looks like rain, which never comes. Ivan Ivanich, the veterinary surgeon, and Bourkin, the schoolmaster, were tired of walking and the fields seemed endless to them. Far ahead they could just see the windmills of the village of Mirousky; to the right stretched away, to disappear behind the village, a line of hills, and they knew that it was the bank of the river; meadows, green willows, farmhouses; and from one of the hills there could be seen a field as endless, telegraph posts, and the train, looking from a distance like a crawling caterpillar, and in clear weather even the town. In the calm weather when all Nature seemed gentle and melancholy, Ivan Ivanich and Bourkin were filled with love for the fields and thought how grand and beautiful the country was.

"Last time, when we stopped in Prokufyi's shed," said Bourkin, "you were going to tell me a story."

"Yes. I wanted to tell you about my brother."

Ivan Ivanich took a deep breath and lighted his pipe before beginning his story, but just then the rain began to fall. And in about five minutes it came pelting down and showed no signs of stopping. Ivan Ivanich stopped and hesitated; the dogs, wet through, stood with their tails between their legs and looked at them mournfully.

"We ought to take shelter," said Bourkin. "Let us go to Aliokhin. It is close by."

"Very well."

They took a short cut over a stubble-field and then bore to the right, until they came to the road. Soon there appeared poplars, a garden, the red roofs of granaries; the river began to glimmer and they came to a wide road with a mill and a white bathing-shed. It was Sophino, where Aliokhin lived.

The mill was working, drowning the sound of the rain, and the dam shook. Round the carts stood wet horses, hanging their heads, and men were walking about with their heads covered with sacks. It was wet, muddy, and unpleasant, and the river looked cold and sullen. Ivan Ivanich and Bourkin felt wet and uncomfortable through and through; their feet were tired with walking in the mud, and they walked past the dam to the barn in silence as though they were angry with each other.

In one of the barns a winnowing-machine was working, sending out clouds of dust. On the threshold stood Aliokhin himself, a man of about forty, tall and stout, with long hair, more like a professor or a painter than a farmer. He was wearing a grimy white shirt and rope belt, and pants instead of trousers; and his boots were covered with mud and straw. His nose and eyes were black with dust. He recognised Ivan Ivanich and was apparently very pleased.

"Please, gentlemen," he said, "go to the house. I'll be with you in a minute."

The house was large and two-storied. Aliokhin lived down-stairs in two vaulted rooms with little windows designed for the farm-hands; the farmhouse was plain, and the place smelled of rye bread and vodka, and leather. He rarely used the reception-rooms, only when guests arrived. Ivan Ivanich and Bourkin were received by a chambermaid; such a pretty young woman that both of them stopped and exchanged glances.

"You cannot imagine how glad I am to see you, gentlemen," said Aliokhin, coming after them into the hall. "I never expected you. Pelagueya," he said to the maid, "give my friends a change of clothes. And I will change, too. But I must have a bath. I haven't had one since the spring. Wouldn't you like to come to the bathing-shed? And meanwhile our things will be got ready."

Pretty Pelagueya, dainty and sweet, brought towels and soap, and Aliokhin led his guests to the bathing-shed.

"Yes," he said, "it is a long time since I had a bath. My bathing-shed is all right, as you see. My father and I put it up, but somehow I have no time to bathe."

He sat down on the step and lathered his long hair and neck, and the water round him became brown.

"Yes. I see," said Ivan Ivanich heavily, looking at his head.

"It is a long time since I bathed," said Aliokhin shyly, as he soaped himself again, and the water round him became dark blue, like ink.

Ivan Ivanich came out of the shed, plunged into the water with a splash, and swam about in the rain, flapping his arms, and sending waves back, and on the waves tossed white lilies; he swam out to the middle of the pool and dived, and in a minute came up again in another place and kept on swimming and diving, trying to reach the bottom. "Ah! how delicious!" he shouted in his glee. "How delicious!" He swam to the mill, spoke to the peasants, and came back, and in the middle of the pool he lay on his back to let the rain fall on his face. Bourkin and Aliokhin were already dressed and ready to go, but he kept on swimming and diving.

"Delicious," he said. "Too delicious!"

"You've had enough," shouted Bourkin.

They went to the house. And only when the lamp was lit in the large drawing-room up-stairs, and Bourkin and Ivan Ivanich, dressed in silk dressing-gowns and warm slippers, lounged in chairs, and Aliokhin himself, washed and brushed, in a new frock coat, paced up and down evidently delighting in the warmth and cleanliness and dry clothes and slippers, and pretty Pelagueya, noiselessly tripping over the carpet and smiling sweetly, brought in tea and jam on a tray, only then did Ivan Ivanich begin his story, and it was as though he was being listened to not only by Bourkin and Aliokhin, but also by the old and young ladies and the officer who looked down so staidly and tranquilly from the golden frames.

"We are two brothers," he began, "I, Ivan Ivanich, and Nicholai Ivanich, two years younger. I went in for study and became a veterinary surgeon, while Nicholai was at the Exchequer Court when he was nineteen. Our father, Tchimsha-Himalaysky, was a cantonist, but he died with an officer's rank and left us his title of nobility and a small estate. After his death the estate went to pay his debts. However, we spent our childhood there in the country. We were just like peasants' children, spent days and nights in the fields and the woods, minded the house, barked the lime-trees, fished, and so on. . . . And you know once a man has fished, or watched the thrushes hovering in flocks over the village in the bright, cool, autumn days, he can never really be a townsman, and to the day of his death he will be drawn to the country. My brother pined away in the Exchequer. Years passed and he sat in the same place, wrote out the same documents, and thought of one thing, how to get back to the country. And little by little his distress became a definite disorder, a fixed idea—to buy a small farm somewhere by the bank of a river or a lake.

"He was a good fellow and I loved him, but I never sympathised with the desire to shut oneself up on one's own farm. It is a common saying that a man needs only six feet of land. But surely a corpse wants that, not a man. And I hear that our intellectuals have a longing for the land and want to acquire farms. But it all comes down to the six feet of land. To leave town, and the struggle and the swim of life, and go and hide yourself in a farmhouse is not life—it is egoism, laziness; it is a kind of monasticism, but monasticism without action. A man needs, not six feet of land, not a farm, but the whole earth, all Nature, where in full liberty he can display all the properties and qualities of the free spirit.

"My brother Nicholai, sitting in his office, would dream of eating his own *schi,* with its savoury smell floating across the farmyard; and of eating out in the open air, and of sleeping in the sun, and of sitting for hours together on a seat by the gate and gazing at the fields and the forest. Books on agriculture and the hints in almanacs were his joy, his favourite spiritual food; and he liked reading newspapers, but only the advertisements of land to be sold, so many acres of arable and grass land, with a farmhouse, river, garden, mill, and mill-pond. And he would dream of garden-walls, flowers, fruits, nests, carp in the pond, don't you know, and all the rest of it. These fantasies of his used to vary according to the advertisements he found, but somehow there was always a gooseberry-bush in every one. Not a house, not a romantic spot could he imagine without its gooseberry-bush.

"'Country life has its advantages,' he used to say. 'You sit on the veranda drinking tea and your ducklings swim on the pond, and everything smells good . . . and there are gooseberries.'

"He used to draw out a plan of his estate and always the same things were shewn on it: *(a)* Farmhouse, *(b)* cottage, (c) vegetable garden, *(d)* gooseberry-bush. He used to live meagrely and never had enough to eat and drink, dressed God knows how, exactly like a beggar, and always saved and put his money into the bank. He was terribly stingy. It used to hurt me to see him, and I used to give him money to go away for a holiday, but he would put that away, too. Once a man gets a fixed idea, there's nothing to be done.

"Years passed; he was transferred to another province. He completed his fortieth year and was still reading advertisements in the papers and saving up his money. Then I heard he was married. Still with the same idea of buying a farmhouse with a gooseberry-bush, he married an elderly, ugly widow, not out of any feeling for her, but because she had money. With her he still lived stingily, kept her half-starved, and put the money into the bank in his own name. She had been the wife of a postmaster and was used to good living, but with her second husband she did not even have enough black bread; she pined away in her new life, and in three years or so gave up her soul to God. And my brother never for a moment thought himself to blame for her death. Money, like vodka, can play queer tricks with a man. Once in our town a merchant lay dying. Before his death he asked for some honey, and he ate all his notes and scrip with the honey so that nobody should get it. Once I was examining a herd of cattle at a station and a horse-jobber fell under the engine, and his foot was cut off. We carried him into the waiting-room, with the blood pouring down—a terrible business—and all the while he kept on asking anxiously for his foot; he had twenty-five roubles in his boot and did not want to lose them."

"Keep to your story," said Bourkin.

"After the death of his wife," Ivan Ivanich continued, after a long pause, "my brother began to look out for an estate. Of course you may search for five years, and even then buy a pig in a poke. Through an agent my brother Nicholai raised a mortgage and bought three hundred acres with a farmhouse, a cottage, and a park, but there was no orchard, no gooseberry-bush, no duck-pond; there was a river but the water in it was coffee-coloured because the estate lay between a brick-yard and a gelatine factory. But my brother Nicholai was not worried about that; he ordered twenty gooseberry-bushes and settled down to a country life.

"Last year I paid him a visit. I thought I'd go and see how things were with him. In his letters my brother called his estate Tchimbarshov Corner, or Himalayskoe. I arrived at Himalayskoe in the afternoon. It was hot. There were ditches, fences, hedges, rows of young fir-trees, trees everywhere, and there was no telling how to cross the yard or where to put your horse. I went to the house and was met by a red-haired dog, as fat as a pig. He tried to bark but felt too lazy.

Out of the kitchen came the cook, barefooted, and also as fat as a pig, and said that the master was having his afternoon rest. I went in to my brother and found him sitting on his bed with his knees covered with a blanket; he looked old, stout, flabby; his cheeks, nose, and lips were pendulous. I half expected him to grunt like a pig.

"We embraced and shed a tear of joy and also of sadness to think that we had once been young, but were now both going grey and nearing death. He dressed and took me to see his estate.

"'Well? How are you getting on?' I asked.

"'All right, thank God. I am doing very well.'

"He was no longer the poor, tired official, but a real landowner and a person of consequence. He had got used to the place and liked it, ate a great deal, took Russian baths, was growing fat, had already gone to law with the parish and the two factories, and was much offended if the peasants did not call him 'Your Lordship.' And, like a good landowner, he looked after his soul and did good works pompously, never simply. What good works? He cured the peasants of all kinds of diseases with soda and castor-oil, and on his birthday he would have a thanksgiving service held in the middle of the village, and would treat the peasants to half a bucket of vodka, which he thought the right thing to do. Ah! Those horrible buckets of vodka. One day a greasy landowner will drag the peasants before the Zemstvo Court for trespass, and the next, if it's a holiday, he will give them a bucket of vodka, and they drink and shout Hooray! and lick his boots in their drunkenness. A change to good eating and idleness always fills a Russian with the most preposterous self-conceit. Nicholai Ivanich, who, when he was in the Exchequer, was terrified to have an opinion of his own, now imagined that what he said was law. 'Education is necessary for the masses, but they are not fit for it.' 'Corporal punishment is generally harmful, but in certain cases it is useful and indispensable.'

"'I know the people and I know how to treat them,' he would say. 'The people love me. I have only to raise my finger and they will do as I wish.'

"And all this, mark you, was said with a kindly smile of wisdom. He was constantly saying: 'We noblemen,' or 'I, as a nobleman.' Apparently he had forgotten that our grandfather was a peasant and our father a common soldier. Even our family name, Tchimsha-Himalaysky, which is really an absurd one, seemed to him full-sounding, distinguished, and very pleasing.

"But my point does not concern him so much as myself. I want to tell you what a change took place in me in those few hours while I was in his house. In the evening, while we were having tea, the cook laid a plateful of gooseberries on the table. They had not been bought, but were his own gooseberries, plucked for the first time since the bushes were planted. Nicholai Ivanich laughed with joy and for a minute or two he looked in silence at the gooseberries with tears in his eyes. He could not speak for excitement, then put one into his mouth, glanced at me in triumph, like a child at last being given its favourite toy, and said:

" 'How good they are!'

"He went on eating greedily, and saying all the while:

" 'How good they are! Do try one!'

"It was hard and sour, but, as Poushkin said, the illusion which exalts us is dearer to us than ten thousand truths. I saw a happy man, one whose dearest dream had come true, who had attained his goal in life, who had got what he wanted, and was pleased with his destiny and with himself. In my idea of human life there is always some alloy of sadness, but now at the sight of a happy man I was filled with something like despair. And at night it grew on me. A bed was made up for me in the room near my brother's and I could hear him, unable to sleep, going again and again to the plate of gooseberries. I thought: 'After all, what a lot of contented, happy people there must be! What an overwhelming power that means! I look at this life and see the arrogance and the idleness of the strong, the ignorance and bestiality of the weak, the horrible poverty everywhere, overcrowding, drunkenness, hypocrisy, falsehood . . . Meanwhile in all the houses, all the streets, there is peace; out of fifty thousand people who live in our town there is not one to kick against it all. Think of the people who go to the market for food: during the day they eat; at night they sleep, talk nonsense, marry, grow old, piously follow their dead to the cemetery; one never sees or hears those who suffer, and all the horror of life goes on somewhere behind the scenes. Everything is quiet, peaceful, and against it all there is only the silent protest of statistics; so many go mad, so many gallons are drunk, so many children die of starvation . . . And such a state of things is obviously what we want; apparently a happy man only feels so because the unhappy bear their burden in silence, but for which happiness would be impossible. It is a general hypnosis. Every happy man should have some one with a little hammer at his door to knock and remind him that there are unhappy people, and that, however happy he may be, life will sooner or later show its claws, and some misfortune will befall him—illness, poverty, loss, and then no one will see or hear him, just as he now neither sees nor hears others. But there is no man with a hammer, and the happy go on living, just a little fluttered with the petty cares of every day, like an aspen-tree in the wind—and everything is all right.'

"That night I was able to understand how I, too, had been content and happy," Ivan Ivanich went on, getting up. "I, too, at meals or out hunting, used to lay down the law about living, and religion, and governing the masses. I, too, used to say that teaching is light, that education is necessary, but that for simple folk reading and writing is enough for the present. Freedom is a boon, I used to say, as essential as the air we breathe, but we must wait. Yes—I used to say so, but now I ask: 'Why do we wait?'" Ivan Ivanich glanced angrily at Bourkin. "Why do we wait, I ask you? What considerations keep us fast? I am told that we cannot have everything at once, and that every idea is realised in time. But who says so? Where is the proof that it is so? You refer me to the natural order of things, to the law of cause and effect, but is there order or natural law in that I, a living, thinking creature, should stand by a ditch until it fills up, or is narrowed, when I could jump it or throw a bridge over it? Tell me, I say, why should we wait? Wait, when we have no strength to live, and yet must live and are full of the desire to live!

"I left my brother early the next morning, and from that time on I found it impossible to live in town. The peace and the quiet of it oppress me. I dare not look in at the windows, for nothing is more dreadful to see than the sight of a happy family, sitting round a table, having tea. I am an old man now and am no good for the struggle. I commenced late. I can only grieve within my soul, and fret and sulk. At night my head buzzes with the rush of my thoughts and I cannot sleep . . . Ah! If I were young!"

Ivan Ivanich walked excitedly up and down the room and repeated:

"If I were young."

He suddenly walked up to Aliokhin and shook him first by one hand and then by the other.

"Pavel Konstantinich," he said in a voice of entreaty, "don't be satisfied, don't let yourself be lulled to sleep! While you are young, strong, wealthy, do not cease to do good! Happiness does not exist, nor should it, and if there is any meaning or purpose in life, they are not in our piddling little happiness, but in something reasonable and grand. Do good!"

Ivan Ivanich said this with a piteous supplicating smile, as though he were asking a personal favour.

Then they all three sat in different corners of the drawing-room and were silent. Ivan Ivanich's story had satisfied neither Bourkin nor Aliokhin. With the generals and ladies looking down from their gilt frames, seeming alive in the firelight, it was tedious to hear the story of a miserable official who ate gooseberries . . . Somehow they had a longing to hear and to speak of charming people, and of women. And the mere fact of sitting in the drawing-room where everything—the lamp with its coloured shade, the chairs, and the carpet under their feet—told how the very people who now looked down at them from their frames once walked, and sat and had tea there, and the fact that pretty Pelagueya was near—was much better than any story.

Aliokhin wanted very much to go to bed; he had to get up for his work very early, about two in the morning, and now his eyes were closing, but he was afraid of his guests saying something interesting without his hearing it, so he would not go. He did not trouble to think whether what Ivan Ivanich had been saying was clever or right; his guests were talking of neither groats, nor hay, nor tar, but of something which had no bearing on his life, and he liked it and wanted them to go on. . . .

"However, it's time to go to bed," said Bourkin, getting up. "I will wish you good night."

Aliokhin said good night and went down-stairs, and left his guests. Each had a large room with an old wooden bed and carved ornaments; in the corner was an ivory crucifix; and their wide, cool beds, made by pretty Pelagueya, smelled sweetly of clean linen.

Ivan Ivanich undressed in silence and lay down.

"God forgive me, a wicked sinner," he murmured, as he drew the clothes over his head.

A smell of burning tobacco came from his pipe which lay on the table, and Bourkin could not sleep for a long time and was worried because he could not make out where the unpleasant smell came from.

The rain beat against the windows all night long.

THE STORM

Kate Chopin

I

THE LEAVES WERE so still that even Bibi thought it was going to rain. Bobinôt, who was accustomed to converse on terms of perfect equality with his little son, called the child's attention to certain sombre clouds that were rolling with sinister intention from the west, accompanied by a sullen, threatening roar. They were at Friedheimer's store and decided to remain there till the storm had passed. They sat within the door on two empty kegs. Bibi was four years old and looked very wise.

"Mama'll be 'fraid, yes," he suggested with blinking eyes.

"She'll shut the house. Maybe she got Sylvie helpin' her this evenin'," Bobinôt responded reassuringly.

"No; she ent got Sylvie. Sylvie was helpin' her yistiday," piped Bibi.

Bobinôt arose and going across to the counter purchased a can of shrimps, of which Calixta was very fond. Then he returned to his perch on the keg and sat stolidly holding the can of shrimps while the storm burst. It shook the wooden store and seemed to be ripping great furrows in the distant field. Bibi laid his little hand on his father's knee and was not afraid.

II

Calixta, at home, felt no uneasiness for their safety. She sat at a side window sewing furiously on a sewing machine. She was greatly occupied and did not notice the approaching storm. But she felt very warm and often stopped to mop her face on which the perspiration gathered in beads. She unfastened her white sacque at the throat. It began to grow dark, and suddenly realizing the situation she got up hurriedly and went about closing windows and doors.

Out on the small front gallery she had hung Bobinôt's Sunday clothes to air and she hastened out to gather them before the rain fell. As she stepped outside, Alcée Laballière rode in at the gate. She had not seen him very often since her marriage, and never alone. She stood there with Bobinôt's coat in her hands, and the big rain drops began to fall. Alcée rode his horse under the shelter of a side projection where the chickens had huddled and there were plows and a harrow piled up in the corner.

"May I come and wait on your gallery till the storm is over, Calixta?" he asked.

"Come 'long in, M'sieur Alcée."

His voice and her own startled her as if from a trance, and she seized Bobinôt's vest. Alcée, mounting to the porch, grabbed the trousers and snatched Bibi's braided jacket that was about to be carried away by a sudden gust of wind. He expressed an intention to remain outside, but it was soon apparent that he might as well have been out in the open: the water beat in upon the boards in driving sheets, and he went inside, closing the door after him. It was even necessary to put something beneath the door to keep the water out.

"My! what a rain! It's good two years since it rain' like that," exclaimed Calixta as she rolled up a piece of bagging and Alcée helped her to thrust it beneath the crack.

She was a little fuller of figure than five years before when she married; but she had lost nothing of her vivacity. Her blue eyes still retained their melting quality; and her yellow hair, dishevelled by the wind and rain, kinked more stubbornly than ever about her ears and temples.

The rain beat upon the low, shingled roof with a force and clatter that threatened to break an entrance and deluge them there. They were in the dining room—the sitting room—the general utility room. Adjoining was her bed room, with Bibi's couch along side her own. The door stood open, and the room with its white, monumental bed, its closed shutters, looked dim and mysterious.

Alcée flung himself into a rocker and Calixta nervously began to gather up from the floor the lengths of a cotton sheet which she had been sewing.

"If this keeps up, *Dieu sait*[1] if the levees goin' to stan' it!" she exclaimed.

"What have you got to do with the levees?"

"I got enough to do! An' there's Bobinôt with Bibi out in that storm—if he only didn' left Friedheimer's!"

"Let us hope, Calixta, that Bobinôt's got sense enough to come in out of a cyclone."

She went and stood at the window with a greatly disturbed look on her face. She wiped the frame that was clouded with moisture. It was stiflingly hot. Alcée got up and joined her at the window, looking over her shoulder. The rain was coming down in sheets obscuring the view of far-off cabins and enveloping the distant wood in a gray mist. The playing of the lightning was incessant. A bolt struck a tall chinaberry tree at the edge of the field. It filled all visible space with a blinding glare and the crash seemed to invade the very boards they stood upon.

Calixta put her hands to her eyes, and with a cry, staggered backward. Alcée's arm encircled her, and for an instant he drew her close and spasmodically to him.

"*Bonté!*"[2] she cried, releasing herself from his encircling arm and retreating from the window, "the house'll go next! If I only knew w'ere Bibi was!" She would not compose herself; she would not be seated. Alcée clasped her shoulders and looked into her face. The contact of her warm, palpitating body when he had unthinkingly drawn her into his arms, had aroused all the old-time infatuation and desire for her flesh.

"Calixta," he said, "don't be frightened. Nothing can happen. The house is too low to be struck, with so many tall trees standing about. There! aren't you going to be quiet? say, aren't you?" He pushed her hair back from her face that was warm and steaming. Her lips were as red and moist as pomegranate seed. Her white neck and a glimpse of her full, firm bosom disturbed him powerfully. As she glanced up at him the fear in her liquid blue eyes had given place to a drowsy gleam that unconsciously betrayed a sensuous desire. He looked down into her eyes and there was nothing for him to do but to gather her lips in a kiss. It reminded him of Assumption.

---

[1] *Dieu sait]* God knows.
[2] *"Bonté!"]* "Goodness!"

"Do you remember—in Assumption, Calixta?" he asked in a low voice broken by passion. Oh! she remembered; for in Assumption he had kissed her and kissed and kissed her; until his senses would well nigh fail, and to save her he would resort to a desperate flight. If she was not an immaculate dove in those days, she was still inviolate; a passionate creature whose very defenselessness had made her defense, against which his honor forbade him to prevail. Now—well, now—her lips seemed in a manner free to be tasted, as well as her round, white throat and her whiter breasts.

They did not heed the crashing torrents, and the roar of the elements made her laugh as she lay in his arms. She was a revelation in that dim, mysterious chamber; as white as the couch she lay upon. Her firm, elastic flesh that was knowing for the first time its birthright, was like a creamy lily that the sun invites to contribute its breath and perfume to the undying life of the world.

The generous abundance of her passion, without guile or trickery, was like a white flame which penetrated and found response in depths of his own sensuous nature that had never yet been reached.

When he touched her breasts they gave themselves up in quivering ecstasy, inviting his lips. Her mouth was a fountain of delight. And when he possessed her, they seemed to swoon together at the very borderland of life's mystery.

He stayed cushioned upon her, breathless, dazed, enervated, with his heart beating like a hammer upon her. With one hand she clasped his head, her lips lightly touching his forehead. The other hand stroked with a soothing rhythm his muscular shoulders.

The growl of the thunder was distant and passing away. The rain beat softly upon the shingles, inviting them to drowsiness and sleep. But they dared not yield.

The rain was over; and the sun was turning the glistening green world into a palace of gems. Calixta, on the gallery, watched Alcée ride away. He turned and smiled at her with a beaming face; and she lifted her pretty chin in the air and laughed aloud.

III

Bobinôt and Bibi, trudging home, stopped without at the cistern to make themselves presentable.

"My! Bibi, w'at will yo' mama say! You ought to be ashame'. You oughtn' put on those good pants. Look at 'em! An' that mud on yo' collar! How you got that mud on yo' collar, Bibi? I never saw such a boy!" Bibi was the picture of pathetic resignation. Bobinôt was the embodiment of serious solicitude as he strove to remove from his own person and his son's the signs of their tramp over heavy roads and through wet fields. He scraped the mud off Bibi's bare legs and feet with a stick and carefully removed all traces from his heavy brogans. Then, prepared for the worst—the meeting with an over-scrupulous housewife, they entered cautiously at the back door.

Calixta was preparing supper. She had set the table and was dripping coffee at the hearth. She sprang up as they came in.

"Oh, Bobinôt! You back! My! but I was uneasy. W'ere you been during the rain? An' Bibi? he ain't wet? he ain't hurt?" She had clasped Bibi and was kissing him effusively. Bobinôt's explanations and apologies which he had been composing all along the way, died on his lips as Calixta felt him to see if he were dry, and seemed to express nothing but satisfaction at their safe return.

"I brought you some shrimps, Calixta," offered Bobinôt, hauling the can from his ample side pocket and laying it on the table.

"Shrimps! Oh, Bobinôt! you too good fo' anything!" and she gave him a smacking kiss on the cheek that resounded. *"J'vous réponds,*[3] we'll have a feas' to-night! umph-umph!"

Bobinôt and Bibi began to relax and enjoy themselves, and when the three seated themselves at table they laughed much and so loud that anyone might have heard them as far away as Laballière's.

IV

Alcée Laballière wrote to his wife, Clarisse, that night. It was a loving letter, full of tender solicitude. He told her not to hurry back, but if she and the babies liked it at Biloxi, to stay a month longer. He was getting on nicely; and though he missed them, he was willing to bear the separation a while longer—realizing that their health and pleasure were the first things to be considered.

---

[3] *"J'vous réponds"*] "You bet!"

V

As for Clarisse, she was charmed upon receiving her husband's letter. She and the babies were doing well. The society was agreeable; many of her old friends and acquaintances were at the bay. And the first free breath since her marriage seemed to restore the pleasant liberty of her maiden days. Devoted as she was to her husband, their intimate conjugal life was something which she was more than willing to forego for a while.

So the storm passed and every one was happy.

WEE WILLIE WINKIE

"An officer and a gentleman"

Rudyard Kipling

HIS FULL NAME was Percival William Williams, but he picked up the other name in a nursery-book, and that was the end of the christened titles. His mother's ayah called him Willie-Baba, but as he never paid the faintest attention to anything that the ayah said, her wisdom did not help matters.

His father was the Colonel of the 195th, and as soon as Wee Willie Winkie was old enough to understand what Military Discipline meant, Colonel Williams put him under it. There was no other way of managing the child. When he was good for a week, he drew good-conduct pay; and when he was bad, he was deprived of his good-conduct stripe. Generally he was bad, for India offers many chances of going wrong to little six-year-olds.

Children resent familiarity from strangers, and Wee Willie Winkie was a very particular child. Once he accepted an acquaintance, he was graciously pleased to thaw. He accepted Brandis, a subaltern of the 195th, on sight. Brandis was having tea at the Colonel's, and Wee Willie Winkie entered strong in the possession of a good-conduct badge won for not chasing the hens round the compound. He regarded Brandis with gravity for at least ten minutes, and then delivered himself of his opinion.

"I like you," said he slowly, getting off his chair and coming over to Brandis. "I like you. I shall call you Coppy, because of your hair. Do you mind being called Coppy? It is because of ve hair, you know."

Here was one of the most embarrassing of Wee Willie Winkie's peculiarities. He would look at a stranger for some time, and then, without warning or explanation, would give him a name. And the name stuck. No regimental penalties could break Wee Willie Winkie of this habit. He lost his good-conduct badge for christening the Commissioner's wife "Pobs"; but nothing that the Colonel could do made the Station forego the nickname, and Mrs. Collen remained "Pobs" till the end of her stay. So Brandis was christened "Coppy," and rose, therefore, in the estimation of the regiment.

If Wee Willie Winkie took an interest in any one, the fortunate man was envied alike by the mess and the rank and file. And in their envy lay no suspicion of self-interest. "The Colonel's son" was idolised on his own merits entirely. Yet Wee Willie Winkie was not lovely. His face was permanently freckled, as his legs were permanently scratched, and in spite of his mother's almost tearful remonstrances he had insisted upon having his long yellow locks cut short in the military fashion. "I want my hair like Sergeant Tumirul's," said Wee Willie Winkie, and, his father abetting, the sacrifice was accomplished.

Three weeks after the bestowal of his youthful affections on Lieutenant Brandis—henceforward to be called "Coppy" for the sake of brevity—Wee Willie Winkie was destined to behold strange things and far beyond his comprehension.

Coppy returned his liking with interest. Coppy had let him wear for five rapturous minutes his own big sword—just as tall as Wee Willie Winkie. Coppy had promised him a terrier puppy; and Coppy had permitted him to witness the miraculous operation of shaving. Nay, more—Coppy had said that even he, Wee Willie Winkie, would rise in time to the ownership of a box of shiny knives, a silver soap-box, and a silver-handled "sputter-brush," as Wee Willie Winkie called it. Decidedly, there was no one except his father, who could give or take away good-conduct badges at pleasure, half so wise, strong, and valiant as Coppy with the Afghan and Egyptian medals on his breast. Why, then, should Coppy be guilty of the unmanly weakness of kissing—vehemently kissing—a "big girl," Miss Allardyce to wit? In the course of a morning ride Wee Willie Winkie had seen Coppy so doing, and, like the gentleman he was, had promptly wheeled round and cantered back to his groom, lest the groom should also see.

Under ordinary circumstances he would have spoken to his father, but he felt instinctively that this was a matter on which Coppy ought first to be consulted.

"Coppy," shouted Wee Willie Winkie, reining up outside that subaltern's bungalow early one morning—"I want to see you, Coppy!"

"Come in, young 'un," returned Coppy, who was at early breakfast in the midst of his dogs. "What mischief have you been getting into now?'

Wee Willie Winkie had done nothing notoriously bad for three days, and so stood on a pinnacle of virtue.

"I've been doing nothing bad," said he, curling himself into a long chair with a studious affectation of the Colonel's languor after a hot parade. He buried his freckled nose in a tea cup and, with eyes staring roundly over the rim, asked: "I say, Coppy, is it pwoper to kiss big girls?"

"By Jove! You're beginning early. Who do you want to kiss?"

"No one. My muvver's always kissing me if I don't stop her. If it isn't pwoper, how was you kissing Major Allardyce's big girl last morning, by ve canal?"

Coppy's brow wrinkled. He and Miss Allardyce had with great craft managed to keep their engagement secret for a fortnight. There were urgent and imperative reasons why Major Allardyce should not know how matters stood for at least another month, and this small marplot had discovered a great deal too much.

"I saw you," said Wee Willie Winkie calmly. "But ve sais didn't see. I said, 'Hut jao!'"

"Oh, you had that much sense, you young Rip," groaned poor Coppy, half amused and half angry. "And how many people may you have told about it?"

"Only me myself. You didn't tell when I twied to wide ve buffalo ven my pony was lame; and I fought you wouldn't like."

"Winkie," said Coppy enthusiastically, shaking the small hand, "you're the best of good fellows. Look here, you can't understand all these things. One of these days—hang it, how can I make you see it!—I'm going to marry Miss Allardyce, and then she'll be Mrs. Coppy, as you say. If your young mind is so scandalised at the idea of kissing big girls, go and tell your father."

"What will happen?" said Wee Willie Winkie, who firmly believed that his father was omnipotent.

"I shall get into trouble," said Coppy, playing his trump card with an appealing look at the holder of the ace.

"Ven I won't," said Wee Willie Winkie briefly. "But my faver says it's un-man-ly to be always kissing, and I didn't fink you'd do vat, Coppy."

"I'm not always kissing, old chap. It's only now and then, and when you're bigger you'll do it too. Your father meant it's not good for little boys."

"Ah!" said Wee Willie Winkie, now fully enlightened. "It's like ve sputter-brush?"

"Exactly," said Coppy gravely.

"But I don't fink I'll ever want to kiss big girls, nor no one, 'cept my muwer. And I must vat, you know."

There was a long pause, broken by Wee Willie Winkie.

"Are you fond of vis big girl, Coppy?"

"Awfully!" said Coppy.

"Fonder van you are of Bell or ve Butcha—or me?"

"It's in a different way," said Coppy. "You see, one of these days Miss Allardyce will belong to me, but you'll grow up and command the Regiment and—all sorts of things. It's quite different, you see."

"Very well," said Wee Willie Winkie, rising. "If you're fond of ve big girl I won't tell any one. I must go now."

Coppy rose and escorted his small guest to the door, adding—"You're the best of little fellows, Winkie. I tell you what. In thirty days from now you can tell if you like—tell any one you like."

Thus the secret of the Brandis-Allardyce engagement was dependent on a little child's word. Coppy, who knew Wee Willie Winkie's idea of truth, was at ease, for he felt that he would not break promises. Wee Willie Winkie betrayed a special and unusual interest in Miss Allardyce, and, slowly revolving round that embarrassed young lady, was used to regard her gravely with unwinking eye. He was trying to discover why Coppy should have kissed her. She was not half so nice as his own mother. On the other hand, she was Coppy's property, and would in time belong to him. Therefore it behoved him to treat her with as much respect as Coppy's big sword or shiny pistol.

The idea that he shared a great secret in common with Coppy kept Wee Willie Winkie unusually virtuous for three weeks. Then the Old Adam broke out, and he made what he called a "camp-fire" at the bottom of the garden. How could he have foreseen that the flying sparks would have lighted the Colonel's little hay-rick and consumed a week's store for the horses? Sudden and swift was the punishment—deprivation of the good-conduct badge and, most sorrowful of all, two days' confinement to barracks—the house and verandah—coupled with the withdrawal of the light of his father's countenance.

He took the sentence like the man he strove to be, drew himself up with a quivering under-lip, saluted, and, once clear of the room, ran to weep bitterly in his nursery—called by him "my quarters." Coppy came in the afternoon and attempted to console the culprit.

"I'm under awwest," said Wee Willie Winkie mournfully, "and I didn't ought to speak to you."

Very early the next morning he climbed on to the roof of the house—that was not forbidden—and beheld Miss Allardyce going for a ride.

"Where are you going?" cried Wee Willie Winkie.

"Across the river," she answered, and trotted forward.

Now the cantonment in which the 195th lay was bounded on the north by a river—dry in the winter. From his earliest years, Wee Willie Winkie had been forbidden to go across the river, and had noted that even Coppy—the almost almighty Coppy—had never set foot beyond it. Wee Willie Winkie had once been read to, out of a big blue book, the history of the Princess and the Goblins—a most wonderful tale of a land where the Goblins were always warring with the children of men until they were defeated by one Curdie. Ever since that date it seemed to him that the bare black and purple hills across the river were inhabited by Goblins, and, in truth, every one had said that there lived the Bad Men. Even in his own house the lower halves of the windows were covered with green paper on account of the Bad Men who might, if allowed clear view, fire into peaceful drawing-rooms and comfortable bedrooms. Certainly, beyond the river, which was the end of all the Earth, lived the Bad Men. And here was Major Allardyce's big girl, Coppy's property, preparing to venture into their borders! What would Coppy say if anything happened to her? If the Goblins ran off with her as they did with Curdie's Princess? She must at all hazards be turned back.

The house was still. Wee Willie Winkie reflected for a moment on the very terrible wrath of his father; and then—broke his arrest! It was a crime unspeakable. The low sun threw his shadow, very large and very black, on the trim garden-paths, as he went down to the stables and ordered his pony. It seemed to him in the hush of the dawn that all the big world had been bidden to stand still and look at Wee Willie Winkie guilty of mutiny. The drowsy sais gave him his mount, and, since the one great sin made all others insignificant, Wee Willie Winkie said that he was going to ride over to Coppy Sahib, and went out at a foot-pace, stepping on the soft mould of the flower-borders.

The devastating track of the pony's feet was the last misdeed that cut him off from all sympathy of Humanity. He turned into the road, leaned forward, and rode as fast as the pony could put foot to the ground in the direction of the river.

But the liveliest of twelve-two ponies can do little against the long canter of a Waler. Miss Allardyce was far ahead, had passed through the crops, beyond the Police-posts, when all the guards were asleep, and her mount was scattering the pebbles of the river-bed as Wee Willie Winkie left the cantonment and British India behind him. Bowed forward and still flogging, Wee Willie Winkie shot into Afghan territory, and could just see Miss Allardyce, a black speck, flickering across the stony plain. The reason of her wandering was simple enough. Coppy, in a tone of too-hastily-assumed authority, had told her overnight that she must not ride out by the river. And she had gone to prove her own spirit and teach Coppy a lesson.

Almost at the foot of the inhospitable hills, Wee Willie Winkie saw the Waler blunder and come down heavily. Miss Allardyce struggled clear, but her ankle had been severely twisted, and she could not stand. Having fully shown her spirit, she wept, and was surprised by the apparition of a white, wide-eyed child in khaki, on a nearly spent pony

"Are you badly, badly hurted?" shouted Wee Willie Winkie, as soon as he was within range. "You didn't ought to be here."

"I don't know," said Miss Allardyce ruefully, ignoring the reproof. "Good gracious, child, what are you doing here?"

"You said you was going acwoss ve wiver," panted Wee Willie Winkie, throwing himself off his pony. "And nobody—not even Coppy—must go acwoss ve wiver, and I came after you ever so hard, but you wouldn't stop, and now you've hurted yourself, and Coppy will be angwy wiv me, and—I've bwoken my awwest! I've bwoken my awwest!"

The future Colonel of the 195th sat down and sobbed. In spite of the pain in her ankle the girl was moved.

"Have you ridden all the way from cantonments, little man? What for?"

"You belonged to Coppy. Coppy told me so!" wailed Wee Willie Winkie disconsolately. "I saw him kissing you, and he said he was fonder of you van Bell or ve Butcha or me. And so I came. You must get up and come back. You didn't ought to be here. Vis is a bad place, and I've bwoken my awwest."

"I can't move, Winkie," said Miss Allardyce, with a groan. "I've hurt my foot. What shall I do?"

She showed a readiness to weep anew, which steadied Wee Willie Winkie, who had been brought up to believe that tears were the depth of unmanliness. Still, when one is as great a sinner as Wee Willie Winkie, even a man may be permitted to break down.

"Winkie," said Miss Allardyce, "when you've rested a little, ride back and tell them to send out something to carry me back in. It hurts fearfully."

The child sat still for a little time and Miss Allardyce closed her eyes; the pain was nearly making her faint. She was roused by Wee Willie Winkie tying up the reins on his pony's neck and setting it free with a vicious cut of his whip that made it whicker. The little animal headed towards the cantonments.

"Oh, Winkie, what are you doing?"

"Hush!" said Wee Willie Winkie. "Veres a man coming—one of ve Bad Men. I must stay wiv you. My faver says a man must always look after a girl. Jack will go home, and ven vey'll come and look for us. Vat's why I let him go."

Not one man but two or three had appeared from behind the rocks of the hills, and the heart of Wee Willie Winkie sank within him, for just in this manner were the Goblins wont to steal out and vex Curdie's soul. Thus had they played in Curdie's garden—he had seen the picture—and thus had they frightened the Princess's nurse. He heard them talking to each other, and recognised with joy the bastard Pushto that he had picked up from one of his father's grooms lately dismissed. People who spoke that tongue could not be the Bad Men. They were only natives after all.

They came up to the boulders on which Miss Allardyce's horse had blundered.

Then rose from the rock Wee Willie Winkie, child of the Dominant Race, aged six and three-quarters, and said briefly and emphatically "Jao!" The pony had crossed the river-bed.

The men laughed, and laughter from natives was the one thing Wee Willie Winkie could not tolerate. He asked them what they wanted and why they did not depart. Other men with most evil faces and crooked-stocked guns crept out of the shadows of the hills, till, soon, Wee Willie Winkie was face to face with an audience some twenty strong. Miss Allardyce screamed.

"Who are you?" said one of the men.

"I am the Colonel Sahib's son, and my order is that you go at once. You black men are frightening the Miss Sahib. One of you must run into cantonments and take the news that the Miss Sahib has hurt herself, and that the Colonel's son is here with her."

"Put our feet into the trap?" was the laughing reply. "Hear this boy's speech!"

"Say that I sent you—I, the Colonel's son. They will give you money."

"What is the use of this talk? Take up the child and the girl, and we can at least ask for the ransom. Ours are the villages on the heights," said a voice in the background.

These were the Bad Men—worse than Goblins—and it needed all Wee Willie Winkie's training to prevent him from bursting into tears. But he felt that to cry before a native, excepting only his mother's ayah, would be an infamy greater than any mutiny. Moreover, he, as future Colonel of the 195th, had that grim regiment at his back.

"Are you going to carry us away?" said Wee Willie Winkie, very blanched and uncomfortable.

"Yes, my little Sahib Bahadur," said the tallest of the men, "and eat you afterwards."

"That is child's talk," said Wee Willie Winkie. "Men do not eat men."

A yell of laughter interrupted him, but he went on firmly—"And if you do carry us away, I tell you that all my regiment will come up in a day and kill you all without leaving one. Who will take my message to the Colonel Sahib?"

Speech in any vernacular—and Wee Willie Winkie had a colloquial acquaintance with three—was easy to the boy who could not yet manage his "r's" and "th's" aright.

Another man joined the conference, crying: "O foolish men! What this babe says is true. He is the heart's heart of those white troops. For the sake of peace let them go both, for if he be taken, the regiment will break loose and gut the valley. Our villages are in the valley, and we shall not escape. That regiment are devils. They broke Khoda Yar's breast-bone with kicks when he tried to take the rifles; and if we touch this child they will fire and rape and plunder for a month, till nothing remains. Better to send a man back to take the message and get a reward. I say that this child is their God, and that they will spare none of us, nor our women, if we harm him."

It was Din Mahommed, the dismissed groom of the Colonel, who made the diversion, and an angry and heated discussion followed. Wee Willie Winkie, standing over Miss Allardyce, waited the upshot. Surely his "wegiment," his own "wegiment," would not desert him if they knew of his extremity.

★ ★ ★

The riderless pony brought the news to the 195th, though there had been consternation in the Colonel's household for an hour before. The little beast came in through the parade-ground in front of the main barracks, where the men were settling down to play Spoil-five till the afternoon. Devlin, the Colour-Sergeant of E Company, glanced at the empty saddle and tumbled through the barrack-rooms, kicking up each Room Corporal as he passed. "Up, you beggars! There's something happened to the Colonel's son," he shouted.

"He couldn't fall off! S'elp me, 'e couldn't fall off," blubbered a drummer-boy "Go an' hunt acrost the river. He's over there if he's anywhere, an' maybe those Pathans have got 'im. For the love o' Gawd don't look for 'im in the nullahs! Let's go over the river."

"There's sense in Mott yet," said Devlin. "E Company, double out to the river—sharp!"

So E Company, in its shirt-sleeves mainly, doubled for the dear life, and in the rear toiled the perspiring Sergeant, adjuring it to double yet faster. The cantonment was alive with the men of the 195th hunting for Wee Willie Winkie, and the Colonel finally overtook E Company, far too exhausted to swear, struggling in the pebbles of the river-bed.

Up the hill under which Wee Willie Winkie's Bad Men were discussing the wisdom of carrying off the child and the girl, a lookout fired two shots.

"What have I said?" shouted Din Mahommed. "There is the warning! The pulton are out already and are coming across the plain! Get away! Let us not be seen with the boy."

The men waited for an instant, and then, as another shot was fired, withdrew into the hills, silently as they had appeared.

"The wegiment is coming," said Wee Willie Winkie confidently to Miss Allardyce, "and it's all wight. Don't cwy!"

He needed the advice himself, for ten minutes later, when his father came up, he was weeping bitterly with his head in Miss Allardyce's lap.

And the men of the 195th carried him home with shouts and rejoicings; and Coppy, who had ridden a horse into a lather, met him, and, to his intense disgust, kissed him openly in the presence of the men.

But there was balm for his dignity. His father assured him that not only would the breaking of arrest be condoned, but that the good-conduct badge would be restored as soon as his mother could sew it on his blouse-sleeve. Miss Allardyce had told the Colonel a story that made him proud of his son.

"She belonged to you, Coppy," said Wee Willie Winkie, indicating Miss Allardyce with a grimy forefinger. "I knew she didn't ought to go acwoss ve wiver, and I knew ve wegiment would come to me if I sent Jack home."

"You're a hero, Winkie," said Coppy—"a pukka hero!"

"I don't know what vat means," said Wee Willie Winkie, "but you mustn't call me Winkie any no more. I'm Percival Will'am Will'ams."

And in this manner did Wee Willie Winkie enter into his manhood.

THE WHITE SILENCE

Jack London

"CARMEN WON'T LAST more than a couple of days." Mason spat out a chunk of ice and surveyed the poor animal ruefully, then put her foot in his mouth and proceeded to bite out the ice which clustered cruelly between the toes.

"I never saw a dog with a highfalutin' name that ever was worth a rap," he said, as he concluded his task and shoved her aside. "They just fade away and die under the responsibility. Did ye ever see one go wrong with a sensible name like Cassiar, Siwash, or Husky? No, sir! Take a look at Shookum here, he's"—

Snap! The lean brute flashed up, the white teeth just missing Mason's throat.

"Ye will, will ye?" A shrewd clout behind the ear with the butt of the dogwhip stretched the animal in the snow, quivering softly, a yellow slaver dripping from its fangs.

"As I was saying, just look at Shookum, here—he's got the spirit. Bet ye he eats Carmen before the week's out."

"I'll bank another proposition against that," replied Malemute Kid, reversing the frozen bread placed before the fire to thaw. "We'll eat Shookum before the trip is over. What d'ye say, Ruth?"

The Indian woman settled the coffee with a piece of ice, glanced from Malemute Kid to her husband, then at the dogs, but vouchsafed no reply. It was such a palpable truism that none was necessary. Two hundred miles of unbroken trail in prospect, with a scant six days' grub for themselves and none for the dogs, could admit no other alternative. The two men and the woman grouped about the fire and began their meagre meal. The dogs lay in their harnesses, for it was a midday halt, and watched each mouthful enviously.

"No more lunches after to-day," said Malemute Kid. "And we've got to keep a close eye on the dogs,—they're getting vicious. They'd just as soon pull a fellow down as not, if they get a chance."

"And I was president of an Epworth once, and taught in the Sunday school." Having irrelevantly delivered himself of this, Mason fell into a dreamy contemplation of his steaming moccasins, but was aroused by Ruth filling his cup. "Thank God, we've got slathers of tea! I've seen it growing, down in Tennessee. What wouldn't I give for a hot corn pone just now! Never mind, Ruth; you won't starve much longer, nor wear moccasins either."

The woman threw off her gloom at this, and in her eyes welled up a great love for her white lord,—the first white man she had ever seen,—the first man whom she had known to treat a woman as something better than a mere animal or beast of burden.

"Yes, Ruth," continued her husband, having recourse to the macaronic jargon in which it was alone possible for them to understand each other; "wait till we clean up and pull for the Outside. We'll take the White Man's canoe and go to the Salt Water. Yes, bad water, rough water,—great mountains dance up and down all the time. And so big, so far, so far away,—you travel ten sleep, twenty sleep, forty sleep" (he graphically enumerated the days on his fingers), "all the time water, bad water. Then you come to great village, plenty people, just the same mosquitoes next summer. Wigwams oh, so high,—ten, twenty pines. Hi-yu skookum!"

He paused impotently, cast an appealing glance at Malemute Kid, then laboriously placed the twenty pines, end on end, by sign language. Malemute Kid smiled with cheery cynicism; but Ruth's eyes were wide with wonder, and with pleasure; for she half believed he was joking, and such condescension pleased her poor woman's heart.

"And then you step into a—a box, and pouf! up you go." He tossed his empty cup in the air by way of illustration, and as he deftly caught it, cried: "And biff! down you come. Oh, great medicine-men! You go Fort Yukon, I go Arctic City,—twenty-five sleep,—big string, all the time,—I catch him string,—I say, 'Hello, Ruth! How are ye?'—and you say, 'Is that my good husband?'—and I say 'Yes,'—and you say, 'No can bake good bread, no more soda,'—then I say, 'Look in cache, under flour; good-by.' You look and catch plenty soda. All the time you Fort Yukon, me Arctic City. Hi-yu medicine-man!"

Ruth smiled so ingenuously at the fairy story, that both men burst into laughter. A row among the dogs cut short the wonders of the Outside, and by the time the snarling combatants were separated, she had lashed the sleds and all was ready for the trail.

"Mush! Baldy! Hi! Mush on!" Mason worked his whip smartly, and as the dogs whined low in the traces, broke out the sled with the gee-pole. Ruth followed with the second team, leaving Malemute Kid, who had helped her start, to bring up the rear. Strong man, brute that he was, capable of felling an ox at a blow, he could not bear to beat the poor animals, but humored them as a dog-driver rarely does,—nay, almost wept with them in their misery.

"Come, mush on there, you poor sore-footed brutes!" he murmured, after several ineffectual attempts to start the load. But his patience was at last rewarded, and though whimpering with pain, they hastened to join their fellows.

No more conversation; the toil of the trail will not permit such extravagance. And of all deadening labors, that of the Northland trail is the worst. Happy is the man who can weather a day's travel at the price of silence, and that on a beaten track.

And of all heart-breaking labors, that of breaking trail is the worst. At every step the great webbed shoe sinks till the snow is level with the knee. Then up, straight up, the deviation of a fraction of an inch being a certain precursor of disaster, the snowshoe must be lifted till the surface is cleared; then forward, down, and the other foot is raised perpendicularly for the matter of half a yard. He who tries this for the first time, if haply he avoids bringing his shoes in dangerous propinquity and measures not his length on the treacherous footing, will give up exhausted at the end of a hundred yards; he who can keep out of the way of the dogs for a whole day may well crawl into his sleeping-bag with a clear conscience and a pride which passeth all understanding; and he who travels twenty sleeps on the Long Trail is a man whom the gods may envy.

The afternoon wore on, and with the awe, born of the White Silence, the voiceless travelers bent to their work. Nature has many tricks wherewith she convinces man of his finity,—the ceaseless flow of the tides, the fury of the storm, the shock of the earthquake, the long roll of heaven's artillery,—but the most tremendous, the most stupefying of all, is the passive phase of the White Silence. All movement ceases, the sky clears, the heavens are as brass; the slightest whisper seems sacrilege, and man becomes timid, affrighted at the sound of his own voice. Sole speck of life journeying across the ghostly wastes of a dead world, he trembles at his audacity, realizes that his is a maggot's life, nothing more. Strange thoughts arise unsummoned, and the mystery of all things strives for utterance. And the fear of death, of God, of the universe, comes over him,—the hope of the Resurrection and the Life, the yearning for immortality, the vain striving of the imprisoned essence,—it is then, if ever, man walks alone with God.

So wore the day away. The river took a great bend, and Mason headed his team for the cut-off across the narrow neck of land. But the dogs balked at the high bank. Again and again, though Ruth and Malemute Kid were shoving on the sled, they slipped back. Then came the concerted effort. The miserable creatures, weak from hunger, exerted their last strength. Up—up—the sled poised on the top of the bank; but the leader swung the string of dogs behind him to the right, fouling Mason's snowshoes. The result was grievous. Mason was whipped off his feet; one of the dogs fell in the traces; and the sled toppled back, dragging everything to the bottom again.

Slash! the whip fell among the dogs savagely, especially upon the one which had fallen.

"Don't, Mason," entreated Malemute Kid; "the poor devil's on its last legs. Wait and we'll put my team on."

Mason deliberately withheld the whip till the last word had fallen, then out flashed the long lash, completely curling about the offending creature's body. Carmen—for it was Carmen—cowered in the snow, cried piteously, then rolled over on her side.

It was a tragic moment, a pitiful incident of the trail,—a dying dog, two comrades in anger. Ruth glanced solicitously from man to man. But Malemute Kid restrained himself, though there was a world of reproach in his eyes, and bending over the dog, cut the traces. No word was spoken. The teams were double-spanned and the difficulty overcome; the sleds were under way again, the dying dog dragging herself along in the rear. As long as an animal can travel, it is not shot, and this last chance is accorded it,—the crawling into camp, if it can, in the hope of a moose being killed.

Already penitent for his angry action, but too stubborn to make amends, Mason toiled on at the head of the cavalcade, little dreaming that danger hovered in the air. The timber clustered thick in the sheltered bottom, and through this they threaded their way. Fifty feet or more from the trail towered a lofty pine. For generations it had stood there, and for generations destiny had had this one end in view,—perhaps the same had been decreed of Mason.

He stooped to fasten the loosened thong of his moccasin. The sleds came to a halt and the dogs lay down in the snow without a whimper. The stillness was weird; not a breath rustled the frost-encrusted forest; the cold and silence of outer space had chilled the heart and smote the trembling lips of nature. A sigh pulsed through the air,—they did not seem to actually hear it, but rather felt it, like the premonition of movement in a motionless void. Then the great tree, burdened with its weight of years and snow, played its last part in the tragedy of life. He heard the warning crash and attempted to spring up, but almost erect, caught the blow squarely on the shoulder.

The sudden danger, the quick death,—how often had Malemute Kid faced it! The pine needles were still quivering as he gave his commands and sprang into action. Nor did the Indian girl faint or raise her voice in idle wailing, as might many of her white sisters. At his order, she threw her weight on the end of a quickly extemporized handspike, easing the pressure and listening to her husband's groans, while Malemute Kid attacked the tree with his axe. The steel rang merrily as it bit into the frozen trunk, each stroke being accompanied by a forced, audible respiration, the "Huh!" "Huh!" of the woodsman.

At last the Kid laid the pitiable thing that was once a man in the snow. But worse than his comrade's pain was the dumb anguish in the woman's face, the blended look of hopeful, hopeless query. Little was said; those of the Northland are early taught the futility of words and the inestimable value of deeds. With the temperature at sixty-five below zero, a man cannot lie many minutes in the snow and live. So the sled-lashings were cut, and the sufferer, rolled in furs, laid on a couch of boughs. Before him roared a fire, built of the very wood which wrought the mishap. Behind and partially over him was stretched the primitive fly,—a piece of canvas, which caught the radiating heat and threw it back and down upon him,— a trick which men may know who study physics at the fount.

And men who have shared their bed with death know when the call is sounded. Mason was terribly crushed. The most cursory examination revealed it. His right arm, leg, and back, were broken;

his limbs were paralyzed from the hips; and the likelihood of internal injuries was large. An occasional moan was his only sign of life.

No hope; nothing to be done. The pitiless night crept slowly by,—Ruth's portion, the despairing stoicism of her race, and Malemute Kid adding new lines to his face of bronze. In fact, Mason suffered least of all, for he spent his time in Eastern Tennessee, in the Great Smoky Mountains, living over the scenes of his childhood. And most pathetic was the melody of his long-forgotten Southern vernacular, as he raved of swimming-holes and coon-hunts and watermelon raids. It was as Greek to Ruth, but the Kid understood and felt,—felt as only one can feel who has been shut out for years from all that civilization means.

Morning brought consciousness to the stricken man, and Malemute Kid bent closer to catch his whispers.

"You remember when we foregathered on the Tanana, four years come next ice-run? I didn't care so much for her then. It was more like she was pretty, and there was a smack of excitement about it, I think. But d'ye know, I've come to think a heap of her. She's been a good wife to me, always at my shoulder in the pinch. And when it comes to trading, you know there isn't her equal. D'ye recollect the time she shot the Moosehorn Rapids to pull you and me off that rock, the bullets whipping the water like hailstones?—and the time of the famine at Nuklukyeto?—or when she raced the ice-run to bring the news? Yes, she's been a good wife to me, better 'n that other one. Didn't know I'd been there? Never told you, eh? Well, I tried it once, down in the States. That's why I'm here. Been raised together, too. I came away to give her a chance for divorce. She got it.

"But that's got nothing to do with Ruth. I had thought of cleaning up and pulling for the Outside next year,—her and I,—but it's too late. Don't send her back to her people, Kid. It's beastly hard for a woman to go back. Think of it!—nearly four years on our bacon and beans and flour and dried fruit, and then to go back to her fish and cariboo. It's not good for her to have tried our ways, to come to know they're better 'n her people's, and then return to them. Take care of her, Kid,—why don't you,—but no, you always fought shy of them,—and you never told me why you came to this country. Be kind to her, and send her back to the States as soon as you can. But fix it so she can come back,—liable to get homesick, you know.

"And the youngster—it's drawn us closer, Kid. I only hope it is a boy. Think of it!—flesh of my flesh, Kid. He mustn't stop in this country. And if it's a girl, why she can't. Sell my furs; they'll fetch at least five thousand, and I've got as much more with the company. And handle my interests with yours. I think that bench claim will show up. See that he gets a good schooling; and Kid, above all, don't let him come back. This country was not made for white men.

"I'm a gone man, Kid. Three or four sleeps at the best. You've got to go on. You must go on! Remember, it's my wife, it's my boy,—O God! I hope it's a boy! You can't stay by me,—and I charge you, a dying man, to pull on."

"Give me three days," pleaded Malemute Kid. "You may change for the better; something may turn up."

"No."

"Just three days."

"You must pull on."

"Two days."

"It's my wife and my boy, Kid. You would not ask it."

"One day."

"No, no! I charge"—

"Only one day. We can shave it through on the grub, and I might knock over a moose."

"No,—all right; one day, but not a minute more. And Kid, don't—don't leave me to face it alone. Just a shot, one pull on the trigger. You understand. Think of it! Think of it! Flesh of my flesh, and I'll never live to see him!

"Send Ruth here. I want to say good-by and tell her that she must think of the boy and not wait till I'm dead. She might refuse to go with you if I didn't. Good-by, old man; good-by.

"Kid! I say—a—sink a hole above the pup, next to the slide. I panned out forty cents on my shovel there.

"And Kid!" he stooped lower to catch the last faint words, the dying man's surrender of his pride. "I'm sorry—for—you know—Carmen."

Leaving the girl crying softly over her man, Malemute Kid slipped into his *parka* and snowshoes, tucked his rifle under his arm, and crept away into the forest. He was no tyro in the stern sorrows of the Northland, but never had he faced so stiff a problem as this. In the abstract, it was a plain, mathematical proposition,—three possible lives as against one doomed one. But now he hesitated. For five years, shoulder to shoulder, on the rivers and trails, in the camps and mines, facing death by field and flood and famine, had they knitted the bonds of their comradeship. So close was the tie, that he had often been conscious of a vague jealousy of Ruth, from the first time she had come between. And now it must be severed by his own hand.

Though he prayed for a moose, just one moose, all game seemed to have deserted the land, and nightfall found the exhausted man crawling into camp, light-handed, heavy-hearted. An uproar from the dogs and shrill cries from Ruth hastened him.

Bursting into the camp, he saw the girl in the midst of the snarling pack, laying about her with an axe. The dogs had broken the iron rule of their masters and were rushing the grub. He joined the issue with his rifle reversed, and the hoary game of natural selection was played out with all the ruthlessness of its primeval environment. Rifle and axe went up and down, hit or missed with monotonous regularity; lithe bodies flashed, with wild eyes and dripping fangs; and man and beast fought for supremacy to the bitterest conclusion. Then the beaten brutes crept to the edge of the firelight, licking their wounds, voicing their misery to the stars.

The whole stock of dried salmon had been devoured, and perhaps five pounds of flour remained to tide them over two hundred miles of wilderness. Ruth returned to her husband, while Malemute Kid cut up the warm body of one of the dogs, the skull of which had been crushed by the axe. Every portion was carefully put away, save the hide and offal, which were cast to his fellows of the moment before.

Morning brought fresh trouble. The animals were turning on each other. Carmen, who still clung to her slender thread of life, was downed by the pack. The lash fell among them unheeded. They cringed and cried under the blows, but refused to scatter till the last wretched bit had disappeared,—bones, hide, hair, everything.

Malemute Kid went about his work, listening to Mason, who was back in Tennessee, delivering tangled discourses and wild exhortations to his brethren of other days.

Taking advantage of neighboring pines, he worked rapidly, and Ruth watched him make a cache similar to those sometimes used by hunters to preserve their meat from the wolverines and dogs.

One after the other, he bent the tops of two small pines toward each other and nearly to the ground, making them fast with thongs of moosehide. Then he beat the dogs into submission and harnessed them to two of the sleds, loading the same with everything but the furs which enveloped Mason. These he wrapped and lashed tightly about him, fastening either end of the robes to the bent pines. A single stroke of his hunting-knife would release them and send the body high in the air.

Ruth had received her husband's last wishes and made no struggle. Poor girl, she had learned the lesson of obedience well. From a child, she had bowed, and seen all women bow, to the lords of creation, and it did not seem in the nature of things for woman to resist. The Kid permitted her one outburst of grief, as she kissed her husband,—her own people had no such custom,—then led her to the foremost sled and helped her into her snowshoes. Blindly, instinctively, she took the gee-pole and whip, and "mushed" the dogs out on the trail. Then he returned to Mason, who had fallen into a coma; and long after she was out of sight, crouched by the fire, waiting, hoping, praying for his comrade to die.

It is not pleasant to be alone with painful thoughts in the White Silence. The silence of gloom is merciful, shrouding one as with protection and breathing a thousand intangible sympathies; but the bright White Silence, clear and cold, under steely skies, is pitiless.

An hour passed,—two hours,—but the man would not die. At high noon, the sun, without raising its rim above the southern horizon, threw a suggestion of fire athwart the heavens, then quickly drew it back. Malemute Kid roused and dragged himself to his comrade's side. He cast one glance about him. The White Silence seemed to sneer, and a great fear came upon him. There was a sharp report; Mason swung into his aerial sepulcher; and Malemute Kid lashed the dogs into a wild gallop as he fled across the snow.

HOW OLD TIMOFEI DIED WITH
A SONG

Rainer Maria Rilke

WHAT A REAL joy it is to tell stories to a paralyzed person! Healthy people are so unreliable; they look at things, now from one viewpoint, now from another, and after you've been walking with them for an hour and they've always been to the right of you, they sometimes answer you from the left all of a sudden, merely because it occurs to them that it's more polite and shows better breeding. With a paralyzed man one need have no fear of that. His immobility makes him resemble inanimate objects, with which he actually has many cordial relationships; it makes him, so to speak, an object far superior to all the rest, an object that not only listens with its taciturnity, but also with its very few, quiet phrases and with its gentle, respectful feelings.

I like best of all to tell stories to my friend Ewald. And I was very happy when he called to me from his daily window: "I must ask you something."

I walked over to him quickly and said hello. "What is the source of the story you told me recently?" he finally asked. "Did it come from a book?" "Yes," I replied sadly, "the scholars have buried it in one ever since it died, which isn't very long ago. A hundred years ago it was still alive, and certainly quite carefree, on many lips. But the words that people now use, these heavy words that are hard to sing to, were hostile to it and stole one mouth after another from it, so that finally it lived on, but very withdrawn and impoverished, only on a few dry lips, as if on a poor widow's farm. There it also died, without leaving any descendants, and, as I mentioned, was buried with all honors in a book, where others of its lineage already lay." "And was it very old when it died?" my friend asked, picking up my metaphor. "Four or five hundred years old," I reported truthfully; "several of its relatives have attained an immeasurably greater age." "What, without ever reposing in a book?" Ewald asked in surprise. I explained: "As far as I know, they were journeying from mouth to mouth the whole time." "And they never slept?" "Oh, yes; arising from the lips of the singer, they surely remained occasionally in someone's heart, where it was warm and dark." "Then, were people so tranquil that songs could sleep in their hearts?" Ewald seemed quite incredulous to me. "It must have been that way. It's claimed that they spoke less, performed slowly accelerating dances that had a cradling motion, and above all, didn't laugh loudly the way you can often hear people do today despite our universally loftier social graces."

Ewald prepared himself to ask another question, but he repressed it and said with a smile: "I keep on asking things—but perhaps you have a story in mind?" He looked at me expectantly.

"A story? I don't know. I merely wanted to say: Those songs were the heirlooms in certain families. That inherited property had been received and handed down again, not quite as good as new, showing the traces of daily use, but nevertheless undamaged, just as an old Bible, let's say, goes from forefather to grandchild. The man without inheritance differed from his siblings who had received their rightful due in that he couldn't sing, or else at least he knew only a small part of his father's and grandfather's songs, and, losing the rest of the songs, he lost that large segment of experience which all those *byliny* and *skazki* mean to the people. And so, for example, Yegor Timofeievich had married a young, beautiful woman against the wishes of his father, old Timofei, and had moved with her to Kiev, the holy city, in which the tombs of the great martyrs of the holy orthodox church have gathered. His father Timofei, who was reputed to be the most knowledgeable singer in a radius of ten days' journey, cursed his son and told his neighbors that he was often convinced that he had never had one. All the same, he grew mute in his grief and sorrow. And he rejected all the young men who crowded into his hut in order to fall heir to the many songs that were shut away in the old man, as in a dust-covered violin. 'Father, little father of ours, just give us one song or another. You see, we'll take it to the villages, and you'll hear it from every courtyard as soon as evening comes and the cattle have become quiet in their stables.' The old man, who constantly sat on the heated platform, shook his head all day long. His hearing was no longer good, and since he didn't know whether one of the lads who were now forever listening around his house had just made another request, he would signal no, no, no with his trembling white head until he fell asleep, and even kept doing it for a while in his sleep. He would gladly have done what the lads wanted; he himself was sorry that his mute, dead dust would lie upon these songs, perhaps very soon now. But if he had tried to teach one of them anything, it would surely have reminded him of his Yegorushka, and then, who knows what might have happened? Because it was only his perpetual silence that kept anyone from seeing him cry. Behind each word of his lay a sob, and he always had to shut his mouth very quickly and carefully to keep it from escaping at the same time.

"From early on, old Timofei had taught his only son, Yegor, a few songs, and when a boy of fifteen he was already able to sing more songs more correctly than any of the fully grown lads in the village or in its vicinity. All the same, the old man used to say to the lad, generally on holidays, when he was slightly drunk: 'Yegorushka, my little dove, I've already taught you to sing many songs, many *byliny*, and also the legends of the saints, one for nearly every day. But, as you know, I'm the most knowledgeable in the whole *guberniya*,[1] and my father knew every song in Russia, so to speak, and Tatar stories, besides. You're still very young, and so I have not yet told you the best *byliny*, in which the words are like icons and can't be compared with everyday words, and you have not yet learned how to sing those melodies which no one yet, be he a Cossack or a peasant, has ever been able to hear without weeping.' Timofei would repeat this to his son on every Sunday and all the many feast days in the Russian calendar; that is, fairly often. Until, after a violent scene with the old man, the boy had vanished together with the beautiful Ustyonka, the daughter of a poor peasant.

"In the third year after that incident, Timofei fell ill, just at the time when one of those numerous bands of pilgrims which constantly converge on Kiev from all sections of the extensive empire was about to set out. Then the sick man's neighbor Osip came to see him: 'I'm leaving with the pilgrims, Timofei Ivanich; permit me

---

[1] A large administrative district.

to embrace you once again.' Osip wasn't friendly with the old man, but now that he was undertaking that distant journey, he felt it needful to take leave of him, as if of a father. 'I've hurt your feelings at times,' he sobbed; 'forgive me, dear heart, it happened while I was drunk and no one can help that, as you know. Now, I'll pray for you and light a candle for you; farewell, Timofei Ivanich, little father; perhaps you'll get well again, if God wishes, then you'll sing to us again. Yes, yes, it's been a long time since you've sung. What songs those were! The one about Dyuk Stepanovich,[2] for instance: do you think I've forgotten it? How foolish you are! I still know it all by heart. Of course, not like you; *you* really and truly knew it, I've got to say! God gave you *that,* to another man he gives other gifts. To me, for example—'

"The old man, who was lying on the heated platform, turned around with a groan and made a gesture as if he wanted to say something. It was as if the name of Yegor could be faintly heard. Perhaps he wanted to send him some news. But when his neighbor, already at the door, asked: 'Did you say something, Timofei Ivanich?' he was already lying there perfectly still and merely shaking his white head gently. Nevertheless, God knows how it happened, scarcely a year after Osip's departure Yegor returned quite unexpectedly. The old man didn't recognize him immediately because it was dark in the hut and his aged eyes didn't easily accept a strange new figure. But after Timofei heard the stranger's voice, he became alarmed and leaped off the heated platform onto his shaky old legs. Yegor caught him, and they hugged each other. Timofei was weeping. The young man kept on asking: 'Have you been sick long, father?' After the old man calmed down a bit, he crept back onto his heated platform and inquired, in a different, severe tone: 'And your wife?' A pause. Yegor spat out the words: 'I've chased her away, you know, along with the child.' He was silent for a while. 'Osip came to see me once. "Osip Nikiforovich?" I said. "Yes," he answered, "it's me. Your father is sick, Yegor. He can't sing anymore. It's completely quiet in the village now, as if it had no more soul, our village. No one knocks, no one budges, no one cries anymore, and there's no real reason for laughing, either." I thought about it. What was to be done? So I called over my wife. "Ustyonka," I said, "I must go home, no one else sings there

---

[2] One of the principal *bylina* heroes.

anymore, it's up to me. My father is sick." "All right," said Ustyonka. "But I can't take you along," I explained to her, "as you know, my father doesn't want you. And I probably won't come back to you, either, once I'm back there singing." Ustyonka understood me: "Well, then, God go with you! There are many pilgrims here now, so people give lots of alms. God will help me, Yegor." And so I left. And now, father, tell me all your songs!'

"Word got around that Yegor had returned and that old Timofei was singing again. But that autumn the wind blew so violently through the village that no passerby could ascertain with any assurance whether there was really singing in Timofei's house or not. And the door wasn't opened to anyone who knocked. The two men wanted to be alone. Yegor sat on the edge of the heated platform on which his father lay, and at times brought his ear right up to the old man's lips; for he was indeed singing. His old voice, somewhat stooped and trembling, carried all the best songs over to Yegor, who often waved his head or moved his dangling feet, exactly as if he were already singing them himself. Things went on that way for many days. Timofei kept finding some even lovelier song in his memory; often he'd awaken his son at night and, while making indistinct gestures with his withered, twitching hands, he'd sing a short song and then another and yet another, until the lazy morning began to stir. Soon after the most beautiful one he died. In the last days he had frequently lamented that he still had a vast number of songs inside him and had no more time to impart them to his son. He lay there with furrowed brow, in strained, anxious thought, and his lips trembled with expectancy. From time to time he sat up, waved his head to and fro for a while, and moved his lips, and finally some quiet song was added to the sum; but now he generally kept repeating the same stanzas about Dyuk Stepanovich that were his special favorites, and his son had to act amazed, as if he were hearing them for the first time, to avoid getting him angry.

"After old Timofei Ivanich died, the house, in which Yegor now lived alone, still remained locked for a time. Then, in early spring, Yegor Timofeievich, who now had a fairly long beard, stepped out of his door and began to wander through the village singing. Afterward he visited the neighboring villages, too, and the peasants were already telling one another that Yegor had become a singer at least as knowledgeable as his father Timofei, for he knew a large number of religious and heroic songs and all those melodies which no one, be he a Cossack or a peasant, could hear without weeping. In addition, he was said to have a soft, sad tone that no other singer had yet possessed. And this tone was always to be heard, quite unexpectedly, in the refrains, which made him particularly effective emotionally. At least, that's what I heard tell."

"So he didn't learn that tone from his father?" my friend Ewald asked after a while. "No," I replied, "no one knows where he got it from." After I had already stepped away from the window, the paralyzed man made another gesture and called after me: "Perhaps he was thinking about his wife and child. Besides, did he never send for them, seeing that his father was now dead?" "No, I don't think so. At any rate, when he died afterward he was alone."

THE PATH TO THE CEMETERY

Thomas Mann

THE PATH TO the cemetery ran always parallel to the highway, always side by side, until it had reached its goal; that is to say, the cemetery. On the other side there were human habitations, new structures of the suburbs, part of which were still in process of completion, and then came fields. As to the highway itself, this was flanked by trees, by knotty beeches of a good old age, and the road was half paved and half bare earth. But the path to the cemetery was thinly strewn with pebbles, which gave it the character of an agreeable foot-path. A small, dry ditch, filled with grass and wildflowers, extended between the two.

It was spring, and almost summer already. The whole world smiled. God's blue skies were covered with masses of small, round, compact little clouds, dotted with many snow-white little clumps which had an almost humorous look. The birds twittered in the beeches, and a mild wind swept across the fields.

A wagon from the neighbouring village crept towards the city; it rolled partly upon the paved, partly upon the unpaved part of the highway. The driver let his legs dangle on both sides of the shaft and whistled execrably. In the back part of the wagon there sat a little yellow dog with its back to him, and along its pointed little nose looked back with an unutterably grave and collected mien at the way it had just come. It was an incomparable, a most diverting little dog, worth its weight in gold; but it plays no part in this affair and so we must turn our faces from it.—A detachment of soldiers went marching by. They came from the garrison near by, marched in their own dust, and sang. A second wagon crept from the direction of the city towards the next village. The driver slept, and there was no little dog, for which reason this vehicle is entirely without interest. Two journeymen came striding along, the one hunched-backed, the other a giant in stature. They went barefooted, carrying their boots on their backs, called out cheerily to the sleeping driver, and strode on bravely. The traffic was moderate, regulating itself without complications or accidents.

The way to the cemetery was trodden by a solitary man; he walked slowly, with lowered head, and supported himself on a black stick. The man was called Piepsam, Lobgott (Praisegod) Piepsam and nothing else. We proclaim his name with a certain emphasis because subsequently he acted in a most peculiar manner.

He was dressed in black, for he was on the way to the graves of his loved ones. He wore a rough, cylindrical silk hat, a frock-coat shiny with age, trousers which were not only too narrow but also too short, and black kid gloves which were shabby all over. His throat, a long, lean throat with a large Adam's apple, lifted itself from a turnover collar which was frayed and displayed corners which had already become a little rough. But when the man raised his head, which he did at times in order to see how far he still was from the cemetery, then one was treated to a strange sight, a remarkable face, a face which beyond all question one was not likely soon to forget.

This face was smooth-shaven and pale. Between the hollowed-out cheeks there protruded a nose which thickened bulbously at the end, a nose which glowed with an irregular, unnatural red and which, quite superfluously, paraded a mass of little excrescences, unhealthy growths which gave it an unconventional and fantastic look. This nose, the dark rubicundity of which contrasted sharply with the dull pallor of the rest of the face, embodied something unreal and picturesque; it looked as though it were merely affixed like a masquerade nose, like a melancholy joke. But it was not this alone. The man kept his mouth, a broad mouth with sunk corners, tightly closed, and whenever he looked up, he lifted his black eyebrows, which were shot through by little white hairs—lifted them beneath the brim of his hat, so that one might see how inflamed his eyes were and what dark circles surrounded them. In short, it was a face to which one could not permanently refuse the deepest sympathy.

Lobgott Piepsam's appearance was not a joyous one; it fitted in but badly with this charming forenoon, and it was even too dismal for one who was about to pay a visit to the graves of his loved ones. But looking into his heart and soul, one was forced to confess that there were sufficient grounds for all this. He was a trifle depressed?— it is difficult to convey this to people so merry as yourselves— perhaps a bit unhappy?—a trifle badly treated? Well, to tell the truth, he was all of these things not only a trifle, but to a high degree; he was, without any exaggeration, in a bad way.

First of all, he drank. But of this more anon. Furthermore he was a widower, had lost both parents, and stood abandoned by every-body; he had not a single soul to love him in all the world. His wife, whose maiden-name had been Lebzelt, had been reft from his side after she had borne him a child little less than half a year ago; it was the third child and it had been still-born. Both of the other children had also died—one of diphtheria, the other of really noth-ing at all—perhaps out of a general ineptitude. But this had not been enough, for soon after this he had lost his job, had been driven out of his petty position; and that bore a close relation to that pas-sion of his which was mightier than Piepsam.

Formerly he had been able to resist it to some degree, although there were periods when he had been intemperately addicted to it. But after wife and children had been taken from him, after he had lost all his friends and stood alone in the world and without a single support or hold, his vice had mastered him and had broken his spiri-tual resistance more and more. He had been an official in the service of an insurance society, a kind of higher copyist with a monthly salary of ninety marks. While in his irresponsible condition, he had become guilty of gross negligence, and after having been repeatedly warned, he had been finally discharged as unreliable.

It is clear that this did not by any manner of means lead to a moral revolt on the part of Piepsam, but that he was thenceforth utterly doomed. For you must know that ill fortune slays the dignity of a man—it is just as well to have a little insight into these things. There is a strange and dreadful concatenation of cause and effect here. There is no use in a man's protesting his own innocence; in most cases he will despise himself for his mis-fortune. But self-contempt and vice have a strange and horrible interrelationship; they feed each other, they play into each other's hands, in a way to make one's blood run cold. And that is the way it was with Piepsam. He drank because he did not respect himself, and he respected himself less and less because the continual shameful defeats of all his good resolutions devoured all his self-confidence. In a wardrobe in his home there usually stood a bottle containing a poisonous yellow fluid, a most pernicious fluid—we must be cautious and not mention its name. Lobgott Piepsam had literally knelt before his wardrobe and almost bitten his tongue in two; and in spite of this he would go down in defeat in the end.—We take no pleasure in relating these facts, but they are, after all, instructive.

And here he was walking along the path to the cemetery and prodding the ground with his black cane. A gentle wind played about his nose, but he did not feel it. His eyebrows elevated, he bent a hollow and turbid look upon the world about him—a lorn and miserable creature.—Suddenly he heard a noise behind him and pricked up his ears; a soft rushing sound was approaching with great rapidity from the distance. He turned about and stood still.— It was a bicycle, the tires of which crunched along the pebble-strewn path. It came on in full career, but then slackened its speed, for Piepsam stood in the middle of the way.

A young man sat in the saddle, a youth, a careless youth on a tour. He himself, great heavens, surely made no pretensions to belonging to the great and glorious one of the world! He rode a machine of middling quality—it does not really matter of what make—a wheel costing, say, about two hundred marks. And with this he went pedalling a bit through the country, fresh from the city, riding with flashing pedals into God's green world—hurray! He wore a coloured shirt and a grey jacket, sports leggings, and the jauntiest little cap in the world—a very joke of a cap, with brown checks and a button on the top. And from under this cap a thick mop of blond hair welled forth and stood up above his forehead. His eyes were of a lightning-blue. He came on like Life itself and tinkled his bell, but Piepsam did not move a hair's breadth out of the way. He stood there and looked at Life with a rigid stare.

It looked angrily at him and rode slowly past him, whereupon Piepsam also began to walk on. But when it was ahead of him, he said slowly and with a weighty emphasis: "Number nine thousand seven hundred and seven."

He then pursed up his lips and stared incontinently at the ground, at the same time feeling that Life's eyes were bent upon him in perplexity.

It had turned round, had seized the saddle from behind with one hand, and rode very slowly.

"What?" it asked.

"Number nine thousand seven hundred and seven," repeated Piepsam. "Oh, nothing. I'll report you."

"You will report me?" Life asked, turned still further round, and rode still more slowly, so that it was obliged to wobble to and fro with the handle-bars.

"Certainly!" replied Piepsam at a distance of five or six steps.

"Why?" asked Life, and dismounted. It stood still and seemed full of expectancy.

"You know why well enough."

"No, I don't know why."

"You must know."

"But I do not know why," said Life, "and moreover I am not at all interested why." With this it was about to mount its wheel again. It was not at all at a loss for words.

"I will report you," said Piepsam, "because you ride here, on this path to the cemetery, and not out there on the high-road."

"But, my dear sir!" Life said, with an impatient and angry laugh, turned round once more, and stood still. "You see tracks of bicycles along the entire path. Everybody rides here."

"That's all one to me," retorted Piepsam; "I'll report you just the same."

"Well, do whatever you like!" Life cried, and mounted its wheel. It really mounted, it did not disgrace itself by making a mess of this; it gave a single thrust with its foot, sat securely on the saddle, and put forth all efforts to reacquire a speed in accordance with its temperament.

"If you keep on riding here, here on the path to the cemetery, I shall most surely report you!" cried Piepsam in a high and trembling voice. But Life really troubled itself very little about this; it rode off with increasing speed.

Had you seen Lobgott Piepsam's face at this moment, you would have been greatly frightened. He pressed his lips so firmly together that his cheeks and even the rubicund nose were twisted quite out of place, and his eyes, from beneath his unnaturally raised eyebrows, stared with an insane expression after the vehicle as it rolled away. Suddenly he dashed forwards. At a run he traversed the short distance which separated him from the machine, and seized the tool-case beneath the saddle. He held on to it with both hands, literally attached himself to it, and with lips still pressed together in an unnatural manner, dumb, and with wild eyes, he tugged with all his strength at the balancing bicycle as it speeded forwards. Anyone seeing him might well have doubted whether he intended, out of malice, to hinder the young man from riding on, or whether he had been seized by the desire to let himself be taken in tow, to jump on behind and ride along with the young man—to go himself riding a bit through the country, riding with flashing pedals into God's green world—hurray!—The wheel was not able to withstand this desperate drag for any length of time; it stood still, it wobbled, it fell over.

And then Life grew wild. It had lighted upon one foot; then it drew back its right arm and gave Herr Piepsam such a blow on the chest that he staggered back several paces. Then, with a voice which swelled into a threatening tone, it said: "You must be drunk, you fool! You must be off your head! If you dare to hold me up again, I'll give you a smash in the jaw—do you hear? I'll break your neck! And don't you forget it!"

With this it turned its back upon Herr Piepsam, gave an indignant tug to its cap, drawing it tighter upon its head, and once more mounted its wheel. No, it was certainly not at a loss for words. And the business of mounting succeeded as well as before. Again it merely thrust down one foot, sat securely in the saddle, and had the machine once more under full control. Piepsam saw its back diminish more and more rapidly.

He stood there panting and stared after Life. It did not take a header, no accident overtook it, no tire burst, and no stone lay in its path; lightly it sailed on. And then Piepsam began to shout and to scold—one might have called it a bellowing, for it was no longer a human voice.

"You shall not ride there!" he cried. "You shall not! You shall ride out there and not on the path to the cemetery, do you hear? You get off—get off at once! Oh, oh! I'll report you! I'll sue you! God! if you would only take a tumble, if you would only fall off, you windy brute, I would kick you, kick you in the face with my boots, you damned rogue! . . ."

Never had the like been seen before! A man calling bad names on the way to the cemetery, a man with a swollen face, bellowing, a man whose scolding renders him hopping mad, who cuts capers, throwing his arms and legs about, and seems unable to control himself. The wheel was really no longer in sight, yet Piepsam still raved and danced in the same spot.

"Hold him! hold him! He is riding on the path to the cemetery! You villain! You impudent clown! You damned ass! If I could only get hold of you, wouldn't I skin you alive, you silly ass, you stupid windbag, you tomfool, you ignorant bounder!—You get off! You get off this very instant! Will nobody kick him into the dirt, the scoundrel?—Riding for pleasure, eh? On the way to the cemetery! Knock him off his wheel, the damned oaf! Oh! Oh! If I only had you, what wouldn't I do? And what else? Eyes blue as lightning, eh? May the devil scratch them out of your face, you ignorant, ignorant, ignorant bounder! . . ."

Piepsam now took to language which is not to be repeated; he foamed, and poured forth in his cracked voice the most shameful terms of reprobation, while the contortions of his body continually increased. A couple of children with a basket and a terrier came over from the high-road; they climbed across the ditch, stood about the screaming man, and looked curiously into his distorted visage. A few labourers, who worked on the new buildings in the vicinity, or had just begun their midday rest, also became attentive, and a number of men as well as some of the women who were mixing mortar came walking towards the group. But Piepsam continued to rave on; he was growing worse and worse. In his blind and insane rage he shook his fists towards heaven and in all directions, shook his legs convulsively, turned himself round and round, bent the knee and leaped into the air again, succumbing to his excessive efforts to shout as loud as possible. He did not pause a single moment in his tirade, he hardly took time to breathe, and it was really astonishing where all his language came from. His face was terribly swollen, his high hat sat far back on his neck, and his false shirt-front, which was not fastened, hung out of his waistcoat. He had long ago arrived at generalities and poured out things which had not the remotest connexion with the subject in hand. They dealt with his dissipated life and with religious matters, uttered in a most unsuitable tone and viciously intermingled with curse-words.

"Come on, come on, all of you!" he bellowed. "Not you, not only you, but the rest of you, you with the bicycle caps and eyes blue as lightning! I'll shout truths into your ear so that your blood will run cold for ever, you windy rogues! . . . You grin, do you? Shrug your shoulders? . . . I drink . . . certainly I drink! I even guzzle, if you care to hear it! What does that mean? It's a long road that knows no turning! The day will come, you good-for-nothing rubbish, when God shall weigh all of us. . . . Oh! oh! The Son of Man will come in the clouds, you innocent *canaille,* and His justice is not of this world! He will cast you into the outermost darkness, you merry wretches, where there is howling and. . ."

He was now surrounded by quite an imposing group of people. A few laughed and a few looked at him with wrinkled brows. More workmen and several more mortar-women had come over from the buildings. A driver had got off his wagon, halting it upon the high-road, and, whip in hand, had also climbed across the ditch. A man took Piepsam by the arm and shook him, but that had no effect. A squad of soldiers marched by and, laughing, craned their necks to look at him. The terrier could no longer hold back, but braced his forelegs against the ground and, with his tail thrust between his legs, howled directly into his face.

Suddenly Lobgott Piepsam cried once more at the top of his voice: "You get off, you get off at once, you ignorant bounder!" described a half-circle with one arm, and then collapsed. He lay there, suddenly struck dumb, a black heap amidst the curious. His cylindrical silk hat flew off, rebounded once from the ground, and also lay there.

Two masons bent over the immovable Piepsam and discussed the case in that whole-hearted and sensible tone common to working-men. Then one of them went off at a quick stride. Those who remained behind undertook a few more experiments with the unconscious one. One man dashed water in his face out of a bucket, another poured some brandy out of a bottle into the palm of his hand and rubbed Piepsam's temples with it. But these efforts were crowned with no success.

A short interval thus elapsed. Then wheels were heard, and a wagon came along the high-road. It was an ambulance, drawn by two pretty little horses and with a gigantic red cross painted on each side. It came to a halt, and two men in neat uniforms climbed down from the driver's seat, and while one went to the back part of the wagon to open it and to draw out the stretcher, the other rushed upon the path to the cemetery, pushed the staring crowd aside, and, with the help of one of the men, carried Herr Piepsam to the wagon. He was laid upon the stretcher and shoved into the wagon like a loaf of bread into an oven, whereupon the door snapped shut and the two uniformed men climbed to the driver's seat again. All this was done with great precision, with a few practised turns of the hand, quick and adroit, as by trained apes.

And then Lobgott Piepsam was driven away.

WITH OTHER EYES

Luigi Pirandello

THOUGH THE LARGE window that opened onto the house's little hanging garden, the pure, fresh morning air made the pretty little room cheerful. An almond branch, which seemed to be all a-blossom with butterflies, projected toward the window; and, mingled with the hoarse, muffled gurgle of the small basin in the center of the garden, was heard the festive peal of faraway churchbells and the chirping of the swallows intoxicated with the air and the sunshine.

As she stepped away from the window, sighing, Anna noticed that her husband that morning had forgotten to rumple his bed, as he used to do each time, so that the servants couldn't tell that he hadn't slept in his room. She rested her elbows on the untouched bed, then stretched out on it with her whole torso, bending her pretty blonde head over the pillows and half-closing her eyes, as if to savor, in the freshness of the linens, the slumbers he was accustomed to enjoy there. A flock of swallows flashed headlong past the window, shrieking.

"You would have done better to sleep here . . .," she murmured languidly after a moment, and got up again wearily.

Her husband was to set out that very evening, and Anna had come into his room to prepare for him the things he needed for the trip.

As she opened the wardrobe, she heard what seemed to be a squeak in the inner drawer and quickly drew back, startled. From a corner of the room she picked up a walking stick with a curved handle and, holding her dress tight against her legs, took the stick by the tip and, standing that way at a distance, tried to open the drawer with it. But as she pulled, instead of the drawer coming out,

451

an insidious gleaming blade emerged smoothly from inside the stick. Anna, who hadn't expected this, felt an extreme repulsion and let the scabbard of the swordstick drop from her hand.

At that moment, a second squeak made her turn abruptly toward the window, uncertain whether the first one as well had come from some rapidly passing swallow.

With one foot she pushed aside the unsheathed weapon and pulled out, between the two open doors of the wardrobe, the drawer full of her husband's old suits that he no longer wore. Out of sudden curiosity she began to rummage around in it and, as she was putting back a worn-out, faded jacket, she happened to feel, in the hem under the lining, a sort of small paper, which had slipped down there through the torn bottom of the breast pocket; she wanted to see what that paper was which had gone astray and been forgotten there who knows how many years ago; and so by accident Anna discovered the portrait of her husband's first wife.

At first she had a start and turned pale; she quickly ran a hand through her hair, which was shaken by a shudder and, with her vision blurred and her heart stopped, she ran to the window, where she remained in astonishment gazing at the unfamiliar image, almost with a feeling of panic.

The bulky hair style and the old-fashioned dress kept her from noticing at first the beauty of that face; but as soon as she was able to concentrate on the features, separating them from the attire, which now, after so many years, looked ludicrous, and to pay special attention to the eyes, she felt wounded by them and, together with her blood, a flush of hatred leaped from her heart to her brain; a hatred as if caused by posthumous jealousy; that hatred mingled with contempt which she had felt for that other woman when she fell in love with Vittore Brivio, eleven years after the marital tragedy that had at one blow destroyed his first household.

Anna had hated that woman, unable to comprehend how she had been capable of betraying the man whom she now worshiped, and in the second place, because her family had objected to her marriage with Brivio, as if *he* had been responsible for the disgrace and violent death of his unfaithful wife.—It was she, yes, it was she beyond a doubt! Vittore's first wife: the one who had killed herself! She found the proof in the dedication written on the back of the portrait: "To my Vittore, his Almira—November 11, 1873."

Anna had very vague information about the dead woman: she knew only that Vittore, when the betrayal was discovered, had, with the impassivity of a judge, forced her to take her own life.

Now with satisfaction she recalled that terrible sentence issued by her husband, and was irritated by that "my" and "his" of the dedication, as if the other woman had wished to flaunt the closeness of the mutual ties that had bound her and Vittore, solely to spite her.

That first flare-up of hatred, ignited, like a will-o'-the-wisp, by a rivalry which by now existed only for her, was succeeded in Anna's mind by feminine curiosity: she desired to examine the features of that face, although she was partially restrained by the odd sorrow one feels at the sight of an object that belonged to a person who died tragically—a sorrow that was sharper now, but not unfamiliar to her, because it permeated her love for her husband, who had formerly belonged to that other woman.

Examining her face, Anna immediately noticed how entirely dissimilar it was to hers, and at the same time there arose in her heart the question of how the husband who had loved that woman, that girl, whom he must have found beautiful, could ever have later fallen in love with *her,* who was so different.

It seemed beautiful, even to her it seemed much more beautiful than hers—that face which, from the portrait, looked swarthy. There!—those lips had joined in a kiss with his lips; but why that sorrowful crease at the corners of the mouth? And why was the gaze in those intense eyes so sad? The entire face spoke of deep suffering; and Anna was moved and almost vexed by the humble and genuine kindness expressed by those features, and after that she felt a twinge of repulsion and disgust, when all at once she believed she had observed in the gaze of those eyes the same expression her own eyes had, whenever, thinking of her husband, she looked at herself in the mirror, in the morning, after arranging her hair.

She had barely enough time to thrust the portrait into her pocket: her husband appeared, fuming, on the threshold to the room.

"What have you been doing? The usual thing? Every time you come into this room to straighten up, you rearrange everything . . ."

Then, seeing the unsheathed swordstick on the floor:

"Have you been fencing with the suits in the wardrobe?"

And he laughed that laugh of his which came only from the throat, as if someone had tickled him there; and, laughing in that fashion, he looked at his wife, as if asking *her* why he himself was laughing. As he looked, his eyelids constantly blinked with extreme rapidity against his sharp, black, restless little eyes.

Vittore Brivio treated his wife like a child capable of nothing but that ingenuous, exclusive and almost childish love with which he felt himself surrounded, frequently to his annoyance, and to which he had determined to pay attention only on due occasion, and even at those times displaying an indulgence partially mixed with light irony, as if he meant to say: "All right, have it your way! For a while I too will become a child along with you: this, too, must be done, but let's not waste too much time!"

Anna had let the old jacket in which she had found the portrait drop to her feet. He picked it up, piercing it with the point of the swordstick; then, through the garden window he called the young servant who also doubled as a coachman and was at that moment harnessing the horse to the cabriolet. As soon as the boy showed up, in his shirt sleeves, in the garden in front of the window, Brivio rudely threw the dangling jacket in his face, accompanying the handout with a: "Take it, it's yours."

"This way, you'll have less to brush," he added, turning toward his wife, "and to straighten up, I hope!"

And again, blinking, he uttered that stentorean laugh of his.

On other occasions her husband had traveled out of the city, and not merely for a few days, also leaving at night like this time; but Anna, still extremely shaken by the discovery of the portrait on that very day, felt a strange fear of being left alone and wept when she said goodbye to him.

Vittore Brivio, in a great rush from fear of being late and evidently preoccupied with his business, reacted ill-manneredly to those uncustomary tears of his wife.

"What! Why? Come on now, come on now, that's so childish!"

And he left in hot haste, without even saying goodbye.

Anna jumped at the sound of the door that he closed behind him with force; she remained in the little room with the lamp in her hand and felt her tears growing cold in her eyes. Then she roused herself and hurriedly withdrew to her room, intending to go to bed at once.

In the room, which was already prepared, the little night light was burning.

"Go to bed," Anna said to the maid who was waiting for her. "I'll take care of things myself. Good night."

She extinguished the lamp, but instead of putting it on the shelf, as she usually did, she put it on the night table, with the feeling—actually against her will—that she might need it later. She started to undress hastily, gazing fixedly at the floor in front of her. When her dress fell around her feet, it occurred to her that the portrait was there, and with acute vexation she felt herself being looked at and pitied by those sorrowful eyes, which had made such an impression on her. With determination she stooped down to pick up the dress from the carpet and, without folding it, she placed it on the arm-chair at the foot of the bed, as if the pocket that hid the portrait and the tangle of the fabric should and could prevent her from reconstructing the image of that dead woman.

As soon as she lay down, she closed her eyes and forced herself to follow her husband mentally along the road leading to the railroad station. She forced this upon herself as a spiteful rebellion against the feeling that had kept her alert all day long observing and studying her husband. She knew where that feeling had come from and she wanted to get rid of it.

In this effort of her will, which caused her acute nervous agitation, she pictured to herself with an extraordinary second sight the long road, deserted at night, illuminated by the streetlamps projecting their wavering light onto the pavement, which seemed to palpitate because of it; at the foot of every lamp, a circle of shadow; the shops, all closed; and there was the carriage in which Vittore was riding: as if she had been lying in wait for it, she started following it all the way to the station: she saw the gloomy train beneath the glass shed; a great many people milling about in that vast, smoky, poorly lit, mournfully echoing interior: now the train was pulling out; and, as if she were really watching it move away and disappear into the darkness, she suddenly came back to herself, opened her eyes in the silent room and felt an anguished feeling of emptiness, as if something were missing inside her. She then felt confusedly, in a flash, becoming bewildered, that for three years perhaps, from the moment in which she had left her parents' home, she had been in that void of which she was only now becoming conscious. She had been unaware of it before, because she had filled that void with herself alone, with her love; she was becoming aware of it now, because all day long she had, as it were, suspended her love in order to look and to observe.

"He didn't even say goodbye to me," she thought; and she started to cry again, as if that thought were the definite reason for her tears.

She sat up in bed: but she suddenly held back the hand she had stretched out, while sitting up, to get her handkerchief from her dress. No, it was no longer any use to forbid herself to take another look at that portrait, to reexamine it! She took it. She put the light back on.

How differently she had pictured that woman! Now, contemplating her real likeness, she felt remorse for the feelings that the imaginary woman had aroused in her. She had pictured a woman rather fat and ruddy, with flashing, smiling eyes, always ready to laugh, enjoying common amusements . . . And instead, now, there she was: a young woman whose cleancut features expressed a profound, sorrowful soul; whose eyes expressed a sort of all-absorbing silence; yes, different from herself, but not in that earlier vulgar sense: just the opposite; no, that mouth looked as if it had never smiled, whereas her own had laughed so often and so gaily; and surely, if that face was swarthy (as it seemed to be from the portrait), it had a less smiling air than her own blonde and rosy face.

Why, why so sad?

A hateful thought flashed across her mind, and all at once with violent repulsion she tore her eyes away from that woman's picture, suddenly discovering in it a snare threatening not only to her peace of mind, to her love, which, as it was, had received more than one wound that day, but also to her proud dignity as an honest woman who had never allowed herself even the remotest thought hostile to her husband.

That woman had had a lover! And perhaps it was because of him she was so sad, because of that adulterous love, and not because of her husband!

She tossed the portrait onto the bedside table and put out the light again, hoping to fall asleep this time without thinking any more about that woman, with whom she could have nothing in common. But, closing her eyes, she suddenly saw, in spite of herself, the dead woman's eyes, and sought in vain to dispel that sight.

"Not because of him, not because of him!" she then murmured with frenzied persistence, as if by insulting her she hoped to be rid of her.

And she made an effort to recall everything she knew about that other man, the lover, as if compelling the gaze and the sadness of those eyes to look no longer at her but at the former lover, whom she knew only by name: Arturo Valli. She knew that he had married a few years later as if to prove his innocence of the blame that Vittore wanted to ascribe to him, that he had vigorously declined Vittore's challenge to a duel, protesting that he would never fight with a mad killer. After this refusal, Vittore had threatened to kill him wherever he came across him, even in church; and then he had left the town with his wife, returning later as soon as Vittore, remarried, had departed.

But from the sadness of those events which she now brought back to mind, from Valli's cowardice and, after so many years, from the way the first wife had been completely consigned to oblivion by her husband, who had been able to resume his life and remarry as if nothing had happened, from the joy that she herself had felt upon becoming Vittore's wife, from those three years she had spent together with him with never a thought about that other woman, unexpectedly a cause of pity for her spontaneously forced itself upon Anna; she saw her image again vividly and it seemed to her that with those eyes, intense from so much suffering, that woman was saying to her:

"But I'm the only one that died as a result! All of you are still living!"

She saw, she felt, that she was alone in the house: she got frightened. Yes, *she* was living; but for three years, since her wedding day, she hadn't seen her parents or sister, not even once. She who adored them, a dutiful daughter, a trusting sister, had had the courage to oppose their wishes out of love for her husband; for his sake, when he was rejected by his own family, she had fallen seriously ill, and would no doubt have died if the doctors hadn't induced her father to accede to her desire. And her father had yielded, but without giving his consent; in fact, he swore that after that wedding she would no longer exist for him or for that household. Besides the difference in age, the husband being eighteen years older than the wife, a more serious obstacle for the father had been Brivio's financial position, which was subject to rapid ups and downs because of the risky undertakings on which this most enterprising and extraordinarily active man was accustomed to embark with foolhardy confidence in himself and his luck.

In three years of marriage Anna, surrounded by comforts, had been able to consider as unjust, or dictated by hostile prejudice, her father's prudent misgivings as to the financial means of her husband, in whom, moreover, in her ignorance, she placed as much confidence as he had in himself; then, as for the difference in their ages, up to then there had been no manifest cause of disappointment for her or surprise for others, because Brivio's advanced years produced in him not the slightest impairment to his small, highly animated and robust body and even less to his mind, which was endowed with tireless energy and restless eagerness.

It was something totally different that Anna, now for the first time, looking into her life (without even realizing it) with the eyes of that dead woman depicted there in the portrait on the bedside table, found to complain of in her husband. Yes, it was true: she had felt hurt at other times by his almost disdainful indifference; but never so much as on that day; and now for the first time she felt so frighteningly alone, separated from her family, who at that moment seemed to her to have abandoned her there, as if, upon marrying Brivio, she already had something in common with that dead woman and was no longer worthy of anyone else's company. And her husband, who ought to have consoled her, it seemed that even her husband was unwilling to give her any credit for the sacrifice of her daughterly and sisterly love that she had offered him, just as if it had cost her nothing, as if he had had a right to that sacrifice and therefore had no obligation now to make it up to her. Yes, he had a right, but it was because she had fallen so totally in love with him at that time; therefore he now had an obligation to repay her. And instead . . .

"It's always been like that!" Anna thought she heard the sorrowful lips of the dead woman sigh to her.

She lit the lamp again and once more, contemplating the picture, she was struck by the expression of those eyes. So then, it was true, she too had suffered on his account? She too, she too, realizing she wasn't loved, had felt that frightening emptiness?

"Yes? Yes?" Anna, choking with tears, asked the picture.

And it then seemed to her that those kindly eyes, intense with passion and heartbreak, were pitying her in their turn, were condoling with her over that abandonment, that unrequited sacrifice, that love which remained locked up in her breast like a treasure in a casket to which he had the keys but would never use them, like a miser.

THE ONLY SON OF AOIFE

Isabella Augusta, Lady Gregory

THE TIME CUCHULAIN came back from Alban, after he had learned the use of arms under Scathach, he left Aoife, the queen he had overcome in battle, with child.

And when he was leaving her, he told her what name to give the child, and he gave her a gold ring, and bade her keep it safe till the child grew to be a lad, and till his thumb would fill it; and he bade her to give it to him then, and to send him to Ireland, and he would know he was his son by that token. She promised to do so, and with that Cuchulain went back to Ireland.

It was not long after the child was born, word came to Aoife that Cuchulain had taken Emer to be his wife in Ireland. When she heard that, great jealousy came on her, and great anger, and her love for Cuchulain was turned to hatred; and she remembered her three champions that he had killed, and how he had overcome herself, and she determined in her mind that when her son would come to have the strength of a man, she would get her revenge through him. She told Conlaoch her son nothing of this, but brought him up like any king's son; and when he was come to sensible years, she put him under the teaching of Scathach, to be taught the use of arms and the art of war. He turned out as apt a scholar as his father, and it was not long before he had learnt all Scathach had to teach.

Then Aoife gave him the arms of a champion, and bade him go to Ireland, but first she laid three commands on him: the first never to give way to any living person, but to die sooner than be made turn back; the second, not to refuse a challenge from the greatest champion alive, but to fight him at all risks, even if he was sure to lose his life; the third, not to tell his name on any account, though he might be threatened with death for hiding it. She put him under *geasa,* that is, under bonds, not to do these things.

Then the young man, Conlaoch, set out, as it was not long before his ship brought him to Ireland, and the place he landed at was Baile's Strand, near Dundealgan.

It chanced that at that time Conchubar, the High King, was holding his court there, for it was a convenient gathering-place for his chief men, and they were settling some business that belonged to the government of that district.

When word was brought to Conchubar that there was a ship come to the strand, and a young lad in it armed as if for fighting, and armed men with him, he sent one of the chief men of his household to ask his name, and on what business he was come.

The messenger's name was Cuinaire, and he went down to the strand, and when he saw the young man he said: "A welcome to you, young hero from the east, with the merry face. It is likely, seeing you come armed as if for fighting, you are gone astray on your journey; but as you are come to Ireland, tell me your name and what your deeds have been, and your victories in the eastern bounds of the world."

"As to my name," said Conlaoch, "it is of no great account; but whatever it is, I am under bonds not to tell it to the stoutest man living."

"It is best for you to tell it at the king's desire," said Cuinaire, "before you get your death through refusing it, as many a champion from Alban and from Britain has done before now." "If that is the order you put on us when we land here, it is I will break it," said Conlaoch, "and no one will obey it any longer from this out."

So Cuinaire went back and told the king what the young lad had said. Then Conchubar said to his people: "Who will go out into the field, and drag the name and the story out of this young man?" "I will go," said Conall, for his hand was never slow in fighting. And he went out, and found the lad angry and destroying, handling his arms, and they attacked one another with a great noise of swords and shouts, and they were gripped together, and fought for a while, and then Conall was overcome, and the great name and the praise that was on Conall, it was on the head of Conlaoch it was now.

Word was sent then to where Cuchulain was, in pleasant, bright-faced Dundealgan. And the messenger told him the whole story, and he said: "Conall is lying humbled, and it is slow the help is in coming; it is a welcome there would be before the Hound."

Cuchulain rose up then and went to where Conlaoch was, and he still handling his arms. And Cuchulain asked him his name and said: "It would be well for you, young hero of unknown name, to loosen yourself from this knot, and not to bring down my hand upon you, for it will be hard for you to escape death." But Conlaoch said: "If I put you down in the fight, the way I put down your comrade, there will be a great name on me; but if I draw back now, there will be mockery on me, and it will be said I was afraid of the fight. I will never give in to any man to tell the name, or to give an account of myself. But if I was not held with a command," he said, "there is no man in the world I would sooner give it to than to yourself, since I saw your face. But do not think, brave champion of Ireland, that I will let you take away the fame I have won, for nothing."

With that they fought together, and it is seldom such a battle was seen, and all wondered that the young lad could stand so well against Cuchulain.

So they fought a long while, neither getting the better of the other, but at last Cuchulain was charged so hotly by the lad that he was forced to give way, and although he had fought so many good fights, and killed so many great champions, and understood the use of arms better than any man living, he was pressed very hard.

And he called for the Gae Bulg, and his anger came on him, and the flames of the hero-light began to shine about his head, and by that sign Conlaoch knew him to be Cuchulain, his father. And just at that time he was aiming his spear at him, and when he knew it was Cuchulain, he threw his spear crooked that it might pass beside him. But Cuchulain threw his spear, the Gae Bulg, at him with all his might, and it struck the lad in the side and went into his body, so that he fell to the ground.

And Cuchulain said: "Now, boy, tell your name and what you are, for it is short your life will be, for you will not live after that wound."

And Conlaoch showed the ring that was on his hand, and he said: "Come here where I am lying on the field, let my men from the east come round me. I am suffering for revenge. I am Conlaoch, son of the Hound, heir of dear Dundealgan; I was bound to this secret in Dun Scathach, the secret in which I have found my grief."

And Cuchulain said: "It is a pity your mother not to be here to see you brought down. She might have stretched out her hand to stop the spear that wounded you." And Conlaoch said: "My curse be on my mother, for it was she put me under bonds; it was she sent me here to try my strength against yours." And Cuchulain said: "My curse be on your mother, the woman that is full of treachery; it is through her harmful thoughts these tears have been brought on us." And Conlaoch said: "My name was never forced from my mouth till now; I never gave an account of myself to any man under the sun. But, O Cuchulain of the sharp sword, it was a pity you not to know me the time I threw the slanting spear behind you in the fight."

And then the sorrow of death came upon Conlaoch, and Cuchulain took his sword and put it through him, sooner than leave him in the pain and the punishment he was in.

And then great trouble and anguish came on Cuchulain, and he made this complaint:

"It is a pity it is, O son of Aoife, that ever you came into the province of Ulster, that you ever met with the Hound of Cuailgne.

"If I and my fair Conlaoch were doing feats of war on the one side, the men of Ireland from sea to sea would not be equal to us together. It is no wonder I to be under grief when I see the shield and the arms of Conlaoch. A pity it is there is no one at all, a pity there are not hundreds of men on whom I could get satisfaction for his death.

"If it was the king himself had hurt your fair body, it is I would have shortened his days.

"It is well for the House of the Red Branch, and for the heads of its fair army of heroes, it was not they that killed my only son.

"It is well for Laegaire of Victories it is not from him you got your heavy pain.

"It is well for the heroes of Conall they did not join in the killing of you; it is well that travelling across the plain of Macha they did not fall in with me after such a fight.

"It is well for the tall, well-shaped Forbuide; well for Dubthach, your Black Beetle of Ulster.

"It is well for you, Cormac Conloingeas, your share of arms gave no help, that it is not from your weapons he got his wound, the hard-skinned shield or the blade.

"It is a pity it was not one of the plains of Munster, or in Leinster of the sharp blades, or at Cruachan of the rough fighters, that struck down my comely Conlaoch.

"It is a pity it was not in the country of the Cruithne, of the fierce Fians, you fell in a heavy quarrel, or in the country of the Greeks, or in some other place of the world, you died, and I could avenge you.

"Or in Spain, or in Sorcha, or in the country of the Saxons of the free armies; there would not then be this death in my heart.

"It is very well for the men of Alban it was not they that destroyed your fame; and it is well for the men of the Gall.

"Och! It is bad that it happened; my grief! it is on me is the misfortune, O Conlaoch of the Red Spear, I myself to have spilled your blood.

"I to be under defeat, without strength. It is a pity Aoife never taught you to know the power of my strength in the fight.

"It is no wonder I to be blinded after such a fight and such a defeat.

"It is no wonder I to be tired out, and without the sons of Usnach beside me.

"Without a son, without a brother, with none to come after me; without Conlaoch, without a name to keep my strength.

"To be without Naoise, without Ainnle, without Ardan; is it not with me is my fill of trouble?

"I am the father that killed his son, the fine green branch; there is no hand or shelter to help me.

"I am a raven that has no home; I am a boat going from wave to wave; I am a ship that has lost its rudder; I am the apple left on the tree; it is little I thought of falling from it; grief and sorrow will be with me from this time."

Then Cuchulain stood up and faced all the men of Ulster. "There is trouble on Cuchulain," said Conchubar; "he is after killing his own son, and if I and all my men were to go against him, by the end of the day he would destroy every man of us. Go now," he said to Cathbad, the Druid, "and bind him to go down to Baile's Strand, and to give three days fighting against the waves of the sea, rather than to kill us all."

So Cathbad put an enchantment on him, and bound him to go down. And when he came to the strand, there was a great white stone before him, and he took his sword in his right hand, and he said: "If I had the head of the woman that sent her son to his death, I would split it as I split this stone." And he made four quarters of the stone.

Then he fought with the waves three days and three nights, till he fell from hunger and weakness, so that some men said he got his death there. But it was not there he got his death, but on the plain of Muirthemne.

THE LEOPARD MAN'S STORY

Jack London

HE HAD A dreamy, far-away look in his eyes, and his sad, insistent voice, gentle-spoken as a maid's, seemed the placid embodiment of some deep-seated melancholy. He was the Leopard Man, but he did not look it. His business in life, whereby he lived, was to appear in a cage of performing leopards before vast audiences, and to thrill those audiences by certain exhibitions of nerve for which his employers rewarded him on a scale commensurate with the thrills he produced.

As I say, he did not look it. He was narrow-hipped, narrow-shouldered, and anaemic, while he seemed not so much oppressed by gloom as by a sweet and gentle sadness, the weight of which was as sweetly and gently borne. For an hour I had been trying to get a story out of him, but he appeared to lack imagination. To him there was no romance in his gorgeous career, no deeds of daring, no thrills—nothing but a gray sameness and infinite boredom.

Lions? Oh, yes! he had fought with them. It was nothing. All you had to do was to stay sober. Anybody could whip a lion to a standstill with an ordinary stick. He had fought one for half an hour once. Just hit him on the nose every time he rushed, and when he got artful and rushed with his head down, why, the thing to do was to stick out your leg. When he grabbed at the leg you drew it back and hit him on the nose again. That was all.

With the far-away look in his eyes and his soft flow of words he showed me his scars. There were many of them, and one recent one where a tigress had reached for his shoulder and gone down to the bone. I could see the neatly mended rents in the coat he had on. His right arm, from the elbow down, looked as though it had gone through a threshing machine, what of the ravage wrought by claws and fangs. But it was nothing, he said, only the old wounds bothered him somewhat when rainy weather came on.

Suddenly his face brightened with a recollection, for he was really as anxious to give me a story as I was to get it.

"I suppose you've heard of the lion-tamer who was hated by another man?" he asked.

He paused and looked pensively at a sick lion in the cage opposite.

"Got the toothache," he explained. "Well, the lion-tamer's big play to the audience was putting his head in a lion's mouth. The man who hated him attended every performance in the hope sometime of seeing that lion crunch down. He followed the show about all over the country. The years went by and he grew old, and the lion-tamer grew old, and the lion grew old. And at last one day, sitting in a front seat, he saw what he had waited for. The lion crunched down, and there wasn't any need to call a doctor."

The Leopard Man glanced casually over his finger nails in a manner which would have been critical had it not been so sad.

"Now, that's what I call patience," he continued, "and it's my style. But it was not the style of a fellow I knew. He was a little, thin, sawed-off, sword-swallowing and juggling Frenchman. De Ville, he called himself, and he had a nice wife. She did trapeze work and used to dive from under the roof into a net, turning over once on the way as nice as you please.

"De Ville had a quick temper, as quick as his hand, and his hand was as quick as the paw of a tiger. One day, because the ring-master called him a frog-eater, or something like that and maybe a little worse, he shoved him against the soft pine background he used in his knife-throwing act, so quick the ring-master didn't have time to think, and there, before the audience, De Ville kept the air on fire with his knives, sinking them into the wood all around the ring-master so close that they passed through his clothes and most of them bit into his skin.

"The clowns had to pull the knives out to get him loose, for he was pinned fast. So the word went around to watch out for De Ville, and no one dared be more than barely civil to his wife. And she was a sly bit of baggage, too, only all hands were afraid of De Ville.

"But there was one man, Wallace, who was afraid of nothing. He was the lion-tamer, and he had the self-same trick of putting his head into the lion's mouth. He'd put it into the mouths of any of them, though he preferred Augustus, a big, good-natured beast who could always be depended upon.

"As I was saying, Wallace—'King' Wallace we called him—was afraid of nothing alive or dead. He was a king and no mistake. I've seen him drunk, and on a wager go into the cage of a lion that'd turned nasty, and without a stick beat him to a finish. Just did it with his fist on the nose.

"Madame De Ville—"

At an uproar behind us the Leopard Man turned quietly around. It was a divided cage, and a monkey, poking through the bars and around the partition, had had its paw seized by a big gray wolf who was trying to pull it off by main strength. The arm seemed stretching out longer and longer like a thick elastic, and the unfortunate monkey's mates were raising a terrible din. No keeper was at hand, so the Leopard Man stepped over a couple of paces, dealt the wolf a sharp blow on the nose with the light cane he carried, and returned with a sadly apologetic smile to take up his unfinished sentence as though there had been no interruption.

"—looked at King Wallace and King Wallace looked at her, while De Ville looked black. We warned Wallace, but it was no use. He laughed at us, and he laughed at De Ville one day when he shoved De Ville's head into a bucket of paste because he wanted to fight.

"De Ville was in a pretty mess—I helped to scrape him off; but he was cool as a cucumber and made no threats at all. But I saw a glitter in his eyes which I had seen often in the eyes of wild beasts, and I went out of my way to give Wallace a final warning. He laughed, but he did not look so much in Madame De Ville's direction after that.

"Several months passed by. Nothing had happened and I was beginning to think it all a scare over nothing. We were West by that time, showing in 'Frisco. It was during the afternoon performance, and the big tent was filled with women and children, when I went looking for Red Denny, the head canvas-man, who had walked off with my pocket-knife.

"Passing by one of the dressing tents I glanced in through a hole in the canvas to see if I could locate him. He wasn't there, but directly in front of me was King Wallace, in tights, waiting for his turn to go on with his cage of performing lions. He was watching with much amusement a quarrel between a couple of trapeze artists.

All the rest of the people in the dressing tent were watching the same thing, with the exception of De Ville, whom I noticed staring at Wallace with undisguised hatred. Wallace and the rest were all too busy following the quarrel to notice this or what followed.

"But I saw it through the hole in the canvas. De Ville drew his handkerchief from his pocket, made as though to mop the sweat from his face with it (it was a hot day), and at the same time walked past Wallace's back. He never stopped, but with a flirt of the hand-kerchief kept right on to the doorway, where he turned his head, while passing out, and shot a swift look back. The look troubled me at the time, for not only did I see hatred in it, but I saw triumph as well.

"De Ville will bear watching," I said to myself, and I really breathed easier when I saw him go out the entrance to the circus grounds and board an electric car for down town. A few minutes later I was in the big tent, where I had overhauled Red Denny. King Wallace was doing his turn and holding the audience spell-bound. He was in a particularly vicious mood, and he kept the lions stirred up till they were all snarling, that is, all of them except old Augustus, and he was just too fat and lazy and old to get stirred up over anything.

"Finally Wallace cracked the old lion's knees with his whip and got him into position. Old Augustus, blinking good-naturedly, opened his mouth and in popped Wallace's head. Then the jaws came together, *crunch,* just like that."

The Leopard Man smiled in a sweetly wistful fashion, and the faraway look came into his eyes.

"And that was the end of King Wallace," he went on in his sad, low voice. "After the excitement cooled down I watched my chance and bent over and smelled Wallace's head. Then I sneezed."

"It . . . it was . . .?" I queried with halting eagerness.

"Snuff—that De Ville dropped on his hair in the dressing tent. Old Augustus never meant to do it. He only sneezed."

A PIECE OF STRING

Guy de Maupassant

ALONG ALL THE roads around Goderville the peasants and their wives were coming toward the burgh because it was market day. The men were proceeding with slow steps, the whole body bent forward at each movement of their long twisted legs, deformed by their hard work, by the weight on the plow which, at the same time, raised the left shoulder and swerved the figure, by the reaping of the wheat which made the knees spread to make a firm "purchase," by all the slow and painful labors of the country. Their blouses, blue, "stiff-starched," shining as if varnished, ornamented with a little design in white at the neck and wrists, puffed about their bony bodies, seemed like balloons ready to carry them off. From each of them a head, two arms, and two feet protruded.

Some led a cow or a calf by a cord, and their wives, walking behind the animal, whipped its haunches with a leafy branch to hasten its progress. They carried large baskets on their arms from which, in some cases, chickens and, in others, ducks thrust out their heads. And they walked with a quicker, livelier step than their husbands. Their spare straight figures were wrapped in a scanty little shawl, pinned over their flat bosoms, and their heads were enveloped in a white cloth glued to the hair and surmounted by a cap.

Then a wagon passed at the jerky trot of a nag, shaking strangely, two men seated side by side and a woman in the bottom of the vehicle, the latter holding on to the sides to lessen the hard jolts.

In the public square of Goderville there was a crowd, a throng of human beings and animals mixed together. The horns of the cattle, the tall hats with long nap of the rich peasant, and the head-gear of the peasant women rose above the surface of the assembly.

And the clamorous, shrill, screaming voices made a continuous and savage din which sometimes was dominated by the robust lungs of some countryman's laugh, or the long lowing of a cow tied to the wall of a house.

All that smacked of the stable, the dairy and the dirt heap, hay and sweat, giving forth that unpleasant odor, human and animal, peculiar to the people of the field.

Maître Hauchecome, of Breaute, had just arrived at Goderville, and he was directing his steps toward the public square, when he perceived upon the ground a little piece of string. Maître Hauchecome, economical like a true Norman, thought that everything useful ought to be picked up, and he bent painfully, for he suffered from rheumatism. He took the bit of thin cord from the ground and began to roll it carefully when he noticed Maître Malandain, the harness-maker, on the threshold of his door, looking at him. They had heretofore had business together on the subject of a halter, and they were on bad terms, being both good haters. Maître Hauchecome was seized with a sort of shame to be seen thus by his enemy, picking a bit of string out of the dirt. He concealed his "find" quickly under his blouse, then in his trousers' pocket; then he pretended to be still looking on the ground for something which he did not find, and he went toward the market, his head forward, bent double by his pains.

He was soon lost in the noisy and slowly moving crowd, which was busy with interminable bargainings. The peasants milked, went and came, perplexed, always in fear of being cheated, not daring to decide, watching the vender's eye, ever trying to find the trick in the man and the flaw in the beast.

The women, having placed their great baskets at their feet, had taken out the poultry which lay upon the ground, tied together by the feet, with terrified eyes and scarlet crests.

They heard offers, stated their prices with a dry air and impassive face, or perhaps, suddenly deciding on some proposed reduction, shouted to the customer who was slowly going away: "All right, Maître Authirne, I'll give it to you for that."

Then little by little the square was deserted, and the Angelus ringing at noon, those who had stayed too long, scattered to their shops.

At Jourdain's the great room was full of people eating, as the big court was full of vehicles of all kinds, carts, gigs, wagons, dump carts, yellow with dirt, mended and patched, raising their shafts to the sky like two arms, or perhaps with their shafts in the ground and their backs in the air.

Just opposite the diners seated at the table, the immense fireplace, filled with bright flames, cast a lively heat on the backs of the row on the right. Three spits were turning on which were chickens, pigeons, and legs of mutton; and an appetizing odor of roast beef and gravy dripping over the nicely browned skin rose from the hearth, increased the jovialness, and made everybody's mouth water.

All the aristocracy of the plow ate there, at Maître Jourdain's, tavern keeper and horse dealer, a rascal who had money.

The dishes were passed and emptied, as were the jugs of yellow cider. Everyone told his affairs, his purchases, and sales. They discussed the crops. The weather was favorable for the green things but not for the wheat.

Suddenly the drum beat in the court, before the house. Everybody rose except a few indifferent persons, and ran to the door, or to the windows, their mouths still full and napkins in their hands.

After the public crier had ceased his drum-beating, he called out in a jerky voice, speaking his phrases irregularly:

"It is hereby made known to the inhabitants of Goderville, and in general to all persons present at the market, that there was lost this morning, on the road to Benzeville, between nine and ten o'clock, a black leather pocketbook containing five hundred francs and some business papers. The finder is requested to return same with all haste to the mayor's office or to Maître Fortune Houlbreque of Manneville; there will be twenty francs reward."

Then the man went away. The heavy roll of the drum and the crier's voice were again heard at a distance.

Then they began to talk of this event discussing the chances that Maître Houlbreque had of finding or not finding his pocketbook.

And the meal concluded. They were finishing their coffee when a chief of the gendarmes appeared upon the threshold.

He inquired:

"Is Maître Hauchecome, of Breaute, here?"

Maître Hauchecome, seated at the other end of the table, replied: "Here I am."

And the officer resumed:

"Maître Hauchecome, will you have the goodness to accompany me to the mayor's office? The mayor would like to talk to you."

The peasant, surprised and disturbed, swallowed at a draught his tiny glass of brandy, rose, and, even more bent than in the morning, for the first steps after each rest were specially difficult, set out, repeating: "Here I am, here I am."

The mayor was awaiting him, seated on an armchair. He was the notary of the vicinity, a stout, serious man, with pompous phrases.

"Maître Hauchecome," said he, "you were seen this morning to pick up, on the road to Benzeville, the pocketbook lost by Maître Houlbreque of Manneville."

The countryman, astounded, looked at the mayor, already terrified, by this suspicion resting on him without his knowing why.

"Me? Me? Me pick up the pocketbook?"

"Yes, you, yourself."

"Word of honor, I never heard of it."

"But you were seen."

"I was seen, me? Who says he saw me?"

"Monsieur Malandain, the harness-maker."

The old man remembered, understood, and flushed with anger.

"Ah, he saw me, the clodhopper, he saw me pick up this string, here, M'sieu' the Mayor." And rummaging in his pocket he drew out the little piece of string.

But the mayor, incredulous, shook his head.

"You will not make me believe, Maître Hauchecome, that Monsieur Malandain, who is a man worthy of credence, mistook this cord for a pocketbook."

The peasant, furious, lifted his hand, spat at one side to attest his honor, repeating:

"It is nevertheless the truth of the good God, the sacred truth, M'sieu' the Mayor. I repeat it on my soul and my salvation."

The mayor resumed:

"After picking up the object, you stood like a stilt, looking a long while in the mud to see if any piece of money had fallen out."

The good old man choked with indignation and fear.

"How anyone can tell—how anyone can tell—such lies to take away an honest man's reputation! How can anyone—"

There was no use in his protesting, nobody believed him. He was confronted with Monsieur Malandain, who repeated and maintained his affirmation. They abused each other for an hour. At his own request, Maître Hauchecome was searched, nothing was found on him.

Finally the mayor, very much perplexed, discharged him with the warning that he would consult the public prosecutor and ask for further orders.

The news had spread. As he left the mayor's office, the old man was surrounded and questioned with a serious or bantering curiosity, in which there was no indignation. He began to tell the story of the string. No one believed him. They laughed at him.

He went along, stopping his friends, beginning endlessly his statement and his protestations, showing his pockets turned inside out, to prove that he had nothing.

They said:

"Old rascal, get out!"

And he grew angry, becoming exasperated, hot, and distressed at not being believed, not knowing what to do and always repeating himself.

Night came. He must depart. He started on his way with three neighbors to whom he pointed out the place where he had picked up the bit of string; and all along the road he spoke of his adventure.

In the evening he took a turn in the village of Breaute, in order to tell it to everybody. He only met with incredulity.

It made him ill at night.

The next day about one o'clock in the afternoon, Marius Paumelle, a hired man in the employ of Maître Breton, husbandman at Ymanville, returned the pocketbook and its contents to Maître Houlbreque of Manneville.

This man claimed to have found the object in the road; but not knowing how to read, he had carried it to the house and given it to his employer.

The news spread through the neighborhood. Maître Hauchecome was informed of it. He immediately went the circuit and began to recount his story completed by the happy climax. He was in triumph.

"What grieved me so much was not the thing itself, as the lying. There is nothing so shameful as to be placed under a cloud on account of a lie."

He talked of his adventure all day long, he told it on the highway to people who were passing by, in the wine-shop to people who were drinking there, and to persons coming out of church the following Sunday. He stopped strangers to tell them about it. He was calm now, and yet something disturbed him without his knowing exactly what it was. People had the air of joking while they listened. They did not seem convinced. He seemed to feel that remarks were being made behind his back.

On Tuesday of the next week he went to the market at Goderville, urged solely by the necessity he felt of discussing the case.

Malandain, standing at his door, began to laugh on seeing him pass. Why?

He approached a farmer from Crequetot, who did not let him finish, and giving him a thump in the stomach said to his face:

"You big rascal."

Then he turned his back on him.

Maître Hauchecome was confused, why was he called a big rascal?

When he was seated at the table in Jourdain's tavern he commenced to explain "the affair."

A horse dealer from Monvilliers called to him:

"Come, come, old sharper, that's an old trick; I know all about your piece of string!"

Hauchecome stammered:

"But since the pocketbook was found."

But the other man replied:

"Shut up, papa, there is one that finds, and there is one that reports. At any rate you are mixed with it."

The peasant stood choking. He understood. They accused him of having had the pocketbook returned by a confederate, by an accomplice.

He tried to protest. All the table began to laugh.

He could not finish his dinner and went away, in the midst of jeers.

He went home ashamed and indignant, choking with anger and confusion, the more dejected that he was capable with his Norman cunning of doing what they had accused him of, and even boasting of it as of a good turn. His innocence to him, in a confused way, was impossible to prove, as his sharpness was known. And he was stricken to the heart by the injustice of the suspicion.

Then he began to recount the adventures again, prolonging his history every day, adding each time, new reasons, more energetic protestations, more solemn oaths which he imagined and prepared in his hours of solitude, his whole mind given up to the story of the string. He was believed so much the less as his defense was more complicated and his arguing more subtle.

"Those are lying excuses," they said behind his back.

He felt it, consumed his heart over it, and wore himself out with useless efforts. He wasted away before their very eyes.

The wags now made him tell about the string to amuse them, as they make a soldier who has been on a campaign tell about his battles. His mind, touched to the depth, began to weaken.

Toward the end of December he took to his bed.

He died in the first days of January, and in the delirium of his death struggles he kept claiming his innocence, reiterating:

"A piece of string, a piece of string,—look—here it is, M'sieu' the Mayor."

HOME SICKNESS

George Moore

HE TOLD THE doctor he was due in the bar-room at eight o'clock in the morning; the bar-room was in a slum in the Bowery; and he had only been able to keep himself in health by getting up at five o'clock and going for long walks in the Central Park.

"A sea voyage is what you want," said the doctor. "Why not go to Ireland for two or three months? You will come back a new man."

"I'd like to see Ireland again."

And then he began to wonder how the people at home were getting on. The doctor was right. He thanked him, and three weeks afterwards he landed in Cork.

As he sat in the railway carriage he recalled his native village—he could see it and its lake, and then the fields one by one, and the roads. He could see a large piece of rocky land—some three or four hundred acres of headland stretching out into the winding lake. Upon this headland the peasantry had been given permission to build their cabins by former owners of the Georgian house standing on the pleasant green hill. The present owners considered the village a disgrace, but the villagers paid high rents for their plots of ground, and all the manual labour that the Big House required came from the village: the gardeners, the stable helpers, the house and the kitchen maids.

He had been thirteen years in America, and when the train stopped at his station, he looked round to see if there were any changes in it. It was just the same blue limestone station-house as it was thirteen years ago. The platform and the sheds were the same, and there were five miles of road from the station to

Duncannon. The sea voyage had done him good, but five miles were too far for him to-day; the last time he had walked the road, he had walked it in an hour and a half, carrying a heavy bundle on a stick.

He was sorry he did not feel strong enough for the walk; the evening was fine, and he would meet many people coming home from the fair, some of whom he had known in his youth, and they would tell him where he could get a clean lodging. But the carman would be able to tell him that; he called the car that was waiting at the station, and soon he was answering questions about America. But Bryden wanted to hear of those who were still living in the old country, and after hearing the stories of many people he had forgotten, he heard that Mike Scully, who had been away in a situation for many years as a coachman in the King's County, had come back and built a fine house with a concrete floor. Now there was a good loft in Mike Scully's house, and Mike would be pleased to take in a lodger.

Bryden remembered that Mike had been in a situation at the Big House; he had intended to be a jockey, but had suddenly shot up into a fine tall man, and had had to become a coachman instead. Bryden tried to recall the face, but he could only remember a straight nose, and a somewhat dusky complexion. Mike was one of the heroes of his childhood, and his youth floated before him, and he caught glimpses of himself, something that was more than a phantom and less than a reality. Suddenly his reverie was broken: the carman pointed with his whip, and Bryden saw a tall, finely-built, middle-aged man coming through the gates, and the driver said:—

"There's Mike Scully."

Mike had forgotten Bryden even more completely than Bryden had forgotten him, and many aunts and uncles were mentioned before he began to understand.

"You've grown into a fine man, James," he said, looking at Bryden's great width of chest. "But you are thin in the cheeks, and you're sallow in the cheeks too."

"I haven't been very well lately—that is one of the reasons I have come back; but I want to see you all again."

Bryden paid the carman, wished him "God-speed," and he and Mike divided the luggage between them, Mike carrying the bag and Bryden the bundle, and they walked round the lake, for the townland was at the back of the demesne; and while they walked,

James proposed to pay Mike ten shillings a week for his board and lodging.

He remembered the woods thick and well-forested; now they were windworn, the drains were choked, and the bridge leading across the lake inlet was falling away. Their way led between long fields where herds of cattle were grazing; the road was broken— Bryden wondered how the villagers drove their carts over it, and Mike told him that the landlord could not keep it in repair, and he would not allow it to be kept in repair out of the rates, for then it would be a public road, and he did not think there should be a public road through his property.

At the end of many fields they came to the village, and it looked a desolate place, even on this fine evening, and Bryden remarked that the county did not seem to be as much lived in as it used to be. It was at once strange and familiar to see the chickens in the kitchen; and, wishing to re-knit himself to the old habits, he begged of Mrs. Scully not to drive them out, saying he did not mind them. Mike told his wife that Bryden was born in Duncannon, and when he mentioned Bryden's name she gave him her hand, after wiping it in her apron, saying he was heartily welcome, only she was afraid he would not care to sleep in a loft.

"Why wouldn't I sleep in a loft, a dry loft! You're thinking a good deal of America over here," said he, "but I reckon it isn't all you think it. Here you work when you like and you sit down when you like; but when you have had a touch of blood-poisoning as I had, and when you have seen young people walking with a stick, you think that there is something to be said for old Ireland."

"Now won't you be taking a sup of milk? You'll be wanting a drink after travelling," said Mrs. Scully.

And when he had drunk the milk Mike asked him if he would like to go inside or if he would like to go for a walk.

"Maybe it is sitting down you would like to be."

And they went into the cabin, and started to talk about the wages a man could get in America, and the long hours of work.

And after Bryden had told Mike everything about America that he thought would interest him, he asked Mike about Ireland. But Mike did not seem to be able to tell him much that was of interest. They were all very poor—poorer, perhaps, than when he left them.

"I don't think anyone except myself has a five pound note to his name."

Bryden hoped he felt sufficiently sorry for Mike. But after all Mike's life and prospects mattered little to him. He had come back in search of health; and he felt better already; the milk had done him good, and the bacon and cabbage in the pot sent forth a savoury odour. The Scullys were very kind, they pressed him to make a good meal; a few weeks of country air and food, they said, would give him back the health he had lost in the Bowery; and when Bryden said he was longing for a smoke, Mike said there was no better sign than that. During his long illness he had never wanted to smoke, and he was a confirmed smoker.

It was comfortable to sit by the mild peat fire watching the smoke of their pipes drifting up the chimney, and all Bryden wanted was to be let alone; he did not want to hear of anyone's misfortunes, but about nine o'clock a number of villagers came in, and their appearance was depressing. Bryden remembered one or two of them—he used to know them very well when he was a boy; their talk was as depressing as their appearance, and he could feel no interest whatever in them. He was not moved when he heard that Higgins the stone-mason was dead; he was not affected when he heard that Mary Kelly, who used to go to do the laundry at the Big House, had married; he was only interested when he heard she had gone to America. No, he had not met her there, America is a big place. Then one of the peasants asked him if he remembered Patsy Carabine, who used to do the gardening at the Big House. Yes, he remembered Patsy well. Patsy was in the poor-house. He had not been able to do any work on account of his arm; his house had fallen in; he had given up his holding and gone into the poor-house. All this was very sad, and to avoid hearing any further unpleasantness, Bryden began to tell them about America. And they sat round listening to him; but all the talking was on his side; he wearied of it; and looking round the group he recognised a ragged hunchback with grey hair; twenty years ago he was a young hunchback, and, turning to him, Bryden asked him if he were doing well with his five acres.

"Ah, not much. This has been a bad season. The potatoes failed; they were watery—there is no diet in them."

These peasants were all agreed that they could make nothing out of their farms. Their regret was that they had not gone to America when they were young; and after striving to take an interest in the fact that O'Connor had lost a mare and foal worth forty pounds

Bryden began to wish himself back in the slum. And when they left the house he wondered if every evening would be like the present one. Mike piled fresh sods on the fire, and he hoped it would show enough light in the loft for Bryden to undress himself by.

The cackling of some geese in the road kept him awake, and the loneliness of the country seemed to penetrate to his bones, and to freeze the marrow in them. There was a bat in the loft—a dog howled in the distance—and then he drew the clothes over his head. Never had he been so unhappy, and the sound of Mike breathing by his wife's side in the kitchen added to his nervous terror. Then he dozed a little; and lying on his back he dreamed he was awake, and the men he had seen sitting round the fireside that evening seemed to him like spectres come out of some unknown region of morass and reedy tarn. He stretched out his hands for his clothes, determined to fly from this house, but remembering the lonely road that led to the station he fell back on his pillow. The geese still cackled, but he was too tired to be kept awake any longer. He seemed to have been asleep only a few minutes when he heard Mike calling him. Mike had come half way up the ladder and was telling him that breakfast was ready. "What kind of breakfast will he give me?" Bryden asked himself as he pulled on his clothes. There were tea and hot griddle cakes for breakfast, and there were fresh eggs; there was sunlight in the kitchen and he liked to hear Mike tell of the work he was going to do in the fields. Mike rented a farm of about fifteen acres, at least ten of it was grass; he grew an acre of potatoes and some corn, and some turnips for his sheep. He had a nice bit of meadow, and he took down his scythe, and as he put the whetstone in his belt Bryden noticed a second scythe, and he asked Mike if he should go down with him and help him to finish the field.

"You haven't done any mowing this many a year; I don't think you'd be of much help. You'd better go for a walk by the lake, but you may come in the afternoon if you like and help to turn the grass over."

Bryden was afraid he would find the lake shore very lonely, but the magic of returning health is the sufficient distraction for the convalescent, and the morning passed agreeably. The weather was still and sunny. He could hear the ducks in the reeds. The hours dreamed themselves away, and it became his habit to go to the lake every morning. One morning he met the landlord, and they walked together, talking of the country, of what it had been, and the ruin it was slipping into. James Bryden told him that ill health had brought him back to Ireland; and the landlord lent him his boat, and Bryden rowed about the islands, and resting upon his oars he looked at the old castles, and remembered the prehistoric raiders that the landlord had told him about. He came across the stones to which the lake dwellers had tied their boats, and these signs of ancient Ireland were pleasing to Bryden in his present mood.

As well as the great lake there was a smaller lake in the bog where the villagers cut their turf. This lake was famous for its pike, and the landlord allowed Bryden to fish there, and one evening when he was looking for a frog with which to bait his line he met Margaret Dirken driving home the cows for the milking. Margaret was the herdsman's daughter, and she lived in a cottage near the Big House; but she came up to the village whenever there was a dance, and Bryden had found himself opposite to her in the reels. But until this evening he had had little opportunity of speaking to her, and he was glad to speak to someone, for the evening was lonely, and they stood talking together.

"You're getting your health again," she said. "You'll soon be leaving us."

"I'm in no hurry."

"You're grand people over there; I hear a man is paid four dollars a day for his work."

"And how much," said James, "has he to pay for his food and for his clothes?"

Her cheeks were bright and her teeth small, white and beautifully even; and a woman's soul looked at Bryden out of her soft Irish eyes. He was troubled and turned aside, and catching sight of a frog looking at him out of a tuft of grass he said:—

"I have been looking for a frog to put upon my pike line."

The frog jumped right and left, and nearly escaped in some bushes, but he caught it and returned with it in his hand.

"It is just the kind of frog a pike will like," he said. "Look at its great white belly and its bright yellow back."

And without more ado he pushed the wire to which the hook was fastened through the frog's fresh body, and dragging it through the mouth he passed the hooks through the hind legs and tied the line to the end of the wire.

"I think," said Margaret, "I must be looking after my cows; it's time I got them home."

"Won't you come down to the lake while I set my line?"

She thought for a moment and said:—

"No, I'll see you from here."

He went down to the reedy tarn, and at his approach several snipe got up, and they flew above his head uttering sharp cries. His fishing-rod was a long hazel stick, and he threw the frog as far as he could into the lake. In doing this he roused some wild ducks; a mallard and two ducks go up, and they flew towards the larger lake. Margaret watched them; they flew in a line with an old castle; and they had not disappeared from view when Bryden came towards her, and he and she drove the cows home together that evening.

They had not met very often when she said, "James, you had better not come here so often calling to me."

"Don't you wish to me to come?"

"Yes, I wish you to come well enough, but keeping company is not the custom of the country, and I don't want to be talked about."

"Are you afraid the priest would speak against us from the altar?"

"He has spoken against keeping company, but it is not so much what the priest says, for there is no harm in talking."

"But if you are going to be married there is no harm in walking out together."

"Well, not so much, but marriages are made differently in these parts; there is not much courting here."

And next day it was known in the village that James was going to marry Margaret Dirken.

His desire to excel the boys in dancing had aroused much gaiety in the parish, and for some time past there had been dancing in every house where there was a floor fit to dance upon; and if the cottager had no money to pay for a barrel of beer, James Bryden, who had money, sent him a barrel, so that Margaret might get her dance. She told him that they sometimes crossed over into another parish where the priest was not so averse to dancing, and James wondered. And next morning at Mass he wondered at their simple fervour. Some of them held their hands above their heads as they prayed, and all this was very new and very old to James Bryden. But the obedience of these people to their priest surprised him. When he was a lad they had not been so obedient, or he had forgotten their obedience; and he listened in mixed anger and wonderment to the priest who was scolding his parishioners, speaking to them by name, saying that he had heard there was dancing going on in their homes. Worse than that, he said he had seen boys and girls loitering about the roads, and the talk that went on was of one kind—love. He said that newspapers containing love-stories were finding their way into the people's houses, stories about love, in which there was nothing elevating or ennobling. The people listened, accepting the priest's opinion without question. And their submission was pathetic. It was the submission of a primitive people clinging to religious authority, and Bryden contrasted the weakness and incompetence of the people about him with the modern restlessness and cold energy of the people he had left behind him.

One evening, as they were dancing, a knock came to the door, and the piper stopped playing, and the dancers whispered:—

"Some one has told on us; it is the priest."

And the awe-stricken villagers crowded round the cottage fire, afraid to open the door. But the priest said that if they did not open the door he would put his shoulder to it and force it open. Bryden went towards the door, saying he would allow no one to threaten him, priest or no priest, but Margaret caught his arm and told him that if he said anything to the priest, the priest would speak against them from the altar, and they would be shunned by the neighbours. It was Mike Scully who went to the door and let the priest in, and he came in saying they were dancing their souls into hell.

"I've heard of your goings on," he said—"of your beer-drinking and dancing. I will not have it in my parish. If you want that sort of thing you had better go to America."

"If that is intended for me, sir, I will go back to-morrow. Margaret can follow."

"It isn't the dancing, it's the drinking I'm opposed to," said the priest, turning to Bryden.

"Well, no one has drunk too much, sir," said Bryden.

"But you'll sit here drinking all night," and the priest's eyes went towards the corner where the women had gathered, and Bryden felt that the priest looked on the women as more dangerous than the porter. "It's after midnight," he said, taking out his watch.

By Bryden's watch it was only half-past eleven, and while they were arguing about the time Mrs. Scully offered Bryden's umbrella to the priest, for in his hurry to stop the dancing the priest had gone out without his; and, as if to show Bryden that he bore him no ill-will, the priest accepted the loan of the umbrella, for he was thinking of the big marriage fee that Bryden would pay him.

"I shall be badly off for the umbrella to-morrow," Bryden said, as soon as the priest was out of the house. He was going with his father-in-law to a fair. His father-in-law was learning him how to buy and sell cattle. And his father-in-law was saying that the country was mending, and that a man might become rich in Ireland if he only had a little capital. Bryden had the capital, and Margaret had an uncle on the other side of the lake who would leave her all he had, that would be fifty pounds, and never in the village of Duncannon had a young couple begun life with so much prospect of success as would James Bryden and Margaret Dirken.

Some time after Christmas was spoken of as the best time for the marriage; James Bryden said that he would not be able to get his money out of America before the spring. The delay seemed to vex him, and he seemed anxious to be married, until one day he received a letter from America, from a man who had served in the bar with him. This friend wrote to ask Bryden if he were coming back. The letter was no more than a passing wish to see Bryden again. Yet Bryden stood looking at it, and everyone wondered what could be in the letter. It seemed momentous, and they hardly believed him when he said it was from a friend who wanted to know if his health were better. He tried to forget the letter, and he looked at the worn fields, divided by walls of loose stones, and a great longing came upon him.

The smell of the Bowery slum had come across the Atlantic, and had found him out in this western headland; and one night he awoke from a dream in which he was hurling some drunken customer through the open doors into the darkness. He had seen his friend in his white duck jacket throwing drink from glass into glass amid the din of voices and strange accents; he had heard the clang of money as it was swept into the till, and his sense sickened for the bar-room. But how should he tell Margaret Dirken that he could not marry her? She had built her life upon this marriage. He could not tell he that he would not marry her . . . yet he must go. He felt as if he were being hunted; the thought that he must tell Margaret that he could not marry her hunted him day after day as a weasel hunts a rabbit. Again and again he went to meet her with the intention of telling her that he did not love her, that their lives were not for one another, that it had all been a mistake, and that happily he had found out it was a mistake soon enough. But Margaret, as if she guessed what he was about to speak of, threw her arms about him and begged him to say he loved her, and that they would be married at once. He agreed that he loved her, and that they would be married at once. But he had not left her many minutes before the feeling came upon him that he could not marry her—that he must go away. The smell of the bar-room hunted him down. Was it for the sake of the money that he might make there that he wished to go back? No, it was not the money. What then? His eyes fell on the bleak country, on the little fields divided by bleak walls; he remembered the pathetic ignorance of the people, and it was these things that he could not endure. It was the priest who came to forbid the dancing. Yes, it was the priest. As he stood looking at the line of the hills the bar-room seemed by him. He heard the politicians, and the excitement of politics was in his blood again. He must go away from this place—he must get back to the bar-room. Looking up he saw the scanty orchard, and he hated the spare road that led to the village, and he hated the little hill at the top of which the village began, and he hated more than all other places the house where he was to live with Margaret Dirken—if he married her. He could see it from where he stood—by the edge of the lake, with twenty acres of pasture land about it, for the landlord had given up part of his demesne land to them.

He caught sight of Margaret, and he called to her to come through the stile.

"I have just had a letter from America."

"About the money?" she said.

"Yes, about the money. But I shall have to go over there."

He stood looking at her, seeking for words; and she guessed from his embarrassment that he would say to her that he must go to America before they were married.

"Do you mean, James, you will have to go at once?"

"Yes," he said, "at once. But I shall come back in time to be married in August. It will only mean delaying our marriage a month."

They walked on a little way talking; every step he took James felt that he was a step nearer the Bowery slum. And when they came to the gate Bryden said:—

"I must hasten or I shall miss the train."

"But," she said, "you are not going now—you are not going to-day?"

"Yes, this morning. It is seven miles. I shall have to hurry not to miss the train."

And then she asked him if he would ever come back.

"Yes," he said, "I am coming back."

"If you are coming back, James, why not let me go with you?"

"You could not walk fast enough. We should miss the train."

"One moment, James. Don't make me suffer; tell me the truth. You are not coming back. Your clothes—where shall I send them?"

He hurried away, hoping he would come back. He tried to think that he liked the country he was leaving, that it would be better to have a farmhouse and live there with Margaret Dirken than to serve drinks behind a counter in the Bowery. He did not think he was telling her a lie when he said he was coming back. Her offer to forward his clothes touched his heart, and at the end of the road he stood and asked himself if he should go back to her. He would miss the train if he waited another minute, and he ran on. And he would have missed the train if he had not met a car. Once he was on the car he felt himself safe—the country was already behind him. The train and the boat at Cork were mere formulae; he was already in America.

The moment he landed he felt the thrill of home that he had not found in his native village, and he wondered how it was that the smell of the bar seemed more natural than the smell of the fields, and the roar of crowds more welcome than the silence of the lake's edge. However, he offered up a thanksgiving for his escape, and entered into negotiations for the purchase of the bar-room.

★ ★ ★

He took a wife, she bore him sons and daughters, the bar-room prospered, property came and went; he grew old, his wife died, he retired from business, and reached the age when a man begins to feel there are not many years in front of him, and that all he has had to do in life has been done. His children married, lonesomeness began to creep about him; in the evening, when he looked into the fire-light, a vague, tender reverie floated up, and Margaret's soft eyes and name vivified the dusk. His wife and children passed out of mind, and it seemed to him that a memory was the only real

thing he possessed, and the desire to see Margaret again grew
intense. But she was an old woman, she had married, maybe she
was dead. Well, he would like to be buried in the village where he
was born.

There is an unchanging, silent life within every man that none
knows but himself, and his unchanging, silent life was his memory
of Margaret Dirken. The bar-room was forgotten and all that concerned it, and the things he saw most clearly were the green hill-
side, and the bog lake and the rushes about it, and the greater lake
in the distance, and behind it the blue lines of wandering hills.

THE OPEN WINDOW

H. H. Munro (Saki)

"MY AUNT WILL be down presently, Mr. Nuttel," said a very self-possessed young lady of fifteen; "in the meantime you must try and put up with me."

Framton Nuttel endeavoured to say the correct something which should duly flatter the niece of the moment without unduly discounting the aunt that was to come. Privately he doubted more than ever whether these formal visits on a succession of total strangers would do very much towards helping the nerve cure which he was supposed to be undergoing.

"I know how it will be," his sister had said when he was preparing to migrate to this rural retreat; "you will bury yourself down there and not speak to a living soul, and your nerves will be worse than ever from moping. I shall just give you letters of introduction to all the people I know there. Some of them, as far as I can remember, were quite nice."

Framton wondered whether Mrs. Sappleton, the lady to whom he was presenting one of the letters of introduction came into the "nice" division.

"Do you know many of the people round here?" asked the niece, when she judged that they had had sufficient silent communion.

"Hardly a soul," said Framton. "My sister was staying here, at the rectory, you know, some four years ago, and she gave me letters of introduction to some of the people here." He made the last statement in a tone of distinct regret.

"Then you know practically nothing about my aunt?" pursued the self-possessed young lady.

"Only her name and address," admitted the caller. He was wondering whether Mrs. Sappleton was in the married or widowed state. An undefinable something about the room seemed to suggest masculine habitation.

"Her great tragedy happened just three years ago," said the child; "that would be since your sister's time."

"Her tragedy?" asked Framton; somehow in this restful country spot tragedies seemed out of place.

"You may wonder why we keep that window wide open on an October afternoon," said the niece, indicating a large French window that opened on to a lawn.

"It is quite warm for the time of the year," said Framton; "but has that window got anything to do with the tragedy?"

"Out through that window, three years ago to a day, her husband and her two young brothers went off for their day's shooting. They never came back. In crossing the moor to their favourite snipe-shooting ground they were all three engulfed in a treacherous piece of bog. It had been that dreadful wet summer, you know, and places that were safe in other years gave way suddenly without warning. Their bodies were never recovered. That was the dreadful part of it."

Here the child's voice lost its self-possessed note and became falteringly human.

"Poor aunt always thinks that they will come back someday, they and the little brown spaniel that was lost with them, and walk in at that window just as they used to do. That is why the window is kept open every evening till it is quite dusk. Poor dear aunt, she has often told me how they went out, her husband with his white waterproof coat over his arm, and Ronnie, her youngest brother, singing 'Bertie, why do you bound?' as he always did to tease her, because she said it got on her nerves. Do you know, sometimes on still, quiet evenings like this, I almost get a creepy feeling that they will all walk in through that window—"

She broke off with a little shudder. It was a relief to Framton when the aunt bustled into the room with a whirl of apologies for being late in making her appearance.

"I hope Vera has been amusing you?" she said.

"She has been very interesting," said Framton.

"I hope you don't mind the open window," said Mrs. Sappleton briskly; "my husband and brothers will be home directly from shooting, and they always come in this way. They've been out for snipe in the marshes today, so they'll make a fine mess over my poor carpets. So like you menfolk, isn't it?"

She rattled on cheerfully about the shooting and the scarcity of birds, and the prospects for duck in the winter.

To Framton it was all purely horrible. He made a desperate but only partially successful effort to turn the talk on to a less ghastly topic, he was conscious that his hostess was giving him only a fragment of her attention, and her eyes were constantly straying past him to the open window and the lawn beyond. It was certainly an unfortunate coincidence that he should have paid his visit on this tragic anniversary.

"The doctors agree in ordering me complete rest, an absence of mental excitement, and avoidance of anything in the nature of violent physical exercise," announced Framton, who laboured under the tolerably widespread delusion that total strangers and chance acquaintances are hungry for the least detail of one's ailments and infirmities, their cause and cure. "On the matter of diet they are not so much in agreement," he continued.

"No?" said Mrs. Sappleton, in a voice which only replaced a yawn at the last moment. Then she suddenly brightened into alert attention—but not to what Framton was saying.

"Here they are at last!" she cried. "Just in time for tea, and don't they look as if they were muddy up to the eyes!"

Framton shivered slightly and turned towards the niece with a look intended to convey sympathetic comprehension. The child was staring out through the open window with a dazed horror in her eyes. In a chill shock of nameless fear Framton swung round in his seat and looked in the same direction.

In the deepening twilight three figures were walking across the lawn towards the window, they all carried guns under their arms, and one of them was additionally burdened with a white coat hung over his shoulders. A tired brown spaniel kept close at their heels. Noiselessly they neared the house, and then a hoarse young voice chanted out of the dusk: "I said, Bertie, why do you bound?"

Framton grabbed wildly at his stick and hat; the hall door, the gravel drive, and the front gate were dimly noted stages in his headlong retreat. A cyclist coming along the road had to run into the hedge to avoid imminent collision.

"Here we are, my dear," said the bearer of the white mackintosh, coming in through the window, "fairly muddy, but most of it's dry. Who was that who bolted out as we came up?"

"A most extraordinary man, a Mr. Nuttel," said Mrs. Sappleton; "could only talk about his illnesses, and dashed off without a word of goodby or apology when you arrived. One would think he had seen a ghost."

"I expect it was the spaniel," said the niece calmly; "he told me he had a horror of dogs. He was once hunted into a cemetery somewhere on the banks of the Ganges by a pack of pariah dogs, and had to spend the night in a newly dug grave with the creatures snarling and grinning and foaming just above him. Enough to make anyone lose their nerve."

Romance at short notice was her speciality.

A WAGNER MATINÉE

Willa Cather

I RECEIVED ONE morning a letter, written in pale ink on glassy, blue-lined note-paper, and bearing the postmark of a little Nebraska village. This communication, worn and rubbed, looking as if it had been carried for some days in a coat pocket that was none too clean, was from my uncle Howard, and informed me that his wife had been left a small legacy by a bachelor relative, and that it would be necessary for her to go to Boston to attend to the settling of the estate. He requested me to meet her at the station and render her whatever services might be necessary. On examining the date indicated as that of her arrival, I found it to be no later than tomorrow. He had characteristically delayed writing until, had I been away from home for a day, I must have missed my aunt altogether.

The name of my Aunt Georgiana opened before me a gulf of recollection so wide and deep that, as the letter dropped from my hand, I felt suddenly a stranger to all the present conditions of my existence, wholly ill at ease and out of place amid the familiar surroundings of my own study. I became, in short, the gangling farmer-boy my aunt had known, scourged with chilblains and bashfulness, my hands cracked and sore from the corn husking. I sat again before her parlour organ, fumbling the scales with my stiff, red fingers, while she, beside me, made canvas mittens for the huskers.

The next morning, after preparing my landlady for a visitor, I set out for the station. When the train arrived I had some difficulty in finding my aunt. She was the last of the passengers to alight, and it was not until I got her into the carriage that she seemed really to recognize me. She had come all the way in a day coach; her linen duster had become black with soot and her black bonnet grey with dust during the journey. When we arrived at my boarding-house the landlady put her to bed at once and I did not see her again until the next morning.

Whatever shock Mrs. Springer experienced at my aunt's appearance, she considerately concealed. As for myself, I saw my aunt's battered figure with that feeling of awe and respect with which we behold explorers who have left their ears and fingers north of Franz-Joseph-Land, or their health somewhere along the Upper Congo. My Aunt Georgiana had been a music teacher at the Boston Conservatory, somewhere back in the latter sixties. One summer, while visiting in the little village among the Green Mountains where her ancestors had dwelt for generations, she had kindled the callow fancy of my uncle, Howard Carpenter, then an idle, shiftless boy of twenty-one. When she returned to her duties in Boston, Howard followed her, and the upshot of this infatuation was that she eloped with him, eluding the reproaches of her family and the criticism of her friends by going with him to the Nebraska frontier. Carpenter, who, of course, had no money, took up a homestead in Red Willow County, fifty miles from the railroad. There they had measured off their land themselves, driving across the prairie in a wagon, to the wheel of which they had tied a red cotton handkerchief, and counting its revolutions. They built a dug-out in the red hillside, one of those cave dwellings whose inmates so often reverted to primitive conditions. Their water they got from the lagoons where the buffalo drank, and their slender stock of provisions was always at the mercy of bands of roving Indians. For thirty years my aunt had not been farther than fifty miles from the homestead.

I owed to this woman most of the good that ever came my way in my boyhood, and had a reverential affection for her. During the years when I was riding herd for my uncle, my aunt, after cooking the three meals—the first of which was ready at six o'clock in the morning—and putting the six children to bed, would often stand until midnight at her ironing-board, with me at the kitchen table beside her, hearing me recite Latin declensions and conjugations, gently shaking me when my drowsy head sank down over a page of irregular verbs. It was to her, at her ironing or mending, that I read my first Shakspere, and her old text-book on mythology was the first that ever came into my empty hands. She taught me my scales and exercises on the little parlour organ which her husband had bought her after fifteen years during which she had not so much as seen a musical instrument. She would sit beside me by the hour, darning and counting, while I struggled with the "Joyous Farmer." She seldom talked to me about music, and I understood why. Once when I had been doggedly beating out some easy passages from an old score of *Euryanthe* I had found among her music books, she came up to me and, putting her hands over my eyes, gently drew my head back upon her shoulder, saying tremendously, "Don't love it so well, Clark, or it may be taken from you."

When my aunt appeared on the morning after her arrival in Boston, she was still in a semi-somnambulant state. She seemed not to realize that she was in the city where she had spent her youth, the place longed for hungrily half a lifetime. She had been so wretchedly train-sick throughout the journey that she had no recollection of anything but her discomfort, and, to all intents and purposes, there were but a few hours of nightmare between the farm in Red Willow County and my study on Newbury Street. I had planned a little pleasure for her that afternoon, to repay her for some of the glorious moments she had given me when we used to milk together in the straw-thatched cowshed and she, because I was more than usually tired, or because her husband had spoken sharply to me, would tell me of the splendid performance of the *Huguenots* she had seen in Paris, in her youth.

At two o'clock the Symphony Orchestra was to give a Wagner program, and I intended to take my aunt; though, as I conversed with her, I grew doubtful about her enjoyment of it. I suggested our visiting the Conservatory and the Common before lunch, but she seemed altogether too timid to wish to venture out. She questioned me absently about various changes in the city, but she was chiefly concerned that she had forgotten to leave instructions about feeding half-skimmed milk to a certain weakling calf, "old Maggie's calf, you know, Clark," she explained, evidently having forgotten how long I had been away. She was further troubled because she had neglected to tell her daughter about the freshly-opened kit of mackerel in the cellar, which would spoil if it were not used directly.

I asked her whether she had ever heard any of the Wagnerian operas, and found that she had not, though she was perfectly familiar with their respective situations, and had once possessed the piano score of *The Flying Dutchman*. I began to think it would be best to get her back to Red Willow County without waking her, and regretted having suggested the concert.

From the time we entered the concert hall, however, she was a trifle less passive and inert, and for the first time seemed to perceive her surroundings. I had felt some trepidation lest she might become aware of her queer, country clothes, or might experience some painful embarrassment at stepping suddenly into the world to which she had been dead for a quarter of a century. But, again, I found how superficially I had judged her. She sat looking about her with eyes as impersonal, almost as stony, as those with which the granite Rameses in a museum watches the froth and fret that ebbs and flows about his pedestal. I have seen this same aloofness in old miners who drift into the Brown hotel at Denver, their pockets full of bullion, their linen soiled, their haggard faces unshaven; standing in the thronged corridors as solitary as though they were still in a frozen camp on the Yukon.

The matinée audience was made up chiefly of women. One lost the contour of faces and figures, indeed any effect of line whatever, and there was only the colour of bodices past counting, the shimmer of fabrics soft and firm, silky and sheer; red, mauve, pink, blue, lilac, purple, écru, rose, yellow, cream, and white, all the colours that an impressionist finds in a sunlit landscape, with here and there the dead shadow of a frock coat. My Aunt Georgiana regarded them as though they had been so many daubs of tube paint on a palette.

When the musicians came out and took their places, she gave a little stir of anticipation, and looked with quickening interest down over the rail at that invariable grouping, perhaps the first wholly familiar thing that had greeted her eye since she had left old Maggie and her weakling calf. I could feel how all those details sank into her soul, for I had not forgotten how they had sunk into mine when I came fresh from ploughing forever and forever between green aisles of corn, where, as in a treadmill, one might walk from daybreak to dusk without perceiving a shadow of change. The clean profiles of the musicians, the gloss of their linen, the dull black of their coats, the beloved shapes of the instruments, the patches of yellow light on the smooth, varnished bellies of the 'cellos and the bass viols in the rear, the restless, wind-tossed forest of fiddle necks and bows—I recalled how, in the first orchestra I ever heard, those long bow-strokes seemed to draw the heart out of me, as a conjurer's stick reels out yards of paper ribbon from a hat.

The first number was the *Tannhauser* overture. When the horns drew out the first strain of the Pilgrim's chorus, Aunt Georgiana clutched my coat sleeve. Then it was I first realized that for her this broke a silence of thirty years. With the battle between the two motives, with the frenzy of the Venusberg theme and its ripping of strings, there came to me an overwhelming sense of the waste and wear we are so powerless to combat; and I saw again the tall, naked house on the prairie, black and grim as a wooden fortress; the black pond where I had learned to swim, its margin pitted with sun-dried cattle tracks; the rain gullied clay banks about the naked house, the four dwarf ash seedlings where the dish-cloths were always hung to dry before the kitchen door. The world there was the flat world of the ancients; to the east, a cornfield that stretched to daybreak; to the west, a corral that reached to sunset; between, the conquests of peace, dearer-bought than those of war.

The overture closed, my aunt released my coat sleeve, but she said nothing. She sat staring dully at the orchestra. What, I wondered, did she get from it? She had been a good pianist in her day, I knew, and her musical education had been broader than that of most music teachers of a quarter of a century ago. She had often told me of Mozart's operas and Meyerbeer's, and I could remember hearing her sing, years ago, certain melodies of Verdi. When I had fallen ill with a fever in her house she used to sit by my cot in the evening—when the cool, night wind blew in through the faded mosquito netting tacked over the window and I lay watching a certain bright star that burned red above the cornfield—and sing "Home to our mountains, O, let us return!" in a way fit to break the heart of a Vermont boy near dead of homesickness already.

I watched her closely through the prelude to *Tristan and Isolde*, trying vainly to conjecture what that seething turmoil of strings and winds might mean to her, but she sat mutely staring at the violin bows that drove obliquely downward, like the pelting streaks of rain in a summer shower. Had this music any message for her? Had she enough left to at all comprehend this power which had kindled the world since she had left it? I was in a fever of curiosity, but Aunt Georgiana sat silent upon her peak in Darien. She preserved this utter immobility throughout the number from *The Flying Dutchman,* though her fingers worked mechanically upon her black dress, as if, of themselves, they were recalling the piano score they had once played. Poor hands! They had been stretched and twisted into mere tentacles to hold and lift and knead with;—on one of them a thin, worn band that had once been a wedding ring. As I pressed and gently quieted one of those groping hands, I remembered with quivering eyelids their services for me in other days.

Soon after the tenor began the "Prize Song," I heard a quick drawn breath and turned to my aunt. Her eyes were closed, but the tears were glistening on her cheeks, and I think, in a moment more, they were in my eyes as well. It never really died, then—the soul which can suffer so excruciatingly and so interminably; it withers to the outward eye only; like that strange moss which can lie on a dusty shelf half a century and yet, if placed in water, grows green again. She wept so throughout the development and elaboration of the melody.

During the intermission before the second half, I questioned my aunt and found that the "Prize Song" was not new to her. Some years before there had drifted to the farm in Red Willow County a young German, a tramp cow-puncher, who had sung in the chorus at Bayreuth when he was a boy, along with the other peasant boys and girls. Of a Sunday morning he used to sit on his gingham-sheeted bed in the hands' bedroom which opened off the kitchen, cleaning the leather of his boots and saddle, singing the "Prize Song," while my aunt went about her work in the kitchen. She had hovered over him until she had prevailed upon him to join the country church, though his sole fitness for this step, in so far as I could gather, lay in his boyish face and his possession of this divine melody. Shortly afterward, he had gone to town on the Fourth of July, been drunk for several days, lost his money at a faro table, ridden a saddled Texas steer on a bet, and disappeared with a fractured collar-bone. All this my aunt told me huskily, wanderingly, as though she were talking in the weak lapses of illness.

"Well, we have come to better things than the old *Trovatore* at any rate, Aunt Georgie?" I queried, with a well meant effort at jocularity.

Her lip quivered and she hastily put her handkerchief up to her mouth. From behind it she murmured, "And you have been hearing this ever since you left me, Clark?" Her question was the gentlest and saddest of reproaches.

The second half of the program consisted of four numbers from the *Ring,* and closed with Siegfried's funeral march. My aunt wept quietly, but almost continuously, as a shallow vessel overflows in a rainstorm. From time to time her dim eyes looked up at the lights, burning softly under their dull glass globes.

The deluge of sound poured on and on; I never knew what she found in the shining current of it; I never knew how far it bore her, or past what happy islands. From the trembling of her face I could well believe that before the last number she had been carried out where the myriad graves are, into the grey, nameless burying grounds of the sea; or into some world of death vaster yet, where, from the beginning of the world, hope has lain down with hope and dream with dream and, renouncing, slept.

The concert was over; the people filed out of the hall chattering and laughing, glad to relax and find the living level again, but my kinswoman made no effort to rise. The harpist slipped the green felt cover over his instrument; the flute-players shook the water from their mouth-pieces; the men of the orchestra went out one by one, leaving the stage to the chairs and music stands, empty as a winter cornfield.

I spoke to my aunt. She burst into tears and sobbed pleadingly. "I don't want to go, Clark, I don't want to go!"

I understood. For her, just outside the concert hall, lay the black pond with the cattle-tracked bluffs; the tall, unpainted house, with weather-curled boards, naked as a tower; the crook-backed ash seedlings where the dish-cloths hung to dry; the gaunt, moulting turkeys picking up refuse about the kitchen door.

THE SET OF POE

George Ade

MR. WATERBY REMARKED to his wife: "I'm still tempted by that set of Poe. I saw it in the window today, marked down to fifteen dollars."

"Yes?" said Mrs. Waterby, with a sudden gasp of emotion, it seemed to him.

"Yes—I believe I'll have to get it."

"I wouldn't if I were you, Alfred," she said. "You have so many books now."

"I know I have, my dear, but I haven't any set of Poe, and that's what I've been wanting for a long time. This edition I was telling you about is beautifully gotten up."

"Oh, I wouldn't buy it, Alfred," she repeated, and there was a note of pleading earnestness in her voice. "It's so much money to spend for a few books."

"Well, I know, but—" and then he paused, for the lack of words to express his mortified surprise.

Mr. Waterby had tried to be an indulgent husband. He took a selfish pleasure in giving, and found it more blessed than receiving. Every salary day he turned over to Mrs. Waterby a fixed sum for household expenses. He added to this an allowance for her spending money. He set aside a small amount for his personal expenses and deposited the remainder in the bank.

He flattered himself that he approximated the model husband.

Mr. Waterby had no costly habits and no prevailing appetite for anything expensive. Like every other man, he had one or two hobbies, and one of his particular hobbies was Edgar Allan Poe. He believed that Poe, of all American writers, was the one unmistakable "genius."

The word "genius" has been bandied around the country until it has come to be applied to a longhaired man out of work or a stout lady who writes poetry for the rural press. In the case of Poe, Mr. Waterby maintained that "genius" meant one who was not governed by the common mental processes, but "who spoke from inspiration, his mind involuntarily taking superhuman flight into the realm of pure imagination," or something of that sort. At any rate, Mr. Waterby liked Poe and he wanted a set of Poe. He allowed himself not more than one luxury a year, and he determined that this year the luxury should be a set of Poe.

Therefore, imagine the hurt to his feelings when his wife objected to his expending fifteen dollars for that which he coveted above anything else in the world.

As he went to his work that day he reflected on Mrs. Waterby's conduct. Did she not have her allowance of spending money? Did he ever find fault with her extravagance? Was he an unreasonable husband in asking that he be allowed to spend this small sum for that which would give him many hours of pleasure, and which would belong to Mrs. Waterby as much as to him?

He told himself that many a husband would have bought the books without consulting his wife. But he (Waterby) had deferred to his wife in all matters touching family finances, and he said to himself, with a tincture of bitterness in his thoughts, that probably he had put himself into the attitude of a mere dependent.

For had she not forbidden him to buy a few books for himself? Well, no, she had not forbidden him, but it amounted to the same thing. She had declared that she was firmly opposed to the purchase of Poe.

Mr. Waterby wondered if it were possible that he was just beginning to know his wife. Was she a selfish woman at heart? Was she complacent and good-natured and kind only while she was having her own way? Wouldn't she prove to be an entirely different sort of woman if he should do as many husbands do—spend his income on clubs and cigars and private amusement, and gave her the pickings of small change?

Nothing in Mr. Waterby's whole experience as a married man had so wrenched his sensibilities and disturbed his faith as Mrs. Waterby's objection to the purchase of the set of Poe. There was but one way to account for it. She wanted all the money for herself, or else she wanted him to put it into the bank so that she could come into it after he—but this was too monstrous.

However, Mrs. Waterby's conduct helped to give strength to Mr. Waterby's meanest suspicions.

Two or three days after the first conversation she asked: "You didn't buy that set of Poe, did you, Alfred?"

. "No, I didn't buy it," he answered, as coldly and with as much hauteur as possible.

He hoped to hear her say: "Well, why don't you go and get it? I'm sure that you want it, and I'd like to see you buy something for yourself once in a while."

That would have shown the spirit of a loving and unselfish wife.

But she merely said, "That's right; don't buy it," and he was utterly unhappy, for he realized that he had married a woman who did not love him and who simply desired to use him as a pack-horse for all household burdens.

As soon as Mr. Waterby had learned the horrible truth about his wife he began to recall little episodes dating back years, and now he pieced them together to convince himself that he was a deeply wronged person.

Small at the time and almost unnoticed, they now accumulated to prove that Mrs. Waterby had no real anxiety for her husband's happiness. Also, Mr. Waterby began to observe her more closely, and he believed that he found new evidences of her unworthiness. For one thing, while he was in gloom over his discovery and harassed by doubts of what the future might reveal to him, she was content and even-tempered.

The holiday season approached and Mr. Waterby made a resolution. He decided that if she would not permit him to spend a little money on himself he would not buy the customary Christmas present for her.

"Selfishness is a game at which two can play," he said.

Furthermore, he determined that if she asked him for any extra money for Christmas he would say: "I'm sorry, my dear, but I can't spare any. I am so hard up that I can't even afford to buy a few books I've been wanting a long time. Don't you remember that you told me that I couldn't afford to buy that set of Poe?"

Could anything be more biting as to sarcasm or more crushing as to logic?

He rehearsed this speech and had it all ready for her, and he pictured to himself her humiliation and surprise at discovering that he had some spirit after all and a considerable say-so whenever money was involved.

Unfortunately for his plan, she did not ask for any extra spending money, and so he had to rely on the other mode of punishment. He would withhold the expected Christmas present. In order that she might fully understand his purpose, he would give presents to both of the children.

It was a harsh measure, he admitted, but perhaps it would teach her to have some consideration for the wishes of others.

It must be said that Mr. Waterby was not wholly proud of his revenge when he arose on Christmas morning. He felt that he had accomplished his purpose, and he told himself that his motives had been good and pure, but still he was not satisfied with himself.

He went to the dining-room, and there on the table in front of his plate was a long paper box, containing ten books, each marked "Poe." It was the edition he had coveted.

"What's this?" he asked, winking slowly, for his mind could not grasp in one moment the fact of his awful shame.

"I should think you ought to know, Alfred," said Mrs. Waterby, flushed, and giggling like a schoolgirl.

"Oh, it was you."

"My goodness, you've had me *so* frightened! That first day, when you spoke of buying them and I told you not to, I was just sure that you suspected something. I bought them a week before that."

"Yes—yes," said Mr. Waterby, feeling the saltwater in his eyes. At that moment he had the soul of a wretch being whipped at the stake.

"I was determined not to ask you for any money to pay for your own presents," Mrs. Waterby continued. "Do you know I had to save for you and the children out of my regular allowance. Why, last week I nearly starved you, and you never noticed it at all. I was afraid you would."

"No, I—didn't notice it," said Mr. Waterby, brokenly, for he was confused and giddy.

This self-sacrificing angel—and he had bought no Christmas present for her!

It was a fearful situation, and he lied his way out of it.

"How did you like *your* present?" he asked.

"Why, I haven't seen it yet," she said, looking across at him in surprise.

"You haven't? I told them to send it up yesterday."

The children were shouting and laughing over their gifts in the next room, and he felt it his duty to lie for their sake.

"Well, don't tell me what it is," interrupted Mrs. Waterby. "Wait until it comes."

"I'll go after it."

He did go after it, although he had to drag a jeweller away from his home on Christmas-day and have him open his great safe. The ring which he selected was beyond his means, it is true, but when a man has to buy back his self-respect, the price is never too high.

THE FURNISHED ROOM

O. Henry

RESTLESS, SHIFTING, FUGACIOUS as time itself is a certain vast bulk of the population of the red brick district of the lower West Side. Homeless, they have a hundred homes. They flit from furnished room to furnished room, transients forever—transients in abode, transients in heart and mind. They sing "Home, Sweet Home" in ragtime; they carry their *lares et penates* in a bandbox; their vine is entwined about a picture hat; a rubber plant is their fig tree.

Hence the houses of this district, having had a thousand dwellers, should have a thousand tales to tell, mostly dull ones, no doubt; but it would be strange if there could not be found a ghost or two in the wake of all these vagrant guests.

One evening after dark a young man prowled among these crumbling red mansions, ringing their bells. At the twelfth he rested his lean hand-baggage upon the step and wiped the dust from his hatband and forehead. The bell sounded faint and far away in some remote, hollow depths.

To the door of this, the twelfth house whose bell he had rung, came a housekeeper who made him think of an unwholesome, surfeited worm that had eaten its nut to a hollow shell and now sought to fill the vacancy with edible lodgers.

He asked if there was a room to let.

"Come in," said the housekeeper. Her voice came from her throat; her throat seemed lined with fur. "I have the third-floor back, vacant since a week back. Should you wish to look at it?"

The young man followed her up the stairs. A faint light from no particular source mitigated the shadows of the halls. They trod noiselessly upon a stair carpet that its own loom would have

forsworn. It seemed to have become vegetable; to have degener-
ated in that rank, sunless air to lush lichen or spreading moss that
grew in patches to the stair-case and was viscid under the foot like
organic matter. At each turn of the stairs were vacant niches in the
wall. Perhaps plants had once been set within them. If so they had
died in that foul and tainted air. It may be that statues of the saints
had stood there, but it was not difficult to conceive that imps and
devils had dragged them forth in the darkness and down to the
unholy depths of some furnished pit below.

"This is the room," said the housekeeper, from her furry
throat. "It's a nice room. It ain't often vacant. I had some most
elegant people in it last summer—no trouble at all, and paid in
advance to the minute. The water's at the end of the hall. Sprowls
and Mooney kept it three months. They done a vaudeville sketch.
Miss B'retta Sprowls—you may have heard of her—Oh, that was
just the stage names—right there over the dresser is where the
marriage certificate hung, framed. The gas is here, and you see
there is plenty of closet room. It's a room everybody likes. It
never stays idle long."

"Do you have many theatrical people rooming here?" asked the
young man.

"They comes and goes. A good proportion of my lodgers is connected with the theatres. Yes, sir, this is the theatrical district. Actor
people never stays long anywhere. I get my share. Yes, they comes
and they goes."

He engaged the room, paying for a week in advance. He was
tired, he said, and would take possession at once. He counted out
the money. The room had been made ready, she said, even to
towels and water. As the housekeeper moved away he put, for
the thousandth time, the question that he carried at the end of
his tongue.

"A young girl—Miss Vashner—Miss Eloise Vashner—do you
remember such a one among your lodgers? She would be singing
on the stage, most likely. A fair girl, of medium height and slender,
with reddish, gold hair and a dark mole near her left eyebrow."

"No, I don't remember the name. Them stage people has names
they change as often as their rooms. They comes and they goes.
No, I don't call that one to mind."

No. Always no. Five months of ceaseless interrogation and the
inevitable negative. So much time spent by day in questioning

managers, agents, schools and choruses; by night among the audiences of theatres from all-star casts down to music halls so low that he dreaded to find what he most hoped for. He who had loved her best had tried to find her. He was sure that since her disappearance from home this great, water-girt city held her somewhere, but it was like a monstrous quicksand, shifting its particles constantly, with no foundation, its upper granules of to-day buried tomorrow in ooze and slime.

The furnished room received its latest guest with a first glow of pseudo-hospitality, a hectic, haggard, perfunctory welcome like the specious smile of a demirep. The sophistical comfort came in reflected gleams from the decayed furniture, the ragged brocade upholstery of a couch and two chairs, a foot-wide cheap pier-glass between the two windows, from one or two gilt picture frames and a brass bedstead in a corner.

The guest reclined, inert, upon a chair, while the room, confused in speech as though it were an apartment in Babel, tried to discourse to him of its divers tenantry.

A polychromatic rug like some brilliant-flowered, rectangular, tropical islet lay surrounded by a billowy sea of soiled matting. Upon the gay-papered wall were those pictures that pursue the homeless one from house to house—The Huguenot Lovers, The First Quarrel, The Wedding Breakfast, Psyche at the Fountain. The mantel's chastely severe outline was ingloriously veiled behind some pert drapery drawn rakishly askew like the sashes of the Amazonian ballet. Upon it was some desolate flotsam cast aside by the room's marooned when a lucky sail had borne them to a fresh port—a trifling vase or two, pictures of actresses, a medicine bottle, some stray cards out of a deck.

One by one, as the characters of a cryptograph became explicit, the little signs left by the furnished room's procession of guests developed a significance. The threadbare space in the rug in front of the dresser told that lovely women had marched in the throng. The tiny fingerprints on the wall spoke of little prisoners trying to feel their way to sun and air. A splattered stain, raying like the shadow of a bursting bomb, witnessed where a hurled glass or bottle had splintered with its contents against the wall. Across the pier-glass had been scrawled with a diamond in staggering letters the name "Marie." It seemed that the succession of dwellers in the furnished room had turned in fury—perhaps tempted beyond forbearance by its garish coldness—and wreaked upon it their passions. The furniture was chipped and bruised; the couch, distorted by bursting springs, seemed a horrible monster that had been slain during the stress of some grotesque convulsion. Some more potent upheaval had cloven a great slice from the marble mantel. Each plank in the floor owned its particular cant and shriek as from a separate and individual agony. It seemed incredible that all this malice and injury had been wrought upon the room by those who had called it for a time their home; and yet it may have been the cheated home instinct surviving blindly, the resentful rage at false household gods that had kindled their wrath. A hut that is our own we can sweep and adorn and cherish.

The young tenant in the chair allowed these thoughts to file, soft-shod, through his mind, while there drifted into the room furnished sounds and furnished scents. He heard in one room a tittering and incontinent, slack laughter; in others the monologue of a scold, the rattling of dice, a lullaby, and one crying dully; above him a banjo tinkled with spirit. Doors banged somewhere; the elevated trains roared intermittently; a cat yowled miserably upon a back fence. And he breathed the breath of the house—a dank savor rather than a smell—a cold, musty effluvium as from underground vaults mingled with the reeking exhalations of linoleum and mildewed and rotten woodwork.

Then suddenly, as he rested there, the room was filled with the strong, sweet odor of mignonette. It came as upon a single buffet of wind with such sureness and fragrance and emphasis that it almost seemed a living visitant. And the man cried aloud: "What, dear?" as if he had been called, and sprang up and faced about. The rich odor clung to him and wrapped him around. He reached out his arms for it, all his senses for the time confused and commingled. How could one be peremptorily called by an odor? Surely it must have been a sound. But, was it not the sound that had touched, that had caressed him?

"She has been in this room," he cried, and he sprang to wrest from it a token, for he knew he would recognize the smallest thing that had belonged to her or that she had touched. This enveloping scent of mignonette, the odor that she had loved and made her own—whence came it?

The room had been but carelessly set in order. Scattered upon the flimsy dresser scarf were half a dozen hairpins—those discreet, indistinguishable friends of womankind, feminine of gender, infinite of mood and uncommunicative of tense. These he ignored, conscious of their triumphant lack of identity. Ransacking the drawers of the dresser he came upon a discarded, tiny, ragged handkerchief. He pressed it to his face. It was racy and insolent with heliotrope; he hurled it to the floor. In another drawer he found odd buttons, a theatre programme, a pawnbroker's card, two lost marshmallows, a book on the divination of dreams. In the last was a woman's black satin hair bow, which halted him, poised between ice and fire. But the black satin hair bow also is femininity's demure, impersonal common ornament and tells no tales.

And then he traversed the room like a hound on the scent, skimming the walls, considering the corners of the bulging matting on his hands and knees, rummaging mantel and tables, the curtains and hangings, the drunken cabinet in the corner, for a visible sign, unable to perceive that she was there beside, around, against, within, above him, clinging to him, wooing him, calling him so poignantly through the finer senses that even his grosser ones became cognizant of the call. Once again he answered loudly: "Yes, dear!" and turned, wild-eyed, to gaze on vacancy, for he could not yet discern form and color and love and outstretched arms in the odor of mignonette. Oh, God! whence that odor, and since when have odors had a voice to call? Thus he groped.

He burrowed in crevices and corners, and found corks and cigarettes. These he passed in passive contempt. But once he found in a fold of the matting a half-smoked cigar, and this he ground beneath his heel with a green and trenchant oath. He sifted the room from end to end. He found dreary and ignoble small records of many a peripatetic tenant; but of her whom he sought, and who may have lodged there, and whose spirit seemed to hover there, he found no trace.

And then he thought of the housekeeper.

He ran from the haunted room downstairs and to a door that showed a crack of light. She came out to his knock. He smothered his excitement as best he could.

"Will you tell me, madam," he besought her, "who occupied the room I have before I came?"

"Yes, sir. I can tell you again. 'Twas Sprowls and Mooney, as I said. Miss B'retta Sprowls it was in the theatres, but Missis Mooney she was. My house is well known for respectability. The marriage certificate hung, framed, on a nail over——"

"What kind of a lady was Miss Sprowls—in looks, I mean?"

"Why, black-haired, sir, short, and stout, with a comical face. They left a week ago Tuesday."

"And before they occupied it?"

"Why, there was a single gentleman connected with the draying business. He left owing me a week. Before him was Missis Crowder and her two children, that stayed four months; and back of them was old Mr. Doyle, whose sons paid for him. He kept the room six months. That goes back a year, sir, and further I do not remember."

He thanked her and crept back to his room. The room was dead. The essence that had vivified it was gone. The perfume of mignon-ette had departed. In its place was the old, stale odor of mouldy house furniture, of atmosphere in storage.

The ebbing of his hope drained his faith. He sat staring at the yellow, singing gaslight. Soon he walked to the bed and began to tear the sheets into strips. With the blade of his knife he drove them tightly into every crevice around windows and door. When all was snug and taut he turned out the light, turned the gas full on again and laid himself gratefully upon the bed.

It was Mrs. McCool's night to go with the can for beer. So she fetched it and sat with Mrs. Purdy in one of those subterranean retreats where housekeepers forgather and the worm dieth seldom.

"I rented out my third-floor-back this evening," said Mrs. Purdy, across a fine circle of foam. "A young man took it. He went up to bed two hours ago."

"Now, did ye, Mrs. Purdy, ma'am?" said Mrs. McCool, with intense admiration. "You do be a wonder for rentin' rooms of that kind. And did ye tell him, then?" she concluded in a husky whisper laden with mystery.

"Rooms," said Mrs. Purdy, in her furriest tones, "are furnished for to rent. I did not tell him, Mrs. McCool."

"'Tis right ye are, ma'am; 'tis by renting rooms we kape alive. Ye have the rale sense for business, ma'am. There be many people will rayjict the rentin' of a room if they be tould a suicide has been after dyin' in the bed of it."

"As you say, we has our living to be making," remarked Mrs. Purdy.

"Yis, ma'am; 'tis true. 'Tis just one wake ago this day I helped ye lay out the third-floor-back. A pretty slip of a colleen she was to be killin' herself wid the gas—a swate little face she had, Mrs. Purdy, ma'am."

"She'd a-been called handsome, as you say," said Mrs. Purdy, assenting but critical, "but for that mole she had a-growin' by her left eyebrow. Do fill up your glass again, Mrs. McCool."

THE GIFT OF THE MAGI

O. Henry

ONE DOLLAR AND eighty-seven cents. That was all. And sixty cents of it was in pennies. Pennies saved one and two at a time by bulldozing the grocer and the vegetable man and the butcher until one's cheeks burned with the silent imputation of parsimony that such close dealing implied. Three times Della counted it. One dollar and eighty-seven cents. And the next day would be Christmas.

There was clearly nothing to do but flop down on the shabby little couch and howl. So Della did it. Which instigates the moral reflection that life is made up of sobs, sniffles, and smiles, with sniffles predominating.

While the mistress of the home is gradually subsiding from the first stage to the second, take a look at the home. A furnished flat at $8 per week. It did not exactly beggar description, but it certainly had that word on the lookout for the mendicancy squad.

In the vestibule below was a letter-box into which no letter would go, and an electric button from which no mortal finger could coax a ring. Also appertaining thereunto was a card bearing the name "Mr. James Dillingham Young."

The "Dillingham" had been flung to the breeze during a former period of prosperity when its possessor was being paid $30 per week. Now, when the income was shrunk to $20, the letters of "Dillingham" looked blurred, as though they were thinking seriously of contracting to a modest and unassuming D. But whenever Mr. James Dillingham Young came home and reached his flat above he was called "Jim" and greatly hugged by Mrs. James Dillingham Young, already introduced to you as Della. Which is all very good.

Della finished her cry and attended to her cheeks with the powder rag. She stood by the window and looked out dully at a gray cat walking a gray fence in a gray backyard. Tomorrow would be Christmas Day, and she had only $1.87 with which to buy Jim a present. She had been saving every penny she could for months, with this result. Twenty dollars a week doesn't go far. Expenses had been greater than she had calculated. They always are. Only $1.87 to buy a present for Jim. Her Jim. Many a happy hour she had spent planning for something nice for him. Something fine and rare and sterling—something just a little bit near to being worthy of the honor of being owned by Jim.

There was a pier-glass between the windows of the room. Perhaps you have seen a pier-glass in an $8 flat. A very thin and very agile person may, by observing his reflection in a rapid sequence of longitudinal strips, obtain a fairly accurate conception of his looks. Della, being slender, had mastered the art.

Suddenly she whirled from the window and stood before the glass. Her eyes were shining brilliantly, but her face had lost its color within twenty seconds. Rapidly she pulled down her hair and let it fall to its full length.

Now, there were two possessions of the James Dillingham Youngs in which they both took a mighty pride. One was Jim's gold watch that had been his father's and his grandfather's. The other was Della's hair. Had the Queen of Sheba lived in the flat across the airshaft, Della would have let her hair hang out the window some day to dry just to depreciate Her Majesty's jewels and gifts. Had King Solomon been the janitor, with all his treasures piled up in the basement, Jim would have pulled out his watch every time he passed, just to see him pluck at his beard from envy.

So now Della's beautiful hair fell about her rippling and shining like a cascade of brown waters. It reached below her knee and made itself almost a garment for her. And then she did it up again nervously and quickly. Once she faltered for a minute and stood still while a tear or two splashed on the worn red carpet.

On went her old brown jacket; on went her old brown hat. With a whirl of skirts and with the brilliant sparkle still in her eyes, she fluttered out the door and down the stairs to the street.

Where she stopped the sign read: "Mme. Sofronie. Hair Goods of All Kinds." One flight up Delia ran, and collected herself, panting. Madame, large, too white, chilly, hardly looked the "Sofronie."

"Will you buy my hair?" asked Della.

"I buy hair," said Madame. "Take yer hat off and let's have a sight at the looks of it."

Down rippled the brown cascade.

"Twenty dollars," said Madame, lifting the mass with a practised hand.

"Give it to me quick," said Della.

Oh, and the next two hours tripped by on rosy wings. Forget the hashed metaphor. She was ransacking the stores for Jim's present.

She found it at last. It surely had been made for Jim and no one else. There was no other like it in any of the stores, and she had turned all of them inside out. It was a platinum fob chain simple and chaste in design, properly proclaiming its value by substance alone and not by meretricious ornamentation—as all good things should do. It was even worthy of The Watch. As soon as she saw it she knew that it must be Jim's. It was like him. Quietness and value—the description applied to both. Twenty-one dollars they took from her for it, and she hurried home with the 87 cents. With that chain on his watch Jim might be properly anxious about the time in any company. Grand as the watch was, he sometimes looked at it on the sly on account of the old leather strap that he used in place of a chain.

When Della reached home her intoxication gave way a little to prudence and reason. She got out her curling irons and lighted the gas and went to work repairing the ravages made by generosity added to love. Which is always a tremendous task, dear friends—a mammoth task.

Within forty minutes her head was covered with tiny, close-lying curls that made her look wonderfully like a truant schoolboy. She looked at her reflection in the mirror long, carefully, and critically.

"If Jim doesn't kill me," she said to herself, "before he takes a second look at me, he'll say I look like a Coney Island chorus girl. But what could I do—oh! what could I do with a dollar and eighty-seven cents?"

At 7 o'clock the coffee was made and the frying-pan was on the back of the stove hot and ready to cook the chops.

Jim was never late. Della doubled the fob chain in her hand and sat on the corner of the table near the door that he always entered. Then she heard his step on the stair away down on the first flight, and she turned white for just a moment. She had a habit of saying little silent prayers about the simplest everyday things, and now she whispered: "Please God, make him think I am still pretty."

The door opened and Jim stepped in and closed it. He looked thin and very serious. Poor fellow, he was only twenty-two—and to be burdened with a family! He needed a new overcoat and he was without gloves.

Jim stopped inside the door, as immovable as a setter at the scent of quail. His eyes were fixed upon Della, and there was an expression in them that she could not read, and it terrified her. It was not anger, nor surprise, nor disapproval, nor horror, nor any of the sentiments that she had been prepared for. He simply stared at her fixedly with that peculiar expression on his face.

Della wriggled off the table and went for him.

"Jim, darling," she cried, "don't look at me that way. I had my hair cut off and sold it because I couldn't have lived through Christmas without giving you a present. It'll grow out again—you won't mind, will you? I just had to do it. My hair grows awfully fast. Say 'Merry Christmas!' Jim, and let's be happy. You don't know what a nice—what a beautiful, nice gift I've got for you."

"You've cut off your hair?" asked Jim, laboriously, as if he had not arrived at that patent fact yet even after the hardest mental labor.

"Cut it off and sold it," said Della. "Don't you like me just as well, anyhow? I'm me without my hair, ain't I?"

Jim looked about the room curiously.

"You say your hair is gone?" he said, with an air almost of idiocy.

"You needn't look for it," said Della. "It's sold, I tell you—sold and gone, too. It's Christmas Eve, boy. Be good to me, for it went for you. Maybe the hairs of my head were numbered," she went on with a sudden serious sweetness, "but nobody could ever count my love for you. Shall I put the chops on, Jim?"

Out of his trance Jim seemed quickly to wake. He enfolded his Della. For ten seconds let us regard with discreet scrutiny some inconsequential object in the other direction. Eight dollars a week or a million a year—what is the difference? A mathematician or a wit would give you the wrong answer. The magi brought valuable gifts, but that was not among them. This dark assertion will be illuminated later on.

Jim drew a package from his overcoat pocket and threw it upon the table.

"Don't make any mistake, Dell," he said, "about me. I don't think there's anything in the way of a haircut or a shave or a shampoo that could make me like my girl any less. But if you'll unwrap that package you may see why you had me going a while at first."

White fingers and nimble tore at the string and paper. And then an ecstatic scream of joy; and then, alas! a quick feminine change to hysterical tears and wails, necessitating the immediate employment of all the comforting powers of the lord of the flat.

For there lay The Combs—the set of combs, side and back, that Della had worshipped for long in a Broadway window. Beautiful combs, pure tortoise shell, with jewelled rims—just the shade to wear in the beautiful vanished hair. They were expensive combs, she knew, and her heart had simply craved and yearned over them without the least hope of possession. And now, they were hers, but the tresses that should have adorned the coveted adornments were gone.

But she hugged them to her bosom, and at length she was able to look up with dim eyes and a smile and say: "My hair grows so fast, Jim!"

And then Della leaped up like a little singed cat and cried, "Oh, oh!"

Jim had not yet seen his beautiful present. She held it out to him eagerly upon her open palm. The dull precious metal seemed to flash with a reflection of her bright and ardent spirit.

"Isn't it a dandy, Jim? I hunted all over town to find it. You'll have to look at the time a hundred times a day now. Give me your watch. I want to see how it looks on it."

Instead of obeying, Jim tumbled down on the couch and put his hands under the back of his head and smiled.

"Dell," said he, "let's put our Christmas presents away and keep 'em a while. They're too nice to use just at present. I sold the watch to get the money to buy your combs. And now suppose you put the chops on."

The magi, as you know, were wise men—wonderfully wise men—who brought gifts to the Babe in the manger. They invented the art of giving Christmas presents. Being wise, their gifts were no doubt wise ones, possibly bearing the privilege of exchange in case of duplication. And here I have lamely related to you the uneventful chronicle of two foolish children in a flat who most unwisely sacrificed for each other the greatest treasures of their house. But in a last word to the wise of these days let it be said that of all who give gifts these two were the wisest. Of all who give and receive gifts, such as they are wisest. Everywhere they are wisest. They are the magi.

THE LAST LEAF

O. Henry

IN A LITTLE district west of Washington Square the streets have run crazy and broken themselves into small strips called "places." These "places" make strange angles and curves. One street crosses itself a time or two. An artist once discovered a valuable possibility in this street. Suppose a collector with a bill for paints, paper and canvas should, in traversing this route, suddenly meet himself coming back, without a cent having been paid on account!

So, to quaint old Greenwich Village the art people soon came prowling, hunting for north windows and eighteenth-century gables and Dutch attics and low rents. Then they imported some pewter mugs and a chafing dish or two from Sixth Avenue, and became a "colony."

At the top of a squatty, three-story brick Sue and Johnsy had their studio. "Johnsy" was familiar for Joanna. One was from Maine; the other from California. They had met at the *table d'hôte* of an Eighth Street "Delmonico's," and found their tastes in art, chicory salad and bishop sleeves so congenial that the joint studio resulted.

That was in May. In November a cold, unseen stranger, whom the doctors called Pneumonia, stalked about the colony, touching one here and there with his icy fingers. Over on the east side this ravager strode boldly, smiting his victims by scores, but his feet trod slowly through the maze of the narrow and moss-grown "places."

Mr. Pneumonia was not what you would call a chivalric old gentleman. A mite of a little woman with blood thinned by California zephyrs was hardly fair game for the red-fisted, short-breathed old duffer. But Johnsy he smote; and she lay, scarcely moving, on her painted iron bedstead, looking through the small Dutch window-panes at the blank side of the next brick house.

One morning the busy doctor invited Sue into the hallway with a shaggy, gray eyebrow.

"She has one chance in—let us say, ten," he said, as he shook down the mercury in his clinical thermometer. "And that chance is for her to want to live. This way people have of lining-up on the side of the undertaker makes the entire pharmacopœia look silly. Your little lady has made up her mind that she's not going to get well. Has she anything on her mind?"

"She—she wanted to paint the Bay of Naples some day," said Sue.

"Paint?—bosh! Has she anything on her mind worth thinking about twice—a man, for instance?"

"A man?" said Sue, with a jew's-harp twang in her voice. "Is a man worth—but, no, doctor; there is nothing of the kind."

"Well, it is the weakness, then," said the doctor. "I will do all that science, so far as it may filter through my efforts, can accomplish. But whenever my patient begins to count the carriages in her funeral procession I subtract 50 per cent from the curative power of medicines. If you will get her to ask one question about the new winter styles in cloak sleeves I will promise you a one-in-five chance for her, instead of one in ten."

After the doctor had gone Sue went into the workroom and cried a Japanese napkin to a pulp. Then she swaggered into Johnsy's room with her drawing board, whistling ragtime.

Johnsy lay, scarcely making a ripple under the bedclothes, with her face toward the window. Sue stopped whistling, thinking she was asleep.

She arranged her board and began a pen-and-ink drawing to illustrate a magazine story. Young artists must pave their way to Art by drawing pictures for magazine stories that young authors write to pave their way to Literature.

As Sue was sketching a pair of elegant horseshow riding trousers and a monocle on the figure of the hero, an Idaho cowboy, she heard a low sound, several times repeated. She went quickly to the bedside.

Johnsy's eyes were open wide. She was looking out the window and counting—counting backward.

"Twelve," she said, and a little later "eleven"; and then "ten," and "nine"; and then "eight" and "seven," almost together.

Sue looked solicitously out of the window. What was there to count? There was only a bare, dreary yard to be seen, and the blank side of the brick house twenty feet away. An old, old ivy vine, gnarled and decayed at the roots, climbed half way up the brick wall. The cold breath of autumn had stricken its leaves from the vine until its skeleton branches clung, almost bare, to the crumbling bricks.

"What is it, dear?" asked Sue.

"Six," said Johnsy, in almost a whisper. "They're falling faster now. Three days ago there were almost a hundred. It made my head ache to count them. But now it's easy. There goes another one. There are only five left now."

"Five what, dear? Tell your Sudie."

"Leaves. On the ivy vine. When the last one falls I must go, too. I've known that for three days. Didn't the doctor tell you?"

"Oh, I never heard of such nonsense," complained Sue, with magnificent scorn. "What have old ivy leaves to do with your getting well? And you used to love that vine, so, you naughty girl. Don't be a goosey. Why, the doctor told me this morning that your chances for getting well real soon were—let's see exactly what he said—he said the chances were ten to one! Why, that's almost as good a chance as we have in New York when we ride on the street cars or walk past a new building. Try to take some broth now, and let Sudie go back to her drawing, so she can sell the editor man with it, and buy port wine for her sick child, and pork chops for her greedy self."

"You needn't get any more wine," said Johnsy, keeping her eyes fixed out the window. "There goes another. No, I don't want any broth. That leaves just four. I want to see the last one fall before it gets dark. Then I'll go, too."

"Johnsy, dear," said Sue, bending over her, "will you promise me to keep your eyes closed, and not look out the window until I am done working? I must hand those drawings in by to-morrow. I need the light, or I would draw the shade down."

"Couldn't you draw in the other room?" asked Johnsy, coldly.

"I'd rather be here by you," said Sue. "Besides, I don't want you to keep looking at those silly ivy leaves."

"Tell me as soon as you have finished," said Johnsy, closing her eyes, and lying white and still as a fallen statue, "because I want to see the last one fall. I'm tired of waiting. I'm tired of thinking.

I want to turn loose my hold on everything, and go sailing down, down, just like one of those poor, tired leaves."

"Try to sleep," said Sue. "I must call Behrman up to be my model for the old hermit miner. I'll not be gone a minute. Don't try to move 'til I come back."

Old Behrman was a painter who lived on the ground floor beneath them. He was past sixty and had a Michael Angelo's Moses beard curling down from the head of a satyr along the body of an imp. Behrman was a failure in art. Forty years he had wielded the brush without getting near enough to touch the hem of his Mistress's robe. He had been always about to paint a masterpiece, but had never yet begun it. For several years he had painted nothing except now and then a daub in the line of commerce or advertising. He earned a little by serving as a model to those young artists in the colony who could not pay the price of a professional. He drank gin to excess, and still talked of his coming masterpiece. For the rest he was a fierce little old man, who scoffed terribly at softness in any one, and who regarded himself as especial mastiff-in-waiting to protect the two young artists in the studio above.

Sue found Behrman smelling strongly of juniper berries in his dimly lighted den below. In one corner was a blank canvas on an easel that had been waiting there for twenty-five years to receive the first line of the masterpiece. She told him of Johnsy's fancy, and how she feared she would, indeed, light and fragile as a leaf herself, float away, when her slight hold upon the world grew weaker.

Old Behrman, with his red eyes plainly streaming, shouted his contempt and derision for such idiotic imaginings.

"Vass!" he cried. "Is dere people in de world mit der foolishness to die because leafs dey drop off from a confounded vine? I haf not heard of such a thing. No, I vill not bose as a model for your fool hermit-dunderhead. Vy do you allow dot silly pusiness to come in der brain of her? Ach, dot poor leetle Miss Yohnsy."

"She is very ill and weak," said Sue, "and the fever has left her mind morbid and full of strange fancies. Very well, Mr. Behrman, if you do not care to pose for me, you needn't. But I think you are a horrid old—old flibbertigibbet."

"You are just like a woman!" yelled Behrman. "Who said I will not bose? Go on. I come mit you. For half an hour I haf peen trying to say dot I am ready to bose. Gott! dis is not any blace in which one so goot as Miss Yohnsy shall lie sick. Some day I vill baint a masterpiece, and ve shall all go away. Gott! yes."

Johnsy was sleeping when they went upstairs. Sue pulled the shade down to the window-sill, and motioned Behrman into the other room. In there they peered out the window fearfully at the ivy vine. Then they looked at each other for a moment without speaking. A persistent, cold rain was falling, mingled with snow. Behrman, in his old blue shirt, took his seat as the hermit miner on an upturned kettle for a rock.

When Sue awoke from an hour's sleep the next morning she found Johnsy with dull, wide-open eyes staring at the drawn green shade.

"Pull it up; I want to see," she ordered, in a whisper.

Wearily Sue obeyed.

But, lo! after the beating rain and fierce gusts of wind that had endured through the livelong night, there yet stood out against the brick wall one ivy leaf. It was the last on the vine. Still dark green near its stem, but with its serrated edges tinted with the yellow of dissolution and decay, it hung bravely from a branch some twenty feet above the ground.

"It is the last one," said Johnsy. "I thought it would surely fall during the night. I heard the wind. It will fall to-day, and I shall die at the same time."

"Dear, dear!" said Sue, leaning her worn face down to the pillow, "think of me, if you won't think of yourself. What would I do?"

But Johnsy did not answer. The lonesomest thing in all the world is a soul when it is making ready to go on its mysterious, far journey. The fancy seemed to possess her more strongly as one by one the ties that bound her to friendship and to earth were loosed.

The day wore away, and even through the twilight they could see the lone ivy leaf clinging to its stem against the wall. And then, with the coming of the night the north wind was again loosed, while the rain still beat against the windows and pattered down from the low Dutch eaves.

When it was light enough Johnsy, the merciless, commanded that the shade be raised.

The ivy leaf was still there.

Johnsy lay for a long time looking at it. And then she called to Sue, who was stirring her chicken broth over the gas stove.

"I've been a bad girl, Sudie," said Johnsy. "Something has made that last leaf stay there to show me how wicked I was. It is a sin to want to die. You may bring me a little broth now, and some milk with a little port in it, and—no; bring me a hand-mirror first, and then pack some pillows about me, and I will sit up and watch you cook."

An hour later she said:

"Sudie, some day I hope to paint the Bay of Naples."

The doctor came in the afternoon, and Sue had an excuse to go into the hallway as he left.

"Even chances," said the doctor, taking Sue's thin, shaking hand in his. "With good nursing you'll win. And now I must see another case I have downstairs. Behrman, his name is—some kind of an artist, I believe. Pneumonia, too. He is an old, weak man, and the attack is acute. There is no hope for him; but he goes to the hospital to-day to be made more comfortable."

The next day the doctor said to Sue: "She's out of danger. You've won. Nutrition and care now—that's all."

And that afternoon Sue came to the bed where Johnsy lay, contentedly knitting a very blue and very useless woollen shoulder scarf, and put one arm around her, pillows and all.

"I have something to tell you, white mouse," she said. "Mr. Behrman died of pneumonia to-day in the hospital. He was ill only two days. The janitor found him on the morning of the first day in his room downstairs helpless with pain. His shoes and clothing were wet through and icy cold. They couldn't imagine where he had been on such a dreadful night. And then they found a lantern, still lighted, and a ladder that had been dragged from its place, and some scattered brushes, and a palette with green and yellow colors mixed on it, and—look out the window, dear, at the last ivy leaf on the wall. Didn't you wonder why it never fluttered or moved when the wind blew? Ah, darling, it's Behrman's masterpiece—he painted it there the night that the last leaf fell."

AN OCCURRENCE AT OWL CREEK BRIDGE

Ambrose Bierce

I

A MAN STOOD upon a railroad bridge in northern Alabama, looking down into the swift water twenty feet below. The man's hands were behind his back, the wrists bound with a cord. A rope closely encircled his neck. It was attached to a stout cross-timber above his head and the slack fell to the level of his knees. Some loose boards laid upon the sleepers supporting the metals of the railway supplied a footing for him and his executioners—two private soldiers of the Federal army, directed by a sergeant who in civil life may have been a deputy sheriff. At a short remove upon the same temporary platform was an officer in the uniform of his rank, armed. He was a captain. A sentinel at each end of the bridge stood with his rifle in the position known as "support," that is to say, vertical in front of the left shoulder, the hammer resting on the forearm thrown straight across the chest—a formal and unnatural position, enforcing an erect carriage of the body. It did not appear to be the duty of these two men to know what was occurring at the centre of the bridge; they merely blockaded the two ends of the foot planking that traversed it.

Beyond one of the sentinels nobody was in sight; the railroad ran straight away into a forest for a hundred yards, then, curving, was lost to view. Doubtless there was an outpost farther along. The other bank of the stream was open ground—a gentle acclivity topped with a stockade of vertical tree trunks, loopholed for rifles, with a single embrasure through which protruded the muzzle of a brass cannon commanding the bridge. Midway of the slope

523

between bridge and fort were the spectators—a single company of infantry in line, at "parade rest," the butts of the rifles on the ground, the barrels inclining slightly backward against the right shoulder, the hands crossed upon the stock. A lieutenant stood at the right of the line, the point of his sword upon the ground, his left hand resting upon his right. Excepting the group of four at the centre of the bridge, not a man moved. The company faced the bridge, staring stonily, motionless. The sentinels, facing the banks of the stream, might have been statues to adorn the bridge. The captain stood with folded arms, silent, observing the work of his subordinates, but making no sign. Death is a dignitary who when he comes announced is to be received with formal manifestations of respect, even by those most familiar with him. In the code of military etiquette silence and fixity are forms of deference.

The man who was engaged in being hanged was apparently about thirty-five years of age. He was a civilian, if one might judge from his habit, which was that of a planter. His features were good—a straight nose, firm mouth, broad forehead, from which his long, dark hair was combed straight back, falling behind his ears to the collar of his well fitting frock-coat. He wore a moustache and pointed beard, but no whiskers; his eyes were large and dark gray, and had a kindly expression which one would hardly have expected in one whose neck was in the hemp. Evidently this was no vulgar assassin. The liberal military code makes provision for hanging many kinds of persons, and gentlemen are not excluded.

The preparations being complete, the two private soldiers stepped aside and each drew away the plank upon which he had been standing. The sergeant turned to the captain, saluted and placed himself immediately behind that officer, who in turn moved apart one pace. These movements left the condemned man and the sergeant standing on the two ends of the same plank, which spanned three of the cross-ties of the bridge. The end upon which the civilian stood almost, but not quite, reached a fourth. This plank had been held in place by the weight of the captain; it was now held by that of the sergeant. At a signal from the former the latter would step aside, the plank would tilt and the condemned man go down between two ties. The arrangement commended itself to his judgement as simple and effective. His face had not been covered nor his eyes bandaged. He looked a moment at his "unsteadfast footing," then let his gaze wander to the swirling water of the stream racing madly beneath his feet. A piece of dancing driftwood caught his attention and his eyes followed it down the current. How slowly it appeared to move! What a sluggish stream!

He closed his eyes in order to fix his last thoughts upon his wife and children. The water, touched to gold by the early sun, the brooding mists under the banks at some distance down the stream, the fort, the soldiers, the piece of drift—all had distracted him. And now he became conscious of a new disturbance. Striking through the thought of his dear ones was a sound which he could neither ignore nor understand, a sharp, distinct, metallic percussion like the stroke of a blacksmith's hammer upon the anvil; it had the same ringing quality. He wondered what it was, and whether immeasurably distant or near by—it seemed both. Its recurrence was regular, but as slow as the tolling of a death knell. He awaited each stroke with impatience and—he knew not why—apprehension. The intervals of silence grew progressively longer; the delays became maddening. With their greater infrequency the sounds increased in strength and sharpness. They hurt his ear like the thrust of a knife; he feared he would shriek. What he heard was the ticking of his watch.

He unclosed his eyes and saw again the water below him. "If I could free my hands," he thought, "I might throw off the noose and spring into the stream. By diving I could evade the bullets and, swimming vigorously, reach the bank, take to the woods and get away home. My home, thank God, is as yet outside their lines; my wife and little ones are still beyond the invader's farthest advance."

As these thoughts, which have here to be set down in words, were flashed into the doomed man's brain rather than evolved from it the captain nodded to the sergeant. The sergeant stepped aside.

II

Peyton Farquhar was a well-to-do planter, of an old and highly respected Alabama family. Being a slave owner and like other slave owners a politician he was naturally an original secessionist and ardently devoted to the Southern cause. Circumstances of an imperious nature, which it is unnecessary to relate here, had prevented him from taking service with the gallant army that had fought the disastrous campaigns ending with the fall of Corinth, and he chafed under the inglorious restraint, longing for the release of his energies, the larger life of the soldier, the opportunity for distinction. That opportunity, he felt, would come, as it comes to all in war time. Meanwhile he did what he could. No service was too humble for him to perform in aid of the South, no adventure too perilous for him to undertake if consistent with the character of a civilian who was at heart a soldier, and who in good faith and without too much qualification assented to at least a part of the frankly villainous dictum that all is fair in love and war.

One evening while Farquhar and his wife were sitting on a rustic bench near the entrance to his grounds, a gray-clad soldier rode up to the gate and asked for a drink of water. Mrs. Farquhar was only too happy to serve him with her own white hands. While she was fetching the water her husband approached the dusty horseman and inquired eagerly for news from the front.

"The Yanks are repairing the railroads," said the man, "and are getting ready for another advance. They have reached the Owl Creek bridge, put it in order and built a stockade on the north bank. The commandant has issued an order, which is posted everywhere, declaring that any civilian caught interfering with the railroad, its bridges, tunnels or trains will be summarily hanged. I saw the order."

"How far is it to the Owl Creek bridge?" Farquhar asked.

"About thirty miles."

"Is there no force on this side of the creek?"

"Only a picket post half a mile out, on the railroad, and a single sentinel at this end of the bridge."

"Suppose a man—a civilian and student of hanging—should elude the picket post and perhaps get the better of the sentinel," said Farquhar, smiling, "what could he accomplish?"

The soldier reflected. "I was there a month ago," he replied. "I observed that the flood of last winter had lodged a great quantity of driftwood against the wooden pier at this end of the bridge. It is now dry and would burn like tow."

The lady had now brought the water, which the soldier drank. He thanked her ceremoniously, bowed to her husband and rode away. An hour later, after nightfall, he repassed the plantation, going northward in the direction from which he had come. He was a Federal scout.

III

As Peyton Farquhar fell straight downward through the bridge he lost consciousness and was as one already dead. From this state he was awakened—ages later, it seemed to him—by the pain of a sharp pressure upon his throat, followed by a sense of suffocation. Keen, poignant agonies seemed to shoot from his neck downward through every fibre of his body and limbs. These pains appeared to flash along well-defined lines of ramification and to beat with an inconceivably rapid periodicity. They seemed like streams of pulsating fire heating him to an intolerable temperature. As to his head, he was conscious of nothing but a feeling of fulness—of congestion. These sensations were unaccompanied by thought. The intellectual part of his nature was already effaced; he had power only to feel, and feeling was torment. He was conscious of motion. Encompassed in a luminous cloud, of which he was now merely the fiery heart, without material substance, he swung through unthinkable arcs of oscillation, like a vast pendulum. Then all at once, with terrible suddenness, the light about him shot upward with the noise of a loud plash; a frightful roaring was in his ears, and all was cold and dark. The power of thought was restored; he knew that the rope had broken and he had fallen into the stream. There was no additional strangulation; the noose about his neck was already suffocating him and kept the water from his lungs. To die of hanging at the bottom of a river!—the idea seemed to him ludicrous. He opened his eyes in the darkness and saw above him a gleam of light, but how distant, how inaccessible! He was still sinking, for the light became fainter and fainter until it was a mere glimmer. Then it began to grow and brighten, and he knew that he was rising toward the surface—knew it with reluctance, for he was now very comfortable. "To be hanged and drowned," he thought, "that is not so bad; but I do not wish to be shot. No; I will not be shot; that is not fair."

He was not conscious of an effort, but a sharp pain in his wrist apprised him that he was trying to free his hands. He gave the struggle his attention, as an idler might observe the feat of a juggler, without interest in the outcome. What splendid effort!—what magnificent, what superhuman strength! Ah, that was a fine endeavor! Bravo! The cord fell away; his arms parted and floated upward, the hands dimly seen on each side in the growing light. He watched them with a new interest as first one and then the other pounced upon the noose at his neck. They tore it away and thrust it fiercely aside, its undulations resembling those of a water-snake. "Put it back, put it back!" He thought he shouted these words to his hands, for the undoing of the noose had been succeeded by the direst pang that he had yet experienced. His neck ached horribly; his brain was on fire, his heart, which had been fluttering faintly, gave a great leap, trying to force itself out at his mouth. His whole body was racked and wrenched with an insupportable anguish! But his disobedient hands gave no heed to the command. They beat the water vigorously with quick, downward strokes, forcing him to the surface. He felt his head emerge; his eyes were blinded by the sunlight; his chest expanded convulsively, and with a supreme and crowning agony his lungs engulfed a great draught of air, which instantly he expelled in a shriek!

He was now in full possession of his physical senses. They were, indeed, preternaturally keen and alert. Something in the awful disturbance of his organic system had so exalted and refined them that they made record of things never before perceived. He felt the ripples upon his face and heard their separate sounds as they struck. He looked at the forest on the bank of the stream, saw the individual trees, the leaves and the veining of each leaf—saw the very insects upon them: the locusts, the brilliant-bodied flies, the gray spiders stretching their webs from twig to twig. He noted the prismatic colors in all the dewdrops upon a million blades of grass. The humming of the gnats that danced above the eddies of the stream, the beating of the dragon-flies' wings, the strokes of the water-spiders' legs, like oars which had lifted their boat—all these made audible music. A fish slid along beneath his eyes and he heard the rush of its body parting the water.

He had come to the surface facing down the stream; in a moment the visible world seemed to wheel slowly round, himself the pivotal point, and he saw the bridge, the fort, the soldiers upon the bridge, the captain, the sergeant, the two privates, his executioners. They were in silhouette against the blue sky. They shouted and gesticulated, pointing at him. The captain had drawn his pistol, but did not fire; the others were unarmed. Their movements were grotesque and horrible, their forms gigantic.

Suddenly he heard a sharp report and something struck the water smartly within a few inches of his head, spattering his face with spray. He heard a second report, and saw one of the sentinels with his rifle at his shoulder, a light cloud of blue smoke rising from the muzzle. The man in the water saw the eye of the man on the bridge gazing into his own through the sights of the rifle. He observed that it was a gray eye and remembered having read that gray eyes were keenest, and that all famous marksmen had them. Nevertheless, this one had missed.

A counter-swirl had caught Farquhar and turned him half round; he was again looking into the forest on the bank opposite the fort. The sound of a clear, high voice in a monotonous singsong now rang out behind him and came across the water with a distinctness that pierced and subdued all other sounds, even the beating of the ripples in his ears. Although no soldier, he had frequented camps enough to know the dread significance of that deliberate, drawling, aspirated chant; the lieutenant on shore was taking a part in the morning's work. How coldly and pitilessly—with what an even, calm intonation, presaging, and enforcing tranquillity in the men—with what accurately measured intervals fell those cruel words:

"Attention, company! . . . Shoulder arms! . . . Ready! . . . Aim! . . . Fire!"

Farquhar dived—dived as deeply as he could. The water roared in his ears like the voice of Niagara, yet he heard the dulled thunder of the volley and, rising again toward the surface, met shining bits of metal, singularly flattened, oscillating slowly downward. Some of them touched him on the face and hands, then fell away, continuing their descent. One lodged between his collar and neck; it was uncomfortably warm and he snatched it out.

As he rose to the surface, gasping for breath, he saw that he had been a long time under water; he was perceptibly farther down stream—nearer to safety. The soldiers had almost finished reloading; the metal ramrods flashed all at once in the sunshine as they were drawn from the barrels, turned in the air, and thrust into their sockets. The two sentinels fired again, independently and ineffectually.

The hunted man saw all this over his shoulder; he was now swimming vigorously with the current. His brain was as energetic as his arms and legs; he thought with the rapidity of lightning.

"The officer," he reasoned, "will not make that martinet's error a second time. It is as easy to dodge a volley as a single shot. He has probably already given the command to fire at will. God help me, I cannot dodge them all!"

An appalling plash within two yards of him was followed by a loud, rushing sound, *diminuendo*, which seemed to travel back through the air to the fort and died in an explosion which stirred the very river to its deeps! A rising sheet of water curved over him, fell down upon him, blinded him, strangled him! The cannon had taken a hand in the game. As he shook his head free from the commotion of the smitten water he heard the deflected shot humming through the air ahead, and in an instant it was cracking and smashing the branches in the forest beyond.

"They will not do that again," he thought; "the next time they will use a charge of grape. I must keep my eye upon the gun; the smoke will apprise me—the report arrives too late; it lags behind the missile. That is a good gun."

Suddenly he felt himself whirled round and round—spinning like a top. The water, the banks, the forests, the now distant bridge, fort and men—all were commingled and blurred. Objects were represented by their colors only; circular horizontal streaks of color—that was all he saw. He had been caught in a vortex and was being whirled on with a velocity of advance and gyration that made him giddy and sick. In a few moments he was flung upon the gravel at the foot of the left bank of the stream—the southern bank—and behind a projecting point which concealed him from his enemies. The sudden arrest of his motion, the abrasion of one of his hands on the gravel, restored him, and he wept with delight. He dug his fingers into the sand, threw it over himself in handfuls and audibly blessed it. It looked like diamonds, rubies, emeralds; he could think of nothing beautiful which it did not resemble. The trees upon the bank were giant garden plants; he noted a definite order in their arrangement, inhaled the fragrance of their blooms. A strange, roseate light shone through the spaces among their trunks and the wind made in their branches the music of æolian harps. He had no wish to perfect his escape—was content to remain in that enchanting spot until retaken.

A whiz and rattle of grapeshot among the branches high above his head roused him from his dream. The baffled cannoneer had fired him a random farewell. He sprang to his feet, rushed up the sloping bank, and plunged into the forest.

All that day he traveled, laying his course by the rounding sun. The forest seemed interminable; nowhere did he discover a break in it, not even a woodman's road. He had not known that he lived in so wild a region. There was something uncanny in the revelation.

By nightfall he was fatigued, footsore, famishing. The thought of his wife and children urged him on. At last he found a road which led him in what he knew to be the right direction. It was as wide and straight as a city street, yet it seemed untraveled. No fields bordered it, no dwelling anywhere. Not so much as the barking of a dog suggested human habitation. The black bodies of the trees formed a straight wall on both sides, terminating on the horizon in a point, like a diagram in a lesson in perspective. Overhead, as he looked up through this rift in the wood, shone great golden stars looking unfamiliar and grouped in strange constellations. He was sure they were arranged in some order which had a secret and malign significance. The wood on either side was full of singular noises, among which—once, twice, and again—he distinctly heard whispers in an unknown tongue.

His neck was in pain and lifting his hand to it he found it horribly swollen. He knew that it had a circle of black where the rope had bruised it. His eyes felt congested; he could no longer close them. His tongue was swollen with thirst; he relieved its fever by thrusting it forward from between his teeth into the cold air. How softly the turf had carpeted the untraveled avenue—he could no longer feel the roadway beneath his feet!

Doubtless, despite his suffering, he had fallen asleep while walking, for now he sees another scene—perhaps he was merely recovered from a delirium. He stands at the gate of his own home. All is as he left it, and all bright and beautiful in the morning sunshine. He must have traveled the entire night. As he pushes open the gate and passes up the wide white walk, he sees a flutter of female garments; his wife, looking fresh and cool and sweet, steps down from the veranda to meet him. At the bottom of the steps she stands waiting, with a smile of ineffable joy, an attitude of matchless grace and dignity. Ah, how beautiful she is! He springs forward with extended arms. As he is about to clasp her he feels a stunning blow upon the back of the neck; a blinding white light blazes all about him with a sound like the shock of a cannon—then all is darkness and silence!

Peyton Farquhar was dead; his body, with a broken neck, swung gently from side to side beneath the timbers of the Owl Creek bridge.

THE ENCHANTED BLUFF

Willa Cather

WE HAD OUR swim before sundown, and while we were cooking our supper the oblique rays of light made a dazzling glare on the white sand about us. The translucent red ball itself sank behind the brown stretches of corn field as we sat down to eat, and the warm layer of air that had rested over the water and our clean sand bar grew fresher and smelled of the rank ironweed and sunflowers growing on the flatter shore. The river was brown and sluggish, like any other of the half-dozen streams that water the Nebraska corn lands. On one shore was an irregular line of bald clay bluffs where a few scrub oaks with thick trunks and flat, twisted tops threw light shadows on the long grass. The western shore was low and level, with corn fields that stretched to the skyline, and all along the water's edge were little sandy coves and beaches where slim cottonwoods and willow saplings flickered.

The turbulence of the river in springtime discouraged milling, and, beyond keeping the old red bridge in repair, the busy farmers did not concern themselves with the stream; so the Sandtown boys were left in undisputed possession. In the autumn we hunted quail through the miles of stubble and fodder land along the flat shore, and, after the winter skating season was over and the ice had gone out, the spring freshets and flooded bottoms gave us our great excitement of the year. The channel was never the same for two successive seasons. Every spring the swollen stream undermined a bluff to the east, or bit out a few acres of corn field to the west and whirled the soil away to deposit it in spumy mud banks some-where else. When the water fell low in midsummer, new sand bars were thus exposed to dry and whiten in the August sun. Sometimes these were banked so firmly that the fury of the next freshet failed to unseat them; the little willow seedlings emerged triumphantly from the yellow froth, broke into spring leaf, shot up into summer growth, and with their mesh of roots bound together the moist sand beneath them against the batterings of another April. Here and there a cottonwood soon glittered among them, quivering in the low current of air that, even on breathless days when the dust hung like smoke above the wagon road, trembled along the face of the water.

It was on such an island, in the third summer of its yellow green, that we built our watch fire; not in the thicket of dancing willow wands, but on the level terrace of fine sand which had been added that spring; a little new bit of world, beautifully ridged with ripple marks, and strewn with the tiny skeletons of turtles and fish, all as white and dry as if they had been expertly cured. We had been careful not to mar the freshness of the place, although we often swam to it on summer evenings and lay on the sand to rest.

This was our last watch fire of the year, and there were reasons why I should remember it better than any of the others. Next week the other boys were to file back to their old places in the Sandtown High School, but I was to go up to the Divide to teach my first country school in the Norwegian district. I was already homesick at the thought of quitting the boys with whom I had always played; of leaving the river, and going up into a windy plain that was all windmills and corn fields and big pastures; where there was nothing wilful or unmanageable in the landscape, no new islands, and no chance of unfamiliar birds—such as often followed the watercourses.

Other boys came and went and used the river for fishing or skating, but we six were sworn to the spirit of the stream, and we were friends mainly because of the river. There were the two Hassler boys, Fritz and Otto, sons of the little German tailor. They were the youngest of us; ragged boys of ten and twelve, with sunburned hair, weather-stained faces, and pale blue eyes. Otto, the elder, was the best mathematician in school, and clever at his books, but he always dropped out in the spring term as if the river could not get on without him. He and Fritz caught the fat, horned catfish and sold them about the town, and they lived so much in the water that they were as brown and sandy as the river itself.

There was Percy Pound, a fat, freckled boy with chubby cheeks, who took half a dozen boys' story-papers and was always being kept in for reading detective stories behind his desk. There was Tip Smith, destined by his freckles and red hair to be the buffoon in all our games, though he walked like a timid little old man and had a funny, cracked laugh. Tip worked hard in his father's grocery store every afternoon, and swept it out before school in the morning. Even his recreations were laborious. He collected cigarette cards and tin tobacco-tags indefatigably, and would sit for hours humped up over a snarling little scroll-saw which he kept in his attic. His dearest possessions were some little pill bottles that purported to contain grains of wheat from the Holy Land, water from the Jordan and the Dead Sea, and earth from the Mount of Olives. His father had bought these dull things from a Baptist missionary who peddled them, and Tip seemed to derive great satisfaction from their remote origin.

The tall boy was Arthur Adams. He had fine hazel eyes that were almost too reflective and sympathetic for a boy, and such a pleasant voice that we all loved to hear him read aloud. Even when he had to read poetry aloud at school, no one ever thought of laughing. To be sure, he was not at school very much of the time. He was seventeen and should have finished the High School the year before, but he was always off somewhere with his gun. Arthur's mother was dead, and his father, who was feverishly absorbed in promoting schemes, wanted to send the boy away to school and get him off his hands; but Arthur always begged off for another year and promised to study. I remember him as a tall, brown boy with an intelligent face, always lounging among a lot of us little fellows, laughing at us oftener than with us, but such a soft, satisfied laugh that we felt rather flattered when we provoked it. In after-years people said that Arthur had been given to evil ways even as a lad, and it is true that we often saw him with the gambler's sons and with old Spanish Fanny's boy, but if he learned anything ugly in their company he never betrayed it to us. We would have followed Arthur anywhere, and I am bound to say that he led us into no worse places than the cattail marshes and the stubble fields. These, then, were the boys who camped with me that summer night upon the sand bar.

After we finished our supper we beat the willow thicket for driftwood. By the time we had collected enough, night had fallen, and the pungent, weedy smell from the shore increased with the coolness. We threw ourselves down about the fire and made another futile effort to show Percy Pound the Little Dipper. We had tried it often before, but he could never be got past the big one.

"You see those three big stars just below the handle, with the bright one in the middle?" said Otto Hassler; "that's Orion's belt, and the bright one is the clasp." I crawled behind Otto's shoulder and sighted up his arm to the star that seemed perched upon the tip of his steady forefinger. The Hassler boys did seine-fishing at night, and they knew a good many stars.

Percy gave up the Little Dipper and lay back on the sand, his hands clasped under his head. "I can see the North Star," he announced, contentedly, pointing toward it with his big toe. "Anyone might get lost and need to know that."

We all looked up at it.

"How do you suppose Columbus felt when his compass didn't point north any more?" Tip asked.

Otto shook his head. "My father says that there was another North Star once, and that maybe this one won't last always. I wonder what would happen to us down here if anything went wrong with it?"

Arthur chuckled. "I wouldn't worry, Ott. Nothing's apt to happen to it in your time. Look at the Milky Way! There must be lots of good dead Indians."

We lay back and looked, meditating, at the dark cover of the world. The gurgle of the water had become heavier. We had often noticed a mutinous, complaining note in it at night, quite different from its cheerful daytime chuckle, and seeming like the voice of a much deeper and more powerful stream. Our water had always these two moods: the one of sunny complaisance, the other of inconsolable, passionate regret.

"Queer how the stars are all in sort of diagrams," remarked Otto. "You could do most any proposition in geometry with 'em. They always look as if they meant something. Some folks say everybody's fortune is all written out in the stars, don't they?"

"They believe so in the old country," Fritz affirmed.

But Arthur only laughed at him. "You're thinking of Napoleon, Fritzey. He had a star that went out when he began to lose battles. I guess the stars don't keep any close tally on Sandtown folks."

We were speculating on how many times we could count a hundred before the evening star went down behind the corn fields, when someone cried, "There comes the moon, and it's as big as a cart wheel!"

We all jumped up to greet it as it swam over the bluffs behind us. It came up like a galleon in full sail; an enormous, barbaric thing, red as an angry heathen god.

"When the moon came up red like that, the Aztecs used to sacrifice their prisoners on the temple top," Percy announced.

"Go on, Perce. You got that out of *Golden Days*. Do you believe that, Arthur?" I appealed.

Arthur answered, quite seriously: "Like as not. The moon was one of their gods. When my father was in Mexico City he saw the stone where they used to sacrifice their prisoners."

As we dropped down by the fire again some one asked whether the Mound–Builders were older than the Aztecs. When we once got upon the Mound–Builders we never willingly got away from them, and we were still conjecturing when we heard a loud splash in the water.

"Must have been a big cat jumping," said Fritz. "They do sometimes. They must see bugs in the dark. Look what a track the moon makes!"

There was a long, silvery streak on the water, and where the current fretted over a big log it boiled up like gold pieces.

"Suppose there ever *was* any gold hid away in this old river?" Fritz asked. He lay like a little brown Indian, close to the fire, his chin on his hand and his bare feet in the air. His brother laughed at him, but Arthur took his suggestion seriously.

"Some of the Spaniards thought there was gold up here somewhere. Seven cities chuck full of gold, they had it, and Coronado and his men came up to hunt it. The Spaniards were all over this country once."

Percy looked interested. "Was that before the Mormons went through?"

We all laughed at this.

"Long enough before. Before the Pilgrim Fathers, Perce. Maybe they came along this very river. They always followed the watercourses."

"I wonder where this river really does begin?" Tip mused. That was an old and a favorite mystery which the map did not clearly explain. On the map the little black line stopped somewhere in western Kansas; but since rivers generally rose in mountains, it was only reasonable to suppose that ours came from the Rockies. Its destination, we knew, was the Missouri, and the Hassler boys always maintained that we could embark at Sandtown in floodtime, follow our noses, and eventually arrive at New Orleans. Now they took up their old argument. "If us boys had grit enough to try it, it wouldn't take no time to get to Kansas City and St. Joe."

We began to talk about the places we wanted to go to. The Hassler boys wanted to see the stockyards in Kansas City, and Percy wanted to see a big store in Chicago. Arthur was interlocutor and did not betray himself.

"Now it's your turn, Tip."

Tip rolled over on his elbow and poked the fire, and his eyes looked shyly out of his queer, tight little face. "My place is awful far away. My Uncle Bill told me about it."

Tip's Uncle Bill was a wanderer, bitten with mining fever, who had drifted into Sandtown with a broken arm, and when it was well had drifted out again.

"Where is it?"

"Aw, it's down in New Mexico somewheres. There aren't no railroads or anything. You have to go on mules, and you run out of water before you get there and have to drink canned tomatoes."

"Well, go on, kid. What's it like when you do get there?"

Tip sat up and excitedly began his story.

"There's a big red rock there that goes right up out of the sand for about nine hundred feet. The country's flat all around it, and this here rock goes up all by itself, like a monument. They call it the Enchanted Bluff down there, because no white man has ever been on top of it. The sides are smooth rock, and straight up, like a wall. The Indians say that hundreds of years ago, before the Spaniards came, there was a village away up there in the air. The tribe that lived there had some sort of steps, made out of wood and bark, hung down over the face of the bluff, and the braves went down to hunt and carried water up in big jars swung on their backs. They kept a big supply of water and dried meat up there, and never went down except to hunt. They were a peaceful tribe that made cloth and pottery, and they went up there to get out of the wars. You see, they could pick off any war party that tried to get up their little steps. The Indians say they were a handsome people, and they had some sort of queer religion. Uncle Bill thinks they were Cliff-Dwellers who had got into trouble and left home. They weren't fighters, anyhow.

"One time the braves were down hunting and an awful storm came up—a kind of waterspout—and when they got back to their rock they found their little staircase had been all broken to pieces, and only a few steps were left hanging away up in the air. While they were camped at the foot of the rock, wondering what to do, a war party from the north came along and massacred 'em to a man, with all the old folks and women looking on from the rock. Then the war party went on south and left the village to get down the best way they could. Of course they never got down. They starved to death up there, and when the war party came back on their way north, they could hear the children crying from the edge of the bluff where they had crawled out, but they didn't see a sign of a grown Indian, and nobody has ever been up there since."

We exclaimed at this dolorous legend and sat up.

"There couldn't have been many people up there," Percy demurred. "How big is the top, Tip?"

"Oh, pretty big. Big enough so that the rock doesn't look nearly as tall as it is. The top's bigger than the base. The bluff is sort of worn away for several hundred feet up. That's one reason it's so hard to climb."

I asked how the Indians got up, in the first place.

"Nobody knows how they got up or when. A hunting party came along once and saw that there was a town up there, and that was all."

Otto rubbed his chin and looked thoughtful. "Of course there must be some way to get up there. Couldn't people get a rope over someway and pull a ladder up?"

Tip's little eyes were shining with excitement. "I know a way. Me and Uncle Bill talked it all over. There's a kind of rocket that would take a rope over—life-savers use 'em—and then you could hoist a rope ladder and peg it down at the bottom and make it tight with guy ropes on the other side. I'm going to climb that there bluff, and I've got it all planned out."

Fritz asked what he expected to find when he got up there.

"Bones, maybe, or the ruins of their town, or pottery, or some of their idols. There might be 'most anything up there. Anyhow, I want to see."

"Sure nobody else has been up there, Tip?" Arthur asked.

"Dead sure. Hardly anybody ever goes down there. Some hunters tried to cut steps in the rock once, but they didn't get higher than a man can reach. The Bluff's all red granite, and Uncle Bill thinks it's a boulder the glaciers left. It's a queer place, anyhow. Nothing but cactus and desert for hundreds of miles, and yet right under the Bluff there's good water and plenty of grass. That's why the bison used to go down there."

Suddenly we heard a scream above our fire, and jumped up to see a dark, slim bird floating southward far above us—a whooping crane, we knew by her cry and her long neck. We ran to the edge of the island, hoping we might see her alight, but she wavered southward along the rivercourse until we lost her. The Hassler boys declared that by the look of the heavens it must be after midnight, so we threw more wood on our fire, put on our jackets, and curled down in the warm sand. Several of us pretended to doze, but I fancy we were really thinking about Tip's Bluff and the extinct people. Over in the wood the ring doves were calling mournfully to one another, and once we heard a dog bark, far away. "Somebody getting into old Tommy's melon patch," Fritz murmured sleepily, but nobody answered him. By and by Percy spoke out of the shadows.

"Say, Tip, when you go down there will you take me with you?"

"Maybe."

"Suppose one of us beats you down there, Tip?"

"Whoever gets to the Bluff first has got to promise to tell the rest of us exactly what he finds," remarked one of the Hassler boys, and to this we all readily assented.

Somewhat reassured, I dropped off to sleep. I must have dreamed about a race for the Bluff, for I awoke in a kind of fear that other people were getting ahead of me and that I was losing my chance. I sat up in my damp clothes and looked at the other boys, who lay tumbled in uneasy attitudes about the dead fire. It was still dark, but the sky was blue with the last wonderful azure of night. The stars glistened like crystal globes, and trembled as if they shone through a depth of clear water. Even as I watched, they began to pale and the sky brightened. Day came suddenly, almost instantaneously. I turned for another look at the blue night, and it was gone. Everywhere the birds began to call, and all manner of little insects began to chirp and hop about in the willows. A breeze sprang up from the west and brought the heavy smell of ripened corn. The boys rolled over and shook themselves. We stripped and plunged into the river just as the sun came up over the windy bluffs.

When I came home to Sandtown at Christmas time, we skated out to our island and talked over the whole project of the Enchanted Bluff, renewing our resolution to find it.

Although that was twenty years ago, none of us have ever climbed the Enchanted Bluff. Percy Pound is a stockbroker in Kansas City and will go nowhere that his red touring car cannot carry him. Otto Hassler went on the railroad and lost his foot braking; after which he and Fritz succeeded their father as the town tailors.

Arthur sat about the sleepy little town all his life—he died before he was twenty-five. The last time I saw him, when I was home on one of my college vacations, he was sitting in a steamer chair under a cottonwood tree in the little yard behind one of the two Sandtown saloons. He was very untidy and his hand was not steady, but when he rose, unabashed, to greet me, his eyes were as clear and warm as ever. When I had talked with him for an hour and heard him laugh again, I wondered how it was that when Nature had taken such pains with a man, from his hands to the arch of his long foot, she had ever lost him in Sandtown. He joked about Tip Smith's Bluff, and declared he was going down there just as soon as the weather got cooler; he thought the Grand Canyon might be worth while, too.

I was perfectly sure when I left him that he would never get beyond the high plank fence and the comfortable shade of the cottonwood. And, indeed, it was under that very tree that he died one summer morning.

Tip Smith still talks about going to New Mexico. He married a slatternly, unthrifty country girl, has been much tied to a perambulator, and has grown stooped and gray from irregular meals and broken sleep. But the worst of his difficulties are now over, and he has, as he says, come into easy water. When I was last in Sandtown I walked home with him late one moonlight night, after he had balanced his cash and shut up his store. We took the long way around and sat down on the schoolhouse steps, and between us we quite revived the romance of the lone red rock and the extinct people. Tip insists that he still means to go down there, but he thinks now he will wait until his boy Bert is old enough to go with him. Bert has been let into the story, and thinks of nothing but the Enchanted Bluff.

THE COTTAGETTE

Charlotte Perkins Gilman

"WHY NOT?" SAID Mr. Mathews. "It is far too small for a house, too pretty for a hut, too—unusual—for a cottage."

"Cottagette, by all means," said Lois, seating herself on a porch chair. "But it is larger than it looks, Mr. Mathews. How do you like it, Malda?"

I was delighted with it. More than delighted. Here this tiny shell of fresh unpainted wood peeped out from under the trees, the only house in sight except the distant white specks on far off farms, and the little wandering village in the river-threaded valley. It sat right on the turf,—no road, no path even, and the dark woods shadowed the back windows.

"How about meals?" asked Lois.

"Not two minutes' walk," he assured her, and showed us a little furtive path between the trees to the place where meals were furnished.

We discussed and examined and exclaimed, Lois holding her pongee skirts close about her—she needn't have been so careful, there wasn't a speck of dust,—and presently decided to take it.

Never did I know the real joy and peace of living, before that blessed summer at "High Court." It was a mountain place, easy enough to get to, but strangely big and still and far away when you were there.

The working basis of the establishment was an eccentric woman named Caswell, a sort of musical enthusiast, who had a summer school of music and the "higher thought." Malicious persons, not able to obtain accommodations there, called the place "High C."

I liked the music very well, and kept my thoughts to myself, both high and low, but "The Cottagette" I loved unreservedly. It was so little and new and clean, smelling only of its fresh-planed boards—they hadn't even stained it.

There was one big room and two little ones in the tiny thing, though from the outside you wouldn't have believed it, it looked so small; but small as it was it harbored a miracle—a real bathroom with water piped from mountain springs. Our windows opened into the green shadiness, the soft brownness, the bird-inhabited quiet flower-starred woods. But in front we looked across whole counties—over a far-off river—into another state. Off and down and away—it was like sitting on the roof of something—something very big.

The grass swept up to the door-step, to the walls—only it wasn't just grass of course, but such a procession of flowers as I had never imagined could grow in one place.

You had to go quite a way through the meadow, wearing your own narrow faintly marked streak in the grass, to reach the town-connecting road below. But in the woods was a little path, clear and wide, by which we went to meals.

For we ate with the highly thoughtful musicians, and highly musical thinkers, in their central boarding-house nearby. They didn't call it a boarding-house, which is neither high nor musical; they called it "The Calceolaria." There was plenty of that growing about, and I didn't mind what they called it so long as the food was good—which it was, and the prices reasonable—which they were.

The people were extremely interesting—some of them at least; and all of them were better than the average of summer boarders.

But if there hadn't been any interesting ones it didn't matter while Ford Mathews was there. He was a newspaper man, or rather an ex-newspaper man, then becoming a writer for magazines, with books ahead.

He had friends at High Court—he liked music—he liked the place—and he liked us. Lois liked him too, as was quite natural. I'm sure I did.

He used to come up evenings and sit on the porch and talk.

He came daytimes and went on long walks with us. He established his workshop in a most attractive little cave not far beyond us,—the country there is full of rocky ledges and hollows,—and sometimes asked us over to an afternoon tea, made on a gipsy fire.

Lois was a good deal older than I, but not really old at all, and she didn't look her thirty-five by ten years. I never blamed her for not mentioning it, and I wouldn't have done so, myself, on any account. But I felt that together we made a safe and reasonable household. She played beautifully, and there was a piano in our big room. There were pianos in several other little cottages about—but too far off for any jar of sound. When the wind was right we caught little wafts of music now and then; but mostly it was still—blessedly still, about us. And yet that Calceolaria was only two minutes off—and with raincoats and rubbers we never minded going to it.

We saw a good deal of Ford and I got interested in him, I couldn't help it. He was big. Not extra big in pounds and inches, but a man with big view and a grip—with purpose and real power. He was going to do things. I thought he was doing them now, but he didn't—this was all like cutting steps in the ice-wall, he said. It had to be done, but the road was long ahead. And he took an interest in my work too, which is unusual for a literary man.

Mine wasn't much. I did embroidery and made designs.

It is such pretty work! I like to draw from flowers and leaves and things about me; conventionalize them sometimes, and sometimes paint them just as they are,—in soft silk stitches.

All about up here were the lovely small things I needed; and not only these, but the lovely big things that make one feel so strong and able to do beautiful work.

Here was the friend I lived so happily with, and all this fairy land of sun and shadow, the free immensity of our view, and the dainty comfort of the Cottagette. We never had to think of ordinary things till the soft musical thrill of the Japanese gong stole through the trees, and we trotted off to the Calceolaria.

I think Lois knew before I did.

We were old friends and trusted each other, and she had had experience too.

"Malda," she said, "let us face this thing and be rational." It was a strange thing that Lois should be so rational and yet so musical—but she was, and that was one reason I liked her so much.

"You are beginning to love Ford Mathews—do you know it?"

I said yes, I thought I was.

"Does he love you?"

That I couldn't say. "It is early yet," I told her. "He is a man, he is about thirty I believe, he has seen more of life and probably loved before—it may be nothing more than friendliness with him."

"Do you think it would be a good marriage?" she asked. We had often talked of love and marriage, and Lois had helped me to form my views—hers were very clear and strong.

"Why yes—if he loves me," I said. "He has told me quite a bit about his family, good western farming people, real Americans. He is strong and well—you can read clean living in his eyes and mouth." Ford's eyes were as clear as a girl's, the whites of them were clear. Most men's eyes, when you look at them critically, are not like that. They may look at you very expressively, but when you look at them, just as features, they are not very nice.

I liked his looks, but I liked him better.

So I told her that as far as I knew it would be a good marriage—if it was one.

"How much do you love him?" she asked.

That I couldn't quite tell,—it was a good deal,—but I didn't think it would kill me to lose him.

"Do you love him enough to do something to win him—to really put yourself out somewhat for that purpose?"

"Why—yes—I think I do. If it was something I approved of. What do you mean?"

Then Lois unfolded her plan. She had been married,—unhappily married, in her youth; that was all over and done with years ago; she had told me about it long since; and she said she did not regret the pain and loss because it had given her experience. She had her maiden name again—and freedom. She was so fond of me she wanted to give me the benefit of her experience—without the pain.

"Men like music," said Lois; "they like sensible talk; they like beauty of course, and all that,— "

"Then they ought to like you!" I interrupted, and, as a matter of fact they did. I knew several who wanted to marry her, but she said "once was enough." I don't think they were "good marriages" though.

"Don't be foolish, child," said Lois, "this is serious. What they care for most after all is domesticity. Of course they'll fall in love with anything; but what they want to marry is a homemaker. Now we are living here in an idyllic sort of way, quite conducive to falling in love, but no temptation to marriage. If I were you—if I really loved this man and wished to marry him, I would make a home of this place."

"Make a home?—why it *is* a home. I never was so happy anywhere in my life. What on earth do you mean, Lois?"

"A person might be happy in a balloon, I suppose," she replied, "but it wouldn't be a home. He comes here and sits talking with us, and it's quiet and feminine and attractive—and then we hear that big gong at the Calceolaria, and off we go slopping through the wet woods—and the spell is broken. Now you can cook." I could cook. I could cook excellently. My esteemed Mama had rigorously taught me every branch of what is now called "domestic science;" and I had no objection to the work, except that it prevented my doing anything else. And one's hands are not so nice when one cooks and washes dishes,—I need nice hands for my needlework. But if it was a question of pleasing Ford Mathews—

Lois went on calmly. "Miss Caswell would put on a kitchen for us in a minute, she said she would, you know, when we took the cottage. Plenty of people keep house up here,—we can if we want to."

"But we don't want to," I said, "we never have wanted to. The very beauty of the place is that it never had any housekeeping about it. Still, as you say, it would be cosy on a wet night, we could have delicious little suppers, and have him stay—"

"He told me he had never known a home since he was eighteen," said Lois.

That was how we came to install a kitchen in the Cottagette. The men put it up in a few days, just a lean-to with a window, a sink and two doors. I did the cooking. We had nice things, there is no denying that; good fresh milk and vegetables particularly, fruit is hard to get in the country, and meat too, still we managed nicely; the less you have the more you have to manage—it takes time and brains, that's all.

Lois likes to do housework, but it spoils her hands for practicing, so she can't; and I was perfectly willing to do it—it was all in the interest of my own heart. Ford certainly enjoyed it. He dropped in often, and ate things with undeniable relish. So I was pleased, though it did interfere with my work a good deal. I always work best in the morning; but of course housework has to be done in the morning too; and it is astonishing how much work there is in the littlest kitchen. You go in for a minute, and you see this thing and that thing and the other thing to be done, and your minute is an hour before you know it.

When I was ready to sit down the freshness of the morning was gone somehow. Before, when I woke up, there was only the clean wood smell of the house, and then the blessed out-of-doors: now I always felt the call of the kitchen as soon as I woke. An oil stove will smell a little, either in or out of the house; and soap, and—well you know if you cook in a bedroom how it makes the room feel differently? Our house had been only bedroom and parlor before.

We baked too—the baker's bread was really pretty poor, and Ford did enjoy my whole wheat, and brown, and especially hot rolls and gems. It was a pleasure to feed him, but it did heat up the house, and me. I never could work much—at my work—baking days. Then, when I did get to work, the people would come with things,—milk or meat or vegetables, or children with berries; and what distressed me most was the wheelmarks on our meadow. They soon made quite a road—they had to of course, but I hated it—I lost that lovely sense of being on the last edge and looking over—we were just a bead on a string like other houses. But it was quite true that I loved this man, and would do more than this to please him. We couldn't go off so freely on excursions as we used, either; when meals are to be prepared someone has to be there, and to take in things when they come. Sometimes Lois stayed in, she always asked to, but mostly I did. I couldn't let her spoil her summer on my account. And Ford certainly liked it.

He came so often that Lois said she thought it would look better if we had an older person with us; and that her mother could come if I wanted her, and she could help with the work of course. That seemed reasonable, and she came. I wasn't very fond of Lois's mother, Mrs. Fowler, but it did seem a little conspicuous, Mr. Mathews eating with us more than he did at the Calceolaria. There were others of course, plenty of them dropping in, but I didn't encourage it much, it made so much more work. They would come in to supper, and then we would have musical evenings. They offered to help me wash dishes, some of them, but a new hand in the kitchen is not much help, I preferred to do it myself; then I knew where the dishes were.

Ford never seemed to want to wipe dishes; though I often wished he would.

So Mrs. Fowler came. She and Lois had one room, they had to,—and she really did a lot of the work, she was a very practical old lady.

Then the house began to be noisy. You hear another person in a kitchen more than you hear yourself, I think,—and the walls were only boards. She swept more than we did too. I don't think much sweeping is needed in a clean place like that; and she dusted all the time; which I know is unnecessary. I still did most of the cooking, but I could get off more to draw, out-of-doors; and to walk. Ford was in and out continually, and, it seemed to me, was really coming nearer. What was one summer of interrupted work, of noise and dirt and smell and constant meditation on what to eat next, compared to a lifetime of love? Besides—if he married me—I should have to do it always, and might as well get used to it.

Lois kept me contented, too, telling me nice things that Ford said about my cooking. "He does appreciate it so," she said.

One day he came around early and asked me to go up Hugh's Peak with him. It was a lovely climb and took all day. I demurred a little, it was Monday, Mrs. Fowler thought it was cheaper to have a woman come and wash, and we did, but it certainly made more work.

"Never mind," he said, "what's washing day or ironing day or any of that old foolishness to us? This is walking day—that's what it is." It was really, cool and sweet and fresh,—it had rained in the night,—and brilliantly clear.

"Come along!" he said. "We can see as far as Patch Mountain I'm sure. There'll never be a better day."

"Is anyone else going?" I asked.

"Not a soul. It's just us. Come."

I came gladly, only suggesting—"Wait, let me put up a lunch."

"I'll wait just long enough for you to put on knickers and a short skirt," said he. "The lunch is all in the basket on my back. I know how long it takes for you women to 'put up' sandwiches and things."

We were off in ten minutes, light-footed and happy: and the day was all that could be asked. He brought a perfect lunch, too, and had made it all himself. I confess it tasted better to me than my own cooking; but perhaps that was the climb.

When we were nearly down we stopped by a spring on a broad ledge, and supped, making tea as he liked to do out-of-doors. We saw the round sun setting at one end of a world view, and the round moon rising at the other; calmly shining each on each.

And then he asked me to be his wife.

We were very happy.

"But there's a condition!" said he all at once, sitting up straight and looking very fierce. "You mustn't cook!"

"What!" said I. "Mustn't cook?"

"No," said he, "you must give it up—for my sake."

I stared at him dumbly.

"Yes, I know all about it," he went on, "Lois told me. I've seen a good deal of Lois—since you've taken to cooking. And since I would talk about you, naturally I learned a lot. She told me how you were brought up, and how strong your domestic instincts were—but bless your artist soul, dear girl, you have some others!" Then he smiled rather queerly and murmured, "surely in vain the net is spread in the sight of any bird."

"I've watched you, dear, all summer;" he went on, "it doesn't agree with you.

"Of course the things taste good—but so do my things! I'm a good cook myself. My father was a cook, for years—at good wages. I'm used to it you see.

"One summer when I was hard up I cooked for a living—and saved money instead of starving."

"O ho!" said I, "that accounts for the tea—and the lunch!"

"And lots of other things," said he. "But you haven't done half as much of your lovely work since you started this kitchen business, and—you'll forgive me, dear—it hasn't been as good. Your work is quite too good to lose; it is a beautiful and distinctive art, and I don't want you to let it go. What would you think of me if I gave up my hard long years of writing for the easy competence of a well-paid cook!"

I was still too happy to think very clearly. I just sat and looked at him. "But you want to marry me?" I said.

"I want to marry you, Malda,—because I love you—because you are young and strong and beautiful—because you are wild and sweet and—fragrant, and—elusive, like the wild flowers you love. Because you are so truly an artist in your special way, seeing beauty and giving it to others. I love you because of all this, because you are rational and highminded and capable of friendship,—and in spite of your cooking!"

"But—how do you want to live?"

"As we did here—at first," he said. "There was peace, exquisite silence. There was beauty—nothing but beauty. There were the clean wood odors and flowers and fragrances and sweet wild wind. And there was you—your fair self, always delicately dressed, with white firm fingers sure of touch in delicate true work. I loved you then. When you took to cooking it jarred on me. I have been a cook, I tell you, and I know what it is. I hated it—to see my wood-flower in a kitchen. But Lois told me about how you were brought up to it and loved it, and I said to myself, 'I love this woman; I will wait and see if I love her even as a cook.' And I do, Darling: I withdraw the condition. I will love you always, even if you insist on being my cook for life!"

"O I don't insist!" I cried. "I don't want to cook—I want to draw! But I thought—Lois said—How she has misunderstood you!"

"It is not true, always, my dear," said he, "that the way to a man's heart is through his stomach; at least it's not the only way. Lois doesn't know everything, she is young yet! And perhaps for my sake you can give it up. Can you, sweet?"

Could I? Could I? Was there ever a man like this?

GERMANS AT MEAT

Katherine Mansfield

BREAD SOUP WAS placed upon the table. "Ah," said the Herr Rat, leaning upon the table as he peered into the tureen, "that is what I need. My *Magen* has not been in order for several days. Bread soup, and just the right consistency. I am a good cook myself"—he turned to me.

"How interesting," I said, attempting to infuse just the right amount of enthusiasm into my voice.

"Oh yes—when one is not married it is necessary. As for me, I have had all I wanted from women without marriage." He tucked his napkin into his collar and blew upon his soup as he spoke. "Now at nine o'clock I make myself an English breakfast, but not much. Four slices of bread, two eggs, two slices of cold ham, one plate of soup, two cups of tea—that is nothing to you."

He asserted the fact so vehemently that I had not the courage to refute it.

All eyes were suddenly turned upon me. I felt I was bearing the burden of the nation's preposterous breakfast—I who drank a cup of coffee while buttoning my blouse in the morning.

"Nothing at all," cried Herr Hoffmann from Berlin. *"Ach,* when I was in England in the morning I used to eat."

He turned up his eyes and his moustache, wiping the soup drippings from his coat and waistcoat.

"Do they really eat so much?" asked Fräulein Stiegelauer. "Soup and baker's bread and pig's flesh, and tea and coffee and stewed fruit, and honey and eggs, and cold fish and kidneys, and hot fish and liver? All the ladies eat too, especially the ladies."

"Certainly. I myself have noticed it, when I was living in a hotel in Leicester Square," cried the Herr Rat. "It was a good hotel, but they could not make tea—now—"

"Ah, that's one thing I *can* do," said I, laughing brightly. "I can make very good tea. The great secret is to warm the teapot."

"Warm the teapot," interrupted the Herr Rat, pushing away his soup plate. "What do you warm the teapot for? Ha! ha! that's very good! One does not eat the teapot, I suppose?"

He fixed his cold blue eyes upon me with an expression which suggested a thousand premeditated invasions.

"So that is the great secret of your English tea? All you do is to warm the teapot."

I wanted to say that was only the preliminary canter, but could not translate it, and so was silent.

The servant brought in veal, with sauerkraut and potatoes.

"I eat sauerkraut with great pleasure," said the Traveller from North Germany, "but now I have eaten so much of it that I cannot retain it. I am immediately forced to—"

"A beautiful day," I cried, turning to Fräulein Stiegelauer. "Did you get up early?"

"At five o'clock I walked for ten minutes in the wet grass. Again in bed. At half past five I fell asleep and woke at seven, when I made an 'overbody' washing! Again in bed. At eight o'clock I had a cold-water poultice, and at half past eight I drank a cup of mint tea. At nine I drank some malt coffee, and began my 'cure.' Pass me the sauerkraut, please. You do not eat it?"

"No, thank you. I still find it a little strong."

"Is it true," asked the Widow, picking her teeth with a hairpin as she spoke, "that you are a vegetarian?"

"Why, yes; I have not eaten meat for three years."

"Im-possible! Have you any family?"

"No."

"There now, you see, that's what you're coming to! Who ever heard of having children upon vegetables? It is not possible. But you never have large families in England now; I suppose you are too busy with your suffragetting. Now I have had nine children, and they are all alive, thank God. Fine, healthy babies—though after the first one was born I had to—"

"How *wonderful!*" I cried.

"Wonderful," said the Widow contemptuously, replacing the hairpin in the knob which was balanced on the top of her head. "Not at all! A friend of mine had four at the same time. Her husband was so pleased he gave a supper-party and had them placed on the table. Of course she was very proud."

"Germany," boomed the Traveller, biting round a potato which he had speared with his knife, "is the home of the Family."

Followed an appreciative silence.

The dishes were changed for beef, red currants and spinach. They wiped their forks upon black bread and started again.

"How long are you remaining here?" asked the Herr Rat.

"I do not know exactly. I must be back in London in September."

"Of course you will visit München?"

"I am afraid I shall not have time. You see, it is important not to break into my 'cure.'"

"But you *must* go to München. You have not seen Germany if you have not been to München. All the Exhibitions, all the Art and Soul life of Germany are in München. There is the Wagner Festival in August, and Mozart and a Japanese collection of pictures—and there is the beer! You do not know what good beer is until you have been to München. Why, I see fine ladies every afternoon, but fine ladies, I tell you, drinking glasses so high." He measured a good washstand pitcher in height, and I smiled.

"If I drink a great deal of München beer I sweat so," said Herr Hoffmann. "When I am here, in the fields or before my baths, I sweat, but I enjoy it; but in the town it is not at all the same thing."

Prompted by the thought, he wiped his neck and face with his dinner napkin and carefully cleaned his ears.

A glass dish of stewed apricots was placed upon the table.

"Ah, fruit!" said Fräulein Stiegelauer, "that is so necessary to health. The doctor told me this morning that the more fruit I could eat the better."

She very obviously followed the advice.

Said the Traveller: "I suppose you are frightened of an invasion too, eh? Oh, that's good. I've been reading all about your English play in a newspaper. Did you see it?"

"Yes." I sat upright. "I assure you we are not afraid."

"Well, then, you ought to be," said the Herr Rat. "You have got no army at all—a few little boys with their veins full of nicotine poisoning."

"Don't be afraid," Herr Hoffmann said. "We don't want England. If we did we would have had her long ago. We really do not want you."

He waved his spoon airily, looking across at me as though I were a little child whom he would keep or dismiss as he pleased.

"We certainly do not want Germany," I said.

"This morning I took a half bath. Then this afternoon I must take a knee bath and an arm bath," volunteered the Herr Rat; "then I do my exercises for an hour, and my work is over. A glass of wine and a couple of rolls with some sardines—"

They were handed cherry cake with whipped cream.

"What is your husband's favourite meat?" asked the Widow.

"I really do not know," I answered.

"You really do not know? How long have you been married?"

"Three years."

"But you cannot be in earnest! You would not have kept house as his wife for a week without knowing that fact."

"I really never asked him; he is not at all particular about his food."

A pause. They all looked at me, shaking their heads, their mouths full of cherry stones.

"No wonder there is a repetition in England of that dreadful state of things in Paris," said the Widow, folding her dinner napkin. "How can a woman expect to keep her husband if she does not know his favourite food after three years?"

"Mahlzeit!"

"Mahlzeit!"

I closed the door after me.

TOBERMORY

H. H. Munro (Saki)

IT WAS A chill, rain-washed afternoon of a late August day, that
indefinite season when partridges are still in security or cold storage,
and there is nothing to hunt—unless one is bounded on the north
by the Bristol Channel, in which case one may lawfully gallop after
fat red stags. Lady Blemley's house-party was not bounded on the
north by the Bristol Channel, hence there was a full gathering of
her guests round the tea-table on this particular afternoon. And, in
spite of the blankness of the season and the triteness of the occasion,
there was no trace in the company of that fatigued restlessness
which means a dread of the pianola and a subdued hankering for
auction bridge. The undisguised open-mouthed attention of the
entire party was fixed on the homely negative personality of Mr.
Cornelius Appin. Of all her guests, he was the one who had come
to Lady Blemley with the vaguest reputation. Some one had said he
was "clever," and he had got his invitation in the moderate expectation, on the part of his hostess, that some portion at least of his
cleverness would be contributed to the general entertainment.
Until tea-time that day she had been unable to discover in what
direction, if any, his cleverness lay. He was neither a wit nor a cro-
quet champion, a hypnotic force nor a begetter of amateur theatricals. Neither did his exterior suggest the sort of man in whom
women are willing to pardon a generous measure of mental deficiency. He had subsided into mere Mr. Appin, and the Cornelius
seemed a piece of transparent baptismal bluff. And now he was
claiming to have launched on the world a discovery beside which
the invention of gunpowder, of the printing-press, and of steam
locomotion were inconsiderable trifles. Science had made

bewildering strides in many directions during recent decades, but this thing seemed to belong to the domain of miracle rather than to scientific achievement.

"And do you really ask us to believe," Sir Wilfrid was saying, "that you have discovered a means for instructing animals in the art of human speech, and that dear old Tobermory has proved your first successful pupil?"

"It is a problem at which I have worked for the last seventeen years," said Mr. Appin, "but only during the last eight or nine months have I been rewarded with glimmerings of success. Of course I have experimented with thousands of animals, but latterly only with cats, those wonderful creatures which have assimilated themselves so marvellously with our civilization while retaining all their highly developed feral instincts. Here and there among cats one comes across an outstanding superior intellect, just as one does among the ruck of human beings, and when I made the acquaintance of Tobermory a week ago I saw at once that I was in contact with a 'Beyond-cat' of extraordinary intelligence. I had gone far along the road to success in recent experiments; with Tobermory, as you call him, I have reached the goal."

Mr. Appin concluded his remarkable statement in a voice which he strove to divest of a triumphant inflection. No one said "Rats," though Clovis's lips moved in a monosyllabic contortion which probably invoked those rodents of disbelief.

"And do you mean to say," asked Miss Resker, after a slight pause, "that you have taught Tobermory to say and understand easy sentences of one syllable?"

"My dear Miss Resker," said the wonder-worker patiently, "one teaches little children and savages and backward adults in that piecemeal fashion; when one has once solved the problem of making a beginning with an animal of highly developed intelligence one has no need for those halting methods. Tobermory can speak our language with perfect correctness."

This time Clovis very distinctly said, "Beyond-rats!" Sir Wilfrid was more polite, but equally sceptical.

"Hadn't we better have the cat in and judge for ourselves?" suggested Lady Blemley.

Sir Wilfrid went in search of the animal, and the company settled themselves down to the languid expectation of witnessing some more or less adroit drawing-room ventriloquism.

In a minute Sir Wilfrid was back in the room, his face white beneath its tan and his eyes dilated with excitement.

"By Gad, it's true!"

His agitation was unmistakably genuine, and his hearers started forward in a thrill of awakened interest.

Collapsing into an armchair he continued breathlessly: "I found him dozing in the smoking-room and called out to him to come for his tea. He blinked at me in his usual way, and I said, 'Come on, Toby; don't keep us waiting'; and, by Gad! he drawled out in a most horribly natural voice that he'd come when he dashed well pleased! I nearly jumped out of my skin!"

Appin had preached to absolutely incredulous hearers; Sir Wilfred's statement carried instant conviction. A Babel-like chorus of startled exclamation arose, amid which the scientist sat mutely enjoying the first fruit of his stupendous discovery.

In the midst of the clamour Tobermory entered the room and made his way with velvet tread and studied unconcern across to the group seated round the tea-table.

A sudden hush of awkwardness and constraint fell on the company. Somehow there seemed an element of embarrassment in addressing on equal terms a domestic cat of acknowledged mental ability.

"Will you have some milk, Tobermory?" asked Lady Blemley in a rather strained voice.

"I don't mind if I do," was the response, couched in a tone of even indifference. A shiver of suppressed excitement went through the listeners, and Lady Blemley might be excused for pouring out the saucerful of milk rather unsteadily.

"I'm afraid I've spilt a good deal of it," she said apologetically.

"After all, it's not my Axminster," was Tobermory's rejoinder.

Another silence fell on the group, and then Miss Resker, in her best district-visitor manner, asked if the human language had been difficult to learn. Tobermory looked squarely at her for a moment and then fixed his gaze serenely on the middle distance. It was obvious that boring questions lay outside his scheme of life.

"What do you think of human intelligence?" asked Mavis Pellington lamely.

"Of whose intelligence in particular?" asked Tobermory coldly.

"Oh, well, mine for instance," said Mavis, with a feeble laugh.

"You put me in an embarrassing position," said Tobermory, whose tone and attitude certainly did not suggest a shred of embarrassment. "When your inclusion in this house-party was suggested Sir Wilfrid protested that you were the most brainless woman of his acquaintance, and that there was a wide distinction between hospitality and the care of the feeble-minded. Lady Blemley replied that your lack of brain-power was the precise quality which had earned you your invitation, as you were the only person she could think of who might be idiotic enough to buy their old car. You know, the one they call 'The Envy of Sisyphus,' because it goes quite nicely up-hill if you push it."

Lady Blemley's protestations would have had greater effect if she had not casually suggested to Mavis only that morning that the car in question would be just the thing for her down at her Devonshire home.

Major Barfield plunged in heavily to effect a diversion.

"How about your carryings-on with the tortoise-shell puss up at the stables, eh?"

The moment he had said it every one realized the blunder.

"One does not usually discuss these matters in public," said Tobermory frigidly. "From a slight observation of your ways since you've been in this house I should imagine you'd find it inconvenient if I were to shift the conversation on to your own little affairs."

The panic which ensued was not confined to the Major.

"Would you like to go and see if cook has got your dinner ready?" suggested Lady Blemley hurriedly, affecting to ignore the fact that it wanted at least two hours to Tobermory's dinner-time.

"Thanks," said Tobermory, "not quite so soon after my tea. I don't want to die of indigestion."

"Cats have nine lives, you know," said Sir Wilfrid heartily.

"Possibly," answered Tobermory; "but only one liver."

"Adelaide!" said Mrs. Cornett,"do you mean to encourage that cat to go out and gossip about us in the servants' hall?"

The panic had indeed become general. A narrow ornamental balustrade ran in front of most of the bedroom windows at the Towers, and it was recalled with dismay that this had formed a favourite promenade for Tobermory at all hours, whence he could watch the pigeons—and heaven knew what else besides. If he intended to become reminiscent in his present outspoken strain the effect would be something more than disconcerting. Mrs. Cornett, who spent much time at her toilet table, and whose

complexion was reputed to be of a nomadic though punctual disposition, looked as ill at ease as the Major. Miss Scrawen, who
wrote fiercely sensuous poetry and led a blameless life, merely
displayed irritation; if you are methodical and virtuous in private
you don't necessarily want every one to know it. Bertie van Tahn,
who was so depraved at seventeen that he had long ago given up
trying to be any worse, turned a dull shade of gardenia white, but
he did not commit the error of dashing out of the room like Odo
Finsberry, a young gentleman who was understood to be reading
for the Church and who was possibly disturbed at the thought of
scandals he might hear concerning other people. Clovis had the
presence of mind to maintain a composed exterior; privately he
was calculating how long it would take to procure a box of fancy
mice through the agency of the *Exchange and Mart* as a species of
hush-money.

Even in a delicate situation like the present, Agnes Resker could
not endure to remain too long in the background.

"Why did I ever come down here?" she asked dramatically.

Tobermory immediately accepted the opening.

"Judging by what you said to Mrs. Cornett on the croquet-lawn
yesterday, you were out for food. You described the Blemleys as
the dullest people to stay with that you knew, but said they were
clever enough to employ a first-rate cook; otherwise they'd find it
difficult to get any one to come down a second time."

"There's not a word of truth in it! I appeal to Mrs. Cornett—"
exclaimed the discomfited Agnes.

"Mrs. Cornett repeated your remark afterwards to Bertie van
Tahn," continued Tobermory, "and said, 'That woman is a regular
Hunger Marcher; she'd go anywhere for four square meals a day,'
and Bertie van Tahn said—"

At this point the chronicle mercifully ceased. Tobermory had
caught a glimpse of the big yellow Tom from the Rectory working
his way through the shrubbery towards the stable wing. In a flash
he had vanished through the open French window.

With the disappearance of his too brilliant pupil Cornelius Appin
found himself beset by a hurricane of bitter upbraiding, anxious
inquiry, and frightened entreaty. The responsibility for the situation
lay with him, and he must prevent matters from becoming worse.
Could Tobermory impart his dangerous gift to other cats? was the
first question he had to answer. It was possible, he replied, that he

might have initiated his intimate friend the stable puss into his new accomplishment, but it was unlikely that his teaching could have taken a wider range as yet.

"Then," said Mrs. Cornett, "Tobermory may be a valuable cat and a great pet; but I'm sure you'll agree, Adelaide, that both he and the stable cat must be done away with without delay."

"You don't suppose I've enjoyed the last quarter of an hour, do you?" said Lady Blemley bitterly. "My husband and I are very fond of Tobermory—at least, we were before this horrible accomplishment was infused into him; but now, of course, the only thing is to have him destroyed as soon as possible."

"We can put some strychnine in the scraps he always gets at dinnertime," said Sir Wilfrid, "and I will go and drown the stable cat myself. The coachman will be very sore at losing his pet, but I'll say a very catching form of mange has broken out in both cats and we're afraid of its spreading to the kennels."

"But my great discovery!" expostulated Mr. Appin; "after all my years of research and experiment—"

"You can go and experiment on the short-horns at the farm, who are under proper control," said Mrs. Cornett, "or the elephants at the Zoological Gardens. They're said to be highly intelligent, and they have this recommendation, that they don't come creeping about our bedrooms and under chairs, and so forth."

An archangel ecstatically proclaiming the Millennium, and then finding that it clashed unpardonably with Henley and would have to be indefinitely postponed, could hardly have felt more crestfallen than Cornelius Appin at the reception of his wonderful achievement. Public opinion, however, was against him—in fact, had the general voice been consulted on the subject it is probable that a strong minority vote would have been in favour of including him in the strychnine diet.

Defective train arrangements and a nervous desire to see matters brought to a finish prevented an immediate dispersal of the party, but dinner that evening was not a social success. Sir Wilfrid had had rather a trying time with the stable cat and subsequently with the coachman. Agnes Resker ostentatiously limited her repast to a morsel of dry toast, which she bit as though it were a personal enemy; while Mavis Pellington maintained a vindictive silence throughout the meal. Lady Blemley kept up a flow of what she hoped was conversation, but her attention was fixed on the doorway. A plateful of carefully dosed fish scraps was in readiness on the sideboard, but sweets and savoury and dessert went their way, and no Tobermory appeared either in the dining-room or kitchen.

The sepulchral dinner was cheerful compared with the subsequent vigil in the smoking-room. Eating and drinking had at least supplied a distraction and cloak to the prevailing embarrassment. Bridge was out of the question in the general tension of nerves and tempers, and after Odo Finsberry had given a lugubrious rendering of "Mélisande in the Wood" to a frigid audience, music was tacitly avoided. At eleven the servants went to bed, announcing that the small window in the pantry had been left open as usual for Tobermory's private use. The guests read steadily through the current batch of magazines, and fell back gradually on the "Badminton Library" and bound volumes of *Punch*. Lady Blemley made periodic visits to the pantry, returning each time with an expression of listless depression which forestalled questioning.

At two o'clock Clovis broke the dominating silence.

"He won't turn up tonight. He's probably in the local newspaper office at the present moment, dictating the first instalment of his reminiscences. Lady What's-her-name's book won't be in it. It will be the event of the day."

Having made this contribution to the general cheerfulness, Clovis went to bed. At long intervals the various members of the house-party followed his example.

The servants taking round the early tea made a uniform announcement in reply to a uniform question. Tobermory had not returned.

Breakfast was, if anything, a more unpleasant function than dinner had been, but before its conclusion the situation was relieved. Tobermory's corpse was brought in from the shrubbery, where a gardener had just discovered it. From the bites on his throat and the yellow fur which coated his claws it was evident that he had fallen in unequal combat with the big Tom from the Rectory.

By midday most of the guests had quitted the Towers, and after lunch Lady Blemley had sufficiently recovered her spirits to write an extremely nasty letter to the Rectory about the loss of her valuable pet.

Tobermory had been Appin's one successful pupil, and he was destined to have no successor. A few weeks later an elephant in the

Dresden Zoological Garden, which had shown no previous signs of irritability, broke loose and killed an Englishman who had apparently been teasing it. The victim's name was variously reported in the papers as Oppin and Eppelin, but his front name was faithfully rendered Cornelius.

"If he was trying German irregular verbs on the poor beast," said Clovis, "he deserved all he got."

HOW PEARL BUTTON WAS KIDNAPPED

Katherine Mansfield

PEARL BUTTON SWUNG on the little gate in front of the House of Boxes. It was the early afternoon of a sunshiny day with little winds playing hide-and-seek in it. They blew Pearl Button's pinafore frill into her mouth, and they blew the street dust all over the House of Boxes. Pearl watched it—like a cloud—like when mother peppered her fish and the top of the pepper-pot came off. She swung on the little gate, all alone, and she sang a small song. Two big women came walking down the street. One was dressed in red and the other was dressed in yellow and green. They had pink handkerchiefs over their heads, and both of them carried a big flax basket of ferns. They had no shoes and stockings on, and they came walking along, slowly, because they were so fat, and talking to each other and always smiling. Pearl stopped swinging, and when they saw her they stopped walking. They looked and looked at her and then they talked to each other, waving their arms and clapping their hands together. Pearl began to laugh. The two women came up to her, keeping close to the hedge and looking in a frightened way towards the House of Boxes. "Hallo, little girl!" said one. Pearl said, "Hallo!" "You all alone by yourself?" Pearl nodded. "Where's your mother?" "In the kitching, ironing-because-its-Tuesday." The women smiled at her and Pearl smiled back. "Oh," she said, "haven't you got very white teeth indeed! Do it again." The dark women laughed, and again they talked to each other with funny words and wavings of the hands. "What's your name?" they asked her. "Pearl Button." "You coming with us, Pearl Button? We got beautiful things to show you," whispered one of the women. So Pearl got down from the gate and she slipped out into the road.

And she walked between the two dark women down the windy road, taking little running steps to keep up, and wondering what they had in their House of Boxes.

They walked a long way. "You tired?" asked one of the women, bending down to Pearl. Pearl shook her head. They walked much further. "You not tired?" asked the other woman. And Pearl shook her head again, but tears shook from her eyes at the same time and her lips trembled. One of the women gave over her flax basket of ferns and caught Pearl Button up in her arms, and walked with Pearl Button's head against her shoulder and her dusty little legs dangling. She was softer than a bed and she had a nice smell—a smell that made you bury your head and breathe and breathe it. . . . They set Pearl Button down in a long room full of other people the same colour as they were—and all these people came close to her and looked at her, nodding and laughing and throwing up their eyes. The woman who had carried Pearl took off her hair ribbon and shook her curls loose. There was a cry from the other women, and they crowded close and some of them ran a finger through Pearl's yellow curls, very gently, and one of them, a young one, lifted all Pearl's hair and kissed the back of her little white neck. Pearl felt shy but happy at the same time. There were some men on the floor, smoking, with rugs and feather mats round their shoulders. One of them made a funny face at her and he pulled a great big peach out of his pocket and set it on the floor, and flicked it with his finger as though it were a marble. It rolled right over to her. Pearl picked it up. "Please can I eat it?" she asked. At that they all laughed and clapped their hands, and the man with the funny face made another at her and pulled a pear out of his pocket and sent it bobbling over the floor. Pearl laughed. The women sat on the floor and Pearl sat down too. The floor was very dusty. She carefully pulled up her pinafore and dress and sat on her petticoat as she had been taught to sit in dusty places, and she ate the fruit, the juice running all down her front. "Oh," she said in a very frightened voice to one of the women, "I've spilt all the juice!" "That doesn't matter at all," said the woman, patting her cheek. A man came into the room with a long whip in his hand. He shouted something. They all got up, shouting, laughing, wrapping themselves up in rugs and blankets and feather mats. Pearl was carried again, this time into a great cart, and she sat on the lap of one of her women with the driver beside her. It was a green cart with a red pony and a black pony. It went very fast out of the town. The driver stood up and waved the whip round his head. Pearl peered over the shoulder of her woman. Other carts were behind like a procession. She waved at them. Then the country came. First fields of short grass with sheep on them and little bushes of white flowers and pink briar rose baskets—then big trees on both sides of the road—and nothing to be seen except big trees. Pearl tried to look through them but it was quite dark. Birds were singing. She nestled closer in the big lap. The woman was warm as a cat, and she moved up and down when she breathed, just like purring. Pearl played with a green ornament round her neck, and the woman took the little hand and kissed each of her fingers and then turned it over and kissed the dimples. Pearl had never been happy like this before. On the top of a big hill they stopped. The driving man turned to Pearl and said, "Look, look!" and pointed with his whip. And down at the bottom of the hill was something perfectly different—a great big piece of blue water was creeping over the land. She screamed and clutched at the big woman. "What is it, what is it?" "Why," said the woman, "it's the sea." "Will it hurt us—is it coming?" "Ai-e, no, it doesn't come to us. It's very beautiful. You look again." Pearl looked. "You're sure it can't come," she said. "Ai-e, no. It stays in its place," said the big woman. Waves with white tops came leaping over the blue. Pearl watched them break on a long piece of land covered with garden-path shells. They drove round a corner. There were some little houses down close to the sea, with wood fences round them and gardens inside. They comforted her. Pink and red and blue washing hung over the fences, and as they came near more people came out, and five yellow dogs with long thin tails. All the people were fat and laughing, with little naked babies holding on to them or rolling about in the gardens like puppies. Pearl was lifted down and taken into a tiny house with only one room and a verandah. There was a girl there with two pieces of black hair down to her feet. She was setting the dinner on the floor. "It *is* a funny place," said Pearl, watching the pretty girl while the woman unbuttoned her little drawers for her. She was very hungry. She ate meat and vegetables and fruit and the woman gave her milk out of a green cup. And it was quite silent except for the sea outside and the laughs of the two women watching her. "Haven't you got any Houses of Boxes?" she said. "Don't you all live in a row? Don't the men go to offices? Aren't there any nasty things?"

They took off her shoes and stockings, her pinafore and dress. She walked about in her petticoat and then she walked outside with the grass pushing between her toes. The two women came out with different sorts of baskets. They took her hands. Over a little paddock, through a fence, and then on warm sand with brown grass in it they went down to the sea. Pearl held back when the sand grew wet, but the women coaxed, "Nothing to hurt, very beautiful. You come." They dug in the sand and found some shells which they threw into the baskets. The sand was wet as mud pies. Pearl forgot her fright and began digging too. She got hot and wet and suddenly over her feet broke a little line of foam. "Oo, oo!" she shrieked, dabbling with her feet, "Lovely, lovely!" She paddled in the shallow water. It was warm. She made a cup of her hands and caught some of it. But it stopped being blue in her hands. She was so excited that she rushed over to her woman and flung her little thin arms round the woman's neck, hugging her, kissing. . . . Suddenly the girl gave a frightful scream. The woman raised herself and Pearl slipped down on the sand and looked towards the land. Little men in blue coats—little blue men came running, running towards her with shouts and whistlings—a crowd of little blue men to carry her back to the House of Boxes.

SMOKE

Djuna Barnes

THERE WAS SWART with his bushy head and Fenken with the half shut eyes and the grayish beard, and there also was Zelka with her big earrings and her closely bound inky hair, who had often been told that "she was very beautiful in a black way."

Ah, what a fine strong creature she had been and what a fine strong creature her father Fenken had been before her, and what a specimen was her husband Swart, with his gentle melancholy mouth and his strange strong eyes and his brown neck.

Fenken in his youth had loaded the cattle boats, and in his twilight of age he would sit in the round-backed chair by the open fireplace, his two trembling hands folded, and would talk of what he had been.

"A bony man I was, Zelka—my two knees as hard as a pavement, so that I clapped them with great discomfort to my own hands; sometimes," he would add, with a twinkle in his old eyes, "I'd put you between them and my hand; it hurt less."

Zelka would turn her eyes on him slowly—they moved around into sight from under her eyebrows like the barrel of a well-kept gun; they were hard like metal and strong, and she was always conscious of them even in sleep. When she would close her eyes before saying her prayers she would remark to Swart, "I draw the hood over the artillery." And Swart would smile, nodding his large head.

In the town these three were called the "Bullets"—when they came down the street little children sprang aside, not because they were afraid, but because they came so fast and brought with them something so healthy, something so potent, something unconquerable. Fenken could make his fingers snap against his palm like the

566

crack of a cabby's whip just by shutting his hand abruptly, and he did this often, watching the gamin and smiling.

★ ★ ★

Swart, too, had his power, but there was a hint at something softer in him, something that made the lips kind when they were sternest, something that gave him a sad expression when he was thinking—something that had drawn Zelka to him in their first days of courting. "We Fenkens," she would say, "have iron in our veins—in yours I fear there's a little blood."

Zelka was cleanly; she washed her linen clean as though she were punishing the dirt. Had the linen been less durable there would have been holes in it from her knuckles in six months. Everything Zelka cooked was tender—she had bruised it with her preparations.

And then Zelka's baby had come. A healthy, fat, little crying thing, with eyes like its father's and with its father's mouth. In vain did Zelka look for something about it that would give it away as one of the Fenken blood—it had a maddeningly tender way of stroking her face, its hair was finer than blown gold, and it squinted up its pale blue eyes when it fell over its nose. Sometimes Zelka would turn the baby around in bed, placing its little feet against her side waiting for it to kick. And when it finally did, it was gently and without great strength and with much good humor. "Swart," Zelka would say, "your child is entirely human. I'm afraid all his veins run blood," and she would add to her father, "Sonny will never load the cattle ships."

When it was old enough to crawl Zelka would get down on hands and knees and chase it about the little ash-littered room. The baby would crawl ahead of her, giggling and driving Zelka mad with a desire to stop and hug him; but when she roared behind him like a lion to make him hurry, the baby would roll over slowly, struggle into a sitting posture, and putting his hand up would sit staring at her as though he would like to study out something that made this difference between them.

When it was seven it would escape from the house and wander down to the shore, and stand for hours watching the boats coming in, being loaded and unloaded. Once one of the men put the cattle belt about him and lowered him into the boat. He went down sadly, his little golden head drooping and his feet hanging down. When they brought him back on shore again and dusted him off they were puzzled at him—he had neither cried nor laughed. They said, "Didn't you like that?" And he had only answered by looking at them fixedly.

And when he grew up he was very tender to his mother, who had taken to shaking her head over him. Fenken had died the Summer of his grandchild's thirtieth year, so that after the funeral Swart had taken the round-backed chair for his own. And now he sat there with folded hands, but he never said what a strong lad he had been. Sometimes he would say, "Do you remember how Fenken used to snap his fingers together like a whip?" and Zelka would answer, "I do."

And finally when her son married, Zelka was seen at the feast dressed in a short blue skirt leaning upon Swart's arm, both of them still strong and handsome and capable of lifting the buckets of cider.

Zelka's son had chosen a strange woman for a wife. A thin little thing, with a tiny waistline and a narrow chest and a small, very lovely throat. She was the daughter of a ship owner and had a good deal of money in her own name. When she married Zelka's son she brought him some ten thousand a year, and so he stopped the shipping of cattle and went in for exports and imports of Oriental silks and perfumes.

When his mother and father died he moved a little inland away from the sea and hired clerks to do his bidding. Still, he never forgot what his mother had said to him:

"There must always be a little iron in the blood, sonny."

He reflected on this when he looked at Lief, his wife. He was a silent, taciturn man as he grew older, and Lief had grown afraid of him, because of his very kindness and his melancholy.

There was only one person to whom he was a bit stern, and this was his daughter, "Little Lief." Toward her he showed a strange hostility, a touch even of that fierceness that had been his mother's—once she had rushed shrieking from his room because he had suddenly roared behind her as his mother had done behind him. When she was gone he sat for a long time by his table, his hands stretched out in front of him, thinking.

He had succeeded well; he had multiplied his wife's money now into the many thousands—they had a house in the country and servants. They were spoken of in the town as a couple who had an existence that might be termed as "pretty soft," and when the carriage drove by of a Sunday with baby Lief up front on her mother's lap and Lief's husband beside her in his gray cloth coat, they stood aside not to be trampled on by the swift legged, slender ankled "pacer" that Lief had bought that day when she had visited the "old home"—the beach that had known her and her husband when they were children. This horse was the very one that she had asked for when she saw how beautiful it was as they fastened the belt to it preparatory to lowering it over the side. It was then that she remembered how when her husband had been a little boy they had lowered him over into the boat with this same belting.

During the Winter that followed, which was a very hard one, Lief took cold and resorted to hot water bottles and thin tea. She became very fretful, and annoyed at her husband's constant questionings as to her health; even Little Lief was a nuisance because she was so noisy. She would steal into the room, and crawling under her mother's bed would begin to sing in a high, thin treble, pushing the ticking with her patent leather boots to see them crinkle. Then the mother would cry out, the nurse would run in and take her away and Lief would spend a half hour in tears. Finally they would not allow Little Lief in the room, so she would steal by the door many times, walking noiselessly up and down the hall; but finally, her youth overcoming her, she would stretch her legs out into a straight goose step, and for this she was whipped because on the day that she had been caught her mother had died.

And so the time passed and the years rolled on, taking their toll. It was now many Summers since that day that Zelka had walked into town with Swart—now many years since Fenken had snapped his fingers like a cabby's whip. Little Lief had never even heard that her grandmother had been called a "beautiful woman in a black sort of way," and she had only vaguely heard of the nickname that had once been given the family, the "Bullets." She came to know that great strength had once been in the family, to such an extent indeed that somehow a phrase was known to her, "Remember always to keep a little iron in the blood." And one night she had pricked her arm to see if there were iron in it, and she had cried because it hurt, and so she knew that there was none.

With her this phrase ended. She never repeated it because of that night when she had made that discovery.

Her father had taken to solitude and the study of sociology. Sometimes he would turn her about by the shoulder and look at her, breathing in a thick way he had with him of late, and once he told her she was a good girl but foolish, and left her alone.

They had begun to lose money, and some of Little Lief's tapestries, given her by her mother, were sold. Her heart broke, but she opened the windows oftener because she needed some kind of beauty. She made the mistake of loving tapestries best and nature second best. Somehow she had gotten the two things mixed—of course it was due to her bringing up. "If you are poor you live out of doors—but if you are rich you live in a lovely house." So to her the greatest of calamities had befallen the house; it was beginning to go away by those imperceptible means, that at first leave a house looking unfamiliar and then bare.

Finally she could stand it no longer and she married a thin, wiry man with a long thin nose and a nasty trick of rubbing it with a finger equally long and thin—a man with a fair income and very refined sisters.

This man Misha wanted to be a lawyer. He studied half the night and never seemed happy unless his head was in his palm. His sisters were like this also, only for another reason: they enjoyed weeping. If they could find nothing to cry about they cried for the annoyance of this dearth of destitution and worry. They held daily councils for future domestic trouble—one the gesture of emotional and one of mental desire.

Sometimes Little Lief's father would come to the big iron gate and ask to see her. He would never come in—why? He never explained. So Little Lief and he would talk over the gate top, and sometimes he was gentle and sometimes he was not. When he was harsh to her Little Lief wept, and when she wept he would look at her steadily from under his eyebrows and say nothing. Sometimes he asked her to take a walk with him. This would set Little Lief into a terrible flutter; the corners of her mouth would twitch and her nostrils tremble, but she always went.

Misha worried little about his wife. He was a very selfish man, with that greatest capacity of a selfish nature, the ability to labor untiringly for some one thing that he wanted and that nature had placed beyond his reach. Some people called this quality excellent, pointing out what a great scholar Misha was, holding him up as an example in their own households, looking after him when he went hurriedly down the street with that show of nervous expectancy that a man always betrays when he knows within himself that he is deficient—a sort of peering in the face of life to see if it has discovered the flaw.

Little Lief felt that her father was trying to be something that was not natural to him. What was it? As she grew older, she tried to puzzle it out. Now it happened more often that she would catch him looking at her in a strange way, and once she asked him half playfully if he wished she had been a boy—and he had answered abruptly, "Yes, I do."

Little Lief would stand for hours at the casement and, leaning her head against the glass, try to solve this thing about her father—and then she discovered it when he had said, "Yes, I do." He was trying to be strong—what was it that was in the family?—oh, yes—iron in the blood—he feared there was no longer any iron left—well, perhaps there wasn't—was that the reason he looked at her like this? No, he was worried about himself. Why?—wasn't he satisfied with his own strength? He had been cruel enough very often. This shouldn't have worried him.

She asked him, and he answered, "Yes, but cruelty isn't strength." That was an admission—she was less afraid of him since that day when he had made that answer, but now she kept peering into his face as he had done into hers and he seemed not to notice it. Well, he was getting to be a very old man.

Then one day her two sisters-in-law pounced upon her so that her golden head shook on its thin, delicate neck.

"Your father has come into the garden," cried one.

"Yes, yes," pursued the elder. "He's even sat himself upon the bench."

She hurried out to him. "What's the matter, father?" Her head was aching.

"Nothing." He did not look up.

She sat down beside him, stroking his hand, at first timidly, then with more courage.

"Have you looked at the garden?"

He nodded.

She burst into tears.

He took his hand away from her and began to laugh.

"What's the matter, child? A good dose of hog-killing would do you good."

"You have no right to speak to me in this way—take yourself off!" she cried sharply, holding her side, and her father rocked with laughter.

She stretched her long, thin arms out, clenching her thin fingers together. The lace on her short sleeves trembled, her knuckles grew white.

"A good pig-killing," he repeated, watching her, and she grew sullen.

"Eh?" He pinched her flesh a little and dropped it. She was passive; she made no murmur. He got up, walked to the gate, opened it and went out, closing it after him. He turned back a step and waved to her. She did not answer for a moment, then she waved back slowly with one of her thin, white hands.

She would have liked to refuse to see him again, but she lacked the courage. She would say to herself, "If I am unkind to him now, perhaps later I shall regret it." In this way she tried to excuse herself. The very next time he had sent word that he wished speech with her she had come.

"Little fool!" he said, in a terrible rage, and walked off. She was quite sure that he was slowly losing his mind—a second childhood, she called it, still trying to make things as pleasant as possible.

She had been ill a good deal that Spring, and in the Fall she had terrible headaches. In the Winter months she took to her bed, and early in May the doctor was summoned.

Misha talked to the physician in the drawing-room before he sent him up to his wife.

"You must be gentle with her; she is nervous and frail." The doctor laughed outright. Misha's sisters were weeping, of course, and perfectly happy.

"It will be such a splendid thing for her," they said. Meaning the beef, iron and wine that they expected the doctor to prescribe.

Toward evening Little Lief closed her eyes.

Her child was still-born.

The physician came downstairs and entered the parlor where Misha's sisters stood together, still shedding tears.

He rubbed his hands.

"Send Misha upstairs."

"He has gone."

"Isn't it dreadful? I never could bear corpses, especially little ones."

"A baby isn't a corpse," answered the physician, smiling at his own impending humor. "It's an interrupted plan."

He felt that the baby, not having drawn a breath in this world, could not feel hurt at such a remark, because it has gathered no feminine pride and, also, as it has passed out quicker than the time it took to make the observation, it really could be called nothing more than the background for medical jocularity.

Misha came into the room with red eyes.

"Out like a puff of smoke," he said.

One of his sisters remarked: "Well, the Fenkens lived themselves thin."

The next Summer Misha married into a healthy Swedish family. His second wife had a broad face, with eyes set wide apart, and with broad, flat, healthy, yellow teeth, and she played the piano surprisingly well, though she looked a little heavy as she sat upon the piano stool.

THE BLIND MAN

James Stephens

HE WAS ONE who would have passed by the Sphinx without seeing it. He did not believe in the necessity for sphinxes, or in their reality, for that matter—they did not exist for him. Indeed, he was one to whom the Sphinx would not have been visible. He might have eyed it and noted a certain bulk of grotesque stone, but nothing more significant.

He was sex-blind, and, so, peculiarly limited by the fact that he could not appreciate women. If he had been pressed for a theory or metaphysic of womanhood he would have been unable to formulate any. Their presence he admitted, perforce: their utility was quite apparent to him on the surface, but, subterraneously, he doubted both their existence and their utility. He might have said perplexedly—Why cannot they do whatever they have to do without being always in the way? He might have said—Hang it, they are everywhere, and what good are they doing? They bothered him, they destroyed his ease when he was near them, and they spoke a language which he did not understand and did not want to understand. But as his limitations did not press on him neither did they trouble him. He was not sexually deficient, and he did not dislike women; he simply ignored them, and was only really at home with men. All the crudities which we enumerate as masculine delighted him—simple things, for, in the gender of abstract ideas, vice is feminine, brutality is masculine, the female being older, vastly older than the male, much more competent in every way, stronger, even in her physique, than he, and, having little baggage of mental or ethical preoccupations to delay her progress, she is still the guardian of evolution, requiring little more from man than to be stroked and petted for a while.

He could be brutal at times. He liked to get drunk at seasonable periods. He would cheerfully break a head or a window, and would bandage the one damage or pay for the other with equal skill and pleasure. He liked to tramp rugged miles swinging his arms and whistling as he went, and he could sit for hours by the side of a ditch thinking thoughts without words—an easy and a pleasant way of thinking, and one which may lead to something in the long run.

Even his mother was an abstraction to him. He was kind to her so far as doing things went, but he looked over her, or round her, and marched away and forgot her.

Sex-blindedness carries with it many other darknesses. We do not know what masculine thing is projected by the feminine consciousness, and civilisation, even life itself, must stand at a halt until that has been discovered or created; but art is the female projected by the male: science is the male projected by the male—as yet a poor thing, and to remain so until it has become art; that is, has become fertilised and so more psychological than mechanical. The small part of science which came to his notice (inventions, machinery, etc.) was easily and delightedly comprehended by him. He could do intricate things with a knife and a piece of string, or a hammer and a saw; but a picture, a poem, a statue, a piece of music—these left him as uninterested as they found him: more so, in truth, for they left him bored and dejected.

His mother came to dislike him, and there were many causes and many justifications for her dislike. She was an orderly, busy, competent woman, the counterpart of endless millions of her sex, who liked to understand what she saw or felt, and who had no happiness in reading riddles. To her he was at times an enigma, and at times again a simpleton. In both aspects he displeased and embarrassed her. One has one's sense of property, and in him she could not put her finger on anything that was hers. We demand continuity, logic in other words, but between her son and herself there was a gulf fixed, spanned by no bridge whatever; there was complete isolation; no boat plied between them at all. All the kindly human things which she loved were unintelligible to him, and his coarse pleasures or blunt evasions distressed and bewildered her. When she spoke to him he gaped or yawned; and yet she did not speak on weighty matters, just the necessary small-change of existence—somebody's cold, somebody's dress, somebody's marriage or death. When she addressed him on sterner subjects, the ground, the weather, the crops, he looked at her as if she were a baby, he listened with stubborn resentment, and strode away a confessed boor. There was no contact anywhere between them, and he was a slow exasperation to her—What can we do with that which is ours and not ours? either we own a thing or we do not, and, whichever way it goes, there is some end to it; but certain enigmas are illegitimate and are so hounded from decent cogitation.

She could do nothing but dismiss him, and she could not even do that, for there he was at the required periods, always primed with the wrong reply to any question, the wrong aspiration, the wrong conjecture; a perpetual trampler on mental corns, a person for whom one could do nothing but apologise.

They lived on a small farm, and almost the entire work of the place was done by him. His younger brother assisted, but that assistance could have easily been done without. If the cattle were sick, he cured them almost by instinct. If the horse was lame or wanted a new shoe, he knew precisely what to do in both events. When the time came for ploughing, he gripped the handles and drove a furrow which was as straight and as economical as any furrow in the world. He could dig all day long and be happy; he gathered in the harvest as another would gather in a bride; and, in the intervals between these occupations, he fled to the nearest public-house and wallowed among his kind.

He did not fly away to drink; he fled to be among men—Then he awakened. His tongue worked with the best of them, and adequately too. He could speak weightily on many things—boxing, wrestling, hunting, fishing, the seasons, the weather, and the chances of this and the other man's crops. He had deep knowledge about brands of tobacco and the peculiar virtues of many different liquors. He knew birds and beetles and worms; how a weazel would behave in extraordinary circumstances; how to train every breed of horse and dog. He recited goats from the cradle to the grave, could tell the name of any tree from its leaf; knew how a bull could be coerced, a cow cut up, and what plasters were good for a broken head. Sometimes, and often enough, the talk would chance on women, and then he laughed as heartily as any one else, but he was always relieved when the conversation trailed to more interesting things.

His mother died and left the farm to the younger instead of the elder son; an unusual thing to do, but she did detest him. She knew her younger son very well. He was foreign to her in nothing. His temper ran parallel with her own, his tastes were hers, his ideas had been largely derived from her, she could track them at any time and make or demolish him. He would go to a dance or a picnic and be as exhilarated as she was, and would discuss the matter afterwards. He could speak with some cogency on the shape of this and that female person, the hat of such an one, the disagreeableness of tea at this house and the goodness of it at the other. He could even listen to one speaking without going to sleep at the fourth word. In all he was a decent, quiet lad who would become a father the exact replica of his own, and whose daughters would resemble his mother as closely as two peas resemble their green ancestors—So she left him the farm.

Of course, there was no attempt to turn the elder brother out. Indeed, for some years the two men worked quietly together and prospered and were contented; then, as was inevitable, the younger brother got married, and the elder had to look out for a new place to live in, and to work in—things had become difficult.

It is very easy to say that in such and such circumstances a man should do this and that well-pondered thing, but the courts of logic have as yet the most circumscribed jurisdiction. Just as statistics can prove anything and be quite wrong, so reason can sit in its padded chair issuing pronouncements which are seldom within measurable distance of any reality. Everything is true only in relation to its centre of thought. Some people think with their heads—their subsequent actions are as logical and unpleasant as are those of the other sort who think only with their blood, and this latter has its irrefutable logic also. He thought in this subterranean fashion, and if he had thought in the other the issue would not have been any different.

Still, it was not an easy problem for him, or for any person lacking initiative—a sexual characteristic. He might have emigrated, but his roots were deeply struck in his own place, so the idea never occurred to him; furthermore, our thoughts are often no deeper than our pockets, and one wants money to move anywhere. For any other life than that of farming he had no training and small desire. He had no money and he was a farmer's son. Without money he could not get a farm; being a farmer's son he could not sink to the degradation of a day labourer; logically he could sink, actually he could not without endangering his own centres and verities—so he also got married.

He married a farm of about ten acres, and the sun began to shine on him once more; but only for a few days. Suddenly the sun went away from the heavens; the moon disappeared from the silent night; the silent night itself fled afar, leaving in its stead a noisy, dirty blackness through which one slept or yawned as one could. There was the farm, of course—one could go there and work; but the freshness went out of the very ground; the crops lost their sweetness and candour; the horses and cows disowned him; the goats ceased to be his friends—It was all up with him. He did not whistle any longer. He did not swing his shoulders as he walked, and, although he continued to smoke, he did not look for a particular green bank whereon he could sit quietly flooded with those slow thoughts that had no words.

For he discovered that he had not married a farm at all. He had married a woman—a thin-jawed, elderly slattern, whose sole beauty was her farm. How her jaws worked! The processions and congregations of words that fell and dribbled and slid out of them! Those jaws were never quiet, and in spite of all he did not say anything. There was not anything to say, but much to do from which he shivered away in terror. He looked at her sometimes through the muscles of his arms, through his big, strong hands, through fogs and fumes and singular, quiet tumults that raged within him. She lessoned him on the things he knew so well, and she was always wrong. She lectured him on those things which she did know, but the unending disquisition, the perpetual repetition, the foolish, empty emphasis, the dragging weightiness of her tongue made him repudiate her knowledge and hate it as much as he did her.

Sometimes, looking at her, he would rub his eyes and yawn with fatigue and wonder—There she was! A something enwrapped about with petticoats. Veritably alive. Active as an insect! Palpable to the touch! And what was she doing to him? Why did she do it? Why didn't she go away? Why didn't she die? What sense was there in the making of such a creature that clothed itself like a bolster, without any freedom or entertainment or shapeliness?

Her eyes were fixed on him and they always seemed to be angry; and her tongue was uttering rubbish about horses, rubbish about cows, rubbish about hay and oats. Nor was this the sum of his

weariness. It was not alone that he was married; he was multitudi-
nously, egregiously married. He had married a whole family, and
what a family—

Her mother lived with her, her eldest sister lived with her, her
youngest sister lived with her—And these were all swathed about
with petticoats and shawls. They had no movement. Their feet
were like those of no creature he had ever observed. One could
hear the flip-flap of their slippers all over the place, and at all hours.
They were down-at-heel, draggle-tailed, and futile. There was no
workmanship about them. They were as unfinished, as unsightly as
a puddle on a road. They insulted his eyesight, his hearing, and his
energy. They had lank hair that slapped about them like wet seaweed, and they were all talking, talking, talking.

The mother was of an incredible age. She was senile with age.
Her cracked cackle never ceased for an instant. She talked to the
dog and the cat; she talked to the walls of the room; she spoke out
through the window to the weather; she shut her eyes in a corner
and harangued the circumambient darkness. The eldest sister was as
silent as a deep ditch and as ugly. She slid here and there with her
head on one side like an inquisitive hen watching one curiously,
and was always doing nothing with an air of futile employment.
The youngest was a semi-lunatic who prattled and prattled without
ceasing, and was always catching one's sleeve, and laughing at one's
face.—And everywhere those flopping, wriggling petticoats were
appearing and disappearing. One saw slack hair whisking by the
corner of one's eye. Mysteriously, urgently, they were coming and
going and coming again, and never, never being silent.

More and more he went running to the public-house. But it was
no longer to be among men, it was to get drunk. One might imagine him sitting there thinking those slow thoughts without words.
One might predict that the day would come when he would realise
very suddenly, very clearly, all that he had been thinking about,
and, when this urgent, terrible thought had been translated into its
own terms of action, he would be quietly hanged by the neck until
he was as dead as he had been before he was alive.

IF I WERE A MAN

Charlotte Perkins Gilman

"IF I WERE a man, . . ." that was what pretty little Mollie Mathewson always said when Gerald would not do what she wanted him to—which was seldom.

That was what she said this bright morning, with a stamp of her little high-heeled slipper, just because he had made a fuss about that bill, the long one with the "account rendered," which she had forgotten to give him the first time and been afraid to the second—and now he had taken it from the postman himself.

Mollie was "true to type." She was a beautiful instance of what is reverentially called "a true woman." Little, of course—no true woman may be big. Pretty, of course—no true woman could possibly be plain. Whimsical, capricious, charming, changeable, devoted to pretty clothes and always "wearing them well," as the esoteric phrase has it. (This does not refer to the clothes—they do not wear well in the least—but to some special grace of putting them on and carrying them about, granted to but few, it appears.)

She was also a loving wife and a devoted mother possessed of "the social gift" and the love of "society" that goes with it, and, with all these was fond and proud of her home and managed it as capably as—well, as most women do.

If ever there was a true woman it was Mollie Mathewson, yet she was wishing heart and soul she was a man.

And all of a sudden she was!

She was Gerald, walking down the path so erect and square-shouldered, in a hurry for his morning train, as usual, and, it must be confessed, in something of a temper.

Her own words were ringing in her ears—not only the "last word," but several that had gone before, and she was holding her lips tight shut, not to say something she would be sorry for. But instead of acquiescence in the position taken by that angry little figure on the veranda, what she felt was a sort of superior pride, a sympathy as with weakness, a feeling that "I must be gentle with her," in spite of the temper.

A man! Really a man—with only enough subconscious memory of herself remaining to make her recognize the differences.

At first there was a funny sense of size and weight and extra thickness, the feet and hands seemed strangely large, and her long, straight, free legs swung forward at a gait that made her feel as if on stilts.

This presently passed, and in its place, growing all day, wherever she went, came a new and delightful feeling of being *the right size*.

Everything fitted now. Her back snugly against the seat-back, her feet comfortably on the floor. Her feet? . . . His feet! She studied them carefully. Never before, since her early school days, had she felt such freedom and comfort as to feet—they were firm and solid on the ground when she walked; quick, springy, safe—as when, moved by an unrecognizable impulse, she had run after, caught, and swung aboard the car.

Another impulse fished in a convenient pocket for change—instantly, automatically, bringing forth a nickel for the conductor and a penny for the newsboy.

These pockets came as a revelation. Of course she had known they were there, had counted them, made fun of them, mended them, even envied them; but she never had dreamed of how it *felt* to have pockets.

Behind her newspaper she let her consciousness, that odd mingled consciousness, rove from pocket to pocket, realizing the armored assurance of having all those things at hand, instantly get-at-able, ready to meet emergencies. The cigar case gave her a warm feeling of comfort—it was full; the firmly held fountain pen, safe unless she stood on her head; the keys, pencils, letters, documents, notebook, checkbook, bill folder—all at once, with a deep rushing sense of power and pride, she felt what she had never felt before in all her life—the possession of money, of her own earned money—hers to give or to withhold, not to beg for, tease for, wheedle for—hers.

That bill—why, if it had come to her—to him, that is—he would have paid it as a matter of course, and never mentioned it—to her.

Then, being he, sitting there so easily and firmly with his money in his pockets, she wakened to his life-long consciousness about money. Boyhood—its desires and dreams, ambitions. Young manhood—working tremendously for the wherewithal to make a home—for her. The present years with all their net of cares and hopes and dangers; the present moment, when he needed every cent for special plans of great importance, and this bill, long overdue and demanding payment, meant an amount of inconvenience wholly unnecessary if it had been given him when it first came; also, the man's keen dislike of that "account rendered."

"Women have no business sense!" she found herself saying. "And all that money just for hats—idiotic, useless, ugly things!"

With that she began to see the hats of the women in the car as she had never seen hats before. The men's seemed normal, dignified, becoming, with enough variety for personal taste, and with distinction in style and in age, such as she had never noticed before. But the women's—

With the eyes of a man and the brain of a man; with the memory of a whole lifetime of free action wherein the hat, close-fitting on cropped hair, had been no handicap; she now perceived the hats of women.

The massed fluffed hair was at once attractive and foolish, and on that hair, at every angle, in all colors, tipped, twisted, tortured into every crooked shape, made of any substance chance might offer, perched these formless objects. Then, on their formlessness the trimmings—these squirts of stiff feathers, these violent outstanding bows of glistening ribbon, these swaying, projecting masses of plumage which tormented the faces of bystanders.

Never in all her life had she imagined that this idolized millinery could look, to those who paid for it, like the decorations of an insane monkey.

And yet, when there came into the car a little woman, as foolish as any, but pretty and sweet-looking, up rose Gerald Mathewson and gave her his seat. And, later, when there came in a handsome red-cheeked girl, whose hat was wilder, more violent in color and eccentric in shape than any other—when she stood nearby and her soft curling plumes swept his cheek once and again—he felt a sense of sudden pleasure at the intimate tickling touch—and she, deep down within, felt such a wave of shame as might well drown a thousand hats forever.

When he took his train, his seat in the smoking car, she had a new surprise. All about him were the other men, commuters too, and many of them friends of his.

To her, they would have been distinguished as "Mary Wade's husband," "the man Belle Grant is engaged to," "that rich Mr. Shopworth," or "that pleasant Mr. Beale." And they would all have lifted their hats to her, bowed, made polite conversation if near enough—especially Mr. Beale.

Now came the feeling of open-eyed acquaintance, of knowing men—as they were. The mere amount of this knowledge was a surprise to her—the whole background of talk from boyhood up, the gossip of barber-shop and club, the conversation of morning and evening hours on trains, the knowledge of political affiliation, of business standing and prospects, of character—in a light she had never known before.

They came and talked to Gerald, one and another. He seemed quite popular. And as they talked, with this new memory and new understanding, an understanding which seemed to include all these men's minds, there poured in on the submerged consciousness beneath a new, a startling knowledge—what men really think of women.

Good, average, American men were there; married men for the most part, and happy—as happiness goes in general. In the minds of each and all there seemed to be a two-story department, quite apart from the rest of their ideas, a separate place where they kept their thoughts and feelings about women.

In the upper half were the tenderest emotions, the most exquisite ideals, the sweetest memories, all lovely sentiments as to "home" and "mother," all delicate admiring adjectives, a sort of sanctuary, where a veiled statue, blindly adored, shared place with beloved yet commonplace experiences.

In the lower half—here that buried consciousness woke to keen distress—they kept quite another assortment of ideas. Here, even in this clean-minded husband of hers, was the memory of stories told at men's dinners, of worse ones overheard in street or car, of base traditions, coarse epithets, gross experiences—known, though not shared.

And all these in the department "woman," while in the rest of the mind—here was new knowledge indeed.

The world opened before her. Not the world she had been reared in—where Home had covered all the map, almost, and the rest had been "foreign," or "unexplored country," but the world as it was—man's world, as made, lived in, and seen, by men.

It was dizzying. To see the houses that fled so fast across the car window, in terms of builders' bills, or of some technical insight into materials and methods; to see a passing village with lamentable knowledge of who "owned it" and of how its Boss was rapidly aspiring in state power, or of how that kind of paving was a failure; to see shops, not as mere exhibitions of desirable objects, but as business ventures, many were sinking ships, some promising a profitable voyage—this new world bewildered her.

She—as Gerald—had already forgotten about that bill, over which she—as Mollie—was still crying at home. Gerald was "talking business" with this man, "talking politics" with that, and now sympathizing with the carefully withheld troubles of a neighbor.

Mollie had always sympathized with the neighbor's wife before.

She began to struggle violently with this large dominant masculine consciousness. She remembered with sudden clearness things she had read, lectures she had heard, and resented with increasing intensity this serene masculine preoccupation with the male point of view.

Mr. Miles, the little fussy man who lived on the other side of the street, was talking now. He had a large complacent wife; Mollie had never liked her much, but had always thought him rather nice—he was so punctilious in small courtesies.

And here he was talking to Gerald—such talk!

"Had to come in here," he said. "Gave my seat to a dame who was bound to have it. There's nothing they won't get when they make up their minds to it—eh?"

"No fear!" said the big man in the next seat. "They haven't much mind to make up, you know—and if they do, they'll change it."

"The real danger," began the Rev. Alfred Smythe, the new Episcopal clergyman, a thin, nervous, tall man with a face several centuries behind the times, "is that they will overstep the limits of their God-appointed sphere."

"Their natural limits ought to hold 'em, I think," said cheerful Dr. Jones. "You can't get around physiology, I tell you."

"I've never seen any limits, myself, not to what they want, anyhow," said Mr. Miles. "Merely a rich husband and a fine house and no end of bonnets and dresses, and the latest thing in motors, and a few diamonds—and so on. Keeps us pretty busy."

There was a tired gray man across the aisle. He had a very nice wife, always beautifully dressed, and three unmarried daughters, also beautifully dressed—Mollie knew them. She knew he worked hard, too, and she looked at him now a little anxiously.

But he smiled cheerfully.

"Do you good, Miles," he said. "What else would a man work for? A good woman is about the best thing on earth."

"And a bad one's the worst, that's sure," responded Miles.

"She's a pretty weak sister, viewed professionally," Dr. Jones averred with solemnity, and the Rev. Alfred Smythe added, "She brought evil into the world."

Gerald Mathewson sat up straight. Something was stirring in him which he did not recognize—yet could not resist.

"Seems to me we all talk like Noah," he suggested drily. "Or the ancient Hindu scriptures. Women have their limitations, but so do we, God knows. Haven't we known girls in school and college just as smart as we were?"

"They cannot play our games," coldly replied the clergyman.

Gerald measured his meager proportions with a practiced eye.

"I never was particularly good at football myself," he modestly admitted, "but I've known women who could outlast a man in all-round endurance. Besides—life isn't spent in athletics!"

This was sadly true. They all looked down the aisle where a heavy ill-dressed man with a bad complexion sat alone. He had held the top of the columns once, with headlines and photographs. Now he earned less than any of them.

"It's time we woke up," pursued Gerald, still inwardly urged to unfamiliar speech. "Women are pretty much *people,* seems to me. I know they dress like fools—but who's to blame for that? We invent all those idiotic hats of theirs, and design their crazy fashions, and, what's more, if a woman is courageous enough to wear common-sense clothes—and shoes—which of us wants to dance with her?

"Yes, we blame them for grafting on us, but are we willing to let our wives work? We are not. It hurts our pride, that's all. We are always criticizing them for making mercenary marriages, but what do we call a girl who marries a chump with no money? Just a poor fool, that's all. And they know it.

"As for Mother Eve—I wasn't there and can't deny the story, but I will say this. If she brought evil into the world, we men have had the lion's share of keeping it going ever since—how about that?"

They drew into the city, and all day long in his business, Gerald was vaguely conscious of new views, strange feelings, and the submerged Mollie learned and learned.

ARABY

James Joyce

NORTH RICHMOND STREET, being blind, was a quiet street except at the hour when the Christian Brothers' School set the boys free. An uninhabited house of two storeys stood at the blind end, detached from its neighbours in a square ground. The other houses of the street, conscious of decent lives within them, gazed at one another with brown imperturbable faces.

The former tenant of our house, a priest, had died in the back drawing-room. Air, musty from having been long enclosed, hung in all the rooms, and the waste room behind the kitchen was littered with old useless papers. Among these I found a few paper-covered books, the pages of which were curled and damp: *The Abbot,* by Walter Scott, *The Devout Communicant* and *The Memoirs of Vidocq.* I liked the last best because its leaves were yellow. The wild garden behind the house contained a central apple-tree and a few straggling bushes under one of which I found the late tenant's rusty bicycle-pump. He had been a very charitable priest; in his will he had left all his money to institutions and the furniture of his house to his sister.

When the short days of winter came dusk fell before we had well eaten our dinners. When we met in the street the houses had grown sombre. The space of sky above us was the colour of ever-changing violet and towards it the lamps of the street lifted their feeble lanterns. The cold air stung us and we played till our bodies glowed. Our shouts echoed in the silent street. The career of our play brought us through the dark muddy lanes behind the houses where we ran the gauntlet of the rough tribes from the cottages, to the back doors of the dark dripping gardens where odours arose from the ashpits, to the dark odorous stables where a coachman smoothed and combed the horse or shook music from the buckled harness. When we returned to the street light from the kitchen windows had filled the areas. If my uncle was seen turning the corner we hid in the shadow until we had seen him safely housed. Or if Mangan's sister came out on the doorstep to call her brother in to his tea we watched her from our shadow peer up and down the street. We waited to see whether she would remain or go in and, if she remained, we left our shadow and walked up to Mangan's steps resignedly. She was waiting for us, her figure defined by the light from the half-opened door. Her brother always teased her before he obeyed and I stood by the railings looking at her. Her dress swung as she moved her body and the soft rope of her hair tossed from side to side.

Every morning I lay on the floor in the front parlour watching her door. The blind was pulled down to within an inch of the sash so that I could not be seen. When she came out on the doorstep my heart leaped. I ran to the hall, seized my books and followed her. I kept her brown figure always in my eye and, when we came near the point at which our ways diverged, I quickened my pace and passed her. This happened morning after morning. I had never spoken to her, except for a few casual words, and yet her name was like a summons to all my foolish blood.

Her image accompanied me even in places the most hostile to romance. On Saturday evenings when my aunt went marketing I had to go to carry some of the parcels. We walked through the flaring streets, jostled by drunken men and bargaining women, amid the curses of labourers, the shrill litanies of shop-boys who stood on guard by the barrels of pigs' cheeks, the nasal chanting of street-singers, who sang a *come-all-you* about O'Donovan Rossa, or a ballad about the troubles in our native land. These noises converged in a single sensation of life for me: I imagined that I bore my chalice safely through a throng of foes. Her name sprang to my lips at moments in strange prayers and praises which I myself did not understand. My eyes were often full of tears (I could not tell why) and at times a flood from my heart seemed to pour itself out into my bosom. I thought little of the future. I did not know whether I would ever speak to her or not or, if I spoke to her, how I could tell her of my confused adoration. But my body was like a harp and her words and gestures were like fingers running upon the wires.

One evening I went into the back drawing-room in which the priest had died. It was a dark rainy evening and there was no sound in the house. Through one of the broken panes I heard the rain impinge upon the earth, the fine incessant needles of water playing in the sodden beds. Some distant lamp or lighted window gleamed below me. I was thankful that I could see so little. All my senses seemed to desire to veil themselves and, feeling that I was about to slip from them, I pressed the palms of my hands together until they trembled, murmuring: "*O love! O love!*" many times.

At last she spoke to me. When she addressed the first words to me I was so confused that I did not know what to answer. She asked me was I going to *Araby*. I forgot whether I answered yes or no. It would be a splendid bazaar, she said she would love to go.

"And why can't you?" I asked.

While she spoke she turned a silver bracelet round and round her wrist. She could not go, she said, because there would be a retreat that week in her convent. Her brother and two other boys were fighting for their caps and I was alone at the railings. She held one of the spikes, bowing her head towards me. The light from the lamp opposite our door caught the white curve of her neck, lit up her hair that rested there and, falling, lit up the hand upon the railing. It fell over one side of her dress and caught the white border of a petticoat, just visible as she stood at ease.

"It's well for you," she said.

"If I go," I said, "I will bring you something."

What innumerable follies laid waste my waking and sleeping thoughts after that evening! I wished to annihilate the tedious intervening days. I chafed against the work of school. At night in my bedroom and by day in the classroom her image came between me and the page I strove to read. The syllables of the word *Araby* were called to me through the silence in which my soul luxuriated and cast an Eastern enchantment over me. I asked for leave to go to the bazaar on Saturday night. My aunt was surprised and hoped it was not some Freemason affair. I answered few questions in class. I watched my master's face pass from amiability to sternness; he hoped I was not beginning to idle. I could not call my wandering thoughts together. I had hardly any patience with the serious work of life which, now that it stood between me and my desire, seemed to me child's play, ugly monotonous child's play.

On Saturday morning I reminded my uncle that I wished to go to the bazaar in the evening. He was fussing at the hallstand, looking for the hat-brush, and answered me curtly:

"Yes, boy, I know."

As he was in the hall I could not go into the front parlour and lie at the window. I left the house in bad humour and walked slowly towards the school. The air was pitilessly raw and already my heart misgave me.

When I came home to dinner my uncle had not yet been home. Still it was early. I sat staring at the clock for some time and, when its ticking began to irritate me, I left the room. I mounted the staircase and gained the upper part of the house. The high cold empty gloomy rooms liberated me and I went from room to room singing. From the front window I saw my companions playing below in the street. Their cries reached me weakened and indistinct and, leaning my forehead against the cool glass, I looked over at the dark house where she lived. I may have stood there for an hour, seeing nothing but the brown-clad figure cast by my imagination, touched discreetly by the lamplight at the curved neck, at the hand upon the railings and at the border below the dress.

When I came downstairs again I found Mrs. Mercer sitting at the fire. She was an old garrulous woman, a pawnbroker's widow, who collected used stamps for some pious purpose. I had to endure the gossip of the tea-table. The meal was prolonged beyond an hour and still my uncle did not come. Mrs. Mercer stood up to go: she was sorry she couldn't wait any longer, but it was after eight o'clock and she did not like to be out late, as the night air was bad for her. When she had gone I began to walk up and down the room, clenching my fists. My aunt said:

"I'm afraid you may put off your bazaar for this night of Our Lord."

At nine o'clock I heard my uncle's latchkey in the hall-door. I heard him talking to himself and heard the hallstand rocking when it had received the weight of his overcoat. I could interpret these signs. When he was midway through his dinner I asked him to give me the money to go to the bazaar. He had forgotten.

"The people are in bed and after their first sleep now," he said.

I did not smile. My aunt said to him energetically:

"Can't you give him the money and let him go? You've kept him late enough as it is."

My uncle said he was very sorry he had forgotten. He said he believed in the old saying: "All work and no play makes Jack a dull boy." He asked me where I was going and, when I had told him a second time he asked me did I know *The Arab's Farewell to his Steed*. When I left the kitchen he was about to recite the opening lines of the piece to my aunt.

I held a florin tightly in my hand as I strode down Buckingham Street towards the station. The sight of the streets thronged with buyers and glaring with gas recalled to me the purpose of my journey. I took my seat in a third-class carriage of a deserted train. After an intolerable delay the train moved out of the station slowly. It crept onward among ruinous houses and over the twinkling river. At Westland Row Station a crowd of people pressed to the carriage doors; but the porters moved them back, saying that it was a special train for the bazaar. I remained alone in the bare carriage. In a few minutes the train drew up beside an improvised wooden platform. I passed out on to the road and saw by the lighted dial of a clock that it was ten minutes to ten. In front of me was a large building which displayed the magical name.

I could not find any sixpenny entrance and, fearing that the bazaar would be closed, I passed in quickly through a turnstile, handing a shilling to a weary-looking man. I found myself in a big hall girdled at half its height by a gallery. Nearly all the stalls were closed and the greater part of the hall was in darkness. I recognised a silence like that which pervades a church after a service. I walked into the centre of the bazaar timidly. A few people were gathered about the stalls which were still open. Before a curtain, over which the words *Café Chantant* were written in coloured lamps, two men were counting money on a salver. I listened to the fall of the coins.

Remembering with difficulty why I had come I went over to one of the stalls and examined porcelain vases and flowered tea-sets. At the door of the stall a young lady was talking and laughing with two young gentlemen. I remarked their English accents and listened vaguely to their conversation.

"O, I never said such a thing!"

"O, but you did!"

"O, but I didn't!"

"Didn't she say that?"

"Yes. I heard her."

"O, there's a . . . fib!"

Observing me the young lady came over and asked me did I wish to buy anything. The tone of her voice was not encouraging; she seemed to have spoken to me out of a sense of duty. I looked humbly at the great jars that stood like eastern guards at either side of the dark entrance to the stall and murmured:

"No, thank you."

The young lady changed the position of one of the vases and went back to the two young men. They began to talk of the same subject. Once or twice the young lady glanced at me over her shoulder.

I lingered before her stall, though I knew my stay was useless, to make my interest in her wares seem the more real. Then I turned away slowly and walked down the middle of the bazaar. I allowed the two pennies to fall against the sixpence in my pocket. I heard a voice call from one end of the gallery that the light was out. The upper part of the hall was now completely dark.

Gazing up into the darkness I saw myself as a creature driven and derided by vanity; and my eyes burned with anguish and anger.

EVELINE

James Joyce

SHE SAT AT the window watching the evening invade the avenue. Her head was leaned against the window curtains and in her nostrils was the odour of dusty cretonne. She was tired.

Few people passed. The man out of the last house passed on his way home; she heard his footsteps clacking along the concrete pavement and afterwards crunching on the cinder path before the new red houses. One time there used to be a field there in which they used to play every evening with other people's children. Then a man from Belfast bought the field and built houses in it—not like their little brown houses but bright brick houses with shining roofs. The children of the avenue used to play together in that field—the Devines, the Waters, the Dunns, little Keogh the cripple, she and her brothers and sisters. Ernest, however, never played: he was too grown up. Her father used often to hunt them in out of the field with his blackthorn stick; but usually little Keogh used to keep *nix* and call out when he saw her father coming. Still they seemed to have been rather happy then. Her father was not so bad then; and besides, her mother was alive. That was a long time ago; she and her brothers and sisters were all grown up; her mother was dead. Tizzie Dunn was dead, too, and the Waters had gone back to England. Everything changes. Now she was going to go away like the others, to leave her home.

Home! She looked round the room, reviewing all its familiar objects which she had dusted once a week for so many years, wondering where on earth all the dust came from. Perhaps she would never see again those familiar objects from which she had never dreamed of being divided. And yet during all those years she had never found out the name of the priest whose yellowing photograph hung on the wall above the broken harmonium beside the coloured print of the promises made to Blessed Margaret Mary Alacoque. He had been a school friend of her father. Whenever he showed the photograph to a visitor her father used to pass it with a casual word:

"He is in Melbourne now."

She had consented to go away, to leave her home. Was that wise? She tried to weigh each side of the question. In her home anyway she had shelter and food; she had those whom she had known all her life about her. Of course she had to work hard, both in the house and at business. What would they say of her in the Stores when they found out that she had run away with a fellow? Say she was a fool, perhaps; and her place would be filled up by advertisement. Miss Gavan would be glad. She had always had an edge on her, especially whenever there were people listening.

"Miss Hill, don't you see these ladies are waiting?"

"Look lively, Miss Hill, please."

She would not cry many tears at leaving the Stores.

But in her new home, in a distant unknown country, it would not be like that. Then she would be married—she, Eveline. People would treat her with respect then. She would not be treated as her mother had been. Even now, though she was over nineteen, she sometimes felt herself in danger of her father's violence. She knew it was that that had given her the palpitations. When they were growing up he had never gone for her, like he used to go for Harry and Ernest, because she was a girl; but latterly he had begun to threaten her and say what he would do to her only for her dead mother's sake. And now she had nobody to protect her. Ernest was dead and Harry, who was in the church decorating business, was nearly always down somewhere in the country. Besides, the invariable squabble for money on Saturday nights had begun to weary her unspeakably. She always gave her entire wages—seven shillings—and Harry always sent up what he could but the trouble was to get any money from her father. He said she used to squander the money, that she had no head, that he wasn't going to give her his hard-earned money to throw about the streets, and much more, for he was usually fairly bad on Saturday night. In the end he would give her the money and ask her had she any intention of buying Sunday's dinner. Then she had to rush out as quickly as she could and do her marketing, holding her black leather purse tightly in her hand as she elbowed her way through the crowds and returning home late under her load of provisions. She had hard work to keep the house together and to see that the two young children who had been left to her charge went to school regularly and got their meals regularly. It was hard work—a hard life— but now that she was about to leave it she did not find it a wholly undesirable life.

She was about to explore another life with Frank. Frank was very kind, manly, open-hearted. She was to go away with him by the night-boat to be his wife and to live with him in Buenos Ayres where he had a home waiting for her. How well she remembered the first time she had seen him; he was lodging in a house on the main road where she used to visit. It seemed a few weeks ago. He was standing at the gate, his peaked cap pushed back on his head and his hair tumbled forward over a face of bronze. Then they had come to know each other. He used to meet her outside the Stores every evening and see her home. He took her to see *The Bohemian Girl* and she felt elated as she sat in an unaccustomed part of the theatre with him. He was awfully fond of music and sang a little. People knew that they were courting and, when he sang about the lass that loves a sailor, she always felt pleasantly confused. He used to call her Poppens out of fun. First of all it had been an excitement for her to have a fellow and then she had begun to like him. He had tales of distant countries. He had started as a deck boy at a pound a month on a ship of the Allan Line going out to Canada. He told her the names of the ships he had been on and the names of the different services. He had sailed through the Straits of Magellan and he told her stories of the terrible Patagonians. He had fallen on his feet in Buenos Ayres, he said, and had come over to the old country just for a holiday. Of course, her father had found out the affair and had forbidden her to have anything to say to him.

"I know these sailor chaps," he said.

One day he had quarrelled with Frank and after that she had to meet her lover secretly.

The evening deepened in the avenue. The white of two letters in her lap grew indistinct. One was to Harry; the other was to her father. Ernest had been her favourite but she liked Harry too. Her father was becoming old lately, she noticed; he would miss her. Sometimes he could be very nice. Not long before, when she had been laid up for a day, he had read her out a ghost story and made toast for her at the fire. Another day, when their mother was alive, they had all gone for a picnic to the Hill of Howth. She remembered her father putting on her mother's bonnet to make the children laugh.

Her time was running out but she continued to sit by the window, leaning her head against the window curtain, inhaling the odour of dusty cretonne. Down far in the avenue she could hear a street organ playing. She knew the air. Strange that it should come that very night to remind her of the promise to her mother, her promise to keep the home together as long as she could. She remembered the last night of her mother's illness; she was again in the close dark room at the other side of the hall and outside she heard a melancholy air of Italy. The organ-player had been ordered to go away and given sixpence. She remembered her father strutting back into the sickroom saying:

"Damned Italians! coming over here!"

As she mused the pitiful vision of her mother's life laid its spell on the very quick of her being—that life of commonplace sacrifices closing in final craziness. She trembled as she heard again her mother's voice saying constantly with foolish insistence:

"Derevaun Seraun! Derevaun Seraun!"

She stood up in a sudden impulse of terror. Escape! She must escape! Frank would save her. He would give her life, perhaps love, too. But she wanted to live. Why should she be unhappy? She had a right to happiness. Frank would take her in his arms, fold her in his arms. He would save her.

★ ★ ★

She stood among the swaying crowd in the station at the North Wall. He held her hand and she knew that he was speaking to her, saying something about the passage over and over again. The station was full of soldiers with brown baggages. Through the wide doors of the sheds she caught a glimpse of the black mass of the boat, lying in beside the quay wall, with illumined portholes. She answered nothing. She felt her cheek pale and cold and, out of a maze of distress, she prayed to God to direct her, to show her what was her duty. The boat blew a long mournful whistle into the mist. If she went, to-morrow she would be on the sea with Frank, steaming towards Buenos Ayres. Their passage had been booked.

Could she still draw back after all he had done for her? Her distress awoke a nausea in her body and she kept moving her lips in silent fervent prayer.

A bell clanged upon her heart. She felt him seize her hand:

"Come!"

All the seas of the world tumbled about her heart. He was drawing her into them: he would drown her. She gripped with both hands at the iron railing.

"Come!"

No! No! No! It was impossible. Her hands clutched the iron in frenzy. Amid the seas she sent a cry of anguish!

"Eveline! Evvy!"

He rushed beyond the barrier and called to her to follow. He was shouted at to go on but he still called to her. She set her white face to him, passive, like a helpless animal. Her eyes gave him no sign of love or farewell or recognition.

SECOND BEST

D. H. Lawrence

"Oh, I'm tired!" Frances exclaimed petulantly, and in the same instant she dropped down on the turf, near the hedge-bottom. Anne stood a moment surprised, then, accustomed to the vagaries of her beloved Frances, said:

"Well, and aren't you always likely to be tired, after travelling that blessed long way from Liverpool yesterday?" and she plumped down beside her sister. Anne was a wise young body of fourteen, very buxom, brimming with common sense. Frances was much older, about twenty-three, and whimsical, spasmodic. She was the beauty and the clever child of the family. She plucked the goose-grass buttons from her dress in a nervous, desperate fashion. Her beautiful profile, looped above with black hair, warm with the dusky-and-scarlet complexion of a pear, was calm as a mask, her thin brown hand plucked nervously.

"It's not the journey," she said, objecting to Anne's obtuseness. Anne looked inquiringly at her darling. The young girl, in her self-confident, practical way, proceeded to reckon up this whimsical creature. But suddenly she found herself full in the eyes of Frances; felt two dark, hectic eyes flaring challenge at her, and she shrank away. Frances was peculiar for these great, exposed looks, which disconcerted people by their violence and their suddenness.

"What's a-matter, poor old duck?" asked Anne, as she folded the slight, wilful form of her sister in her arms. Frances laughed shakily, and nestled down for comfort on the budding breasts of the strong girl.

"Oh, I'm only a bit tired," she murmured, on the point of tears.

"Well, of course you are, what do you expect?" soothed Anne. It was a joke to Frances that Anne should play elder, almost mother to her. But then, Anne was in her unvexed teens; men were like big dogs to her: while Frances, at twenty-three, suffered a good deal.

The country was intensely morning-still. On the common everything shone beside its shadow, and the hillside gave off heat in silence. The brown turf seemed in a low state of combustion, the leaves of the oaks were scorched brown. Among the blackish foliage in the distance shone the small red and orange of the village.

The willows in the brook-course at the foot of the common suddenly shook with a dazzling effect like diamonds. It was a puff of wind. Anne resumed her normal position. She spread her knees, and put in her lap a handful of hazel nuts, whity-green leafy things, whose one cheek was tanned between brown and pink. These she began to crack and eat. Frances, with bowed head, mused bitterly.

"Eh, you know Tom Smedley?" began the young girl, as she pulled a tight kernel out of its shell.

"I suppose so," replied Frances sarcastically.

"Well, he gave me a wild rabbit what he'd caught, to keep with my tame one—and it's living."

"That's a good thing," said Frances, very detached and ironic.

"Well, it *is!* He reckoned he'd take me to Ollerton Feast, but he never did. Look here, he took a servant from the rectory; I saw him."

"So he ought," said Frances.

"No, he oughtn't! and I told him so. And I told him I should tell you—an' I have done."

Click and snap went a nut between her teeth. She sorted out the kernel, and chewed complacently.

"It doesn't make much difference," said Frances.

"Well, 'appen it doesn't; but I was mad with him all the same."

"Why?"

"Because I was; he's no right to go with a servant."

"He's a perfect right," persisted Frances, very just and cold.

"No, he hasn't, when he'd said he'd take me."

Frances burst into a laugh of amusement and relief.

"Oh, no; I'd forgot that," she said, adding, "And what did he say when you promised to tell me?"

"He laughed and said, 'She won't fret her fat over that.'"

"And she won't," sniffed Frances.

There was silence. The common, with its sere, blonde-headed thistles, its heaps of silent bramble, its brown-husked gorse in the glare of sunshine, seemed visionary. Across the brook began the immense pattern of agriculture, white chequering of barley stubble, brown squares of wheat, khaki patches of pasture, red stripes of fallow, with the woodland and the tiny village dark like ornaments, leading away to the distance, right to the hills, where the check-pattern grew smaller and smaller, till, in the blackish haze of heat, far off, only the tiny white squares of barley stubble showed distinct.

"Eh, I say, here's a rabbit hole!" cried Anne suddenly. "Should we watch if one comes out? You won't have to fidget, you know."

The two girls sat perfectly still. Frances watched certain objects in her surroundings: they had a peculiar, unfriendly look about them: the weight of greenish elderberries on their purpling stalks; the twinkling of the yellowing crab-apples that clustered high up in the hedge, against the sky: the exhausted, limp leaves of the primroses lying flat in the hedge-bottom: all looked strange to her. Then her eyes caught a movement. A mole was moving silently over the warm, red soil, nosing, shuffling hither and thither, flat, and dark as a shadow, shifting about, and as suddenly brisk, and as silent, like a very ghost of *joie de vivre*. Frances started, from habit was about to call on Anne to kill the little pest. But, to-day, her lethargy of unhappiness was too much for her. She watched the little brute paddling, snuffing, touching things to discover them, running in blindness, delighted to ecstasy by the sunlight and the hot, strange things that caressed its belly and its nose. She felt a keen pity for the little creature.

"Eh, our Fran, look there! It's a mole."

Anne was on her feet, standing watching the dark, unconscious beast. Frances frowned with anxiety.

"It doesn't run off, does it?" said the young girl softly. Then she stealthily approached the creature. The mole paddled fumblingly away. In an instant Anne put her foot upon it, not too heavily. Frances could see the struggling, swimming movement of the little pink hands of the brute, the twisting and twitching of its pointed nose, as it wrestled under the sole of the boot.

"It *does* wriggle!" said the bonny girl, knitting her brows in a frown at the eerie sensation. Then she bent down to look at her trap. Frances could now see, beyond the edge of the boot-sole, the heaving of the velvet shoulders, the pitiful turning of the sightless face, the frantic rowing of the flat, pink hands.

"Kill the thing," she said, turning away her face.

"Oh—I'm not," laughed Anne, shrinking. "You can, if you like."

"I *don't* like," said Frances, with quiet intensity.

After several dabbing attempts, Anne succeeded in picking up the little animal by the scruff of its neck. It threw back its head, flung its long blind snout from side to side, the mouth open in a peculiar oblong, with tiny pinkish teeth at the edge. The blind, frantic mouth gaped and writhed. The body, heavy and clumsy, hung scarcely moving.

"Isn't it a snappy little thing," observed Anne twisting to avoid the teeth.

"What are you going to do with it?" asked Frances sharply.

"It's got to be killed—look at the damage they do. I s'll take it home and let dadda or somebody kill it. I'm not going to let it go."

She swaddled the creature clumsily in her pocket-handkerchief and sat down beside her sister. There was an interval of silence, during which Anne combated the efforts of the mole.

"You've not had much to say about Jimmy this time. Did you see him often in Liverpool?" Anne asked suddenly.

"Once or twice," replied Frances, giving no sign of how the question troubled her.

"And aren't you sweet on him any more, then?"

"I should think I'm not, seeing that he's engaged."

"Engaged? Jimmy Barrass! Well, of all things! I never thought *he'd* get engaged."

"Why not, he's as much right as anybody else?" snapped Frances.

Anne was fumbling with the mole.

"'Appen so," she said at length; "but I never thought Jimmy would, though."

"Why not?" snapped Frances.

"*I* don't know—this blessed mole, it'll not keep still!—who's he got engaged to?"

"How should I know?"

"I thought you'd ask him; you've known him long enough. I s'd think he thought he'd get engaged now he's a Doctor of Chemistry."

Frances laughed in spite of herself.

"What's that got to do with it?" she asked.

"I'm sure it's got a lot. He'll want to feel *somebody* now, so he's got engaged. Hey, stop it; go in!"

But at this juncture the mole almost succeeded in wriggling clear. It wrestled and twisted frantically, waved its pointed blind head, its mouth standing open like a little shaft, its big, wrinkled hands spread out.

"Go in with you!" urged Anne, poking the little creature with her forefinger, trying to get it back into the handkerchief. Suddenly the mouth turned like a spark on her finger.

"Oh!" she cried, "he's bit me."

She dropped him to the floor. Dazed, the blind creature fumbled round. Frances felt like shrieking. She expected him to dart away in a flash, like a mouse, and there he remained groping; she wanted to cry to him to be gone. Anne, in a sudden decision of wrath, caught up her sister's walking-cane. With one blow the mole was dead. Frances was startled and shocked. One moment the little wretch was fussing in the heat, and the next it lay like a little bag, inert and black—not a struggle, scarce a quiver.

"It is dead!" Frances said breathlessly. Anne took her finger from her mouth, looked at the tiny pinpricks, and said:

"Yes, he is, and I'm glad. They're vicious little nuisances, moles are."

With which her wrath vanished. She picked up the dead animal.

"Hasn't it got a beautiful skin," she mused, stroking the fur with her forefinger, then with her cheek.

"Mind," said Frances sharply. "You'll have the blood on your skirt!"

One ruby drop of blood hung on the small snout, ready to fall. Anne shook it off on to some harebells. Frances suddenly became calm; in that moment, grown-up.

"I suppose they have to be killed," she said, and a certain rather dreary indifference succeeded to her grief. The twinkling crab-apples, the glitter of brilliant willows now seemed to her trifling, scarcely worth the notice. Something had died in her, so that things lost their poignancy. She was calm, indifference overlying her quiet sadness. Rising, she walked down to the brook course.

"Here, wait for me," cried Anne, coming tumbling after.

Frances stood on the bridge, looking at the red mud trodden into pockets by the feet of cattle. There was not a drain of water left, but everything smelled green, succulent. Why did she care so little for anyone? She did not know, but she felt a rather stubborn pride in her isolation and indifference.

They entered a field where stooks of barley stood in rows, the straight, blonde tresses of the corn streaming on to the ground. The stubble was bleached by the intense summer, so that the expanse glared white. The next field was sweet and soft with a second crop of seeds; thin, straggling clover whose little pink knobs rested prettily in the dark green. The scent was faint and sickly. The girls came up in single file, Frances leading.

Near the gate a young man was mowing with the scythe some fodder for the afternoon feed of the cattle. As he saw the girls he left off working and waited in an aimless kind of way. Frances was dressed in white muslin, and she walked with dignity, detached and forgetful. Her lack of agitation, her simple, unheeding advance made him nervous. She had loved the far-off Jimmy for five years, having had in return his half-measures. This man only affected her slightly.

Tom was of medium stature, energetic in build. His smooth, fair-skinned face was burned red, not brown, by the sun, and this ruddiness enhanced his appearance of good humour and easiness. Being a year older than Frances, he would have courted her long ago had she been so inclined. As it was, he had gone his uneventful way amiably, chatting with many a girl, but remaining unattached, free of trouble for the most part. Only he knew he wanted a woman. He hitched his trousers just a trifle self-consciously as the girls approached. Frances was a rare, delicate kind of being, whom he realized with a queer and delicious stimulation in his veins. She gave him a slight sense of suffocation. Somehow, this morning, she affected him more than usual. She was dressed in white. He, however, being matter-of-fact in his mind, did not realize. His feeling had never become conscious, purposive.

Frances knew what she was about. Tom was ready to love her as soon as she would show him. Now that she could not have Jimmy, she did not poignantly care. Still, she would have something. If she could not have the best—Jimmy, whom she knew to be something of a snob—she would have the second best, Tom. She advanced rather indifferently.

"You are back, then!" said Tom. She marked the touch of uncertainty in his voice.

"No," she laughed, "I'm still in Liverpool," and the undertone of intimacy made him burn.

"This isn't you, then?" he asked.

Her heart leapt up in approval. She looked in his eyes, and for a second was with him.

"Why, what do you think?" she laughed.

He lifted his hat from his head with a distracted little gesture. She liked him, his quaint ways, his humour, his ignorance, and his slow masculinity.

"Here, look here, Tom Smedley," broke in Anne.

"A moudiwarp! Did you find it dead?" he asked.

"No, it bit me," said Anne.

"Oh, aye! An' that got your rag out, did it?"

"No, it didn't!" Anne scolded sharply. "Such language!"

"Oh, what's up wi' it?"

"I can't bear you to talk broad."

"Can't you?"

He glanced at Frances.

"It isn't nice," Frances said. She did not care, really. The vulgar speech jarred on her as a rule; Jimmy was a gentleman. But Tom's manner of speech did not matter to her.

"I like you to talk *nicely,*" she added.

"Do you," he replied, tilting his hat, stirred.

"And generally you *do,* you know," she smiled.

"I s'll have to have a try," he said, rather tensely gallant.

"What?" she asked brightly.

"To talk nice to you," he said. Frances coloured furiously, bent her head for a moment, then laughed gaily, as if she liked this clumsy hint.

"Eh now, you mind what you're saying," cried Anne, giving the young man an admonitory pat.

"You wouldn't have to give yon mole many knocks like that," he teased, relieved to get on safe ground, rubbing his arm.

"No indeed, it died in one blow," said Frances, with a flippancy that was hateful to her.

"You're not so good at knockin' 'em?" he said, turning to her.

"I don't know, if I'm cross," she said decisively.

"No?" he replied, with alert attentiveness.

"I could," she added, harder, "if it was necessary."

He was slow to feel her difference.

"And don't you consider it *is* necessary?" he asked, with misgiving.

"W—ell—is it?" she said, looking at him steadily, coldly.

"I reckon it is," he replied, looking away, but standing stubborn.

She laughed quickly.

"But it isn't necessary for *me,*" she said, with slight contempt.

"Yes, that's quite true," he answered.

She laughed in a shaky fashion.

"I *know it is,*" she said; and there was an awkward pause.

"Why, would you *like* me to kill moles then?" she asked tentatively, after a while.

"They do us a lot of damage," he said, standing firm on his own ground, angered.

"Well, I'll see the next time I come across one," she promised, defiantly. Their eyes met, and she sank before him, her pride troubled. He felt uneasy and triumphant and baffled, as if fate had gripped him. She smiled as she departed.

"Well," said Anne, as the sisters went through the wheat stubble; "I don't know what you two's been jawing about, I'm sure."

"Don't you?" laughed Frances significantly

"No, I don't. But, at any rate, Tom Smedley's a good deal better to my thinking than Jimmy, so there—and nicer."

"Perhaps he is," said Frances coldly.

And the next day, after a secret, persistent hunt, she found another mole playing in the heat. She killed it, and in the evening, when Tom came to the gate to smoke his pipe after supper, she took him the dead creature.

"Here you are then!" she said.

"Did you catch it?" he replied, taking the velvet corpse into his fingers and examining it minutely. This was to hide his trepidation.

"Did you think I couldn't?" she asked, her face very near his.

"Nay, I didn't know."

She laughed in his face, a strange little laugh that caught her breath, all agitation, and tears, and recklessness of desire. He looked frightened and upset. She put her hand to his arm.

"Shall you go out wi' me?" he asked, in a difficult, troubled tone.

She turned her face away, with a shaky laugh. The blood came up in him, strong, overmastering. He resisted it. But it drove him down, and he was carried away. Seeing the winsome, frail nape of her neck, fierce love came upon him for her, and tenderness.

"We s'll 'ave to tell your mother," he said. And he stood, suffering, resisting his passion for her.

"Yes," she replied, in a dead voice. But there was a thrill of pleasure in this death.

THE SIGNAL

Vsevolod M. Garshin

SEMYON IVANOV WAS a track-walker. His hut was ten versts away from a railroad station in one direction and twelve versts away in the other. About four versts away there was a cotton mill that had opened the year before, and its tall chimney rose up darkly from behind the forest. The only dwellings around were the distant huts of the other track-walkers.

Semyon Ivanov's health had been completely shattered. Nine years before he had served right through the war as servant to an officer. The sun had roasted him, the cold frozen him, and hunger famished him on the forced marches of forty and fifty versts a day in the heat and the cold and the rain and the shine. The bullets had whizzed about him, but, thank God! none had struck him.

Semyon's regiment had once been on the firing line. For a whole week there had been skirmishing with the Turks, only a deep ravine separating the two hostile armies; and from morn till eve there had been a steady cross-fire. Thrice daily Semyon carried a steaming samovar and his officer's meals from the camp kitchen to the ravine. The bullets hummed about him and rattled viciously against the rocks. Semyon was terrified and cried sometimes, but still he kept right on. The officers were pleased with him, because he always had hot tea ready for them.

He returned from the campaign with limbs unbroken but crippled with rheumatism. He had experienced no little sorrow since then. He arrived home to find that his father, an old man, and his little four-year-old son had died. Semyon remained alone with his wife. They could not do much. It was difficult to plough with rheumatic arms and legs. They could no longer stay in their village, so they started off to seek their fortune in new places. They stayed for a short time on the line, in Kherson and Donshchina, but nowhere found luck. Then the wife went out to service, and Semyon continued to travel about. Once he happened to ride on an engine, and at one of the stations the face of the station-master seemed familiar to him. Semyon looked at the station-master and the station-master looked at Semyon, and they recognized each other. He had been an officer in Semyon's regiment.

"You are Ivanov?" he said.

"Yes, your Excellency."

"How do you come to be here?"

Semyon told him all.

"Where are you off to?"

"I cannot tell you, sir."

"Idiot! What do you mean by 'cannot tell you?'"

"I mean what I say, your Excellency. There is nowhere for me to go to. I must hunt for work, sir."

The station-master looked at him, thought a bit, and said: "See here, friend, stay here a while at the station. You are married, I think. Where is your wife?"

"Yes, your Excellency, I am married. My wife is at Kursk, in service with a merchant."

"Well, write to your wife to come here. I will give you a free pass for her. There is a position as track-walker open. I will speak to the Chief on your behalf."

"I shall be very grateful to you, your Excellency," replied Semyon.

He stayed at the station, helped in the kitchen, cut firewood, kept the yard clean, and swept the platform. In a fortnight's time his wife arrived, and Semyon went on a hand-trolley to his hut. The hut was a new one and warm, with as much wood as he wanted. There was a little vegetable garden, the legacy of former track-walkers, and there was about half a desyatin of ploughed land on either side of the railway embankment. Semyon was rejoiced. He began to think of doing some farming, of purchasing a cow and a horse.

He was given all necessary stores—a green flag, a red flag, lanterns, a horn, hammer, screw-wrench for the nuts, a crow-bar, spade, broom, bolts, and nails; they gave him two books of regulations and a timetable of the trains. At first Semyon could not sleep at night, and learnt the whole time-table by heart. Two hours before a train was due he would go over his section, sit on the bench at his hut, and look and listen whether the rails were trembling or the rumble of the train could be heard. He even learned the regulations by heart, although he could only read by spelling out each word.

It was summer; the work was not heavy; there was no snow to clear away, and the trains on that line were infrequent. Semyon used to go over his verst twice a day, examine and screw up nuts here and there, keep the bed level, look at the water-pipes, and then go home to his own affairs. There was only one drawback— he always had to get the inspector's permission for the least little thing he wanted to do. Semyon and his wife were even beginning to be bored.

Two months passed, and Semyon commenced to make the acquaintance of his neighbors, the track-walkers on either side of him. One was a very old man, whom the authorities were always meaning to relieve. He scarcely moved out of his hut. His wife used to do all his work. The other track-walker, nearer the station, was a young man, thin, but muscular. He and Semyon met for the first time on the line midway between the huts. Semyon took off his hat and bowed. "Good health to you, neighbor," he said.

The neighbor glanced askance at him. "How do you do?" he replied; then turned around and made off.

Later the wives met. Semyon's wife passed the time of day with her neighbor, but neither did she say much.

On one occasion Semyon said to her: "Young woman, your husband is not very talkative."

The woman said nothing at first, then replied: "But what is there for him to talk about? Every one has his own business. Go your way, and God be with you."

However, after another month or so they became acquainted. Semyon would go with Vasily along the line, sit on the edge of a pipe, smoke, and talk of life. Vasily, for the most part, kept silent, but Semyon talked of his village, and of the campaign through which he had passed.

"I have had no little sorrow in my day," he would say; "and goodness knows I have not lived long. God has not given me happiness, but what He may give, so will it be. That's so, friend Vasily Stepanych."

Vasily Stepanych knocked the ashes out of his pipe against a rail, stood up, and said: "It is not luck which follows us in life, but human beings. There is no crueller beast on this earth than man. Wolf does not eat wolf, but man will readily devour man."

"Come, friend, don't say that; a wolf eats wolf."

"The words came into my mind and I said it. All the same, there is nothing crueller than man. If it were not for his wickedness and greed, it would be possible to live. Everybody tries to sting you to the quick, to bite and eat you up."

Semyon pondered a bit. "I don't know, brother," he said; "perhaps it is as you say, and perhaps it is God's will."

"And perhaps," said Vasily, "it is waste of time for me to talk to you. To put everything unpleasant on God, and sit and suffer, means, brother, being not a man but an animal. That's what I have to say." And he turned and went off without saying good-bye.

Semyon also got up. "Neighbor," he called, "why do you lose your temper?" But his neighbor did not look round, and kept on his way.

Semyon gazed after him until he was lost to sight in the cutting at the turn. He went home and said to his wife: "Arina, our neighbor is a wicked person, not a man."

However, they did not quarrel. They met again and discussed the same topics.

"Ah, friend, if it were not for men we should not be poking in these huts," said Vasily, on one occasion.

"And what if we are poking in these huts? It's not so bad. You can live in them."

"Live in them, indeed! Bah, you! . . . You have lived long and learned little, looked at much and seen little. What sort of life is there for a poor man in a hut here or there? The cannibals are devouring you. They are sucking up all your life-blood, and when you become old, they will throw you out just as they do husks to feed the pigs on. What pay do you get?"

"Not much, Vasily Stepanych—twelve rubles."

"And I, thirteen and a half rubles. Why? By the regulations the company should give us fifteen rubles a month with firing and lighting. Who decides that you should have twelve rubles, or I thirteen and a half? Ask yourself! And you say a man can live on that? You understand it is not a question of one and a half rubles or three rubles—even if they paid us each the whole fifteen rubles.

I was at the station last month. The director passed through. I saw him. I had that honor. He had a separate coach. He came out and stood on the platform. . . . I shall not stay here long; I shall go somewhere, anywhere, follow my nose."

"But where will you go, Stepanych? Leave well enough alone. Here you have a house, warmth, a little piece of land. Your wife is a worker."

"Land! You should look at my piece of land. Not a twig on it—nothing. I planted some cabbages in the spring, just when the inspector came along. He said: 'What is this? Why have you not reported this? Why have you done this without permission? Dig them up, roots and all.' He was drunk. Another time he would not have said a word, but this time it struck him. Three rubles fine! . . ."

Vasily kept silent for a while, pulling at his pipe, then added quietly: "A little more and I should have done for him."

"You are hot-tempered."

"No, I am not hot-tempered, but I tell the truth and think. Yes, he will still get a bloody nose from me. I will complain to the Chief. We will see then!" And Vasily did complain to the Chief.

Once the Chief came to inspect the line. Three days later important personages were coming from St. Petersburg and would pass over the line. They were conducting an inquiry, so that previous to their journey it was necessary to put everything in order. Ballast was laid down, the bed was levelled, the sleepers carefully examined, spikes were driven in a bit, nuts screwed up, posts painted, and orders given for yellow sand to be sprinkled at the level crossings. The woman at the neighboring hut turned her old man out to weed. Semyon worked for a whole week. He put everything in order, mended his *caftan,* cleaned and polished his brass plate until it fairly shone. Vasily also worked hard. The Chief arrived on a trolley, four men working the handles and the levers making the six wheels hum. The trolley traveled at twenty versts an hour, but the wheels squeaked. It reached Semyon's hut, and he ran out and reported in soldierly fashion. All appeared to be in repair.

"Have you been here long?" inquired the Chief.

"Since the second of May, your Excellency."

"All right. Thank you. And who is at hut No. 164?"

The traffic inspector (he was traveling with the Chief on the trolley) replied: "Vasily Spiridov."

"Spiridov, Spiridov. . . . Ah! is he the man against whom you made a note last year?"

"He is."

"Well, we will see Vasily Spiridov. Go on!" The workmen laid to the handles, and the trolley got under way. Semyon watched it, and thought, "There will be trouble between them and my neighbor."

About two hours later he started on his round. He saw some one coming along the line from the cutting. Something white showed on his head. Semyon began to look more attentively. It was Vasily. He had a stick in his hand, a small bundle on his shoulder, and his cheek was bound up in a handkerchief.

"Where are you off to?" cried Semyon.

Vasily came quite close. He was very pale, white as chalk, and his eyes had a wild look. Almost choking, he muttered: "To town—to Moscow—to the head office."

"Head office? Ah, you are going to complain, I suppose. Give it up! Vasily Stepanych, forget it."

"No, mate, I will not forget. It is too late. See! He struck me in the face, drew blood. So long as I live I will not forget. I will not leave it like this!"

Semyon took his hand. "Give it up, Stepanych. I am giving you good advice. You will not better things. . . . "

"Better things! I know myself I shan't better things. You were right about Fate. It would be better for me not to do it, but one must stand up for the right."

"But tell me, how did it happen?"

"How? He examined everything, got down from the trolley, looked into the hut. I knew beforehand that he would be strict, and so I had put everything into proper order. He was just going when I made my complaint. He immediately cried out: 'Here is a Government inquiry coming, and you make a complaint about a vegetable garden. Here are privy councillors coming, and you annoy me with cabbages!' I lost patience and said something—not very much, but it offended him, and he struck me in the face. I stood still; I did nothing, just as if what he did was perfectly all right. They went off; I came to myself, washed my face, and left."

"And what about the hut?"

"My wife is staying there. She will look after things. Never mind about their roads."

Vasily got up and collected himself. "Good-bye, Ivanov. I do not know whether I shall get any one at the office to listen to me."

"Surely you are not going to walk?"

"At the station I will try to get on a freight train, and to-morrow I shall be in Moscow."

The neighbors bade each other farewell. Vasily was absent for some time. His wife worked for him night and day. She never slept, and wore herself out waiting for her husband. On the third day the commission arrived. An engine, luggage-van, and two first-class saloons; but Vasily was still away. Semyon saw his wife on the fourth day. Her face was swollen from crying and her eyes were red.

"Has your husband returned?" he asked. But the woman only made a gesture with her hands, and without saying a word went her way.

★ ★ ★

Semyon had learnt when still a lad to make flutes out of a kind of reed. He used to burn out the heart of the stalk, make holes where necessary, drill them, fix a mouthpiece at one end, and tune them so well that it was possible to play almost any air on them. He made a number of them in his spare time, and sent them by his friends amongst the freight brakemen to the bazaar in the town. He got two kopeks apiece for them. On the day following the visit of the commission he left his wife at home to meet the six o'clock train, and started off to the forest to cut some sticks. He went to the end of his section—at this point the line made a sharp turn—descended the embankment, and struck into the wood at the foot of the mountain. About half a verst away there was a big marsh, around which splendid reeds for his flutes grew. He cut a whole bundle of stalks and started back home. The sun was already dropping low, and in the dead stillness only the twittering of the birds was audible, and the crackle of the dead wood under his feet. As he walked along rapidly, he fancied he heard the clang of iron striking iron, and he redoubled his pace. There was no repair going on in his section. What did it mean? He emerged from the woods, the railway embankment stood high before him; on the top a man was squatting on the bed of the line busily engaged in something. Semyon commenced quietly to crawl up towards him. He thought it was some one after the nuts which secure the rails. He watched,

and the man got up, holding a crow-bar in his hand. He had loosened a rail, so that it would move to one side. A mist swam before
Semyon's eyes; he wanted to cry out, but could not. It was Vasily!
Semyon scrambled up the bank, as Vasily with crow-bar and
wrench slid headlong down the other side.

"Vasily Stepanych! My dear friend, come back! Give me the
crowbar. We will put the rail back; no one will know. Come back!
Save your soul from sin!"

Vasily did not look back, but disappeared into the woods.

Semyon stood before the rail which had been torn up. He threw
down his bundle of sticks. A train was due; not a freight, but a
passenger-train. And he had nothing with which to stop it, no flag.
He could not replace the rail and could not drive in the spikes with
his bare hands. It was necessary to run, absolutely necessary to run
to the hut for some tools. "God help me!" he murmured.

Semyon started running towards his hut. He was out of breath,
but still ran, falling every now and then. He had cleared the forest;
he was only a few hundred feet from his hut, not more, when he
heard the distant hooter of the factory sound—six o'clock! In two
minutes' time No. 7 train was due. "Oh, Lord! Have pity on innocent souls!" In his mind Semyon saw the engine strike against the
loosened rail with its left wheel, shiver, careen, tear up and splinter
the sleepers—and just there, there was a curve and the embankment seventy feet high, down which the engine would topple—
and the third-class carriages would be packed . . . little children. . . .
All sitting in the train now, never dreaming of danger. "Oh, Lord!
Tell me what to do! . . . No, it is impossible to run to the hut and
get back in time."

Semyon did not run on to the hut, but turned back and ran faster
than before. He was running almost mechanically, blindly; he did
not know himself what was to happen. He ran as far as the rail
which had been pulled up; his sticks were lying in a heap. He bent
down, seized one without knowing why, and ran on farther. It
seemed to him the train was already coming. He heard the distant
whistle; he heard the quiet, even tremor of the rails; but his strength
was exhausted, he could run no farther, and came to a halt about
six hundred feet from the awful spot. Then an idea came into his
head, literally like a ray of light. Pulling off his cap, he took out of
it a cotton scarf, drew his knife out of the upper part of his boot,
and crossed himself, muttering, "God bless me!"

He buried the knife in his left arm above the elbow; the blood spurted out, flowing in a hot stream. In this he soaked his scarf, smoothed it out, tied it to the stick and hung out his red flag.

He stood waving his flag. The train was already in sight. The driver would not see him—would come close up, and a heavy train cannot be pulled up in six hundred feet.

And the blood kept on flowing. Semyon pressed the sides of the wound together so as to close it, but the blood did not diminish. Evidently he had cut his arm very deep. His head commenced to swim, black spots began to dance before his eyes, and then it became dark. There was a ringing in his ears. He could not see the train or hear the noise. Only one thought possessed him. "I shall not be able to keep standing up. I shall fall and drop the flag; the train will pass over me. Help me, oh Lord!"

All turned black before him, his mind became a blank, and he dropped the flag; but the blood-stained banner did not fall to the ground. A hand seized it and held it high to meet the approaching train. The engineer saw it, shut the regulator, and reversed steam. The train came to a standstill.

People jumped out of the carriages and collected in a crowd. They saw a man lying senseless on the footway, drenched in blood, and another man standing beside him with a blood-stained rag on a stick.

Vasily looked around at all. Then, lowering his head, he said: "Bind me. I tore up a rail!"

THE WHITE MOTHER

Theodor Sologub

I

EASTER WAS DRAWING near. Esper Konstantinovitch Saksaulov was in a worried, weary mood. It began, seemingly, from the moment when at the Gorodishchevs' he was asked, "Where are you spending the festival?"

Saksaulov for some reason delayed his reply.

The hostess, a stout, short-sighted, bustling lady, said, "Come to us."

Saksaulov was annoyed. Was it with the girl, who, at her mother's words, glanced at him quickly and instantly withdrew her gaze as she continued her conversation with the young assistant professor?

Saksaulov was eligible in the eyes of mothers of grown-up daughters, and this fact irritated him. He regarded himself as an old bachelor, and he was only thirty-seven. He replied curtly: "Thank you. I always spend this night at home."

The girl glanced at him, smiled, and said, "With whom?"

"Alone," Saksaulov replied, with a slight surprise in his voice.

"What a misanthrope!" said Madame Gorodishchev with a sour smile.

Saksaulov liked his freedom. There were occasions when he wondered how at one time he had nearly come to marry. He was now used to his small flat, furnished in severe style, used to his own valet, the aged, sedate Fedot, and to his no less aged wife, Christine, who cooked his dinner—and was thoroughly convinced that he did not marry because he wished to remain true to his first love. In reality his heart had grown cold from indifference resulting from his solitary, aimless life. He had independent means, his father and mother were long since dead, and of near relations he had none. He lived an assured, tranquil life, was attached to some department, intimately acquainted with contemporary literature and art, and took an Epicurean pleasure in the good things of life, while life itself seemed to him empty and meaningless. Were it not for a solitary bright and pure dream that came to him sometimes, he would have grown quite cold, as so many other men have done.

II

His first and only love, that had ended before it had blossomed, in the evening sometimes made him dream sad sweet dreams. Five years ago he had met the young girl who had produced such a lasting impression on him. Pale, delicate, with slender waist, blue-eyed, fair-haired, she had seemed to him an almost celestial creature, a product of air and mist, accidentally cast by fate for a short span into the city din. Her movements were slow; her clear, tender voice sounded soft, like the murmur of a stream rippling gently over stones.

Saksaulov—was it by accident or design?—always saw her in a white dress. The impression of white became to him inseparable from his thought of her. Even her name, Tamara, seemed to him always white, like the snow on the mountain tops. He began to visit Tamara's parents. On more than one occasion had he resolved to speak those words to her that bind the fate of one human being with that of another. But she always eluded him; fear and anguish were reflected in her eyes. Of what was she afraid? Saksaulov saw in her face the signs of girlish love; her eyes lighted up when he appeared, and a faint blush spread over her cheeks.

But on one never-to-be-forgotten evening she listened to him. The time was early spring. It was not long since the river had broken up and the trees had clothed themselves in a soft green gown. In a flat in town Tamara and Saksaulov sat by the open window facing the Neva. Without troubling himself about what to say and how to say it, he spoke sweet, for her terrifying, words. She turned pale, smiled absently, and got up. Her delicate hand trembled on the carved back of the chair.

"To-morrow," Tamara said softly, and went out.

Saksaulov, with a tense expectancy, sat for a long time staring at the door that had hidden Tamara. His head was in a whirl. A sprig of white lilac caught his eye; he took it and went away without bidding good-bye to his hosts.

At night he could not sleep. He stood by the window staring into the dark street that grew lighter towards the morning, smiling and toying with the sprig of white lilac. When it grew light he saw that the floor of the room was littered with petals of white lilac. This struck him as naive and ridiculous. He took a bath, which made him feel as though he had almost regained his composure, and went to Tamara.

He was told that she was ill, she had caught a chill somewhere. And Saksaulov never saw her again. In two weeks she was dead. He did not go to her funeral. Her death left him almost unshaken. Already he could not tell whether he had loved her or if it were merely a brief passing fascination.

Sometimes in the evening he would dream of her; then her image began to fade. Saksaulov had no portrait of Tamara. It was only after several years had gone by, during last spring, that he was reminded of Tamara by a sprig of white lilac in the window of a restaurant, sadly out of place amidst the rich food. And from that day he again liked to think of Tamara in the evenings. Sometimes when he dozed off, he dreamt that she had come and sat down opposite him and looked at him with a fixed, caressing gaze, seeming to want something. It oppressed and hurt him sometimes to feel Tamara's expectant gaze.

Now, as he left the Gorodishchevs, he thought apprehensively: "She will come to give me the Easter greeting."

The fear and loneliness were so oppressive that he thought: "Why shouldn't I marry? I need not be alone then on holy mystic nights."

Valeria Michailovna—the Gorodishchev girl—came into his mind. She was not beautiful, but she always dressed well. It seemed to Saksaulov that she liked him and would not refuse him if he proposed.

In the street the noise and crowd distracted his attention; his thoughts of the Gorodishchev girl became tinged with the usual cynicism. Moreover, could he be untrue to Tamara's memory for anyone? The whole world seemed to him so petty and commonplace that he longed for Tamara—and Tamara only—to come and give him the Easter greeting.

"But," he reflected, "she will again fix on me that expectant gaze. Pure, gentle Tamara, what does she want? Will her soft lips kiss mine?"

III

With tormenting thoughts of Tamara, Saksaulov wandered about the streets, peering into the faces of the passers-by; the coarse faces of the men and women disgusted him. He reflected that there was no one with whom he would care to exchange the Easter greeting with any pleasure or love. There would be many kisses on the first day—coarse lips, tangled beards, an odor of wine.

If one had to kiss anyone at all it should be a child. The faces of children became pleasing to Saksaulov.

He walked about for a long time; he grew tired and went into a churchyard off the noisy street. A pale boy, sitting on a seat, glanced up at Saksaulov apprehensively and then sat on motionless, staring straight in front of him. His blue eyes were sad and caressing, like Tamara's. He was so tiny that his feet were not long enough to dangle, but projected straight in front of the seat. Saksaulov sat down beside him and regarded him with a sympathetic curiosity. There was something about this lonely little boy that stirred sweet memories. To look at he was the most ordinary child; in torn, ragged clothes, a white fur cap on his fair little head, and dirty, worn boots on his feet.

For a long time he sat on the seat, then he got up and began to cry pitifully. He ran out of the gate and along the street, stopped, set off in the opposite direction and stopped again. It was clear that he did not know which way to go. He cried softly to himself, the big tears dropping down his cheeks. A crowd gathered. A policeman came up. The boy was asked where he lived.

"Gluikhov House," he lisped in the manner of very young children.

"In what street?" the policeman asked.

But the boy did not know the street, and only repeated, "Gluikhov House."

The policeman, a jolly young fellow, reflected for a moment, and decided that there was no such house in the immediate neighborhood.

"Whom do you live with?" asked a gloomy-looking workman; "have you got a father?"

"I haven't got a father," the boy replied, looking at the crowd with tearful eyes.

"Got no father! dear, dear," the workman said solemnly, shaking his head. "Have you got a mother?"

"Yes, I have a mother," the boy replied.

"What is her name?"

"Mother," the boy replied, then reflecting for a moment added, "Black Mother."

"Black? Is that her name?" the gloomy workman asked.

"First I had a white mother and now I have a black mother," the boy explained.

"Well, my boy, we shall never make head or tail of you," the policeman said decisively. "I had better take you to the police-station. They can find out where you live on the telephone."

He went up to the gate and rang. At this moment a porter, catching sight of the policeman, came out with a broom in his hand. The policeman told him to take the boy to the police-station, but the boy bethought himself and cried, "Let me go; I will find the way myself!"

Was he frightened by the porter's broom, or had he indeed remembered something? At any rate, he ran away so quickly that Saksaulov nearly lost sight of him. Soon, however, the boy slackened his pace. He went up the street, running from one side to the other, trying in vain to find the house he lived in. Saksaulov followed him silently. He did not know how to speak to children.

At last the boy became tired. He stopped by a lamp-post and leant against it. The tears glistened in his eyes.

"Well, my boy," Saksaulov began, "can't you find the house?"

The boy looked at him with his sad, gentle eyes, and suddenly Saksaulov realized what had made him follow the boy so persistently.

In the gaze and mien of the little wanderer there was something very like Tamara.

"What is your name, my dear?" Saksaulov asked gently.

"Lesha," the boy replied.

"Do you live with your mother, Lesha?"

"Yes, with mother—but she is a black mother; I used to have a white mother."

Saksaulov thought that by black mother he must mean a nun.

"How did you get lost?"

"I walked with mother, and we walked and walked. She told me to sit down and wait, and then she went away. And I got frightened."

"Who is your mother?"

"My mother? She is black and angry."

"What does she do?"

The boy thought a while.

"She drinks coffee," he said.

"What else does she do?"

"She quarrels with the lodgers," Lesha replied after a pause.

"And where is your white mother?"

"She was carried away. She was put into a coffin and carried away. And father was carried away, too."

The boy pointed into the distance somewhere and burst into tears.

"What can I do with him?" Saksaulov thought.

Then suddenly the boy began to run again. After having run round a few street-corners he slackened his pace. Saksaulov caught him up a second time. The boy's face expressed a strange mixture of fear and joy.

"Here is the Gluikhov House," he said to Saksaulov, as he pointed to a big, five-storied, ugly building.

At this moment there appeared at the gates of the Gluikhov House a black-haired, black-eyed woman in a black dress, on her head a black kerchief with white spots. The boy shrank back in fear.

"Mother!" he whispered.

His step-mother looked at him in astonishment.

"How did you get here, you rascal?" she cried. "I told you to stop on the seat, didn't I?"

She would have struck him, but observing a gentleman of solemn dignified mien who seemed to be watching them, she lowered her voice.

"Can't you be left for half an hour without running away? I've tired myself out looking for you, you rascal!"

She snatched the boy's little hand in her big one and dragged him within the gate.

Saksaulov made a note of the street and went home.

IV

Saksaulov liked to listen to Fedot's sound judgments. When he reached home he told him about the boy Lesha.

"She had left him on purpose," Fedot announced. "What a wicked woman, to take the boy so far from home!"

"What made her do it?" Saksaulov asked.

"One can't tell. Silly woman—no doubt she thought the boy would wander about the streets until someone or other would pick him up. What can you expect from a step-mother? What use is the child to her?"

"But the police would have found her," Saksaulov said incredulously.

"Perhaps; but she may be leaving the town altogether, and how could they find her then?"

Saksaulov smiled. "Really," he thought, "Fedot should have been an examining magistrate."

However, sitting near the lamp with a book, he dozed off. In his dreams he saw Tamara—gentle and white—she came and sat beside him. Her face was wonderfully like Lesha's. She gazed at him incessantly, persistently, seeming to expect something. It was oppressive for Saksaulov to see her bright, pleading eyes and not to know what it was that she wanted. He got up quickly and walked over to the chair where Tamara appeared to be sitting. Standing before her he implored aloud:

"What do you want? Tell me."

But she was no longer there.

"It was only a dream," Saksaulov thought sadly.

V

Coming out of the Academy exhibition on the following day, Saksaulov met the Gorodishchevs.

He told the girl about Lesha.

"Poor boy!" Valeria Michailovna said softly: "his step-mother simply wants to get rid of him."

"That is by no means certain," Saksaulov replied, annoyed that both Fedot and the girl should take such a tragic view of a simple incident.

"It is quite obvious. The boy has no father and lives with his stepmother. She finds him a nuisance. If she can't get rid of him decently she will cast him off altogether."

"You take too gloomy a view," said Saksaulov with a smile.

"Why don't you adopt him?" Valeria Michailovna suggested.

"I?" Saksaulov asked in surprise.

"You live alone," she persisted; "you have no one belonging to you. Do a good deed at Easter. You will have someone with whom to exchange the greeting, at any rate."

"But what could I do with a child, Valeria Michailovna?"

"Get a nurse for it. Fate seems to have sent the child to you."

Saksaulov looked at the flushed, animated face of the girl in wonder, and with an unconscious gentleness.

When Tamara again appeared to him in his dreams that evening it seemed to him that he knew what she wanted. And in the stillness of his room the words seemed to ring softly: "Do as she has told you."

Saksaulov got up rejoicing, and passed his hand over his sleepy eyes. He caught sight of a sprig of white lilac on the table. Where had it come from? Had Tamara left it in token of her will?

And suddenly it occurred to him that by marrying the Gorodishchev girl and adopting Lesha he would fulfill Tamara's wish. Gladly he breathed in the fragrant perfume of the lilac.

He recollected that he had bought the flower himself that day, but instantly thought, "It makes no difference that I bought it myself. There is an omen in the fact that I wished to buy it and then forgot that I had bought it."

VI

In the morning he set out to find Lesha. The boy met him at the gate and showed him where he lived. Lesha's mother was drinking coffee and quarreling with her red-nosed lodger. This is what Saksaulov was able to learn about Lesha.

His mother had died when he was three years old. His father had married this dark woman and had also died within the year. The dark woman, Irena Ivanovna, had a year-old child of her own. She was about to marry again. The wedding was to take place in a few days, and immediately afterwards they were to go into the "provinces." Lesha was a stranger to her and in her way.

"Give him to me," Saksaulov suggested.

"With pleasure," Irena Ivanovna said with malicious joy. Then after a pause added, "Only you must pay me for his clothes."

And thus Lesha was installed in Saksaulov's home. The Gorodishchev girl helped him to find a nurse and with the other details in connection with Lesha's installment at the flat. For this purpose she had to visit Saksaulov's home. Occupied thus she seemed quite a different being to Saksaulov. The door of her heart seemed to have opened to him. Her eyes became tender and radiant. Altogether she was permeated with the same gentleness that had emanated from Tamara.

VII

Lesha's stories of his white mother touched Fedot and his wife. On Passion Saturday, when putting him to bed, they hung a white sugar egg at the end of his bed.

"This is from your white mother," Christine said. "But you mustn't touch it, dear, until the Lord has risen and the bells are ringing."

Lesha lay down obediently. For a long time he stared at the lovely egg, then he fell asleep.

And Saksaulov on this evening sat at home alone. About midnight an uncontrollable feeling of drowsiness closed his eyes and he was glad, because soon he would see Tamara. And she came, clothed in white, radiant, bringing with her the joyful distant sound of church bells. With a gentle smile she bent over him, and—unutterable joy!—Saksaulov felt a gentle touch on his lips. A gentle voice pronounced softly, "Christ has risen!"

Without opening his eyes Saksaulov stretched out his arms and embraced a tender slim body. This was Lesha, who had climbed on to his knee to give him the Easter greeting.

The church bells had wakened the boy. He had seized the white egg and run in to Saksaulov.

Saksaulov awoke. Lesha laughed and held up his white egg.

"White Mother has sent it," he lisped; "I will give it you and you must give it to Auntie Valeria."

"Very well, dear, I will do as you say," Saksaulov replied.

He put Lesha to bed and then went to Valeria Michailovna with Lesha's white egg, a present from the white mother. But it seemed to Saksaulov at the moment to be a present from Tamara.

THE PLOUGHING OF
LEACA-NA-NAOMH

Daniel Corkery

WITH WHICH SHALL I begin—man or place? Perhaps I had better first tell of the man; of him the incident left so withered that no sooner had I laid eyes on him than I said: Here is one whose blood at some terrible moment of his life stood still, stood still and never afterwards regained its quiet, old-time ebb-and-flow. A word or two then about the place—a sculped-out shell in the Kerry mountains, an evil-looking place, green-glaring like a sea when a storm has passed. To connect man and place together, even as they worked one with the other to bring the tragedy about, ought not then to be so difficult.

I had gone into those desolate treeless hills searching after the traces of an old-time Gaelic family that once were lords of them. But in this mountainy glen I forgot my purpose almost as soon as I entered it.

In that round-ended valley—they call such a valley a coom—there was but one farmhouse, and Considine was the name of the householder—Shawn Considine, the man whose features were white with despair; his haggard appearance reminded me of what one so often sees in war-ravaged Munster—a ruined castle-wall hanging out above the woods, a grey spectre. He made me welcome, speaking slowly, as if he was not used to such amenities. At once I began to explain my quest. I soon stumbled; I felt that his thoughts were far away. I started again. A daughter of his looked at me—Nora was her name—looked at me with meaning; I could not read her look aright. Haphazardly I went through old family names and recalled old-world incidents; but with no more success.

He then made to speak; I could catch only broken phrases, repeated again and again. "In the presence of God." "In the Kingdom of God." "All gone for ever." "Let them rest in peace"—(I translate from the Irish). Others, too, there were of which I could make nothing. Suddenly I went silent. His eyes had begun to change. They were not becoming fiery or angry—that would have emboldened me, I would have blown on his anger; a little passion, even an outburst of bitter temper would have troubled me but little if in its sudden revelation I came on some new fact or even a new name in the broken story of that ruined family. But no; not fiery but cold and terror-stricken were his eyes becoming. Fear was rising in them like dank water. I withdrew my gaze, and his daughter ventured on speech:

"If you speak of the cattle, noble person, or of the land, or of the new laws, my father will converse with you; but he is dark about what happened long ago." Her eyes were even more earnest than her tongue—they implored the pity of silence.

So much for the man. A word now about the place where his large but neglected farmhouse stood against a bluff of rock. To enter that evil-looking green-mountained glen was like entering the jaws of some slimy, cold-blooded animal. You felt yourself leaving the sun, you shrunk together, you hunched yourself as if to bear an ugly pressure. In the far-back part of it was what is called in the Irish language a *leaca*—a slope of land, a lift of land, a bracket of land jutting out from the side of a mountain. This leaca, which the daughter explained was called Leaca-na-Naomh—the Leaca of the Saints—was very remarkable. It shone like a gem. It held the sunshine as a field holds its crop of golden wheat. On three sides it was pedestalled by the sheerest rock. On the fourth side it curved up to join the parent mountain-flank. Huge and high it was, yet height and size took some time to estimate, for there were mountains all around it. When you had been looking at it for some time you said aloud: "That leaca is high!" When you had stared for a longer time you said: "That leaca is immensely high—and huge!" Still the most remarkable thing about it was the way it held the sunshine. When all the valley had gone into the gloom of twilight—and this happened in the early afternoon—the leaca was still at mid-day. When the valley was dark with night and the lamps had been long alight in the farmhouse, the leaca had still the red gleam of sunset on it. It hung above the misty valley like a velarium—as they used to call that awning-cloth which hung above the emperor's seat in the amphitheatre.

"What is it called, do you say?" I asked again.

"Leaca-na-Naomh," she replied.

"Saints used to live on it?"

"The Hermits," she answered, and sighed deeply.

Her trouble told me that that leaca had to do with the fear that was burrowing like a mole in her father's heart. I would test it. Soon afterwards the old man came by, his eyes on the ground, his lips moving.

"That leaca," I said, "what do you call it?"

He looked up with a startled expression. He was very white; he couldn't abide my steady gaze.

"Nora," he cried, raising his voice suddenly and angrily, "cas isteach iad, cas isteach iad!" He almost roared at the gentle girl.

"Turn in—what?" I said, roughly, "the cattle are in long ago."

" 'Tis right they should," he answered, leaving me.

Yes, this leaca and this man had between them moulded out a tragedy, as between two hands.

Though the sun had gone still I sat staring at it. It was far off, but whatever light remained in the sky had gathered to it. I was wondering at its clear definition among all the vague and misty mountain-shapes when a voice, quivering with age, high and untuneful, addressed me:

" 'Twould be right for you to see it when there's snow on it."

"Ah!"

" 'Tis blinding!" The voice had changed so much as his inner vision strengthened that I gazed up quickly at him. He was a very old man, somewhat fairy-like in appearance, but he had the eyes of a boy! These eyes told me he was one who had lived imaginatively. Therefore I almost gripped him lest he should escape; from him would I learn of Leaca-na-Naomh. Shall I speak of him as a vassal of the house, or as a tatter of the family, or as a spall of the rough landscape? He was native to all three. His homespun was patched with patches as large and as straight-cut as those you'd see on a fisherman's sail. He was, clothes and all, the same colour as the aged lichen of the rocks; but his eyes were as fresh as dew.

Gripping him, as I have said, I searched his face, as one searches a poem for a hidden meaning.

"When did it happen, this dreadful thing?" I said.

He was taken off his guard. I could imagine, I could almost feel his mind struggling, summoning up an energy sufficient to express his idea of how as well as when the thing happened. At last he spoke deliberately.

"When the master,"—I knew he meant the householder—"was at his best, his swiftest and strongest in health, in riches, in force and spirit." He hammered every word.

"Ah!" I said; and I noticed the night had begun to thicken, fitly I thought, for my mind was already making mad leaps into the darkness of conjecture. He began to speak a more simple language:

"In those days he was without burden or ailment—unless maybe every little biteen of land between the rocks that he had not as yet brought under the plough was a burden. This, that, yonder, all those fine fields that have gone back again into heather and furze, it was he made them. There's sweat in them! But while he bent over them in the little dark days of November, dropping his sweat, he would raise up his eyes and fix them on the leaca. *That* would be worth all of them, and worth more than double all of them if it was brought under the plough."

"And why not?" I said.

"Plough the bed of the saints?"

"I had forgotten."

"You are not a Gael of the Gaels maybe?"

"I had forgotten; continue; it grows chilly."

"He had a serving-man; he was a fool; they were common in the country then; they had not been as yet herded into asylums. He was a fool; but a true Gael. That he never forgot; except once."

"Continue."

"He had also a sire horse, Griosach he called him, he was so strong, so high and princely."

"A plough horse?"

"He had never been harnessed. He was the master's pride and boast. The people gathered on the hillsides when he rode him to Mass. You looked at the master; you looked at the horse; the horse knew the hillsides were looking at him. He made music with his hoofs, he kept his eyes to himself, he was so proud.

"What of the fool?"

"Have I spoken of the fool?"

"Yes, a true Gael."

"'Tis true, that word. He was as strong as Griosach. He was what no one else was: he was a match for Griosach. The master petted the horse. The horse petted the master. Both of them knew they went well together. But Griosach the sire horse feared Liam Ruadh the fool; and Liam Ruadh the fool feared Griosach the sire horse. For neither had as yet found out that he was stronger than the other. They would play together like two strong boys, equally matched in strength and daring. They would wrestle and throw each other. Then they would leave off; and begin again when they had recovered their breath.

"Yes," I said, "the master, the horse Griosach, the fool Liam—now, the Leaca, the Leaca."

"I have brought in the leaca. It will come in again, now! The master was one day standing at a gap for a long time; there was no one near him. Liam Ruadh came near him. 'It is not lucky to be so silent as that,' he said. The master raised his head and answered:

"'The Leaca for wheat.'

"The fool nearly fell down in a sprawling heap. No one had ever heard of anything like that.

"'No,' he said like a child.

"'The Leaca for wheat,' the master said again, as if there was someone inside him speaking.

"The fool was getting hot and angry.

"'The Leaca for prayer!' he said.

"'The Leaca for wheat,' said the master, a third time.

"When the fool heard him he gathered himself up and roared—a loud 'O-oh!' it went around the hills like sudden thunder; in the little breath he had left he said: 'The Leaca for prayer!'

"The master went away from him; who could tell what might have happened?

"The next day the fool was washing a sheep's diseased foot—he had the struggling animal held firm in his arms when the master slipped behind him and whispered in his ear:

"'The Leaca for wheat.'

"Before the fool could free the animal the master was gone. He was a wild, swift man that day. He laughed. It was that self-same night he went into the shed where Liam slept and stood a moment looking at the large face of the fool working in his dreams. He watched him like that a minute. Then he flashed the lantern quite close into the fool's eyes so as to dazzle him, and he cried out harshly, 'The Leaca for wheat,' making his voice appear far off, like a trumpet-call, and before the fool could understand where he was, or whether he was asleep or awake, the light was gone and the master was gone.

"Day after day the master put the same thought into the fool's ear. And Liam was becoming sullen and dark. Then one night long after we were all in our sleep we heard a wild crash. The fool had gone to the master's room. He found the door bolted. He put his shoulder to it. The door went in about the room, and the arch above it fell in pieces around the fool's head—all in the still night.

'"Who's there? What is it?' cried the master, starting up in his bed.

'"Griosach for the plough!' said the fool.

"No one could think of Griosach being hitched to a plough. The master gave him no answer. He lay down in his bed and covered his face. The fool went back to his straw. Whenever the master now said 'The Leaca for wheat' the fool would answer 'Griosach for the plough.'

"The tree turns the wind aside, yet the wind at last twists the tree. Like wind and tree master and fool played against each other, until at last they each of them had spent their force.

'"I will take Griosach and Niamh and plough the leaca,' said the fool; it was a hard November day.

'"As you wish,' said the master. Many a storm finishes with a little sob of wind. Their voices were now like a little wind.

"The next night a pair of smiths were brought into the coom all the way from Aunascawl. The day after the mountains were ringing with their blows as the ploughing-gear was overhauled. Without rest or laughter or chatter the work went on, for Liam was at their shoulders, and he hardly gave them time to wipe their sweaty hair. One began to sing: "Tis my grief on Monday now,' but Liam struck him one blow and stretched him. He returned to his work quiet enough after that. We saw the fool's anger rising. We made way for him; and he was going back and forth the whole day long; in the evening his mouth began to froth and his tongue to blab. We drew away from him; wondering what he was thinking of. The master himself began to grow timid; he hadn't a word in him; but he kept looking up at us from under his brow as if he feared we would turn against him. Sure we wouldn't; wasn't he our master— even what he did?

"When the smiths had mounted their horses that night to return to Aunascawl one of them stooped down to the master's ear and whispered: 'Watch him, he's in a fever.'

"'Who?'

"'The fool.' That was a true word.

"Some of us rode down with the smiths to the mouth of the pass, and as we did so snow began to fall silently and thickly. We were glad; we thought it might put back the dreadful business of the ploughing. When we returned towards the house we were talking. But a boy checked us.

"'Whisht!' he said.

"We listened. We crept beneath the thatch of the stables. Within we heard the fool talking to the horses. We knew he was putting his arms around their necks. When he came out, he was quiet and happy-looking. We crouched aside to let him pass. Then we told the master.

"'Go to your beds,' he said, coldly enough.

"We played no cards that night; we sang no songs; we thought it too long until we were in our dark beds. The last thing we thought of was the snow falling, falling, falling on Leaca-na-Naomh and on all the mountains. There was not a stir or a sigh in the house. Everyone feared to hear his own bed creak. And at last we slept.

"What awoke me? I could hear voices whispering. There was fright in them. Before I could distinguish one word from another I felt my neck creeping. I shook myself. I leaped up. I looked out. The light was blinding. The moon was shining on the slopes of new snow. There was none falling now; a light, thin wind was blowing out of the lovely stars.

"Beneath my window I saw five persons standing in a little group, all clutching one another like people standing in a flooded river. They were very still; they would not move even when they whispered. As I wondered to see them so fearfully clutching one another a voice spoke in my room:

"'For God's sake, Stephen, get ready and come down.'

"'Man, what's the matter with ye?'

"'For God's sake come down.'

"'Tell me, tell me!'

"'How can I? Come down!'

"I tried to be calm; I went out and made for that little group, putting my hand against my eyes, the new snow was so blinding.

' "Where's the master?' I said.

" 'There!' They did not seem to care whether or not I looked at the master.

"He was a little apart; he was clutching a jut of rock as if the land was slipping from his feet. His cowardice made me afraid. I was hard put to control my breath.

' "What are ye, are ye all staring at?' I said.

' "Leaca-na———'—the voice seemed to come from over a mile away, yet it was the man beside me had spoken.

"I looked. The leaca was a dazzling blaze, it was true, but I had often before seen it as a bright and wonderful. I was puzzled.

"Is it the leaca ye're all staring——' I began; but several of them silently lifted up a hand and pointed towards it. I could have stared at them instead; whether or not it was the white moonlight that was on them, they looked like men half-frozen, too chilled to speak. But I looked where those outstretched hands silently bade me. Then I, too, was struck dumb and became one of that icy group, for I saw a little white cloud moving across Leaca, a feathery cloud, and from the heart of it there came every now and then a little flash of fire, a spark. Sometimes, too, the little cloud would grow thin, as if it were scattering away, at which times it was a moving shadow we saw. As I blinked at it I felt my hand groping about to catch something, to catch someone, to make sure of myself; for the appearance of every-thing, the whiteness, the stillness, and then that moving cloud whiter than everything else, whiter than anything in the world, and so like an angel's wing moving along the leaca, frightened me until I felt like fainting away. To make things worse, straight from the little cloud came down a whisper, a long, thin, clear, silvery cry: 'Griosach! Ho-o-o-oh! Ho-o-o-oh!' a ploughing cry. We did not move; we kept our silence: everyone knew that that cry was going through everyone else as through himself, a stroke of coldness. Then I understood why the master was hanging on to a rock; he must have heard the cry before anyone else. It was terrible, made so thin and silvery by the distance; and yet it was a cry of joy—the fool had conquered Griosach!

"I do not know what wild thoughts had begun to come into my head when one man in the group gasped out 'Now!' and then another, and yet another. Their voices were breath, not sound. Then they all said 'Ah!' and I understood the fear that had moved their tongues. I saw the little cloud pause a moment on the edge of the leaca, almost hang over the edge, and then begin to draw back from it. The fool had turned his team on the verge and was now ploughing up against the hill.

" 'O-o-h,' said the master, in the first moment of relief; it was more like a cry of agony. He looked round at us with ghastly eyes; and our eyeballs turned towards his, just as cold and fixed. Again that silvery cry floated down at us 'Griosach! Ho-o-o-oh!' And again the stroke of coldness passed through every one of us. The cry began to come more frequently, more triumphantly, for now again the little cloud was ploughing down the slope, and its pace had quickened. It was making once more for that edge beneath which was a sheer fall of hundreds of feet.

"Behind us, suddenly, from the direction of the thatched stables came a loud and high whinny—a call to a mate. It was so unexpected, and we were all so rapt up in what was before our eyes, that it shook us, making us spring from one another. I was the first to recover.

" 'My God,' I said, 'that's Niamh, that's Niamh!'

"The whinny came again; it was Niamh surely.

" 'What is he ploughing with, then? What has he with Griosach?'

"A man came running from the stables; he was trying to cry out: he could hardly be heard:

" 'Griosach and Lugh! Griosach and Lugh!'

"Lugh was another sire horse; and the two sires would eat each other; they always had ill-will for each other. The master was staring at us.

" ' 'Tisn't Lugh?' he said, with a gurgle in his voice.

"No one could answer him. We were thinking if the mare's cry reached the sires their anger would blaze up and no one could hold them; but why should Liam have yoked such a team?

" 'Hush! hush!' said a woman's voice.

"We at once heard a new cry; it came down from the leaca:

" 'Griosach, Back! Back!' It was almost inaudible, but we could feel the swiftness and terror in it. 'Back! Back!' came down again. 'Back, Griosach, back!'

" 'They're fighting, they're fighting—the sires!' one of our horse-boys yelled out—the first sound above a breath that had come from any of us, for he was fonder of Lugh than of the favourite Griosach, and had forgotten everything else. And we saw that the little cloud was almost at a stand-still; yet that it was disturbed; sparks were flying from it; and we heard little clanking sounds, very faint, coming from it. They might mean great leaps and rearings.

"Suddenly we saw the master spring from that rock to which he had been clinging as limp as a leaf in autumn, spring from it with great life and roar up towards the leaca:

"'Liam! Liam! Liam Ruadh!' He turned to us, 'Shout, boys, and break his fever,' he cried, 'Shout, shout!'

"We were glad of that.

"'Liam! Liam! Liam Ruadh!' we roared.

"'My God! My God!' we heard as we finished. It was the master's voice; he then fell down. At once we raised our voices again; it would keep us from seeing or hearing what was happening on the leaca.

"'Liam! Liam! Liam Ruadh!'

"There was wild confusion.

"'Liam! Liam! Liam! Ruadh! Ruadh! Ruadh!' the mountains were singing back to us, making the confusion worse. We were twisted about—one man staring at the ground, one at the rock in front of his face, another at the sky high over the leaca, and one had his hand stretched out like a sign-post on a hilltop, I remember him best; none of us were looking at the leaca itself. But we were listening and listening, and at last they died, the echoes, and there was a cold silence, cold, cold. Then we heard old Diarmuid's passionless voice begin to pray:

"'Abhaile ar an sioruidheacht go raibh a anam.' At home in Eternity may his soul——.' We turned round, one by one, without speaking a word, and stared at the leaca. It was bare! The little cloud was still in the air—a white dust, ascending. Along the leaca we saw two thin shadowy lines—they looked as if they had been drawn in very watery ink on its dazzling surface. Of horses, plough, and fool there wasn't a trace. They had gone over the edge while we roared."

"Noble person, as they went over I'm sure Liam Ruadh had one fist at Lugh's bridle, and the other at Griosach's, and that he was swinging high in the air between them. Our roaring didn't break his fever, say that it didn't, noble person? But don't question the master about it. I have told you all!"

* * *

"I will leave this place to-night," I said.

"It is late, noble person."

"I will leave it now, bring me my horse."

That is why I made no further inquiries in that valley as to the fate of that old Gaelic family that were once lords of those hills. I gave up the quest. Sometimes a thought comes to me that Liam Ruadh might have been the last of an immemorial line, no scion of which, if God had left him his senses, would have ploughed the Leaca of the Saints, no, not even if it were to save him from begging at fairs and in public houses.

THE JUDGMENT

Franz Kafka

IT WAS ON a Sunday morning in the loveliest part of the spring. Georg Bendemann, a young merchant, sat in his room on the second floor of one of the low, lightly built houses that extended along the river in a long line, differing, if at all, only in height and coloration. He had just finished a letter to a childhood friend who was living abroad; he sealed the letter with playful slowness and then, leaning his elbow on the desk, looked out the window at the river, the bridge and the pale-green hills on the far bank.

He thought about how this friend, dissatisfied with his advancement at home, had, years ago now, literally fled to Russia. Now this friend was running a business in St. Petersburg that had been very promising at the start, but for a long time now seemed to be at a standstill, as he complained during his increasingly infrequent visits to Georg. And so he was wearing himself out uselessly far from home; his foreign-style beard failed to disguise the face Georg had known so well since they were children, a face whose yellow complexion was apparently the sign of a developing illness. As he told Georg, he had no close relations with the colony of his compatriots in that place, but, in addition, practically no social intercourse with native families, and thus was in a fair way to remain a bachelor always.

What was one to write to a man like that, who had obviously taken a wrong course, whom one could pity but not help? Should one perhaps advise him to come home, resume his life back here, restore all his old friendships (there was no obstacle to this) and, for all the rest, rely on his friends' assistance? But that would mean nothing less than to tell him at the same time—hurting him more, the more one wished to spare his feelings—that his efforts up to now had been unsuccessful, that he should finally abandon them, that he had to return and be gaped at by everyone as a man who had come back as a failure. It would mean telling him that his friends were the only ones with any sense, and that he was just a grown-up child who should merely obey his successful friends that had stayed at home. And was it even certain that all the pain that would have to be inflicted on him would be to any purpose? Maybe they wouldn't even succeed in bringing him home at all— for he himself said that he no longer understood the conditions back home—and so he would remain abroad in spite of everything, embittered by their suggestions and all the more alienated from his friends. But if he actually followed their advice and were to come to grief here—not intentionally, of course, but through circumstances—if he failed to find a proper footing either with or without his friends, if he suffered humiliation, if he then really had no home or friends left, wasn't it much better for him to remain abroad just as he was? In such circumstances, was it possible to believe that he would actually make a go of it here?

For these reasons, if one was to maintain communication by letter at all, one could not send him any real news, as one would unhesitatingly do even to the most casual acquaintances. Now, it was more than three years since Georg's friend had been home, giving as a quite flimsy excuse for his absence the instability of political conditions in Russia, which according to him did not allow a small businessman to leave his work for even the briefest period—while hundreds of thousands of Russians were calmly traveling all over. In the course of those three years, however, much had changed for Georg in particular. The death of Georg's mother, which had occurred about two years earlier, since which time Georg had been sharing the household with his old father, had, of course, still been communicated to his friend. The friend had expressed his sympathy in a letter so dry that the only possible explanation for it was that mourning over such an event becomes quite unimaginable when one is abroad. But, in addition, since that time Georg had taken charge of the family business with greater decisiveness, as he had done with everything else. Perhaps, while his mother was alive, his father had hindered Georg from taking a really active part in the business by insisting that only *his* views were valid; perhaps, since the death of Georg's mother, his father, while still working in the business, had become more withdrawn; perhaps—and this was extremely probable—lucky accidents played a far more important role. But at any rate, in these two years the business had grown at a quite unexpected rate, they had had to double their personnel, the returns had increased fivefold, and further expansion was undoubtedly due in the future.

But Georg's friend had no idea of this change. Earlier, perhaps most recently in that letter of sympathy, he had tried to persuade Georg to emigrate to Russia and had expatiated on the prospects in St. Petersburg for Georg's line of business in particular. The figures he quoted were infinitesimal compared with the volume of business Georg was now doing. But Georg had not felt like writing his friend about his business successes, and if he were to have done so belatedly now, it would really have looked odd.

And so Georg confined himself to continually writing his friend about nothing but insignificant events, as they accumulate disorderedly in one's memory when one thinks back on a quiet Sunday. His only wish was to leave undisturbed the mental picture of his hometown that his friend must have created during the long interval, a picture he could live with. And so it happened that three times, in letters written fairly far apart, Georg informed his friend of the engagement of a man of no consequence to an equally inconsequential girl, until his friend, quite contrary to Georg's intentions, really began to be interested in this curious fact.

But Georg far preferred to write him about things like that than to admit that he himself, a month earlier, had become engaged to a Miss Frieda Brandenfeld, a girl from a well-to-do family. He often spoke to his fiancée about that friend and their special relationship as correspondents. "Now, he won't come to our wedding," she said, "and I do have the right to meet all your friends." "I don't want to bother him," Georg replied; "mind you, he probably would come—at least, I think so—but he would feel constrained and injured; perhaps he would envy me, and he would surely go back again alone, discontented and incapable of ever overcoming that discontentment. Alone—do you know what that means?" "Yes, but couldn't he come to hear about our marriage in some other way?" "Naturally I can't prevent that, but, given his mode of life, it's not likely." "If you have friends like that, Georg, you shouldn't have become engaged at all." "Yes, that's the fault of both of us; but even so I wouldn't have wanted it any other way."

And when she then, breathing rapidly as he kissed her, still managed to say: "And yet it does really make me sad," he decided it would really do no harm to write his friend about everything. "That's how I am and that's how he's got to accept me," he said to himself; "I can't remake myself into a person who might be more suited to be his friend than I am."

And, in fact, in the long letter he composed on that Sunday morning he informed his friend of the engagement that had taken place, writing as follows: "I have saved the best news for the end. I have become engaged to a Miss Frieda Brandenfeld, a girl from a well-to-do family that did not move here until long after your departure, and whom you thus can hardly be expected to know. There will be further opportunities to tell you details about my fiancée; let it suffice for today that I am very happy and that the only change in the relationship between you and me is that, in place of a very ordinary friend, you will now have in me a happy friend. In addition, in my fiancée, who sends warmest regards and who will soon write to you herself, you are acquiring a sincere female friend, which is not totally insignificant for a bachelor. I know that all sorts of things prevent you from visiting us, but wouldn't my wedding, of all things, be the right occasion for you to cast all obstacles to the winds? However that may be, though, don't make any special allowances but act only as you see fit."

With this letter in his hand Georg had sat at his desk for a long time, his face turned toward the window. When an acquaintance had greeted him from the street passing by, he had barely responded with an absent smile.

Finally he put the letter in his pocket and stepped from his room across a small corridor into his father's room, which he had not been in for months. Nor was there any particular need for him to go there, because he saw his father constantly in their office and they took their lunch in a restaurant at the same hour; in the evening, to be sure, each of them saw to his own needs as he wished, but then usually (unless Georg, as happened most often, was together with friends or, as things were now, visited his fiancée) each would sit with his newspaper for another little while in the living room that they shared.

Georg was surprised at how dark his father's room was even on this sunny morning. So the high wall that rose beyond the narrow yard cast such a great shadow! His father was sitting by the window in a corner that was decorated with various mementos of his late mother, and was reading the newspaper, which he held off to one side in front of his face, attempting to correct some eye condition. On the table were the leftovers of his breakfast, not much of which seemed to have been eaten.

"Ah, Georg!" said his father and walked right over to him. His heavy bathrobe opened as he walked, the tails flapping around him—"My father is *still* a giant," Georg said to himself.

"But it's unbearably dark here," he said then.

"Yes, it is dark, isn't it?" his father answered.

"You shut the window, too?"

"I like it better this way."

"But it's quite warm outside," said Georg, as an addition to his earlier remark, and sat down.

His father cleared away the breakfast dishes and put them on a chest.

"All that I really wanted to tell you," continued Georg, who was following the old man's movements in great perplexity, "is that, after all, I have written to St. Petersburg announcing my engagement." He drew the letter a little way out of his pocket and let it slide back.

"What do you mean, to St. Petersburg?" asked his father.

"To my friend, of course," said Georg and tried to meet his father's eyes.—"At work he's quite different," he thought; "the way he sits here, filling out the chair, with his arms folded over his chest!"

"Yes. To your friend," said his father with a special emphasis.

"You know, of course, Father, that at first I wanted to keep my engagement a secret from him. Out of consideration for his feelings, for no other reason. You know yourself, he's a difficult man. I said to myself that he could find out about my engagement in some other way, even though, given his lonely way of life, that's hardly likely—I couldn't prevent that—but that he definitely wasn't going to find out about it from me."

"And now you've changed your mind?" asked his father, laid his voluminous paper down on the windowsill and put his glasses, which he covered with his hand, on top of the paper.

"Yes, now I have changed my mind. If he is a good friend of mine, I said to myself, then my happy engagement is a bit of happiness for him too. And therefore I no longer hesitated to tell him about it. But before I mailed the letter I wanted to tell you."

"Georg," said his father and drew the corners of his toothless mouth out wide, "listen! You came to me with this matter to consult with me. That doubtless does you honor. But it is meaningless, it is worse than meaningless, if you don't tell me the whole truth now. I don't wish to stir up matters that don't pertain to this. Since the death of your dear mother, certain unpleasant things have occurred. Perhaps the time is coming for them, too, and perhaps it is coming sooner than we think. At work a lot escapes me; perhaps it isn't intentionally hidden from me—for the moment I shall definitely assume that it is not hidden from me—I am no longer strong enough, my memory is going, I can no longer keep up with all the particulars. For one thing, that is perfectly natural for my age, and, for another, your mother's death took a much greater toll of me than of you.—But since we are discussing this matter, this letter, I implore you, Georg, don't deceive me. It's a trifle, it's not worth mentioning, so don't deceive me. Do you really have this friend in St. Petersburg?"

Georg stood up in embarrassment. "Let's forget about my friends. A thousand friends are no substitute for my father. Do you know what I think? You don't take good enough care of yourself. But old age demands its due. I can't do without you in the business, you know that very well, but if the business were to threaten your health, I would shut it down forever tomorrow. This is no good. We must institute a new way of life for you. And thoroughly. You sit here in the dark while you would have fine light in the living room. You nibble at your breakfast instead of nourishing yourself properly. You sit by a closed window while the air would do you so much good. No, Father! I am going to get the doctor and we'll follow his advice. We'll exchange rooms; you'll move into the front room, I'll move in here. It won't mean any change for you, all your possessions will be brought in with you. But there's time for all that; for the moment do lie down in bed for a while, you definitely need rest. Come, I'll help you undress; you'll see, I can. Or if you want to go to the front room at once, then you can lie down on my bed for the time being. In fact, that would be very sensible."

Georg was standing close by his father, who had let his head, with its disheveled white hair, drop onto his breast.

"Georg," said his father quietly, without moving.

Georg immediately knelt down beside his father; in his father's weary face he saw that the unnaturally large pupils in the corners of the eyes were directed at himself.

"You have no friend in St. Petersburg. You've always been a practical joker and you haven't spared even me. How could you have a friend there, of all places! I can't believe that at all."

"Just try to remember, Father," said Georg, lifting his father from the armchair and drawing off his bathrobe as the old man now stood there in great debility; "it's now almost three years ago that my friend was here on a visit. I still recall that you didn't particularly like him. At least twice I told you that he wasn't here, although he was sitting in my room at the moment. Of course, I could understand your dislike of him very well: my friend does have his peculiarities. But then after all you got along very well with him again. I was still so proud at the time that you listened to him, nodded and asked him questions. If you think about it, you must remember. At the time he told us unbelievable stories about the Russian revolution. For example, how, on a business trip to Kiev, during a riot he had seen a priest on a balcony cutting a wide bloody cross into the palm of his hand, raising that hand and addressing the crowd. You yourself repeated that story from time to time."

Meanwhile Georg had succeeded in sitting his father down again and carefully pulling off the long knitted drawers he wore over his linen underpants, as well as his socks. At sight of the not especially clean underwear, he reproached himself for having neglected his father. It surely would also have been his duty to watch over his father's changes of underwear. He had not yet spoken expressly with his fiancée about how they wished to arrange his father's future, for they had tacitly presupposed that his father would remain alone in the old house. But now he quickly decided, with full determination, to take his father along into his future household. Indeed, it almost seemed, upon examining the situation more closely, that the care that would be given his father there might come too late.

He carried his father to bed in his arms. He had a frightening feeling when he noticed, during the few paces over to the bed, that his father was playing with the watch chain on his chest. He couldn't put him right into bed because he was holding onto that watch chain so tightly.

But scarcely was he in bed when all seemed well. He covered himself and then pulled the blanket extremely far up over his shoulders. He looked up at Georg in a not unfriendly way.

"Then, you remember him now?" asked Georg and nodded to him encouragingly.

"Am I completely covered up now?" asked his father, as if he couldn't see whether his feet were sufficiently covered.

"So you're already pleased to be in bed," said Georg and tucked him in more thoroughly.

"Am I completely covered up?" asked his father again, and seemed to wait for the answer with particular attention.

"Relax, you're all covered up."

"No!" shouted his father, running his reply into his preceding remark, then threw the blanket back with such force that it completely unfolded for a moment as it flew through the air, and stood upright on the bed. He merely touched the ceiling lightly with one hand. "You wanted to cover me up, I know, offspring of mine, but I'm not covered up yet. And even if I am doing this with my last strength, it is enough for you—too much for you. Of course I know your friend. He would have been a son after my own heart. And that's why you have cheated him all these years. Why else? Do you think I haven't wept over him? Isn't that why you lock yourself into your office, so no one will disturb you—'the boss is busy'—just so you can write your treacherous little letters to Russia. But fortunately no one needs to teach a father how to see through his son. Now that you believed you had got the better of him, got the better of him to such an extent that you can seat yourself on him with your backside and he won't move, this fine son of mine has decided to get married!"

Georg looked up at the frightening image his father presented. His St. Petersburg friend, whom his father suddenly knew so well, stirred his emotions as never before. He saw him lost in far-off Russia. He saw him at the door of his empty, plundered establishment. He was still standing amid the ruins of the shelves, the mangled merchandise, the falling gas brackets. Why did he have to travel so far away!

"But look at me!" shouted his father, and Georg ran almost absent-mindedly toward the bed, in order to grasp everything, but came to a sudden halt midway.

"Because she lifted her skirts," his father began to pipe, "because she lifted her skirts that way, the disgusting ninny," and, in order to depict this, he lifted his nightshirt so high that the scar from his war years could be seen on his upper thigh; "because she lifted her skirts so and so and so, you went for her, and in order to satisfy yourself with her without being disturbed, you profaned your mother's memory, betrayed your friend and stuck your father in bed so he couldn't move. But can he move or can't he?"

And he stood completely unsupported and flung out his legs. He was radiant with insight.

Georg stood in a corner, as far from his father as possible. A long time ago he had firmly decided to observe everything with complete thoroughness, so that he might not be somehow taken by surprise in a roundabout way, from behind, from above. Now he once more remembered that long-forgotten decision and forgot it, as one draws a short thread through the eye of a needle.

"But my friend is *not* betrayed!" shouted his father, and his index finger, moving to and fro, confirmed this. "I was his local representative here."

"Play actor!" Georg could not help calling out, immediately recognized the harm he had done himself, and, with staring eyes—but too late—bit his tongue so hard that he doubled up with pain.

"Yes, of course I was playing a part! Play actor! What a good expression! What other comfort remained for an old, bereaved father? Tell me—and, for the moment that it takes you to reply, be my living son yet—what else could I do, in my back room, persecuted by my faithless staff, old to my very bones? And my son went everywhere exultantly, closed business deals that I had set up, turned somersaults from joy, and moved about in front of his father with the poker face of a man of honor! Do you think I wouldn't have loved you, I who gave you your being?"

"Now he'll lean forward," thought Georg; "if he would only fall and smash himself!" This sentence hissed through his mind.

His father leaned forward, but did not fall. Since Georg did not come closer, as he had expected, he straightened up again.

"Stay where you are, I don't need you! You think you still have the strength to come over here, and are merely hanging back because you want to. Don't make a mistake! I am still by far the stronger. On my own I might have had to retreat, but your mother passed her strength along to me, I made a wonderful alliance with your friend, I have your clientele here in my pocket!"

"He even has pockets in his nightshirt!" Georg said to himself, and thought that he could obliterate him with that remark. He thought so only for a moment, because he kept forgetting everything.

"Just lock arms with your fiancée and come over to me. I'll sweep her away from your side before you know it!"

Georg made grimaces as if he didn't believe that. His father merely nodded toward Georg's corner, in asseveration of the truth of what he said.

"How you did amuse me today when you came and asked whether you should write your friend about your engagement. He knows everything, foolish boy, he knows everything! I wrote to him because you forgot to take away my writing supplies. That's why he hasn't come for years now, he knows everything a hundred times better than you do; he crumples up your letters in his left hand without reading them, while he holds my letters in front of him in his right hand to read them!"

In his enthusiasm he swung his arm above his head. "He knows everything a thousand times better!" he shouted.

"Ten thousand times!" said Georg, meaning to mock his father, but while still on his lips the words took on a deadly serious tone.

"For years I've been watching and waiting for you to come along with that question! Do you think I care about anything else? Do you think I read newspapers? There!" and he threw over to Georg a sheet of the newspaper that had somehow been carried into the bed along with him. An old paper, with a name now completely unknown to Georg.

"How long you hesitated before your time was ripe! Mother had to die, she couldn't live until the happy day; your friend is going to ruin in his Russia, even three years ago his face was yellow enough to throw away; and I—well, you see how things stand with me. That you have eyes for!"

"So you were lying in wait for me!" shouted Georg.

In a sympathetic tone his father said parenthetically: "You probably wanted to say that before. Now it's no longer fitting."

And in a louder voice: "So now you know what existed outside yourself; up to now you knew only about yourself! You were truly an innocent child, but even more truly you were a fiendish person!—And therefore know this: I now condemn you to death by drowning!"

Georg felt himself driven from the room; the crash with which his father collapsed onto the bed behind him was still in his ears as he went. On the staircase, as he dashed down the steps as if down an inclined plane, he knocked over his maid, who was about to go upstairs to tidy up the house after the night. "Jesus!" she cried and covered her face with her apron, but he was already gone. He leapt past the gate and across the roadway, impelled to reach the water. Now he clutched the railing as a hungry man clutches food. He vaulted over like the accomplished gymnast he had been in his youth, to his parents' pride. He was still holding tight with hands that were growing weaker; between the bars of the railing he caught sight of a bus that would easily smother the noise of his fall; he called softly: "Dear parents, I *did* always love you," and let himself fall.

At that moment a simply endless stream of traffic was passing over the bridge.

THE COFFIN-MAKER

Alexander Pushkin

THE LAST OF the effects of the coffin-maker, Adrian Prokhoroff, were placed upon the hearse, and a couple of sorry-looking jades dragged themselves along for the fourth time from Basmannaia to Nikitskaia,[1] whither the coffin-maker was removing with all his household. After locking up the shop, he posted upon the door a placard announcing that the house was to be let or sold, and then made his way on foot to his new abode. On approaching the little yellow house, which had so long captivated his imagination, and which at last he had bought for a considerable sum, the old coffin-maker was astonished to find that his heart did not rejoice. When he crossed the unfamiliar threshold and found his new home in the greatest confusion, he sighed for his old hovel, where for eighteen years the strictest order had prevailed. He began to scold his two daughters and the servant for their slowness, and then set to work to help them himself. Order was soon established; the ark with the sacred images, the cupboard with the crockery, the table, the sofa, and the bed occupied the corners reserved for them in the back room; in the kitchen and parlour were placed the articles comprising the stock-in-trade of the master—coffins of all colours and of all sizes, together with cupboards containing mourning hats, cloaks and torches.

Over the door was placed a sign representing a fat Cupid with an inverted torch in his hand and bearing this inscription: "Plain and coloured coffins sold and lined here; coffins also let out on hire, and old ones repaired."

---

[1] Streets in Moscow.

The girls retired to their bedroom; Adrian made a tour of inspection of his quarters, and then sat down by the window and ordered the tea-urn to be prepared.

The enlightened reader knows that Shakespeare and Walter Scott have both represented their grave-diggers as merry and facetious individuals, in order that the contrast might more forcibly strike our imagination. Out of respect for the truth, we cannot follow their example, and we are compelled to confess that the disposition of our coffin-maker was in perfect harmony with his gloomy occupation. Adrian Prokhoroff was usually gloomy and thoughtful. He rarely opened his mouth, except to scold his daughters when he found them standing idle and gazing out of the window at the passers by, or to demand for his wares an exorbitant price from those who had the misfortune—and sometimes the good fortune—to need them. Hence it was that Adrian, sitting near the window and drinking his seventh cup of tea, was immersed as usual in melancholy reflections. He thought of the pouring rain which, just a week before, had commenced to beat down during the funeral of the retired brigadier. Many of the cloaks had shrunk in consequence of the downpour, and many of the hats had been put quite out of shape. He foresaw unavoidable expenses, for his old stock of funeral dresses was in a pitiable condition. He hoped to compensate himself for his losses by the burial of old Trukhina, the shopkeeper's wife, who for more than a year had been upon the point of death. But Trukhina lay dying at Rasgouliai,[2] and Prokhoroff was afraid that her heirs, in spite of their promise, would not take the trouble to send so far for him, but would make arrangements with the nearest undertaker.

These reflections were suddenly interrupted by three masonic knocks at the door.

"Who is there?" asked the coffin-maker.

The door opened, and a man, who at the first glance could be recognized as a German artisan, entered the room, and with a jovial air advanced towards the coffin-maker.

"Pardon me, respected neighbour," said he in that Russian dialect which to this day we cannot hear without a smile: "pardon me for disturbing you. . . . I wished to make your acquaintance as soon as possible. I am a shoemaker, my name is Gottlieb Schultz, and I

---

[2] [Locality in Moscow.]

live across the street, in that little house just facing your windows. Tomorrow I am going to celebrate my silver wedding, and I have come to invite you and your daughters to dine with us."

The invitation was cordially accepted. The coffin-maker asked the shoemaker to seat himself and take a cup of tea, and thanks to the open-hearted disposition of Gottlieb Schultz, they were soon engaged in friendly conversation.

"How is business with you?" asked Adrian.

"Just so so," replied Schultz; "I cannot complain. My wares are not like yours: the living can do without shoes, but the dead cannot do without coffins."

"Very true," observed Adrian; "but if a living person hasn't anything to buy shoes with, you cannot find fault with him, he goes about barefooted; but a dead beggar gets his coffin for nothing."

In this manner the conversation was carried on between them for some time; at last the shoemaker rose and took leave of the coffin-maker, renewing his invitation.

The next day, exactly at twelve o'clock, the coffin-maker and his daughters issued from the doorway of their newly-purchased residence, and directed their steps towards the abode of their neighbour. I will not stop to describe the Russian *caftan* of Adrian Prokhoroff, nor the European toilettes of Akoulina and Daria, deviating in this respect from the usual custom of modern novelists. But I do not think it superfluous to observe that they both had on the yellow cloaks and red shoes, which they were accustomed to don on solemn occasions only.

The shoemaker's little dwelling was filled with guests, consisting chiefly of German artisans with their wives and foremen. Of the Russian officials there was present but one, Yourko the Finn, a watchman, who, in spite of his humble calling, was the special object of the host's attention. For twenty-five years he had faithfully discharged the duties of postilion of Pogorelsky. The conflagration of 1812, which destroyed the ancient capital, destroyed also his little yellow watch-house. But immediately after the expulsion of the enemy, a new one appeared in its place, painted grey and with white Doric columns, and Yourko began again to pace to and fro before it, with his axe and grey coat of mail. He was known to the greater part of the Germans who lived near the Nikitskaia Gate, and some of them had even spent the night from Sunday to Monday beneath his roof.

Adrian immediately made himself acquainted with him, as with a man whom, sooner or later, he might have need of, and when the guests took their places at the table, they sat down beside each other. Herr Schultz and his wife, and their daughter Lotchen, a young girl of seventeen, did the honours of the table and helped the cook to serve. The beer flowed in streams; Yourko ate like four, and Adrian in no way yielded to him; his daughters, however, stood upon their dignity. The conversation, which was carried on in German, gradually grew more and more boisterous. Suddenly the host requested a moment's attention, and uncorking a sealed bottle, he said with a loud voice in Russian:

"To the health of my good Louise!"

The champagne foamed. The host tenderly kissed the fresh face of his partner, and the guests drank noisily to the health of the good Louise.

"To the health of my amiable guests!" exclaimed the host, uncorking a second bottle; and the guests thanked him by draining their glasses once more.

Then followed a succession of toasts. The health of each individual guest was drunk; they drank to the health of Moscow and to quite a dozen little German towns; they drank to the health of all corporations in general and of each in particular; they drank to the health of the masters and foremen. Adrian drank with enthusiasm and became so merry, that he proposed a facetious toast to himself. Suddenly one of the guests, a fat baker, raised his glass and exclaimed:

"To the health of those for whom we work, our customers!"

This proposal, like all the others, was joyously and unanimously received. The guests began to salute each other; the tailor bowed to the shoemaker, the shoemaker to the tailor, the baker to both, the whole company to the baker, and so on. In the midst of these mutual congratulations, Yourko exclaimed, turning to his neighbour:

"Come, little father! Drink to the health of your corpses!"

Everybody laughed, but the coffin-maker considered himself insulted, and frowned. Nobody noticed it, the guests continued to drink, and the bell had already rung for vespers when they rose from the table.

The guests dispersed at a late hour, the greater part of them in a very merry mood. The fat baker and the bookbinder, whose face seemed as if bound in red morocco, linked their arms in those of

Yourko and conducted him back to his little watch-house, thus observing the proverb: "One good turn deserves another."

The coffin-maker returned home drunk and angry.

"Why is it," he exclaimed aloud, "why is it that my trade is not as honest as any other? Is a coffin-maker brother to the hangman? Why did those heathens laugh? Is a coffin-maker a buffoon? I wanted to invite them to my new dwelling and give them a feast, but now I'll do nothing of the kind. Instead of inviting them, I will invite those for whom I work: the orthodox dead."

"What is the matter, little father?" said the servant, who was engaged at that moment in taking off his boots: "why do you talk such nonsense? Make the sign of the cross! Invite the dead to your new house! What folly!"

"Yes, by the Lord! I will invite them," continued Adrian, "and that, too, for to-morrow! . . . Do me the favour, my benefactors, to come and feast with me to-morrow evening; I will regale you with what God has sent me."

With these words the coffin-maker turned into bed and soon began to snore.

It was still dark when Adrian was awakened out of his sleep. Trukhina, the shopkeeper's wife, had died during the course of that very night, and a special messenger was sent off on horseback by her bailiff to carry the news to Adrian. The coffin-maker gave him ten copecks to buy brandy with, dressed himself as hastily as possible, took a *droshky* and set out for Rasgouliai. Before the door of the house in which the deceased lay, the police had already taken their stand, and the trades-people were passing backwards and forwards, like ravens that smell a dead body. The deceased lay upon a table, yellow as wax, but not yet disfigured by decomposition. Around her stood her relatives, neighbours and domestic servants. All the windows were open; tapers were burning; and the priests were reading the prayers for the dead. Adrian went up to the nephew of Trukhina, a young shopman in a fashionable surtout, and informed him that the coffin, wax candles, pall, and the other funeral accessories would be immediately delivered with all possible exactitude. The heir thanked him in an absent-minded manner, saying that he would not bargain about the price, but would rely upon him acting in everything according to his conscience. The coffin-maker, in accordance with his usual custom, vowed that he would not charge him too much, exchanged significant glances with the bailiff, and then departed to commence operations.

The whole day was spent in passing to and fro between Rasgouliai and the Nikitskaia Gate. Towards evening everything was finished, and he returned home on foot, after having dismissed his driver. It was a moonlight night. The coffin-maker reached the Nikitskaia Gate in safety. Near the Church of the Ascension he was hailed by our acquaintance Yourko, who, recognizing the coffin-maker, wished him goodnight. It was late. The coffin-maker was just approaching his house, when suddenly he fancied he saw some one approach his gate, open the wicket, and disappear within.

"What does that mean?" thought Adrian. "Who can be wanting me again? Can it be a thief come to rob me? Or have my foolish girls got lovers coming after them? It means no good, I fear!"

And the coffin-maker thought of calling his friend Yourko to his assistance. But at that moment, another person approached the wicket and was about to enter, but seeing the master of the house hastening towards him, he stopped and took off his three-cornered hat. His face seemed familiar to Adrian, but in his hurry he had not been able to examine it closely.

"You are favouring me with a visit," said Adrian, out of breath. "Walk in, I beg of you."

"Don't stand on ceremony, little father," replied the other, in a hollow voice; "you go first, and show your guests the way."

Adrian had no time to spend upon ceremony. The wicket was open; he ascended the steps followed by the other. Adrian thought he could hear people walking about in his rooms.

"What the devil does all this mean!" he thought to himself, and he hastened to enter. But the sight that met his eyes caused his legs to give way beneath him.

The room was full of corpses. The moon, shining through the windows, lit up their yellow and blue faces, sunken mouths, dim, half-closed eyes, and protruding noses. Adrian, with horror, recognized in them people that he himself had buried, and in the guest who entered with him, the brigadier who had been buried during the pouring rain. They all, men and women, surrounded the coffin-maker, with bowings and salutations, except one poor fellow lately buried gratis, who, conscious and ashamed of his rags, did not venture to approach, but meekly kept aloof in a corner. All the others were decently dressed: the female corpses in caps and ribbons, the officials in uniforms, but with their beards unshaven, the tradesmen in their holiday *caftans*.

"You see, Prokhoroff," said the brigadier in the name of all the honourable company, "we have all risen in response to your invitation. Only those have stopped at home who were unable to come, who have crumbled to pieces and have nothing left but fleshless bones. But even of these there was one who hadn't the patience to remain behind—so much did he want to come and see you. . . ."

At this moment a little skeleton pushed his way through the crowd and approached Adrian. His fleshless face smiled affably at the coffin-maker. Shreds of green and red cloth and rotten linen hung on him here and there as on a pole, and the bones of his feet rattled inside his big jackboots, like pestles in mortars.

"You do not recognize me, Prokhoroff," said the skeleton. "Don't you remember the retired sergeant of the Guards, Peter Petrovitch Kourilkin, the same to whom, in the year 1799, you sold your first coffin, and that, too, of deal instead of oak?"

With these words the corpse stretched out his bony arms towards him; but Adrian, collecting all his strength, shrieked and pushed him from him. Peter Petrovitch staggered, fell, and crumbled all to pieces. Among the corpses arose a murmur of indignation; all stood up for the honour of their companion, and they overwhelmed Adrian with such threats and imprecations, that the poor host, deafened by their shrieks and almost crushed to death, lost his presence of mind, fell upon the bones of the retired sergeant of the Guards, and swooned away.

For some time the sun had been shining upon the bed on which lay the coffin-maker. At last he opened his eyes and saw before him the servant attending to the tea-urn. With horror, Adrian recalled all the incidents of the previous day. Trukhina, the brigadier, and the sergeant, Kourilkin, rose vaguely before his imagination. He waited in silence for the servant to open the conversation and inform him of the events of the night.

"How you have slept, little father Adrian Prokhorovitch!" said Aksinia, handing him his dressing-gown. "Your neighbour, the tailor, has been here, and the watchman also called to inform you that to-day is his name-day; but you were so sound asleep, that we did not wish to wake you."

"Did anyone come for me from the late Trukhina?"

"The late? Is she dead, then?"

"What a fool you are! Didn't you yourself help me yesterday to prepare the things for her funeral?"

"Have you taken leave of your senses, little father, or have you not yet recovered from the effects of yesterday's drinking-bout? What funeral was there yesterday? You spent the whole day feasting at the German's, and then came home drunk and threw yourself upon the bed, and have slept till this hour, when the bells have already rung for mass."

"Really!" said the coffin-maker, greatly relieved.

"Yes, indeed," replied the servant.

"Well, since that is the case, make the tea as quickly as possible and call my daughters."

MRS. FROLA AND MR. PONZA,
HER SON-IN-LAW

Luigi Pirandello

BUT AFTER ALL, can you imagine? Everybody may really go mad because they can't decide which of the two is the crazy one, that Mrs. Frola or that Mr. Ponza, her son-in-law. Things like this only happen in Valdana, an unlucky town that attracts every kind of eccentric outsider!

She is crazy or *he* is crazy; there's no middle ground: one of the two *must* be crazy. Because what's involved is nothing less than this . . . No, it's better to start off explaining things in their proper order.

I assure you, I'm seriously alarmed by the anxiety in which the inhabitants of Valdana have been living for three months, and I'm not much concerned for Mrs. Frola and Mr. Ponza, her son-in-law. Because, even if it's true that a grave misfortune has befallen them, it's no less true that one of them, at least, has had the good luck to be driven crazy by it and the other one has aided and is continuing to aid the victim, in such a way that, I repeat, no one can manage to know for sure which of the two is really crazy; and, certainly, they couldn't have comforted each other in a better way than that. But I ask you, do you think it's nothing to keep the entire citizenry under such a nightmarish burden, knocking out all the props of their reasoning capacity so that they can no longer distinguish between illusion and reality? It's anguish, perpetual dismay. Everyone sees those two daily, looks at their faces, knows that one of the two is crazy, studies them, scrutinizes them, spies on them and—no use! Impossible to discover which of the two it is; where illusion lies, where reality lies. Naturally, there arises in each mind the pernicious suspicion that, in that case, reality counts for no more than illusion does, and that every reality may very well be an illusion, and vice versa. You think it's nothing? If I were in the governor's[1] shoes, for the mental well-being of the inhabitants of Valdana I wouldn't hesitate to give Mrs. Frola and Mr. Ponza, her son-in-law, their walking papers.

But let's proceed in an orderly fashion.

This Mr. Ponza arrived in Valdana three months ago as a secretary in the governor's office. He took lodgings in the new apartment house at the edge of town, the one called "the Honeycomb." There. On the top floor, a tiny flat. Three windows looking out at the countryside, high, sad windows (because the housefront on that side, exposed to the north wind, facing all those pallid market gardens, although it's new, has become so deteriorated, who knows why?), and three inner windows, on this side, facing the courtyard, which is encircled by the railing of the top gallery, divided into sections by grated partitions. Hanging from that railing, all the way up, are a large number of little baskets ready to be lowered on ropes as needed.

At the same time, however, to everyone's amazement, Mr. Ponza rented another small furnished flat, three rooms and kitchen, in the center of town, Number 15 Via dei Santi, to be exact. He said it was to be used by his mother-in-law, Mrs. Frola. And she did indeed arrive five or six days later; and Mr. Ponza, all alone, went to meet her at the station, took her to the apartment and left her there by herself.

Now, please! You can understand it if a daughter, on getting married, leaves her mother's house to go and live with her husband, even in another town; but when that mother, not bearing to remain far from her daughter, leaves her hometown, her own house, and follows her, and when, in the town where both she and her daughter are strangers, she goes to live in a separate house, *that* is no longer so easily understood; or else one must assume such a strong incompatibility between mother-in-law and son-in-law that their all living together is impossible, even under these circumstances.

---

[1] *Prefetto,* chief officer of a *provincia* (Italy is divided into "provinces" administratively).

Naturally, that's what people in Valdana thought at first. And certainly the one who came off the worst in everyone's opinion because of this was Mr. Ponza. When it came to Mrs. Frola, if someone granted that she might perhaps be partly to blame in this, either through a lack of indulgence or through some obstinacy or intolerance, everybody was favorably impressed by the maternal love that drew her close to her daughter, even though condemned not to be able to live by her side.

A great part was played in this favoring of Mrs. Frola and in the image of Mr. Ponza that was immediately stamped on everyone's mind—namely, that he was a hard, no! a cruel man—by their physical appearance as well, it must be said. Thickset, neckless, dark as an African, with thick, coarse hair hanging over his low forehead, dense, bristly eyebrows that meet over his nose, a big shiny mustache like a policeman's, and in his eyes—melancholy, staring, almost without any white—a violent, exasperated, barely restrained intensity—whether from sad pain or from irritation at other people's glances, it was hard to say—Mr. Ponza is certainly one whose looks don't make him readily liked or trusted. On the other hand, Mrs. Frola is a frail, pale little old lady, with elegant, very noble features and an air of melancholy, but a weightless, vague and sweet melancholy that doesn't keep her from being affable to everyone.

Now, as soon as she came to town, Mrs. Frola exhibited this affability, so natural in her, and, because of that, the aversion for Mr. Ponza immediately increased in everybody's mind; because everyone clearly perceived her character—as not only gentle, humble, tolerant, but also full of indulgent understanding for the wrong that her son-in-law is doing her; and also because it came to be known that Mr. Ponza is not satisfied to relegate that poor mother to a separate house, but also pushes his cruelty to the point of forbidding her to see her daughter.

Except that, on her visits to the ladies of Valdana, Mrs. Frola immediately protests: "Not cruelty, not cruelty," thrusting out her little hands, sincerely distressed that people can think such a thing about her son-in-law. And she hurriedly praises all his virtues, saying all the good about him that's possible and imaginable: how much love, how much care, how many attentions he lavishes not only on her daughter but also on her, yes, yes, also on her; solicitous, selfless . . . Oh, not cruel, no, for heaven's sake! There's only this: that Mr. Ponza wants to have his wife entirely to himself, to such an extent that he wants even the love she must have for her mother (and he admits it, of course) to reach her not directly but through him, as intermediary, that's it! Yes, this may look like cruelty, but it's not; it's something else, something that she, Mrs. Frola, understands perfectly and is anguished at being unable to express. His nature, that's what . . . but no, perhaps a kind of illness . . . how to put it? My goodness, you just have to look at his eyes. At first those eyes may make a bad impression; but they say it all to anyone who can read them as she can: they speak of the sealed-up fullness of a whole world of love within him, in which his wife must live without ever leaving it for a moment, and into which no one else, not even her mother, must enter. Jealousy? Yes, perhaps; but only if you want to give a cheap name to this exclusive totality of love. Selfishness? If so, it's a selfishness that makes him give all of himself, like a world, to his own lady! When you get to the bottom of it, you might call it selfishness in *her* that she desires to break open this closed world of love, to make her way into it by force, when she knows that her daughter is happy and so adored . . . That should be enough for a mother! Besides, it's not at all true that she doesn't see her daughter. She sees her two or three times a day: she goes into the courtyard of the building; she rings the bell and immediately her daughter comes to the window up there.

"How are you, Tildina?"

"Fine, Mother. And you?"

"As God wishes, daughter. Send down the basket!"

And in the basket there's always a short note with the events of the day. There! that's enough for her. This life has been going on for four years now, and Mrs. Frola has already gotten used to it. Yes, she's resigned to it. And she practically no longer suffers from it.

As you can easily understand, this resigned attitude of Mrs. Frola's, her saying that she has gotten used to her torment, redounds all the more to the discredit of Mr. Ponza, her son-in-law, the more that she strains herself to excuse him in that long speech of hers.

Therefore it is with real indignation and, I may add, even with fear, that the ladies of Valdana to whom Mrs. Frola paid her first visit receive the notice on the following day of another unexpected visit, from Mr. Ponza, who begs them to grant him just two minutes of audience, for a "dutiful declaration," if it's not inconvenient.

Red in the face, almost as if he were having a stroke, with his eyes harder and sadder than ever, in his hand a handkerchief whose whiteness, like that of his cuffs and shirt collar, clashes with the darkness of his skin, body hair and suit, Mr. Ponza, continually wiping away the perspiration dripping from his low forehead and stubbly, purplish cheeks—not from the heat, but from the very evident violence of the control he is exerting over himself, which also causes a trembling in his large hands with their long nails—in this parlor and in that, in front of those ladies staring at him as if in fright, first asks whether Mrs. Frola, his mother-in-law, came to visit them the day before; then, with his sorrow, effort and agitation constantly increasing, asks whether she spoke to them about her daughter and told them that he absolutely forbids her to see her and go up to his apartment.

The ladies, seeing him so upset, as you may easily imagine, quickly reply that it's true, yes, Mrs. Frola did tell them about being forbidden to see her daughter, but also said all the good about him that's possible and imaginable, to the extent of not only excusing him, but also not giving him a shred of blame for that very prohibition.

Except that, instead of calming down at this reply from the ladies, Mr. Ponza gets even more upset; his eyes become harder, more staring, sadder; the big drops of sweat fall more heavily; and finally, making an even more violent effort at self-control, he comes to his "dutiful declaration."

Which is simply this: that Mrs. Frola, poor woman, doesn't look it, but she's crazy.

Yes, she's been crazy for four years. And her madness takes this very form: her belief that he refuses to allow her to see her daughter. What daughter? She's dead, her daughter died four years ago; and it was precisely from her grief at that death that Mrs. Frola went mad; yes, and it's a good thing she went mad, because for her, madness was the release from her desperate sorrow. Naturally she could only escape it in this manner; namely, by believing that it wasn't true her daughter had died, and that instead it's he, her son-in-law, who won't let her see her any more.

Purely out of a duty of charity toward an unhappy creature, he, Mr. Ponza, has for four years, at the cost of many serious sacrifices, been humoring that pathetic delusion: at an expense beyond his means, he maintains two households, one for him and one for her; and he makes his second wife, who by good luck is charitably willing to go along, humor that delusion, too. But charity, duty—look, they can go only so far: in his capacity as a civil servant as well, Mr. Ponza can't permit the people in town to think such a cruel and improbable thing about him; namely, that out of jealousy or any other reason, he forbids a poor mother to see her own daughter.

After this declaration, Mr. Ponza makes a bow to those bewildered ladies, and leaves. But this bewilderment of the ladies doesn't even have the time to diminish a little, when there appears Mrs. Frola again with her gentle air of vague melancholy, asking forgiveness if, on her account, the kind ladies were somewhat frightened by the visit of Mr. Ponza, her son-in-law.

And Mrs. Frola, with the greatest simplicity and naturalness in the world, declares in her turn, but in strict confidence, for heaven's sake! because Mr. Ponza is a civil servant and for that very reason she refrained from saying this the first time, yes, because this could seriously damage his career; Mr. Ponza, poor man—an excellent, excellent irreproachable secretary at the governor's office, perfect, precise in all his actions, in all his thoughts, full of so many good qualities—Mr. Ponza, poor man, in this matter alone is no longer . . . no longer in his right mind; there you have it; the crazy one is he, poor man; and his madness takes this very form: his belief that his wife died four years ago and his going around saying that the crazy one is she, Mrs. Frola, who believes her daughter is still alive. No, he isn't doing this in order somehow to justify to others that almost maniacal jealousy of his and that cruelty of forbidding her to see her daughter; no, the poor man believes, seriously believes that his wife is dead, and the one he has with him is a second wife. A most pitiful case! Because, to tell the truth, with his excessive love this man at first ran the risk of destroying, of killing his young, fragile little wife, so much so that it was necessary to get her out of his hands secretly and put her into a nursing home without his knowledge. Well, the poor man, whose mind had already been seriously weakened by this frenzied love, went mad from this; he thought his wife had really died: and this idea became so fixed in his mind that there was no longer any way to remove it, not even when his wife, back home after about a year, and as healthy as before, was brought before him. He thought she was a different woman; so that, with the aid of everybody, relatives and friends, it was necessary to simulate a second wedding, which fully restored the balance of his mental faculties.

Now, Mrs. Frola believes she has some right to suspect that for some time her son-in-law has been completely himself again and that he is pretending, only pretending to believe that his wife is a second wife, in order to keep her entirely to himself, without contact with anyone, because perhaps from time to time he nevertheless is smitten with the fear that she may be secretly taken away from him again.

Yes! Otherwise, how could you explain all the care, all the solicitude, he has for her, his mother-in-law, if he really believes that the woman he has with him is a second wife? He ought not to feel the obligation of so much consideration for a woman who in fact would no longer be his mother-in-law, right? Note that Mrs. Frola says this, not to give an even better proof that *he* is the crazy one; but to prove even to herself that her suspicion is well founded.

"And meanwhile," she concludes with a sigh that on her lips assumes the form of a sweet, very sad smile, "meanwhile my poor daughter has to pretend she's not herself but someone else; and I am also obliged to pretend I'm crazy to believe my daughter is still alive. It doesn't cost me much, thank God, because my daughter is there, well and full of life; I see her, I speak to her; but I'm condemned not to be able to live with her, and also to see her and speak to her only from a distance, so that he can keep on believing, or pretending to believe, that my daughter, God forbid, is dead and the woman he has with him is a second wife. But I say once more, what's the difference if, on these terms, we have succeeded in restoring peace of mind to both of them? I know that my daughter is adored, contented; I see her; I speak to her; and I resign myself, out of love for her and for him, to live this way and even to be considered a madwoman, madam—patience! . . ."

I ask you, don't you think that things are at such a pass in Valdana that we will go around with open mouths, looking each other in the eye, like lunatics? Who of the two is to be believed? Who is the crazy one? Where is the reality, where the illusion?

Mr. Ponza's wife would be able to tell us. But there's no trusting her when, in his presence, she says she is the second wife; just as there's no trusting her when, in Mrs. Frola's presence, she confirms the statement that she's her daughter. It would be necessary to take her aside and make her tell the truth privately. But that's impossible. Mr. Ponza—whether or not he's the crazy one—is really very jealous and doesn't let anybody see his wife. He keeps her up there, as if in prison, under lock and key; and without a doubt this fact is in Mrs. Frola's favor; but Mr. Ponza says he is compelled to do this, in fact that his wife herself makes him do it, for fear that Mrs. Frola will unexpectedly come into the house. That may be an excuse. But it's also a fact that Mr. Ponza doesn't even have one maid in the house. He says he does it to save money, obliged as he is to pay rent on two apartments; and in the meantime he himself assumes the burden of doing the daily marketing; and his wife, who according to her own statements is not Mrs. Frola's daughter, out of pity for her—that is, for a poor old woman who was formerly her husband's mother-in-law—also takes it upon herself to attend to all the household chores, even the most humble, doing without the aid of a servant. It seems a bit much to everybody. But it's also true that if this state of affairs can't be explained by pity, it can be explained by his jealousy.

Meanwhile, the governor of Valdana has been satisfied with Mr. Ponza's declaration. But surely the latter's appearance and in large part his conduct do not speak in his favor, at least for the ladies of Valdana, who are all more inclined to give credence to Mrs. Frola. Indeed, that lady comes solicitously to show them the loving notes that her daughter sends down to her in the little basket, as well as many other private documents, the credibility of which, however, is totally denied by Mr. Ponza, who says that they were delivered to her to bolster the pious deception.

One thing is certain anyway: that both of them manifest a marvelous, deeply moving spirit of sacrifice for each other; and that each of them has the most exquisitely compassionate consideration for the presumed madness of the other. Both of them state their case with wonderful rationality; so that it would never have occurred to anyone in Valdana to say that either of them was crazy, if they hadn't said it themselves: Mr. Ponza about Mrs. Frola, and Mrs. Frola about Mr. Ponza.

Mrs. Frola often goes to see her son-in-law at the governor's office to get some advice from him, or waits for him when he comes out so he can accompany her to do some shopping; and very often, for his part, in his free time and every evening Mr. Ponza goes to visit Mrs. Frola in her little furnished flat; and every time they accidentally run into each other in the street they immediately continue on together with the greatest cordiality; he lets her walk on the right and, if she's tired, he offers his arm, and so they go off together, amid the sullen anger, amazement and dismay of the people who study them, scrutinize them, spy on them, but—no use!—cannot yet in any way manage to understand which of the two is the crazy one, where the illusion is, where the reality.

THE BLIND ONES

Isaak Babel

THE SIGNBOARD READ: "Shelter for Blind Soldiers." I rang at the tall oak doors. No one answered. The door seemed open. I went in and saw this:

Down a wide staircase walked a big black-haired fellow in dark glasses. He waved a reed cane before him. After he had successfully conquered the staircase, there lay in front of the blind man multiple ways—blind alleys, dark alleys, steps, side-rooms. His cane quietly tapped the smooth, dimly shining walls. His still head was tilted up. He moved slowly, felt for the step with his foot, stumbled and fell. A streak of blood cut his prominent white forehead, ran down around his temple, and disappeared under his dark glasses. The black-haired fellow lifted up and wetting his finger in the blood, softly called, "Kablukov." The door of the neighboring room opened soundlessly. Before me flitted more reed canes. The blind ones went to help their fallen comrade. Some did not find him, pressing themselves to the walls and looking up with unseeing eyes, while others took him by the arm, lifted him from the floor and, their heads drooping, awaited a nurse or orderly.

A nurse came. She led the soldiers to their rooms, then explained to me:

"Every day such things happen. This house doesn't suit us, really doesn't suit. We need a level, one-floor house with long corridors. Our shelter—it's a booby trap. All the stairs, stairs! . . . The men fall every day."

Our government, as is known, exhibits an administrative energy in only two events—when it is necessary to flee or whine. In the

664

periods of all of our evacuations and disastrous mass-resettlements, the government's work takes on an attitude of busy, creative liveliness and efficient passion.

I was told about the process of evacuating the blind from the shelter.

The initiative for the transfer came from the wounded themselves. The Germans were closely approaching, and their fear of this occupation drove them into complete agitation. The reasons for their agitation were many. The first of them is that any kind of alarm is sweet for the blind. The excitement seizes them quickly and irresistibly, and their nervous anxiety to reach an imaginary goal overwhelms their despondent bodies for a while.

The second reason for fleeing was a particular fear of the Germans.

The majority of the men in the wards had been sent back from captivity. They were firmly convinced that if the Germans came they would again be forced to serve, forced to work, forced to starve.

The nurses told them: "You're blind—no one needs you, there's nothing they'll make you do."

They answered: "A German doesn't let up, a German gives everyone work. We lived among the Germans, nurse."

This alarm was touching and was apparent in the psychology of all the returning prisoners.

The blind ones asked to be led into the depths of Russia. As evacuations were already anticipated, the decision was quickly given. And here began the main thing.

With the imprint of decisiveness on their thin faces, the wrapped-up blind ones stretched themselves along to the train station.

The guides then told the story of their adventures.

The whole day it rained. Clumped in a heap, the downcast men waited the whole night under a landing. Then in cold, dark boxcars, they made their way across the face of our motherland. They went to councils, into the dirty reception halls, then awaited the distribution of rations. Dismayed, direct, silent, they submissively walked after the tired, vexed guards. Some pushed on into villages. The villages had no use of them. No one did. The worthless particles of human dust, needed by no one, wandered like blind puppies through the empty stations and looked for a home. No home turned up. Everyone returned to Petrograd. In Petrograd, it was quiet, so quiet.

Beside the main building crouched a one-story hovel. In it lived the particular people of a particular time—the families of blind ones.

I chatted with one of the women—a fleshy young woman in a housecoat with Kavkazi slippers. There sat her husband—an old, bony Pole with an orange face from the poison gas.

I asked and quickly took it in: she was a Russian woman of our time, sent spinning by the whirlwind of war, by shock, by migration.

In the beginning of the war she joined the nurses "out of patriotism."

She had gone through a lot: mutilated "soldier-boys," German air-strikes, evening dances at officers' gatherings, officers in jodhpurs, a female disease, love for some kind of man in authority, then—the Revolution, the campaign, another love, evacuation and subcommittees.

Somewhere, at some point, her parents had been in Simbirsk along with her sister Varya, and her cousin was in the rail service . . . But for a year and a half her parents hadn't written, her sister Varya was far away, so her warm memories of home had evaporated.

All she had now was weariness, a body falling apart, a seat by a window, a fondness for lethargy, a dull gaze idly shifting from one object to another, and her husband—the blind Pole with an orange face.

There were several such women at the shelter. They did not leave because there was nowhere to go and no reason to. The supervising nurse often said to them:

"I don't understand what we have here . . . Everyone piled in a heap and so we live, but you're not supposed to be living here. . . . I can't refer to this as a shelter anymore, because we're a public establishment, but now . . . nothing now can be understood."

In a dark cramped room sat two pale bearded peasants across from each other on narrow beds. Their glassy eyes did not move. With quiet voices they spoke about the land, about wheat, about the going price for piglets.

In another room a creaky and apathetic old man was teaching a tall strong soldier to play the fiddle. The pathetic screechy sounds wavered from the bow on the trembling strings.

I went on further.

In one of the rooms a woman was moaning. I looked and saw a girl about seventeen years old with a crimson little face who was writhing from pain on a wide bed. Her dark husband sat in the corner on a small stool, his hand plaiting a basket in wide motions while he attentively but coldly listened to her moans.

The girl married him half a year ago.

Soon in a particular hovel for particular people a little one will be born.

This child will be, truly, a child of our times.

A MALEFACTOR

Anton Chekhov

An EXCEEDINGLY LEAN little peasant, in a striped hempen shirt and patched drawers, stands facing the investigating magistrate. His face overgrown with hair and pitted with smallpox, and his eyes scarcely visible under thick, overhanging eyebrows have an expression of sullen moroseness. On his head there is a perfect mop of tangled, unkempt hair, which gives him an even more spider-like air of moroseness. He is barefooted.

"Denis Grigoryev!" the magistrate begins. "Come nearer, and answer my questions. On the seventh of this July the railway watchman, Ivan Semyonovitch Akinfov, going along the line in the morning, found you at the hundred-and-forty-first mile engaged in unscrewing a nut by which the rails are made fast to the sleepers. Here it is, the nut! . . . With the aforesaid nut he detained you. Was that so?"

"Wha-at?"

"Was this all as Akinfov states?"

"To be sure, it was."

"Very good; well, what were you unscrewing the nut for?"

"Wha-at?"

"Drop that 'wha-at' and answer the question; what were you unscrewing the nut for?"

"If I hadn't wanted it I shouldn't have unscrewed it," croaks Denis, looking at the ceiling.

"What did you want that nut for?"

"The nut? We make weights out of those nuts for our lines."

"Who is 'we'?"

"We, people. . . . The Klimovo peasants, that is."

"Listen, my man; don't play the idiot to me, but speak sensibly. It's no use telling lies here about weights!"

"I've never been a liar from a child, and now I'm telling lies . . ." mutters Denis, blinking. "But can you do without a weight, your honour? If you put live bait or maggots on a hook, would it go to the bottom without a weight? . . . I am telling lies," grins Denis. . . . "What the devil is the use of the worm if it swims on the surface! The perch and the pike and the eel-pout always go to the bottom, and a bait on the surface is only taken by a shillisper, not very often then, and there are no shillispers in our river. . . . That fish likes plenty of room."

"Why are you telling me about shillispers?"

"Wha-at? Why, you asked me yourself! The gentry catch fish that way too in our parts. The silliest little boy would not try to catch a fish without a weight. Of course anyone who did not understand might go to fish without a weight. There is no rule for a fool."

"So you say you unscrewed this nut to make a weight for your fishing line out of it?"

"What else for? It wasn't to play knuckle-bones with!"

"But you might have taken lead, a bullet . . . a nail of some sort. . . ."

"You don't pick up lead in the road, you have to buy it, and a nail's no good. You can't find anything better than a nut. . . . It's heavy, and there's a hole in it."

"He keeps pretending to be a fool! as though he'd been born yesterday or dropped from heaven! Don't you understand, you blockhead, what unscrewing these nuts leads to? If the watchman had not noticed it the train might have run off the rails, people would have been killed—you would have killed people."

"God forbid, your honour! What should I kill them for? Are we heathens or wicked people? Thank God, good gentlemen, we have lived all our lives without ever dreaming of such a thing. . . . Save, and have mercy on us, Queen of Heaven! . . . What are you saying?"

"And what do you suppose railway accidents do come from? Unscrew two or three nuts and you have an accident."

Denis grins, and screws up his eye at the magistrate incredulously.

"Why! how many years have we all in the village been unscrewing nuts, and the Lord has been merciful; and you talk of accidents, killing people. If I had carried away a rail or put a log across the line, say, then maybe it might have upset the train, but . . . pouf! a nut!"

"But you must understand that the nut holds the rail fast to the sleepers!"

"We understand that. . . . We don't unscrew them all . . . we leave some. . . . We don't do it thoughtlessly . . . we understand. . . ."

Denis yawns and makes the sign of the cross over his mouth.

"Last year the train went off the rails here," says the magistrate. "Now I see why!"

"What do you say, your honour?"

"I am telling you that now I see why the train went off the rails last year. . . . I understand!"

"That's what you are educated people for, to understand, you kind gentlemen. The Lord knows to whom to give understanding. . . . Here you have reasoned how and what, but the watchman, a peasant like ourselves, with no understanding at all, catches one by the collar and hauls one along. . . . You should reason first and then haul me off. It's a saying that a peasant has a peasant's wit. . . . Write down, too, your honour, that he hit me twice—in the jaw and in the chest."

"When your hut was searched they found another nut. . . . At what spot did you unscrew that, and when?"

"You mean the nut which lay under the red box?"

"I don't know where it was lying, only it was found. When did you unscrew it?"

"I didn't unscrew it; Ignashka, the son of one-eyed Semyon, gave it me. I mean the one which was under the box, but the one which was in the sledge in the yard Mitrofan and I unscrewed together."

"What Mitrofan?"

"Mitrofan Petrov. . . . Haven't you heard of him? He makes nets in our village and sells them to the gentry. He needs a lot of those nuts. Reckon a matter often for each net."

"Listen. Article 1081 of the Penal Code lays down that every wilful damage of the railway line committed when it can expose the traffic on that line to danger, and the guilty party knows that an accident must be caused by it . . . (Do you understand? Knows! And you could not help knowing what this unscrewing would lead to . . .) is liable to penal servitude."

"Of course, you know best. . . . We are ignorant people. . . . What do we understand?"

"You understand all about it! You are lying, shamming!"

"What should I lie for? Ask in the village if you don't believe me. Only a bleak is caught without a weight, and there is no fish worse than a gudgeon, yet even that won't bite without a weight."

"You'd better tell me about the shillisper next," said the magistrate, smiling.

"There are no shillispers in our parts. . . . We cast our line without a weight on the top of the water with a butterfly; a mullet may be caught that way, though that is not often."

"Come, hold your tongue."

A silence follows. Denis shifts from one foot to the other, looks at the table with the green cloth on it, and blinks his eyes violently as though what was before him was not the cloth but the sun. The magistrate writes rapidly.

"Can I go?" asks Denis after a long silence.

"No. I must take you under guard and send you to prison."

Denis leaves off blinking and, raising his thick eyebrows, looks inquiringly at the magistrate.

"How do you mean, to prison? Your honour! I have no time to spare, I must go to the fair; I must get three roubles from Yegor for some tallow! . . ."

"Hold your tongue; don't interrupt."

"To prison. . . . If there was something to go for, I'd go; but just to go for nothing! What for? I haven't stolen anything, I believe, and I've not been fighting. . . . If you are in doubt about the arrears, your honour, don't believe the elder. . . . You ask the agent . . . he's a regular heathen, the elder, you know."

"Hold your tongue."

"I am holding my tongue, as it is," mutters Denis; "but that the elder has lied over the account, I'll take my oath for it. . . . There are three of us brothers: Kuzma Grigoryev, then Yegor Grigoryev, and me, Denis Grigoryev."

"You are hindering me. . . . Hey, Semyon," cries the magistrate, "take him away!"

"There are three of us brothers," mutters Denis, as two stalwart soldiers take him and lead him out of the room. "A brother is not responsible for a brother. Kuzma does not pay, so you, Denis, must answer for it. . . . Judges indeed! Our master the general is dead—the Kingdom of Heaven be his—or he would have shown you judges. . . . You ought to judge sensibly, not at random. . . . Flog if you like, but flog someone who deserves it, flog with conscience."

A CHRISTMAS TREE AND A WEDDING

A STORY

Fyodor Dostoyevsky

THE OTHER DAY I saw a wedding . . . but no, I had better tell you about the Christmas tree. The wedding was nice, I liked it very much; but the other incident was better. I don't know how it was that, looking at that wedding, I thought of that Christmas tree. This was what happened. Just five years ago, on New Year's Eve, I was invited to a children's party. The giver of the party was a well-known and business-like personage, with connections, with a large circle of acquaintance, and a good many schemes on hand, so that it may be supposed that this party was an excuse for getting the parents together and discussing various interesting matters in an innocent, casual way. I was an outsider; I had no interesting matter to contribute, and so I spent the evening rather independently. There was another gentleman present who was, I fancied, of no special rank or family, and who, like me, had simply turned up at this family festivity. He was the first to catch my eye. He was a tall, lanky man, very grave and very correctly dressed. But one could see that he was in no mood for merrymaking and family festivity; whenever he withdrew into a corner he left off smiling and knitted his bushy black brows. He had not a single acquaintance in the party except his host. One could see that he was fearfully bored, but that he was valiantly keeping up the part of a man perfectly happy and enjoying himself. I learned afterwards that this was a gentleman from the provinces, who had a critical and perplexing piece of business in Petersburg, who had brought a letter of introduction to our host, for whom our host was, by no means *con amore,* using his interest, and whom he had invited, out of civility, to his children's party. He did not play cards, cigars were not offered him, every one avoided entering into conversation with him, most likely recognising the bird from its feathers; and so my gentleman was forced to sit the whole evening stroking his whiskers simply to have something to do with his hands. His whiskers were certainly very fine. But he stroked them so zealously that, looking at him, one might have supposed that the whiskers were created first and the gentleman only attached to them in order to stroke them.

In addition to this individual who assisted in this way at our host's family festivity (he had five fat, well-fed boys), I was attracted, too, by another gentleman. But he was quite of a different sort. He was a personage. He was called Yulian Mastakovitch. From the first glance one could see that he was an honoured guest, and stood in the same relation to our host as our host stood in relation to the gentleman who was stroking his whiskers. Our host and hostess said no end of polite things to him, waited on him hand and foot, pressed him to drink, flattered him, brought their visitors up to be introduced to him, but did not take him to be introduced to any one else. I noticed that tears glistened in our host's eyes when he remarked about the party that he had rarely spent an evening so agreeably. I felt as it were frightened in the presence of such a personage, and so, after admiring the children, I went away into a little parlour, which was quite empty, and sat down in an arbour of flowers which filled up almost half the room.

The children were all incredibly sweet, and resolutely refused to model themselves on the "grown-ups," regardless of all the admonitions of their governesses and mammas. They stripped the Christmas tree to the last sweetmeat in the twinkling of an eye, and had succeeded in breaking half the playthings before they knew what was destined for which. Particularly charming was a black-eyed, curly-headed boy, who kept trying to shoot me with his wooden gun. But my attention was still more attracted by his sister, a girl of eleven, quiet, dreamy, pale, with big, prominent, dreamy eyes, exquisite as a little Cupid. The children hurt her feelings in some way, and so she came away from them to the same empty parlour in which I was sitting, and played with her doll in the corner. The visitors respectfully pointed out her father, a wealthy contractor, and some one whispered that three hundred thousand roubles were already set aside for her dowry. I turned round to glance at the group who were interested in such a circumstance, and my eye fell on Yulian Mastakovitch, who, with his hands behind his back and his head on one side, was listening with the greatest attention to these gentlemen's idle gossip. Afterwards I could not help admiring the discrimination of the host and hostess in the distribution of the children's presents. The little girl, who had already a portion of three hundred thousand roubles, received the costliest doll. Then followed presents diminishing in value in accordance with the rank of the parents of these happy children; finally, the child of lowest degree, a thin, freckled, red-haired little boy of ten, got nothing but a book of stories about the marvels of nature and tears of devotion, etc., without pictures or even wood-cuts. He was the son of a poor widow, the governess of the children of the house, an oppressed and scared little boy. He was dressed in a short jacket of inferior nankin. After receiving his book he walked round the other toys for a long time; he longed to play with the other children, but did not dare; it was evident that he already felt and understood his position. I love watching children. Their first independent approaches to life are extremely interesting. I noticed that the red-haired boy was so fascinated by the costly toys of the other children, especially by a theatre in which he certainly longed to take some part, that he made up his mind to sacrifice his dignity. He smiled and began playing with the other children, he gave away his apple to a fat-faced little boy who had a mass of goodies tied up in a pocket-handkerchief already, and even brought himself to carry another boy on his back, simply not to be turned away from the theatre, but an insolent youth gave him a heavy thump a min-ute later. The child did not dare to cry. Then the governess, his mother, made her appearance, and told him not to interfere with the other children's playing. The boy went away to the same room in which was the little girl. She let him join her, and the two set to work very eagerly dressing the expensive doll.

I had been sitting more than half an hour in the ivy arbour, lis-tening to the little prattle of the red-haired boy and the beauty with the dowry of three hundred thousand, who was nursing her doll, when Yulian Mastakovitch suddenly walked into the room. He had taken advantage of the general commotion following a quarrel among the children to step out of the drawing-room. I had noticed him a moment before talking very cordially to the future heiress's papa, whose acquaintance he had just made, of the superiority of one branch of the service over another. Now he stood in hesitation and seemed to be reckoning something on his fingers.

"Three hundred . . . three hundred," he was whispering. "Eleven . . . twelve . . . thirteen," and so on. "Sixteen—five years! Supposing it is at four per cent.—five times twelve is sixty; yes, to that sixty . . . well, in five years we may assume it will be four hundred. Yes! . . . But he won't stick to four per cent., the rascal. He can get eight or ten. Well, five hundred, let us say, five hundred at least . . . that's certain; well, say a little more for frills. H'm! . . ."

His hesitation was at an end, he blew his nose and was on the point of going out of the room when he suddenly glanced at the little girl and stopped short. He did not see me behind the pots of greenery. It seemed to me that he was greatly excited. Either his calculations had affected his imagination or something else, for he rubbed his hands and could hardly stand still. This excitement reached its utmost limit when he stopped and bent another resolute glance at the future heiress. He was about to move forward, but first looked round, then moving on tiptoe, as though he felt guilty, he advanced towards the children. He approached with a little smile, bent down and kissed her on the head. The child, not expecting this attack, uttered a cry of alarm.

"What are you doing here, sweet child?" he asked in a whisper, looking round and patting the girl's cheek.

"We are playing."

"Ah! With him?" Yulian Mastakovitch looked askance at the boy. "You had better go into the drawing-room, my dear," he said to him.

The boy looked at him open-eyed and did not utter a word. Yulian Mastakovitch looked round him again, and again bent down to the little girl.

"And what is this you've got—a dolly, dear child?" he asked.

"Yes, a dolly," answered the child, frowning and a little shy.

"A dolly . . . and do you know, dear child, what your dolly is made of?"

"I don't know . . ." the child answered in a whisper, hanging her head.

"It's made of rags, darling. You had better go into the drawing-room to your playmates, boy," said Yulian Mastakovitch, looking sternly at the boy. The boy and girl frowned and clutched at each other. They did not want to be separated.

"And do you know why they gave you that doll?" asked Yulian Mastakovitch, dropping his voice to a softer and softer tone.

"I don't know."

"Because you have been a sweet and well-behaved child all the week."

At this point Yulian Mastakovitch, more excited than ever, speaking in most dulcet tones, asked at last, in a hardly audible voice choked with emotion and impatience—

"And will you love me, dear little girl, when I come and see your papa and mamma?"

Saying this, Yulian Mastakovitch tried once more to kiss "the dear little girl," but the red-haired boy, seeing that the little girl was on the point of tears, clutched her hand and began whimpering from sympathy for her. Yulian Mastakovitch was angry in earnest.

"Go away, go away from here, go away!" he said to the boy. "Go into the drawing-room! Go in there to your playmates!"

"No, he needn't, he needn't! You go away," said the little girl. "Leave him alone, leave him alone," she said, almost crying.

Some one made a sound at the door. Yulian Mastakovitch instantly raised his majestic person and took alarm. But the red-haired boy was even more alarmed than Yulian Mastakovitch; he abandoned the little girl and, slinking along by the wall, stole out of the parlour into the dining-room. To avoid arousing suspicion, Yulian Mastakovitch, too, went into the dining-room. He was as red as a lobster, and, glancing into the looking-glass, seemed to be ashamed at himself. He was perhaps vexed with himself for his impetuosity and hastiness. Possibly, he was at first so much impressed by his calculations, so inspired and fascinated by them, that in spite of his seriousness and dignity he made up his mind to behave like a boy, and directly approach the object of his attentions, even though she could not be really the object of his attentions for another five years at least. I followed the estimable gentleman into the dining-room and there beheld a strange spectacle. Yulian Mastakovitch, flushed with vexation and anger, was frightening the red-haired boy, who, retreating from him, did not know where to run in his terror.

"Go away; what are you doing here? Go away, you scamp; are you after the fruit here, eh? Get along, you naughty boy! Get along, you sniveller, to your playmates!"

The panic-stricken boy in his desperation tried creeping under the table. Then his persecutor, in a fury, took out his large batiste handkerchief and began flicking it under the table at the child, who kept perfectly quiet. It must be observed that Yulian Mastakovitch was a little inclined to be fat. He was a sleek, red-faced, solidly built man, paunchy, with thick legs; what is called a fine figure of a man, round as a nut. He was perspiring, breathless, and fearfully flushed. At last he was almost rigid, so great was his indignation and perhaps—who knows?—his jealousy. I burst into loud laughter. Yulian Mastakovitch turned round and, in spite of all his consequence, was overcome with confusion. At that moment from the opposite door our host came in. The boy crept out from under the table and wiped his elbows and his knees. Yulian Mastakovitch hastened to put to his nose the handkerchief which he was holding in his hand by one end.

Our host looked at the three of us in some perplexity; but as a man who knew something of life, and looked at it from a serious point of view, he at once availed himself of the chance of catching his visitor by himself.

"Here, this is the boy," he said, pointing to the red-haired boy, "for whom I had the honour to solicit your influence."

"Ah!" said Yulian Mastakovitch, who had hardly quite recovered himself.

"The son of my children's governess," said our host, in a tone of a petitioner, "a poor woman, the widow of an honest civil servant; and therefore . . . and therefore, Yulian Mastakovitch, if it were possible . . ."

"Oh, no, no!" Yulian Mastakovitch made haste to answer; "no, excuse me, Filip Alexyevitch, it's quite impossible. I've made inquiries; there's no vacancy, and if there were, there are twenty applicants who have far more claim than he. . . . I am very sorry, very sorry. . . ."

"What a pity," said our host. "He is a quiet, well-behaved boy."

"A great rascal, as I notice," answered Yulian Mastakovitch, with a nervous twist of his lip. "Get along, boy; why are you standing there? Go to your playmates," he said, addressing the child.

At that point he could not contain himself, and glanced at me out of one eye. I, too, could not contain myself, and laughed straight in his face. Yulian Mastakovitch turned away at once, and in a voice calculated to reach my ear, asked who was that strange young man? They whispered together and walked out of the room. I saw Yulian Mastakovitch afterwards shaking his head incredulously as our host talked to him.

After laughing to my heart's content I returned to the drawing-room. There the great man, surrounded by fathers and mothers of families, including the host and hostess, was saying something very warmly to a lady to whom he had just been introduced. The lady was holding by the hand the little girl with whom Yulian Mastakovitch had had the scene in the parlour a little while before. Now he was launching into praises and raptures over the beauty, the talents, the grace and the charming manners of the charming child. He was unmistakably making up to the mamma. The mother listened to him almost with tears of delight. The father's lips were smiling. Our host was delighted at the general satisfaction. All the guests, in fact, were sympathetically gratified; even the children's games were checked that they might not hinder the conversation: the whole atmosphere was saturated with reverence. I heard afterwards the mamma of the interesting child, deeply touched, beg Yulian Mastakovitch, in carefully chosen phrases, to do her the special honour of bestowing upon them the precious gift of his acquaintance, and heard with what unaffected delight Yulian Mastakovitch accepted the invitation, and how afterwards the guests, dispersing in different directions, moving away with the greatest propriety, poured out to one another the most touchingly flattering comments upon the contractor, his wife, his little girl, and, above all, upon Yulian Mastakovitch.

"Is that gentleman married?" I asked, almost aloud, of one of my acquaintances, who was standing nearest to Yulian Mastakovitch. Yulian Mastakovitch flung a searching and vindictive glance at me.

"No!" answered my acquaintance, chagrined to the bottom of his heart by the awkwardness of which I had intentionally been guilty. . . .

I passed lately by a certain church; I was struck by the crowd of people in carriages. I heard people talking of the wedding. It was a cloudy day, it was beginning to sleet. I made my way through the crowd at the door and saw the bridegroom. He was a sleek, well-fed, round, paunchy man, very gorgeously dressed up. He was running fussily about, giving orders. At last the news passed through the crowd that the bride was coming. I squeezed my way through the crowd and saw a marvellous beauty, who could scarcely have reached her first season. But the beauty was pale and melancholy. She looked preoccupied; I even fancied that her eyes were red with recent weeping. The classic severity of every feature of her face gave a certain dignity and seriousness to her beauty. But through that sternness and dignity, through that melancholy, could be seen the look of childish innocence; something indescribably naive, fluid, youthful, which seemed mutely begging for mercy.

People were saying that she was only just sixteen. Glancing attentively at the bridegroom, I suddenly recognised him as Yulian Mastakovitch, whom I had not seen for five years. I looked at her. My God! I began to squeeze my way as quickly as I could out of the church. I heard people saying in the crowd that the bride was an heiress, that she had a dowry of five hundred thousand . . . and a trousseau worth ever so much.

"It was a good stroke of business, though!" I thought as I made my way into the street.

THE PEASANT MAREY

Fyodor Dostoyevsky

IT WAS THE second day in Easter week. The air was warm, the sky was blue, the sun was high, warm, bright, but my soul was very gloomy. I sauntered behind the prison barracks. I stared at the palings of the stout prison fence, counting the mover; but I had no inclination to count them, though it was my habit to do so. This was the second day of the "holidays" in the prison; the convicts were not taken out to work, there were numbers of men drunk, loud abuse and quarrelling was springing up continually in every corner. There were hideous, disgusting songs and card-parties installed beside the platform-beds. Several of the convicts who had been sentenced by their comrades, for special violence, to be beaten till they were half dead, were lying on the platform-bed, covered with sheepskins till they should recover and come to themselves again; knives had already been drawn several times. For these two days of holiday all this had been torturing me till it made me ill. And indeed I could never endure without repulsion the noise and disorder of drunken people, and especially in this place. On these days even the prison officials did not look into the prison, made no searches, did not look for vodka, understanding that they must allow even these outcasts to enjoy themselves once a year, and that things would be even worse if they did not. At last a sudden fury flamed up in my heart. A political prisoner called M. met me; he looked at me gloomily, his eyes flashed and his lips quivered. *"Je haïs ces brigands!"* he hissed to me through his teeth, and walked on. I returned to the prison ward, though only a quarter of an hour before I had rushed out of it, as though I were crazy, when six stalwart fellows had all together flung themselves upon the drunken

Tatar Gazin to suppress him and had begun beating him; they beat him stupidly, a camel might have been killed by such blows, but they knew that this Hercules was not easy to kill, and so they beat him without uneasiness. Now on returning I noticed on the bed in the furthest corner of the room Gazin lying unconscious, almost without sign of life. He lay covered with a sheepskin, and every one walked round him, without speaking; though they confidently hoped that he would come to himself next morning, yet if luck was against him, maybe from a beating like that, the man would die. I made my way to my own place opposite the window with the iron grating, and lay on my back with my hands behind my head and my eyes shut. I liked to lie like that; a sleeping man is not molested, and meanwhile one can dream and think. But I could not dream, my heart was beating uneasily, and M.'s words, "*Je hais ces brigands!*" were echoing in my ears. But why describe my impressions; I sometimes dream even now of those times at night, and I have no dreams more agonising. Perhaps it will be noticed that even to this day I have scarcely once spoken in print of my life in prison. *The House of the Dead* I wrote fifteen years ago in the character of an imaginary person, a criminal who had killed his wife. I may add by the way that since then, very many persons have supposed, and even now maintain, that I was sent to penal servitude for the murder of my wife.

Gradually I sank into forgetfulness and by degrees was lost in memories. During the whole course of my four years in prison I was continually recalling all my past, and seemed to live over again the whole of my life in recollection. These memories rose up of themselves, it was not often that of my own will I summoned them. It would begin from some point, some little thing, at times unnoticed, and then by degrees there would rise up a complete picture, some vivid and complete impression. I used to analyse these impressions, give new features to what had happened long ago, and best of all, I used to correct it, correct it continually, that was my great amusement. On this occasion, I suddenly for some reason remembered an unnoticed moment in my early childhood when I was only nine years old—a moment which I should have thought I had utterly forgotten; but at that time I was particularly fond of memories of my early childhood. I remembered the month of August in our country house: a dry bright day but rather cold and windy; summer was waning and soon we should have to go to Moscow to be bored all the winter over French lessons, and I was so sorry to leave the country. I walked past the threshing-floor and, going down the ravine, I went up to the dense thicket of bushes that covered the further side of the ravine as far as the copse. And I plunged right into the midst of the bushes, and heard a peasant ploughing alone on the clearing about thirty paces away. I knew that he was ploughing up the steep hill and the horse was moving with effort, and from time to time the peasant's call "come up!" floated upwards to me. I knew almost all our peasants, but I did not know which it was ploughing now, and I did not care who it was, I was absorbed in my own affairs. I was busy, too; I was breaking off switches from the nut trees to whip the frogs with. Nut sticks make such fine whips, but they do not last; while birch twigs are just the opposite. I was interested, too, in beetles and other insects; I used to collect them, some were very ornamental. I was very fond, too, of the little nimble red and yellow lizards with black spots on them, but I was afraid of snakes. Snakes, however, were much more rare than lizards. There were not many mushrooms there. To get mushrooms one had to go to the birch wood, and I was about to set off there. And there was nothing in the world that I loved so much as the wood with its mushrooms and wild berries, with its beetles and its birds, its hedgehogs and squirrels, with its damp smell of dead leaves which I loved so much, and even as I write I smell the fragrance of our birch wood: these impressions will remain for my whole life. Suddenly in the midst of the profound stillness I heard a clear and distinct shout, "Wolf!" I shrieked and, beside myself with terror, calling out at the top of my voice, ran out into the clearing and straight to the peasant who was ploughing.

It was our peasant Marey. I don't know if there is such a name, but every one called him Marey—a thick-set, rather well-grown peasant of fifty, with a good many grey hairs in his dark brown, spreading beard. I knew him, but had scarcely ever happened to speak to him till then. He stopped his horse on hearing my cry, and when, breathless, I caught with one hand at his plough and with the other at his sleeve, he saw how frightened I was.

"There is a wolf!" I cried, panting.

He flung up his head, and could not help looking round for an instant, almost believing me.

"Where is the wolf?"

"A shout . . . some one shouted: 'wolf . . .'" I faltered out.

"Nonsense, nonsense! A wolf? Why, it was your fancy! How could there be a wolf?" he muttered, reassuring me. But I was trembling all over, and still kept tight hold of his smock frock, and I must have been quite pale. He looked at me with an uneasy smile, evidently anxious and troubled over me.

"Why, you have had a fright, *aïe, aïe!*" He shook his head. "There, dear. . . . Come, little one, *aïe!*"

He stretched out his hand, and all at once stroked my cheek.

"Come, come, there; Christ be with you! Cross yourself!"

But I did not cross myself. The corners of my mouth were twitching, and I think that struck him particularly. He put out his thick, black-nailed, earth-stained finger and softly touched my twitching lips.

"*Aïe,* there, there," he said to me with a slow, almost motherly smile. "Dear, dear, what is the matter? There; come, come!"

I grasped at last that there was no wolf, and that the shout that I had heard was my fancy. Yet that shout had been so clear and distinct, but such shouts (not only about wolves) I had imagined once or twice before, and I was aware of that. (These hallucinations passed away later as I grew older.)

"Well, I will go then," I said, looking at him timidly and inquiringly.

"Well, do, and I'll keep watch on you as you go. I won't let the wolf get at you," he added, still smiling at me with the same motherly expression. "Well, Christ be with you! Come, run along then," and he made the sign of the cross over me and then over himself. I walked away, looking back almost at every tenth step. Marey stood still with his mare as I walked away, and looked after me and nodded to me every time I looked round. I must own I felt a little ashamed at having let him see me so frightened, but I was still very much afraid of the wolf as I walked away, until I reached the first barn half-way up the slope of the ravine; there my fright vanished completely, and all at once our yard-dog Voltchok flew to meet me. With Voltchok I felt quite safe, and I turned round to Marey for the last time; I could not see his face distinctly, but I felt that he was still nodding and smiling affectionately to me. I waved to him; he waved back to me and started his little mare. "Come up!" I heard his call in the distance again, and the little mare pulled at the plough again.

All this I recalled all at once, I don't know why, but with extraordinary minuteness of detail. I suddenly roused myself and sat up on the platform-bed, and, I remember, found myself still smiling quietly at my memories. I brooded over them for another minute.

When I got home that day I told no one of my "adventure" with Marey. And indeed it was hardly an adventure. And in fact I soon forgot Marey. When I met him now and then afterwards, I never even spoke to him about the wolf or anything else; and all at once now, twenty years afterwards in Siberia, I remembered this meeting with such distinctness to the smallest detail. So it must have lain hidden in my soul, though I knew nothing of it, and rose suddenly to my memory when it was wanted; I remembered the soft motherly smile of the poor serf, the way he signed me with the cross and shook his head. "There, there, you have had a fright, little one!" And I remembered particularly the thick earth-stained finger with which he softly and with timid tenderness touched my quivering lips. Of course any one would have reassured a child, but something quite different seemed to have happened in that solitary meeting; and if I had been his own son, he could not have looked at me with eyes shining with greater love. And what made him like that? He was our serf and I was his little master, after all. No one would know that he had been kind to me and reward him for it. Was he, perhaps, very fond of little children? Some people are. It was a solitary meeting in the deserted fields, and only God, perhaps, may have seen from above with what deep and humane civilised feeling, and with what delicate, almost feminine tenderness, the heart of a coarse, brutally ignorant Russian serf, who had as yet no expectation, no idea even of his freedom, may be filled. Was not this, perhaps, what Konstantin Aksakov meant when he spoke of the high degree of culture of our peasantry?

And when I got down off the bed and looked around me, I remembered I suddenly felt that I could look at these unhappy creatures with quite different eyes, and that suddenly by some miracle all hatred and anger had vanished utterly from my heart. I walked about, looking into the faces that I met. That shaven peasant, branded on his face as a criminal, bawling his hoarse, drunken song, may be that very Marey; I cannot look into his heart.

I met M. again that evening. Poor fellow! he could have no memories of Russian peasants, and no other view of these people but: *"Je haïs ces brigands!"* Yes, the Polish prisoners had more to bear than I.

PINK FLANNEL

Ford Madox Ford

W. L. JAMES waved his penny candle round the dark tent and the shadow of the pole moved in queer angles on the canvas sides.

It was a great worry—it was more than a worry! to have lost Mrs. Wilkinson's letter. There was very little in the tent—and still less that the letter could be in. When Caradoc Morris had brought him the letter in the front line, W. L. James had had with him, of what the tent now contained, only his trench coat, his tunic, and his shirts, of things that could contain letters. It could not be in the dirty collection of straps and old clothes that were in his valise; it could not be in his wash-basin or in his flea-bag. And he had not even read Mrs. Wilkinson's letter! Caradoc Morris had come down from the first Line Transport, and had given it to him at the very beginning of the strafe that had lasted two days. The sentry on the right had called out: "Rum Jar, left," and he and Morris had bolted up the communication trench at the very moment when, holding in his hand the longed-for envelope, he had recognised the handwriting of the address. He knew he had put it somewhere for safety.

But where? Where the devil *could* you put a letter for safety in a beastly trench? In your trench coat—in your tunic—in your breeches pocket. There *was* not anywhere else.

He was tired: he was dog-tired. He was always dog-tired, anyhow, when he came out of the Front Line. Now he felt relaxed all over: dropping, for next morning he was going on ninety-six hours' leave and, for the moment, that seemed like an eternity of slackness. So that he could let himself go.

He could have let himself go altogether if he had not lost Mrs. Wilkinson's letter—or even if he had known what it contained. . . .

He did not suppose, even if he had dropped it in the trench, that anyone would who picked it up would make evil use of it— forward it to Mrs. Wilkinson's husband, say? On the other hand, they might? . . .

He took off his tunic, his boots, and his puttees, and let himself, feet forward into his flea-bag. He blew out the candle that he had stuck on to the top of his tin hat. A triangle of stars became important before his eyes. The night was full of the babble of voices. He heard one voice call: "The major wants: *Mr. Britling Sees It Through.*" . . . The machine-guns said: "Wukka! Wukka!" under the pale stars, as if their voices were part of the stillness. The stars rose swiftly in the triangle of sky; they hung for a long time, then descended or went out. Much noise existed for a moment. He said to himself that the Hun had got the wind up, and, whilst he began to worry once more about the letter, as it were, with nearly all his brain, one spot of it said: "That insistent 'Wukka! Wukka!' to the right is from Wytschaete: the intermittent one is our 'G' trenches . . . There's an HE going to the top of Kemmel Hill. . . ."

So his mind made before his eyes pictures of the Flanders plain; the fact that the Germans were alarmed at the idea of a sudden raid—that our machine-guns were answering theirs—that their gunners were putting over some random shells from 4.2s. Presently our own 99-pounders or naval guns or something would shut them up. Then they would all be quiet. . . . A sense of deep and voluptuous security had descended on him. Out there, when you have nothing else to worry you, you calculate the chances: rifle fire 20 to 1 against MGs 30: Rum Jars 40; FA 70 against a shot of flying iron. Now his mind registered the fact that the chances of direct hits was nil, or bits of flying iron, 250 to 1 against—and his mind put the idea to sleep, as it were . . . He was in support. . . .

The noise continued—there were some big thumps away to the right. Our artillery was waking up. But the voices from the tents were audible: tranquil conversations about strafes, about Cardiff, about ship owners' profits, about the Divisional "Follies" . . . The Divisional "Follies"!

He would be going to the "Ambassadors"—with Mrs. Wilkinson—within twenty-four hours if he had any luck . . . GSO II had promised to run him from Bailleul to Boulogne: he would catch the one-o'clock leave boat; he would be in Town—Town— Town!—by six. Mrs. Wilkinson would meet him on the platform.

He would keep her waiting twenty minutes in the vestibule of his hotel while he had a quick bath. By 6.45 they would be dining together; she would be looking at him across the table with her exciting eyes that had dark pupils and yellow-brown iris! Her chin would be upon her hands with the fingers interlocked. Then they would be in the dress circle of the theatre—looking down on the nearly darkened stage from which, nevertheless, a warm light would well upwards upon her face. . . . And she would be warm, beside him, her hand touching his hand amongst her furs. . . . And her white shoulders. . . . And they would whisper, her hair just touching his ear. . . . And be warm. . . . Warm!

And then. . . . Damn! Damn! Oh, damnation! . . . He had lost her letter. . . . He did not know if she would meet him. . . . If she cared. . . . If she cared still—or had ever cared. . . . He rolled over and writhed in the long grass in which his flea-bag was laid. . . . The pounding outside grew furious. . . . There seemed to be hundreds of stars—and more and more and more shooting up into the triangle of the tent-flap. He could see a pallid light shining down the blanket that covered his legs. . . . And then, like a piece of madness, the earth moved beneath him as if his bed had been kicked, and a hard sound seemed to hammer his skull. . . . An immense, familiar sound—august as if a God had spoken benevolently, the echoes going away among the woodlands. And the immense shell whined over his head, as if a railway train or the Yeth hounds were going on a long journey. . . .

The Very lights died down, the shell whined further and further towards the plains; it seemed as if a dead silence fell. A voice said: "Somebody's ducking out there!" and the voices began to talk again in the dead silence that fell on the battle-field.

But his thoughts raged blackly. He was certain that Mrs. Wilkinson would not meet him. . . . Then all his leave would be mucked up. He imagined himself—he felt himself—arriving at Victoria, in the half-light of the great barn, in the jostling crowd, with all the black shadows, all sweeping up towards the barrier. And there would be a beastly business with three coppers in a cramped telephone box. And the voice of her maid saying that her mistress was out. . . . Where, in God's name, had he put the letter? . . .

He tried to memorise exactly what had happened—but it ended at that. . . . Caradoc Morris who had come back from a course, had brought the letter down to the trench from the 1st Line Transport.

He had just looked at the envelope. Then the sentry had yelled out. And he remembered distinctly that he had done something with the letter. But what? What?

The rum jar had bumped off: then gas had come over: then a Hun raid. They had got into the front line and it had taken hours to bomb and bayonet them out, and to work the beastly sandbags of that Godforsaken line into some semblance of a parapet again—a period of sweating and swearing, and the stink of gas, and shoving corpses out of the way. . . . His mind considered with horror what he could do if Mrs. Wilkinson refused to see him altogether. And it went on and on. . . .

He couldn't sleep. Then he said a prayer to St. Anthony—a thing he had not done since he had been a little boy in the Benedictine School at Ramsgate. The pale stars surveyed him from their triangle. One Very light ascended slowly over the dark plain. . . .

He was standing in Piccadilly, looking into a window from which there welled a blaze of light. Skirts brushed him then receded. An elderly, fat man in a brown cassock, with a bald head, a rope around the waist and a crook from which depended a gourd, was gazing into the window beside him. This saint remarked:

"You perceive? Pink flannel!"

The whole window, the whole shop—which was certainly Swan and Edgar's—was a deluge of pink—a rather odious pink with bluey suggestions. A pink that was unmistakable if ever you had seen anything like it. . . .

"Pink!" the saint said: "Bluey pink!"

Yes: there were pink monticules, pink watersheds, cascades of pink flannel, deserts, wild crevasses, perspectives. . . .

W. L. James looked at St. Anthony with deep anxiety: he was excited, he was bewildered. The saint continued to point a plump finger, and the crowd all around tittered.

The saint slowly ascended towards a black heaven that was filled with the beams from searchlights. . . .

And W. L. James found himself running madly in his stockinged feet, in the long grass beside the ditch to the tent at the head of the line. "Caradoc!" he was calling out, "Caradoc Morris! Where the hell is my Field Service Pocket-Book?"

He got it out of the tunic pocket of his friend, who was in a dead sleep. He pulled a letter from the pocket that is under the pink flannel intended to hold a supply of pins. Holding the letter towards the candle that was at Caradoc's head, he read—as a man drinks after long hours on a hot road. . . .

And, as he stumbled slowly among tent ropes, he remembered that forgotten moment of his life. He remembered saying to himself—even as the sentry shouted "Rum jar: left," in the harsh Welsh accent that is like the croak of a raven—saying to himself: "I *must* put this letter safely away." And, before he had run, he had pulled out the FSPB, had undone the rubber bands, and had placed the unopened envelope in the little pocket that is under the pink flannel, "intended," as the inscription says, "to hold a supply of pins" . . .

He stood still beside his fleabag for a minute as the full remembrance came back to him. And a queer, as it were clean and professional satisfaction crept over him. Before, he had remembered only the, as it were, panic of running—though it was perfectly correct to run—up the communication trench. Now he saw that, even under that panic, he had been capable of a collected—ordered, and as it were, generous action. For he had tried to shield to the best of his ability the woman he loved at the cost of quite great danger to himself.

For the rum jar had flattened out the wretched sandbags of the trench exactly where he had been standing.

Later, of course, he had lent the pocket-book to Caradoc Morris—who was the sort of chap who never would have a pocket-book—for the purpose of writing a report to BHQ. . . . But he had certainly behaved well. . . .

He said to himself:

"By jove, I may be worthy of her even yet," and getting back into his fleabag, after he had pulled off his socks, which had been wetted by the dewy grass, he fell into pleasurable fancies of softly lighted restaurants, of small orchestras, of gentle contacts of hands and the soft glances of eyes that had dark pupils and brown iris. . . .

That is, mostly, the way war goes!

A COUNTRY DOCTOR

Franz Kafka

I WAS IN a most awkward predicament: I needed to leave at once on an urgent journey; a seriously ill patient was waiting for me in a village ten miles away; a heavy snowstorm filled the wide interval between him and me; I had a carriage, light, with large wheels, perfectly suited to our country roads; wrapped in my fur coat, my instrument bag in my hand, I was already standing in the yard ready to go; but I lacked a horse, a horse. The previous night my own horse had died as a result of overwork in this glacial winter; my maid was now running all over the village trying to borrow a horse; but it was hopeless, I knew, and with more and more snow piling up on me, becoming more and more immobile, I stood there aimlessly. The maid showed up at the gate alone, swinging her lantern; naturally, who would lend his horse for such a ride? I walked across the yard once again; I could see no possibility; distracted, tormented, I kicked at the ramshackle door of the pigpen, which hadn't been used for years. It opened and swung back and forth on its hinges. Warmth and a smell like that of horses came out of it. A murky stable lantern was swinging by a rope inside. A man, crouching in the low shed, showed his candid, blue-eyed face. "Shall I hitch up?" he asked, creeping out on all fours. I could think of nothing to say, and only stooped down to see what else was in the pen. The maid stood next to me. "People don't know what they've got available in their own house," she said, and we both laughed. "Hey there, Brother! Hey there, Sister!" called the groom, and two horses, powerful animals with strong flanks, their legs drawn up tight to their bodies, lowering their well-formed heads like camels, slid out of the door one after the other solely by

690

twisting their bodies to and fro, and occupied the doorway completely with not an inch to spare. But immediately they stood up on tall legs, their bodies steaming with dense vapor. "Help him," I said, and the willing maid ran to hand the groom the carriage harness. But the moment she has reached him, the groom embraces her and shoves his face against hers. She yells out and escapes over to me; two rows of teeth have left their red marks on the girl's cheek. "You beast," I shout furiously, "would you like to feel my whip?" But I instantly recall that he's a stranger, that I don't know where he has come from, and that he's volunteering to help me when all the rest are failing me. As if he knew my thoughts, he isn't vexed by my threat, but still busy with the horses, merely turns once to face me. "Get in," he then says, and truly: everything is in readiness. I observe that I have never before handled such a beautiful team, and I get in cheerfully. "I'll do the driving, you don't know the way," I say. "Sure," he says, "I'm not going along at all, I'm staying with Rosa." "No!" yells Rosa and with a true foreboding that her fate is inevitable, she runs into the house; I hear the door chain rattle as she draws it tight; I hear the lock snap shut; I watch as, in addition, she turns off all the lights, first in the vestibule and then racing through the rooms, so she won't be found. "You're coming along," I say to the groom, "or I'm giving up the trip, no matter how urgent it is. I have no wish to hand the maid over to you as fare for the ride." "Giddy-up!" he says and claps his hands; the carriage is swept away like a piece of wood in a current; I can still hear the door of my house cracking and splintering as the groom assaults it, then my eyes and ears are filled with a rustling wind that penetrates all my senses uniformly. But even that lasts only a moment, because, as if my patient's farmyard opened up directly in front of the gate of my own yard, I am already there; the horses are standing calmly; the snowfall has ended; moonlight all around; the parents of the patient rush out of the house; his sister after them; they practically lift me out of the carriage; I can't make out any of their confused talk; in the sickroom the air is barely breathable; the stove, which hadn't been tended to, is smoking. I intend to open the window; but first I want to see the patient. Then, with no fever, not cold, not warm, with expressionless eyes, without a shirt, the boy raises himself up under the feather bed, embraces my neck and whispers in my ear: "Doctor, let me die." I look around; no one has heard; his parents are standing in silence,

bending forward in expectation of my medical opinion; the sister
has brought a chair for my bag. I open the bag and look through
my instruments; the boy continues to grope toward me from his
bed in order to remind me of his request; I take hold of some twee-
zers, examine them in the candlelight and put them down again.
"Yes," I think blasphemously, "in such cases, the gods come to
your aid; they send the missing horse; because of the urgency, they
add a second one; and in their bounty they then grant you the
groom—" It is only then that I think of Rosa again; what am I to
do, how can I rescue her, how can I pull her out from under that
groom when I am ten miles away from her and unmanageable
horses are harnessed to my carriage? Those horses, which somehow
have now loosened the reins and in some unknown way have
opened the windows from outside! Each one has thrust its head in
through a window and, heedless of the family's outcry, is scrutiniz-
ing the patient. "I'll ride right back," I think, as if the horses are
inviting me to go, but I allow the sister, who believes I am numb
from the heat, to take off my fur coat. A glass of rum is prepared
for me, the old man pats me on the shoulder; the surrender of this
treasure of his justifies that familiarity. I shake my head; I would
grow ill within the old man's circumscribed way of thinking; for
that reason alone, I refuse the drink. The mother stands by the bed
and entices me over; I obey and, while a horse neighs loudly at the
ceiling, I place my head on the chest of the boy, who shivers at the
touch of my wet beard. What I know is confirmed: the boy is
healthy, with somewhat poor circulation, glutted with coffee[1] by
his anxious mother, but healthy, so that the best thing would be to
shove him out of bed. But I'm not out to improve the world, and
I let him lie there. I'm an employee of the district government and
I do my duty to the hilt, to the point where it's almost too much.
Though badly paid, I'm generous and helpful to the poor. I still
must take care of Rosa, then the boy may be right and I, too, shall
die. What am I doing here in this endless winter? My horse is dead,
and there's no one in the village who'll lend me his. I have to find
my team in the pigpen; if, by chance, they weren't horses, I'd have
to drive with sows. That's the way it is. And I nod at the family.
They know nothing about it, and if they knew, they wouldn't

---

[1] Untranslatable wordplay here: for "with . . . circulation" the German has
durchblutet; for "glutted," *durchtränkt.*—TRANS.

believe it. Writing prescriptions is easy, but, otherwise, communicating with people is hard. Well, this seems to be the end of my call here, once again I've been annoyed for nothing; I'm used to that, with the help of my night bell the whole district tortures me; but having to give up Rosa, too, this time, that beautiful girl who has lived in my house for years, and whom I scarcely noticed—that sacrifice is too great, and I must somehow square it temporarily in my own mind through sophistries if I'm not to make an all-out attack on this family, because, even with the best will in the world, they can't give me back Rosa. But as I am closing my bag and signaling to have my coat brought over, as the family stands there together, the father sniffing at the glass of rum in his hand, the mother, whom I have most likely disappointed—what do the people expect of me?—biting her lips tearfully, and the sister waving a blood-soaked towel, I am somehow ready to admit on certain conditions that the boy is perhaps ill after all. I go over to him, he smiles at me as I approach as if I were bringing him, say, the most invigorating soup—oh, now both horses are neighing; the noise, ordained by some lofty powers, is probably meant to facilitate my examination—and I find: yes, the boy is ill. On his right side, around the hip, a wound as large as the palm of one's hand has opened up. Pink,[2] in many shades, dark as it gets deeper, becoming light at the edges, softly granular, with irregular accumulations of blood, wide open as the surface entrance to a mine. That's how it looks from some distance. But, close up, a complication can be seen, as well. Who can look at it without giving a low whistle? Worms as long and thick as my little finger, naturally rose-colored and in addition spattered with blood, firmly attached to the inside of the wound, with white heads and many legs, are writhing upward into the light. Poor boy, there's no hope for you. I have discovered your great wound; you will be destroyed by this flower on your side. The family is happy; it sees me active; the sister tells it to the mother, the mother to the father, the father to a few guests who are entering the open door through the moonlight on tiptoe, balancing with outstretched arms. "Will you save me?" the boy whispers with a sob, completely dazzled by the life in his wound. That's how the people are in my area. Always asking the doctor for the impossible. They've lost their old faith; the priest sits home and

---

[2] In German, *Rosa*. A wordplay?—TRANS.

picks his vestments to pieces, one after another; but the doctor is supposed to accomplish everything with his gentle, surgical hands. Well, have it any way you like: I didn't offer my services; if you misuse me for religious purposes, I'll go along with that, too; what better can I ask for, an old country doctor, robbed of my maid! And they come, the family and the village elders, and they undress me; a school choir led by their teacher is standing in front of the house and singing an extremely simple setting of these words:

> Undress him, then he will cure,
> And if he doesn't cure, then kill him!
> It's only a doctor, it's only a doctor.

Then I'm undressed and, my fingers in my beard, I look at the people calmly with head bowed. I am completely composed and superior to them all, and remain so, too, even though it doesn't help me, because now they take me by the head and feet and carry me into the bed. They lay me against the wall, on the side where the wound is. Then they all leave the room; the door is closed; the singing dies away; clouds pass in front of the moon; the bedclothes lie warmly on top of me, the horses' heads in the window openings waver like shadows. "Do you know," I hear, spoken into my ear, "I don't have much confidence in *you*. You just drifted in here from somewhere, you didn't come on your own two feet. Instead of helping, you're just crowding me out of my deathbed. I'd like most of all to scratch your eyes out." "Right," I say, "it's a disgrace. But I'm a doctor, you see. What should I do? Believe me, it's not easy for me, either." "Am I supposed to be contented with that excuse? Oh, I guess I must, I'm always forced to be contented. I came into the world with a fine wound; that was my entire portion in life." "My young friend," I say, "your mistake is this: you don't have the big picture. I, who have already been in all sickrooms, far and wide, tell you: your wound isn't that bad. Brought on by two hatchet blows at an acute angle. Many people offer their sides and scarcely hear the hatchet in the forest, let alone having it come closer to them." "Is it really so, or are you fooling me in my fever?" "It's really so, take a government doctor's word of honor into the next world with you." And he took it, and fell silent. But now it was time to think about how to save myself. The horses still stood faithfully in their places. Clothing, fur coat and bag were quickly seized and bundled together; I didn't want to waste time getting dressed; if the horses made the same good time as on the way over, I would, so to speak, be jumping out of this bed into mine. Obediently a horse withdrew from the window; I threw the bundle into the carriage; the fur coat flew too far, it just barely caught on to a hook with one sleeve. Good enough. I leaped onto the horse. The reins loosely trailing along, one horse just barely attached to the other, the carriage meandering behind, the fur coat bringing up the rear in the snow. "Giddy-up, and look lively," I said, but the ride wasn't lively; as slowly as old men we proceeded across the snowy waste; for a long time there resounded behind us the new, but incorrect, song of the children:

> Rejoice, O patients,
> The doctor has been put in bed alongside you!

Traveling this way, I'll never arrive home; my flourishing practice is lost; a successor is robbing me, but it will do him no good, because he can't replace me; in my house the loathsome groom is rampaging; Rosa is his victim; I don't want to think of all the consequences. Naked, exposed to the frost of this most unhappy era, with an earthly carriage and unearthly horses, I, an old man, roam about aimlessly. My fur coat is hanging in back of the carriage, but I can't reach it, and no one among the sprightly rabble of my patients lifts a finger to help. Betrayed! Betrayed! Having obeyed the false ringing of the night bell just once—the mistake can never be rectified.

THE EGG

Sherwood Anderson

MY FATHER WAS, I am sure, intended by nature to be a cheerful, kindly man. Until he was thirty-four years old he worked as a farm-hand for a man named Thomas Butterworth whose place lay near the town of Bidwell, Ohio. He had then a horse of his own and on Saturday evenings drove into town to spend a few hours in social intercourse with other farm-hands. In town he drank several glasses of beer and stood about in Ben Head's saloon—crowded on Saturday evenings with visiting farmhands. Songs were sung and glasses thumped on the bar. At ten o'clock father drove home along a lonely country road, made his horse comfortable for the night and himself went to bed, quite happy in his position in life. He had at that time no notion of trying to rise in the world.

It was in the spring of his thirty-fifth year that father married my mother, then a country school-teacher, and in the following spring I came wriggling and crying into the world. Something happened to the two people. They became ambitious. The American passion for getting up in the world took possession of them.

It may have been that mother was responsible. Being a school-teacher she had no doubt read books and magazines. She had, I presume, read of how Garfield, Lincoln, and other Americans rose from poverty to fame and greatness and as I lay beside her—in the days of her lying-in—she may have dreamed that I would some day rule men and cities. At any rate she induced father to give up his place as a farm-hand, sell his horse and embark on an independent enterprise of his own. She was a tall silent woman with a long nose and troubled grey eyes. For herself she wanted nothing. For father and myself she was incurably ambitious.

The first venture into which the two people went turned out badly. They rented ten acres of poor stony land on Griggs's Road, eight miles from Bidwell, and launched into chicken raising. I grew into boyhood on the place and got my first impressions of life there. From the beginning they were impressions of disaster and if, in my turn, I am a gloomy man inclined to see the darker side of life, I attribute it to the fact that what should have been for me the happy joyous days of childhood were spent on a chicken farm.

One unversed in such matters can have no notion of the many and tragic things that can happen to a chicken. It is born out of an egg, lives for a few weeks as a tiny fluffy thing such as you will see pictured on Easter cards, then becomes hideously naked, eats quantities of corn and meal bought by the sweat of your father's brow, gets diseases called pip, cholera, and other names, stands looking with stupid eyes at the sun, becomes sick and dies. A few hens and now and then a rooster, intended to serve God's mysterious ends, struggle through to maturity. The hens lay eggs out of which come other chickens and the dreadful cycle is thus made complete. It is all unbelievably complex. Most philosophers must have been raised on chicken farms. One hopes for so much from a chicken and is so dreadfully disillusioned. Small chickens, just setting out on the journey of life, look so bright and alert and they are in fact so dreadfully stupid. They are so much like people they mix one up in one's judgments of life. If disease does not kill them they wait until your expectations are thoroughly aroused and then walk under the wheels of a wagon—to go squashed and dead back to their maker. Vermin infest their youth, and fortunes must be spent for curative powders. In later life I have seen how a literature has been built up on the subject of fortunes to be made out of the raising of chickens. It is intended to be read by the gods who have just eaten of the tree of the knowledge of good and evil. It is a hopeful literature and declares that much may be done by simple ambitious people who own a few hens. Do not be led astray by it. It was not written for you. Go hunt for gold on the frozen hills of Alaska, put your faith in the honesty of a politician, believe if you will that the world is daily growing better and that good will triumph over evil, but do not read and believe the literature that is written concerning the hen. It was not written for you.

I, however, digress. My tale does not primarily concern i~ with the hen. If correctly told it will centre on the egg. F~

years my father and mother struggled to make our chicken farm pay and then they gave up that struggle and began another. They moved into the town of Bidwell, Ohio and embarked in the restaurant business. After ten years of worry with incubators that did not hatch, and with tiny—and in their own way lovely—balls of fluff that passed on into semi-naked pullethood and from that into dead henhood, we threw all aside and packing our belongings on a wagon drove down Griggs's Road toward Bidwell, a tiny caravan of hope looking for a new place from which to start on our upward journey through life.

We must have been a sad looking lot, not, I fancy, unlike refugees fleeing from a battlefield. Mother and I walked in the road. The wagon that contained our goods had been borrowed for the day from Mr. Albert Griggs, a neighbor. Out of its sides stuck the legs of cheap chairs and at the back of the pile of beds, tables, and boxes filled with kitchen utensils was a crate of live chickens, and on top of that the baby carriage in which I had been wheeled about in my infancy. Why we stuck to the baby carriage I don't know. It was unlikely other children would be born and the wheels were broken. People who have few possessions cling tightly to those they have. That is one of the facts that make life so discouraging.

Father rode on top of the wagon. He was then a bald-headed man of forty-five, a little fat and from long association with mother and the chickens he had become habitually silent and discouraged. All during our ten years on the chicken farm he had worked as a laborer on neighboring farms and most of the money he had earned had been spent for remedies to cure chicken diseases, on Wilmer's White Wonder Cholera Cure or Professor Bidlow's Egg Producer or some other preparations that mother found advertised in the poultry papers. There were two little patches of hair on father's head just above his ears. I remember that as a child I used to sit looking at him when he had gone to sleep in a chair before the stove on Sunday afternoons in the winter. I had at that time already begun to read books and have notions of my own and the bald path that led over the top of his head was, I fancied, something like a broad road, such a road as Caesar might have made on which to lead his legions out of Rome and into the wonders of an unknown world. The tufts of hair that grew above father's ears were, I thought, like forests. I fell into a half-sleeping, half-waking state and dreamed I was a tiny thing going along the road into a far beautiful place where there were no chicken farms and where life was a happy eggless affair.

One might write a book concerning our flight from the chicken farm into town. Mother and I walked the entire eight miles—she to be sure that nothing fell from the wagon and I to see the wonders of the world. On the seat of the wagon beside father was his greatest treasure. I will tell you of that.

On a chicken farm where hundreds and even thousands of chickens come out of eggs surprising things sometimes happen. Grotesques are born out of eggs as out of people. The accident does not often occur—perhaps once in a thousand births. A chicken is, you see, born that has four legs, two pairs of wings, two heads or what not. The things do not live. They go quickly back to the hand of their maker that has for a moment trembled. The fact that the poor little things could not live was one of the tragedies of life to father. He had some sort of notion that if he could but bring into henhood or roosterhood a five-legged hen or a two-headed rooster his fortune would be made. He dreamed of taking the wonder about to county fairs and of growing rich by exhibiting it to other farm-hands.

At any rate he saved all the little monstrous things that had been born on our chicken farm. They were preserved in alcohol and put each in its own glass bottle. These he had carefully put into a box and on our journey into town it was carried on the wagon seat beside him. He drove the horses with one hand and with the other clung to the box. When we got to our destination the box was taken down at once and the bottles removed. All during our days as keepers of a restaurant in the town of Bidwell, Ohio, the grotesques in their little glass bottles sat on a shelf back of the counter. Mother sometimes protested but father was a rock on the subject of his treasure. The grotesques were, he declared, valuable. People, he said, liked to look at strange and wonderful things.

Did I say that we embarked in the restaurant business in the town of Bidwell, Ohio? I exaggerated a little. The town itself lay at the foot of a low hill and on the shore of a small river. The railroad did not run through the town and the station was a mile away to the north at a place called Pickleville. There had been a cider mill and pickle factory at the station, but before the time of our coming they had both gone out of business. In the morning and in the evening busses came down to the station along a road called Turner's from the hotel on the main street of Bidwell. Our going to the out of the way place to embark in the restaurant business was mother's idea. She talked of it for a year and then one day went off and rented an empty store building opposite the railroad station. It was her idea that the restaurant would be profitable. Travelling men, she said, would be always waiting around to take trains out of town and town people would come to the station to await incoming trains. They would come to the restaurant to buy pieces of pie and drink coffee. Now that I am older I know that she had another motive in going. She was ambitious for me. She wanted me to rise in the world, to get into a town school and become a man of the towns.

At Pickleville father and mother worked hard as they always had done. At first there was the necessity of putting our place into shape to be a restaurant. That took a month. Father built a shelf on which he put tins of vegetables. He painted a sign on which he put his name in large letters. Below his name was the sharp command— "EAT HERE" that was so seldom obeyed. A show case was bought and filled with cigars and tobacco. Mother scrubbed the floor and the walls of the room. I went to school in the town and was glad to be away from the farm and from the presence of the discouraged, sad-looking chickens. Still I was not very joyous. In the evening I walked home from school along Turner's Pike and remembered the children I had seen playing in the town school yard. A troop of little girls had gone hopping about and singing. I tried that. Down along the frozen road I went hopping solemnly on one leg. "Hippity Hop To The Barber Shop," I sang shrilly. Then I stopped and looked doubtfully about. I was afraid of being seen in my gay mood. It must have seemed to me that I was doing a thing that should not be done by one who, like myself, had been raised on a chicken farm where death was a daily visitor.

Mother decided that our restaurant should remain open at night. At ten in the evening a passenger train went north past our door followed by a local freight. The freight crew had switching to do in Pickleville and when the work was done they came to our restaurant for hot coffee and food. Sometimes one of them ordered a fried egg. In the morning at four they returned north-bound and again visited us. A little trade began to grow up. Mother slept at night and during the day tended the restaurant and fed our boarders while father slept. He slept in the same bed mother had occupied during the night and I went off to the town of Bidwell and to school. During the long nights, while mother and I slept, father cooked meats that were to go into sandwiches for the lunch baskets of our boarders. Then an idea in regard to getting up in the world came into his head. The American spirit took hold of him. He also became ambitious.

In the long nights when there was little to do father had time to think. That was his undoing. He decided that he had in the past been an unsuccessful man because he had not been cheerful enough and that in the future he would adopt a cheerful outlook on life. In the early morning he came upstairs and got into bed with mother. She woke and the two talked. From my bed in the corner I listened.

It was father's idea that both he and mother should try to entertain the people who came to eat at our restaurant. I cannot now remember his words, but he gave the impression of one about to become in some obscure way a kind of public entertainer. When people, particularly young people from the town of Bidwell, came into our place, as on very rare occasions they did, bright entertaining conversation was to be made. From father's words I gathered that something of the jolly inn-keeper effect was to be sought. Mother must have been doubtful from the first, but she said nothing discouraging. It was father's notion that a passion for the company of himself and mother would spring up in the breasts of the younger people of the town of Bidwell. In the evening bright happy groups would come singing down Turner's Pike. They would troop shouting with joy and laughter into our place. There would be song and festivity. I do not mean to give the impression that father spoke so elaborately of the matter. He was as I have said an uncommunicative man. "They want some place to go. I tell you they want some place to go," he said over and over. That was as far as he got. My own imagination has filled in the blanks.

For two or three weeks this notion of father's invaded our house. We did not talk much, but in our daily lives tried earnestly to make smiles take the place of glum looks. Mother smiled at the boarders and I, catching the infection, smiled at our cat. Father became a little feverish in his anxiety to please. There was no doubt, lurking somewhere in him, a touch of the spirit of the showman. He did not waste much of his ammunition on the railroad men he served at night but seemed to be waiting for a young man or woman from

Bidwell to come in to show what he could do. On the counter in the restaurant there was a wire basket kept always filled with eggs, and it must have been before his eyes when the idea of being entertaining was born in his brain. There was something pre-natal about the way eggs kept themselves connected with the development of his idea. At any rate an egg ruined his new impulse in life. Late one night I was awakened by a roar of anger coming from father's throat. Both mother and I sat upright in our beds. With trembling hands she lighted a lamp that stood on a table by her head. Downstairs the front door of our restaurant went shut with a bang and in a few minutes father tramped up the stairs. He held an egg in his hand and his hand trembled as though he were having a chill. There was a half insane light in his eyes. As he stood glaring at us I was sure he intended throwing the egg at either mother or me. Then he laid it gently on the table beside the lamp and dropped on his knees beside mother's bed. He began to cry like a boy and I, carried away by his grief, cried with him. The two of us filled the little upstairs room with our wailing voices. It is ridiculous, but of the picture we made I can remember only the fact that mother's hand continually stroked the bald path that ran across the top of his head. I have forgotten what mother said to him and how she induced him to tell her of what had happened downstairs. His explanation also has gone out of my mind. I remember only my own grief and fright and the shiny path over father's head glowing in the lamp light as he knelt by the bed.

As to what happened downstairs. For some unexplainable reason I know the story as well as though I had been a witness to my father's discomfiture. One in time gets to know many unexplainable things. On that evening young Joe Kane, son of a merchant of Bidwell, came to Pickleville to meet his father, who was expected on the ten o'clock evening train from the South. The train was three hours late and Joe came into our place to loaf about and to wait for its arrival. The local freight train came in and the freight crew were fed. Joe was left alone in the restaurant with father.

From the moment he came into our place the Bidwell young man must have been puzzled by my father's actions. It was his notion that father was angry at him for hanging around. He noticed that the restaurant keeper was apparently disturbed by his presence and he thought of going out. However, it began to rain and he did not fancy the long walk to town and back. He bought a five-cent cigar and ordered a cup of coffee. He had a newspaper in his pocket and took it out and began to read. "I'm waiting for the evening train. It's late," he said apologetically.

For a long time father, whom Joe Kane had never seen before, remained silently gazing at his visitor. He was no doubt suffering from an attack of stage fright. As so often happens in life he had thought so much and so often of the situation that now confronted him that he was somewhat nervous in its presence.

For one thing, he did not know what to do with his hands. He thrust one of them nervously over the counter and shook hands with Joe Kane. "How-de-do," he said. Joe Kane put his newspaper down and stared at him. Father's eye lighted on the basket of eggs that sat on the counter and he began to talk. "Well," he began hesitatingly, "well, you have heard of Christopher Columbus, eh?" He seemed to be angry. "That Christopher Columbus was a cheat," he declared emphatically. "He talked of making an egg stand on its end. He talked, he did, and then he went and broke the end of the egg."

My father seemed to his visitor to be beside himself at the duplicity of Christopher Columbus. He muttered and swore. He declared it was wrong to teach children that Christopher Columbus was a great man when, after all, he cheated at the critical moment. He had declared he would make an egg stand on end and then when his bluff had been called he had done a trick. Still grumbling at Columbus, father took an egg from the basket on the counter and began to walk up and down. He rolled the egg between the palms of his hands. He smiled genially. He began to mumble words regarding the effect to be produced on an egg by the electricity that comes out of the human body. He declared that without breaking its shell and by virtue of rolling it back and forth in his hands he could stand the egg on its end. He explained that the warmth of his hands and the gentle rolling movement he gave the egg created a new centre of gravity, and Joe Kane was mildly interested. "I have handled thousands of eggs," father said. "No one knows more about eggs than I do."

He stood the egg on the counter and it fell on its side. He tried the trick again and again, each time rolling the egg between the palms of his hands and saying the words regarding the wonders of electricity and the laws of gravity. When after a half hour's effort he did succeed in making the egg stand for a moment he looked up to find that his visitor was no longer watching. By the time he had succeeded in calling Joe Kane's attention to the success of his effort the egg had again rolled over and lay on its side.

Afire with the showman's passion and at the same time a good deal disconcerted by the failure of his first effort, father now took the bottles containing the poultry monstrosities down from their place on the shelf and began to show them to his visitor. "How would you like to have seven legs and two heads like this fellow?" he asked, exhibiting the most remarkable of his treasures. A cheerful smile played over his face. He reached over the counter and tried to slap Joe Kane on the shoulder as he had seen men do in Ben Head's saloon when he was a young farm-hand and drove to town on Saturday evenings. His visitor was made a little ill by the sight of the body of the terribly deformed bird floating in the alcohol in the bottle and got up to go. Coming from behind the counter father took hold of the young man's arm and led him back to his seat. He grew a little angry and for a moment had to turn his face away and force himself to smile. Then he put the bottles back on the shelf. In an outburst of generosity he fairly compelled Joe Kane to have a fresh cup of coffee and another cigar at his expense. Then he took a pan and filling it with vinegar, taken from a jug that sat beneath the counter, he declared himself about to do a new trick. "I will heat this egg in this pan of vinegar," he said. "Then I will put it through the neck of a bottle without breaking the shell. When the egg is inside the bottle it will resume its normal shape and the shell will become hard again. Then I will give the bottle with the egg in it to you. You can take it about with you wherever you go. People will want to know how you got the egg in the bottle. Don't tell them. Keep them guessing. That is the way to have fun with this trick."

Father grinned and winked at his visitor. Joe Kane decided that the man who confronted him was mildly insane but harmless. He drank the cup of coffee that had been given him and began to read his paper again. When the egg had been heated in vinegar father carried it on a spoon to the counter and going into a back room got an empty bottle. He was angry because his visitor did not watch him as he began to do his trick, but nevertheless went cheerfully to work. For a long time he struggled, trying to get the egg to go through the neck of the bottle. He put the pan of vinegar back on the stove, intending to reheat the egg, then picked it up and burned his fingers. After a second bath in the hot vinegar the shell of the egg had been softened a little but not enough for his purpose. He worked and worked and a spirit of desperate determination took possession of him. When he thought that at last the trick was about to be consummated the delayed train came in at the station and Joe Kane started to go nonchalantly out at the door. Father made a last desperate effort to conquer the egg and make it do the thing that would establish his reputation as one who knew how to entertain guests who came into his restaurant. He worried the egg. He attempted to be somewhat rough with it. He swore and the sweat stood out on his forehead. The egg broke under his hand. When the contents spurted over his clothes, Joe Kane, who had stopped at the door, turned and laughed.

A roar of anger rose from my father's throat. He danced and shouted a string of inarticulate words. Grabbing another egg from the basket on the counter, he threw it, just missing the head of the young man as he dodged through the door and escaped.

Father came upstairs to mother and me with an egg in his hand. I do not know what he intended to do. I imagine he had some idea of destroying it, of destroying all eggs, and that he intended to let mother and me see him begin. When, however, he got into the presence of mother something happened to him. He laid the egg gently on the table and dropped on his knees by the bed as I have already explained. He later decided to close the restaurant for the night and to come upstairs and get into bed. When he did so he blew out the light and after much muttered conversation both he and mother went to sleep. I suppose I went to sleep also, but my sleep was troubled. I awoke at dawn and for a long time looked at the egg that lay on the table. I wondered why eggs had to be and why from the egg came the hen who again laid the egg. The question got into my blood. It has stayed there, I imagine, because I am the son of my father. At any rate, the problem remains unsolved in my mind. And that, I conclude, is but another evidence of the complete and final triumph of the egg—at least as far as my family is concerned.

THE MARK ON THE WALL

Virginia Woolf

PERHAPS IT WAS the middle of January in the present year that I first looked up and saw the mark on the wall. In order to fix a date it is necessary to remember what one saw. So now I think of the fire; the steady film of yellow light upon the page of my book; the three chrysanthemums in the round glass bowl on the mantelpiece. Yes, it must have been the winter time, and we had just finished our tea, for I remember that I was smoking a cigarette when I looked up and saw the mark on the wall for the first time. I looked up through the smoke of my cigarette and my eye lodged for a moment upon the burning coals, and that old fancy of the crimson flag flapping from the castle tower came into my mind, and I thought of the cavalcade of red knights riding up the side of the black rock. Rather to my relief the sight of the mark interrupted the fancy, for it is an old fancy, an automatic fancy, made as a child perhaps. The mark was a small round mark, black upon the white wall, about six or seven inches above the mantelpiece.

How readily our thoughts swarm upon a new object, lifting it a little way, as ants carry a blade of straw so feverishly, and then leave it. . . . If that mark was made by a nail, it can't have been for a picture, it must have been for a miniature—the miniature of a lady with white powdered curls, powder-dusted cheeks, and lips like red carnations. A fraud of course, for the people who had this house before us would have chosen pictures in that way—an old picture for an old room. That is the sort of people they were—very interesting people, and I think of them so often, in such queer places, because one will never see them again, never know what happened next. They wanted to leave this house because they wanted to

706

change their style of furniture, so he said, and he was in process of saying that in his opinion art should have ideas behind it when we were torn asunder, as one is torn from the old lady about to pour out tea and the young man about to hit the tennis ball in the back garden of the suburban villa as one rushes past in the train.

But as for that mark, I'm not sure about it; I don't believe it was made by a nail after all; it's too big, too round, for that. I might get up, but if I got up and looked at it, ten to one I shouldn't be able to say for certain; because once a thing's done, no one ever knows how it happened. Oh! dear me, the mystery of life; The inaccuracy of thought! The ignorance of humanity! To show how very little control of our possessions we have—what an accidental affair this living is after all our civilization—let me just count over a few of the things lost in one lifetime, beginning, for that seems always the most mysterious of losses—what cat would gnaw, what rat would nibble—three pale blue canisters of book-binding tools? Then there were the bird cages, the iron hoops, the steel skates, the Queen Anne coal-scuttle, the bagatelle board, the hand organ—all gone, and jewels, too. Opals and emeralds, they lie about the roots of turnips. What a scraping paring affair it is to be sure! The wonder is that I've any clothes on my back, that I sit surrounded by solid furniture at this moment. Why, if one wants to compare life to anything, one must liken it to being blown through the Tube at fifty miles an hour—landing at the other end without a single hairpin in one's hair! Shot out at the feet of God entirely naked! Tumbling head over heels in the asphodel meadows like brown paper parcels pitched down a shoot in the post office! With one's hair flying back like the tail of a race-horse. Yes, that seems to express the rapidity of life, the perpetual waste and repair; all so casual, all so haphazard. . . .

But after life. The slow pulling down of thick green stalks so that the cup of the flower, as it turns over, deluges one with purple and red light. Why, after all, should one not be born there as one is born here, helpless, speechless, unable to focus one's eyesight, groping at the roots of the grass, at the toes of the Giants? As for saying which are trees, and which are men and women, or whether there are such things, that one won't be in a condition to do for fifty years or so. There will be nothing but spaces of light and dark, intersected by thick stalks, and rather higher up perhaps, rose-shaped blots of an indistinct colour—dim pinks and blues—which will, as time goes on, become more definite, become—I don't know what. . . .

And yet that mark on the wall is not a hole at all. It may even be caused by some round black substance, such as a small rose leaf, left over from the summer, and I, not being a very vigilant house-keeper—look at the dust on the mantelpiece, for example, the dust which, so they say, buried Troy three times over, only fragments of pots utterly refusing annihilation, as one can believe.

The tree outside the window taps very gently on the pane. . . . I want to think quietly, calmly, spaciously, never to be interrupted, never to have to rise from my chair, to slip easily from one thing to another, without any sense of hostility, or obstacle. I want to sink deeper and deeper, away from the surface, with its hard separate facts. To steady myself, let me catch hold of the first idea that passes. . . . Shakespeare. . . . Well, he will do as well as another. A man who sat himself solidly in an arm-chair, and looked into the fire, so—A shower of ideas fell perpetually from some very high Heaven down through his mind. He leant his forehead on his hand, and people, looking in through the open door,—for this scene is supposed to take place on a summer's evening—But how dull this is, this historical fiction! It doesn't interest me at all. I wish I could hit upon a pleasant track of thought, a track indirectly reflecting credit upon myself, for those are the pleasantest thoughts, and very frequent even in the minds of modest mouse-coloured people, who believe genuinely that they dislike to hear their own praises. They are not thoughts directly praising oneself; that is the beauty of them; they are thoughts like this:

"And then I came into the room. They were discussing botany. I said how I'd seen a flower growing on a dust heap on the site of an old house in Kingsway. The seed, I said, must have been sown in the reign of Charles the First. What flowers grew in the reign of Charles the First?" I asked—(but I don't remember the answer). Tall flowers with purple tassels to them perhaps. And so it goes on. All the time I'm dressing up the figure of myself in my own mind, lovingly, stealthily, not openly adoring it, for if I did that, I should catch myself out, and stretch my hand at once for a book in self-protection. Indeed, it is curious how instinctively one protects the image of one-self from idolatry or any other handling that could make it ridiculous, or too unlike the original to be believed in any longer. Or is it not so very curious after all? It is a matter of great importance. Suppose the looking glass smashes, the image disappears, and the romantic figure with the green of forest depths all about it is there no longer, but only that shell of a person which is seen by other people—what an airless, shallow, bald, prominent world it becomes! A world not to be lived in. As we face each other in omnibuses and underground railways we are looking into the mirror; that accounts for the vagueness, the gleam of glassiness, in our eyes. And the novelists in future will realize more and more the importance of these reflections, for of course there is not one reflection but an almost infinite number; those are the depths they will explore, those the phantoms they will pursue, leaving the description of reality more and more out of their stories, taking a knowledge of it for granted, as the Greeks did and Shakespeare perhaps—but these generalizations are very worthless. The military sound of the word is enough. It recalls leading articles, cabinet ministers—a whole class of things indeed which as a child one thought the thing itself, the standard thing, the real thing, from which one could not depart save at the risk of nameless damnation. Generalizations bring back somehow Sunday in London, Sunday afternoon walks, Sunday luncheons, and also ways of speaking of the dead, clothes, and habits—like the habit of sitting all together in one room until a certain hour, although nobody liked it. There was a rule for everything. The rule for tablecloths at that particular period was that they should be made of tapestry with little yellow compartments marked upon them, such as you may see in photographs of the carpets in the corridors of the royal palaces. Tablecloths of a different kind were not real tablecloths. How shocking, and yet how wonderful it was to discover that these real things, Sunday luncheons, Sunday walks, country houses, and tablecloths were not entirely real, were indeed half phantoms, and the damnation which visited the disbeliever in them was only a sense of illegitimate freedom. What now takes the place of those things I wonder, those real standard things? Men perhaps, should you be a woman; the masculine point of view which governs our lives, which sets the standard, which establishes Whitaker's Table of Precedency, which has become, I suppose, since the war half a phantom to many men and women, which soon, one may hope, will be laughed into the dustbin where the phantoms go, the mahogany sideboards and the Landseer prints, Gods and Devils, Hell and so forth, leaving us all with an intoxicating sense of illegitimate freedom—if freedom exists. . . .

In certain lights that mark on the wall seems actually to project from the wall. Nor is it entirely circular. I cannot be sure, but it seems to cast a perceptible shadow, suggesting that if I ran my finger

down that strip of the wall it would, at a certain point, mount and
descend a small tumulus, a smooth tumulus like those barrows on
the South Downs which are, they say, either tombs or camps. Of
the two I should prefer them to be tombs, desiring melancholy like
most English people, and finding it natural at the end of a walk to
think of the bones stretched beneath the turf. . . . There must be
some book about it. Some antiquary must have dug up those bones
and given them a name. . . . What sort of a man is an antiquary, I
wonder? Retired Colonels for the most part, I daresay, leading parties of aged labourers to the top here, examining clods of earth and
stone, and getting into correspondence with the neighbouring
clergy, which, being opened at breakfast time, gives them a feeling
of importance, and the comparison of arrowheads necessitates
cross-country journeys to the county towns, an agreeable necessity
both to them and to their elderly wives, who wish to make plum
jam or to clean out the study, and have every reason for keeping
that great question of the camp or the tomb in perpetual suspension, while the Colonel himself feels agreeably philosophic in accu-
mulating evidence on both sides of the question. It is true that he
does finally incline to believe in the camp; and, being opposed,
indites a pamphlet which he is about to read at the quarterly meeting of the local society when a stroke lays him low, and his last
conscious thoughts are not of wife or child, but of the camp and
that arrowhead there, which is now in the case at the local museum,
together with the foot of a Chinese murderess, a handful of
Elizabethan nails, a great many Tudor clay pipes, a piece of Roman
pottery, and the wine-glass that Nelson drank out of—proving I
really don't know what.

No, no, nothing is proved, nothing is known. And if I were to
get up at this very moment and ascertain that the mark on the wall
is really—what shall we say?—the head of a gigantic old nail, driven
in two hundred years ago, which has now, owing to the patient
attrition of many generations of housemaids, revealed its head
above the coat of paint, and is taking its first view of modern life in
the sight of a white-walled fire-lit room, what should I gain?—
Knowledge? Matter for further speculation? I can think sitting still
as well as standing up. And what is knowledge? What are our
learned men save the descendants of witches and hermits who
crouched in caves and in woods brewing herbs, interrogating
shrew-mice and writing down the language of the stars? And the

less we honour them as our superstitions dwindle and our respect for beauty and health of mind increases. . . . Yes, one could imagine a very pleasant world. A quiet, spacious world, with the flowers so red and blue in the open fields. A world without professors or specialists or house-keepers with the profiles of policemen, a world which one could slice with one's thought as a fish slices the water with his fin, grazing the stems of the water-lilies, hanging suspended over nests of white sea eggs. . . . How peaceful it is down here, rooted in the centre of the world and gazing up through the grey waters, with their sudden gleams of light, and their reflections—if it were not for Whitaker's Almanack—if it were not for the Table of Precedency!

I must jump up and see for myself what that mark on the wall really is—a nail, a rose-leaf, a crack in the wood?

Here is nature once more at her old game of self-preservation. This train of thought, she perceives, is threatening mere waste of energy, even some collision with reality, for who will ever be able to lift a finger against Whitaker's Table of Precedency? The Archbishop of Canterbury is followed by the Lord High Chancellor; the Lord High Chancellor is followed by the Archbishop of York. Everybody follows somebody, such is the philosophy of Whitaker; and the great thing is to know who follows whom. Whitaker knows, and let that, so Nature counsels, comfort you, instead of enraging you; and if you can't be comforted, if you must shatter this hour of peace, think of the mark on the wall.

I understand Nature's game—her prompting to take action as a way of ending any thought that threatens to excite or to pain. Hence, I suppose, comes our slight contempt for men of action—men, we assume, who don't think. Still, there's no harm in putting a full stop to one's disagreeable thoughts by looking at a mark on the wall.

Indeed, now that I have fixed my eyes upon it, I feel that I have grasped a plank in the sea; I feel a satisfying sense of reality which at once turns the two Archbishops and the Lord High Chancellor to the shadows of shades. Here is something definite, something real. Thus, waking from a midnight dream of horror, one hastily turns on the light and lies quiescent, worshipping the chest of drawers, worshipping solidity, worshipping reality, worshipping the impersonal world which is a proof of some existence other than ours. That is what one wants to be sure of. . . . Wood is a pleasant thing to think about. It comes from a tree; and trees grow, and we don't know how they grow. For years and years they grow, with-out paying any attention to us, in meadows, in forests, and by the side of rivers—all things one likes to think about. The cows swish their tails beneath them on hot afternoons; they paint rivers so green that when a moorhen dives one expects to see its feathers all green when it comes up again. I like to think of the fish balanced against the stream like flags blown out; and of water-beetles slowly raising domes of mud upon the bed of the river. I like to think of the tree itself:—first the close dry sensation of being wood; then the grinding of the storm; then the slow, delicious ooze of sap. I like to think of it, too, on winter's nights standing in the empty field with all leaves close-furled, nothing tender exposed to the iron bullets of the moon, a naked mast upon an earth that goes tumbling, tum-bling, all night long. The song of birds must sound very loud and strange in June; and how cold the feet of insects must feel upon it, as they make laborious progresses up the creases of the bark, or sun themselves upon the thin green awning of the leaves, and look straight in front of them with diamond-cut red eyes. . . . One by one the fibres snap beneath the immense cold pressure of the earth, then the last storm comes and, falling, the highest branches drive deep into the ground again. Even so, life isn't done with; there are a million patient, watchful lives still for a tree, all over the world, in bedrooms, in ships, on the pavement, lining rooms, where men and women sit after tea, smoking cigarettes. It is full of peaceful thoughts, happy thoughts, this tree. I should like to take each one separately—but something is getting in the way. . . . Where was I? What has it all been about? A tree? A river? The Downs? Whitaker's Almanack? The fields of asphodel? I can't remember a thing. Everything's moving, falling, slipping, vanishing. . . . There is a vast upheaval of matter. Someone is standing over me and saying—

"I'm going out to buy a newspaper."

"Yes?"

"Though it's no good buying newspapers. . . . Nothing ever happens. Curse this war; God damn this war! . . . All the same, I don't see why we should have a snail on our wall."

Ah, the mark on the wall! It was a snail.

A HUNGER ARTIST

Franz Kafka

IN THE LAST decades interest in hunger artists has declined considerably. Whereas in earlier days there was good money to be earned putting on major productions of this sort under one's own management, nowadays that is totally impossible. Those were different times. Back then the hunger artist captured the attention of the entire city. From day to day while the fasting lasted, participation increased. Everyone wanted to see the hunger artist at least daily. During the final days there were people with subscription tickets who sat all day in front of the small barred cage. And there were even viewing hours at night, their impact heightened by torchlight. On fine days the cage was dragged out into the open air, and then the hunger artist was put on display particularly for the children. While for grown-ups the hunger artist was often merely a joke, something they participated in because it was fashionable, the children looked on amazed, their mouths open, holding each other's hands for safety, as he sat there on scattered straw—spurning a chair—in a black tights, looking pale, with his ribs sticking out prominently, sometimes nodding politely, answering questions with a forced smile, even sticking his arm out through the bars to let people feel how emaciated he was, but then completely sinking back into himself, so that he paid no attention to anything, not even to what was so important to him, the striking of the clock, which was the single furnishing in the cage, merely looking out in front of him with his eyes almost shut and now and then sipping from a tiny glass of water to moisten his lips.

Apart from the changing groups of spectators there were also constant observers chosen by the public—strangely enough they were usually butchers—who, always three at a time, were given the task of observing the hunger artist day and night, so that he didn't get something to eat in some secret manner. It was, however, merely a formality, introduced to reassure the masses, for those who understood knew well enough that during the period of fasting the hunger artist would never, under any circumstances, have eaten the slightest thing, not even if compelled by force. The honour of his art forbade it. Naturally, none of the watchers understood that. Sometimes there were nightly groups of watchers who carried out their vigil very laxly, deliberately sitting together in a distant corner and putting all their attention into playing cards there, clearly intending to allow the hunger artist a small refreshment, which, according to their way of thinking, he could get from some secret supplies. Nothing was more excruciating to the hunger artist than such watchers. They depressed him. They made his fasting terribly difficult. Sometimes he overcame his weakness and sang during the time they were observing, for as long as he could keep it up, to show people how unjust their suspicions about him were. But that was little help. For then they just wondered among themselves about his skill at being able to eat even while singing. He much preferred the observers who sat down right against the bars and, not satisfied with the dim backlighting of the room, illuminated him with electric flashlights. The glaring light didn't bother him in the slightest. Generally he couldn't sleep at all, and he could always doze under any lighting and at any hour, even in an overcrowded, noisy auditorium. With such observers, he was very happily prepared to spend the entire night without sleeping. He was very pleased to joke with them, to recount stories from his nomadic life and then, in turn, to listen to their stories—doing everything just to keep them awake, so that he could keep showing them once again that he had nothing to eat in his cage and that he was fasting as none of them could.

He was happiest, however, when morning came and a lavish breakfast was brought for them at his own expense, on which they hurled themselves with the appetite of healthy men after a hard night's work without sleep. True, there were still people who wanted to see in this breakfast an unfair means of influencing the observers, but that was going too far, and if they were asked whether they wanted to undertake the observers' night shift for its own sake, without the breakfast, they excused themselves. But nonetheless they stood by their suspicions.

However, it was, in general, part of fasting that these doubts were inextricably associated with it. For, in fact, no one was in a position to spend time watching the hunger artist every day and night, so no one could know, on the basis of his own observation, whether this was a case of truly uninterrupted, flawless fasting. The hunger artist himself was the only one who could know that and, at the same time, the only spectator capable of being completely satisfied with his own fasting. But the reason he was never satisfied was something different. Perhaps it was not fasting at all which made him so very emaciated that many people, to their own regret, had to stay away from his performance, because they couldn't bear to look at him. For he was also so skeletal out of dissatisfaction with himself, because he alone knew something that even initiates didn't know—how easy it was to fast. It was the easiest thing in the world. About this he did not remain silent, but people did not believe him. At best they thought he was being modest. Most of them, however, believed he was a publicity seeker or a total swindler, for whom, at all events, fasting was easy, because he understood how to make it easy, and then had the nerve to half admit it. He had to accept all that. Over the years he had become accustomed to it. But this dissatisfaction kept gnawing at his insides all the time and never yet— and this one had to say to his credit—had he left the cage of his own free will after any period of fasting.

The impresario had set the maximum length of time for the fast at forty days—he would never allow the fasting go on beyond that point, not even in the cosmopolitan cities. And, in fact, he had a good reason. Experience had shown that for about forty days one could increasingly whip up a city's interest by gradually increasing advertising, but that then the people turned away—one could demonstrate a significant decline in popularity. In this respect, there were, of course, small differences among different towns and among different countries, but as a rule it was true that forty days was the maximum length of time.

So then on the fortieth day the door of the cage—which was covered with flowers—was opened, an enthusiastic audience filled the amphitheatre, a military band played, two doctors entered the cage, in order to take the necessary measurements of the hunger artist, the results were announced to the auditorium through a megaphone, and finally two young ladies arrived, happy about the fact that they were the ones who had just been selected by lot, seeking to lead the hunger artist down a couple of steps out of the cage, where on a small table a carefully chosen hospital meal was laid out. And at this moment the hunger artist always fought back. Of course, he still freely laid his bony arms in the helpful outstretched hands of the ladies bending over him, but he did not want to stand up. Why stop right now after forty days? He could have kept going for even longer, for an unlimited length of time. Why stop right now, when he was in his best form, indeed, not yet even in his best fasting form? Why did people want to rob him of the fame of fasting longer, not just so that he could become the greatest hunger artist of all time, which he probably was already, but also so that he could surpass himself in some unimaginable way, for he felt there were no limits to his capacity for fasting. Why did this crowd, which pretended to admire him so much, have so little patience with him? If he kept going and kept fasting longer, why would they not tolerate it? Then, too, he was tired and felt good sitting in the straw. Now he was supposed to stand up straight and tall and go to eat, something which, when he just imagined it, made him feel nauseous right away. With great difficulty he repressed mentioning this only out of consideration for the women. And he looked up into the eyes of these women, apparently so friendly but in reality so cruel, and shook his excessively heavy head on his feeble neck.

But then happened what always happened. The impresario came and in silence—the music made talking impossible—raised his arms over the hunger artist, as if inviting heaven to look upon its work here on the straw, this unfortunate martyr, something the hunger artist certainly was, only in a completely different sense, then grabbed the hunger artist around his thin waist, in the process wanting with his exaggerated caution to make people believe that here he had to deal with something fragile, and handed him over—not without secretly shaking him a little, so that the hunger artist's legs and upper body swung back and forth uncontrollably—to the women, who had in the meantime turned as pale as death. At this point, the hunger artist endured everything. His head lay on his chest—it was as if it had inexplicably rolled around and just stopped there—his body was arched back, his legs, in an impulse of self-preservation, pressed themselves together at the knees, but scraped the ground, as if they were not really on the floor but were looking for the real ground, and the entire weight of his body, admittedly very small, lay against one of the women, who appealed for help with flustered breath, for she had not imagined her post of honour would be like this, and then stretched her neck as far as possible, to keep her face from the least contact with the hunger artist, but then, when she couldn't manage this and her more fortunate companion didn't come to her assistance but trembled and remained content to hold in front of her the hunger artist's hand, that small bundle of knuckles, she broke into tears, to the delighted laughter of the auditorium, and had to be relieved by an attendant who had been standing ready for some time. Then came the meal. The impresario put a little food into the mouth of the hunger artist, now half unconscious, as if fainting, and kept up a cheerful patter designed to divert attention away from the hunger artist's condition. Then a toast was proposed to the public, which was supposedly whispered to the impresario by the hunger artist, the orchestra confirmed everything with a great fanfare, people dispersed, and no one had the right to be dissatisfied with the event, no one except the hunger artist—he was always the only one.

He lived this way, taking small regular breaks, for many years, apparently in the spotlight, honoured by the world, but for all that his mood was usually gloomy, and it kept growing gloomier all the time, because no one understood how to take him seriously. But how was he to find consolation? What was there left for him to wish for? And if a good-natured man who felt sorry for him ever wanted to explain to him that his sadness probably came from his fasting, then it could happen that the hunger artist responded with an outburst of rage and began to shake the bars like an animal, frightening everyone. But the impresario had a way of punishing moments like this, something he was happy to use. He would make an apology for the hunger artist to the assembled public, conceding that the irritability had been provoked only by his fasting, something quite intelligible to well-fed people and capable of excusing the behaviour of the hunger artist without further explanation. From there he would move on to speak about the equally hard to understand claim of the hunger artist that he could go on fasting for much longer than he was doing. He would praise the lofty striving, the good will, and the great self-denial no doubt contained in this claim, but then would try to contradict it simply by producing photographs, which were also on sale, for in the pictures one could see the hunger artist on the fortieth day of his fast, in bed, almost dead from exhaustion. Although the hunger artist was very familiar with this perversion of the truth, it always strained his nerves again and was too much for him. What was a result of the premature ending of the fast people were now proposing as its cause! It was impossible to fight against this lack of understanding, against this world of misunderstanding. In good faith he always listened eagerly to the impresario at the bars of his cage, but each time, once the photographs came out, he would let go of the bars and, with a sigh, sink back into the straw, and a reassured public could come up again and view him.

When those who had witnessed such scenes thought back on them a few years later, often they were unable to understand themselves. For in the meantime that change mentioned above had set it. It happened almost immediately. There may have been more profound reasons for it, but who bothered to discover what they were? At any rate, one day the pampered hunger artist saw himself abandoned by the crowd of pleasure seekers, who preferred to stream to other attractions. The impresario chased around half of Europe one more time with him, to see whether he could still rediscover the old interest here and there. It was all futile. It was as if a secret agreement against the fasting performances had developed everywhere. Naturally, it couldn't really have happened all at once, and people later remembered some things which in the days of intoxicating success they hadn't paid sufficient attention to, some inadequately suppressed indications, but now it was too late to do anything to counter them. Of course, it was certain that the popularity of fasting would return once more someday, but for those now alive that was no consolation. What was the hunger artist to do now? A man whom thousands of people had cheered on could not display himself in show booths at small fun fairs. The hunger artist was not only too old to take up a different profession, but was fanatically devoted to fasting more than anything else. So he said farewell to the impresario, an incomparable companion on his life's road, and let himself be hired by a large circus. In order to spare his own feelings, he didn't even look at the terms of his contract at all.

A large circus with its huge number of men, animals, and gimmicks, which are constantly being let go and replenished, can use anyone at any time, even a hunger artist, provided, of course, his demands are modest. Moreover, in this particular case it was not only the hunger artist himself who was engaged, but also his old and famous name. In fact, given the characteristic nature of his art, which was not diminished by his advancing age, one could never claim that a worn out artist, who no longer stood at the pinnacle of his ability, wanted to escape to a quiet position in the circus. On the contrary, the hunger artist declared that he could fast just as well as in earlier times—something that was entirely credible. Indeed, he even affirmed that if people would let him do what he wanted—and he was promised this without further ado—he would really now legitimately amaze the world for the first time, an assertion which, however, given the mood of the time, which the hunger artist in his enthusiasm easily overlooked, only brought smiles from the experts.

However, basically the hunger artist had not forgotten his sense of the way things really were, and he took it as self-evident that people would not set him and his cage up as the star attraction somewhere in the middle of the arena, but would move him outside in some other readily accessible spot near the animal stalls. Huge brightly painted signs surrounded the cage and announced what there was to look at there. During the intervals in the main performance, when the general public pushed out towards the menagerie in order to see the animals, they could hardly avoid moving past the hunger artist and stopping there a moment. They would perhaps have remained with him longer, if those pushing up behind them in the narrow passage way, who did not understand this pause on the way to the animal stalls they wanted to see, had not made a longer peaceful observation impossible. This was also the reason why the hunger artist began to tremble at these visiting hours, which he naturally used to long for as the main purpose of his life. In the early days he could hardly wait for the pauses in the performances. He had looked forward with delight to the crowd pouring around him, until he became convinced only too quickly—and even the most stubborn, almost deliberate self-deception could not hold out against the experience—that, judging by their intentions, most of these people were, again and again without exception, only visiting the menagerie. And this view from a distance still remained his most beautiful moment. For when they had come right up to him, he immediately got an earful from the shouting of the two steadily increasing groups, the ones who wanted to take their time looking at the hunger artist, not with any understanding but on a whim or from mere defiance—for him these ones were soon the more painful—and a second group of people whose only demand was to go straight to the animal stalls.

Once the large crowds had passed, the late comers would arrive, and although there was nothing preventing these people any more from sticking around for as long as they wanted, they rushed past with long strides, almost without a sideways glance, to get to the animals in time. And it was an all-too-rare stroke of luck when the father of a family came by with his children, pointed his finger at the hunger artist, gave a detailed explanation about what was going on here, and talked of earlier years, when he had been present at similar but incomparably more magnificent performances, and then the children, because they had been inadequately prepared at school and in life, always stood around still uncomprehendingly. What was fasting to them? But nonetheless the brightness of the look in their searching eyes revealed something of new and more gracious times coming. Perhaps, the hunger artist said to himself sometimes, everything would be a little better if his location were not quite so near the animal stalls. That way it would be easy for people to make their choice, to say nothing of the fact that he was very upset and constantly depressed by the stink from the stalls, the animals' commotion at night, the pieces of raw meat dragged past him for the carnivorous beasts, and the roars at feeding time. But he did not dare to approach the administration about it. In any case, he had the animals to thank for the crowds of visitors among whom, here and there, there could be one destined for him. And who knew where they would hide him if he wished to remind them of his existence and, along with that, of the fact that, strictly speaking, he was only an obstacle on the way to the menagerie.

A small obstacle, at any rate, a constantly diminishing obstacle. People got used to the strange notion that in these times they would want to pay attention to a hunger artist, and with this habitual awareness the judgment on him was pronounced. He might fast as well as he could—and he did—but nothing could save him any more. People went straight past him. Try to explain the art of fasting to anyone! If someone doesn't feel it, then he cannot be made to understand it. The beautiful signs became dirty and illegible. People tore them down, and no one thought of replacing them. The small table with the number of days the fasting had lasted, which early on had been carefully renewed every day, remained unchanged for a long time, for after the first weeks the staff grew tired of even this small task. And so the hunger artist kept fasting on and on, as he once had dreamed about in earlier times, and he had no difficulty succeeding in achieving what he had predicted back then, but no one was counting the days—no one, not even the hunger artist himself, knew how great his achievement was by this point, and his heart grew heavy. And when once in a while a person strolling past stood there making fun of the old number and talking of a swindle, that was in a sense the stupidest lie which indifference and innate maliciousness could invent, for the hunger artist was not being deceptive—he was working honestly—but the world was cheating him of his reward.

Many days went by once more, and this, too, came to an end. Finally the cage caught the attention of a supervisor, and he asked the attendant why they had left this perfectly useful cage standing here unused with rotting straw inside. Nobody knew, until one man, with the help of the table with the number on it, remembered the hunger artist. They pushed the straw around with a pole and found the hunger artist in there. "Are you still fasting?" the supervisor asked. "When are you finally going to stop?" "Forgive me everything," whispered the hunger artist. Only the supervisor, who was pressing his ear up against the cage, understood him. "Certainly," said the supervisor, tapping his forehead with his finger in order to indicate to the spectators the state the hunger artist was in, "we forgive you." "I always wanted you to admire my fasting," said the hunger artist. "But we do admire it," said the supervisor obligingly. "But you shouldn't admire it," said the hunger artist. "Well then, we don't admire it," said the supervisor, "but why shouldn't we admire it?" "Because I had to fast. I can't do anything else," said the hunger artist. "Just look at you," said the supervisor, "why can't you do anything else?" "Because," said the hunger artist, lifting his head a little and, with his lips pursed as if for a kiss, speaking right into the supervisor's ear so that he wouldn't miss anything, "because I couldn't find a food which I enjoyed. If I had found that, believe me, I would not have made a spectacle of myself and would have eaten to my heart's content, like you and everyone else." Those were his last words, but in his failing eyes there was the firm, if no longer proud, conviction that he was continuing to fast.

"All right, tidy this up now," said the supervisor. And they buried the hunger artist along with the straw. But in his cage they put a young panther. Even for a person with the dullest mind it was clearly refreshing to see this wild animal throwing itself around in this cage, which had been dreary for such a long time. It lacked nothing. Without thinking about it for any length of time, the guards brought the animal food. It enjoyed the taste and never seemed to miss its freedom. This noble body, equipped with everything necessary, almost to the point of bursting, also appeared to carry freedom around with it. That seem to be located somewhere or other in its teeth, and its joy in living came with such strong passion from its throat that it was not easy for spectators to keep watching. But they controlled themselves, kept pressing around the cage, and had no desire to move on.

THE GOLDEN HONEYMOON

Ring Lardner

MOTHER SAYS THAT when I start talking I never know when to
stop. But I tell her the only time I get a chance is when she ain't
around, so I have to make the most of it. I guess the fact is neither
one of us would be welcome in a Quaker meeting, but as I tell
Mother, what did God give us tongues for if He didn't want we
should use them? Only she says He didn't give them to us to say
the same thing over and over again, like I do, and repeat myself.
But I say:

"Well, Mother," I say, "when people is like you and I and been
married fifty years, do you expect everything I say will be something you ain't heard me say before? But it may be new to others,
as they ain't nobody else lived with me as long as you have."

So she says:

"You can bet they ain't, as they couldn't nobody else stand you
that long."

"Well," I tell her, "you look pretty healthy."

"Maybe I do," she will say, "but I looked even healthier before
I married you."

You can't get ahead of Mother.

Yes, sir, we was married just fifty years ago the seventeenth day
of last December and my daughter and son-in-law was over from
Trenton to help us celebrate the Golden Wedding. My son-in-law
is John H. Kramer, the real estate man. He made $12,000 one year
and is pretty well thought of around Trenton; a good, steady, hard
worker. The Rotarians was after him a long time to join, but he
kept telling them his home was his club. But Edie finally made him
join. That's my daughter.

Well, anyway, they come over to help us celebrate the Golden Wedding and it was pretty crimpy weather and the furnace don't seem to heat up no more like it used to and Mother made the remark that she hoped this winter wouldn't be as cold as the last, referring to the winter previous. So Edie said if she was us, and nothing to keep us home, she certainly wouldn't spend no more winters up here and why didn't we just shut off the water and close up the house and go down to Tampa, Florida? You know we was there four winters ago and staid five weeks, but it cost us over three hundred and fifty dollars for hotel bill alone. So Mother said we wasn't going no place to be robbed. So my son-in-law spoke up and said that Tampa wasn't the only place in the South, and besides we didn't have to stop at no high price hotel but could rent us a couple rooms and board out somewheres, and he had heard that St. Petersburg, Florida, was the spot and if we said the word he would write down there and make inquiries.

Well, to make a long story short, we decided to do it and Edie said it would be our Golden Honeymoon and for a present my son-in-law paid the difference between a section and a compartment so as we could have a compartment and have more privatecy. In a compartment you have an upper and lower berth just like the regular sleeper, but it is a shut in room by itself and got a wash bowl. The car we went in was all compartments and no regular berths at all. It was all compartments.

We went to Trenton the night before and staid at my daughter and son-in-law and we left Trenton the next afternoon at 3:23 p.m. This was the twelfth day of January. Mother set facing the front of the train, as it makes her giddy to ride backwards. I set facing her, which does not affect me. We reached North Philadelphia at 4:03 p.m. and we reached West Philadelphia at 4:14, but did not go into Broad Street. We reached Baltimore at 6:30 and Washington, D.C., at 7:25. Our train laid over in Washington two hours till another train come along to pick us up and I got out and strolled up the platform and into the Union Station. When I come back, our car had been switched on to another track, but I remembered the name of it, the La Belle, as I had once visited my aunt out in Oconomowoc, Wisconsin, where there was a lake of that name, so I had no difficulty in getting located. But Mother had nearly fretted herself sick for fear I would be left.

"Well," I said, "I would of followed you on the next train."

"You could of," said Mother, and she pointed out that she had the money.

"Well," I said, "we are in Washington and I could of borrowed from the United States Treasury. I would of pretended I was an Englishman."

Mother caught the point and laughed heartily.

Our train pulled out of Washington at 9:40 p.m. and Mother and I turned in early, I taking the upper. During the night we passed through the green fields of old Virginia, though it was too dark to tell if they was green or what color. When we got up in the morning, we was at Fayetteville, North Carolina. We had breakfast in the dining car and after breakfast I got in conversation with the man in the next compartment to ours. He was from Lebanon, New Hampshire, and a man about eighty years of age. His wife was with him, and two unmarried daughters and I made the remark that I should think the four of them would be crowded in one compartment, but he said they had made the trip every winter for fifteen years and knowed how to keep out of each other's way. He said they was bound for Tarpon Springs.

We reached Charleston, South Carolina, at 12:50 p.m. and arrived at Savannah, Georgia, at 4:20. We reached Jacksonville, Florida, at 8:45 p.m. and had an hour and a quarter to lay over there, but Mother made a fuss about me getting off the train, so we had the darky make up our berths and retired before we left Jacksonville. I didn't sleep good as the train done a lot of hemming and hawing, and Mother never sleeps good on a train as she says she is always worrying that I will fall out. She says she would rather have the upper herself, as then she would not have to worry about me, but I tell her I can't take the risk of having it get out that I allowed my wife to sleep in an upper berth. It would make talk.

We was up in the morning in time to see our friends from New Hampshire get off at Tarpon Springs, which we reached at 6:53 a.m.

Several of our fellow passengers got off at Clearwater and some at Belleair, where the train backs right up to the door of the mammoth hotel. Belleair is the winter headquarters for the golf dudes and everybody that got off there had their bag of sticks, as many as ten and twelve in a bag. Women and all. When I was a young man we called it shinny and only needed one club to play with and about one game of it would of been a-plenty for some of these dudes, the way we played it.

The train pulled into St. Petersburg at 8:20 and when we got off the train you would think they was a riot, what with all the darkies barking for the different hotels.

I said to Mother, I said:

"It is a good thing we have got a place picked out to go to and don't have to choose a hotel, as it would be hard to choose amongst them if every one of them is the best."

She laughed.

We found a jitney and I give him the address of the room my son-in-law had got for us and soon we was there and introduced ourselves to the lady that owns the house, a young widow about forty-eight years of age. She showed us our room, which was light and airy with a comfortable bed and bureau and washstand. It was twelve dollars a week, but the location was good, only three blocks from Williams Park.

St. Pete is what folks calls the town, though they also call it the Sunshine City, as they claim they's no other place in the country where they's fewer days when Old Sol don't smile down on Mother Earth, and one of the newspapers gives away all their copies free every day when the sun don't shine. They claim to of only give them away some sixty-odd times in the last eleven years. Another nickname they have got for the town is "the Poor Man's Palm Beach," but I guess they's men that comes there that could borrow as much from the bank as some of the Willie boys over to the other Palm Beach.

During our stay we paid a visit to the Lewis Tent City, which is the headquarters for the Tin Can Tourists. But maybe you ain't heard about them. Well, they are an organization that takes their vacation trips by auto and carries everything with them. That is, they bring along their tents to sleep in and cook in and they don't patronize no hotels or cafeterias, but they have got to be bona fide auto campers or they can't belong to the organization.

They tell me they's over 200,000 members to it and they call themselves the Tin Canners on account of most of their food being put up in tin cans. One couple we seen in the Tent City was a couple from Brady, Texas, named Mr. and Mrs. Pence, which the old man is over eighty years of age and they had come in their auto all the way from home, a distance of 1,641 miles. They took five weeks for the trip, Mr. Pence driving the entire distance.

The Tin Canners hails from every State in the Union and in the summer time they visit places like New England and the Great Lakes region, but in the winter the most of them comes to Florida and scatters all over the State. While we was down there, they was a national convention of them at Gainesville, Florida, and they elected a Fredonia, New York, man as their president. His title is Royal Tin Can Opener of the World. They have got a song wrote up which everybody has got to learn it before they are a member:

> The tin can forever! Hurrah, boys! Hurrah!
> Up with the tin can! Down with the foe!
> We will rally round the campfire, we'll rally once again,
> Shouting, "We auto camp forever!"

That is something like it. And the members has also got to have a tin can fastened on to the front of their machine.

I asked Mother how she would like to travel around that way and she said:

"Fine, but not with an old rattle brain like you driving."

"Well," I said, "I am eight years younger than this Mr. Pence who drove here from Texas."

"Yes," she said, "but he is old enough to not be skittish."

You can't get ahead of Mother.

Well, one of the first things we done in St. Petersburg was to go to the Chamber of Commerce and register our names and where we was from as they's great rivalry amongst the different States in regards to the number of their citizens visiting in town and of course our little State don't stand much of a show, but still every little bit helps, as the fella says. All and all, the man told us, they was eleven thousand names registered, Ohio leading with some fifteen hundred-odd and New York State next with twelve hundred. Then come Michigan, Pennsylvania and so on down, with one man each from Cuba and Nevada.

The first night we was there, they was a meeting of the New York-New Jersey Society at the Congregational Church and a man from Ogdensburg, New York State, made the talk. His subject was Rainbow Chasing. He is a Rotarian and a very convicting speaker, though I forget his name.

Our first business, of course, was to find a place to eat and after trying several places we run on to a cafeteria on Central Avenue that suited us up and down. We eat pretty near all our meals there and it averaged about two dollars per day for the two of us, but the food was well cooked and everything nice and clean. A man don't mind paying the price if things is clean and well cooked.

On the third day of February, which is Mother's birthday, we spread ourselves and eat supper at the Poinsettia Hotel and they charged us seventy-five cents for a sirloin steak that wasn't hardly big enough for one.

I said to Mother: "Well," I said, "I guess it's a good thing every day ain't your birthday or we would be in the poorhouse."

"No," says Mother, "because if every day was my birthday, I would be old enough by this time to of been in my grave long ago."

You can't get ahead of Mother.

In the hotel they had a card-room where they was several men and ladies playing five hundred and this new fangled whist bridge. We also seen a place where they was dancing, so I asked Mother would she like to trip the light fantastic too and she said no, she was too old to squirm like you have got to do now days. We watched some of the young folks at it awhile till Mother got disgusted and said we would have to see a good movie to take the taste out of our mouth. Mother is a great movie heroyne and we go twice a week here at home.

But I want to tell you about the Park. The second day we was there we visited the Park, which is a good deal like the one in Tampa, only bigger, and they's more fun goes on here every day than you could shake a stick at. In the middle they's a big bandstand and chairs for the folks to set and listen to the concerts, which they give you music for all tastes, from Dixie up to classical pieces like Hearts and Flowers.

Then all around they's places marked off for different sports and games—chess and checkers and dominoes for folks that enjoys those kind of games, and roque and horse-shoes for the nimbler ones. I used to pitch a pretty fair shoe myself, but ain't done much of it in the last twenty years.

Well, anyway, we bought a membership ticket in the club which costs one dollar for the season, and they tell me that up to a couple years ago it was fifty cents, but they had to raise it to keep out the riff-raff.

Well, Mother and I put in a great day watching the pitchers and she wanted I should get in the game, but I told her I was all out of practice and would make a fool of myself, though I seen several men pitching who I guess I could take their measure without no practice. However, they was some good pitchers, too, and one boy from Akron, Ohio, who could certainly throw a pretty shoe. They told me it looked like he would win them championship of the United States in the February tournament. We come away a few days before they held that and I never did hear if he win. I forget his name, but he was a clean cut young fella and he has got a brother in Cleveland that's a Rotarian.

Well, we just stood around and watched the different games for two or three days and finally I set down in a checker game with a man named Weaver from Danville, Illinois. He was a pretty fair checker player, but he wasn't no match for me, and I hope that don't sound like bragging. But I always could hold my own on a checker-board and the folks around here will tell you the same thing. I played with this Weaver pretty near all morning for two or three mornings and he beat me one game and the only other time it looked like he had a chance, the noon whistle blowed and we had to quit and go to dinner.

While I was playing checkers, Mother would set and listen to the band, as she loves music, classical or no matter what kind, but anyway she was setting there one day and between selections the woman next to her opened up a conversation. She was a woman about Mother's own age, seventy or seventy-one, and finally she asked Mother's name and Mother told her her name and where she was from and Mother asked her the same question, and who do you think the woman was?

Well, sir, it was the wife of Frank M. Hartsell, the man who was engaged to Mother till I stepped in and cut him out, fifty-two years ago!

Yes, sir!

You can imagine Mother's surprise! And Mrs. Hartsell was surprised, too, when Mother told her she had once been friends with her husband, though Mother didn't say how close friends they had been, or that Mother and I was the cause of Hartsell going out West. But that's what we was. Hartsell left his town a month after the engagement was broke off and ain't never been back since. He had went out to Michigan and become a veterinary, and that is where he had settled down, in Hillsdale, Michigan, and finally married his wife.

Well, Mother screwed up her courage to ask if Frank was still living and Mrs. Hartsell took her over to where they was pitching horse-shoes and there was old Frank, waiting his turn. And he knowed Mother as soon as he seen her, though it was over fifty years. He said he knowed her by her eyes.

"Why, it's Lucy Frost!" he says, and he throwed down his shoes and quit the game.

Then they come over and hunted me up and I will confess I wouldn't of knowed him. Him and I is the same age to the month, but he seems to show it more, some way. He is balder for one thing. And his beard is all white, where mine has still got a streak of brown in it. The very first thing I said to him, I said:

"Well, Frank, that beard of yours makes me feel like I was back north. It looks like a regular blizzard."

"Well," he said, "I guess yourn would be just as white if you had it dry cleaned."

But Mother wouldn't stand that.

"Is that so!" she said to Frank. "Well, Charley ain't had no tobacco in his mouth for over ten years!"

And I ain't!

Well, I excused myself from the checker game and it was pretty close to noon, so we decided to all have dinner together and they was nothing for it only we must try their cafeteria on Third Avenue. It was a little more expensive than ours and not near as good, I thought. I and Mother had about the same dinner we had been having every day and our bill was $1.10. Frank's check was $1.20 for he and his wife. The same meal wouldn't of cost them more than a dollar at our place.

After dinner we made them come up to our house and we all set in the parlor, which the young woman had give us the use of to entertain company. We begun talking over old times and Mother said she was a-scared Mrs. Hartsell would find it tiresome listening to we three talk over old times, but as it turned out they wasn't much chance for nobody else to talk with Mrs. Hartsell in the company. I have heard lots of women that could go it, but Hartsell's wife takes the cake of all the women I ever seen. She told us the family history of everybody in the State of Michigan and bragged for a half hour about her son, who she said is in the drug business in Grand Rapids, and a Rotarian.

When I and Hartsell could get a word in edgeways we joked one another back and forth and I chafed him about being a horse doctor.

"Well, Frank," I said, "you look pretty prosperous, so I suppose they's been plenty of glanders around Hillsdale."

"Well," he said, "I've managed to make more than a fair living. But I've worked pretty hard."

"Yes," I said, "and I suppose you get called out all hours of the night to attend births and so on."

Mother made me shut up.

Well, I thought they wouldn't never go home and I and Mother was in misery trying to keep awake, as the both of us generally always takes a nap after dinner. Finally they went, after we had made an engagement to meet them in the Park the next morning, and Mrs. Hartsell also invited us to come to their place the next night and play five hundred. But she had forgot that they was a meeting of the Michigan Society that evening, so it was not till two evenings later that we had our first card game.

Hartsell and his wife lived in a house on Third Avenue North and had a private setting room besides their bedroom. Mrs. Hartsell couldn't quit talking about their private setting room like it was something wonderful. We played cards with them, with Mother and Hartsell partners against his wife and I. Mrs. Hartsell is a miserable card player and we certainly got the worst of it.

After the game she brought out a dish of oranges and we had to pretend it was just what we wanted, though oranges down there is like a young man's whiskers; you enjoy them at first, but they get to be a pesky nuisance.

We played cards again the next night at our place with the same partners and I and Mrs. Hartsell was beat again. Mother and Hartsell was full of compliments for each other on what a good team they made, but the both of them knowed well enough where the secret of their success laid. I guess all and all we must of played ten different evenings and they was only one night when Mrs. Hartsell and I come out ahead. And that one night wasn't no fault of hern.

When we had been down there about two weeks, we spent one evening as their guest in the Congregational Church, at a social give by the Michigan Society. A talk was made by a man named Bitting of Detroit, Michigan, on "How I Was Cured of Story Telling." He is a big man in the Rotarians and give a witty talk.

A woman named Mrs. Oxford rendered some selections which Mrs. Hartsell said was grand opera music, but whatever they was my daughter Edie could of give her cards and spades and not made such a hullaballoo about it neither.

Then they was a ventriloquist from Grand Rapids and a young woman about forty-five years of age that mimicked different kinds of birds. I whispered to Mother that they all sounded like a chicken, but she nudged me to shut up.

After the show we stopped in a drug store and I set up the refreshments and it was pretty close to ten o'clock before we finally turned in. Mother and I would of preferred tending the movies, but Mother said we mustn't offend Mrs. Hartsell, though I asked her had we came to Florida to enjoy ourselves or to just not offend an old chatter-box from Michigan.

I felt sorry for Hartsell one morning. The women folks both had an engagement down to the chiropodist's and I run across Hartsell in the Park and he foolishly offered to play me checkers.

It was him that suggested it, not me, and I guess he repented himself before we had played one game. But he was too stubborn to give up and set there while I beat him game after game and the worst part of it was that a crowd of folks had got in the habit of watching me play and there they all was, hooking on, and finally they seen what a fool Frank was making of himself, and they began to chafe him and pass remarks. Like one of them said: "Who ever told you you was a checker player!"

And: "You might maybe be good for tiddle-de-winks, but not checkers!"

I almost felt like letting him beat me a couple games. But the crowd would of knowed it was a put up job.

Well, the women folks joined us in the Park and I wasn't going to mention our little game, but Hartsell told about it himself and admitted he wasn't no match for me.

"Well," said Mrs. Hartsell, "checkers ain't much of a game anyway, is it?" She said: "It's more of a children's game, ain't it? At least, I know my boy's children used to play it a good deal."

"Yes, ma'am," I said. "It's a children's game the way your husband plays it, too."

Mother wanted to smooth things over, so she said: "Maybe they's other games where Frank can beat you."

"Yes," said Mrs. Hartsell, "and I bet he could beat you pitching horse-shoes."

"Well," I said, "I would give him a chance to try, only I ain't pitched a shoe in over sixteen years."

"Well," said Hartsell, "I ain't played checkers in twenty years."

"You ain't never played it," I said.

"Anyway," says Frank, "Lucy and I is your master at five hundred."

Well, I could of told him why that was, but had decency enough to hold my tongue.

It had got so now that he wanted to play cards every night and when I or Mother wanted to go to a movie, any one of us would have to pretend we had a headache and then trust to goodness that they wouldn't see us sneak into the theater. I don't mind playing cards when my partner keeps their mind on the game, but you take a woman like Hartsell's wife and how can they play cards when they have got to stop every couple seconds and brag about their son in Grand Rapids?

Well, the New York-New Jersey Society announced that they was goin' to give a social evening too and I said to Mother, I said: "Well, that is one evening when we will have an excuse not to play five hundred."

"Yes," she said, "but we will have to ask Frank and his wife to go to the social with us as they asked us to go to the Michigan social."

"Well," I said, "I had rather stay home than drag that chatterbox everywheres we go."

So Mother said: "You are getting too cranky. Maybe she does talk a little too much but she is good hearted. And Frank is always good company."

So I said: "I suppose if he is such good company you wished you had of married him."

Mother laughed and said I sounded like I was jealous. Jealous of a cow doctor!

Anyway we had to drag them along to the social and I will say that we give them a much better entertainment than they had given us.

Judge Lane of Paterson made a fine talk on business conditions and a Mrs. Newell of Westfield imitated birds, only you could really tell what they was the way she done it. Two young women from Red Bank sung a choral selection and we clapped them back and they gave us "Home to Our Mountains," and Mother and Mrs. Hartsell both had tears in their eyes. And Hartsell, too.

Well, some way or another the chairman got wind that I was there and asked me to make a talk and I wasn't even going to get up, but Mother made me, so I got up and said:

"Ladies and gentlemen," I said. "I didn't expect to be called on for a speech on an occasion like this or no other occasion as I do not set myself up as a speech maker, so will have to do the best I can, which I often say is the best anybody can do."

Then I told them the story about Pat and the motorcycle, using the brogue, and it seemed to tickle them and I told them one or two other stories, but altogether I wasn't on my feet more than twenty or twenty-five minutes and you ought to of heard the clapping and hollering when I set down. Even Mrs. Hartsell admitted that I am quite a speechifier and said if I ever went to Grand Rapids, Michigan, her son would make me talk to the Rotarians.

When it was over, Hartsell wanted we should go to their house and play cards, but his wife reminded him that it was after 9:30 p.m., rather a late hour to start a card game, but he had went crazy on the subject of cards, probably because he didn't have to play partners with his wife. Anyway, we got rid of them and went home to bed.

It was the next morning, when we met over to the Park, that Mrs. Hartsell made the remark that she wasn't getting no exercise so I suggested that why didn't she take part in the roque game.

She said she had not played a game of roque in twenty years, but if Mother would play she would play. Well, at first Mother wouldn't hear of it, but finally consented, more to please Mrs. Hartsell than anything else.

Well, they had a game with a Mrs. Ryan from Eagle, Nebraska, and a young Mrs. Morse from Rutland, Vermont, who Mother had met down to the chiropodist's. Well, Mother couldn't hit a flea and they all laughed at her and I couldn't help from laughing at her myself and finally she quit and said her back was too lame to stoop over. So they got another lady and kept on playing and soon Mrs. Hartsell was the one everybody was laughing at, as she had a long shot to hit the black ball, and as she made the effort her teeth fell out on to the court. I never seen a woman so flustered in my life. And I never heard so much laughing, only Mrs. Hartsell didn't join in and she was madder than a hornet and wouldn't play no more, so the game broke up.

Mrs. Hartsell went home without speaking to nobody, but Hartsell stayed around and finally he said to me, he said: "Well, I played you checkers the other day and you beat me bad and now what do you say if you and me play a game of horseshoes?"

I told him I hadn't pitched a shoe in sixteen years, but Mother said: "Go ahead and play. You used to be good at it and maybe it will come back to you."

Well, to make a long story short, I give in. I oughtn't to of never tried it, as I hadn't pitched a shoe in sixteen years, and I only done it to humor Hartsell.

Before we started, Mother patted me on the back and told me to do my best, so we started in and I seen right off that I was in for it, as I hadn't pitched a shoe in sixteen years and didn't have my distance. And besides, the plating had wore off the shoes so that they was points right where they stuck into my thumb and I hadn't throwed more than two or three times when my thumb was raw and it pretty near killed me to hang on to the shoe, let alone pitch it.

Well, Hartsell throws the awkwardest shoe I ever seen pitched and to see him pitch you wouldn't think he would ever come nowheres near, but he is also the luckiest pitcher I ever seen and he made some pitches where the shoe lit five and six feet short and then schoonered up and was a ringer. They's no use trying to beat that kind of luck.

They was a pretty fair size crowd watching us and four or five other ladies besides Mother, and it seems like, when Hartsell pitches, he has got to chew and it kept the ladies on the anxious seat as he don't seem to care which way he is facing when he leaves go.

You would think a man as old as him would of learnt more manners.

Well, to make a long story short, I was just beginning to get my distance when I had to give up on account of my thumb, which I showed it to Hartsell and he seen I couldn't go on, as it was raw and bleeding. Even if I could of stood it to go on myself, Mother wouldn't of allowed it after she seen my thumb. So anyway I quit and Hartsell said the score was nineteen to six, but I don't know what it was. Or don't care, neither.

Well, Mother and I went home and I said I hoped we was through with the Hartsells as I was sick and tired of them, but it seemed like she had promised we would go over to their house that evening for another game of their everlasting cards.

Well, my thumb was giving me considerable pain and I felt kind of out of sorts and I guess maybe I forgot myself, but anyway, when we was about through playing Hartsell made the remark that he wouldn't never lose a game of cards if he could always have Mother for a partner.

So I said: "Well, you had a chance fifty years ago to always have her for a partner, but you wasn't man enough to keep her."

I was sorry the minute I had said it and Hartsell didn't know what to say and for once his wife couldn't say nothing. Mother tried to smooth things over by making the remark that I must of had something stronger than tea or I wouldn't talk so silly. But Mrs. Hartsell had froze up like an iceberg and hardly said good night to us and I bet her and Frank put in a pleasant hour after we was gone.

As we was leaving, Mother said to him: "Never mind Charley's nonsense, Frank. He is just mad because you beat him all hollow pitching horseshoes and playing cards."

She said that to make up for my slip, but at the same time she certainly riled me. I tried to keep ahold of myself, but as soon as we was out of the house she had to open up the subject and begun to scold me for the break I had made.

Well, I wasn't in no mood to be scolded. So I said: "I guess he is such a wonderful pitcher and card player that you wished you had married him."

"Well," she said, "at least he ain't a baby to give up pitching because his thumb has got a few scratches."

"And how about you," I said, "making a fool of yourself on the roque court and then pretending your back is lame and you can't play no more!"

"Yes," she said, "but when you hurt your thumb I didn't laugh at you, and why did you laugh at me when I sprained my back?"

"Who could help from laughing!" I said.

"Well," she said, "Frank Hartsell didn't laugh."

"Well," I said, "why didn't you marry him?"

"Well," said Mother, "I almost wished I had!"

"And I wished so, too!" I said.

"I'll remember that!" said Mother, and that's the last word she said to me for two days.

We seen the Hartsells the next day in the Park and I was willing to apologize, but they just nodded to us. And a couple days later we heard they had left for Orlando, where they have got relatives.

I wished they had went there in the first place.

Mother and I made it up setting on a bench.

"Listen, Charley," she said. "This is our Golden Honeymoon and we don't want the whole thing spoilt with a silly old quarrel."

"Well," I said, "did you mean that about wishing you had married Hartsell?"

"Of course not," she said, "that is, if you didn't mean that you wished I had, too." So I said:

"I was just tired and all wrought up. I thank God you chose me instead of him as they's no other woman in the world who I could of lived with all these years."

"How about Mrs. Hartsell?" says Mother.

"Good gracious!" I said. "Imagine being married to a woman that plays five hundred like she does and drops her teeth on the roque court!"

"Well," said Mother, "it wouldn't be no worse than being married to a man that expectorates towards ladies and is such a fool in a checker game."

So I put my arm around her shoulder and she stroked my hand and I guess we got kind of spoony.

They was two days left of our stay in St. Petersburg and the next to the last day Mother introduced me to a Mrs. Kendall from Kingston, Rhode Island, who she had met at the chiropodist's.

Mrs. Kendall made us acquainted with her husband, who is in the grocery business. They have got two sons and five grandchildren and one great-grandchild. One of their sons lives in Providence and is way up in the Elks as well as a Rotarian.

We found them very congenial people and we played cards with them the last two nights we was there. They was both experts and I only wished we had met them sooner instead of running into the Hartsells. But the Kendalls will be there again next winter and we will see more of them, that is, if we decide to make the trip again.

We left the Sunshine City on the eleventh day of February, at 11 a.m. This give us a day trip through Florida and we seen all the country we had passed through at night on the way down.

We reached Jacksonville at 7 p.m. and pulled out of there at 8:10 p.m. We reached Fayetteville, North Carolina, at nine o'clock the following morning, and reached Washington, D.C., at 6:30 p.m., laying over there half an hour.

We reached Trenton at 11:01 p.m. and had wired ahead to my daughter and son-in-law and they met us at the train and we went to their house and they put us up for the night. John would of made us stay up all night, telling about our trip, but Edie said we must be tired and made us go to bed. That's my daughter.

The next day we took our train for home and arrived safe and sound, having been gone just one month and a day.

Here comes Mother, so I guess I better shut up.

A RAID NIGHT

H. M. Tomlinson

SEPTEMBER 17, 1915. I had crossed from France to Fleet Street, and was thankful at first to have about me the things I had proved, with their suggestion of intimacy, their look of security; but I found the once familiar editorial rooms of that daily paper a little more than estranged. I thought them worse, if anything, than Ypres. Ypres is within the region where, when soldiers enter it, they abandon hope, because they have become sane at last, and their minds have a temperature a little below normal. In Ypres, whatever may have been their heroic and exalted dreams, they awake, see the world is mad, and surrender to the doom from which they know a world bereft will give them no reprieve.

There was a way in which the office of that daily paper was familiar. I had not expected it, and it came with a shock. Not only the compulsion, but the bewildering inconsequence of war was suggested by its activities. Reason was not there. It was ruled by a blind and fixed idea. The glaring artificial light, the headlong haste of the telegraph instruments, the wild litter on the floor, the rapt attention of the men scanning the news, their abrupt movements and speed when they had to cross the room, still with their gaze fixed, their expression that of those who dreaded something worse to happen; the suggestion of tension, as though the Last Trump were expected at any moment, filled me with vague alarm. The only place where that incipient panic is not usual is the front line, because there the enemy is within hail and is known to be another unlucky fool. But I allayed my anxiety. I leaned over one of the still figures, and scanned the fateful document which had given its reader the aspect of one who was staring at what the Moving Finger had done. Its message was no more than the excited whisper of a witness who had just left a keyhole. But I realized in that moment of surprise that this office was an essential feature of the War; without it, the War might become Peace. It provoked the emotions which assembled civilians in ecstatic support of the sacrifices, just as the staff of a corps head-quarters, at some comfortable leagues behind the trenches, maintains its fighting men in the place where gas and shells tend to engender common sense and irresolution.

I left the glare of that office, its heat and half-hysterical activity, and went into the coolness and quiet of the darkened street, and there the dread left me that it could be a duty of mine to keep hot pace with patriots in full stampede. The stars were wonderful. It is such a tranquillizing surprise to discover there are stars over London. Until this War, when the street illuminations were doused, we never knew it. It strengthens one's faith to discover the Pleiades over London; it is not true that their delicate glimmer has been put out by the remarkable incandescent energy of our power stations. As I crossed London Bridge the City was as silent as though it had come to the end of its days, and the shapes I could just make out under the stars were no more substantial than the shadows of its past. Even the Thames was a noiseless ghost. London at night gave me the illusion that I was really hidden from the monstrous trouble of Europe, and, at least for one sleep, had got out of the War. I felt that my suburban street, secluded in trees and unimportance, was as remote from the evil I knew of as though it were in Alaska. When I came to that street I could not see my neighbors' homes. It was with some doubt that I found my own. And there, with three hours to go to midnight, and a book, and some circumstances that certainly had not changed, I had retired thankfully into a fragment of that world I had feared we had completely lost.

"What a strange moaning the birds in the shrubbery are making!" my companion said once. I listened to it, and thought it was strange. There was a long silence, and then she looked up sharply. "What's that?" she asked. "Listen!"

I listened. My hearing is not good.

"Nothing!" I assured her.

"There it is again." She put down her book with decision, and rose, I thought, in some alarm.

"Trains," I suggested. "The gas bubbling. The dog next door. Your imagination." Then I listened to the dogs. It was curious, but they all seemed awake and excited.

"What is the noise like?" I asked, surrendering my book on the antiquity of man.

She twisted her mouth in a comical way most seriously, and tried to mimic a deep and solemn note.

"Guns," I said to myself, and went to the front door.

Beyond the vague opposite shadows of some elms, lights twinkled in the sky, incontinent sparks, as though glow lamps on an invisible pattern of wires were being switched on and off by an idle child. That was shrapnel. I walked along the empty street a little to get a view between and beyond the villas. I turned to say something to my companion, and saw then my silent neighbors, shadowy groups about me, as though they had not approached but had materialized where they stood. We watched those infernal sparks. A shadow lit its pipe and offered me its match. I heard the guns easily enough now, but they were miles away.

A slender finger of brilliant light moved slowly across the sky, checked, and remained pointing, firmly accusatory, at something it had found in the heavens. A Zeppelin!

There it was, at first a wraith, a suggestion on the point of vanishing, and then illuminated and embodied, a celestial maggot stuck to the round of a cloud like a caterpillar to the edge of a leaf. We gazed at it silently, I cannot say for how long. The beam of light might have pinned the bright larva to the sky for the inspection of interested Londoners. Then somebody spoke: "I think it is coming our way."

I thought so too. I went indoors, calling out to the boy as I passed his room upstairs, and went to where the girls were asleep. Three miles, three minutes! It appears to be harder to waken children when a Zeppelin is coming your way. I got the elder girl awake, lifted her, and sat her on the bed, for she had become heavier, I noticed. Then I put her small sister over my shoulder, as limp and indifferent as a half-filled bag. By this time the elder one had snuggled into the foot of her bed, resigned to that place if the other end were disputed, and was asleep again. I think I became annoyed, and spoke sharply. We were in a hurry. The boy was waiting for us at the top of the stairs.

"What's up?" he asked with merry interest, hoisting his slacks.

"Come on down," I said.

We went into a central room, put coats round them, answering eager and innocent questions with inconsequence, had the cellar door and a light ready, and then went out to inspect affairs. There were more searchlights at work. Bright diagonals made a living network on the overhead dark. It was remarkable that those rigid beams should not rest on the roof of night, but that their ends should glide noiselessly about the invisible dome. The nearest of them was followed, when in the zenith, by a faint oval of light. Sometimes it discovered and broke on delicate films of high fair-weather clouds. The shells were still twinkling brilliantly, and the guns were making a rhythm-less baying in the distance, like a number of alert and indignant hounds. But the Zeppelin had gone. The firing diminished and stopped.

They went to bed again, and as I had become acutely depressed, and the book now had no value, I turned in myself, assuring everyone, with the usual confidence of the military expert, that the affair was over for the night. But once in bed I found I could see there only the progress humanity had made in its movement heavenwards. That is the way with us; never to be concerned with the newest clever trick of our enterprising fellow-men till a sudden turn of affairs shows us, by the immediate threat to our own existence, that that cleverness has added to the peril of civilized society, whose house has been built on the verge of the pit. War now would be not only between soldiers. In future wars the place of honor would be occupied by the infants, in their cradles. For war is not murder. Starving children is war, and it is not murder. What treacherous lying is all the heroic poetry of battle! Men will now creep up after dark, ambushed in safety behind the celestial curtains, and drop bombs on sleepers beneath, for the greater glory of some fine figment or other. It filled me, not with wrath at the work of Kaisers and Kings, for we know what is possible with them, but with dismay at the discovery that one's fellows are so docile and credulous that they will obey any order, however abominable. The very heavens had been fouled by this obscene and pallid worm, crawling over those eternal verities to which eyes had been lifted for light when night and trouble were over-dark. God was dethroned by science. One looked startled at humanity, seeing not the accustomed countenance, but, for a moment, glimpsing instead the baleful lidless stare of the evil of the slime, the unmentionable of a nightmare . . .

A deafening crash brought us out of bed in one movement. I must have been dozing. Someone cried, "My children!" Another rending uproar interrupted my effort to shepherd the flock to a lower floor. There was a raucous avalanche of glass. We muddled down somehow—I forget how. I could not find the matches. Then in the dark we lost the youngest for some eternal seconds while yet another explosion shook the house. We got to the cellar stairs, and at last there they all were, their backs to the coals, sitting on lumber.

A candle was on the floor. There were more explosions, somewhat muffled. The candle-flame showed a little tremulous excitement, as if it were one of the party. It reached upwards curiously in a long intent flame, and then shrank flat with what it had learned. We were accompanied by grotesque shadows. They stood about us on the white and unfamiliar walls. We waited. Even the shadows seemed to listen with us; they hardly moved, except when the candle-flame was nervous. Then the shadows wavered slightly. We waited. I caught the boy's eye, and winked. He winked back. The youngest, still with sleepy eyes, was trembling, though not with cold, and this her sister noticed, and put her arms about her. His mother had her hand on her boy's shoulder.

There was no more noise outside. It was time, perhaps, to go up to see what had happened. I put a raincoat over my pajamas, and went into the street. Some of my neighbors, who were special constables, hurried by. The enigmatic night, for a time, for five minutes, or five seconds (I do not know how long it was), was remarkably still and usual. It might have been pretending that we were all mistaken. It was as though we had been merely dreaming our recent excitements. Then, across a field, a villa began to blaze. Perhaps it had been stunned till then, and had suddenly jumped into a panic of flames. It was wholly involved in one roll of fire and smoke, a sudden furnace so consuming that, when it as suddenly ceased, giving one or two dying spasms, I had but an impression of flames rolling out of windows and doors to persuade me that what I had seen was real. The night engulfed what may have been an illusion, for till then I had never noticed a house at that point.

Whispers began to pass of tragedies that were incredible in their incidence and craziness. Three children were dead in the rubble of one near villa. The ambulance that was passing was taking their father to the hospital. A woman had been blown from her bed into the street. She was unhurt, but she was insane. A long row of humbler dwellings, over which the dust was still hanging in a faint mist, had been demolished, and one could only hope the stories about that place were far from true. We were turned away when we would have assisted; all the help that was wanted was there. A stranger offered me his tobacco pouch, and it was then I found my rainproof was a lady's, and therefore had no pipe in its pocket.

The sky was suspect, and we watched it, but saw only vacuity till one long beam shot into it, searching slowly and deliberately the whole mysterious ceiling, yet hesitating sometimes, and going back on its path as though intelligently suspicious of a matter which it had passed over too quickly. It peered into the immense caverns of a cloud to which it had returned, illuminating to us unsuspected and horrifying possibilities of hiding-places above us. We expected to see the discovered enemy boldly emerge then. Nothing came out. Other beams by now had joined the pioneer, and the night became bewildering with a dazzling mesh of light. Shells joined the wandering beams, those sparks of orange and red. A world of fantastic chimneypots and black rounds of trees leaped into being between us and the sudden expansion of a fan of yellow flame. A bomb! We just felt, but hardly heard, the shock of it. A furious succession of such bursts of light followed, a convulsive opening and shutting of night. We saw that when midnight is cleft asunder it has a fiery inside.

The eruptions ceased. Idle and questioning, not knowing we had heard the last gun and bomb of the affair, a little stunned by the maniacal rapidity and violence of this attack, we found ourselves gazing at the familiar and shadowy peace of our suburb as we have always known it. It had returned to that aspect. But something had gone from it for ever. It was not, and never could be again, as once we had known it. The security of our own place had been based on the goodwill or indifference of our fellow-creatures everywhere. Tonight, over that obscure and unimportant street, we had seen a celestial portent illuminate briefly a little of the future of mankind.

THE BROKEN BOOT

John Galsworthy

THE ACTOR, GILBERT Caister, who had been "out" for six months, emerged from his East Coast seaside lodging about noon in the day, after the opening of "Shooting the Rapids," on tour, in which he was playing Dr. Dominick in the last act. A salary of four pounds a week would not, he was conscious, remake his fortunes, but a certain jauntiness had returned to the gait and manner of one employed again at last.

Fixing his monocle, he stopped before a fishmonger's and, with a faint smile on his face, regarded a lobster. Ages since he had eaten a lobster! One could long for a lobster without paying, but the pleasure was not solid enough to detain him. He moved upstreet and stopped again, before a tailor's window. Together with the actual tweeds, in which he could so easily fancy himself refitted, he could see a reflection of himself, in the faded brown suit wangled out of the production of "Marmaduke Mandeville" the year before the war. The sunlight in this damned town was very strong, very hard on seams and buttonholes, on knees and elbows! Yet he received the ghost of aesthetic pleasure from the reflected elegance of a man long fed only twice a day, of an eyeglass well rimmed out from a soft brown eye, of a velour hat salved from the production of "Educating Simon" in 1912; and, in front of the window he removed that hat, for under it was his new phenomenon, not yet quite evaluated, his *mèche blanche*. Was it an asset, or the beginning of the end? It reclined backwards on the right side, conspicuous in his dark hair, above that shadowy face always interesting to Gilbert Caister. They said it came from atrophy of the—er—something nerve, an effect of the war, or of under-nourished tissue. Rather distinguished, perhaps, but——!

He walked on, and became conscious that he had passed a face he knew. Turning, he saw it also turned on a short and dapper figure—a face rosy, bright, round, with an air of cherubic knowledge, as of a getter-up of amateur theatricals.

Bryce-Green, by George!

"Caister? It is! Haven't seen you since you left the old camp. Remember what sport we had over 'Gotta Grampus'? By Jove! I am glad to see you. Doing anything with yourself? Come and have lunch with me."

Bryce-Green, the wealthy patron, the moving spirit of entertainment in that South Coast convalescent camp. And, drawling slightly, Caister answered:

"Shall be delighted." But within him something did not drawl: "By God, you're going to have a feed, my boy!"

And—elegantly threadbare, roundabout and dapper—the two walked side by side.

"Know this place? Let's go in here! Phyllis, cocktails for my friend Mr. Caister and myself, and caviare on biscuits. Mr. Caister is playing here! you must go and see him."

The girl who served the cocktails and the caviare looked up at Caister with interested blue eyes. Precious! He had been "out" for six months!

"Nothing of a part," he drawled; "took it to fill a gap." And below his waistcoat the gap echoed: "Yes, and it'll take some filling."

"Bring your cocktail along, Caister; we'll go into the little further room, there'll be nobody there. What shall we have—a lobstah?"

And Caister murmured: "I love lobstahs."

"Very fine and large here. And how are you, Caister? So awfully glad to see you—only real actor we had."

"Thanks," said Caister, "I'm all right." And he thought: "He's a damned amateur, but a nice little man."

"Sit here. Waiter, bring us a good big lobstah and a salad; and then—er—a small fillet of beef with potatoes fried crisp, and a bottle of my special hock. Ah! and a rum omelette—plenty of rum and sugah. Twig?"

And Caister thought: "Thank God, I do."

They had sat down opposite each other at one of the two small tables in the little recessed room.

"Luck!" said Bryce-Green.

"Luck!" replied Caister; and the cocktail trickling down him echoed: "Luck!"

"And what do you think of the state of the drama?" Oh! ho! A question after his own heart. Balancing his monocle by a sweetish smile on the opposite side of his mouth, Caister drawled his answer: "Quite too bally awful!"

"H'm! Yes," said Bryce-Green; "nobody with any genius, is there?"

And Caister thought: "Nobody with any money."

"Have you been playing anything great? You were so awfully good in 'Gotta Grampus'!"

"Nothing particular. I've been—er—rather slack." And with their feel around his waist his trousers seemed to echo: "Slack!"

"Ah!" said Bryce-Green. "Here we are! Do you like claws?"

"Tha-a-nks. Anything!" To eat—until warned by the pressure of his waist against his trousers! Huh! What a feast! And what a flow of his own tongue suddenly released—on drama, music, art; mellow and critical, stimulated by the round eyes and interjections of his little provincial host.

"By Jove, Caister! You've got a *mêche blanche*. Never noticed. I'm awfully interested in *mêches blanches*. Don't think me too frightfully rude—but did it come suddenly?"

"No, gradually"

"And how do you account for it?"

"Try starvation," trembled on Caister's lips.

"I don't."

"I think it's ripping. Have some more omelette? I often wish I'd gone on the regular stage myself. Must be a topping life, if one has talent, like you."

Topping?

"Have a cigar. Waiter! Coffee and cigars. I shall come and see you tonight. Suppose you'll be here a week?"

Topping! The laughter and applause—"Mr. Caister's rendering left nothing to be desired; its——and its——are in the true spirit of——!"

Silence recalled him from his rings of smoke. Bryce-Green was sitting, with cigar held out and mouth a little open, and bright eyes round as pebbles, fixed—fixed on some object near the floor, past the corner of the tablecloth. Had he burnt his mouth? The eyelids fluttered; he looked at Caister, licked his lips like a dog, nervously, and said:

"I say, old chap, don't think me a beast, but are you at all—er—er—rocky? I mean—if I can be of any service, don't hesitate! Old acquaintance, don't you know, and all that——"

His eyes rolled out again towards the object, and Caister followed them. Out there above the carpet he saw it—his own boot. It dangled, because his knees were crossed, six inches off the ground—split—right across, twice, between lace and toecap. Quite! He knew it. A boot left him from the role of Bertie Carstairs, in "The Dupe," just before the war. Good boots. His only pair, except the boots of Dr. Dominick, which he was nursing. And from the boot he looked back at Bryce-Green, sleek and concerned. A drop, black when it left his heart, suffused his eye behind the monocle; his smile curled bitterly; he said:

"Not at all, thanks! Why?"

"Oh! n-n-nothing. It just occurred to me." His eyes—but Caister had withdrawn the boot. Bryce-Green paid the bill and rose.

"Old chap, if you'll excuse me; engagement at half-past two. So awf'ly glad to have seen you. Good-bye!"

"Good-bye!" said Caister. "And thanks!"

He was alone. And, chin on hand, he stared through his monocle into an empty coffee cup. Alone with his heart, his boot, his life to come. . . . "And what have you been in lately, Mr. Caister?" "Nothing very much lately. Of course I've played almost everything." "Quite so. Perhaps you'll leave your address; can't say anything definite, I'm afraid." "I—I should—er—be willing to rehearse on approval; or—if I could read the part?" "Thank you, afraid we haven't got as far as that." "No? Quite! Well, I shall hear from you, perhaps." And Caister could see his own eyes looking at the manager. God! What a look. . . . A topping life! A dog's life! Cadging—cadging—cadging for work! A life of draughty waiting, of concealed beggary, of terrible depressions, of want of food!

The waiter came skating round as if he desired to clear. Must go! Two young women had come in and were sitting at the other table between him and the door. He saw them look at him, and his sharpened senses caught the whisper:

"Sure—in the last act. Don't you see his *mêche blanche?*"

"Oh! yes—of course! Isn't it—wasn't he——!"

Caister straightened his back; his smile crept out, he fixed his monocle. They had spotted his Dr. Dominick!

"If you've quite finished, sir, may I clear?"

"Certainly. I'm going." He gathered himself and rose. The young women were gazing up. Elegant, with faint smile, he passed them close, managing—so that they could not see—his broken boot.